BLACK
KNIGHT

SVETLANA IVANOVA

ISBN-13: 978-1537543819
ISBN-10:1537543814

DEDICATION

To all the homosexual girls, bisexual girls, heterosexual girls, queer girls, still-questioning-their-sexuality girls and all the transgender babes out there, this book is written especially for you.

PROLOGUE

At the edge of an unknown galaxy, a baby girl was born on a planet called Arzuria. She possessed the delicacy of a girl and the purity of a boy. She was given a mission that would determine the fate of her people. Along with two guardians, the girl sailed through the vast empty space to the planet Earth where life sucked the most in the middle of the Milky Way. Needless to say, she had to safeguard a secret too, and a big one at that. Her one and only purpose was to find a special Earthling among the seven billion humans on this lonely planet.

But then there were a few complications.

And all of them were because of me.

CHAPTER 1

My FATHER DROPPED me off at the *Domodedovo* airport. It was freezing outside and even inside his beat-up Nissan. The Moscow skies turned a perfect cloudless gray. I pulled over the hood of my brown parka to keep warm.

Pyotr, my dad, had personally volunteered to kick me out of his house this morning. It was America where my butt would land in the next seventeen hours and a stop later.

"Nina," he called to me for the fifteenth time after I crammed all my stuff into the car. I was waiting for him to say, *'I'm sorry, we can work this out together. You don't have to go.'* or something along that line, but he seemed to have a frog stuck in his throat every time he opened his mouth, so I just gave up and let this hope die.

After we parked, I got out of the passenger seat.

"Call me when you get there," he said as he loaded everything I owned onto a cart and then with a small unmanly voice, he added, "Take care."

I slung my bag which contained my passport and plane ticket over my shoulder and walked off into the busiest waiting areas without looking back again.

As I boarded the plane, I knew Pyotr was already on his merry way, and I tried not to cry.

The next day, I woke up in the sky domain of the United States. Everything went smoothly after my plane landed. And before I knew it, I came out of the revolving glass doors of the Los Angeles airport. I pushed my cart to the curb and looked around myself.

While I was waiting, my thoughts wandered to my old home, which led me to think about Dominika, who sucked my father's soul through his you-know-what and then got herself knocked up with the devil's spawn.

Dominika would have liked to strangle me in my sleep, or poisoned my drink and let me die in agony if I were to have stayed there long enough. Dad had to send me off to live with my aunt in the states while he and his hot young wife went on to celebrate their new family with me out of the picture.

1

Now looking at the land I barely knew with its beautiful sunshine, I felt completely lost. My eyes scanned the area for a middle-aged woman. She was my dad's younger sister, Aunt Viktoriya, who was married to an American businessman. They were now living in a big house somewhere in LA.

But after half an hour passed, there was still no one that looked like Aunt Vikki.

Great, I was exiled from my country and got abandoned in another one.

Then I noticed this uniformed man approaching me. He could be in his fifties, a bit too thin for his sleek black suit.

"You must be Miss. Antonina Volkova, right?" The old man said to me.
"Yes?"

"I'm John, your aunt's personal driver. I'm here to pick you up since she couldn't make it."

He handed me his ID card and a signed note from Aunt Vikki saying she apologized for not being able to receive me herself and that she would see me at dinner time.

"We should go now, Miss Volkova," he said. The old man had a kind sincere face that made it impossible not to trust him. I couldn't help feeling relieved to have someone found me at last.

"Please, just call me Nina, " I said, sounding somewhat awkward speaking in a foreign tongue for the first time. "Nice to meet you, Mr. John."

"Just call me John," he said with a warm beam, which brought out his laughing wrinkles even more.

We got my luggage into the trunk of a black BMW and then I got into the front seat with John. The old man simply started the car and drove off.

The afternoon sun shone through the tinted window of the car. I looked at stores and buildings, traffic signs and people, and big cars and small cars. I saw a bunch of high-school kids getting out of Starbucks, laughing and joking. When we stopped at a red light, we heard blasting music booming from a white Jeep next to us. Some guys with sunglasses bobbed their heads to the beats.

Everything seemed so hyped here. I was still trying to get my head around all this.

"You'll get used to it," John said even though I hadn't said anything out loud. I guessed it was a good thing I educated myself about American culture before I came over here — thanks to Hollywood movies. But to be completely honest, all of this was still taking me by surprise.

After a long while later, we arrived at my aunt's house.

It was a beautiful house with red tiled roofs that reminded me of a Mediterranean holiday villa. The rest of it was painted pure white. It had a large manicured garden and a cobbled driveway snaked through to the front door.

John told me to go inside while he took care of my belongings, which wasn't much. I sucked in the air and walked up to the glossy front door. But before I could knock on it, it burst opened and a tall dark-haired guy stepped out. He was wearing an American football jacket and chewing a mint gum with open mouth. The guy gave me a once over.

"Who are you?" he asked.

"Oh, I'm—I'm Mrs. Black's—niece—I—er—"

His laughter cut me off. Then he extended his hand to me.

"I'm just kidding. I'm your cousin, Jason," he said. "Mom told me to wait for you. Your English needs more improvement, but I like the accent. Keep it! Now please come on in. And by the way, you can call me Jay. I don't like my real name."

He shook my hand as soon as I took his and looked at me with a wide grin. Then Jay-not-Jason motioned for me to get inside.

The interior was just as splendid and cozy. The furniture of the living room looked like it was fresh out of a modern decor magazine.

Then we heard footsteps coming down the stairs. A girl about my age appeared. She had a pretty face that reminded me of Aunt Vikki, and she wore a short denim skirt with a black rock band t-shirt.

"Hey Piper, look! Who's here?" Jay said and turned to me. "This is my twin sister, Piper."

It took me a while to notice their similarities and differences. Piper had blonde hair —almost platinum blonde. Jay had dark hair with brown eyes while his sister's were deep blue. I wouldn't have guessed they were twins.

"Oh, hi!" she said as if she didn't expect to see me there. "You're my cousin, Antonina, right?"

"Yes, hello," I said and smiled back. "You can call me Nina."

"Alas, I finally found someone who hates real names in this house," Jay said. "I'm sure we're going to get along so well, cousin Nina."

Piper came forward and knocked her brother on the forehead.

"You better not let dad hear this, or he'll disown your unappreciative ass." Piper then turned to me. "Come on, I'll show you your room."

I nodded. The girl turned to walk back upstairs and I followed her. The house wasn't too big, but if you spent almost all of your seventeen years living in a small apartment, then it was the biggest you had ever been in. I tried not to be all starry-eyed. I didn't want my cousin to think that kids from Russia weren't as cool as kids in America where they had cars and lived in a big nice house and wore fashionable clothes and all that jazz.

Piper took me to a room at the other end of the hallway, which seemed like the kind of room a monk would live. It was isolated and far away from the others. But when she opened the door, a great burst of brightness greeted us with the sunny view from the windows. Outside, there were oak trees, willow trees along with aspens and chestnuts, dotting over the green hills with other houses.

"Mom and dad will be back to have dinner with us," Piper told me. "Make yourself at home, Nina. And if you need anything, just ask."

"Thank you, Piper." I smiled in gratitude.

"Well, you must be so jet-lagged and tired now. Get some sleep," she said. I nodded as she turned to leave. At least, my cousins seemed so nice.

Yet when I looked around the room, an empty feeling enveloped me. I was going to stay here for—who knows how long? But at last, I was away from my old troubled life for now.

~*~

I didn't mean to fall asleep practically the whole day. When I woke up, I thought I was still in my bed back in Russia thousands of miles away.

The sun might have just set. There was still the slightest bit of orangy sky over the green hill. I looked out the window at the beautiful landscape that appeared so still and perfect, a unicorn might as well trot into view at night, but I didn't see anything except a few birds flying home after a long hard day.

I grabbed my bag of toiletry and went to the bathroom to freshen up. I washed my pale face and brushed my bed hair, smoothing out the chocolate brown tangles into place. My eyes were puffy and a bit hazy as I looked at myself in the mirror. The irises were sparkling with light but as black as my soul.

Facing my pallid self, I wondered what I would be doing next. I felt too shy to get out of my room, but I couldn't hide forever. After I finished cleaning up, I unpacked my clothes and got changed into a simple t-shirt and jeans before going downstairs. I found Piper half way.

"Oh, I was going to go to your room," she said. "Mom and Dad are already here. Come. Dinner is ready."

Jay was standing by the entrance when we got to the dining hall. He looked at me with unblinking eyes and smiled at me in his own boyish way.

"See you again, cousin, I thought you turned into Snow White already," he said in a mischievous voice, which earned him a blush from my cheeks and an elbow from Piper in his gut as she walked past him.

"What?" Jay said, rubbing his tummy. "I'm just teasing."

Aunt Viktoriya was there. Once she saw me, she walked right up and put her arms around me. Then she stepped back and looked at my face and just said, "Nina," like it was all she could muster up to say. After a while, she added, "You're as beautiful as your mother," which obviously wasn't true since my mother was really beautiful and I was not.

Mr. Robert Black, her husband, was a large bald man with a smiling face. He was at the head of the table. He stood up and held out his hand like I was his business client.

"What a pleasure to have you here," he said as I shook his outstretched hand.

After we settled around the table, a maid came in with plates of food. They served clam chowder, meatloaf, and chicken soup with a side dish of macaroni and salad.

After we exchanged some pleasantries, everyone began to eat.

"By the way, how about telling us a little about Russia," Mr. Black said.

But before I could reply, the twins started bombarding me with a million questions. Piper asked me about Russian models and whether it was true that most girls in Russia smoke to keep themselves slim or that they won't get out of the house without makeups. Jay asked me if I knew about mafia kings and drug lords. But Aunt Vikki gave them a disapproving look, so they stopped.

I did tell them about my town, which wasn't as nice as this one and about my school. Aunt Vikki asked about my father and Dominika. They asked me a lot about Dominika and their new heir and everything else that led up to me sitting there with them. I could tell that they felt kind of sorry for me. Aunt Vikki asked me privately, and by private I meant she spoke in Russian, which I knew none of her American-born children understood and neither did her husband.

She asked how my father was doing and whether he was doing alright financially. I told her he was fine except for his taste in women, and that he was probably feeling a lot better now that I wasn't around to remind him about it day and night.

Aunt Vikki gave a kind of funny look like she couldn't decide whether to keep from laughing or crying.

"Well, their loss is our gain," she said at last. "Anyway, Robert and I have registered you as a member of our family already. From now on, you are Antonina Black."

I looked up from my plate in surprise. So my father had secretly disowned me for real? A pang of sadness and hurt ran through me like a blade. I swallowed the lump in my throat.

"But I don't know if it's a good idea, Aunt Vikki," I said.

"Oh dear, we would love to have you in our family. Why did you say that?" Aunt Vikki said with a concerned frown. Everyone looked at me silently. I had to take a sip of iced water to calm my nerves. My hand shook as I put the glass down. I looked back at them again, thinking if I didn't tell them now, they would be crushed by disappointment just like my father. I took a deep breath and told myself, *'It's now or never!'*

"Because another reason why I was sent here is the fact that—" I gulped. "—I'm gay."

If they couldn't accept it, I would just have to get out of this beautiful cozy house and drop dead somewhere else. I was sick and tired of hiding who I was for all those years. I had to let them know and make it crystal clear, and to hell with it!

There was a silence at the table. It was so quiet you could hear a fly fart.

Jay dropped his silver fork on his porcelain plate, making a loud clanking noise.

Piper just stared at me wide eyed. Robert and Aunt Vikki looked like Medusa had just turned them into stone.

Piper was the first to speak.

"You're...*gay?*"

I nodded. Jay had his jaw hanging open.

"But—but—" he stuttered, "You don't look like a les—"

"Jason!" Robert hushed him sternly.

"That's alright Mr. Black," I said. ""I know this is quite a shock to all of you, but I guess you don't have to do this for me. Thank you for taking me in and all, but I think I better go and get packed now."

I just wanted to say that I couldn't live with people who would house my body but reject my soul. As I pushed my chair back and stood up to leave, my aunt reached out to grip my hand.

"Where are you going, Nina?" Aunt Vikki asked. Her eyes darted to her husband as if asking for him to intervene. Robert cleared his throat awkwardly.

"Nina, don't be silly. You can stay here," he said, but it sounded more like a command.

"Yes, dear. Let's sit down and finish your meal. Tomorrow, Piper and Jason will show you your new school." Aunt Vikki quickly changed the subject and tried to be cheerful again. "We have registered you and everything. Are you ready to go to school or is it too soon?"

"I'm fine with it," I said and sat back down. Everyone continued to eat in an awkward silence. Then Robert announced that he had a business trip to Las Vegas the next day and would like to go to bed early. After he excused himself from the table, Piper and Jay also came up with their own reasons to leave.

Then there was just Aunt Vikki and me. She looked at me as if she was trying to figure out something about me, but not in a judging way most adults would do with their homosexual relatives. She was just genuinely curious. She asked me a lot of questions. And later, she put her hand on mine and said she wished my mother were here to see what a vivid person I was. I thought *'vivid'* was a pretty strange choice of words. I asked if she meant to say *'messed up in the head'* but she just laughed. Then she stroked my cheek and it made me feel sad and happy all at once.

"Pyotr was so wrong not to choose you, Nina," she said.

CHAPTER 2

BREAKFAST WITH THE BLACKS was a quiet affair. Robert left the house early. When I asked about the bus system in the neighborhood, Aunt Vikki told me I could go with Piper. Jay acted like a brat this morning. He kept complaining about his burned bacon and answering his mom with one-syllable words before sulking out of the house and was gone.

Aunt Vikki wondered what was wrong with her son today.

When I stepped out of the house, Piper was waiting for me inside her silver Porsche. I walked towards her shiny sport car that gleamed under the Californian sun. But Piper was quieter than usual when I got inside.

"How far is the school?" I asked to break the silence. She fumbled around in her Prada and fished out the car key.

"Not very far," she said flatly, but I could detect a hint of discomfort in her voice. This was more than enough for a 'vivid' person like me to understand.

"Then maybe I should walk," I said and was ready to open the door when Piper gripped my elbow.

"Wait, are you crazy?" she said. "You can't walk there by yourself. You don't even know the area."

"That's what Google Maps is for, isn't it?" I said. She didn't know what to say. "Look, cousin, you don't have to put on a smiley face if you don't feel comfortable being around me. I'm not asking you to step on egg shells when it comes to anything concerning my situation or even my sexuality. So if you don't like it, you don't have to give me a cold shoulder like that. I'm not here to make things difficult for you."

Piper's blue eyes widened at me, speechless. I made an attempt to move again, but she stopped me one more time.

"Nina!"

"What is your problem, Piper?" I snapped. I wasn't in the best of mood the entire time I was here, and this was starting to get under my skin.

"I'm sorry," she said softly. "It's just—this is so new to me and I don't know how to react to something like this. I mean, your being—gay. Our family is pretty normal as you can see. This is kind of..."

"Unusual to have me?" I said. "I understand that. That's why I don't want to burden you with me around."

"But we're cousins," she said again. "I just need time to adjust to it. I'm sorry, Nina, please don't be mad."

I heaved out a sigh.

"That's alright," I said.

"And please, don't tell my mom I said this to you," Piper said and she put another hand on my arm pleadingly. "But is it okay if we just pretend we don't know each other at school?"

I thought I had enough experiences with discrimination, but nothing is ever okay when people say hurtful things to you, no matter how many times you have heard it. I was prepared to face such treatment ever since I came out, but it still kind of hurt.

Is it ever okay to be treated like that?

Nien, ora, non, nyet.

Anyway, it wasn't her fault that Piper was born straight just as I was born gay. She wouldn't understand it.

"Fine," I said quietly at last. "If that's what you want."

Piper let out a sigh of relief. She patted my hand with a grateful smile and then started the car. The engine purred to life. Piper seemed to relax a little. I sat back and closed my eyes, trying to drown out every thought that tried to ignite my brain with self-pity.

After about ten minutes of our silent ride, Piper spoke up again.

"By the way, I love your clothes. Never seen this fashion here. It makes you look different," Piper said.

Maybe she just said that to cheer me up.

"Thanks," I said.

"Well," she breathed and gave a nervous laugh. "I'm surprised you don't wear that lesbian lingerie."

"What is lesbian lingerie?"

"Oh! Well, welcome to America," Piper said and grinned sideways at me. "I was referring to flannels. I've heard lesbians love flannels and beanies and sandals to death. It's like lingerie to them, isn't it, Nina?"

I looked at Piper in disbelief and for a moment, I was trying so hard not to strangle her with the seat-belt.

At last, we reached our school none too soon.

The campus was bigger than I expected. New shiny Jeeps, and Porsches were common in the student lot—obviously a school for rich kids. Piper cut the engine as soon as she found a space.

Piper had given me a map of the buildings and told me everything that I needed to know. It would have been nice of her if I hadn't figured out that just so I wouldn't have to bother her again.

"See you after school," she said and walked away quickly.

I saw a group of girls standing by the entrance's staircase. They waved at her to join them.

I sighed and stuffed everything in my bag then slung the leather strap over my shoulder. Inhaling the fresh morning air, I convinced myself that no one was going to accuse me of being a Russian spy or worse bully me for being gay.

Skirting around the main building, I found another double glass doors and slipped inside. When the bell rang with a nasal buzzing noise, I walked to the registrar office. There was a tall boy with clear skin and oil slick black hair in front of me at the counter. I walked up and talked to a young woman behind the computer screen. The woman told me to wait and left the desk for a moment, and while I waited for my papers to be signed, the guy turned to me.

"Hey, I haven't seen you around here before?" he said overly friendly. The guy towered over me with his tall muscular body. I wore a low cut t-shirt and had to hold my document papers over my chest. With a dry smile, I shook my head back.

The woman gave me the slips.

"Oh, you're new, I see," the guy said. "Well, I can show you to your class if you'd like. What's your first period?"

Because I was new and hated being late, I had to agree.

"Mmm, Advanced Language Arts, Room 102, Building C," I said as I read through my schedule.

"Cool, I'm going to the same building," he said. "I could show you the way."

"Thank you." I smiled and we began to walk.

"I'm Jack Connor by the way," he said and when I didn't say anything back, he added, "And you are—?"

"Oh," I breathed. "I'm Nina Volk—er—Nina Black."

It felt sort of weird saying my new name out loud for the first time, but I figured my former name would sound even weirder. I guessed I wanted to be a new person now, and Pytor's name just didn't feel like mine anymore.

From the corner of my eyes, I saw Jack nodded at a group of guys hovering around on the other side of the hall. They chuckled and hooted among their peers.

Everything looked like it was coming straight out of a typical American movie—a typical American high school with janitors and students roaming the halls, talking through the corridors by their glossy red lockers. It was different from my old school back in Russia. Students wore whatever they wanted here whereas I had to wear my uniform. The energy was also different. I couldn't tell whether the place was depressing or exciting.

I hoped I wasn't feeling too overwhelmed by all that.

"So where are you from?" Jack asked a while later.

"I've just moved here from Moscow," I replied. Jack's eyes widened in utter surprise.

"No kidding? That explained the accent!" he said and I smiled back, but half of me wanted to roll my eyes at him.

"You came here with your family then?"

"No, it's just me," I said.

"So you live with any relatives?"

"Yes, my aunt."

"Oh, I see. Well, I know lots of places to hang out in town. If you don't mind, we can—" he started to offer but I cut him off by pointing to a classroom door.

"Hey, that's my class!" I said and started to run off towards it. "Thank you, Joe!"

He looked confused.

"It's Jack—but okay—see you around!" he called after me.

My morning class passed by in the same vague fashion. Mrs. Smith introduced me to my classmates, and I blushed like crazy when everyone started to gasp after they found out where I came from. Pytor said I would love the school here. *'You're so smart,'* he said. *'It would all come easily for you over there. It's going to be the best year of your life.'* I hated it when he said that.

After the first period, I got to know a few people who took the same ALA class with me. They helped me find my way around the campus. Although they were welcoming and helpful, I tried to keep the conversation short without being rude.

I used to care about making friends. But now looking back, I realized that being popular in high school was like sitting at a cool table inside an asylum. I wanted to finish it as soon as possible and move out of Robert's house then go to college and get a life elsewhere. I had learned quite recently that no matter how much people love you, they aren't going to be there for you forever.

I had to depend on myself.

I sat alone near the window in science class when some students cried out as they gathered at the windows. I turned to see what the fuss it was about.

That was when I saw a very unusual sport car pulling up into the parking lot across from the building. It looked like it belonged to Batman or some sci-fi action movies. With all the sleek black tinted windows and black metal designs, I would be disappointed if the driver wasn't as impressive.

We could hear the growling engine before it was cut off. Then the car doors were lifted open. A tall silver hair dude stepped out. The bulky guy wore a black sleeveless shirt, showing his weird tattoos, which spiraled over both of his arms like little snakes. A moment later, we saw a long slim leg popped out from the other side. The trees and grassy hill almost hid the person away from my view.

More people came over to the window, all gawking at the spectacle.

At last, I saw a tall blonde girl appeared.

I had never seen anyone, who caught and held my attention like this one in my entire life. It was the first moment you realize you have formed an unhealthy obsession towards a stranger—or as my best friend Klara had put it— your ultimate crush.

The girl wore all black —black leather jacket, black t-shirt, black skinny jeans with a pair of heavy combat boots. And when she walked, it reminded me of a black panther. Her long messy blonde hair gently swayed to the wind. At the same moment, the sunlight broke through the clouds and bathed the blonde angel like a halo.

Several gasps issued from the people around me. I, myself, was bewitched, intrigued, and above all confused. Something about her was impossible to describe.

But then we saw another girl wearing a fitted jacket and zipper leggings walked up to them. She was about the same size as me with short jet-black hair. As she joined the duo, they exchanged a few words and then walked together towards the building. It was like watching some supermodels on a catwalk.

I was still mesmerized by their unusual beauties. Their facial features were so different — so strangely proportional and singular that I now understood why it caused such an unduly reaction, especially with the blonde one. She seemed more inhumanly perfect and even intimidating.

"I bet they must be some ancient gods coming down to Earth," a girl sighed dreamily beside me.

"Who are those kids?" I asked. I didn't realize I was actually dying of curiosity until then. The girl looked at me for a moment before she remembered I was new.

"That's Triton and Xenon Knight," she told me, pointing to the short-haired girl and the big guy.

"And the blonde one?"

The girl leaned in and said in a theatrical voice as if she'd been waiting for that question.

"Her name is Allecra Knight."

CHAPTER 3

I LEARNED LATER on that the trio was siblings. They just got transferred to this school two months ago. Their unusual appearances and intimidating personality scared people off, but they never caused any trouble so the teachers just left them alone. Maybe they scared the teachers, too.

Anyway, it was counterproductive for me to suddenly take an interest in those strangers. I shook my head to clear the image of the blonde girl and opened my science textbook to read before the class started. The book was full of colorful pictures of galaxies, planets, and other scientific information.

I was so absorbed in my reading that I didn't know when the noises in the class had died down. It wasn't until a moment later that I heard the sound of heavy boots approaching my table. I felt a presence of someone standing beside me so I looked up.

My heart almost exploded out of my chest. I recognized that perfectly chiseled face immediately.

Oh, my god.

Allecra Knight was looking down at me with a deep frown. My mouth fell open like a goldfish's. Then her eyes also widened and twinkled like lit jewels when they met mine. I couldn't make out what color they were since it was more than one. It was like looking at a kaleidoscope or a greenish blue galaxy.

Wow, hybrid much?

The blonde girl said nothing and just stared and stared at me.

"I'm—I'm sorry—I must have taken your seat," I stammered. Her intense eyes made my hands shake as I closed the book and put it back into my bag. She had the strangest look on her face. It almost seemed restrained.

But then Mrs. Cowell, our science teacher came into the room.

"Alright children, please take a seat," she said in a clear strong voice. "Time to discover the wonder and joy of science!"

"Mrs. Cowell, we have a new student from Russia," some guy yelled, causing my head to turn away from that antagonistic stare.

"Who's that?" the teacher asked. I timidly raised my hand.

"Oh, may I see your slip, please?" she said.

At last, I had an excuse to escape that unsettling pair of blazing eyes. But when I was about to move away from the table, the teacher walked over and took the slip for herself. I was still left in my undeserving spot.

Mrs. Cowell signed the slip without making a fuss. But still felt uneasy standing there.

"Welcome to my class, Antonina Black, right?" the teacher handed me back the signed paper with a smile. "I guess you and Allecra are going to be partners from now on. Please take a seat so we can start our lesson."

My stomach did a somersault. Great, now I had no choice and neither had the girl. Keeping my eyes down, I took my seat again. There was this swagger-handsomeness in her posture when she turned and slumped herself on the chair. She crossed her arms and leaned herself back, resting her feet on the footrest of the table.

Then I heard her mumbling something I didn't understand. My hands balled into fists on my lap. Who does she think she is? I thought resentfully. It wasn't like I was dying to be near her or anything.

People turned their heads away from our table as Mrs. Cowell started the lesson. I dropped my eyes to my book and tried to read again, ignoring the tension.

We learned about stars. Now the teacher was discussing some light year distances and time.

"The light from the nearest stars to our earth takes four years to reach your eyes," Mrs. Cowell said. "Some of the stars might already die hundreds if not thousands of years ago. What you see now may just be their past."

A student raised his hand and asked, "Mrs. Cowell, so based on this theory, if an alien in a galaxy million light years away is looking at us through a telescope right now, what do they see?"

"I know!" another kid said. "They will see dinosaurs!"

A burst of laughter rang around the class.

"It's not possible," a brunette girl spoke up in protest. "Dinosaurs don't project light. The earth isn't a star that radiates light either, so they can't see anything."

"But did you know—" a glass-wearing guy who looked like a true science nerd said, "—that when you look in the mirror, you are seeing yourself a nanosecond ago?"

"So if I stand three feet away, do I look younger?" another student chimed in.

The goofy back row kids laughed and one of them said, "By my Einstein point of view, even from a million light years away, you're still one ugly dude!"

My lips twitched in amusement as I listened to them.

"Alright, kids, that's enough!" Mrs. Cowell said to hush her boisterous class. "For those of you who failed physics last year, I will explain to you again. It takes millions of years for an image to travel that far through space. So by the time the image of the earth gets to the alien, it would have been millions of years since. Plus, time and space are on the same continuum, so if you are traveling through or looking out into space, you're also traveling or looking out either backward or forwards in time."

I took note of that.

After a while, I felt Allecra's stare on the back of my head. I quickly stole a glance from the corner of my eyes and sure enough, she was looking at me, with no shame to hide the fact that she was being rude. My cheeks blushed hot. I bit my bottom lip. Then I heard her sort of groaned from the depth of her throat. I turned to the girl again. She had one hand on her lower stomach. Her beautiful blonde brows knitted together. She looked like she was in pain.

"Are you okay?" I found myself asking out of concern. She shook her head.

"I'm fine," she said. Her voice made my heart falter. I had never heard a voice like this. Each word rolled off her tongue like harmonic music.

Can she be a little less perfect?

"You have a cramp?" I said again.

"Hmm."

"Are you on your period?" I asked in a low whisper, but she shot me an annoyed look. I was startled by her expression and also embarrassed by my

17

own carelessness. I had to remind myself that some people were not that open about stuff like that.

After the lecture was over, the bell rang loudly, signaling the end of the lesson. I felt the weight of the tension rolled off my shoulders at last. The students rose from their seats and started stretching and yelling. I turned to Allecra Knight again, but she was not in her seat anymore. Then I caught a glimpse of her by the door. She moved away fluidly like a graceful ballerina and was gone.

~*~

Piper took me shopping after school. She said that was what she'd always dreamed of doing with a sister since Jay wasn't much of a sister to her. Pytor had given me loads of money before I came here, but my cousin insisted on buying me the things I wanted.

'For friendship's sake,' she said, but I guessed she was just feeling guilty about last morning.

We bought new clothes, shoes and make-up we didn't even plan on buying. At the end of the day, I was the one who felt guilty. Money probably grew on trees in the backyard of the Black's house. One thing I noticed about my cousin was that she would give me compliments on something, but at the same time, she criticized herself.

"I like your legs," she had said. "Mine are too big."

"No, they're not," I said. "They look just fine as long as you could walk."

Piper laughed, but I wasn't trying a joke.

"Have you made any friends?"

"Not really." I shrugged as my hand brushed through a rack of summer t-shirts.

"Well," she said a bit hesitantly. "I heard from my friends' friends that you talked to Allecra Knight."

"Oh, you know her, too?" I asked, turning my head to look at her. Piper huffed and rolled her eyes.

"Please, everyone knows that girl and her siblings," she said. "I meant they're totally weird, aren't they? I know they are damn gorgeous and all that, but still! They never talk to anyone."

18

Even so, her tone had a touch of jealousy in it. But I admitted she was right. Piper looked at me again.

"What did you two talk about?" she asked.

"Nothing much," I said. "I asked her about her period cramp and she almost bit my head off."

My cousin burst out laughing.

"I told you, that girl is not even human," she said, still sniffing. "I bet she's not gonna get a boyfriend dressing and acting like that."

I just wanted to groan. Right, a teenage life is so boring, a boy has to make it better. Because that is the only way anything gets better in life — with boys.

"Anyway, Nina, have you ever dated a boy before?" she asked. I knew my answer would shock her, so I just nodded, hoping she would get the hint, but Piper Black seemed to be living in the world of need-to-know basis.

"Really? You have dated a guy?" she said. "I thought you were gay!"

A staff and a few other customers gave us an eavesdropping glance.

I turned to Piper again.

"Piper, you make it sound like homosexuality is a disability," I said. "But it's just the natural feeling you were born with. It just happens like the color of your eyes. Of course, I have had three boyfriends in the past, but that doesn't stop me from being gay."

"Oh." She just blinked at me.

I waved my hand off and turned away from her. After we finished shopping a while later, we both drove back home in silence. Piper kept peering at me from the side. Her hands grabbed and released the steering wheel nervously.

"What else do you want to ask me, Piper?" I said without looking at her. "I guess it's an honest hour now."

My cousin seemed to blush for getting caught.

"Oh—well—I'm sorry if I have offended you, Nina. But I just wonder—you know—" she said and cleared her throat again. "What is like having sex with a girl?"

I kind of saw that coming.

"I have never had sex with a girl," I said flatly.

"What?" she squeaked. "Never?"

I was pretty sure she was thinking, *'what kind of a lesbian are you?'*

"You don't need to have sex with a girl to know you're a lesbian," I said. "Why does a girl have to have sex with a girl to be considered gay, but a virgin straight girl doesn't get asked how she's straight even if she's never had sex with a guy? What's the difference?"

Piper pursed her lips.

"Then what about sex with guys?"

"Not either."

"I can't believe it!" she said. "So you're a virgin?"

I turned to look at her at last.

"You said it like it's disgusting — like it's a sin or taboo or something," I said. Piper blushed really hard.

"Well, my dad is a full-blown Christian, you know," she murmured. "I think I'm more of a sinner than you, considering that I've already done it."

"Oh," I breathed, ignoring what she had implied that being gay was supposed to be a sin. I let out a sigh, not knowing what to say.

"Just a few times when my boyfriend insisted, though," Piper added like she needed to explain herself.

"Well Piper, people make their own choices with their bodies, I'm not going to judge you," I said a while later. "But I think you should never feel obligated to have sex for someone else's pleasure. It has to mean the same for both of you."

"I know, Nina," she said. "I just don't want to disappoint him."

"You will find yourself disappointing people, no matter how hard you try to please them," I said. "But the person you must never disappoint in this world is yourself. You don't need to use your body as security to make you feel that someone needs you."

Piper's eyes began to tear up. I wasn't sure if my words had affected her or whether it was just the reflection of the streetlight. We were quiet again until she pulled up into the driveway. I was gathering the shopping bags under my feet when I felt Piper's hand touching my shoulder. I looked at her again.

"I wish we had grown up together, Nina," she said.

"If we had, would we still pretend like we don't know each other at school?" I said and then opened the door to get out.

20

_*_

The next day was a Saturday. I had come to school on Friday, which was kind of ridiculous. As usual, the sky was a perfect blue although there were some opaque clouds here and there and the air was hot and humid. I had to get used to not being in a constant cold.

Aunt Vikki had asked me about school and whether the kids were nice to me and if my jetlag was still there. I reassured her with all the positive things I could come up with.

Then I spent most of my time in my room, avoiding Jay. He would frown at me now whenever he saw me, and sometimes he shouted mean things to the people on the TV. In my room, I arranged clothes that I had unpacked into the closet. I put some of the books I had brought with me on the empty shelf and tidied the room up a little. When I was left with nothing else to do, I sat down and wrote things in my notebook.

I got into a habit of writing because of my best friend, Klara, who constantly told me I had a way with words. Then I was hooked, like a fish to the bait. And I would go off on my own to the park and sat by the honeysuckle vines and watched the squirrels and birds. I wrote short stories about them. Sometimes I gave my writing to Klara to read. They were what got me through middle school.

That night, I sat down and wrote about a girl in black.

The weekend passed by at a drop of a hat. My school day started with me sitting in biology class studying flowers. Ms. Peterson spent half an hour teaching us the different flower parts. Inside her class, plants were growing like it was in a greenhouse.

The students in the back almost dosed off. Then Ms. Peterson mentioned that flowers needed bees to procreate. Their ears suddenly perked up and soon the class was roaring with a discussion of how many times a queen bee had orgasms in one day. Most of the girls looked disgusted, while some of the boys blushed in embarrassment. Ms. Peterson hushed them.

My partner was a quiet girl, named Jordan. We both were the quietest people in the class. I had difficulty reading words at first, but Jordan helped me out and things made sense after you looked at them long enough.

During pair work, I found a seed of apple in a pot near my window. It had split open, showing a white stem inside. I picked it up and looked at it like a curious scientist.

"Biology is so cool, isn't it?" I said with a smile. Jordan looked up and then smiled back.

"Yeah." She shrugged.

"An apple tree grows from an apple seed that grows inside an apple from an apple tree," I added.

Jordan giggled.

"Like the chicken and eggs, eh?" she said.

"Mother Nature is so cool, isn't she?" I said. "She always finds a way to make things *procreate*."

Jordan snickered again, louder, causing a few students to look at us. I smiled.

"But maybe not for me," I murmured to myself afterward. "I'm different."

~*~

I hadn't seen a certain blonde since the first day we met. But I figured we only had one class in common anyway. Besides, I didn't look forward to meeting her either.

After school, when the other students were playing sports, in a band, or a drama class, or going somewhere and doing illegal things, I went off to look for a place I could write. I thought of going to the library but dismissed the idea.

I went around a few buildings, past the football field where I spotted Jay and his friends practicing. I learned later that Jay was a quarterback. I didn't know what a quarterback was supposed to do, but it sounded important when he said it.

"Mom, I'm a quarterback! My friends need me to go practice with them. I promise it's not a party." He would say to Aunt Vikki. Although she wasn't convinced, she would let him have his way. All day he would do nothing but complained about everything. Jay needed to spend some time in Russia to learn how lucky he was.

I walked past the tennis courts and got inside a glass building, which housed an indoor swimming pool. It was quiet with no one around. I walked to the back of the building and found a metal stair that led to the rooftop. The wind was blowing gently as I climbed up. There was another door to another building which I ignored, thinking it was probably locked anyway.

I dropped my bag on the floor and sat down with my back against the wall. Then I opened my notebook.

"It was a dark and stormy night," I said out loud and chuckled to myself. Sometimes, I would start with this sentence just for a laugh. I was writing about a girl who was trapped in a coconut, and the thought of Allecra Knight floated into my mind again. I had a feeling that something about her was a mystery wrapped in a banana leaf of ordinariness.

I just wanted to creak open that hard shell of hers and see who she was inside. But the taste of the coconut juice could be sweet or sour.

Then the wind started to pick up. My page kept flipping. I didn't want to stop writing yet so I turned towards the door. I wondered if I could open it and get inside. With that thought, I rose to my feet, brushed off my pants, and picked up my bag again.

Surprisingly, the door was not locked. It opened and closed with a loud metal screech. The door really needed serious oiling. Then I realized it was the attic of a dark storage room. The attic had a small glass window that provided enough light to see through. When my eyes adjusted to the darkness, I walked to a corner and sat down by the window.

About two feet below me was school equipment. There were some stakes for old floats, carts full of basket balls, and some old cardboard boxes that the school might have thrown in.

After sitting there writing for a while, I heard movements coming inside. There were soft voices talking in the shadow but clear enough to be heard in this quiet place.

"You think it's her?" a girl voice's spoke. I looked up from my book and peered through the dark.

"Her name is Antonina Black," answered a familiar angelic voice. I closed my book gently. I would have sneaked out of there if it wasn't because of the mention of my name. I should have crawled out, but it felt like my body was frozen with curiosity.

"Are you sure she's the one?"

That was when I saw them — the beautiful short-haired girl and the blonde mystery. With a jolt of additional shock, I realized I was eavesdropping on them by accident. Allecra's back was turned to me. I could only see the other one's face over her shoulder.

"I'm not sure yet, but she gave me the sensation," Allecra said and I just wanted to ask, *What sensation?* but I knew I couldn't.

"How many times do we have to look for the right one, Alle?" the dark-haired girl said almost with a sigh. "If she isn't the one, then we will have to move out if here."

"I know," Allecra said, sounding tired. The girl in front of her looked sympathetic. She stepped over and ran her fingers through that messy blonde lock. The gesture was like a lover would do more than a sister. My heart leaped forward as I watched them.

"That's alright," Xenon said. "We'll try one more time."

What are they talking about? Why was I mentioned in their conversation? The questions kept running through my mind. Then Xenon came to wrap her arms around Allecra and kissed her cheek over and over.

"Are you still tensed from meeting her?" she whispered softly. Allecra gave a slight nod.

"I can relieve you," Xenon said.

"It's fine," the blonde said. "I can handle it."

"Come on, we all know it hurts," she said and then slowly slipped her hand inside Allecra's pants. I almost squeaked. Allecra let out a groan when Xenon started moving her hand.

"No—Don't!" Allecra tried to speak but her tall frame doubled over by the impact of her sister's touch. I put my hand over my mouth. My breathing was getting too loud, I was afraid they would hear me.

"Be still," Xenon said and lowered herself until she was kneeling between Allecra's legs. She unzipped her pants. The sound of that sharp sliding was unmistakable.

What are they doing?

I wanted to get out of there, but the situation didn't allow it. They would hear me if I dared move, let alone open that stupid rusty door to escape.

Before I realized it myself, I was stuck watching them. Allecra's laborious breathing grew louder in the dark storage room. The girl between her legs tilted her head slightly. There were slurping sounds. I almost died right there in the corner.

'Go!' My mind screamed at me. *'Get the hell out of here!'*

Instead, I was paralyzed by what I saw. I was bound by a spell of shock.

Allecra was groaning now. She said something in a language I had never heard of. It sounded ancient.

"Please, stop—" she said once again. Then she cursed and threw her head back. I almost jumped at her reaction.

"You're out." Xenon was licking her lips. "Come here. I'm ready."

She pulled Allecra by the waist, coaxing her to come closer. Xenon leaned herself back against a pile of boxes. Allecra walked over to her. Xenon reached her hands out and peeled the leather jacket off of the blonde's shoulders, revealing her tattooed arms.

Even in the dark, I could see the strange outlines of ink curving all around her exposed skin. Each stroke looked like a Maori tribal tattoo or some ancient symbols.

Her supposed sister rolled up her short skirt and opened her legs. Allecra slowly went between them and seemed to be guiding something. A moan echoed from their throats at the same time. Their bodies seemed to join together. I took a deep intake of air through my nose and felt my stomach churn.

Xenon wrapped one of her arms around the blonde's shoulders; the other went around to her back. Then she lifted a leg up to the taller girl like she was climbing a tree. She bit her lips and moaned in obvious pleasure. A sensual look on her face became more evident. Allecra was moving the way a guy would do when he does it. Their gasps came out in tandem with one another. Xenon closed her eyes and arched her trembling body against her sister.

"Please, Alle, don't stop," she whimpered. I couldn't see Allecra's face, but I could hear her moans in response. Blood drained from my face. I lost my ability to think. I felt like throwing up, yet I couldn't even move.

Then Xenon looked like she was coming. She started wailing and shuddering, clawing at her sister's back with her nails.

After a minute passed, something stranger happened. It hit me like a wave of otherworldly madness. Allecra's visible tattoos started to glow in a deep neon-like blue light. It spread along her arms and shoulders, following the inked patterns.

My eyes went wide.

And a burst of scream exploded out of my lungs.

CHAPTER 4

I WOKE UP IN THE MIDST of a painful headache. It was a sharp and intense pounding. But then it was gone even before I could check to see whether I had busted my head with something. My notebook was still lying on my lap. The unfinished writing glared at me. I was surprised to see how much I had written on the page. I didn't remember having gone through these lines before. That was strange.

The sky was getting dark as the sun had already set. I wondered how I could fall asleep unceremoniously on the rooftop just like that. I gathered my bag, put my book aside and rose to my feet. My legs felt wobbly and were on pins and needles. I didn't know how long I had been sleeping.

The school campus began to switch the lights on. I gripped the railing for support. My eyes glanced at the door of the other building. For a moment, I got a weird feeling just by looking at it — a strong sense of déjà vu — and I didn't know why. I walked over to the rusty door and tried to open it, but it was locked.

Another stronger feeling flooded through me. I couldn't grasp what it was - something felt like fear or shock? My heart was telling me something my mind couldn't seem to comprehend or remember.

I had woken up with a splitting headache. Obviously, my brain overworked, probably from all the writing. This had never happened before. I shook my head to clear the inconceivable thoughts and left the rooftop.

Once I reached the parking lot, I saw Piper there. She was on the phone and looked as pissed as when she got stuck in the traffic. But I felt eyes following me from behind. It was a chilling sensation. I looked over my shoulder and found three dark figures hovering by a familiar black car. It was the Knight trio.

The big guy stood resting his elbow on the roof of their car while the short-haired girl stood closely beside the blonde one.

Allecra Knight and her siblings were staring at me. Her very presence knocked the breath out of my lungs. She bore the kind of stare that sent a woman's heart hammering by instinct. The other two had a curious expression on their faces.

"Where have you been, Nina?" Piper yelled from across the lot. "I've been trying to call you all day!"

As she was babbling about the long wait and how I made her anxious, my eyes were still glued to the three siblings. I tore my gaze away from them and turned to my fuming cousin.

"I thought you had gone home, but the maid said you weren't there," she said, "Where have you been?"

"I'm sorry. I fell asleep," I said. Piper stepped back and squinted her eyes as if she was staring at something too bright.

"You what?" she said.

"My jet lag," I lied.

"Oh," Piper breathed and then her face muscle relaxed a little. She looked past me. "Are they the Knight kids?"

I fought the urge to look at them and just gripped Piper's hand and steered her away from the spot.

"Don't look at them! Let's go home," I whispered. I didn't know why I had to whisper. It felt like I was reacting to some dangerous predators in the jungle.

"Are you having a problem with them or something?" Piper asked as we walked over to her car. She pressed a button on the remote and the engine automatically hummed to life.

"I don't know," I said once we got inside.

"Yeah, but people say they seem to have this clothe-ripping magnetism about them, don't they?" she said, meaning to be funny, but I didn't laugh. The darkness of the car interior and the familiar perfume from Piper eased my nerves a bit.

Why did they have such a strong effect on me? No, there was only one of them who had such a strong unidentifiable effect on me. I still had a feeling that they were waiting for something— like a predator waiting to catch a prey.

With my jumbled thoughts, my eyes suddenly lost their focus. It was like a vinyl record that had been scratched or the burnt film that played images in a disoriented view. I thought I saw two girls in the dark and eyes glowing in deep unnatural blue. Then it was over. I pressed my thumb and index finger to my eyelids as the headache returned.

"What's wrong, Nina? Are you okay?" Piper asked after she backed the car out. I looked through the tinted window and the Knights were gone.

"Nothing—sorry, I'm just tired," I said with a weak shrug. Piper frowned but she nodded and drove away.

~*~

I was walking through a forest. It was just after sunset and the horizon turned rosy pink. The rest of the sky was a deep, fabulous violet. Stars were already visible, twinkling like fantastic diamonds. Their lights were puny in comparison to the brilliant crescent moon overhead.

I strolled through the small footpath. The moonlight pierced through the trees, casting its pale silvery glow over my thin white dress. In the distance, I heard the trickling of water. It sounded delightfully cool, and I felt thirsty.

I left the beaten path to follow the sound and soon found myself in front of a clearing before a strange cave. The cave entrance was made of blue jade and crystal, which sparkled against the moon and stars in the sky.

I went farther into the beautiful cavern without hesitation. Inside, I found a spring of mineral water. The water streamed out of the rocks. Its laughing sound echoed off the jagged ceiling. The spring seemed to glow with aquatic light.

I knelt by the edge and cupped a handful of cool water to my lips. It was refreshing with a light mineral taste that satisfied my thirst.

Feeling alone and strangely safe in a concealing place, I rose to my feet again and removed my dress. I wriggled out of my underwear, letting each piece fall to the cave floor. Then I kicked off my shoes and unclasped my hair-tie.

With a soft sigh, I stepped into the tickling water.

It felt so good to be free and exposed to the night air. And the cool spring was alluring me to submerge my nakedness.

A feeling of peace washed over my body once the water reached my bare shoulders and neck. The cave was a place of tranquility. It relaxed not only my tensed body but also my troubled mind.

After a while, I languidly rested my back against the steep wall of a smooth boulder and closed my eyes. But the calmness of the spring was interrupted by a burst of air bubbles rising from the bottom.

Something was in the water!

I recoiled from the strange happening. But then I saw the crown of a blonde head emerged. A naked girl appeared with a pair of pale lock-covered breasts.

I gasped at those piercing eyes of greenish blue.

"Allecra?" I heard myself speaking amidst the fear. My heart fluttered and pounded faster as her nude presence surprised me.

"Hello, Nina," she said, her silken voice was low and laced with an internal struggle. For some unknown reason, I was glad to see her, impossibly extremely glad, as if my life was all about her. My reaction was not what I expected. I didn't feel like myself anymore.

"I have been waiting for you for a very long time," she said again as she slowly closed the distance between us. We were nose to nose now. Her breasts were round and beautiful, pressing against mine. She put both hands over the stone wall on either side of me. Her cold breath brushed lightly against my cheeks. Allecra smelled of wonderful spring and exquisite flowery scent.

"I knew one day I would find you," she said. And I nodded back against my will. My heart was still aflutter by her nakedness. My toes tingled and my spine surged with chills.

With an impulsive desire, it was I who threw my arms around Allecra Knight— the intimidating beautiful girl I had come to fear. My hands felt along her spiraling tattoos that ran over her arms and disappeared behind her long blonde hair covering thickly over her back. They were strange beautiful patterns.

Her smooth golden skin glittered with water. I was practically giving myself up to the strong current of lust I had never realized existed within me. Wasting no time, Allecra claimed my mouth with hers. Her taste flowed through me like delicious summer honey. I craved her more than anything. Our kiss was ravenous and passionate. We gasped and moaned in unison.

Her hands squeezed and roamed over my wet skin, sending sparks of sensation over my trembling form. I began to feel a hot throb below my belly. I was getting aroused. Allecra held me like she wanted to merge our bodies into one. I gasped for air once she released my mouth to suck on my neck and collarbones, and down my bare chest. I shuddered in the heat of passion. It was unbelievably surreal.

Allecra twirled me around and effortlessly lifted me up. My legs wrapped around her hourglass waist possessively. She moved us to the shallow water. Then she put me down on the cave floor where my hips were only slightly above the rippling waves.

Our lips came apart wetly, letting our craving eyes locked. I saw the movement of Allecra's slender shoulders and felt a hand over my private. It felt warm and soft, gently fondling and teasing me there. My jaw fell open to the surprisingly wonderful sensation. No one had ever touched me like that. I had never allowed anyone to do this to me. I was speechless at how everything started. Half of me wanted her to stop but the other half longed for her burning touch. My cheeks flushed hot. I was having trouble breathing evenly as I became embarrassingly and ridiculously wet.

Allecra's other hand curved around my waist and adjusted me. All the while, she was gazing at my facial expression. Her bright eyes observed my reaction, which was obviously a positive one. She joined our lips again, this time slowly and sensually. Her tongue wagged everywhere inside my mouth, and it felt rather long. Several times she almost choked me.

And when I was least expected, the blonde slipped a finger inside me, filling me with an intense pleasure. I let out a sharp gasp.

"No," I whimpered. "Don't!"

She moved. I clenched my teeth and gripped her tattooed arms with my clawing hands, but she kept on moving anyway. I whimpered and heaved out of breath.

It felt so undeniably good.

Then she withdrew her hand and embraced me. Allecra lowered her hips a bit and I felt something else nestling between my legs. When she slowly rose up again, it startled me out of my wit.

Something firm and soft was penetrating me, widening me and filling me all at once. My voice got stuck in my throat.

Allecra's hands moved to my waist, pulling me closer to her. I felt myself sheathing over a long fleshy rigid thing. It felt so wrong and yet so amazingly right. I wanted to cry and moan at the same time, but Allecra's mouth soon claimed my lips, silencing me.

She was groaning now. The thing between my legs kept sliding in slowly, causing my heart to race and skip with a wild tingling sensation.

"Allecra...Allecra," I said in a strangled voice. She didn't seem to hear me. Her body shivered in a pleasurable reaction. I felt her hands around my waist tightened as if to prevent me from escaping. And oddly, I felt powerless.

At last, we were joined at the hips. My mind left my body then. My thighs widely spread and wrapped around her elegant waist. I could no longer form any thought, let alone protest her. She had claimed my territory.

I felt so tight and full and deliriously incredible. It took a while to realize how slippery I got when Allecra began to move again, this time with her whole goddess-like body. She held me tighter, and the thing felt hot inside me, throbbing and pulsing like it was alive.

"No..." I managed to speak through my clenched teeth. But she kept moving faster. The pleasure had become increasingly maddening, my body started writhing with pleasure. "Allecra, no!"

There was no doubt what was inside me. Everything started to blur in my vision. My eyesight began to darken and the sound of water splashing slowly ebbed away from my ears. The last bizarre thing I saw was the bright burning turquoise eyes— eyes like glowing galaxies, gazing hypnotically into mine.

The tingling sensual pleasure intensified. There was a wonderful smell that was new to me. I felt Allecra pulsing and growing, driving wave after wave of otherworldly euphoria. Each stroke of that powerful improbable length going deep into my core sent me wailing.

Allecra's strange tattoos began to glow. The bright blue patterns danced like the sparkling light of the crystal cave.

I snapped wide awake and realized I was in my own bed, panting from the orgasmic dream. My body was covered in sweat. I could still feel the waves of pleasure wracked me with sparks of electrical ecstasy.

It was just bizarre. I felt the slippery wetness between my legs and quickly got off my bed to clean up. I had to change into a fresh pair of underwear.

It was almost dawn. But I couldn't go back to sleep out of embarrassment. The dream of Allecra doing unimaginable things to me was still vivid in my mind. I didn't know why I dreamed of her like that.

"That was a stupid, stupid dream!" I hissed to myself, burying my head into the pillow to muffle a scream.

I admitted that I found Allecra Knight extraordinarily fascinating. But my goodness, I couldn't believe I fantasized about her in such a perverted way.

What's wrong with me?

CHAPTER 5

AUNT VIKKI HAD TO VISIT some friends and left early. It was a spring day with a light drizzle in the morning. Piper would have given me a ride if she hadn't promised to pick her friends up. And the way she offered it, "I can still give you a ride, you know," was like she was afraid I would say *Yes*, so I said *'No*. I had already worked out the bus system in this small rich neighborhood and would like to try my luck.

On the bus, I managed to act normal and took a seat with the rest of the strangers. After the bus let us out near the school, I walked the rest of the way. My hair was half damped and plastered on my forehead as I was walking through the campus. Other students sheltered themselves under their umbrellas, I realized I should've brought one too.

Now I was freezing.

Then a growling black car whizzed passed me. I sort of gasped when it almost splashed the water on my feet. I jumped away just in time. It was that Batman car. Piper had told me it was the latest Lamborghini or something. Its backlight glowed bright red as the driver stopped to notice me on the sidewalk. But then the car zoomed off again. I frowned and bit my lips at the rudeness.

Along the hallway, a wall of bulletin board was overflowed with posters and announcements. I wondered if there were job ads there, but I couldn't linger around to look. The first bell already buzzed. Students who hovered around their lockers began to move to their classes.

"Nina!" a male voice called down the hall. I had to make sure it wasn't someone else with the same name as me, but the voice kept calling until I turned. The guy came towards me with a blinding all-American toothpaste commercial smile.

"Hey!" he breathed. "I finally found you again."

I smiled back, trying to put the name to that face. I didn't mean to come off as a stuck-up snob, but I was just terrible at remembering faces and names at the same time. Well, except a certain kind that didn't seem to go away even if I tried to forget.

"Yeah?" I swept my wet hair to one side, a gesture that seemed to freeze the dude a little.

"Where have you been?" he said cheerfully.

"Er—around?" I said, but the guy chuckled back. That was when I remembered his name: Jack Conner. I had practically ditched him on the first day of school here.

"I was trying to catch you after class but you seemed to disappear like a smoke," Jack said.

"Oh," I said. "Why?"

"I just found out that one of my teammates had a cousin from Russia," he told me excitedly as if he had just discovered the law of gravity. "Isn't it a coincidence?"

I didn't think so, but I nodded.

"Anyway, we have a party this weekend, I was wondering..."

Oh gosh — not that good old cliché teenage gathering again. All of a sudden, I felt so ancient. When was the last time I felt the perk of going to one of those parties? I realized I had grown too fast in the past ten months. Ever since Dominika poked her head through my front door, suddenly this fun stuff didn't excite me anymore.

"I'm sorry but I have a class to go. Can we talk about it later?" I said, making a turn to leave. Jack looked a bit hurt, and I felt a little sorry but not sorry at the same time.

"Oh, okay," he said. "I guess I'll see you around then."

In Language Arts, Mrs. Smith had to raise her voice to get everyone's attention. She began to talk about an integral concept of Alchemy.

"This is the secret key to manifesting the Philosopher's Stone, Elixir of Life and immortality in myths. Alchemy is still being used in fictions," she was saying and pointing to the slide show. "This idea is represented in the image of Hermaphroditus - the demigod who holds the assets of both genders."

My ears perked up almost over the top of my head at that. I didn't know why it fascinated me.

"Is that the same name they used in biology for an intersex organism?" someone in the front row asked. At least no one was making any dirty jokes in Mrs. Smith's class.

"Yes," the teacher said. "The name came from a Greek myth. Hermaphroditus was the son of Aphrodite and Hermes. He was a remarkably handsome boy, nursed by Naiads. At the age of fifteen, he grew bored with his surroundings and traveled about the city. It was in the woods of Caria, that he encountered the nymph, Salmacis, in her spring."

My face flushed at the thought of my embarrassing dream in the spring. By now everyone was listening with great interest. No one interrupted or made a snickering noise of amusement.

The teacher paused. We were waiting for her to continue but she just smiled and said, "If you want to know the rest of the story, you better do your own research."

A few of us let out a groan. I tried to swallow back mine.

Mrs. Smith simply moved on to talk about 'Shakespeare's women'. We discussed Portia, Desdemona, Lady Macbeth, all of whom I had no idea about except Juliet. I didn't grow up reading English classics like the kids here. At my old school, we read Asimov, Chekhov, Tolstoy, and Nabokov. Yet my mind was still intrigued by the brand new tale of Hermaphroditus.

A few seconds later, the door swung open. And in came a striking figure, tall and slender like one of those supermodels you envy on the media. Everyone sort of gawked at her. With a raven black shirt, black leather jacket, and messy sandy blonde lock, she walked in like a ghost— just drifting in as if it didn't matter if she was in the wrong class. I kind of suspected that she was.

She mumbled something to Mrs. Smith and handed her a pink slip then drifted to a seat on the other side. I felt the acid inside my stomach churned, and I was afraid I would let out an unladylike burp in the class.

Oh my god, of all the classes in the building and she chose to be in this one?

"Miss. Knight," Mrs. Smith said after a while. "Can I partner you with Nina?"

I almost fainted in my chair.

Mrs. Smith explained later that I was the odd one out in the room since everyone had an editing partner.

"Would you mind, Nina?" she asked.

Yes, actually I would, though I didn't say that to her. Allecra didn't respond beyond a sketchy shrug. Then she turned to me. Her crystalline eyes seemed to stir with inner light as pierced into mine. I felt the heat rose to my cheeks. An alarm began to clang inside my body the way a bronze bell was struck. I went hot all over. I had to turn away from that brilliant stare.

At that moment, I wished I could disappear through the tiny crack of the window.

When the class ended, Allecra saved me the troubles of facing her and just vanished. A huge sigh of relief escaped my lungs. I felt like I had been sitting in an aquarium tank with my thoughts swimming around like fish.

I didn't know if I could survive the tension of having Allecra as my partner.

At lunch break, I was finally desperate enough to go the library. It was huge and well-kept. The windows allowed columns of sunbeam to shine over the bookshelves and reading tables. Small corridors wrapped around the second floor of the library. There were comfy chair and lamps with bright yellow glow dotting every corner.

You would think I would go browsing through piles of ancient books like a nerd in the movie, but I found a computer section and consulted Google instead. I typed the first word I remembered. After a few clicks later, the Hermaphroditus story appeared on the screen. There were a few nude images of Greek characters. I had to minimize the window so that people couldn't look over my shoulders and think it was porn.

"There dwelt a Nymph, not up for hunting or archery:
Unfit for footraces. She the only Naiad not in Diana's band.
Often her sisters would say: "Pick up a javelin, or
bristling quiver, and interrupt your leisure for the chase!"
But she would not pick up a javelin or arrows,
nor trade leisure for the chase.
Instead, she would bathe her beautiful limbs and tend to her hair,
With her waters as a mirror."

I continued to read with a keen interest. Salmacis then saw a brilliant lad like a god walking towards the water. Of course, his godly presence motivated her to do something other than lying about like a potato. The nymph watched him undressing and jumping into the water. Unable to contain her desire, the nymph followed him. She wrapped herself around the boy, forcibly kissing him and touching him. While Hermaphroditus struggled, she called out to the gods and asked that there would never be a day they would ever be apart. Her wish was granted and so their bodies blended into one, becoming a creature of both sexes.

And that was how it started with the first rapist nymph in Greek mythology.

That was it. I was feeling a little jittery with no reason. My heart thumped in my chest. Why am I here researching this ridiculous myth? I thought. Then I left the computer and walked out of the library. Maybe I should've nicely accepted Jack Conner's invitation to his party and just be normal like everyone else.

~*~

Nothing went right the next morning.

No matter how many times I reapplied my eyeliners, those stubborn wings didn't curve the way I wanted.

I tried to put a little of an Egyptian eye. But I looked as if I loved cats too much I wanted everyone to know that through my makeup.

I couldn't decide whether to straighten my hair or curl it, or even to wear maroon lipstick or pink lip-gloss. I didn't know why I even bothered all of a sudden. But the truth behind it was like a cat hiding its claws, waiting to scratch my flesh. I had read somewhere that evolution had installed in females the instinct to find a mate. She would have to attract the one who would fight for her and breed with her.

I never thought about it until I, Antonina Volkova (now Nina Black), who pride myself as a strong independent girl, was now trying to attract a potential mate. Well, except in my case, it was another girl. Not that I was desperate for Allecra Knight to notice me. Maybe a little bit. But somehow, for the first time in a long time, I didn't just want to show up in class but also make an entrance. Geez, I didn't know who I was anymore.

When I got downstairs for breakfast, there was a series of interesting reactions. Piper noticed me and raised an eyebrow. Jay noticed me and pursed his lips. Aunt Vikki, who was drinking her tea while reading the Time magazine, noticed me and smiled.

Maybe, I overdid my dress code a little. My aunt gave me a knowing look when I took a seat opposite her.

"*Dobreya utra, krasivitsa*," Aunt Vikki greeted me good-morning in Russian, but I sort of blushed when she used the last word '*beautiful*'.

"*Dobreya utra*," I replied.

Jay, as usual, looked at me like I was a stone stuck in his shoes. He scowled and stabbed his bacon noisily until Aunt Vikki whacked him with her folded Time.

"Bad *mal'chik*," she said. "What is wrong with you?"

"Mom! What was that for?" Jay cried, rubbing his shoulder with an annoyed look. "And why did you call me a chick?!"

It made me laugh. Then Jay scowled at me again before going back to his meal. It was so nice of my aunt to try and amuse me. She reminded me of my dad. Once upon a time, when I was still the apple of his eyes, he would tell jokes to make me laugh. But I guessed that apple had long rotten and was now replaced by a new seed.

Piper drove me to school as usual.

I thought it was because she didn't want Aunt Vikki to question her about my taking a bus. She had to drop me off in a hurry and swirled around to her friends' house.

In the hallway, I navigated through the honor-roll students. They were in honor of everything and planned to go to Harvard after graduation.

After them came the artsy kids. They were creative in art, music, and drama while I was just there—like talentless.

Then there were the jocks and the cheerleaders. Although I wasn't exactly a lazy bum, my enthusiasm would drop dramatically if I had to do anything physical. So I had no high hope of being a part of the sisterhood.

And after that there was the kind of kids who did community service. They preached the words of god with the capital G. I appreciated their hard work, but I just knew I could never get passed the Pearly Gate anyway.

But what made up the majority were the regular ones. They looked and dressed and thought like everyone else. Their world was two-dimensional. These background kids were best if a movie director wanted to cast them in a zombie movie or in a stampede scene. They didn't stand out nor had perfected themselves in any skill. They annoyed me the most because they acted like a herd of sheep, boring and passive. I would rather hug a cactus than being near those kids. That was why I had lost interests in hanging out in a crowd. Or maybe I was designed to be alone.

I was fortunate that I discovered writing. Writing was the only thing that treated me so kindly in this world. People relish in things that take the pain away.

Before it was time for my first class, I went to my locker and took the books out. But when I turned around again, Jack was right there, grinning his thirty-two teeth at me.

"*Privet!*" he said, trying to impress me with the language.

"Hi, Jack," I said, shifting my bag over my shoulder. "What are you doing here?"

"I wanna know your answer about the party," he said, looking hopeful. "Will you join?"

"I don't know, Jack, I don't know anyone," I said and started to walk.

"But you know me!" he said.

Yeah, barely.

"Come on, Nina," he pleaded. "I will introduce you to new friends. They are going to like you heaps."

I was going to say *'no'* when I saw her standing with her back against the locker. She was laughing at something her brother said.

It was a rare sight to see her smile, let alone laugh.

I watched her messy blonde lock brushed over her shoulders. Her peaked angelic face was glowing. She looked adorable like a child when she was like that. I realized then that Allecra Knight was not as intimidating as she pretended to be. Beneath her poise and stiff posture was another face full of mischief and mirth. Everything about her seemed like a faceted diamond caught in the light.

I wondered why she had to live inside a hard coconut shell.

The thought of her cramming inside a coconut cracked me up. Jack looked at me in confusion.

"What's so funny?" he said.

"Oh, nothing," I said. "Look, Jack, I will think about the party but I can't make any promise since I don't have a ride and I live with my aunt. So if I don't go, just know that it's not you. Are we clear?"

Jack wanted to say something more but the bell rang. I turned back to look at the spot where Allecra stood again, but they were gone.

I clumsily waved goodbye to Jack and took off without a second glance.

Mrs. Smith was already in the class when I entered and so was the blonde mystery. Allecra sat oh-so-majestically on her throne at my table while looking out the window.

How dare she took my window side!

I forgot about making an entrance and stormed towards the ignorant girl.

Then I remembered how I had also taken her seat the first time we met. But that was an honest mistake. Was she doing it on purpose?

But Mrs. Smith started doing a roll call, and I had to forget about being snarky with the girl and sat down.

Her lean body turned half way from me, so I couldn't see her face. But I could have sworn she was smiling.

The teacher began to talk about today's activities. We were going to write a poem about romance. Almost everyone in class cringed.

When I took out my notebook to write, she glanced at it for a brief moment and turned away as if it bothered her. I frowned and ignored her as much as my mind could manage.

I didn't know if Allecra listened to what was being said, but soon she began her writing too.

As we were scribbling away, I glanced at her hands. The fingers of her left hand were tapping in contemplation. Allecra had the most delicate hands I'd ever seen. The fingers were like sea-smoothed shells and long like orange thorns. I just wanted to hold them and kiss each fingertip. Just looking at her hands was doing the same wild things to the secret places of my body. And the remembrance of the dream did not help at all.

Stay focused, Nina!

I tried to concentrate on my work again. Poetry wasn't my forte, but I could come up with two rhyming lines that were packed with imagery of romance or sadness. Some lines didn't have to make any sense and then a final one.

'*When the seagulls fly over the sea,*
They carry the message from me,
It says that we will never be apart,
Even while you are away,
And the seagulls weep for the day,

We come back to each other's heart."

Okay, that was lame.

But you couldn't blame poetry. Poetry is always beautiful even my poem had a delusion of faithful love that made me want to gag.

Mrs. Smith then said we had to read to our partners and let them comment. My heart dropped to my stomach. What did she just say?

I felt Allecra turned to face me at last. My palms were sweaty as I gripped my notebook.

"You first," she said coolly, her bright eyes half shut. My face obviously flushed as I cleared my throat. In the dullest tone, I read the poem in one breath and finished it.

Allecra was silent for a minute and then said, "What's that supposed to mean?"

"A lover is being far away," I explained.

"Then why are the gulls crying?" Allecra asked.

"It's a figure of speech," I said, feeling a little defensive. "You can't state the meaning too plainly."

Allecra arched her perfect blonde brows at me.

"I don't get this thing," she said with a confused look. "Why don't you say what you mean?"

"It's poetry," I told her. "People use it to express their hidden feelings."

"Who invented this writing? It's such a waste of time."

"What? No, it's not!" I protested.

"I bet there's not a single bird out there boohooing about some lovers being away."

"Forget about the seagulls then," I muttered. "Tell me about the rest."

"I forget."

I gritted my teeth to keep from screaming at her. But I reread the whole poem to her.

"I thought you were going to forget about the seagulls."

"No, *you* forget about the seagulls. Now tell me how it is with the rest."

She shrugged and said, "It doesn't make sense."

I looked at her in frustration and exasperation. I didn't know which emotion was the strongest. Allecra just sat there as if she hadn't done anything to ruin my state of mind.

Before I could ask her to show me her poem, the bell rang. The blonde girl just gathered her stuff and got up then left. I wanted to scream.

CHAPTER 6

WHEN I GOT BACK HOME, Aunt Vikki told me that Pyotr had called. He apologized for not checking up on me earlier because Dominika went into labor right after I had left. What a perfect timing. And then the whole baby thing took his overpopulated mind. I couldn't blame him for that. I also had a similar issue and didn't have the heart to even think of him either.

Robert came back from Las Vegas in a good mood. It was like he just came back from a fishing trip with a big fish. He was one of the board members of a shipping company. Robert married my aunt after he lost his heart to her during a business trip to Moscow. My dad said my aunt was really close to my mother before she moved away. Dad wasn't one to talk about my mother much. She died giving birth to me. In fact, I was supposed to be dead before I was even born, and by being alive, I was her murderer.

If she hadn't had me, they could still have another child later and would have lived happily ever after. I used to question why my mom didn't give up on me when she hadn't even seen me yet.

I tried to imagine the pain that raged through her — how I refused to leave her body while trying to split her into halves. And not until she shed her last tear and took her last breath that I was brought into the coldness of this world. But she was gone. Maybe the occurrence of this death and birth that had taken place at the same time was what made me feel different from other people.

At dinner with the family, I stayed quiet and only answered when my aunt asked me. The foods were prepared by the maid. You wouldn't believe how costly it was to hire a cook in this country. I was self-conscious to even eat. Piper was chatting away easily with her dad. And before we knew it, she was asking permission to go to some friend's party.

"I promise I will be back like a Cinderella," she said.

"Then I should ask John to drive you," Robert said. "You don't want to drive that late."

"No, dad! That's embarrassing!" She made a face. "Jason is going to be there, too, right Jason?"

She nudged her twin brother with her elbow. Jay nodded vigorously.

"Yeah, it's a celebration of my team winning the rival high school the other week," he said. "Our coach will join us too, so you don't have to worry."

"Well," Robert said, scratching his double chin in consideration and then nodded. "Alright, you kids can go, but don't break my trust or do something stupid. I won't bail you two out of jail the next day, understand?"

"Yes, sir!" Jay said and mirrored his sister's big grin.

"Honey!" Aunt Vikki turned to her husband. "You're spoiling them again!"

"Oh, mom!" Piper whined. "All my friends go!"

"I'll take care of Piper," Jay added reassuringly. "If she's a bad kid, I'll make sure to change her password on her Candy Crush."

"Oh, since when you take the role of a big brother so seriously?" Piper scoffed. "It should be me to keep you on the leash."

Jay reached his hand out and tousled her hair. Piper shrieked, shielded her head and kicked him under the table.

"Don't fight at the table! You're not five anymore," my aunt hushed them.

"So, when is the party?" my uncle-in-law asked.

"This weekend," Piper turned to say excitedly.

"Oh." Robert looked at his wife. "Honey, did you tell the kids yet?"

Aunt Vikki shook her head.

"Tell us what?" Jay asked.

"Actually, we were planning our anniversary this weekend," my aunt said a bit shyly.

"Oh my god!" Piper gasped. "Your anniversary! I totally forgot."

"Will we have a celebration on a cruise ship again?" Jay asked curiously.

"Well, no, your mom and I just want to have a getaway vacation this time," his father said. "We've always wanted to have a quiet time for once. We're thinking about Fiji or Hawaii, but we haven't decided yet."

"And now I'm a bit worried about leaving you kids for a whole week," Aunt Vikki said.

"No, mom, don't be! We're old enough to take care of ourselves," Jay said with a puffed chest. "Remember that one summer you left to Florida and we didn't burn down the house or anything?"

I pushed my broccoli into my mouth as I listened to the conversation. The taste was a bit blunt for my liking.

"I'm just afraid when the cat is away, the mice will play," Aunt Vikki said.

"Geez, mom!" Jay groaned. "You need to quit using all that cheesy sayings!"

"I think you two should go. You deserve a break," Piper said in encouragement. "If there is anything wrong, I will hold Jason responsible."

"Hey!"

Robert chuckled and then looked at my aunt. I knew he was the first to give in.

"Maybe we should let them learn how to be independent, darling," he said. "Strict parents only produce rebellious kids."

"But honey, Nina just got here not that long. I don't think it's a good idea to leave her like that," she said. Suddenly, everyone's heads turned to me as if they just remembered I was there.

"Oh, don't worry about me," I said. "I'm totally fine with that. Pyo—I meant my dad let me stay home by myself all the times."

"Yes, mom, she'll be with me anyway," Piper said.

Robert had a slight look of discomfort when he heard that, but only I noticed. Aunt Vikki seemed like she was in a deep thought. I kept my eyes on my hot buttery pasta.

"Oh and Nina can also come to the party with us," Jay said all of a sudden, making me look up from my plate. "So she won't get bored at home, you know."

I narrowed my eyes at him, but Jay pretended not to notice. After a long while later, Aunt Vikki nodded.

"Alright then," she said at last. "But you will have a lot of rules from me, are we clear?"

The twins smiled back, simply overjoyed.

After the meal, I went back to my room and started doing my homework. I finished an evolution paper for Bio II and a printed report for European History. Now I was trying to tackle five problems for my math homework. I thought that math was probably the reason why teens go into depression, but Mr. Oliveira made it funny. He talked about limits, logarithm, and linear like they were beautiful women. It was hard not to feel his passion with math even it still frustrated me the way Allecra frustrated me.

Thinking about that one blonde always made my heart beat a little faster, and I hated myself for that. Then I realized I had to write a diary entry for Mrs. Smith's class. I didn't know what to write about.

As I was thinking, I heard a knock on the door. I opened it and found Jay standing there.

"Yes?" My tone was sharp, even I hadn't meant to.

Jay looked nervous. He scratched the back of his neck, but when he didn't say anything, I yanked the door to close.

"Nina, wait!" he said, stopping me. "I just want to talk to you about the whole party thing."

"Don't worry. I'm not going," I said. "You and Piper can go ahead and have fun."

"No, it's not that," Jay said, licking his dry lips. "I—er—sort of told my friends about you coming from Russia, and they asked me to invite you."

"So that you can display your Russian gay cousin around?" I said without breaking my stare.

Jay's eyes grew wide and his ears went red.

"No! God, no! That's not what I meant!"

"Well, tell them I can't go," I said and started to close the door again when Jay arrested it with his strong hand.

"No, please, Nina, I know we haven't been on a good term lately. But please, do me a favor. I already said you would join us," he pleaded, looking at me with his big cow-like eyes. "They just want to make friends."

"Why?" I asked.

"Look, I'm sorry for how I have been acting around you," he said. "I knew I'm a total jerk but I was just a little upset that—that—you—"

"You're a homophobic beef brain, you know that?" I said.

Jay looked at me, blinking.

"A homophobic what?" he said and tried to muffle a laugh. "Nina, where did you learn to curse like that?"

"From the children books I read while I was learning English," I said. "And there is no amount of cootie shot in the world could cure you of this phobia, I tell you."

Jay burst out laughing. Watching my cousin in his ridiculous hysteria, I had to press my lips together to hide my smile. I sort of agreed that my cursing ability would make even a five-year-old roll eyes.

After Jay got his breath back, he wiped his tears and looked at me again.

"I'm so sorry for everything that wedged its way between us, Nina. We could have had a lot of bonding time together if I wasn't much of a beef brain to you."

"A homophobic one, don't you forget that," I said.

"Yes, yes, I know!" He put his hands together like he was praying. "But please, you're my cousin. Let's rejoice and start over again. I will be more open-minded this time, and I swear, you won't regret it, please!"

I looked back at him. Jay tried to appear miserable and all sincere. I yanked the door close on his face. But after a few seconds, I opened it again.

"I'll think about your party invitation," I said to him. "Now, good night."

Jay, who had looked disappointed just a moment ago, lit up again.

"Thank you, Ni—"

I slammed the door shut.

~*~

Klara's email arrived this morning. It was more entertaining than a copy of People magazine, with all the juicy gossips from my old school. Not that I cared about that stuff, but then she also wrote that Yuliya and Erik were getting together. She even capitalized the headline. Well, Erik was my ex-boyfriend. He was nice at first, but when he started complaining to his friends that I didn't satisfy his needs, I right out dumped him in the face.

Yuliya's family was the world's professional old-fashion people. I guessed Erik would have to satisfy his needs all by himself again.

In biology, I handed my report to Ms. Peterson.

She looked at it and smiled at me.

"The Flaws of Evolution?" she said with a raised brow. "Sounds like an interesting topic. I'm looking forward to hearing your presentation, Nina."

"Wait, I have to present it?" I asked. Jordan giggled at the horrified look on my face.

"Don't worry. You're going to do great, Nina," the teacher said and turned away. Jordan patted my back.

"Didn't know you were shy," she said.

I wasn't shy, but sometimes people didn't know the difference between being shy and not wanting attentions.

"So what false image did you have of me?" I asked her.

"You have no false images, but you're like a chameleon," she said. "You don't want people to know much about you. But my mom told me that quiet people are strong people."

Klara used to tell me the same thing when she first met me. On that day, when a cockroach crawled over her desk, she instantly turned opera singer. I found an empty plastic cup and covered the cockroach with it then inserted a paper underneath. She looked at me like I had single-handedly taken down a fire-breathing dragon. I was scared, too, but sometimes when you look past your fear, even if you are frightened down to your tail bone, you can do what is required of you.

Ms. Peterson was talking about female genes.

"Inside of each one of your cell, there are two meters of DNA— two meters in every single cell!" she said as if she had never heard anything as wonderful.

She rolled down a cut-out picture of the chromosome, showing twenty-two of them that found their matching pairs except for the twenty-third ones. Without a doubt, I knew what the pair was, the sex chromosome.

"It isn't lined up in order like what you see on the picture. In reality, your DNA gets tangled up worse than a headphone in your bags. You got twenty-three chromosomes from you mom mixed with twenty-three from you dad," she said, pointing at the image. "We learned that two Xs make you female and an X to a Y makes you male. For a male, sex chromosome is always active for life, but for female, one of her X chromosomes has to be deactivated for proper development."

"Why is that?" someone asked.

"It's just the natural thing for our species so that women can survive to adulthood," she said. "If you could look at a woman skin and really see where the X chromosome has been inactivated, you will see stripy patterns all over her body."

"Really? Why don't I see any patterns on my skin then?" another girl said as she turned her hand over in front of her.

"Of course not! You couldn't see that on humans unless you're like a Calico cat," the teacher said. "Haven't you noticed that only female Calico cats have more than one color on their coats?"

"If women really have patterns, then that's another way to link them to cat personality, mysterious and make no sense," Michael said and started laughing until one of the girls stuffed his mouth with a paper ball.

"Just shut up."

And the whole class burst out laughing, including the teacher.

~*~

In science class, my heart raced again because I knew whom I was going to put up with. I walked in and took my seat by the window. Allecra hadn't arrived yet. More students kept pouring in as the clock ticked away.

Without meaning to, I found myself glancing at the door more often than usual. To distract myself, I took out my notebook, but I wasn't in the mood to write anything, or that I just couldn't think straight (no pun intended). Instead, I started doodling an ugly little cartoon girl, wearing a black jacket with wild hair. A flock of seagulls flew over her head and a bubble that screamed, 'It doesn't make sense!'

I giggled to myself.

"What's that?" a voice said beside me. I jumped up with an uncharacteristic gasp and turned to see pools of stirring galaxies. Allecra's eyes twinkled as she was peering over my shoulder. I could feel her breath on my heated cheek. My heart beat all the way to my throat.

How could I not sense her coming? I almost always sensed people when they invaded my personal space. It was like built-in radar for me, but Allecra Knight made all the functions in my body jumble like parched peas.

She leaned in closer to look at my doodles, and her perfect jawline distracted me for a minute. Before I could cover the page with my hands, Allecra scooped the book up faster than I could blink.

"That's me, isn't it?" she said, still looking at my cartoons. My face had gone from red to ghost color. She was going to kill me, wasn't she? Then the girl did something that surprised me. She pulled out her black ink pen and drew another bubble next to one of the seagulls then wrote, 'Booo hooo hooo!'

"That's more like it," she said after she finished. Was that her way of saying 'sorry' after brutally mocked my poem? My lips turned up into a betraying smile. Allecra turned around and handed my notebook back.

She gave me a small smile, which made me drop the book. It bounced off my chair and skidded on the floor under the desk.

We looked at each other and then wordlessly bent to retrieve the book at the same time. Our heads tilted. I didn't know how it all started, but the next thing I knew, my lips were brushing against Allecra's neck. We both froze with my lips rested there on her skin. My nose caught the unique scent of her fragrant blonde hair.

I jerked myself back from her. Allecra was staring at me. Her eyes seemed to get brighter than usual. My face reddened like ripe cherries.

Then she picked the book up and handed it to me again. We sat back on our chairs as if nothing had happened. No one in the class seemed to notice anything. They were laughing and chatting away among themselves. But my face was still hot.

Did I just kiss her neck? How the heck did I end up kissing her neck?

I had never found any real attraction towards a girl before even I was gay. It was unmistakable that something about Allecra bewitched me.

I didn't dare look at her again. We both sat in silence until Mrs. Cowell barged into the room and apologized for being a little late today.

As my mind kept rewinding the moment my lips were on Allecra's skin, she was just staring blankly ahead. When my eyes fell on the side of her neck, I got a glimpse of her strange tattoo peeping out of the collar of her jacket. Then a bright flash burst into my retinas out of nowhere. It was like when you look up at the sun and the brightness attacks your vision. I closed my eyes in pain, but behind them, I saw some glowing patterns on a smooth back of someone. I saw two pairs of glowing eyes and heard my own piercing scream. I dropped my head in my hands as a wave of dizziness hit me.

"Are you okay?" Allecra's voice sounded close by. As soon as she said it, the scene began to clear away. I waved my hand to reassure her that I was fine.

"Just the headache," I said. When I opened my eyes again, I found Allecra staring at me. There was a look on her face that I couldn't seem to understand. It wasn't just a concern but also something else.

When the bell rang at the end of the class, she simply stood up and walked away without another word.

CHAPTER 7

I WENT QUIETLY DOWNSTAIRS to knock on Aunt Vikki's office. There was light under the door, and I heard my aunt approaching from the inside.

"Piper, is that you?" she said.

"No, it's me," I replied. When my aunt opened the door and saw me, she smiled.

"Oh, Nina, please come on in," she said and held the door wider for me. Aunt Vikki was her husband's personal accountant. She worked from home most of the time and only went out to meetings if need be.

Inside the room, there was a smaller fireplace, which didn't burn real fire. It was an electronic heating system.

"Sit down with me," she said, gesturing to the couch. "I haven't had any time alone with you much."

I huddled up close to the fire for it was freezing cold at night in this big house. Aunt Vikki put her work away.

"I'm sorry to interrupt you," I said, but she just shook her head.

"No worries. My work can wait." She smiled again. "How are you doing with school and everything?"

"I've caught up with most of my classes," I told her. "It's a bit easier here than back at home actually."

"I'm glad you don't feel too much pressure," she said and smoothed my hair. "If there is anything I can help you with, don't keep quiet."

I nodded back. I hadn't seen my aunt in person for many years, saved that one winter she visited us in Moscow. I was only twelve at that time. My aunt was a beautiful woman and so caring. When she saw I was shivering, she got up to grab a blanket and wrapped it around my shoulders. Her arms were around me the whole time with a kind honest look. I felt like that was what my mother would do to me.

Before I knew it, Aunt Vikki started telling me about mom. It took me awhile to realize she understood how I must have felt. She told me things I never knew about her— how my mom was a total nerd and had set her

53

heart to go to a university and study Russian Literature. But then she fell in love with my father and dropped her dream and married him.

I wondered what was so special about Pyotr Volkov.

From the top drawer of her desk, Aunt Vikki took out a framed picture of two young women in their sky gears and sleds.

"It was taken during a heavy winter in Moscow," she told me and handed me the photo to look. I stared at the beautiful woman beside my aunt, and I could feel my tears burning from the inside of my head. Aunt Vikki rubbed one hand across her eyes.

"I'm sorry if that saddens you, Nina," she apologized, but I shook my head.

"I'm glad you still have this picture."

"I will make a copy for you if you want," she offered.

"That's okay." I smiled back. "I have seen her pictures. It's just this one is not with my dad."

"Your father loves you, Nina," my aunt said in a rather pity tone. "He just has a lot on his plate right now, but I'm sure he thinks better of your future. That's why he sent you here."

I didn't say anything. I wished I could believe my aunt, but I just couldn't. I heard her sigh and got up from the couch again.

"It's late now. You better get back to bed."

I looked up from the picture and remembered why I was here.

"Actually, Aunt Vikki, I wanted to talk to you about something else," I said, causing her to raise an eyebrow.

"Oh, what is it?"

"Er...I just think that the cost to hire a cook is quite outrageous here," I started a little awkwardly. "I think during your absence, we don't need to spend much money on the cook. I've been pretty good at reading recipes, and I know how to cook quite well if I dare say so myself. I think if you allow me, I can make do with that."

My aunt just stood there and looked sort of amused hearing my proposal.

"You remind me so much of your mother," she said at last. "She always tried make people's lives easier."

I felt a blush on my cheeks at her compliment. Aunt Vikki came forward to hug me. I held her back in my arms.

"When your mother called to tell me she was pregnant with you," my aunt said, "she sounded happier than she'd ever sounded in her whole life."

~*~

The next day, I gave a presentation on my bio II report. Everyone looked at me with hopeful eyes. I swallowed and began to speak. It was harder than when I did it in my own language, but I had no choice.

"My report is about the Flaws of Evolution," I started in a shortened breath and paused for a moment. "We all know that through evolution, humans can adapt to their environment and reproduce."

All eyes were on me, blinking and listening. Jordan gave me an encouraging nod.

"But my report is about the hidden imperfection of human race, mainly, of women," I said with a little more force of confidence after I had started.

A few girls sitting at the front exchanged a curious look, but I carried on.

"Now, we know why women would not survive ten months of pregnancy for they could die giving birth. The first stage of human development starts with the head, which has to grow big for intellectual and survival purposes. But the woman's pelvic bones are not well-developed enough to push anything with that size. That's why it's extremely painful during labor." I clicked on the slide show that had a picture of a baby inside the womb. I glanced briefly at Ms. Peterson, who wore a slight smile on her lips.

"So babies have to be born even they actually need longer time to develop, it's why they're such a mess. Human mothers have not evolved enough to have an easy labor like most mammals. It's kind of a huge and secret flaw in our evolution that we don't really notice. So if a woman's body can't cope with this insane pain during childbirth, she can die. And if you think it's normal to give birth, it's actually not. It's natural, but it's not normal."

I finished my report. No one asked questions. Or they didn't know what to ask.

"Well done, Nina," Ms. Peterson said after a while later.

I strode back to my desk and plopped down in my chair as if my energy was all drained.

"You did great," Jordan said, smiling sweetly.

"Thank you," I said.

"You sounded passionate about this," she added. "It's a very interesting topic."

"My mom died giving birth to me," I told her. Jordan's mouth fell open. She looked at me long and hard as if she didn't know what to say. I shouldn't have said that, but it just came out. I gave her a weak smile and waved her look away. The last thing I wanted was sympathy.

In Language Arts, I didn't feel quite as snarky as I wanted to with Allecra Knight. I got to where she was sitting by the window and sat down. Allecra had always been like a stone, but now she seemed even more unresponsive. I still thought of the neck-kissing incident. I couldn't tell if she had minded and decided to ignore me for that.

Mrs. Smith started the class as soon as the bell rang.

"Listen, class!" she said. "You're supposed to give your editing partner your stuff to read and comment on with constructive criticism, alright? You are to write a personal creative essay. It's whatever you want to write about. Now, let's get to work."

I didn't quite know anything personal and creative to write about, so I just wrote things off the top of my head. Feet crossed, Allecra turned to work with her eyes half-shut as usual. I was dying to know what she was going to write about and ready to be one hell of a critic to her. The class went so silent with students concentrating on their writing.

It continued like that until the teacher said to give the writing to our partners. Allecra's long white hand reached for my pages unapologetically. But in turn, she handed me back hers.

I started to read her writing but immediately put it down.

"What kind of language is this?" I said to her. I had to wave her papers to get her attention. "I can't read this."

"It's Arzurian," she said.

"What?" I blinked stupidly back, but Allecra didn't say anything and just turned her gaze back at my writing. I wrote about a man, who was trapped inside an acorn — sort of a brother to the girl in the coconut.

Then the bell went off.

"Alright class, give your partners back their writing and we will come back to discuss it later," the teacher said.

Allecra and I hadn't even finished ours. She just handed back my papers. I was still frowning at what she had said. Instead of leaving, as usual, she seemed to linger there. After I got my books in my bag and was ready to go to lunch. Allecra stood up, too. I lifted my face to see her staring back at me. I froze on my track.

"Come with me," she said and reached her hand out to take mine. The moment our skins touched it was like a million volts of electricity zapped through my body. If it was real electricity, I would be dead by now. Allecra towed me along without saying anything. I couldn't find a word to speak, let alone asking where she was taking me.

We weaved through the crowded hallways. Some students stared at us while other whispered to each other. Of course, it was Allecra Knight I was holding hand with. They must be surprised.

Not until I realized we were out of people's sight that I mustered up the courage to ask her.

"Where are you taking me?" I said in a panic.

"Somewhere you might know," she said and kept speed-walking. Allecra went past the baseball field and the gym, going towards the pool building. We went around it and climbed up the metal stairs to the rooftop.

I was having trouble catching my breath when she finally stopped.

Gosh, was she a mountain goat in her past life or what?

"Here," she said without a desperate gasp for air or anything. I noticed she was pointing to the small rusty door at a corner of the wall.

"Ye—yes?" I said, still breathing heavily. We were on the rooftop where I had come to sit and write on my notebook.

"Remember anything?" Allecra asked.

"How do you know this place?" I said, staring back at her in confusion. But she turned to the door and opened it effortlessly. Wasn't the door locked the last time I had tried it? Allecra motioned for me to follow her. I stepped forward hesitantly. Once my eyes adjusted to the dark, I discovered that it was an attic. Below were school equipment, carts of valley balls and floats, and cardboard boxes.

"Why did you bring me here?" I asked in suspicion. Allecra slowly turned around to look at me. Her lips pressed together as if she was trying to hold back some secret from crawling out. We stood like that in a long stretching silence. Then she stepped towards me. The darkness around us made her quite intimidating. I took a step back, holding my bag in front of me like it was my only protection.

"Nina," she said in a soft tone, so soft, it sounded like a plea. Her eyes sparkled like glittering diamonds. Her smooth face looked tensed with inner conflicts. My heart began to pound wildly, and my knees started trembling. I had forgotten about how scary she could be. Maybe it was the effect of my crazy dreams that added to it.

"I think we should go back," I said and turned to the small door when her strong hands pulled me to her. Allecra spun me around to face her and wrapped her arms over my body. My bag dropped onto the dusty floor with a muffled thud.

Then all I could feel was her lips and tongue all over my mouth. I had no voice left, not even my breath. She had taken it all, including my strength. My struggle was unsurprisingly feeble. I came to realize how strong she was— so strong that I couldn't even move in her death-like grip.

Allecra delved her tongue deeper into my mouth, filling it with sleek softness. I felt like I was reliving the dream all over again. Only this time, it was real. Her taste made the nerves in my body tingle, and that embarrassed me to no end. It was a strange intoxicating feeling — to feel wanted by Allecra Knight.

It excited me.

Her long tongue was like a live eel in my mouth. I could barely breathe. Allecra's hands wound around my body, pressing me against hers. My eyes fluttered and then closed from her passionate kiss. There were only the quiet noises of heavy breathing between us. I began to melt like hot butter. With that merciless tongue of hers inside my mouth, I could do nothing but surrender. Despite my confused whimpers, I was kissing her back sooner than I would like to. My hands felt the outlines of her slender body. Each part was so perfectly formed.

After a moment later, Allecra broke our kiss, making a wet sound from my blushed lips.

"Xenon is going to kill me," she said in a breathless whisper. "But I just couldn't help it."

"What—what do you mean?" I whispered back.

"I wasn't supposed to—you're not ready—"

"Ready for what?"

She pushed me against the wall and brought her face to mine and kissed me again. But she pulled away quickly. Her hands cupped my cheeks, keeping my head still. Our noses almost touched. Allecra was staring at me with those beautiful brilliant eyes. They were neither green nor blue, but somewhere between. And in that moment, I swear I could see strange light ignited like blue fire from the tissues of her irises. Something else began to stir up inside her body, but I couldn't place what it was.

Just like that, Allecra released me and stepped away. For the first time, she was breathing hard. My own mind was unreliable. I understood nothing of what was going on.

Allecra looked at me, frowning as if it was my fault that she had done what she had done. I just stood there, speechless. After a while, she turned her perfect torso away and walked out of the dark attic, leaving me to the shock and confusion all by myself.

CHAPTER 8

THERE MUST BE AN UNSPOKEN rule out there that says you don't leave a girl like that after you've kissed her senseless. I wished I had learned how to cope with someone like Allecra Knight before I came here.

The day that followed the incident, I didn't see her again at school. Besides, we didn't have any other class together except Language Art and Science.

But every once in a blue moon, I would spot her and her siblings outside the school building, but they were constantly talking. I never saw them in the cafeteria at lunch break, and I knew myself better than to muster up the courage to confront Allecra about *the kiss*.

I wondered if she had regretted it. I wanted so badly to understand the motive of her intimacy towards me, but I found no clue.

Why did she do that to me and said stuff that made no sense?

Yet the feeling of our lips melting into each other still burned in my memory. With a sunken heart, I knew deep down that Allecra's touch would mark me for the rest of my life.

There were other things about her that I couldn't stop molding around in my mind. There was something unusual that I had come to notice later. I tried to convince myself that what I saw was just a reflection of the light. Her eyes couldn't have glowed, could they? And her tongue was perfectly fine. My mind might have overworked, which made me temporary delusional.

Yet again, when we kissed, I could feel her body changed. Something was aching and craving inside her. It was unmistakable how she wanted me in that moment. Thinking back, this thought terrified me, what could she have done if she didn't break it off? Would she and I have gone further? My body flushed all over just thinking about it. Did I want it if she were to take me? I felt my heart clenched at the answer. Yes, I wanted it. It was embarrassing how I wanted her already while we had barely known each other.

That left me completely and utterly miserable.

Aunt Vikki and Robert were preparing for their vacation. Jay and Piper were excited for them although I knew they were also excited for a different reason. But what shocked me more than anything thing was when my aunt told me she had bought me a car.

"A car?" I said.

"I knew it was hard for you to ride with Piper," she said a bit apologetically. I tried not to correct her that it was hard for Piper, not me. But my aunt reassured me that she already talked about it with her husband and that it was mostly her money. She almost made me cry right there at the table during dinner.

Nobody seemed overly surprised when the car was delivered to their front garden, except me. I felt like I had never seen a car so new in my life. It was a very cute and very red Mini Cooper with two white lines going across the hood. While the dealer talked to my aunt and her husband about the license and stuff, my cousins were feeling around the Cooper. They teased about wanting to switch theirs with mine.

"Now you don't have to take a bus when I have to pick up my friends anymore," Piper whispered to me with a relieved smile. I smiled back for it was hard to be sarcastic with her in a moment like this.

During that week, Jack Conner was becoming increasingly impossible to avoid. He waited for me outside the class and made excuses to walk with me to the parking lot.

For the two classes I had been looking forward to with Allecra, it turned out she wasn't there. I was getting upset and angry, but there was nothing I could do. It was obvious she was avoiding me.

But after a whole week passed by, she reappeared like a zombie walking into the room. She would be sitting at her desk and practically ignored me for the rest of the period. Soon after the class was over, she would just perfect her invisibility and disappeared.

No words could describe how frustrated and disappointed I was.

What was I to her? A toy-girl she could go around kissing and tossing aside after she had tried it? She left me cold and depressed, and I wasn't even the one to come her for crying out loud!

I usually ate my lunch alone outside under a dark pine tree where there were green grass and fresher air. The cafeteria was only excited when you wanted to make an impression. I had out-grown this teenage phase. In fact, after Allecra literally ignored my whole existence, I even lost my appetite. It wasn't long until Jack asked me to join his table with his group of friends. I tried to refuse but he was, again, impossible.

Jack introduced me to his clan one day. I only remembered a few of them, because they were also in some of my classes. But they made an effort to talk to me and being nice. The boys looked like some sport model-wannabes with their gelled hair and aftershave smell.

"I like your hair," Nathan, the guy from my math class said. "You could pass as a real-life Rapunzel, you know."

I smiled. Jack frowned at his friend. His other friend, Andrew, rested his chin on his folded arms and looked at me like some kind of mutt that wished you would take him home. Only I would never take him home.

The other girls, Phoebe, Claudia and Jessica laughed at some jokes. They all had high ponytails and perfect makeup. They were the cheerleaders. After a while, we were joined by another girl. But when I looked up from my lunch tray, I realized it was my cousin. Without anyone noticing, we both froze at the same time.

"Hey, Piper, come and meet Nina, she's just moved from Russia. I also invited her to our party this weekend," Jack said excitedly. Piper responded with a stiff grin and murmured a soft, "Hi".

She actually didn't plan on telling them that I was her cousin, and I just played along. Giving her a fake smile back, I stayed quiet as she sat down at the farthest chair of the table. The whole lunch break, we didn't make any eye contact. She was probably resenting me for being there.

After the bell rang, releasing us from the awkwardness, I stood up and retrieved my bag. But when I glanced at my cousin again, a shock hit me like a lightning. Piper leaned in to kiss Jack, but he briefly turned away pretending not to notice. I knew he didn't want me to see it, and a look of hurt registered on Piper's face. I balled my hands into fists. But before I could do anything to save my cousin from that potential player, I dashed out of there. It was none of my business.

Jack called out to me, but I didn't turn.

In biology, I sat with Jordan as usual. We hadn't talked much since the day I gave my oral report. I knew I shouldn't have told her about my mom. It must have made her uncomfortable. But Jordan didn't bring it up again, which was a good thing. We carried out our work with little to no conversation at all.

Today, as we were taking notes, Jordan turned to me.

"Don't cut it," she said, reaching out to touch my hair. Normally girls would do that to me like they wished it were theirs, but she seemed to just appreciate what she saw.

"Your hair, I mean," she added and withdrew her hand with a smile. Her dark eyelashes were long and feathery, but she hardly wore any makeup. I realized Jordan had a pleasant face that needed no extra help anyway. With her big greenish eyes and sun-bleached hair, she was like most Californian beach girls.

Jordan was not what I would describe as beautiful. But she was pretty in her own way. The main impression I got from her was she didn't mind being plain and ordinary, and that she didn't bother to wear anything mainstream.

Maybe I should surround myself with more ordinariness rather than chase after the mystery.

That night after successfully avoiding Piper, I went to my room and started writing in my notebook. The images of a certain blonde always seemed to poke their ways into my mind. I wrote the title of the writing, *"Trapped"*.

"All my life I lived in an acorn.
It was cramped and dark.
But what pained me was I had no way. The outside world seemed scary to be exposed to. If no one out there happened to find the acorn, if no one cracked it, then I would be forever trapped.
To live all my life in the nut, and maybe even die there alone and lonely.
I died in the acorn years later, though.
Then they found the nut and cracked it and found me shrunk and crumpled inside.
"What a pity!"
"If only we had known it earlier..."
"Then maybe we could save her..."
"Maybe there are more of them trapped in like that..."
'We should try to save them from their shells."
"No used! A waste of time! There are too many of them!"

They might be right or they might wrong. A person who chooses to live in a coconut is even worse, the shell is hard and the taste might be sour."

_*_

The next morning, Piper confronted me on my way to my car.

"We need to talk," she said.

"I didn't know they were your friends, Piper." I stepped around her.

"It doesn't matter anymore," she said, following me. "I just want you to know that I can't lose my boyfriend."

I stopped and turned to look at my cousin again.

"What are you talking about?"

"I'm blonde, but I'm not dumb, Nina," she said. "Jack is my boyfriend. He keeps mentioning you. We're having a rough time lately, but I don't want to break up with him."

"Isn't that what between you and him?" I said. "Look, Piper, you can do better than that."

I walked off and got in the car before driving away.

It was Friday.

The last day I got to see Allecra again since our last unspoken contact. When I got to Language Arts, she was already there. Her face looked straight out of the window in an attempt to ignore me as usual. I wasn't going to let her treat me like that anymore.

I sat down, willing her to turn to me. She didn't move, not until Mrs. Smith arrived. And when she did notice me, she acted like I wasn't there — like I was transparent or something she didn't care.

Nice try, Allecra.

The class proceeded slowly. Mrs. Smith told us to edit each other's writing. I didn't feel like writing anything new, so I just half-heartedly handed Allecra's the writing I did last night. I didn't expect her to give me back anything, but this time, she surprised me once again. Her beautiful hand slid a neatly typed page over to me.

I looked at it like it was a time-bomb.

"Read," she said, almost like a command and then turned away again. My eyebrows still knitted together as I looked back at her. She kept on reading my writing. I turned back and picked up her work.

64

It was a relief that everything was actually written in English and not some weird Picasso-ish symbols. I started reading whatever Allecra finally decided to contribute to our partnership, though she still had no sense of decency to give me a proper apology whatsoever.

But then I forgot the time and that I was reading her writing at all. It was just like I only let myself being carried by the voice that seemed to echo off the page. A dark, sure voice talked in pure poetry about the space and constellations and the black holes and the galaxies. The voice transferred me through a wormhole into the different universe.

How could she do that?

The way she wrote was sharp and raw, yet beautiful like a star was beautiful. The idea was deep even the language was simple. The words came together smoothly like the surface of a waveless sea. Each of her prose was written like spoken haiku. Every sentence made your mind sing and your heart dance.

I was blown away by her ability to place the best words in the right places and made it so effortless and perfect. How could she write off the entire universe and the tiny things that made up life so beautifully?

And all this came out of Allecra Knight?

She was a better writer than *me*.

I knew that it sounded kind of snobbish to say, but when you can write quite well yourself, the knowledge of how hard it is to do it, how much effort it takes to get things right, makes you a better judge of someone else's work. It makes me realize when to appreciate writing that is good.

Just like I appreciated Allecra's now.

So when it was time to give it back, all I could do was giving her a look of utter surprise.

"Where did you learn to write like that?" I asked curiously.

"Boredom." She shrugged with a nonchalant look.

I couldn't help feeling a little jealous. At last, she turned her face to me.

"Yours is not bad," she said and handed me back the book. When I reached my hand out to get it, our fingers brushed. I pretended not to notice, but she still didn't turn away.

"I'm sorry about that day," she said quietly like she really meant it. The heat of my anger for the past week instantly vaporized.

"Never mind," I said brashly. "Just don't kiss me again if you never wanted to."

Allecra frowned then it followed by an amused smile.

"I never recall not wanting to do that with you," she said. It made my skin prickle. My face blushed again as I looked back at her. The smile was gone, replaced by a kind of hungry look I once saw back in the attic.

Allecra reached her hand out and grabbed my wrist. I flinched and held back my gasp. My eyes stared at our joined hands.

"You've never let anyone touch you before?" She asked.

"What—what do you mean by that?" I stammered.

"You flinched," she pointed out. "I just wondered."

"I did not."

She took her hand away and rested it on my knee. This time, my breath hitched loudly. My other hand went to cover my mouth, fearing that people would hear me.

"Hmm..." Allecra nodded like a doctor examining a patient. "You need more physical contact."

~*~

The day before school was closed for that weekend, I made my way to classes as usual, yet my mind was elsewhere. It drifted back to the blonde girl, who had entered my world and filled it with intense curiosity.

I didn't expect to see Allecra while I walked down the quiet hallway, but she was there standing by my locker. With her messy blonde lock around her shoulders, she tilted her head to look at me as if she was daring me to come closer.

I stopped for a moment. She held up her index finger and wagged it at me to follow her.

Curiosity kills the cat.

I walked after her. My heels clicked sharply on the floor. The sound gave an eerie echo against the silence. My feet obeyed her unspoken summon. There was no one around as I followed the mysterious blonde up the empty stairwell. Allecra turned the corner and disappeared.

I ran after her. Looking around, I saw a door opened to what looked like a janitor closet. My hands were trembling at my sides with each step I took. Turning the knob slowly, I pushed my way in. Then a hand grabbed my elbow and pulled me inside. The door slammed shut, and I heard the lock clicked, but I could not see anyone. When my eyes adjusted to the semi-darkness, a pair of bright unnatural eyes emerged from the shadow. Then her angelic face appeared.

"Allecra?"

She didn't answer me and simply rushed over to push me against the wall. Her hands turned me around, pressing my front against the cold concrete. I let out a yelp and felt the weight of her body pinned me from behind.

Allecra's voice spoke something in my ear, but I couldn't understand it. She chuckled and started stripping my clothes.

A terror shot through me. My heart pounded like there was a drummer in my chest. I tried to turn myself around, but the pressure on me only intensified. I was trapped between the wall and Allecra's unusual strength. Her hands worked their ways through my panties and tore it from under my skirt like it was made of thin paper. I gasped in shock. A soft cold hand went around my waist and down between my legs. Her fingers sensually rubbed over my startled femininity.

"What are you doing?" My voice came in a shocked protest. "Stop it!"

She wasn't listening and seemed to be busy grinding herself against my rear. Something warm pressed against my backside, and it seemed to grow.

My mind could no longer process any thought. Her animalistic behavior caused the heat to burn in my body. Allecra bucked her hips into me and held me there while her hands seemed to fumble around.

A moment later, I was startled once again by a smooth slippery feeling of something firm and soft touching my heated folds. It nestled its way into me eagerly. I heard Allecra groaned over my shoulder as she rubbed the thing against my softness. My body felt too hot and too weak I could barely stand. I gasped from the contact that was taking place between my girlhood. It choked me in a crescendo of sensation. The smell of my arousal enveloped the tiny darkness. All I could hear was the sound of our heavy breathings.

Allecra pushed her hips hard into me. And I felt a long slippery length of that thing sliding through my sensitive passage. My eyes went wide as my mouth flung open in shock.

"What's that?!" I cried, feeling its smooth hard tip wedging its way through the wetness of my inner depth.

"My secret you're longing to know," Allecra whispered hoarsely from behind. Then she gave me one hard thrust, ending the whole length up to the base. Electricity zapped through my core.

My eyes squeezed shut, and my jaw snapped open in a voiceless cry. The pain mixed with indescribable pleasure caused my tears to well up.

What the hell is this?

The sound of my pounding heart was as frantic as the frenzy struggle of an impaled moth. I could feel the muscles around my hips shivering as the pleasure rolled like crushing waves. Allecra moaned and put her nose into my neck. Her arms locked me around the waist as she began stirring her hips.

The sensation she brought me was of sensual madness.

"Allecra—please—don't do that! Please, take it out now!" I begged her breathlessly, but every cell in my body was dancing.

"But you want me, don't you, Nina?" she grunted against my neck and began to move that rigid length between my legs, over and over.

"But I don't want— this thing in me!" I tried to speak when the lustful motion increased. She went faster and harder, sending spark after blissful spark through my burning core.

"It's part of me, can't you tell?" she said, drawing herself deeper into me. "You have to take all of me. All of it."

With that, she pounded until I felt my own juice dripping down my inner thighs. My legs trembled and my knees jerked.

Her moans mixed with my gasping little cries every time she rocked my body. I found myself moaning along.

No, this is wrong!

A vibrant frenzy wave of climax began to rise from the depth of my belly. The building and tightening of my youthful womb robbed me off my ability to think. Allecra held me tighter as she was taking me, dragging me higher up the cliff of ecstasy. I bit my lips and endured the tormenting pleasure. Then I felt her body shuddered against me. She groaned and seethed into my neck. At the same time, I felt her pulsating, and a rush of hot thick fluid surging through me. It came as a shock that my walls went into spasm and then contracted; gathering all her juices.

My eyes flew open wide, and I sat bolt upright, causing my pulse to beat furiously in my throbbing head. My heart thumped against my rib cages as if it was a bird trying to get out.

I didn't know what the hell was wrong with me.

My bed was damped with sweat. With a realization that I had gone through another episode of my own delusion, I buried my face in my pillow and screamed.

Allecra Knight had driven me insane!

I rolled onto my back and waited until my heart calmed down again. My eyes stared at the ceiling. If the blonde was a witch, I would have believed it without a doubt. How else could she have mentally tortured a person even in her sleep?

My mind was filled with the thoughts of her day and night.

Although for the first time in my life, she had brought me a strange kind of excitement like the sun lighted up a new day, she was also something else darker.

Of course, I couldn't deny it. Allecra could make my heart flutter like the wings of a thousand butterflies. And her brilliant stare never failed to send the chill through my bones. Yet I had no idea what power she possessed to cause all these flowing emotions in my heart. It coursed through the secret parts of my body and aroused the ones I had never known existed.

For the last several weeks, my mind was spinning with her image, her name, her touch, and her piercing turquoise eyes.

Then there was this stupid delusional dream of her!

Allecra was so cruel.

She had invaded my mind and entered my nightmare to torture me. She knew what effect she could instill in my body. She was cruel and sadistic, and I knew I should stay away from her.

But at the same time, I still felt drawn to her like a moth flying towards the flame.

What is she exactly?

CHAPTER 9

THE WEEKEND TOOK my aunt and her husband away on their trip. Without actually thinking that I had been abandoned again, I tried to run the household with my two cousins. I had the groceries refilled to last the whole week and started to take over the kitchen front after school.

Yet, trying to make something special out of American frozen foods needed real talents. For our dinner, I made *Okroshka* soup, Caesar salad, and *Pirozhki* made with onion and mushroom, including meat stuffed with rice. For breakfast, I delighted the twins with my favorite *Vatruska*, a kind of cake with a ring of dough and cottage cheese in the middle. I added some raisins and bits of fruit in them for good measure.

My cousins couldn't shut up about how delicious it was. Somehow, it pleased me.

I still had enough cash to spend for at least another month. Before Aunt Vikki left, she also handed me a credit card, a sleek black kind of card with an Indian on the front. I had refused to take it, but she insisted that it was in the case of emergency.

Saturday night came. I was lying in my bed under the soft humps of the blanket and twisted sheets, trying to write something, but nothing could be put into words.

Every time I closed my eyes, the unsmiling angelic face would haunt me.

Then I heard two quick knocked on my door. I got up and went over to open it. Jay was all dressed up and smelled of choking man cologne.

He frowned at me.

"Why are you not dressed up?" he asked. That was when I remembered about the party.

"Oh, I forgot," I said.

"What?! You forgot? Come on, we're waiting!" he said then he raised his hand as if to excuse himself and fished out the phone from his pocket. The screen flashed Piper's photo with her tongue sticking out. Jay talked to her for a minute before he looked at me again.

"Get dressed, Nina," he said. "Piper is taking her own car to pick up some friends. I'll drive you."

But another buzz came from his phone. He answered the call. A few moments later, he turned to me again.

"My friends are waiting. I have to pick them up, too," he said in an apologetic voice. "How about I give you the direction and you drive there by yourself? It's not that far from here."

He showed me where on the Google map.

"Call me if you couldn't find it," he said in a hurry, "I gotta go!"

With that, he left. The whole time, I hadn't said a word back. I sighed, then closed the door and dropped myself onto the bed. All I wanted to do was to be alone.

Half an hour later, I felt decent enough to get out of the house.

I looked around the quiet neighborhood while driving slowly.

The party was only a couple of blocks away from our school. But it was deep inside a private property with big oak trees lining along a small unpaved lane. It was hard to miss when there was a sign hanging with colorful balloons at the entrance. I drove in and passed cars lining up the sidewalk. I found a space to park under a dark oak tree.

All around the estate were tall uneven grasses and bushes. Sat in the middle of the lot was a big house. Loud music was blasting and the smell of beers and barbecued meat reached my nose even before I walked out of the car.

It was full of people roaming around. My cell buzzed. I picked it up and saw Jay's number.

"Where are you, Nina? Can you find the place?" His voice came through the loud music in the background.

"I'm already here," I told him.

"Oh cool, I'll go and get you," he said and hung up.

A few minute later, he appeared, and I stepped out to meet him.

"Glad you made it, cousin!" he said excitedly. "Come on in. My friends are eager to meet you."

I put my hand up as if to stop him.

"I'm not here as an exhibition for your straight people, Jay," I said.

"What? I didn't say that! I just want you to have some fun," he said, "Come on, loosen up, Nina. They're fun people. Nothing serious."

He smiled and gestured for me to go inside. I sighed and followed him.

The house was swarming with teens. The beat of the music seemed to echo right through my chest. If it was any louder, I would have mistaken it as a heart attack. Guys were all over the place. They were shouting, laughing, smoking, drinking beer, and eating chips, candy, and pretzels. There were two girls holding up with their feet against the wall, twerking.

I found Piper sitting on the couch. She looked stunning in some red backless and a short. I wanted to go over to her, but I was still racked with guilt. Then out of nowhere, Jack Conner walked in. He looked at me as if he'd just seen Jesus.

"Nina!?" he shouted in surprise. His voice was loud enough to be heard above the noises, causing everyone to look at me.

Piper turned her face to us. I gave Jack an awkward smile. I just prayed that he wouldn't get any closer. Luckily, before he could come over to me, Andrew and Nathan walked into the room. They hollered like some wild boars. One of them shoved a bottle of beer in my hand. I took it only because I didn't want to drop it to the floor. The rug looked a little moist and squishy already. The place was actually a madhouse full of hormonal teenagers.

"You know my cousin?" Jay asked Jack, leaning into his ear.

"Oh! She's your cousin that you told us about?"

Jay nodded. There was a look of discomfort in Jack Conner's eyes as he looked at me again. Now he knew I was also Piper's cousin.

Piper had disappeared when I looked over at the couch again. That didn't stop Jack from showing me the food table and drinks. I wanted to find Piper, yet it was not easy to actually see anybody because it was pretty dark and smoky. The mixed smell of food and something fragrant hung in the room. Then Jay also disappeared with some friends and that left me with Jack. He was grinning. A brunette girl offered me things to eat.

There were girls with tanned skins in short shorts and tank tops. They danced sensually against each other as the guys sat staring from the corners. Another bunch of girls and guys surrounded a pool table, hollering at two girls lapping vodka off each other's body. I tried not to shake my head at their male-teasing 'body shot' display.

As I looked around, I caught a few guys eyeing me from a dark room. One of the bulky guys was staring right at me and grinning. It was creepy, and I turned away.

"You just did me a world of good by coming here tonight," Jack said as I took a bite of pepperoni pizza. His sweet words almost choked me. Later, Phoebe, Claudia, and Jessica walked in and joined us at the pizza table. They shared some jokes with me and asked me about Russia. Soon I felt less uncomfortable being here. Maybe Jay was right - I should loosen up and let myself socialize again.

I drank some sweet fruity wine instead of beer and felt relaxed enough to tell a joke my dad had told me. It was something about a man who asked the Genie to make him a thousand times smarter than any man on earth. The Genie turned him into a woman.

The girls laughed so hard, they snorted beer up their noses. The music turned from rap music to electro beats and then to rock metal. I thought I might get brain hemorrhage after this.

"Do you want to dance?" Jack asked me. His breath smelled too much of beer.

"No, thanks." I shook my head.

"Would you like to have a seat then?" He tried again. Since it sounded like a harmless thing to do, I nodded.

"Alright," I said.

"Cool, let's have a seat outside." Jack grabbed my hand and led me out the back door before I could say another word. There was a swing set on the porch. There was no one there. Suddenly, I felt awkward, standing alone with my cousin's boyfriend.

Jack went to sit on the swing and beckoned to me. I took a deep breath and walked over to him and sat down. Jack was smiling, trying to look charming under the glowing light.

"I was trying to catch you in school again, but you just vanished," he said, giving me a pouty look. "I was so heartbroken, you know."

"Listen to me Jack, before you get any wild ideas." I looked at him. His ears perked up as he stared back at me. "I'm Piper's cousin. You know that, don't you?"

"Yeah—I—I just realized that now," he said. "But Nina, I'm totally single. Piper and I already broke up."

"What?" I said in disbelief.

"We have been off and on for two years. She just refuses to accept the fact that our relationship isn't working out," he said and reached his hand

73

out to take mine. "If you're worried about that, I can guarantee you, we're really over. I want to ask you out. I like you a lot, Nina. Please, if you give me a chance..."

"Jack," I cut him off in a solemn tone. "There is something you need to know about me."

"Yes?" He looked at me, waiting and hoping.

"I'm gay."

There was a long stretching silence. I could hear the moths fluttering their wings around the light bulb. Jack kept staring at me, blinking. But after a while, he started giggling to himself.

"You lied," he said. "I don't believe you."

I rolled my eyes.

"Oh well."

"Aw, come on, Nina, don't do that just to get rid of me," he said. "A lot of girls would line up to date me. What else do you want? I'm the captain of the football team. I have the looks and the money. Besides, I can make you happy."

"I'm sorry, Mister, but that long list of girls who want to date you just doesn't have me on it," I said and got up. I was about to leave when he pulled me back by the wrist.

"Tell me why you don't want me?"

"You're drunk, Jack," I said, trying to pry my hand from his tight grip. But it only got tighter.

Jack hurled me against his chest and wrapped his strong arms around my body. He leaned over to kiss me, but I turned my face away from him.

"What the hell are you doing, Jack?" I cried.

His wet sloppy mouth landed on my neck. I pushed him back, but his grip only tightened.

But then we heard a girl's voice cried out.

"Jack!" It was my cousin Piper. I wrenched myself free from him and stood up.

"Piper..." I said, staring at her with wide eyes. Piper came over to us, and I stepped away from her boyfriend.

"What are you two doing here?!" she snapped in a fury. Jack got up from the swing and glared back at her.

"We are not in a relationship anymore, Piper! It's over now, just let me go!"

Standing in the middle of some stranger's sunken porch, I realized what a big mistake I had made by coming here. Piper started yelling something incomprehensible. With a burst of anger, she stormed over to Jack and slapped him in the face. His head snapped to the side. Piper continued to attack her boyfriend in frenzy until he grabbed her wrists and pushed her away. Piper tripped over her heels and fell on the floor.

"Piper!" I came to help her up, but she pushed me off.

"Get away from me, you dyke!"

My hands balled into fists. Jack stood there, looking at me and his crying girlfriend. I rose to my feet again and clenched my teeth. Piper was crying with her head in her hands. My other cousin appeared along with Nathan and Andrew.

"What the hell is going on? What did you do to her?" he cried and rushed over to his sister. I realized that almost everyone in the house had come out the back door to watch us. I tried to keep a straight face without looking at anyone.

Then Jason walked up to his friend and raised his clenched fist. But before any punches were thrown, the other guys rushed over to hold him back. There were some yellings and name callings afterward. Unable to bear it anymore, I turned to walk back into the house, pushing through the crowd.

In the dark hallway, the creepy guy I saw earlier came to block me. He was grinning with his eyelid half shut. A stench of alcohol reeked from his mouth as he spoke to a few of his friends behind him. They were chuckling to each other. The guy flicked his cigarette and puffed out the smoke.

"Is that the Russian girl Jack was bragging that he was going to bang one of these days?" he said. His other friends started laughing.

My body froze. A hot burst of rage rose like lava inside of me.

"Get out of my way," I muttered through my gritted teeth. My entire being was shaking. I felt like the whole house was a ship in the storm.

"Oh, she speaks English!" He laughed. "I've heard pretty Russian girls like you would have sex for a discount coupon, is that true? Because I have many and if you'd like, my boy is waiting."

He moved his hand to his crotch and his friends howled like mad wolves. Hot tears began to burn in my eyes.

"Aw, no, don't cry! We're just joking!" The bulky guy came closer to me and reached his hand out to tip my chin up. With a rush of adrenaline, I grabbed his hand and head-butted him right on his freaking nose. The guy fell to the floor and passed the hell out. The rest of his friends stepped back, but then they burst out laughing at him. They were too high to even care.

"Your joke isn't funny," I said and dared anyone else to come close to me again. They just stepped back like I was a female version of the hulk.

I stepped over the lying man and was out of there.

CHAPTER 10

I WAS UP ON THE HILL overlooking the valley. It was a little cold but I didn't care. Below me, the city stretched out like sparkling golden sea.

I had driven aimlessly along an empty street for what seemed like forever and then ended up here. My mind was still fighting with nagging thoughts to even care where I was.

The stink of alcohol and smoke still clung to my hair and clothes. I wiped the tears off my face. It was quiet up on the hill. I didn't see anyone, except the outstretched flower bushes and swaying trees. It wasn't how my day should have started.

I tried not to think of Piper's words that wedged deep into my chest like thorns, bright steel thorns. I tried not to think of the insult those American kids said to me, but it was impossible. I thought of my father thousands of miles away having the time of his life, and of my mother, especially my mother. I started to cry again. How could there be more tears in me? They flowed like slow rivers, burning my eyes and were hot on my skin.

The night was getting colder under the starlit sky. My fingers were too numb and I couldn't bend them anymore. I shivered from the constant chilling breeze.

I didn't want to move, but I shouldn't stay here. I left the vista and return to my car. But when I started the engine, it sounded like it was choking then it went dead. That was unexpected from a brand new vehicle. I tried to ignite the car again, but it wouldn't start. Then I noticed the bright neon needle pointing to the letter E. My forehead banged against the steering wheel with a groan.

"Well done, Nina," I murmured at my own stupidity.

After a while, I took out my phone from my purse. I needed to call someone for help. But then who? I didn't know anybody. Obviously, I wouldn't want to call Jay. He probably didn't want anything to do with me now. I had just become a plague that ruined his sister's love life. There was no one I could depend on.

I felt depressed, scared, and exhausted. Then my thought flickered to Allecra and all my despair doubled.

She wouldn't know that I was here all alone crying a river. Maybe there wouldn't be a fragment of me in her thought, would there? For the life of me, I didn't know how and when I became so attached to her. I was trying my hardest not to think of her and the complexities she brought into my life, but I was losing the battle.

Now I was stuck in a foreign land, like a person who got stranded on a desert island and the world she knew was lost forever.

If I called the cops, they would ask me where I lived and want to see my license and ID card or stuff that I didn't bring along with me. They would call my aunt and Robert in the midst of their holiday. Robert would think I was a crazy delinquent, who they shouldn't have taken under their wings.

There was no taxi or bus at this hour. I ran my hand through my hair and took a deep breath. The street lights were on, but it got so dark beyond that field. I leaned my head back over the steering wheel and chuckled at my own ridiculous predicament.

Allecra, help me! I wanted to scream.

I sat there for a while, and just as I thought all hope was lost, a bright headlight flashed through my window. I looked up and saw a black shiny Lambo zoomed over and screeched to a stop a few feet away. The doors automatically lifted up and a heavy black boot stepped out from the driver side.

Allecra turned elegant body around. My jaw dropped. I had never felt so relieved in my life. Her beautiful face turned to me, and our eyes met. My heart skipped a whole long beat.

Another bulky figure emerged from the other side. It was her brother Triton.

In ten graceful steps, Allecra was by my car. I stepped out with tears on my face. She reached out for me, and I reached over for her like we were two survivors in a drowning sea. Relief filled my chest to the brim, and I couldn't speak.

"You're alright?" She whispered. I nodded.

I held her waist and burrowed my face into her warm body. Allecra rubbed my back, drawing me closer to her.

After a moment, she took a step back. Her warm breath brushed faintly against my cheeks. I realized how desperate I was to have our lips connected again. But Triton was watching us.

"I couldn't go home...my car..." I chocked. My voice didn't sound like my own. It was croaky, clogged and wet and heavy with fear. Allecra smooth my hair as if to calm me down.

"I know. It's alright. You're safe now," she reassured me then turned me away from the door. She bent over into my car and retrieved my purse. She turned to her brother again.

"Take care of it, Triton," she said to the smiling man. We walked away with our arms around each other like two wounded soldiers getting off the battlefield. The door of her Lambo lifted open, and she escorted me in. Allecra leaned over to yank the seatbelt and strapped me in like I was a baby. She slammed the door shut.

The car was so dark and low inside. The interior looked like an alien space ship with all the lit screens. But the smell of mild exotic perfume calmed me. It was clean and fresh with some traces of Allecra's intriguing scent.

She got into the car soon after and tossed my purse to the back. The ocean green of her eyes gleamed in the dark. When she turned to me, those eyes dimmed down a little, but her elegant brows furrowed.

"We're not done talking yet," she said and expertly shifted the gear. And I swear no man could do that so attractively like Allecra.

The car eased out of the cliff and sped onto the highway. I sat in silence. The whole time, Allecra didn't look at me again. I was kind of afraid even to breathe too loudly. I didn't know if I was being an inconvenience to her.

We stopped at an intersection as the light turned red. She revved the engine a few times with a deafening crackling. Then she turned her face to me. It made my heart pound at a frantic tempo again. I was also blushing under her steady scrutiny. Her flawless angelic face looked tensed with conflicting thoughts.

"Tell me where your house is, I'll take you there," she said. At the thought of me parting from her so soon, my brain's functionality returned.

"I don't want to go home," I murmured and looked down at my fidgeting hands. If I was being honest, I actually missed seeing her.

"You're not making it easy for me," she said, but it was more to herself. When the light turned green, she stepped on the accelerator again. I was jolted back into my seat. I glanced at Allecra. A slight frown marred her face. The light from the street did little to help me see her expression in the dark.

"There's no one home," I said again. "Please take me somewhere else."

"Why were you out at night all alone?" she asked.

"I went to someone's party and then I left early," I told her without giving any details.

"What happened, Nina?" she said. I realized she must have noticed my miserable state a while ago.

"I don't want to talk about it," I said with a shrug. Allecra's hands on the wheel tightened.

"Alright," she sighed. "I will find out eventually."

We stopped at another traffic light. She turned to me once more. This time, her eyes softened and her brows smoothed back.

"You feel better now?" she said with concern, which made my heart flutter at the caring tone of her voice.

"Buy me a drink," I said boldly. It made her laugh. She shook her head in amusement, but she didn't refuse.

"Okay," she said. "But you also need food."

"I'm not hungry."

"But I am," she replied.

The next thing I knew, Allecra brought me to a traditional Japanese restaurant. It wasn't a normal family-friendly one. The customers there wore a grim expression. It looked like they would draw out samurai swords at any moment and start slaying each other into sushi. Most of them were in their black suits. Some had casual Hawaiian shirts with a few buttons undone to show their colorful tattoos. They were either eating or drinking tea, but hardly talking.

I might have head-butted a man twice my size, but I was still afraid being in such environment. It wasn't like I could head-butt every freaking idiot that wished to harm me. The horrified look on my face made Allecra smile and pat my hand. I didn't even realize my hands had looped around her arm to seek her protection. I pulled away quickly and blushed again.

The waitresses in their lovely pink *Kimonos* ushered us to a secluded part of the restaurant. They opened a *Shoji* door to a private room. There we sat on the flat cushions with a polished wooden table in the middle. I felt relieved to be out of sight at last, but I was also a bit nervous to be left alone with Allecra.

She was now looking over the menu and started ordering *Tempura*, *Sashimi*, *miso* soup, and of course, some expensive-looking *sushi* and other dishes I didn't know.

The waitress took the orders then she bowed at us again and left, sliding the shoji door shut behind her.

I looked around the room. There were Japanese paintings hanging on the walls. Some were rather sexual with naked women and men going at it in a more artistic kind of position.

There was an image painted in light modest shades the way the Japanese art was, depicting a woman enveloped in the tentacles of two octopuses. The larger of the two performed some sort of sexual act on her. The smaller octopus assisted it to the left by fondling her mouth and left nipple. The woman and the creatures seemed to express their mutual pleasure together.

I had to avert my eyes away after I understood what the pictures really were. I realized Allecra was also looking at me. Her lips arched with a trace of a smile and her eyes twinkled in amusement.

"You like that painting?" she said.

"It's an interesting work, but I wouldn't say I do," I said. She smirked and came over to my side. My body froze. I could see the delicious charge from her brilliant eyes on me.

"That painting is a copy of the original painting called, *The Dream of the Fisherman's Wife*. It is the most famous work during the Edo period."

"You know about Japanese art?"

"I spent a year there," she said casually. "Japan is a world of bizarre creativity and abnormality hidden underneath the sophisticated surface."

I wanted to know why she was there, but it would be too snoopy to ask.

"The Japanese never cease to amaze me," I simply said, "...like that painting, for an example."

"It's the reflection of human's sexual desires," Allecra said, still staring at me. "Deep within that timid unassuming exterior lays a dark sexual perversion waiting to be unleashed."

I blushed scarlet. I knew she was talking about the painting, but her penetrating stare never left mine. I felt self-conscious. The dreams I had of Allecra and me were still vivid in my mind. Then we heard a soft call and the door slid open again.

The waitress and two other female helpers brought the foods over. They started arranging our meal on the table. There were myriad plates and side dishes everywhere. It was like looking at a colorful garden of foods. The decoration was insane.

The waitresses left us but not without stealing a glance at the dreamy blonde girl beside me. I figured that Allecra Knight was just universally attractive.

Allecra turned her attention back to me.

"We should start," she said and began to mix a small portion of Wasabi into my soy source. Then she watched me pick up my chopstick clumsily.

"You must say *'Itadakimasu'* before you eat," Allecra said, her eyes were alight with humor. She actually looked her age like this. I was always used to her brashness and her stern expression that seeing this side of her mesmerized me.

"What does that mean?" I asked.

"*'Bon appetite'* in Japanese." She smiled. Her smile took my breath away.

"I see," I said with a dazed nod.

Allecra giggled and turned to the food again before saying the word.

"Itadakimasu!"

"Itada—*Priyatnava appetita!*"

"What's that?" her head snapped back at me with a questioning frown.

"*'Bon appetite'* in Russian." I stuck my tongue out at her and simply began to eat. Allecra muttered something about uncultured table manners. But she started to eat as well. The salmon was fresh and chewy like it had just jumped out of the ocean. There were some bites I was too afraid to put in my mouth, like the *Natto* stuff that looked like sticky gooey slime.

Allecra picked up an oyster. I went stiff as I stared at her sideways. I was sure she was aware of me watching her. She took her time and seductively ran her tongue around the slimy oyster. Her tongue was bright pink and long. It caught my attention.

"Your tongue," I blurted out.

"Yeah?"

"Well, it just seems longer than average."

She tilted her head and looked at me. "So you've measured it with yours?"

I blinked hard. *How could she ask such a thing?*

"I—we—" I stammered. My face felt hot again. Allecra laughed at my reaction.

"It's not that long, trust me," she said. "But I believe it could do many wonders aside from tasting good oysters."

I felt every part of my body went tingling with heat. My face must look like a ripe cherry, but I tried to give her a look. Allecra merely smirked back. I turned my attention to the food again.

"So will you tell me about why you ended up on the street alone?" Allecra asked.

I let out a sigh and put my chopsticks down.

"It's a long story," I said.

"We've got time."

"Well, I knocked the light out of someone."

Allecra raised her perfect eyebrows in genuine surprise.

"You don't come off as a fighter," she commented, sounding rather amused and impressed at the same time.

"He thought I was a hooker," I said.

Her face hardened. I noticed Allecra's hands had balled into fists on the table. I quickly regretted what I just said.

"What's his name?" Her voice came out like a death sentence. It gave me a chill of fear.

"I—I don't know."

"What does he look like?" she asked again, turning her hard stare at me.

"Allecra, it's alright. It's over."

"No, it's not! I'm going to skin him alive!"

"Allecra!"

I stared at her with wide eyes. She looked away. The way she said those words held no false promise. Then she pinched the bridge of her nose.

"I'm sorry, Nina. To think of how they have treated you, I just—" she said and trailed off. The anger in her voice was still flaring, but it had softened somewhat.

"You scared me sometimes," I admitted.

"You should be," she said and turned to me again. Her jaw tightened. "Why couldn't you go home like any sane girl?"

"How did you find me?" I asked instead. Allecra scowled at my question. Then she picked up her rice wine and downed it before looking at me again.

"Just know that I'm now affected by you in more ways than you can imagine, Nina," she said.

I frowned at her enigmatic words. Her genuine tone left my head spinning. I looked at her with my hands twitching over the table.

Allecra slowly moved towards me like a graceful panther.

"I'm glad you thought of me," she whispered. "I hate to imagine you being all by yourself at night. Anything could have happened to you and I would never forgive myself."

"It's not your fault. And I'm always thinking of you, Allecra," I said, but that was an understatement. I was always fantasizing about her and dreaming about her even in my waking hours.

"I know," she said, "but I'm still sorry."

We held each other's gaze. The sexual tension pulsed through every nerve in my body. Allecra seemed to feel it, too. Her eyes darkened and I knew what was coming next. With a low hiss, she lunged at me.

My back landed on the Tatami floor with Allecra pinning me down with her weight. This time, I didn't squirm. I didn't move. And just like that, her lips were hot on my own. She kept my hands in her death-like grip above my head. Her lower half wedged between my thighs, and it was so overwhelming.

I opened my mouth for her slithering delicious tongue. It filled me with her taste and passion. Our ragged breaths and kissing lips brought a fiery heat to our bodies. I had never been so satisfied by a kiss before. It was like an out-of-the-body experience. Her mouth devoured mine time after time, transporting me to another world.

I realized then that I was the unassuming fisherman's wife and she was the octopus.

CHAPTER 11

Allecra parked her black car in the driveway in front of the house. The thought of her sleek ravenous tongue inside my mouth wouldn't leave my mind. Allecra could make every fiber of my being effervesce at will. And I didn't think I could ever get used to her random outburst of passion.

After we left the Japanese restaurant, we hadn't said anything to each other again, except when I told her my address. Allecra had grown especially quiet throughout the ride, and I was too shy to speak.

After we arrived at my aunt's house, I glanced at her in apprehension. Allecra's turquoise eyes stared straight through the windshield. I wondered if I had upset her with anything. She was so hard to understand sometimes.

"Allecra," I said at last. "Are you alright?"

"This is all messed up." Her velvety tone sounded conflicted. She turned her anguished face to me. "I am not someone you're looking for, Nina."

Her words startled me. I looked away from her like an angry child. She didn't know how much that hurt me. She couldn't tell me what to think of her at this point now, could she?

"It's too late," I told her.

"Why?" she asked, her voice laced with frustration and curiosity.

"Because I decided that it is."

"Because you decided it?" she echoed my words.

"That's so ironic, don't you think?" I snapped back. "After everything you have done to me, you've got me hooked on whatever it is that you are. But now you're trying to push me away?"

Allecra let out a sigh of exasperation. This time, she turned away from my gaze. Her eyes were darker as she stared into space. She knew what I said was right, but she seemed to be torn up inside by something unbeknown to me.

We sat like that for a moment before she suddenly leaned over to me again. Her face was inches away from mine. I could smell the exquisite scent of her flawless skin. Her eyes paralyzed me in my seat and I couldn't look away from them.

"You don't know what you're getting yourself into when you're with me," she said in a slow and clear voice. "For the first time, I'm afraid to break a heart like yours. I don't have time to entertain your idea of romance. I can't make you any promise, Nina. I want something else you can offer me. You might or might not have it, and if you can't give me what I need, I will have to leave you. Are you okay with that?"

"Allecra, you sound like a guy!" I cried and glared at her in tears of anger. "What do you want from me? My body?"

"No, not just your body although that's also the case," Allecra said calmly and then she paused. "I want something more."

"What is it?"

"I can't tell you yet."

"You're so complicated," I snapped. "Weren't you the one who said people don't say what they mean? Now you're just like them."

"I'm trying to protect you, Nina," Allecra said. "I'm not normal like other people."

"Of course, you're not!" I spoke in the angriest voice I could muster. "The moment I met you, my intuition already told me that you were trouble. You were like the chain that would tie me and hold me down for eternity, but the messed up part is, I am willing!"

"Then you should have trusted your intuition more." Her words cut at me like cold jagged ice.

"Allecra, what are you trying to scare me away from?" I bit my lips from crying.

"I can't tell you," she said. "Not yet."

"Then let me tell you this— whatever you say to make me forget about everything that has happened between us, it doesn't work."

"I'm just stating the facts."

"Well, that doesn't work either," I said stubbornly. Allecra laughed and shook her head.

"Tomorrow." She turned to say instead, which confused me. "We will talk about it again tomorrow. It's late. You need your beauty sleep."

I considered it for a moment and decided to let it go for now.

"You promise?"

"I promise."

"Fine." I nodded but not without a sigh.

"Your car will be delivered to you the next day," she told me. "But I will pick you up in the morning if you want."

"Really?" I said, trying not to sound perky about it.

Allecra nodded, but she didn't smile. I was still unable to look away from her captivating face. I didn't want to look away from her. It was like I was afraid if I did, she would vanish.

Gosh, I really got it bad.

"There's a lot of things you don't know about me," she reminded me. "After you know the whole truth, you can decide for yourself."

"So, it's now or never— deal or no deal?" I said.

"Yes, Miss. Antonina Black," she said, giving me a dazzling smile at last.

"Well, good night then, Miss Allecra Knight," I said.

Allecra's bright eyes kept staring at me as I reluctantly unbuckled my seatbelt. I stepped out of the comfort of her presence.

The night air was cold on my skin. The black shiny Lambo growled and revved up again. Then I watched it rolling out of the driveway, taking Allecra away from me.

I felt deprived and sad as if I had just woken up from a fairytale dream and came to face my reality again. Maybe that was how Cinderella felt after the night with the prince. Allecra Knight was like a prince who came to rescue me out of nowhere.

Walking into the big empty house, I wondered where my cousins were. And just to complicate things even more, I was starting to feel responsible for their safety and got paranoid at the idea of them being corrupted by the outside world.

But after a long while later, I heard Jay's car pulling up through the front garden. If he was home, then maybe Piper was alright. At last, I could rest with the thought that they were safe.

When I finished my bath and was ready to go to bed, my head was kind of spinning, probably from trying to unscramble all thoughts in my mind. I wished I had someone to talk to about it, but since my fate had linked me with Allecra Knight's, it seemed no one would ever understand.

This was the strangest night. It was all miraculous yet confusing. The fact that I began to fall deeper for a girl who might probably cause me great pain didn't help either. I could feel it in my bones, but for some strange reason, I was already prepared to fight against the odds.

Maybe I was no different than Piper. We both put love first.

My heart fluttered at the word 'love'. Was I that quick to fall in love? I had never thought I became that kind of girl who let love blind her eyes. But now, I felt helpless against Allecra's spell.

Maybe it was true that being in love means you give someone the power to destroy you, and hope that they wouldn't.

For the first time, I knew for certain in all the years I had been on earth, that as long as I was going to be with Allecra, I would sacrifice anything for her. Probably that was the nature of women. My mother was a perfect example of that. Now, I kind of understood why she did what she did.

But will I be like her? I thought.

I stumbled towards the bed. My unsettling mind was exhausted from all the emotions of tonight. Then a familiar flash of a vivid ten-second image came back to me without a warning. It was projected directly onto the screen of my consciousness. The air grew thin, and I had trouble breathing all of a sudden. The scene was not my own imagination.

It was a hidden file in a locked drawer of my memory.

I sat myself down on the bed. The dizzying flashback gripped me like an iron clasp. Then the scene became clearer like a camera was finally coming into focus.

Allecra was standing in a dark building with her sister, having sex.

It wasn't just how two girls would do it. Allecra had something else that I knew was different from any other girls. I knew what it was. This one wasn't a delusional dream. I was sure because I was there. In all my dreams, my subconscious had pieced together the clues to Allecra's mystery.

My trembling hands went to my mouth, trying to smother the gasp that already escaped my lips. The image continued on to where Allecra and her sister found me shaking like a leaf on the floor. I looked at them in fear and shock. The blond rushed over to pull me up against her warm body. Her eyes and tattoos were still aglow as she stared at my frightened face.

"You shouldn't have found out too soon," she said. "I'm sorry, Nina, but I have to do this."

As she spoke, the glow brightened from those stirring turquoise eyes. I had struggled against her grip, but she was inhumanly strong. Then the scene was gone. It was as if the film got ripped out of the projector of my mind and everything went blank.

Only now it came back to me, and I remembered everything.

~*~

It was sunny as usual the next morning. The sky was pale blue and the air was crisp and fresh like an apple plucked straight from the tree. I didn't want to get out of bed but I had to. After a quick bath, I dressed in a black skirt and a white top under a denim jacket. The warm ray of golden sun shone through my window and made my hair look almost bronze as I brushed it.

I used some eye drops because my eyes were still sore and dry. I had never cried so hard over anything until last night. The only girl I'd ever found myself falling in love with turned out to be something else entirely.

What I was positive about Allecra Knight was that she wasn't a normal human or a normal girl even. Another thing was that she committed incest with her sister. It made me sick although I had no solid ground to prove how accurate my assumption was.

But I wasn't scared as I was supposed to be. If anything, I was more hurt than scared. Why did she do this to me?

Then I heard Jay's voice calling from downstairs. I grabbed my purse and left the room. My heart pounded and clenched simultaneously. I had to stop in the hallway to breathe. Jay was standing there and frowning at me quizzically. He was still in his old clothes. It looked like he had been sleeping on the couch all night.

"Why is there a Knight kid in our driveway, Nina?" he asked.

"She's here to pick me up for school. My car had a little problem," I told him, "How's Piper?"

"She's at a friend's house," Jay said.

"Is she okay?"

"I don't know."

"I'm sorry about last night, Jay," I said honestly. "I didn't mean to ruin your friend's party."

89

"He's not my friend anymore!" Jay growled bitterly, "I don't want to know about the drama between you and my sister, but it would be better if you just try to be normal like everyone else."

With that, he stormed off. I swallowed back the pain and took a deep long breath. Then I turned to walk over to the front door. Leaning on her Lambo like a cover girl was Allecra. She was looking right at me. Instead of wearing all black today, she wore a red maroon jacket with black leather sleeves. A pair of sunglasses hung on the neck of her ultra-white T-shirt handsomely. Her long messy sun-drenched hair covered her shoulders as she stood with her arms crossed. Allecra could put any male models to shame. Even at this point, I still found myself marveled at her flawless presence.

My red cooper was already parked in the front garden.

I walked up to her car, unable to look her in the eyes.

"Good morning, Nina," her voice contradicted her words. It was unsure and dark. When I stood there like an idiot, looking down at my shoes, she sighed. "It's alright if you don't want to come with me."

My head shot up at her. It was unfair how the thought of us being apart wrecked me. It would be much easier if it were all about a chaste and a normal love life between two girls against the whole wide world. But the truth was there was nothing normal about us at all.

"We need to have a talk," I said, at last, my tone sounded weird to me, like an echoing chamber of an empty castle. I hated saying that to her, but I had no choice.

"After school," Allecra said. Her voice was steady and collected, but her words were uncertain. She knew I was troubled by something. I could feel her mood changed.

"I don't want to go to school today," I said helplessly.

"But you have to," she said in a heavy tone and then stepped back to open the door for me. I felt a slight sting in my chest as I got into her car.

At school, Allecra dropped me off, but she didn't come along.

"You're not going to class with me?" I mumbled, almost disappointed. She just shook her head. Her face was smooth like a marble statue. I couldn't see her beautiful brilliant eyes behind her sunglasses. In fact, she didn't even look at me again. The pain grew sharper, spreading throughout my body like needles in my veins.

"Will I see you after school?"

"Yes."

One word set like a stone on my shoulders. But I nodded and finally stepped out of her car. Allecra zoomed off immediately.

In biology, I sat still like a ghost next to Jordan. She didn't try to ask me anything. She let me be in my confused, unrealistic world. There no longer was any real world for me.

I drifted off to Language Arts, trying to stop myself from hoping yet I didn't succeed. The window seat was empty. What did I expect? Finding Allecra smiling at me and saying, 'everything is just a joke'? A black hole manifested itself in my chest. It was horrible, I realized. Everything without Allecra was horrible. Was this how her absence felt like? It terrified me to live like this every day.

What was I going to do with myself if there was no Allecra in my life anymore?

Mrs. Smith talked about the plot twist in the stories from classical mythology.

"How many of you have heard of the story of Pandora?"

A number of hands went up, but mine didn't even if I knew the tale.

"You meant Pandora of the Greek myth or in Avatar movie?" some kids asked jokingly.

"The Greek myth, of course," Mrs. Smith said. "Most people think that Pandora was sent to man as a punishment, but she was also sent as a gift."

The teacher went on about how Zeus ordered Hephaestus to mold a girl out of clay and to have Aphrodite pose for it to make sure it was beautiful. He breathed life into the clay figure and the clay turned to flesh as she lay sleeping all anew. Then he summoned the gods and asked them each to give her a gift. Apollo taught her to sing and play the lyre. Athena taught her how to spin. Demeter taught her how to tend to the garden. Aphrodite taught her how to look at a man without him noticing and gave her the power of persuasion. Poseidon gave her a pearl necklace. And finally, Hermes gave her a beautiful golden box, which he told her not to open. Because of those gifts, Zeus named her Pandora, which meant "the gift of all".

"But there are two more gifts that are the plot twist in this story. Does anyone know?" Mrs. Smith asked.

"I do!" Mary Jones said enthusiastically. "One of them was curiosity given by Hera."

"Is that why all women are snoopy? Because the first woman was given the gift of curiosity?" Ben asked.

"You should be thankful," Mary Jones hissed. "Man would have gone crazy with loneliness if he had a mute and boring Pandora."

The teacher cleared her throat and they turned back.

"The most important gift was a beautiful box covered in gold and jewels. And this is the main plot," she said. "The box was the very secret of life itself. Pandora was forbidden to open it."

"But she was too curious that she must look inside or die," Mary Jones added excitedly.

"And opened it she did," the teacher said and nodded.

I imagined what was inside the golden box. Of course, they were ills that beset mankind, the spites, diseases in its thousand shapes, old age, famine, insanity, and all their foul kins, flying out like a black shadow and mist. Pandora was frightened, and she tried to shut the box, but it was too late.

"And that's why there are all the hatred, envy, jealousy, and sadness in the world," Mrs. Smith concluded. "But there was one last thing inside the box. Without it, everyone on earth would have been told what a misfortune it was every day of our lives, and that would be the end of humanity."

"What is it?"

There was a brief silence in the class.

"It's hope." I heard myself speaking for the first time. Everyone looked at me and then let out a long 'oh' as they understood.

"That's right, Nina. 'Hope' is the last thing in the box," the teacher smiled, "We can bear endless troubles, but we cannot bear to live without hope at all."

After class, I kept thinking about Pandora's Box. I couldn't help but compare the plot twists of Pandora's story to my life. Imagine if there were gods in my own story. They breathed life into my clay form but then made me gay—you know, just for a laugh. They gave me a similar gift to the golden box but in the form of a girl and she also wasn't an ordinary gift. They told me to stay away from her, but Hera instilled in me a great curiosity, and I really, really wanted to know who that beautiful mysterious girl was. But just like Pandora's Box, my gift could cause me pain, sorrow, and heartbreak, and I could end up with the same regret.

Could Allecra contain the same misery and grief for me if I dare to be with her?

But would there be one good thing about Allecra like there was hope at the bottom of the bad box?

I hoped it was love.

CHAPTER 12

THE OUTSIDE WORLD was cloudy with lots of little clouds spreading out in ripples. It was a 'mackerel sky', my father once told me. I walked listlessly out of the school building and headed to the parking lot. My hand brushed over the well-trimmed bushes of the pathway, which snaked through the grassy hill of the campus.

Then I remembered I didn't bring my car today. I wondered if Allecra would still see me after school as she had promised. I could only hope that she would.

After all the thinking and crying, I had decided to ask Allecra about everything, once and for all. I wanted to know the truth about someone I was so emotionally involved with. The questions had been drafted inside my head. Where did she come from and why was she here? I was dying with curiosity to know who or what she really was, and most importantly, what did she want from me?

"I want something more."

If it was not just my body, then what was that *'something more'* she spoke of?

I passed a clump of trees standing tall and dark along the school borders. There was one particular tree that I liked. Among a grove of eucalyptus was a pepper tree. It stood with graceful drooping branches adorned with clusters of beautiful red berries. I remembered a poem someone wrote about the pepper tree in a children's book. Although I never recalled who wrote it, but it had stuck with me.

The pleasantest place for a child to be,
Is under my tent, the old pepper tree.
Its fern-like branches droop clear to the ground,
Its red and green berries peep in all around,
The shiny brown grasses have woven a mat,
No gypsy queen has a carpet like that.

This poem comforted me as a kid while I ostracized myself from the ordinary world. I kept staring at the pepper tree for a while, indulging in this nostalgic thinking. My eyes tried to spot any bird's nest, but there was none.

When I reached the parking lot, there was no sight of the shiny black car. One by one, the students came and went in their cars. They were either in pairs or groups, talking and laughing. Their cars blasted out funky music. Everyone was ready for the fun after a school day. Some of them did glance at me as if they knew me, but not enough to say 'hi' or 'goodbye.' A few students walked by me and peeked over their shoulders again. Then they turned back to whisper in each other's ear. They thought I didn't hear them, but I did.

"The Russian girl who stole her cousin's boyfriend at the party." I heard them say. I knew what they meant. Everything about me that day must have been broadcast faster than birds chirping gossips from tree to tree.

I watched the students leaving the campus until the lot was nearly empty. Yet there was no Allecra. The mackerel sky began to darken. The evening air grew rough and chilly, and I wondered why I was still waiting.

She promised.

That was all it took to keep me there and nurse my hope. She would come eventually. The wind ruffled the blades of green grass on the hill, swirling dead leaves about my feet. The trees swayed, making a dry rustling sound. I hugged myself and hunched my shoulders as my hair was swept by a gust of wind.

Then I heard the crispy noises of dry leaves under someone's footfalls. A smile tugged on my lips. I turned around excitedly. To my utter shock, it wasn't the person I had been expecting.

"Hello, Russian girl."

My breath hitched in my throat. Terrors shot thought me. It was the same bulky man from the party. His nose had an ugly gauze on it. But his bruised face spotted a wicked look. It was enough to set my adrenaline in motion, except this time it wasn't to fight but to take flight.

I turned on my heels sharply and dashed out of there. My feet sprinted through the too quiet lot. I felt my heart thumping inside my chest. It was like a fire alarm to warn me to go faster, but I wasn't fast enough. A strong hand grabbed my shoulder and turned me around. The guy pushed me against the side of a nearby car.

"You think you can get away from me? Do you see this thing you put on my face?!" The man sneered, pointing to his broken nose. One of his hands clasped over my mouth. I clutched his big wrist, trying to pry his iron grip off, but he was way stronger than me. I stared into his furious eyes. They were the color of a gray storm. My mind tried to think of ways to escape from this beast of a man, but nothing came. I couldn't scream or bite him with his hand on my face like that.

I was doomed.

But then she was there.

I didn't even see her coming. She was simply there. Allecra grabbed the man by the back of his neck and tore him away from me before smashing his face onto the hood of the car. Then she did it again harder. The loud crushing made me jump and step away in shock and confusion. Allecra's eyes blazed like blue-green fire.

I stood there watching her pinning the guy's head against the car. A small dent on the metal hood was evident under the pressure. With all the screaming I heard, I was afraid the guy's head might burst like a watermelon.

Gosh, she was strong!

"What the hell!" The bulky man seemed powerless against her hold. His protest was futile. He swung his arms helplessly like a blind crab. I started to fear for his life.

"Which of his hands touched you, Nina?" Allecra said to me through her clenched jaw. Her face bore the most murderous expression I had never seen. She was terrifying this way, but strangely, I felt protected.

"Allecra—" I stuttered in alarm, sensing the violence raging through her system.

"Which hand?!" she growled again, making me gasped sharply. Yet I couldn't speak. Allecra spun the man around and reached for his right hand. A piercing, almost girly scream, echoed through the darkened sky. Allecra was gripping his hand in an odd angle. He cried and dropped to his knees in front of her. All he could do was pleading for her mercy. His head had a red swelling bump the size of tennis ball. His already broken nose now oozed fresh blood.

"Allecra, please! He didn't harm me. Just let him go!" I cried.

"I need him to apologize!" Allecra hissed and tightened her grip even more. It caused the crying guy to yelp and nodded in acceptance.

"I'm ssss—so sorry. I didn't know...*Aaaaahhhh!* Oh god...my hand!"

I went over to tug at Allecra's arm and gently pulled her away from him. I was amazed at the strength that existed in the blonde's elegant figure. It was like pulling on a marble statue that wouldn't budge.

But after a moment, her tensed posture began to loosen up at last. Then without another word, Allecra released him. I watched the poor dude put his injured hand to his chest. He rolled over and sobbed on the ground.

Allecra turned to me and hastily pulled me along by the elbow. She walked me away from the scene without looking back.

"What did you do to him?" I asked, peering over my shoulder to the bulky guy.

"Don't worry, he still has the use of his limb," she muttered back, almost sounding disappointed. In front of us parked her black car. The door was lifted open for me, and Allecra herded me into the Lambo. Her blazing turquoise eyes had softened a little, but her smooth face was stone-like. She still bore that dangerous look when she got into the car. The tires squealed and swerved out of the campus. As the car raced forward, all my shock and choking fear soon vanished. Now they were replaced by deep concerns for the girl next to me. Allecra whizzed around other vehicles, going too fast on the highway street.

"Allecra..." I said. My lips went dry.

My voice came out in a plea, but she didn't respond. Her white knuckles held firm on the steering wheel. I decided to reach out and stroke her arm. The gesture seemed to relax her a little. Allecra let out a long heavy sigh.

"Was he the one at the party that you told me about?" she asked. Her tone was calculating as if she was planning something I wouldn't want to know.

"Y-yes—but—" I stammered.

"Tomorrow, he's dead," she declared.

"No!" I cried. "Allecra, don't do anything stupid!"

"You may have to excuse me for that. I don't have that much self-control," she said, turning briefly to look at me. "I was made to protect my—"

She didn't finish her sentence and looked straight ahead.

"Please," I said again, "just leave it. I beg you."

Allecra took a deep breath to ease her temper. Her face turned to me again, noticing my concerned look. She exhaled.

"Fine," she said at last. I was finally able to sigh in relief.

"I hope I don't get to see that again," I murmured to myself.

"I'm sorry to have you witnessed it," she said. "Did I scare you?"

I shook my head to reassure her.

"Not really," I lied in hope that it might cheer her up a bit. "I was just glad to see you there."

She looked at me and a tiny smile curved up at the corners of her lips. We then came to the traffic light and slowed down. I noticed Allecra was wearing a black blazer over a white blouse. Both sleeves rolled up stylishly, exposing her beautiful tattoos.

"I'm sorry I made you wait," Allecra spoke in a soft quiet voice. "I didn't think you would stay."

"Of course, I would stay," I said. "You promised me."

Allecra didn't say anything. The light turned green and the car rolled forward again.

"Are you hungry?" she asked instead as if to avoid talking about it. I had to think for a moment to answer her new question.

"I don't know," I said honestly.

"You don't know?" Allecra said in a mocking surprise.

"I just don't feel like eating, okay?"

"But I do," she said. "I'm so hungry, I could eat you."

I glared at her. But it only caused the tiny smile on her lips to grow wider.

~*~

Allecra took me to a fancy French restaurant on a quiet block. A young valet was almost too eager to take the Lambo after Allecra and I stepped out. We walked through the carved marble entrance together. She gave her name at the door and they ushered us to a secluded private room. On the walls of the small quiet place was hung only a painting of the unspoiled countryside landscape. That was a relief.

We took a seat at a silk-clothed table. The waiter couldn't stop gawking at us as he took our orders. Allecra asked for hors d'oeuvres, shrimps, some French soup and beef steak, and a bottle of red wine. Then the waiter left, not bothering about asking for our age. I figured they must know Allecra.

"You come here often?" I asked her just to break the heavy silence.

"Sometimes," she said. I was secretly relieved that she seemed to be back to her normal mood again.

"It's an expensive place," I noted.

"I assumed you might like it better," Allecra said. I blushed at the memory of the Japanese restaurant and the heated moment we shared together.

"You don't have to do that." I averted my eyes away to hide my embarrassment. "I'm just a simple girl."

"Not to me," she said in a matter of fact way. I looked back at her. How Allecra could drop words like that and expect my heart not to flutter.

"Do you always treat girls to a snooty place like this?"

"Whyever not?" she said. The thought of her bringing anyone else other than me made my chest tightened a little. What made me think I was any more special? I just nodded and didn't say anything.

The drinks arrived first. The waiter poured the wine into two glasses and then left again. I watched Allecra taking a swig of her wine. Her luscious lips pressed against the crystal glass. Those beautiful pools of stirring galaxies flashed like gems in the dark.

"They serve great wine here," she said. "Why don't you try it?"

"You drive, Allecra," I reminded her but she just giggled back.

"I almost killed a man with my bare hands," she said. "And you think a few drinks would do so much as to blur my supervision?"

"Oh."

"I guess you have been waiting for this moment to ask me," she said, putting her glass down and resting her elbows on the table. Her eyes fell on me again.

"Yes, I do have so many questions," I admitted.

"If you think you're ready to ask, then ask."

"Well, where were you this evening?" I started with a light one. "I didn't mean to blame anything on you. I was just curious."

"I was debating with myself whether to come or not," Allecra answered much to my surprise.

"But why?" I asked. "You promised me..."

"I know," she cut me off and turned to swirl the wine in her glass without looking at me. "I was just—scared."

"What?"

"Please ask me something else," Allecra said. My face fell a bit. Why would she avoid answering me this?

"Okay...so tell me about yourself. Do you have any parent?"

"No," she said. There was no emotion or hidden sadness in her tone unlike those who lost their parents would. Certainly, not the way I would tell people about my mother.

"And what's your real name?" I asked.

"Allecra," she answered quickly.

"Knight is your real name, too?"

"No," she admitted. "Triton picked it for us when he was reading a book about King Arthur, and we just went with it."

"Oh." I nodded in amusement. "So how old are you now?"

"Eighteen," she said then her eyebrows furrowed, as if she was suddenly curious about the age, too. "You?"

"Seventeen," I told her. "Eighteen in May."

"Three more months," she mused to herself.

"Does age matter to you?" I asked.

"Sometimes."

Allecra downed her wine in one gulp and refilled the glass again. Just the sound of her swallowing was loud enough in an all too quiet room, but it felt oddly intimate. It was insane how everything she did fascinated me. It almost became a dangerous addiction to my emotional health.

The food arrived at a leisure pace. I could smell the delicious aroma from across the room. We started to eat in a serene atmosphere.

"My turn." Allecra leaned over the table again.

"I'm not done with my questions yet," I told her.

"Remember the first time I kissed you?" she asked anyway. My heart skipped at the mention of our first kiss.

"I did," I said with a blush. "You said something crazy. You told me I wasn't ready."

"And you're still not," she whispered.

"How?" I said as our gaze entwined. A small part of me wished there would be another episode of our intimacy in this room. But Allecra leaned back into her seat again. She picked a small pea from her plate and stared at it like it was the most interesting thing in the world. I kind of envied the pea for that much attention.

"You haven't completely adapted to me yet," she said. "That's why I still hesitate."

"I'm uncomfortable not only with you, Allecra. I'm always like that. I have never been close to anybody like this before. Maybe, I've been living inside an acorn for too long," I said. The metaphor made Allecra look up at me and then a slow brilliant smile followed. She remembered reading my writing.

"So that's why you were too stiff when I touched you," she said.

"I won't flinch if you do it again," I told her, but it sounded more like a dare. Then I dropped my gaze as I could see her plump pink lips turned up into a smirk again. I didn't know why I said that.

Then her gentle fingers came to wrap around my wrist. Allecra coaxed me from my chair. I got up and gingerly walked over to her. She wrapped her arm around my waist, pulling me to sit on her lap. My heart drummed so loud against my rib cage, and I wondered if she could hear it. By the look on her face, she probably could.

I watched Allecra's perfect lips pressed together as if to restrain herself. She put a careful hand on the small of my back, and I was instantaneously delirious. I felt her other hand on my bare thigh, going up slightly beneath my plaid skirt. I willed myself to breathe and stay calm.

"I can see the improvement," she noted, but her bright eyes gleamed with a slight wickedness.

"I told you," I said. "You can't make me flinch anymore."

"Oh, don't get your hope up yet." She smiled. "I can still make you flinch —just not from pain."

My ears and cheeks felt too hot all of a sudden.

"Do you really want me?" I asked her in a whisper.

"What if I say 'yes?" she challenged.

"Then I guess I don't mind."

"You don't mind?" she said. "Even if I'm not normal? Even if I could hurt you?"

My thoughts raced a million miles per second, flying through logical reasons and rational answers, debating and discussing. But at the end, they all disappeared from my mind because I knew that my heart would win.

My heart wanted her.

I lost track of time as I stared back into those hypnotic eyes. The taste could be sweet or it could be sour. The only way to know is to drink it.

"No, I don't mind even if you could hurt me," I decided. "Even if I remember everything." She knew that I knew what she did with her sister that day.

"The memory has come back to you." She nodded. "I already figured that out when I saw you this morning."

We kept staring at each other in silence. Allecra reached out to stroke my cheek with those long delicate fingers.

"Why did you do that?" I asked, unable to suppress my hurt that was now crawling its way to the surface. I remembered what she did with her sister, and I wished I could unsee it.

Allecra's eyes seemed to darken in color as she looked at me.

"Which part? The part where I screwed my sister or the part where I forced you to forget?" she asked in a bleak sadistic tone.

In a matter of seconds, Allecra could be so cold and mean. It almost shocked me. My tears already threatened to burn in the back of my head.

"Both," I said in a small trembling voice.

"You already knew the answer, Nina."

I turned away from her gaze. I didn't know why I couldn't bear to look at that beautiful face in that moment. Maybe that was what she kept warning me about, that she could truly hurt me, emotionally or maybe physically too. I honestly didn't know.

"Do you hate me because of what I did?" she asked again.

"I don't even know how to feel about it."

"Fair enough." Allecra nodded. "You're not afraid of the things you know now, are you? That's why you're still here with me."

"No," I said. "I'm not afraid of you, Allecra."

She looked dissatisfied with my quick answer.

"Maybe not yet," she decided for me. I frowned back, noticing her change in demeanor.

"What are you exactly, Allecra?"

"You already figured that part out."

"I want you to tell me," I insisted. "I know you're not human, and you have that—that *thing*."

Allecra became rigid under me. There was no way she could deny what I saw that day. Her glowing neon-like tattoos and turquoise eyes were enough proof, not to mention what was hiding inside her pants.

"Right, I'm not human," she said at last. "But there is something else about me."

I nodded and took a deep breath, trying to let the truth set in slowly.

"So based on your confirmation, are you an alien transgender?" I asked.

Allecra's eyes widened at me for a moment and then she threw her head back and laughed. Her whole body shook. I felt so embarrassed. I didn't know what was so funny.

"You're not an alien trans?" I asked again.

"Oh, Nina," Allecra giggled some more. "You are way too imaginative for your own good."

"What? I'm wrong?"

"No no, you are right about the alien part," she said and stopped herself from laughing. "But Nina, where did the trans part come from?"

"You're an alien and—and—you have a boy's thing," I said to clarify my point. "What else could you be?"

"Really?" she said. "An alien transgender?"

"Then tell me!" I insisted.

"Alright," she said with a sniff. "Just so you know, I was born like this. All natural. No transition. And you missed my girl's part."

"You have both!?" I gasped in disbelief. "Oh my goodness, Allecra, then you are a hermaphrodite!"

"The Japanese would call that, *'Futanari'*," she told me with an amused smile. I stared at her long and hard, trying not to remind myself that I was still sitting on her lap—close to that thing.

"Okay." I cleared my throat. "Then do you identify yourself as a boy or a girl?"

"I identify myself as me." Allecra frowned. "You can't define me based on my sex."

"Or sexes," I murmured.

"You don't seem that surprised that I have two sex organs?" Allecra said, sounding uncertain, yet I could also hear a slight edge of relief in her voice. I guessed the dreams might have helped to prepare me for what was coming my way after all.

"I'm still a little scared about all this," I admitted. "But as I told you before, it's already too late, and I couldn't go back to the old Nina anymore. My mind has evolved to accept you as you are, and I would still drink you even if you taste sour."

"Hmm...the last part sounds pretty sexual," she said with a wide grin. I bit my lips to keep from screaming at her.

Allecra's stare fixed on my blushed face. Then her eyes got suddenly intense for some reason. She leaned over to me.

"Once you're with me," she whispered, her voice dripped with lust. "All your lips are mine."

My body grew weak at her words. My nerve ends went prickling under that powerful stare. Allecra reached for my hands, lacing our fingers together. The act startled me and melted me at the same time. Our heads drew in towards each other. But as our lips began to meet, I paused with my hand on her shoulder, stopping us both.

"There is one thing I need to tell you, Allecra," I whispered, eyes gazing deep into those turquoise seas.

"Yes?" she asked softly back.

"I'm still a virgin."

"That I already know," she said and closed the space between our lips again and we kissed until my breath caught in my throat. I felt the same butterfly feeling.

This time, Allecra used less tongue and more of soft nipping and licking. Yet before I lost my mind completely to her hypnotizing kiss, I pulled my mouth away from hers again wetly. Allecra's eyes flared open. She scowled at the interruption the way a child was deprived of her favorite lolly.

"How did you know I'm a virgin?" I asked.

"Because you wouldn't have given me a sensation if you were not," she said.

"Is that an alien thing?" I frowned at her. Allecra sighed and leaned herself back. I was kind of disappointed, but I was too curious. Well, blame it on Hera.

"I was bred with a special DNA from Arzuria, my home planet," she told me. "My body is like radar constantly detecting genetic waves from humans whose genes are the most compatible with mine."

"Why is that?"

"Because in this way, I could find a potential one."

"A potential one?"

"It means you're a perfect match to my species." Allecra turned away from my gaze. She didn't seem to want to tell me more, so I asked again.

"A potential one for what?"

She looked back at me with an expression I couldn't read.

"Nina, you are a potential one for me," she said, looking right into my eyes before she added, "to breed with."

CHAPTER 13

THE AIR IN THE ROOM shifted and grew heavy as my chest tightened. I could barely breathe or even remember to. My lips pressed together in a hard line. I was afraid I might puke the fancy food all over the table.

As I sat there staring at that seraphic face in front of me, it was like I had just snapped out of a coma or a trance. I realized now how servile and pathetic I was. My heart had been so besotted by Allecra Knight that I couldn't see her ostensible goal.

"Is that why you want me?" I said. My voice grew cold like ice. Her eyes never left mine, but for the first time, they seemed confused and alarmed by my reaction. Allecra hesitated — not the way someone was weighing words to see how she should deliver them. It was more like she felt conflicted with thoughts she couldn't express.

"Answer me, Allecra," I demanded.

"Yes," she said at last. "But listen...Nina..."

I didn't want to hear any more of it. I was on my feet again. Allecra looked at me with a slight flash of shock in her turquoise eyes. The floor swayed for a tiny moment as my balance was still troubled by the push and pull of my heart

She reached for my hand, but I stepped away from her.

"What you just said," I started, trying to keep my voice from trembling, "it's not going to happen—not with me."

Then I turned on my heels and ran to the door.

"Nina!"

I got out into the hall of the busy restaurant again. A sea of unfamiliar faces turned like waves towards me. I ignored those curious patrons and weaved around the tables. Everything was like a funhouse-mirror, blurring through my tears, hot tears like napalm burning my face. But I couldn't stop my feet from running and taking me out of there, away from everything, away from Allecra. I blocked out the velvety honey-dripping voice calling me like a siren.

I had to run, or I could never escape her again.

"Nina!" Allecra cried. "Stop running!"

Even now she still thought she had the power over me. I gritted my teeth, weaving my way through the passing waiters and tables. Finally, I exited the depressing fancy place. Outside, I couldn't see anything else except the sidewalk and my sprinting legs.

My lungs felt like it had expanded and then shrunk inside my chest. I was choking with tears. The sound of whizzing cars and horn honking filled my ears. I must look crazy to the eyes of the passersby. A few of them even stopped to look at me with concern.

The cold night air hit my tear-stricken face. I ran until I couldn't run anymore. It was at the end of a block that I stopped on the sidewalk at the corner. My hand rested on the wall as I bended over to gasp for air.

"Hey girl, are you okay?" a man called out from the side.

I waved my hand over to reassure him. He gave a suspicious look before moving on. I turned the corner, but then she was right in front of me. I gasped when Allecra's hands reached for me, holding me back against the wall. A burst of fury rushed through my veins, causing hot tears to stream down my cheeks.

"Let me go! Don't touch me!" I cried and tried to shrug her hands off, but she kept me still. I struggled harder against her hold, yet it was fruitless.

"Shh...Nina. It's alright... I'm not going to hurt you. Nina, please listen to me!" she said, rubbing my arms to calm me down. My loud panting breath was mixed with soft whimpering. I felt her gentle hand wiped the tears from my cheeks.

Allecra's eyes gleamed in the dark corner as they met mine again. She stared at me with a questioning frown, as if she didn't know what she had done.

My mind went back to our conversation at the restaurant.

"Tell me, Nina, what is wrong?" she whispered. She was looking at me with the same concerns etched on her perfect brows. Her tall figure towered over mine in a protective stance. Yet it also confined me from attempting to free myself from her.

"Let me tell you, Allecra, you're not going to get your deed done with me, and I'm not going to bear any child for you," I said in an acerbic voice. "Not now, not ever!"

107

Her mind was trying to comprehend the hidden distress and fear that ensnared me. She couldn't pinpoint the aspect that transpired my reaction. Allecra seemed genuinely curious and apparently worried and confused. Of course, she must be worried, because her potential baby-maker had just refused to breed with her. I felt my inside churn at the word again, and the urge to throw up bubbled in my stomach.

"Why?" Allecra's voice was gentle and rather helpless. Her jaw clenched as she gazed at me with her blazing intense eyes. If I wasn't mistaken, she almost looked hurt. But I scoffed at the idea since Allecra Knight was someone with grace and confidence and all the wonders of both worlds. She wouldn't get hurt over a loveless relationship with me, would she? I didn't know if what we had could even be called a 'relationship' anyway.

"Because I am not! You don't really care about me but what I could offer you from between my legs!" I said and looked away from the enthralling beauty of her face. I wouldn't let it fool me again.

"I have warned you that I can't promise you any romance... " she said. "But for you, I can try."

"I don't want you to try!" I spat back.

"So, tell me what you want, Nina? Tell me!" she growled, pressing herself against my body, closing the space between us completely. I arched my back to push her away, but she didn't budge.

"Save your sympathy for someone else!" I said. "Maybe with another potential girl, who is better than me and more submissive...I'm not worth your try!"

But just like that, she grabbed my face in her hands and merged our lips together. I tried to push her chest away, but she wrapped her strong arms around my body and pulled me to her even more. The sleek long tongue invaded my mouth, slithering like a vicious thing. Allecra kissed me fiercely and desperately with a faint hint of frustration. My blood turned cold, and I shivered in her tight embrace. Instead of the heat of passion, I felt the icy fear up my spine. My knees nearly gave way from under me. I thought my heart would pound to the point it might stop. Allecra was trying to make me surrender to her. I groaned from the hot white pain that burned through me. I wouldn't let her do this to me anymore. She had tortured my confused heart and enslaved my weakened mind enough.

I gripped her collar and summoned all my strength to wrench my lips away from hers. Allecra tried to reach for my mouth again, but I turned my head away.

"Stop it!" I cried and then broke into a heart-wrecking sob. Everything was silent for a long moment as our chests pounded.

"Nina..." Allecra's voice came out in a soft whisper.

"I hate you! I was enough before I met you! I was my own person until you showed up. You did this to me!" I glared at her again. "Now I feel stupid to believe there was still hope for us."

"Nina, I know I'm being selfish to you, but I have no choice," she said.

"But I do have a choice," I hissed. "Since I am nothing but a mean to your end, I can be convinced that I don't deserve to go through this. I have accepted what you are, but I will never do this to myself. Never!"

Allecra looked utterly shocked, but I didn't care. She wouldn't understand the hidden guilt and fear that pained me all my life. Nobody would.

At last, I pushed her away. She didn't stumble under the force, but she did step aside for me to slip out of her grasp.

I rushed to the sidewalk again and hailed a taxi. Allecra stood a few feet away, looking at me from the dark corner. A bright yellow cab pulled over. I walked towards it. A tiny clingy part of me wished she would do something to make me stay. But even if she did, I knew I would never accede to her will.

Once inside the car, I gave my address to the driver in a hurried voice. I was afraid that if I didn't get myself away from her now, I could never muster up the same courage again.

The car began to drive off.

As I leaned back, I glanced at stunned blonde through the window. I saw her still watching me. Her face looked conflicted. I turned my eyes away. Then the gripping sadness and loss overcame me, and I buried my face in my hands. Silent tears spilled from my closed eyelids as the car began to roll away.

CHAPTER 14

I SPENT MOST OF my weekend learning math. Yes, I really did. It seemed like a self-punishment at first, but it turned out math made me feel better. There was no 'if' or 'but' or even a 'maybe.' Either I got it right or I didn't get it at all. I wished my life was so precise and well-defined like this, but sadly, life was the only equation that had some right answers and far too many wrong ones.

Since that night, I felt like I was living in a glass box. Everything was going on outside in the world around me, but I was not a part of it. I remembered making myself get up in the morning. I remembered brushing my teeth, getting dressed, and fixing meals for the twins, but it didn't feel like I was the one doing all these mundane things. Piper was home, but we never talked to each other. Aunt Vikki called to check up on us that Sunday night. She told us about her flight being delayed due to bad weather on the island.

My mind was still a complete wreck with my thoughts thrown about like debris in a storm. Then the dreaded Monday came. I lifted my head up to a cold morning air, but all I saw was a void in the world that was as empty as my chest.

I had written everything down about that night. I wrote in choppy fragments about the part of me that refused to let go. But I also promised myself not to reminisce a single detail of it again. It was for better or for worse — for better because I was not interested in starving, slashing, moping, or even crying anymore, and for worse because there was no reason for me to relish the prospect of living the days to come.

As I walked into school, I felt like a ghost of myself. I heard my feet in the corridors among others, walking but unfeeling.

This morning in Biology, I didn't meet anyone's eyes— not even Jordan's. By the look on her face, I knew she had never seen me like this. Today, we were supposed to learn about mitosis and mitochondria and other cell types. Jordan covered for me and did most of the pair work when the teacher walked by. I just sat there staring blankly at my hands like a statue.

"It will pass, Nina, whatever it is," she whispered in a low voice. Then she reached for my hand and I let her warm palm comfort me. Inside, I was holding onto a fragile thread of my sanity. I was too afraid that at any moment, I could lose that meager grip and everything would fall apart. Maybe that was why Allecra had warned me because she didn't feel the same way. I was nothing compared to her. Allecra was too handsome and perfect and beautiful for a girl like me. If I wasn't marked as her potential one, she would never have looked at me twice.

After class, Jordan walked me to the locker as if I needed an escort.

Then I saw *her* standing there. Allecra looked the same— always the epitome of grace and allure. My heart just stopped. She was talking to her 'sister' at the other end of the hallway. Triton stood with his back against the wall and his arms folded over his chest. I saw Xenon purposely turned around, but Allecra gripped her elbow and pulled her back. They looked like they were arguing over something. I watched them giving each other an intense look. Standing here now, it was hard to believe that I used to be a part of their world.

As if on cue, all three of them looked in my direction. I quickly turned away and hid my face behind the curtain of my hair.

"You have a problem with them?" Jordan noticed and her eyes held unnecessary concern.

"No," I lied. My voice croaked from being quiet for too long, but I could still feel their eyes on me.

"That girl you were talking to," Jordan said again, "...she's looking at you."

"Please don't look at her," I said. But my eyes drifted back to them. I didn't want to, yet I couldn't help it. The instant my eyes met those turquoise ones, I felt like my soul was being sucked out of my body. My bloodstream wobbled. My stomach twisted. I bit my lips from the overflowing emotions. It took every fiber of my being to not rush over and hurl myself at Allecra. I wanted to hear her voice saying my name again. I wanted to know how she had been for the past few days, and—

No, bad Nina!

I squeezed my eyes shut and shook my head to dispel the thought.

"Nina," Jordan said in a suspicious tone and her frown deepened with worries. "What's wrong?"

"Nothing." I shook my head at her, not wanting to talk about it. I felt as if the world was spinning back and forth where I stood. I gave a surreptitious glance their way and realized Allecra and her siblings were gone.

"I'll see you again, Jordan," I said as I started to make my way to the opposite side of the building.

"I'm sorry if I'm intruding into your personal life, Nina," Jordan was saying, "I'm just worried about you."

I stopped to look at the girl standing beside me. It had crossed my mind a few times before, but I was just too blind to see it. Jordan was a nice person. She was a human being with no complications. She was a real girl with no extra parts. And most importantly, she wouldn't want to impregnate me. Why could I not forget about Allecra and go back to being normal? I could have a normal girlfriend like Jordan, and the thread of life would be less tangled and knotty.

"Jordan," I said, causing her to look at me again. "Would you like to have a drink with me after school?"

Her brows rose at the sudden question. Then slowly, she gave me a small nod and smiled.

"If you pay," she said.

It made me chuckle a little, and that surprised me. I could still be happy without Allecra Knight. Yes, that feeling was really something to hold on to.

"See you after school then," I said and we bid each other goodbye.

At the end of lunch period, my life was still going on slowly, one minute at a time. I thought it couldn't get any better, but at least it didn't get worse. That was a sign that I had survived the first stage of heartbreak. It was a miracle that I had made it through the horrible Monday morning and was still able to plan to go out with Jordan.

I dreaded going to Language Arts, though it wasn't for long. I sat down at an empty desk all by myself. On the table was a yellow post-it note with a poem written on it.

Don't fall in love with a sailor boy,
He won't set your heart free,
Oh, don't fall in love with a sailor boy,

He'll take your heart to sea.

It was apropos to my old poem that I read to Allecra. My tears welled up in my eyes, but I fought to keep them from flowing. I had cried enough for her.

Not half an hour had passed and I was soon haunted by Allecra's face and her honey-coated voice. I could still picture her beautiful slender fingers scribbling away, the way she stood and how she looked at me, especially how she looked at me. No one had looked at me that way.

When the last school bell sounded, I waited for the hallway to be cleared of students. Then I received a text from Jordan. We had agreed that I would drive back to my aunt's house to leave my car there before riding in hers.

As I headed down the corridor to my locker again, I bumped into Jack, of all people.

"Nina!" he said when I turned away from him. "Nina, wait!"

He came to block me with his arms extended out.

"What do you want?" My voice was low like a growl of an animal ready to bite and tear.

"Look, Nina, I just want to apologize for what had happened," he said.

"Then you've found the wrong person," I said.

"You know Piper and I are not in a relationship anymore," he tried to explain and his face was pleading. "Piper has agreed to end it with me for real this time. I swear I will treat you better than anyone you've ever been with, girls or guys alike."

"I don't care about your relationship status, Jack," I said. "I don't like you. I don't want anything to do with you, and you better stop following me!"

I skirted around him and walked in the direction of my locker. I heard him follow behind me.

"You should be thankful that I noticed you, Nina," he snarled. Jack was trying to get my attention again, but I ignored his acrimonious remark. I put away my books as quickly as I could so that I'd be ready to leave.

"You'll regret it," he said again.

"No, I won't," I said. "I have dated guys like you before. I could see the same patterns."

"Girls will always be just girls," he said suddenly. "You will eventually come back to men."

This time, I stopped whatever I was doing and turned sharply to face him. "What did you just say?"

Jack recoiled at the fury in my eyes. What was it with the male species? What gave them the idea that a woman is destined to satisfy their emotional and physical needs?

"Listen carefully, Jack Conner, I will never be just a girl. I refuse to be as simple as guys like you want me to be because I am important and I will be unapologetic about myself. Screw you for trying to make me feel otherwise!"

Jack looked at me with wide eyes. He was stunned by all my frustrated streams of emotions.

"I'm...I'm sorry, Nina," he said, holding his hands up as if guilty. "It's just...It's just I have never felt this way towards anyone before. I promise I will change for you."

I scoffed and shook my head to myself in utter dismay.

"You should change for someone who loves you back, Jack. One day you'll find that person, but I'm not the one for you," I said and then walked away.

_*_

Jordan and I went to a nightclub called Crysis. I didn't know why she picked this place. Maybe the name sounded like 'crisis, which kind of suited the mood. We each started off with two vodka and tonics, followed by some cocktails. The music wasn't too loud. Maybe, it was still early so people weren't too eager to dance and go wild just yet.

"I come here once in a while," she told me. "They don't bother to card you even if they know you're underage."

"Oh," I said.

Jordan rattled the ice in her glass.

"You ought to unwind, Nina," she said, turning to look at me. "Girlfriend, family, school—just throw them all out the window."

"Did you notice that you said 'girlfriend' instead of 'boyfriend'?" I asked, feigning offended. "You think I'm gay?"

"I saw the way you looked at Allecra Knight. Girls who look at her like that are not completely straight," she said. The mention of Allecra sent me a pang of sadness.

I drank my third glass of vodka. Jordan ate pistachio as her eyes kept looking at me.

"Tell me what is troubling you, Nina," she asked.

"It's not worth telling." I shook my head.

"It's not worth bottling up your feelings inside either," she said. "Come on, let's talk about whatever that comes to your mind. It doesn't have to be your problems."

"Can I ask you something then?" I asked, earning a nod from Jordan while she was still busy cracking nutshells. "If you fall in love with someone with a physical abnormality, say... if he or she has six fingers, do you mind being with that person?"

Jordan stopped chewing. She pursed her lips.

"I don't think I mind," she said at last.

"What if that person has three breasts?"

Jordan almost choked. She stared at me like she was trying to tell if I was still right in the head. I didn't even know if I was still right in the head myself.

"Well...I don't know," she said slowly.

"Why not?" I said. "You don't mind being with someone with six fingers, but why not someone with three breasts?"

"Because it's hard to imagine, Nina, unless you're talking about some kind of alien," she said. I frowned at how spot-on it was.

"What if it's someone with two sexes?"

"Oh, god, Nina!"

"Just answer me, please," I said.

"It depends," she said. "If that person can make me fall in love, I think they deserve that same amount of happiness they have given to me. I will do whatever that makes them happy, too."

"What about making yourself happy?"

"If your feeling is reciprocated, then what goes around comes around." She shrugged.

"And will you do something you don't want to do just for that person, too?"

"If that person really loves me, I don't think they will make me do something I don't want to," she said and turned to me. "But Nina, if you can experience the feeling of doing something you don't understand just for love, then you have found the true essence of it."

Jordan may be right, except I knew my feelings would never be reciprocated. How egotistical I was to think that I could affect her that much. Thinking about it made me want to have another drink. I called to the waiter and ordered a fourth round of vodka.

"You know if you get too drunk, the morning after won't be all sunshine and flowers," Jordan reminded me.

"There won't be any sunshine and flowers even if I'm sober."

"Nina, how bad are you feeling right now?" she asked rather seriously.

"Bad enough to melt all the tigers in the world to butter," I said and Jordan laughed.

"Oh, great! Now we better go," she said and signaled to the waiter to get the tab.

"Are we leaving now?"

"I don't think I could carry you all the way to my car after this."

"But I'm not drunk!"

"Oh yeah, one of the biggest lies in the world," she said. "Now, come!"

She pulled me from the stool, and in a minute, we left the place. Outside, we strolled along a lighted pathway in the park.

"Are you okay?" she said.

"Hey, I came from the land of vodka. A few shots do nothing," I said and missed a step, but Jordan steadied me back.

"Sure," she said. "Not drunk at all!"

"You don't believe me, Jordan? You don't believe me?" I said. "I can climb the tree to prove it."

Unfortunately, there was not a single tree nearby. Jordan reassured me that she believed my ability to climb trees, so I decided to drop it. Then we reached a wooden bench in the park. Jordan sat me down and magically produced a bottle of water and told me to drink the content slowly. After a long while later, the earth felt less unstable and I stopped seeing double.

"Whoa, I'm a wreck," I murmured.

"Any drunk person is a wreck, don't worry," she said and placed a wet towel over my forehead.

"My first time getting wasted, though," I said.

"You're quite strong for a first-timer," she said as she kneeled in front of me. "Now, please tell me what turned you into this?"

"You really want to know my dirty little secret?"

She nodded and her eyes were fixed on mine.

"I am in love with an alien girl," I said, "and she wants me to have her baby."

"I'm not sure whether I should spank your butt or laugh my head off first," Jordan said and then she broke into laughter and I joined her. After all, my life felt like a joke. We laughed until we couldn't breathe and then we stopped.

"No, I'm serious," I said but then I started hiccupping. Jordan laughed again.

"Come on, let's get you home, princess," she said. "I'm not the knight you're expecting, but as of now, I will have to assume the role."

"No, I don't want to go home," I protested and staggered to my feet. Jordan put an arm around my waist.

"It's the Knight girl, isn't it?" she asked suddenly. "The hot blonde one, I might add."

"How did you know?"

"When you looked at her this morning, I just knew something wasn't right," she said. "What did that girl do to you?"

I shivered and wrapped my arms around her neck. In that moment, I was suddenly in need of human warmth.

"I love her, Jordan. I love her, but I also hate her. Do you understand? Do you?" I said and broke into uncontrollable sobs in her arms. Jordan smoothed my hair and rubbed my back gently.

"I do, Nina. I do," she comforted me. "It might sound crazy, but all I want is to see you happy again. You seem like someone who could be loved by just about anybody in the world. That girl has to be stupid to reject you."

"It's the other way around," I whispered and pulled away. "I was the one who rejected her."

Jordan looked confused.

117

"But...why?"

"Because I'm a coward," I said and then cried again. We stood holding each other like that for a long moment.

By the time we got back to Jordan's car, it was around ten o'clock. I felt better after a bottle of water and a good hearty cry later.

"I'm hungry," I said. "Let's have pizza."

There was a small Italian pizza joint around the corner.

"Not a bad idea," she said and we turned to head there together. We ordered pizza Margherita and soda. We went back to the car again. Jordan searched for the car keys while I was eating from the pizza box.

Then we got inside the car.

"You sure made a fast recovery," Jordan noted as I was sipping my drink.

"Russian girls are tough, you know. Besides the pizza was so good, it unclogged me." I grinned and sipped my soda.

"Yeah, tough girl, you've got tomato source on your face," she said with a giggle.

"Oh, where?" I wiped my mouth with the back of my hand. Jordan pulled out a tissue and dabbed it on my lips. But when she was done, Jordan still gazed at my face. Her hand gently caressed my cheek.

"Jordan..."

"I will never hurt you like her," she whispered. Our eyes met in silence. Both heads began to tilt as our faces drew closer. Just before our lips touched, I heard the door opened at my side. My head turned when a hand pulled me by the wrist out of the car. Out of instinct, I struggled against the vise-like grip, but only to find myself crushed against the soft chest of a tall figure. Allecra's face stood out like the moon in the sky. Her eyes blazed like a deep glowing sea.

"Allecra?" I said amidst the shock. She seemed to have the knack of finding me in unexpected places. Was she stalking me? I heard Jordan got out from the other side.

"What are you doing?" my friend said.

Allecra turned to her and then back at me. Her expression was the same one I spotted the day she almost killed the guy who had harassed me. I twisted my body around and broke away from her hold, but Allecra wrapped her hands around my waist and pulled me back against her roughly.

"Nina!" Jordan was going to walk over to me. "Let her go!"

"Tell your friend, you're coming with me," the smooth voice whispered in my ear. Suddenly, I felt the chilling terror and feared for the safety of my innocent friend.

"It's—It's okay, Jordan," I said, too startled to give any more explanation. "I will see you at school."

After I said that, I felt Allecra's strong hands steer me around, almost dragging me like a ragdoll away from the car.

"Nina!" Jordan called after us. I looked over my shoulder to her.

"I'll be fine. Please go home, Jordan! I'm sorry," I said.

The next thing I knew I was inside the black car again. What was worse was Allecra's cold eyes glaring at me.

"You will never do that again, you hear me?" she said.

"That's none of your concern!" I snapped.

"Everything about you concerns me!" she retorted back.

I fell silent. She turned away as her hand swiftly started the engine. The car revved deafeningly for a good two seconds before it jerked forward. If that wasn't a sign of jealousy, I didn't know what was. But why should she be jealous? Surely she had no care about me. And now all I could do was staring at her in confusion.

"Where are you taking me?" My words came out less hostile than I had intended. I heard Allecra took a deep breath for a second before glancing at me again.

"I'd like to have a talk with you again," she said. "But first, we have to go somewhere quiet."

CHAPTER 15

"Please, stop the car now," I demanded. "I need to go home."

Allecra ignored me. Her lips still pressed together into a tight line. Her bright turquoise eyes kept staring ahead. The car was accelerating way too fast down an empty highway street. Was she trying to get us killed or something? I bit my lips in exasperation, glaring at her with extra force to get her attention.

"If you keep going at this speed to God knows where I have to assume you're kidnapping me," I said again in a threatening voice, but the car didn't decelerate. If anything, the needle on the speedometer dial kept rising, and it scared me.

"If I'm kidnapping you now, what can you do about that, huh?" Allecra asked, turning her gaze sideway at me. Her brows knitted in the midst of mockery and frustration. It was hard to believe in a time like this I still found her shockingly attractive.

"Pull over, Allecra, or I'll call the police," I tried to speak with a considerable amount of boldness.

Allecra let out a laugh and just shook her head.

"As much as my sister insisted, I wouldn't do that. Maybe not yet."

"Wait, your sister wanted you to kidnap me?"

The prickling fear began to creep into my body like chilling frost. Allecra didn't answer my question. I remembered seeing both of them arguing this morning. Was it something in that regard? Allecra wasn't one of those psycho aliens with impregnation fetish, was she?

"Stop staring at me like that, you could burn holes." She scoffed without looking at me. Then her hand pushed the clutch expertly as she steered the car off the road. The pebbles under the tires made crunching sounds when we came to a crawl.

I realized it was where she had found me that night. Below us was the golden sea of tiny houses and streets. Allecra pressed on a certain button next to the dashboard and the roof fell away, folding automatically into the rear trunk. She cut off the engine. The quietness of the cold night pervaded us.

"I just want to talk about you and me again." Allecra's voice was very low against the night breeze.

"There is nothing to talk about," I told her. "Whatever it is that you think we have is over."

"Is it because you wanted so badly to be in bed with that girl?" she said acidly.

My jaw flung open as I looked at her. I almost didn't believe my ears.

"Jordan and I are just friends!" I growled.

"Didn't look like that when she tried to shove her tongue in your mouth," she shot back, her eyes still glaring like bright jewels. I gritted my teeth.

"If I want to sleep with her, it's still none of your business," I hissed and then raised my chin up daringly. "At least, she genuinely cares about me."

"I'll make sure she cares no more." Allecra's cold words hinted a dark intention, and I recoiled from the idea of Jordan getting hurt.

"Don't you do anything to her," I muttered protectively. "She's my friend."

"I still won't let anyone touch you like that."

"Oh, so only you can?"

The light in her eyes shifted as she glared at me. She reached over and grabbed my shoulders, pulling me forcefully towards her. Our noses almost touched. I tried to pry her hands off, but it was like wriggling out of a lioness's grip. Those gem-like eyes bored with heat into mine. I fought against the fear that tried to overpower me.

"You've tormented me enough, Nina," she muttered in a low frustrated tone. "It could have been easier if I just let my sister handle you in the first place."

"What were you going to do to me?" I snapped back. "Abduct me to your spaceship and force yourself on me?"

Allecra's jaw tightened at my words. The look on her face morphed from anger to pain. Her piercing turquoise eyes glittered with moisture. She looked genuinely hurt. Allecra Knight in her most vulnerable state was something I never expected to see. Then she let go of me and turned her face away. With her arms on the steering wheel, Allecra leaned her forehead against it and gave a long drawn out sigh. For the first time, she looked exhausted and defeated. A spark of worries ignited in my heart.

121

"Allecra..." I called out, but she kept quiet for a long while. I could hear her soft panting. Her long blonde lock fell loosely like a waterfall around her shoulders, and I felt the urge to run my fingers through those silky strands, but I restrained myself and kept my emotions at bay.

Allecra let out a humorless chuckle.

"I should have left long ago," she said. "I don't know what to make of you. It's not what we've planned."

I frowned, unable to understand it.

"If you wish to leave, surely no one's stopping you," I said.

"That is where the complication started, Nina," Allecra said bitterly, looking up at me now. Her eyes were softer but still bright with intensity. They kept me frozen like a mouse in the eyes of a snake. "The first time I saw you, it was a tremendous shock to me. Then when we were in the dark attic, I came so very close to nearly take you then, but I couldn't bring myself to hurt you like that."

I shivered under her intense, glowing gaze. Allecra looked away again as if she was ashamed.

"You were trying to make me remember what I saw between you and your sister," I said. "Why did you want me to remember it again?"

"I wanted you to hate me and be scared of me so that you would stay away," she said. "I was hoping to rely on your willpower, and it worked. But then this happened. I'm just too weak to let you go."

"But—why me?" I whispered softly.

"Remember what I told you?" she asked. "I would have to leave you if you couldn't give me what I wanted. It would hurt you. But now I can't make myself leave even when you rejected me. I crave your company too much I can't keep myself away from you anymore."

My mouth went dry.

"What am I to you exactly, Allecra, other than the potential one to breed with?" I said. I was proud of myself for sounding unaffected and detached enough.

"I wish I could understand human emotions better," she said. "I know it's extremely important for you to decide whether to mate with me. But Nina, if we're together, we can talk it out. We don't have to rush."

Her voice sounded astonishingly convincing. I already felt my heart soften by her words, but I tried to recompose myself.

"No, I meant what I said, Allecra," I reminded her. "I can't make babies for you, and that's that."

"You can't?" she asked.

"Actually, I won't," I clarified.

"But why? Is it because of me? Do you mind that I'm not human, or that I'm neither a boy nor a girl?"

"No, it's nothing to do with you being you," I said.

"Then why?"

"I just don't, okay?" I retorted. "If you don't like that, it's your problem— not mine."

"Oh Nina," Allecra breathed. Then her gaze met mine again. I had to look away. I knew that angel's face was the end of my unbreakable vow. Silence descended on us once again. I could hear the leaves on the nearby trees rattled softly in the wind.

After a while, Allecra leaned herself back against the seat and looked up at the stars in the sky. I couldn't help but do the same. It was exhausting to me as well. We both looked up at the serene night together — a black canvas of velvet had been laid over and sprinkled with twinkling gems. We let the tranquil atmosphere eased away the tension of our earlier chagrin for what seemed like a long time.

"I am the Endling, Nina," Allecra spoke again. "You know what an Endling is?"

My heart sort of froze. I knew what it was from biology class. An Endling is referred to an organism that is the last of its species. Once the endling dies, the species becomes extinct.

"You're the last of your kind?" I sat up straighter to look at her.

"Yes." She nodded weakly. "I am the last Arzurian now."

"What about your brother and sister?" I asked.

"They're not my biological siblings. They were created to accompany me to Earth," she said. "Triton and Xenon are the products of cloning, a genetic engineering, alteration, manipulation, or whatever the word they called. But like everyone else on my planet, they can't reproduce."

"Why is that?" I said. "How did it happen?"

"I will tell you another time," Allecra said with a long exhale. "But Nina, I was made from the best DNA there is. I came from the strongest and healthiest of the Arzurian gene pool. I was supposed to carry these genes and travel through the galaxy just to find the potential one. My entire existence is to breed so that I could continue the Arzurian bloodline. I am my species' last hope, but now I guess—it doesn't matter anymore."

She turned and looked at me meaningfully and I finally understood. I was the thing that went wrong.

"Were there other potential ones before me?" I asked.

"You're not the first human girl that we have found, or that I have attempted to breed with," she said and then paused to glance at my face.

"How many?" I said in a bold tone.

"Seven."

I kept myself composed.

"What happened to those seven potentials?"

"It is still extremely difficult to find the one that is my match," she just told me. "None of the Earthlings I have been with bore me any child."

"What did you do when you found out they weren't the right one for you?" I asked.

"Just like I have warned you, Nina," she sighed softly. "If it doesn't work..."

"You leave," I concluded.

"That's why I was trying to protect you from me," Allecra said. "For the first time I am afraid. None of the potential girls I met made me afraid. But with you, it terrifies me."

"You're afraid of what?"

"Of having to lose you, Nina," she said softly.

"But I can't give you what you want," I said. "You should try to look for someone else."

"No, it's already too late," she said. "The thought of not being near you again made everything suddenly unbearable. And to see you with someone else is far worse."

I dropped my eyes to my hands that rested limply on my lap. Then gentle fingers brushed my hair back behind my ear and stroked my cheek. Allecra tipped my chin up and turned my face back to her. She leaned over until our foreheads were inches apart. Her bright enigmatic eyes gazed into mine.

"You seemed so happy with that girl," she said softly. "In that moment, I never wanted anything so badly than to be in her place."

I heard my pulse humming through my veins as I stared at her. Allecra looked miserable. She then tilted her head and placed her face at the curve of my neck.

"Allecra, I..." I tried to say something but trailed off. I listened to her breathing and felt the tickling of soft blonde hair as the wind brushed through it. Gingerly, I put my arms around her. With deliberate gentleness, she slid her hands down to my sides and enveloped my waist. Her nose drifted over my throat, skimming across my collarbone. I shivered from both the sensation and the cold air, but I felt strangely comforted by her warmth. Allecra let out a heavy sigh again. She came to rest her head on my chest, listening to my heartbeat.

"I don't know how to feel about all this yet," she whispered. "All I know is I miss our kisses as soon as they end. Something that I can't define makes me crave you. I crave your voice, your hands, your lips, everything. There is not a single part of you that is not worth kissing. It leaves me sleepless at night. You can't imagine how hard it is for me. I don't care if I'm an Endling anymore as long as I have you."

CHAPTER 17

IT WAS PAST MIDNIGHT when Allecra parked her car in front of my aunt's house. Before I turned to leave, she pulled me back by my elbow gently and took my hands in hers.

"Nina." Her voice saying my name shouldn't have been so alluring and familiar. It was as if I had heard that melodious tone all my life while we'd only met for barely a couple months. I looked up reluctantly at that inhumanly stunning face. Allecra seemed to brighten a little after the talk. But I still felt a bit nervous as she stared at me imploringly.

"Yes?" I said.

"I just want you to know that I'm not pressuring you. You don't have to do anything with me, and I mean anything," she said gently and stroked my hand with her thumbs in a circular motion.

"Do what exactly?" I asked, although deep down I kind of knew what she was referring to. Allecra almost looked sheepish before she answered in a quiet tone.

"You don't have to have sex with me."

I tried to remind myself to suck in the air through my nose and not my mouth.

Allecra looked concerned when she heard me gasp.

"Are you okay?"

"Well." I gulped, feeling my face heated up a little. "Why the change?"

I was still trying to calm my heartbeat when Allecra startled me by lifting my hand to her face and pressed my palm to her cheek. Her face was so smooth and soft, I had to resist to the urge to trace my fingers over her flawless skin. I watched her eyelids closed and saw those long black lashes curved.

"Because I want you more, Nina," she whispered, and I felt my breath leaving me again. "If it scares you so much to make you wish to leave me, then I don't want it at all. It doesn't matter anymore. None of it matters if it's not about you."

All of a sudden, I could almost conjure up a physical pain just to think about being separated from her.

"No, Allecra." I shook my head. "It's not just the sex with you that frightens me. I mean, yes, the mere thought of doing it does scare me a little, but it's because I have never done anything like that with anyone. Besides, I'm not a normal girl."

"You're not into boys, you mean?" she said. "That's what makes you hesitate because I have a boy's part."

Sometimes, Allecra's ability to understand human internal conflict was too impressive. It gave me a fresh surge of admiration.

"Right." I nodded. "But it's not just the sex with—your boy's thing itself. There's something else I can't do with you."

"I see. It's the breeding, isn't it?" she added.

I bit my lips and looked away. I felt Allecra graze my cheek with the back of her fingers gently.

"Don't worry," she said. "I won't do that to you if that's what push you away. This, being around you, is enough."

"Am I worth it?" I said. "You have come a long way for something important to your race, and you are willing to give it all up because of me?"

"I would give up the entire universe just for you, Nina."

She brought my hand to her lips and kissed it softly. I watched her perfectly sculpted mouth pursed over my skin before releasing me again. The cold tingling sensation was pleasant where her lips touched.

"Goodnight, Nina," she said. It took me a while to recover. I had to tear my eyes away from the finest curves of her lips and those brilliantly piercing turquoise eyes.

"Goodnight, Allecra," I replied softly before getting out of the car.

I watched her until she was gone, then entered the house in a daze once again. What still shocked me was Allecra's willingness to give up her future generation and even the pleasure of having (you know) just to be with me. I found that incredibly touching, yet also terrifying. Because of me, she would go to this great length while I wouldn't have done the same for her.

Was I being selfish?

No, no, stop it, Nina. You shouldn't feel like that.

Allecra might look sincere enough to melt the hearts of every human virgin girls, but I couldn't just throw caution to the wind. How could I tell whether she said all this just to lure me in and have her way with me before she dumps me? Allecra must have done it so many times since she had been with those seven potential ones prior. What made the eighth any different?

Besides, if I let her have a hold on my heartstring again, I might end up being her willing puppet, serving her needs day and night. And the next thing I knew, I would be brainwashed and feel obligated to even go further as to carry her baby. I'd also have to abandon all my dreams and future, my only chance of spreading my wings and be free.

No, I couldn't let that happen. That was what had happened to my mother. I wouldn't let Allecra Knight rob me of my freedom in life like my dad did to my mom.

_*_

That night, I had a dream about Allecra again just before dawn. It was extremely realistic and sexually charged. But I knew it was a dream — one of those dreams that are so vivid it's hard to distinguish it from reality.

In the dream, we were lying on a large flat rock. It was polished smooth and cold. The sky was a perfect light purple. There were white clouds hanging low. I could see a very big pale grayish moon just above us. Yet there was also another aqua-blue moon hovering over the horizon. The grass was tall and swaying, even though there wasn't any wind. It felt like twilight and some large featherless birds were hurrying off to their nests. It was a strange place, different than anywhere I'd ever seen on earth. So there the two of us lying under the violet sky, silently had sex.

My body was entangled with Allecra's beautiful feminine form. The only thing that stood out was the soft bulge nesting between our pelvises. I felt my wetness and smelled the sweet musky scent. My core was burning for something. I felt an indescribable pleasure when Allecra pushed herself against me and then slipped into me. Now to think of it, I would never have given in to a desire like this with Allecra. It only made sense that this happened in a dream. But for the first time, I had thrown away all restraints and hesitation and succumbed to my lust.

I felt the friction inside me. It was deliriously delicious. She was so hard, and I was so soft. We both were slippery and burning with passion. My heart was pounding and I found it hard to breathe. I didn't know what I was doing, but in that moment, I didn't really care, as if I had no sense of self anymore and every part of me was Allecra's. I was hers to take and I was wildly going at it with her in pure joy. Strangely, in the dream, I never saw her infamous secret. All I had was the feeling of that invisible member inside me. I tried to see it, but I never got a glimpse.

Allecra's skin was pale like milk and her tattoos were glowing bright blue. She looked at me with hungry eyes and they, too, were glowing. I wanted to touch her face, but I couldn't move my hands. It was as if I was paralyzed. Her hips kept moving against mine, and I felt her thing deep in my core. I was gasping and whimpering in her arms, but Allecra didn't stop. Over and over, I felt her all the way until I climaxed.

It all was so strange and so new to me. It also scared me. I wanted Allecra inside me, but at the same time, I wanted to run away from her and all this. It was so confusing and a complication at its worst.

When I opened my eyes, it was still dim outside, and I felt very odd. My panties were drenched in slipperiness, and it felt as if I had just been penetrated. The idea made me cringe in embarrassment.

It was not until after dawn that I got up. I drew the curtain back and looked out at the morning sky. It seemed like it had just stopped raining since everything was still wet and drippy. Clouds to the east were sharply etched into the sky, each one framed by light. The sky looked ominous one moment and alluring the next. It all depended on the angle, like everything else in the world. I wondered why it had to be like that, even something dirty like sex.

I decided to banish the thought of my dream and went to the bathroom. For some shameful reason, I kind of let myself marvel in that sweet erotic feeling that came afterward. Was it how it felt like having sex with Allecra? If the dream happened again, it would be my secret, my guilty pleasure, and no one else had to know, not even Allecra herself.

As I expected, I was experiencing a mild hangover. My head pounded a little as I stepped down the stairs, but it wasn't that bad. I could have used some aspirins but didn't. I figured my headache would be gone by itself anyway. Then I found Piper in the kitchen, rummaging through the fridge. She turned when she heard me.

"Hey," she greeted with a small smile. It was the first time since the party night that my cousin spoke to me.

"Morning, Piper," I murmured, trying not to be so surprised about it.

"I'm hungry and I just—" She gestured to the content inside the fridge as if she needed to explain herself. I nodded and walked over to the stove.

"Sit down. I'll make you something," I said as I got the toaster and took some whole wheat bread out of the cupboard.

"Where's Jason?" Piper asked after she took a seat on the island. I had to pause to see whether I knew where her own brother was right now.

"I don't know," I said. Piper turned to look out the window facing the garage and returned to her stool.

"His car's here. Probably sleeping, that sleepyhead. So where have you been last night?" Piper swirled around to ask me. She seemed strangely conversational today.

"I was out with a friend," I told her while I wrapped aluminum foil over the bread. I was making some grilled cheese sandwiches. Then I felt Piper coming to stand beside the counter.

"Uncle Peter called, and he asked for you," she said. "But I didn't know where you were, so I told him you were sleeping."

"Who?"

"Your dad, my uncle, remember?" she said.

I had to keep in mind that Piper couldn't say my father's Russian name, so she chose an English equivalent for his name.

"Your uncle's name is pronounced, *'Pi-ooh-ter*. Take note," I said. "And thank you. I'll get back to him—which is never."

I mumbled the last part, so my cousin didn't hear. What did my dad expect to hear from me? That I missed my step-mom and his newborn baby? I didn't even want to know if the new apple was a girl or a boy, which proved that I was a terrible sister and would never make a good mother, which served me right.

I sensed Piper coming to stand beside me.

"So was it the Knight girl you went out with last night?" she asked nosily. "I saw you and her in the car by chance when I got down for water. Are you guys—you know— dot dot dot?"

I turned and gave her a disapproving look. Piper put her hands up apologetically. I sighed and went back to slicing cheese again.

"Shouldn't you concern with your love life instead, Piper?" I said. From the corner of my eyes, Piper pouted.

"Well, I just want us to make up and be cousin-friends again and forget about what happened," she said at last and then she took my hand, causing me to stop my work and look at her. "I'm sorry for what I said and how I treated you that night, Nina. I have been thinking and thinking. It wasn't your fault. My relationship took a nose dive long before you came, and I should have known it better than to blame you. I meant, you are gay, for crying out loud, and you are not into guys, right? So it was just Jack. He is the biggest jerk I've ever met. All my friends kept telling me he's not a keeper, but I didn't believe them. Looking back, I couldn't get why I was obsessed with him. I mean he's handsome and all, but he's an a-hole. I guess I was just afraid to be single and lonely and horny—"

"Piper, I get it," I cut her off.

"Sorry," she murmured. "Now I understand. Until I'm comfortable being by myself that I know whether I want someone because I'm in love or because I'm just desperate to be loved. Gosh, I'm such an idiot!"

"No, you're just straight and blonde," I said sarcastically, which caused Piper to frown in confusion.

"Huh?"

"My point exactly," I said under my breath. "Anyway, never mind." I waved her off with my free hand.

"So, are we cool?" she asked, swinging my arm a little. The movement made my head dizzy. I had to nod in acceptance.

"Okay—okay, we're cool."

Piper squealed cheerily and bounced forward to kiss me on the cheek. My eyebrows automatically rose at her.

"Now I can't wait to go shopping with you again!" She clapped her hands together and laughed. I just rolled my eyes.

When I put the grilled sandwiches in front of her, Piper inhaled and sighed.

"I have missed your cooking," she said and began to chomp down on her sandwich delightfully.

"Was it why you wanted to make up with me?" I teased.

"Partly, yes," she said, but it made me smile. Piper wasn't that bad after all. While we were eating, she went on about how guys were a disappointment throughout her entire history of dating, and how she was tired of relationships and being cheated on and whatnots.

I was only half-listening as my mind was still pondering about last night.

Then Jordan popped into my head like a bubble. I felt my heart sunk at the thought of my friend. It was rude and terrible of me to leave her like that, and I was still mad at Allecra about it. It was obvious that I needed to apologize to Jordan today.

"You know, the only thing guys know how to do is lie to you," Piper still complained energetically.

"Not all guys are like that," I commented. "There are plenty of the good ones out there, too."

"Aren't you supposed to hate men or something, Nina?" she asked.

I put my sandwich down for this was one of the facepalm-worthy moments with Piper.

"What? You think there has to be a clog in my brain to prevent me from appreciating good people with the Y chromosome?"

"Well, that's not what I meant, but—you know—*lesbians?*" she said.

"Piper, you say 'lesbian' one more time and you'll never see your grilled cheese sandwich again," I said and reached out to take her plate away.

"Hey, no!" she cried, coming to pry my hand from her plate. "I'm sorry! I won't say it again."

"There's a lot you need to learn about homosexuality," I said and let go.

"I know, sometimes I wish I were a les—I mean—gay. They seem pretty chill and lovey-dovey-gooey when they're in love. I want a relationship like that. Maybe things would be so much easier."

"Right, except for the hate crimes, bullying, higher suicide rates, workplace harassment and discrimination, possibility of being stoned to death or flogged in some countries, Russia's violent crackdown on gay people, assault, depression, familial persecution, having to come out every time you meet a new person, threats of being disowned by loved ones, and having to field the above questions over and over again until the day you die. Other than that, it is pretty great and you get to enjoy the Ellen show."

Piper looked at me and didn't talk for a long time, which made me a bit worry at her unusual quietness.

"Piper?"

"Oh," she finally breathed. "Oh wow. It just hit me. That's scary. It must be so hard being you."

"You have no idea," I said and gathered our empty plates to put in the sink. "Just stay straight if you can."

But before I left, Piper grabbed my hand. I looked at my cousin again.

"You are very brave, Nina," she said, "and very strong, too."

I wanted to tell her that I wasn't, that I had things that terrified me, like losing my virginity to a hermaphrodite alien girl and having a hybrid child and dying of childbirth. But of course, I didn't tell Piper all that.

"It's just worth being who you are," I simply said. "You love whoever you love, just sometimes they have the same body parts like you."

Or sometimes they have same-same but different body parts. I thought to myself.

"Yeah, although it's kinda weird to say this," Piper bit her lips shyly. "But who knows? If one day I meet someone I love, who happens to be a girl, my straightness probably goes out the window, too. I mean, hey, I was in love with a guy whose brain is the size of a peanut, so why is it harder to love a girl if she's everything I've ever wanted, right?"

A girl who's everything I've ever wanted. Right, why is it so hard?

Piper smiled at me, and I smiled back.

"You learn fast, cousin."

CHAPTER 19

PIPER SEEMED TO BE in a good mood, almost more than her usual good mood because she actually asked me if I wanted to ride with her today.

"I just want to spend more time with you - that's all," she had said.

We left the house together. It was sunny again after the rain. The grass looked greener with twinkling dew reflected the sunlight. I only dressed in jeans and a casual t-shirt. My hair was up in a loose bun since I expected the day to be foggy and humid, but it wasn't.

Halfway down the driveway, I froze because a familiar shiny black car was parking in front of the house. My heart thumped and clenched at the same time. Piper turned to look at me when I just stood there then she followed my gaze.

"Wow! What a goddamn car," she breathed beside me.

The tinted window rolled down, revealing the driver with sunglasses. The smooth angelic face seemed to shine like a star from within the dark interior.

"Is she here to pick you up?" Piper asked.

"I—I don't know."

Allecra did nothing but stared and stared. While I stood there like an idiot, looking back at her, Piper surprised me by starting to walk towards the car.

"Piper?" I gasped, trying to pull her back, but she already bounced off like a perky schoolgirl she was.

I had to trot after my cousin, not knowing what she was up to.

"Hi!" Piper said as she casually stuck her head into the Lambo through the window with her hands folded over the door. I stood back, holding my breath. Allecra didn't seem to react to anything. Her sunglasses were metallic that mirrored back everything in miniature. She took off her shade and threw me a quick glance before directing her beautiful turquoise eyes to Piper.

"Hello," Allecra responded in the silkiest voice that sent a chill through my spine. I bet Piper also got the same effect on full blast. My cousin looked stunned and her playful daredevil demeanor suddenly vanished.

Piper leaned back from the car a little and blinked a few times as if to get her mind working again.

Oh my goodness, even Piper, the straightest of the straight girls, wasn't immune to Allecra!

"Well—mmm—I just—wanna ask if you're here for my cousin," she stammered out. Her cheeks suddenly looked redder.

"Indeed, I am," Allecra said and then flashed her perfect smile at her. The smile though was Piper's undoing. My cousin's jaw seemed to drop slightly as she looked at the blonde girl. Then Piper snapped herself out of it and stepped away from the Lambo as if it was hot. She turned to me with a troubled, almost panicky look on her face.

"Oh wow...this is weird," she mumbled to herself and grabbed my hand. "Nina, I think we don't get to ride to school together today. You can go with her. It's cool. No prob."

"Wait, what?"

"See you later!"

"Piper, wait!" I called after her, but she already jogged away.

I swirled myself around to look at Allecra with a frown. The corners of her crimson lips turned up in a smirk. Then the passenger door lifted open for me. Before I could let myself think twice, I stepped into the black car. It was filled with her exquisite scent. I noticed Allecra was wearing a black V-neck t-shirt and a black leather jacket with sleeves covering her tattooed arms. Everything Allecra put on looked just right all the times. She dressed better than all the guys I had seen and still managed to look feminine enough to draw air out of my lungs.

"I hope I'm not scaring your cousin or anything," she said in an apologetic voice. Her eyes still gazed at me, observing me. "I just couldn't wait to see you again."

A spontaneous blush rushed up my neck. I cleared my throat in an attempt to distract myself from everything that was Allecra Knight.

"That's—alright. You probably just messed up her straightness a little," I said then averted my gaze away from that Vogue cover-worthy face.

"I did?" Allecra asked in surprise.

"As if you haven't done that to anyone before," I murmured back. There was a tone in my voice I didn't recognize, and I wasn't fond of the feeling I was having either. It made the throbbing in my skull worsen. I rubbed my forehead to ease the pain and wished I hadn't ignored taking the medicine earlier.

"Are you okay?" Allecra asked softly.

"I'm fine."

"You don't look fine to me," she said with her eyes shining with concerns.

"Just a headache." I shrugged.

"Then come here," Allecra said. I looked back at her in shock as she began to lean in. Her long hands went up to both sides of my face and pulled me to her.

"What are you doing?!"

I put my hands on Allecra's shoulders to stop her advancement. Those perfect brows creased into an annoyed frown at me.

"Don't worry Nina, I'm not gonna do anything with you in my car," she scoffed at my nervousness.

And before I could say anything else, Allecra's face was barely inches away from mine. The look of a strange focus in her eyes made me stay still. I gazed back into the stirring galaxies that began to glow in a bright greenish blue. I gasped, but the glow dimmed back. The dull pounding inside my head slowly lessened and disappeared. I shook my head a little in surprise.

"What was that?" I breathed. "What did you do to me?"

"Relax," Allecra said and pulled way with an easy smile. "I was just regenerating your brain cells."

"What?" I squeaked.

"What? You don't know your brain gets a little wonky every time you get drunk?" Allecra said as she started the car's engine.

"Said by a person who has tattoos and drinks like a fish," I said which made her laugh. Her laughter was as pleasant as a morning bird's song. It left me tongue-tied with joy just to hear that.

"Just so you know, the patterns you see on me are not tattoos," she said. I shot her a questioning look, but she didn't explain.

We drove through the sun-bathed streets in silence. I kept looking at Allecra. I thought about how she had acted last night. When all her solid walls crumbled down, she had let a flood of hidden emotions spinning around me like a whirlpool.

136

"How are you feeling now?" she asked suddenly. I paused to think for a moment. My mind was clear and refreshed. My emotions were somehow stable. If I didn't count the messy part that involved Piper and Allecra earlier, I almost felt terrific.

"Good," I said. "And you?"

She smirked. "Never better."

I frowned. "What brought you here today?"

"I don't want to let you know how much power you have over me," she admitted and my heart seized at her words again. Allecra turned the corner leading in the school's direction. I didn't know what to say. I wondered if whatever she said was true or just the lines she repeated every time she met a potential one.

Soon after, we parked in the student lot and got out of the car. Allecra walked towards me like a professional catwalker. It was still a wonder watching her move. Allecra was tall, but not by far, lean but not bone skinny. I was too busy being caught up in all the impacts and amazement that I hadn't gotten the time to really observe her properly. An ancient goddess coming down to earth wasn't an exaggeration after all.

"Do you remember that today we have science together?" Allecra asked with an impish smile. She reached her white hand out and ran her delicate fingers along a strand of my hair, wounding it away from my face. I could feel the heat spreading across my cheeks.

"Oh." I nodded. How could I forget? She was the one who hardly ever showed up. She came to place a hand on my lower back. I felt the familiar chill shot through me again. Allecra seemed to notice my discomfort and removed her hand.

"I'm sorry if I'm getting too close," she murmured. I almost protested that it wasn't the case, but I kept my mouth shut. Maybe it was better this way. We strode towards the school building together.

I heard a soft hissing of a bike and looked up to find Allecra's siblings. Xenon got off the motorcycle with Triton as the rider following after. I didn't know much about bikes, but the one they rode was so big and futuristic. Triton flashed a smile and waved at us after taking off his helmet. For some reason, he seemed pleased. Xenon hadn't bothered to glance at us. Her jet-black hair was longer now, almost reaching her shoulder blades as she turned away.

"Your sister doesn't like me, does she?" I said to Allecra.

"She's just curious, that's all." Allecra shrugged.

"Curious about what?"

"Let's talk about it later," she sighed and led the way. We arrived to class together, which was already filled with students. All heads turned towards us as if we were some sort of celebrities. I tried to convince myself that it was just the person walking beside me they were looking at.

Soon after, Mrs. Cowell entered the class. The students directed their attention back to the teacher. Mrs. Cowell then started to roll call and prepared her slides. Allecra sat silently beside me, but this time, she kept a certain angle of her torso turned so that she was always facing me. I looked straight ahead; otherwise, I would start hyperventilating.

"Class!" Mrs. Cowell started after she flicked off some lights in the room. "Tell me how many people live on earth now?"

"That's too easy," Michael said. "We all know it's seven billions."

"No, it's 7.125 billion people," Mary Jone corrected him.

"Ugh—who cares?" He made a face at her.

"Alright kids," the teacher raised her hands up. "If you couldn't be in the same room together without fighting, the good news is that there may be a planet out there just for each of you."

A round of laughter echoed in the class.

"Given that there are just over seven billions of us on this planet," she said again. "That means there is a planet for each of us plus some spares for your annoying neighbors, a vacation planet for your parents."

"You mean in the Milky Way?" a student said.

"Well, there are more than ten billion planets just like earth located in our galaxy," she said. "So what do you think?"

"I bet aliens do exist," Michael said with a vehement look. I glanced at Allecra and thought if only they knew that some already walked among us.

"Is that true, Mrs. Cowell? Because I can't wait to move out of this planet. Humans suck."

Some more laughter rang from the students.

"I don't know about that. But when you look up at the thousands of stars in the night sky..." she clicked on a starry image, zooming it in slow-motion on planets of various kinds on her computer. "...you might see the nearest sun-like star with an Earth-size planet in its goldilocks zone. Some of them are probably only twelve light years away and can be seen with the naked eyes. Isn't that amazing?"

Afterward, we were asked to watch a NASA documentary. While everyone was engrossed in it, I turned to Allecra again. She was now very close to me that I could practically hear her faint breathing. Her delightful scent almost gave me a crazy impulse to inhale her like a fresh daisy.

She was watching the movie, pretending it was something interesting to her. Her gorgeous face seemed enticed by whatever it was on the screen. Her eyes somehow managed to shimmer. My mind began to jumble with the overwhelming needs to touch her. I wanted to stroke her perfect form, holding her elegant self in my arm and tracing my fingertips over her authentic tattoos. I was aching to do these things. The overflowing desire to feel Allecra up surprised me. And the dream about her last night kept floating back into my mind. I wished I could be fearless like I was in the dream. Maybe I wouldn't be so uptight with Allecra all the damn times.

No, I was losing myself again. I had to get over this love-crazed phase. It was unhealthy. I tried to take a low deep breath and concentrate on the screen.

Not until the movie ended that I could distract myself with other stuff.

"Now I have a project for you to work on with your partner," Mrs. Cowell said, looking more enthusiastic than the majority of her students. "You are going to create your own planet and write about each factor that helps sustain life. You can make up things as long as you have good premises. You can use your knowledge of earth to help with your report."

Allecra and I exchanged a look. Then she grinned, showing off her extra-white teeth wickedly. Well, needless to say, I was going to be stuck with an actual alien for this project.

After the class was over, Allecra rose from her seat and took my hand. It wasn't like the last time when we ended up in the attic and her tonguing down my throat. It was a polite gesture, almost like courting.

She fluidly walked me out of the class and into the hall as people continued to stare at us. Then her eyes shifted to a certain thing or rather a certain person. Jordan was looking at us with an unreadable expression. My heart dropped. I didn't know what to say to her.

"Aren't you going to say *'hi'* to your friend?" Allecra whispered low in my ear. I suppressed a hiss in my throat. Suddenly, she pulled me along by the hand. My eyes widened as I didn't know what she was going to do.

"You must be Jordan," Allecra said in a polite tone when we reached my friend, who stood stiffly. My embarrassment began to strangle me little by little.

"Hey," Jordan spoke at last.

"I believe I might have caused some sort of misunderstanding last night," Allecra said in her smooth voice. "So I want to apologize to you for my rude behavior."

Jordan looked taken aback. Her eyes drifted between me and Allecra. After a minute, a look of disappointment crossed her face, but she nodded.

"It's alright," she said. "I was just concerned about Nina."

"I promise nothing bad will ever happen to her while she's with me. You can rest assured," Allecra said and gave a small smile before she turned to me again. "You might have something to catch up with your classmate, I suppose. We'll see each other again after school."

With that Allecra walked away, leaving me somewhat perplexed. Jordan looked over her shoulder to the retreating blonde and back at me.

"So," Jordan said as she puffed out the air from her chest. "You're still alive, hmm? I was so worried."

My face crumbled in shame. "I'm so sorry, Jordan. I knew I should have called you last night, but I had too much on my mind. I don't know what to say except that I'm just so sorry."

"Nah, that's fine." She waved me off. "I knew I shouldn't have pushed my luck with you. I should be the one to apologize, Nina."

"Oh, no, Jordan," I said. "Don't say that. You just helped comfort me when I needed a friend. It was just a bad timing."

"Yeah, it was," Jordan said and giggled a little. We stood there without saying anything for a while. People moved around us.

"Can we just stay friends, Jordan?" I said, looking at her hopefully. She chewed on her bottom lip.

"Does that include drinking vodka and eating pizza together sometimes?" she asked. I laughed, and a bright smile lightened up her pleasant face.

"Of course!" I bounced off to give her a hearty hug, which she returned but only briefly.

"Be careful! I don't want your girlfriend to tear me to shreds."

"What? No—Allecra and I are not—" I tried to explain as we pulled away.

"Oh, please, Nina," Jordan rolled her eyes. "Didn't you see the look on her face when I tried to kiss you last night? She was like a human hurricane ready to destroy everything in sight. I almost wet myself!"

"Seriously?" I couldn't help giggling at her.

"She's too intimidating. I have never seen a girl like that," Jordan said again.

"Yeah, me, too," I agreed wholeheartedly. I didn't tell her I had witnessed that first hand.

"But I'm just relieved that she's being protective of you. That must be something, eh?"

"Well, I'm not so sure." I shrugged.

"What? Didn't you notice how she marked her territory with me?" Jordan said. "*That 'I promise nothing bad will ever happen to Nina while she's with me. You can rest assured.'* It screams, *'Back off, she's mine.'*"

"No kidding?" I looked cluelessly at her.

"Oh, Nina." Jordan sighed and shook her head. "The sky might fall and the earth might crumble and you still wouldn't feel a thing!"

"Aw, Jordan, stop!" I smacked her lightly on her arm. She laughed and I laughed with her.

"So are you going to be serious with Allecra Knight now?" she asked later.

"I can't tell that yet," I sighed. "It's complicated."

"Nina," Jordan said, making me look at her. "To like is to want, but to love is to give. It's just that simple."

I looked at my friend long and hard.

"You know what, Jordan, you should have been an amazing love expert," I said. She laughed.

"Such a shame I missed my true calling."

We laughed again.

"Alright, let's go to class."

She nodded and we turned to leave together.

After my classes were over, Jordan went to the cafeteria with some other friends. I told her I already brought my lunch and would like to eat outside. Jordan understood and let me be. She wasn't like most people. That was the thing I liked most about Jordan. She didn't hover or pressure me into things.

As I walked along a quiet sidewalk of the school building, a sharp whistle startled me. My head snapped to the direction of the piercing sound. To my utter shock, Allecra was sitting high up on a window sill, looking down at me. Her long slim legs dangled over the edge. Her messy blonde hair fell over her face, swaying in the afternoon breeze. A tiny smile curved on her perfect pink lips.

"Oh, my god! What on earth are you doing up there?!" I cried from the ground with worries.

Allecra just smirked. Then she jumped right off. I clasped my hands over my mouth, ready to scream. Instead, I froze in wonderment. Allecra landed onto the ground with a cat-like ease. She straightened herself back and grinned at me. I should have expected the unexpected with Allecra Knight by now.

I tried holding back the overwhelming urge to hurt her. How many things could she do that I have to lose my mind over?

"Sorry if I scared you," she said sheepishly and came to my side. She was careful not to get too close as if there was an unspoken rule between us.

"You better stop that alien behavior of yours. I don't want my hair to turn prematurely gray."

I began to walk again and Allecra followed me.

"Where are you going?"

"Somewhere that gives me a little peace of mind," I muttered back and strode on.

"I know such a place," she said. "We can discuss our project together."

"Oh really?" I scoffed.

"Don't you want to get an A with this?" She pointed to herself, smiling so beautifully I couldn't think straight again. Wait, was I actually thinking straight right now, considering it was Allecra? I brushed the thought aside before my head started to spin in confusion again.

"How do I know you won't kidnap me this time?" I said.

"Why can't you accept the fact that I have no wish to harm you in any way? And stop being so paranoid and pessimistic already!" Allecra rolled her eyes at me.

"How could I not when you walk around with that thing between your legs?"

Allecra stopped walking and turned her face to me with a glare. Her eyes froze me on my track. My heart jumped at the look on her face.

"I'm sorry, Allecra," I said in a small voice.

Allecra pinched the bridge of her nose and squeezed her eyes shut. Then she let out a loud exhale and looked at me again.

"For the last time, Nina, you have to believe that I will never ever do anything to hurt you," she said. "I thought we were over that."

I nodded like a misbehaving child. Allecra sighed again and lifted her hand to my cheek, stroking it gently. Her expression was almost pleading. I felt horrible for having said what I said.

The trees blocked the sunray, casting dancing shadows on the ground around us.

"You brought your lunch along with you, right?" Allecra said to change the subject.

"Yes."

"Good, share it with me," she said. "I'm hungry."

After that, we sat down on the dry grass under the big pepper tree. The other trees and flower bushes surrounded us. We could see the sky and little clouds above. It was a perfect day. The sun had dried the moisture from the land and the grass we sat on as we ate my lunch. I made ham sandwiches and brought a bottle of grape juice with me, all of which Allecra had half of.

"How did you know I like this tree?" I asked when we finished eating and taking turn sipping the remaining juice. Allecra shook her head.

"No, I didn't know you like it," she said, gazing up at the flowing canopy of leaves hanging above us. "It happens to be the tree I like the most here, so I wanted to share it with you."

"Oh." I nodded, blushing slightly again.

"Trees here are so different from where I was from," she said. "They have good shapes and nice leaves, some of them look like women. It's beautiful."

I realized I'd never found anyone who talked about trees in that way. Hell, no one would even want to share their appreciation of something like this.

I sat there listening to her and looking at her. Then Allecra turned to me and our eyes met. The silence deepened.

"Tell me something about you and your home planet," I said.

"Want to get ahead of the class already?" she teased.

"I want to know it for myself," I snapped. Allecra chuckled softly and then she lay down on her back, folding her hands behind her head as a pillow. She closed her eyes as if to recall the memories.

"We landed on Earth when I was twelve. Our planet, Arzuria, is pretty much like Earth. We also have our sun to orbit around, but Arzuria is much bigger than your planet. It has four moons."

"Four moons?" I said in astonishment.

"Yes." She smiled, enjoying the impressed tone in my voice. "Ceyron, Piero, Acera, and Oraes are our moons. Each rises at different times. They have different colors, too. The pastel-pink one comes out in the morning, aqua blue in the afternoon, violet in the evening, and pale silver at night. Sometimes, when the sky was clear enough, we could see two moons at the same time."

"Wow, it must be beautiful there."

It was pretty strange that what Allecra said seemed too parallel with my dream. But how could I dream of Arzuria without having been there?

"How did you meet your first potential then?" I asked before I could chicken out from hearing the answer. "What was she like?"

Allecra looked at me with a frown. She obviously did not want to talk about it.

"Maybe I'll tell you their stories later," she said and she sat up again, facing me this time. She took my hand in hers.

"Why not now?"

"Nina," she sighed. "I need you to know that you are the first human I feel this way with. It might sound odd, but where I came from, this complicated feeling doesn't exist."

"So are you sure you can be in a complete sexual abstinence with me?" I said, turning to look at her directly in the eyes.

"Not that I am not tempted, Nina. You have no idea. I was born purely for this one ultimate goal. It's still difficult even while I'm talking to you right now, but it got easier over time."

She gave me a sad smile. I remembered her untimely outburst of affection and understood.

"It got easier? How did it really make you feel before?"

"A bit uncomfortable," she said with a helpless shrug. After she said that, I remembered the day we first met and I asked Allecra about her cramp.

"Oh! That thing hurts you!" I blurted out.

Allecra lowered her face and let those impossibly long black lashes hide her iridescent eyes from mine.

"Please, Nina," she said. "That 'thing' you keep calling is a part of me."

"That's why you did it with your sister?" I went on and suddenly felt irritated. "So now that I wouldn't have sex with you, you could do it with her instead, right?"

"No!" Allecra's eyes widened in alarm. "No, Nina...Gosh! How could you say that? It's—it's hard to explain. You just don't understand!"

"Right, Allecra, I don't," I said and pulled my hands away from her roughly.

"Oh, Nina, please, don't be like that again," she said pleadingly, looking pained and afraid. "I did what I did with her because that's how it has always been for me. My body is genetically designed for doing this breeding thing. It's like a cow that has to get milked or it'd die. Same way with me. It would be unbearably hard if I didn't...if I didn't...get off."

"So what makes you think you could stand it with me?"

"Because it doesn't matter that much anymore," she said, "especially since there are other pains."

"Other pains?"

"Like this pain right here." Allecra pointed to her heart. "But it's a good kind of pain, so sweet and warm. Yet it also agonizes me. It's been aching ever since I saw you. It used to scare me out of my mind. I didn't know what kind of a disease I had caught. It keeps troubling me in my sleep and haunting in my wake. My heart no longer feels like my own, and the strangest thing is, it's you who seems to have more control over it. It's like you own me, and I just want to be completely and utterly yours."

Everything went silent. I could hear her heavy breathing mixed with mine. I sighed and went to wrap my arms around her. I wished one thing she could have done to preserve my sanity was to be a little less perfect so that I could concentrate on keeping my resistance.

But now, I was so far gone.

She hugged me back tighter. Her hands roamed over my back. Then she pulled me with her, and we both let ourselves fall to the ground. Allecra lay there looking up at my face. The craving, that had been caged inside me like a bird for so long was now free and wild and strong. It made me dizzy with joy. Allecra raised her head to kiss me on the lips, so softly and sweetly, but she pulled away too soon, which left me a little disappointed.

"The way your cheeks blush, how your eyes shine when you look at me. It makes the pain grow sharper," she whispered. "But oh, Nina, if the sweet throbbing stops, I think I could die."

This time, I kissed her again, only not quite so sweetly yet with more passionate feelings. Her sweet delicious mouth opened under mine. I devoured her lips as every inch of me that was alive was consumed by hunger.

And I was still craving, craving, and craving for Allecra Knight.

CHAPTER 20

WHO WOULD'VE THOUGHT a physic lesson could ever come in handy? It turned out to be true that an object in motion stays in motion. Now understand that my falling into emotional thrall with an alien hermaphrodite hadn't exactly been on my list of what to expect when I moved here.

But I was coming around to embrace the belief that whether I liked it or not, things happen. And once they start happening, you pretty much just have to hold on for dear life and see where the motion drops you when it stops. I believed no one with half a toehold on reality would think my life was ordinary anymore.

The feeling I got when I was around Allecra was so intense, I was afraid she could hear the hum coming from me. Now, I had come to a conclusion that maybe I wasn't that persistent in the first place. I guessed I should just let myself go through the motion.

Allecra drove me home. After what had happened under the pepper tree, she didn't actually try to touch me or tease me again. I considered the silence as her way of not wanting to interrupt my thoughts.

The car finally stopped. I looked up and was surprised that we were already at my aunt's house. When I turned towards Allecra, she was staring at me with her measuring gem-like eyes.

"I'm sorry if I upset you," she said, her golden voice laced with so much sincerity it wreaked havoc with the rhythm of my heart. "I won't come to pick you up randomly anymore. Don't stress out over what I said."

I felt the back of her slender fingers came to brush over my cheek. I looked up at her again and noticed a kind smile dancing on her lips. After all her confessions, it went without a doubt that she was in love with me.

"Allecra," I said. "It's not you. I was being so mean to you this whole time. It's just my inability to decide what I truly want with you."

As if to testify my statement, my hands reached around her neck and pulled her head in until our lips merged together again. Like always, our kiss made my mind woozy and my nerves prickling. Allecra was startled by my sudden boldness, but she returned my unannounced affection. Then came the heavy breathing and gasping between our frantic sliding lips, which were soon joined by wrestling probing tongues. Neither of us intended the kiss to be deep and desperate, but some passionate force inside us seemed to be at work.

I could sense the familiar hunger begin to awaken from the pit of my stomach again. It was like a dying ember that could always be rekindled or some witch's curse where the more I tried to suppress my craving, the more starved I became. With great reluctant effort, I broke away from Allecra's lips soundly.

We were both staring into each other's bewildered eyes. Our chests heaved in a simultaneous rhythm.

"Please—just give me time," I told her promisingly. Her face was warm against my palms. "It won't be long until I am sure this is what I want."

"You don't have to ask me for the time," she said. "I told you I'm not pressuring you into doing anything with me."

"But this isn't fair, especially to you."

"As long as you're happy, I don't care."

"But I do," I insisted. "Just wait until I'm ready and I'll let you know, okay?"

Allecra put her hands over mine, squeezed them a little, and then she nodded. Although I knew time was just an excuse to help me adjust myself to her, it was already crystal clear that I wanted Allecra — no 'if', no 'but', and not even a 'maybe' anymore. After all, wasn't I the one who hoped for something as miraculous and cliché as love at the bottom of a bad box?

Now that love had presented itself, all I could do was to grab it by the horns and lived it to the fullest.

As soon as I entered the house, my reality came back to me. The house, the feeling of normalcy floated in and wrapped itself around me. It was as if I existed in two different worlds. The world I saw before me here looked as it always had been. There was no sign of change, yet it ought to have been the world distinctly different from the one where Allecra existed. It was where my dark and untamed desire came into existence. Somehow, it was hard for me to believe that I could maintain such a fair balance between those two realities. I could end up in either world. It was just a matter of where my foot happened to fall.

I finished my bath and was ready to go make dinner. When I got downstairs, there was a phone call all the way from Moscow.

"Robert Black's residence," I spoke into the cordless receiver.

"Nina?" said a familiar male voice. "Nina, it's me!"

"Me who?" I said, knowing full well it was my dad.

"Pyotr Volkov," he said. "Your father, remember?"

I gritted my teeth at his sarcasm.

"Who do you wish to speak to, sir?" I said. "No one is home at the moment I'm afraid."

"Nina, please." My dad breathed. "I just want to talk to you to see if everything is okay. So how's America?"

"The country is doing fine," I said.

"Nina..." he was about to say something else but then let out a sigh instead. There was a long silence on both ends. I was thinking about putting the receiver down, but the voice sounded out again. This time, it was more resigned.

"I miss you, my little *devushka*," he murmured. "I'm sorry. I know you're still mad at me, but this is for your best interest. I wish things can be reversible. I promise when everything settles down again, we can get back together as a family..."

"Forget it, dad. You chose her over me— it's already too late," I cut him off in a bitter tone. What I hated the most was how he didn't stand up and fight for me.

"Nina, don't say that," my dad groaned. "You know it's not how I want you to feel."

"You want me to feel that you're ashamed to have a gay daughter," I spat, the anger flaring up again as I remembered Dominika's look of disgust and his helplessness in defending me. "That's why you sent me away so that you can have your new family all perfect with no spoilt part."

"God, Nina!" he cried. "Do we have to go through this again?"

I heard some movements in the background. My dad was pacing as he always did when he was upset.

"I will call you later if you don't want to talk to me right now," he finally said, his voice strained with control. "But I want to let you know that I'm always thinking of you. You're my daughter and will always be. And I still love you no matter what."

149

I wanted to point out that he had a new child to love now. There was no need to think of me, but I held back my tongue. Then he sighed.

"Goodbye, Nina," he said and waited for a moment before he finally hung up.

I put the receiver down and looked at it for a while. But just as I was about to walk away, another ringing sounded. I picked it up and noticed it was my aunt by her voice. We exchanged pleasantries and then she told me they were at the airport ready to come home from their delayed trip. I told her I would ask John to pick them up, but she said she already informed him.

That evening, I prepared dinner for the whole family. There was nothing but some chicken and salmon in the fridge, so I fried the fish and made a chicken enchilada. Seeing it was still little food, I made steam rice and scavenged around to put together a decent bowl of mixed salad, which used the rest of the cottage cheese that was left.

Soon afterward, Piper and Jay returned home surprisingly early like a mouse sensing the presence of a returning cat. Piper came to help me cook or at least tried to, while Jay tidied up the house as if to rid of all evidence of a crime.

My aunt and her husband arrived home an hour later just as we were finishing up. Piper ran to hug her dad first, which reminded me of the dead relationship between me and my father. Our phone conversation still left a bitter taste in my mouth. Aunt Vikki just came and kissed each of us and smiled. She told us how relieved she was that the house was still standing. There was something about the way she didn't even miss a beat when it came to kissing me and hugging me that made me feel a whole lot better.

They bought us each souvenir from the island and showed us tons of pictures. Robert talked about the trip when the twins asked how it went. They listened like a couple of well-behaved children. I went back to the kitchen and started setting the table. My aunt came in to help me. I pulled up the edge of a chicken enchilada with a fork to check the sides. Then I topped the remaining taco sauce and sprinkled with shredded cheese over it.

At times, my aunt would look at me with scrutinizing gaze.

"Are you feeling alright, Nina?" she asked. I looked up at her and gave her a smile and reassured her that I was pretty good, but there was still a flash in her eyes that meant she knew it better.

I sighed.

"Actually, my Dad called me just an hour ago," I told her, which caused my aunt to look up while arranging the silverware.

"Oh, what did you say to him?"

"Nothing much." I shrugged. It might as well mean 'nothing nice' to Aunt Vikki, but she just nodded.

"You know you two are still family," she said. "Just give each other time."

I thought about her words without saying anything else.

While we were seated at the dining table, my aunt engaged each of us in giving details of our lives during the past two weeks. Jay talked nothing but football matches with his dad and before I knew it, Piper was talking about me.

"Did you know Nina has made a friend?" she said, sending a playful glance at me. I shot her daggers, but her announcement already drew everyone's attention. By the tone of her voice, she already implied that there was something more to that friend title. Robert pretended to be eating. He was always in his neutral state when the subject of me popped up. I guessed he wasn't as uncomfortable as he was before, but that didn't mean he felt pleasant or concerned about my homosexual welfare either.

"That's great!" my aunt said enthusiastically. "I was worried that you were lonely here."

"Is that friend a girl or a guy?" Jay asked.

"Jason," Aunt Vikki said with a frown at her son.

"Well, I'm just asking since she's..." he said but trailed off.

Now, I had one of those murderous thoughts towards Jay. Why would people expect a gay person to be socially impaired when it came to the opposite sex?

"It's a girl," I sighed to end the confusion. "We just have a science project together, that's all."

Which was partly true.

"Maybe you can bring her here for dinner sometimes," my aunt suggested. I couldn't imagine the scenario where Allecra was sitting at the table among us with all her tattoos and androgynous clothing.

But I just nodded.

Afterward, they thanked me for a delicious welcome home meal. Then my aunt and Robert retired to bed, saying they were too exhausted after the long hour flight. I returned to my room and did my biology homework. Did you know that fish was the first organism to have sex on this planet? I was in the middle of reviewing my math lesson for tomorrow test when I heard a knock at the door. It was Piper. She let herself in and plopped down on my bed.

"Is that true?" she asked, looking flabbergasted.

"Is what true?" I frowned at her incoherency as I turned around to face her.

"That you and Allecra Knight are a couple?" she prompted.

"Where did you hear that from?"

"Dude, that girl and her siblings have been the topic of every conversation for months!" she went on. "Surely, if one of them is dating, it's hot news!"

"Why are you interested in this?" I asked, still trying to get her point.

"Why? Don't you get it, Nina? It's Allecra Knight! She was in front of our house this morning. She was just there all dreamy and unbelievable!"

"Unbelievable?" I raised my eyebrows at her choice word.

"Yeah! If that could even be more possible, she is shockingly attractive up close! And damn, her eyes! I had always thought she wore contacts! Allecra is freaking perfect, like out of this world perfect. Well, there I said it, but Nina, there is something else I can't explain about her."

CHAPTER 21

THEN MY COUSIN turned red like a tomato.

"Wow, someone is interested in Allecra Knight."

"Aw, no!" Piper said and fervently shook her head. "I know I'm totally straight! But you know if she were a boy, I would at least try to have my way with her for sure!"

"Don't tell me you're having that bi-curious symptom," I said to her with an amused smile.

"Well, I don't know. It's just there's something about her, I can't explain it," Piper said. "She's so...so overwhelming, so vibrant, and strangely well-put together. Sometimes, it's hard to believe she is a human."

Well, it seemed people would always find Allecra different. I guessed she hadn't been a hundred percent successful in the art of camouflage after all.

"I couldn't agree more," I simply said.

"You're extremely lucky, you know," Piper sighed. "I wish I had someone who would look at me like the way she looks at you."

I fiddled with the edges of my sleeves. My thoughts drifted back to the evening I spent with Allecra.

"Can I ask you something personal?" I said, looking at my cousin again. She gave it some thinking before she nodded.

"If I could answer it," she said.

"What is it like having sex with a guy for the first time?"

Piper looked surprised at my question, but then she huffed and rolled her eyes at the memory.

"It was super awkward and uncomfortable, to say the least," she said. "It hurt, too, like you almost couldn't tell what's tearing at you. I just wished it to be over, but it was my first time anyway."

I inwardly cringed. I wondered if Allecra could hurt me that much. Of course, she wouldn't mean to, but the pain was still expected. I honestly had no clues what to think of that.

"Then why did you do it?" I asked Piper.

"I thought I had found the right person," she said. I saw a flash of remorse glittering in her eyes. Then I remembered her ex-boyfriend was Jack Conner, the most pathetic guy.

"I'm sorry," I said apologetically.

"Nah, that's okay. I got over it already," she said and shrugged. "Anyway, why did you ask me that out of a sudden?"

"I'm just curious," I said.

"If I didn't know you, Nina, I would have thought you were planning to have your first time with a guy!"

I didn't want to tell her that it wasn't that far from the truth, except it wasn't a guy, but a girl who had a guy's part — as if that wasn't confusing enough.

~*~

The next morning, Allecra didn't show up in front of the house again. For that, I was relieved. The two worlds shouldn't be so close to each other.

I reached school in my car. And after checking myself in the rear-view mirror for the fifth time, I decided that I was decent enough to get out. As I stepped into the sun, she was right there by the door, smiling at me. Her face startled me by its fierce comeliness. I began to think that Allecra was growing more and more attractive each time I saw her. Or was this how being in love made me feel?

She was wearing a simple white t-shirt and a blue denim jacket. I was always struck by how well she dressed. Allecra could wear the plainest articles of clothing and manage, with the roll of the sleeves or the curl of the collar, to transform them into something spectacular. She made a girl like me envy that inborn sense of fashion.

"Good morning," she said. She moved fluidly to my side, keeping a certain distance between us. Her turquoise eyes flicked against the sun. The electric current that was radiating from somewhere within my body didn't seem to slack. I sucked in the morning air.

"Morning, Allecra," I said.

"Shall we go?" she asked and I nodded. There was no need for small talks between us. For some reason, we both deemed it unnecessary.

Whoever happened to be around watched us walk through the campus. I felt the urge to reach out and hold Allecra's hand, like a real couple. I had never felt that way with anyone I'd dated. But I felt self-conscious to touch her and afraid that I would come off as clingy. How she was always so pleasant, graceful and golden was beyond me. Piper was right — Allecra was something else. I watched the way she carried herself.

"Why do you move like that?" I asked out of curiosity.

"Like what?" Allecra looked at me, confused.

"Like that." I gestured in her general direction. "You don't move like humans."

"Because I am—*not?*" Allecra raised a perfectly shaped eyebrow.

"That's not what I mean." I shook my head. "You don't move like me."

"Well, I just don't want to waste my time and energy by being clumsy."

"So you think I'm clumsy?" I said and was ready to spit fire back.

"You're not clumsy," she said. "You're just delicate—like a dainty flower."

My heart fluttered at that, and I felt my cheeks redden as I stared at her smiling angelic face. I snapped my head back and started to walk again, otherwise, I would turn into a human-shaped jello right there. All the while, I could feel Allecra amused stare on me.

We entered the building together. She walked me to my locker and carried my books for me, even though I insisted that I could hold them myself. Then we walked to Language Arts class. The students looked at us as usual when we went to our seats. Allecra pulled the chair out for me. We sat down, but she still looked at me with a hint of amusement in her eyes.

"Why are you staring at me like that?" I asked after a while.

"I'm hoping to hear one of your poems again," she said.

"Didn't you say poetry doesn't make any sense?"

"With you, it does now." She grinned. I turned my head back, ignoring the heat that crept up my cheeks. Then I remembered the poem Allecra wrote to me, the one about the sailor. Unzipping my bag, I pulled the notebook out and opened the page until I found the yellow post-it note, which contained her poem.

"I would like to have it back," Allecra said. Her face suddenly turned serious. Her white slender hand reached out, but I pushed it away.

"If you don't want me to keep it then why did you write it to me?"

Allecra glared at me with conflict raging in her eyes. It was still hard to deal with her sudden mood change. But good grief - that annoyed look on her face was utterly adorable!

"Have you ever cared about someone so much you have to distance yourself for fear of hurting that person?" she said and then turned away towards the window. I didn't know what to say. I wanted to console her but I didn't know how. After a while, the teacher sailed into the room and called the class to order.

"Today you are supposed to write a poem about someone you love," Mrs. Smith said to our surprise. "It's a joy to be able to express this feeling with the most beautiful words possible, isn't it? You don't have to put your name, so no one knows it's you."

Everyone stared at her blankly until the teacher pointed to the clock and said, "You've gotten ten minutes."

There was a buzz around the room. The hand on the clock was ticking away. I wasted five minutes just staring at the blank page. Allecra didn't seem to be anxious or anything. But as my pen hit the paper, I decided to stop thinking for there was no time to think. When the teacher called 'Stop!' everyone looked up in a daze.

"I would like to share the poems with the class," Mrs. Smith said. Jenny asked if she could go the bathroom and Michelle said she felt sick and begged to see the nurse. But the teacher ignored their reactions and simply went around the room, snatching the work from their unwilling hands. People were squirming all over the place. By the time the teacher got to me, I got a sunken feeling about what I had written, but it was too late to hide it now. After she had collected all the poems, Mrs. Smith smiled at each anxious face.

"Not to worry, I will change the name if there's any mention and keep it anonymous," she said, but everyone was sitting poised and tense as if the teacher was to announce someone's death sentence. Mrs. Smith selected a poem from the bunch and began to read.

'I think Jimmy is a flirt,
But his skin is always pink,
And his hair is always shiny,

But really, he's just a jerk.'

I thought Mary Jone was going to fall out of her chair. A guy named Taylor who sat next to her was turning bright pink. He looked at Mary Jone as if she had punched him in the gut.

"No—I—no," she stuttered in alarm.

Mrs. Smith liked the poem because it showed conflicting feeling about someone. Then she shuffled the papers and picked out another one and started to read.

'I love her,
Her eyes are like thunderstorms,
Her smile is like rainbow,
She is cute, she smells so good,
Oh, I love her, I love her.'

I looked at the boys, who cowered in their seats - some looked embarrassed, some snickered in amusement. But every girl in the class was smiling. The teacher said she liked it because it was straight from the heart. Allecra was just gazing nonchalantly at Mrs. Smith as the teacher went on to another one.

'When darkness falls and we're apart,
Can love heal this lonely heart?
I love you dearly that I do.
Sleep is good when dreaming of you.'

I looked carefully at Allecra. She was snickering to herself. I frowned sideway at her. She was probably thinking it was mine since the poem was plagued with the same romantic naivety like the one I had written before. Suddenly I wondered who she had written about. Was it one of her seven potentials?

Mrs. Smith flipped to another poem and began to read. I got a prickly feeling up and down my arms. My heart was clobbering so hard it might leap out of my chest. I realized what a terrible mistake I had made to write that poem in the class.

'Mother, are you gone forever
To the land so bright and fair?
While your daughter weeps, unstopping.
Do you hear me? Do you care?'

Silence invaded the room. For a long moment, no one made any sound. I almost died right then and there. Mrs. Smith didn't look up from the paper.

"Well," she breathed. "Looks like we've got a natural here."

"It sounds pretty sad, though," Michael commented.

I couldn't look up from my hands. All of a sudden, I found it hard to breathe. Allecra must have noticed me. Her gaze returned to my face.

"Are you alright?" she asked in a low voice that only I could hear.

I nodded and remained silent for the rest of the lesson until the bell rang.

Then I rose up from my seat and whizzed out of the class. Allecra's quickened steps were behind me. I dodged around the passing students and down the hallways. She didn't try to stop me. The whole time Allecra just followed. Once I got out of the building, I continued to stride in silence until I reached a football field. No one was there at this hour. I climbed the metal stairs and then sat on one of those empty benches.

The sky had become cloudy and gray, like a poorly painted canvas. I felt the tall figure stood by my side. She didn't say anything and just sat next to me. Her hand wound a strand of hair from my face as I stared at the empty greenness of the field. The distant trees that surrounded the campus stood like dark soldiers going to war. We both didn't speak. Allecra waited and waited. Then when I finally let my guard down, I gave into a quiet sob. Allecra put her arms around me and pulled me into her. My face buried in her chest as she rubbed my back.

"You wrote that poem," she said, not as a question but more of a statement.

"She died giving birth to me," I said through the flowing tears, "Even she was gone, I'm still sad when I think about her. People would put on the sickening kind of face and say *'Oh, I'm so sorry'* like it was their fault. Or they would ask a perfectly normal question like *'Where is your mother?'* and I might have managed to answer with some vagueness. But it still pains me to look them in the eyes when they say these things. It's like a curse to start out your first day on earth as a murderer, isn't it?"

I felt Allecra's lips brushed over my hair.

"You are wrong, Nina," she said softly. "You were brought into the world by a love so deep, it can't be measured. If your mother exists in some other universe, she needs not worry because from this moment on I will take care of you."

I pulled away and looked up at her turquoise eyes. As usual, they were perfect and beautiful to a hypnotizing degree. I felt better just by looking at them.

"Call it psychological thing, but I can't mother your child, Allecra," I said in a scratchy tone. "I'm just scared."

"I understand," she said. "And you don't have to."

Allecra pulled me back in her embrace and smoothed my hair. I wrapped my arms around her and breathed in her exquisite scent into my heavy lungs. We sat like that for a long moment.

"Please take me somewhere else, I don't want to stay here anymore," I said. Allecra turned her head slightly downward to peek at me.

"Where do you want to go?" she asked.

"Somewhere away from all this dullness of the world," I said.

"Mmm, you've got quite a request." She chuckled. "Lucky you, I'm in the mood of spoiling some crying baby today. Alright, let's get going then."

"Where to?" I said curiously. She beamed at me.

"You'll see."

_*_

The aquarium was where Allecra took me. I had never seen an aquarium in my life. A childish excitement began to seep into my nerves once we entered the enormous place. It was like another world entirely. The interior was cold and dark when we walked inside, except for the aqua blue light from the glass windows, which were actually fish tanks.

The tanks were so large; they took up an entire wall. There were so many displays of sea creatures. I had never seen a great variety of fish like this aside from the ones at the markets. It literally took my breath away.

We watched different schools of aquatic life swimming together leisurely. The tanks were decorated with multi-colored corals and seaweeds to resemble the natural habitat of these deep water species.

We were told that the place itself was maintained by aquarists, who also work to ensure that some of these fishes didn't go extinct using good captive husbandry so they could breed in captivity. I really didn't want to get too strictly ethical over it. For now, I just wanted to forget all of that and enjoyed the trip.

Allecra smiled when she saw the look of amazement on my face. We saw dolphins, sea turtles and even killer sharks, but what intrigued me the most was the whales. As we stood there before the enormous window, one of the whales sailed across the gigantic tank like some kind of submarine. I could see its belly and fins and the tail the size of a big ship's masts. Never in my life had I seen any living things this huge and this close.

"Wow," I breathed. "I can't believe such a giant thing exist in the world!"

"I like to come here once in a while because it reminds me of home," she told me. I turned to look at Allecra.

"They have an aquarium like this over there?" I asked.

"No, in fact, Arzuria is much like a giant aquarium in itself. It's just that there is only one continent there," she said to my total surprise.

"One continent?" I said.

"Yes." She smiled. "The land has coral-like trees with whatever shapes and colors imaginable. Some even glow at night. They also produce oxygen and yield fruits — some edible, some poisonous."

"It sounds familiar but still different," I said.

"Earth is not the only Water Planet in the Milky Way. The ocean in Arzuria is three times bigger than the Pacific. What do your people say— that only ten percent of your seas have been discovered? Try the oceans there! Many strange fishes, and of course, there are big ones just like the whales here, but the evolution had made them evolve so much that they grow wings and can fly across lands."

My jaw just dropped.

"You're not kidding, right?"

Allecra chuckled and shook her head. She seemed to enjoy my awe-struck face.

"The whales would migrate to other seas every season, and when that happens, you could see them sail like some flock of flying ships in the sky."

I guessed you couldn't find anywhere in the universe that had four moons and flying fishes like where Allecra came from.

"Are you sure you're not from Wonderland?" I asked with astonishment. She laughed melodiously. My heart perked up at the fact that I could amuse her.

"There are a lot of places here that are beautiful and strange," she said. "You just haven't seen them yet, Nina."

"You are right," I said with a nod of agreement. "It occurs to me now that what we see before us is just one tiny part of the world — just the surface or the skin. People get used to thinking, this is the world, but it's not true. The real world is in a much darker and deeper place than what we see every day. I suddenly feel too small and my problems seemed insignificant."

Allecra looked at me and smiled. I smiled back. As we strolled around the aquarium, I felt like the child in me was showing up more and more. I would point to this and that and gasp in joy at what I found. Once in a while, I would catch an amused smile on Allecra's lips. She followed me around with her hands jammed into the pockets of her jacket like that glamorous fashion model, but for some reason, it seemed like she was just trying to keep them to herself. I felt a bit disappointed that she didn't try to touch me again. I could imagine the rush and thrill every time our bodies made contact. The thought sent a shivery jolt to all the secret places in my being. I tried to shake the feeling off my head.

It wasn't crowded as it was a weekday. We went through a special display of jellyfish. They were from all parts of the world. We watched them floating in their tanks, from a tiny cotton puff to monster size.

"Isn't it amazing?" I exclaimed. "They just keep wobbling along like this until they've been to every ocean!"

Allecra smiled and nodded back. Then we went to see the star-fishes and the sea horses. They were my favorite oceanic species.

"Look at those strange chessman-like guys!" I said, still gazing through the tank filled with colorful seaweed and coral. "Did you know, Allecra, seahorses stay in a long-term monogamous partnership and tend to mate under full moons? They even make musical sounds while doing it!"

"Well, I'm jealous. I can't make any musical sounds during sex," Allecra said. I turned and gave her a look.

"You don't need to tell me that," I said, fighting back the blush that threatened to form on my face.

She shrugged and grinned playfully at me.

"Just in case, you have any unusual expectation of me."

"Why would I expect that from you?" I said with a glare. "Are you a sea horse?"

Allecra laughed. I had to bite my lips from laughing, too, but I didn't succeed.

Afterward, we went to see a video of male seahorses giving birth. Of course, male seahorses are the ones to become pregnant. They're not only carrying but fertilizing and nourishing the developing eggs with their fluid secretions.

It was mind-blowing how their babies were born. A turbid liquid burst forth from the brood pouch, and like magic, minuscule but fully formed sea horses appear out of the cloud. I was amazed at how nature could come up with something like this.

"Isn't it wonderful?!" I said to Allecra, who was just as fascinated by the process. The light that came from the tank intensified her turquoise eyes even more, and they were sparkling with a kind of amazement bordering on longing.

As if forgetting herself, she came to wrap her arms around my waist from behind and pulled my back against her front. Her chest was soft and comforting. I ignored the heat on my face and leaned myself into her. I wondered how the universe could come up with Allecra.

"You know, I wish we were like seahorses," she whispered into my hair.
"Why?"

"So that I could carry babies for you instead."

In that moment, I understood the longing in her voice. I could feel her heart beating against her chest. It made me sad. I turned around in her arms and stared at her face. Then I pulled her down by the front her jacket and kissed her. She melted into my mouth, and we kissed like that in front of the glowing light of the aquarium.

_*_

After that day, Allecra and I had realized something for the first time. It was not one of those strong, impulsive feelings that can hit two hormonal teenagers like an electric shock when they first fall in love, but something quieter and gentler, like two tiny lights traveling in tandem through a vast darkness and drawing imperceptibly closer to each other as they go. As our meeting became more frequent, I felt not so much as I had met someone new but as I had chanced upon a dear old friend.

She would ask me relentlessly about every trivial detail of my existence — even something as small as what popcorn flavor I preferred.

At first, I thought she was just trying to know me as a person, but then it seemed she was genuinely curious about whatever I thought and felt. She also wanted to know the world as I saw it. I had told her about my childhood, my father, my aunt, my favorite music, and the books I had read. I told her about Klara, who was the first person to keep a reality check on me if she sensed that I had drifted too far from the real world. Allecra didn't find it odd at all with the ways I perceived things. I had always been insecure about expressing myself to other people. I didn't think they could understand me or even care. Now it was a new kind of feeling of having someone who was truly absorbed in whatever that was on my mind.

With Allecra, endless thoughts and ideas that were kept buried inside my head came streaming out like rivers. Sometimes, I tried to stop something I was saying, thinking it was boring or unimportant, but Allecra wouldn't allow me to.

"No, no, please, just go on," she would encourage me, and when she turned those beautiful brilliant eyes on you, you felt as if her whole purpose in life was just to sit there and listen to you and you alone. I could even talk about the craziest things I had never voiced to anyone for fear of being made fun of or judged, like how starry the night sky would have been a thousand years ago without light pollution or how come sloths didn't go extinct, even though they are so damn slow and why do humans have five fingers instead of three or six???

Suddenly, it hit me like a spark of lightning. I realized then that no one, not even my best friend, could make me feel unafraid of being completely honest with myself.

I discovered more about Allecra as well, like she was inhumanly intelligent. Of course, she didn't tell me that, but the day I insisted on ditching school and we went to the aquarium, I had missed my math test. The teacher gave me extra work to make up for it, but it was something I had to study before I could solve the problems. In the science lab, Allecra caught me doing math assignment and with just a glance at the page, she said, "How did you get a 'negative one'? It's not correct."

I wanted to snap at her for shunning my mathematical ability, but it turned out, she was right. The most shocking thing was that Allecra never learned a thing about math.

"Then how do you know all these?" I had asked and she just shrugged back.

"I don't know the answers. I see them," she replied.

"How?" I asked again. She seemed to think for a second before she tried to explain it to me in the simplest way I could follow. She picked up three pens and dropped them onto the table and asked me how many.

"Three?" I said with a curious frown at her. Then Allecra smiled and grabbed a box full of matches from the lab table drawer before spilling the matches slowly out of the box. This time, she asked the same question, but I couldn't answer it and just looked back like she was insane.

"It's seventy-nine matches in total," she told me.

"What? How could you possibly know that?" I gasped.

"Like I said, I didn't know, I just saw," she said. "You also saw seventy-nine matches the same way you saw three pens, but your brain couldn't grasp it all like the way mine did. It's the same to me with everything else. The shadow of a tree, the shape of a box, the curve of a blackberry bush. I see it in more precise dimensions and accuracy. It might sound crazy to you, but when I looked at your math work, it was as if the numbers and symbols and stuff jumped out at me. I just saw the answer. I don't need to learn a thing."

Well, I should have known that someone who had dropped off from space wouldn't have a shitty brain. But I also remembered what Allecra had told me about being made from the best DNAs there were. No wonder she wasn't just a beauty but also a genius.

"You know what, Allecra, you should be my personal tutor from now on," I said, which caused her to chuckle.

"With pleasure, Miss Antonina Black." She grinned widely.

We started doing a lot of school stuff together. She was a great teacher, too, who always knew how to connect the dots for me. And I learned from the world through her eyes a little more while she did the same through mine.

But most importantly, I started to feel like I could trust Allecra with anything, and that was a very important milestone in any relationship. This unsullied feeling held the key. It was like the secret to a food recipe. The main ingredient in any relationship was trust. If you didn't have trust, everything tasted blunt and the whole dish was ruined.

So when trust itself finally blossomed, all the fear ceased to exist.

For the first time, I understood what true freedom meant. It was not just being liberated and free from the bond placed by societies, but also being liberated and free from the bond within oneself.

Allecra and I grew closer together as the days passed by. We would talk about innocuous things, but if we should happen to touch, I felt a stronger fluttering in my chest and the same tingling in my stomach.

Soon I started to find it difficult when the weekends were drawing near and I would desperately wish for Monday to come. I would make extra lunch for her and make sure I had put all my heart into it. That afternoon while we sat eating lunch together under our favorite pepper tree, I decided to ask about her past relationships with the potential girls.

"Tell me," I said in a demanding voice, though I knew I could have gotten the answer through persuasion.

"What do you want to know?" she asked, sounding annoyed at my determination like it was a bug.

"How did you meet your potentials? Everything from start to finish in fine details. Don't spare me," I said and then continued in a softer tone. "Please, Allecra, I have to know."

"Are you sure you want to hear everything even if what you might hear will bother you?" she asked.

I nodded solemnly.

"You will hate me after this." Allecra sighed.

"I won't."

"Alright then," she said. Her face looked as if she was confessing on a trail. "It was when I turned thirteen that I met the first one."

"Thirteen?" I couldn't help my surprise.

"What? It wasn't my fault I hit puberty early," she said.

"Sorry, please go on."

"We met her in Africa."

"Africa?"

"Why are you so surprised, Nina?" Allecra frowned at me.

"No, it's not in a bad way," I reassured her and sidestepped the minefield. "Please continue. I won't interrupt you again."

She let out a long exhale before she went on.

"That year we lived at the edge of a beautiful town. Behind our house was the country view. We had a vineyard and orchard garden. Green fields and woodland stretched far to the mountains. I loved it there. I was still young at that time when I met Nattia. She was a daughter of a rancher, who raised cattle and horses," she said. "Triton helped her father repair his beloved truck by chance, and he invited us to his house. Then I saw her. She was three years older than me, but I was tall for my age, and I was instantly aware that I was sexually attracted to her that day. We got to know each other, and we went riding together every day. She told me about horses and how they are tremendously influenced by the phases of the moon - both physically and emotionally. Their brain waves go wild as full moon approaches, and they would start having all kinds of physical problems. When the full moon arrives, some of them die. No one knows why this happen. I told her where I came from had no horses, and if there were, they would all be extinct since the full moons were quite frequent. I thought we were close enough to talk about it. I knew she liked me a lot, too. She asked me where I came from and I told her the truth. At first, she thought I was joking, but as the sun began to set and we were alone, I showed her my tattoos that had recently shown up on my body."

"Your tattoos are natural?" I said, even when I knew I shouldn't interrupt, but Allecra just nodded.

"It's our patterns. Every Arzurian has it, just like a tiger has stripes," she said.

I wanted to tell her that in fact, humans also have patterns, but it's invisible and only the females bear the marks. *See how strange that is! In some world, people have stripes while in other world, the males carry babies?!?*

"And what happened after you told her?"

"Nattia said she didn't mind who or what I was. I was so happy," Allecra said. "That night we decided to make love."

There was a long pause from Allecra. Her eyes dissected my expression and her usual easy demeanor faded. She almost looked guilty. I let her know that I wanted her to continue.

"We went to our secret hut inside the woods. There was a full moon in the sky that night and we kissed for a while. We were both already naked. Then when she started touching me, I began to feel something weird inside my body. There was a great pressure between my legs. I thought I was just too aroused."

I shivered, imagining too vividly to myself what Allecra had described — the small straw hut in the wood, the shape of the trees, a full moon that could kill horses, and Allecra, like a glorious goddess with her creamy nude form, as she bathed in the moonlight. I imagine seeing beautiful Nattia in her arms and I felt a pang of jealousy rose from somewhere I didn't want to acknowledge.

"But before I realized what was happening, something sprang out from within me. I screamed then. Nattia didn't know what was wrong. She held me as I curled into a ball. My hands were over my private part."

I later realized Allecra didn't know that she was born with both sexes either. It might have happened when she hit puberty.

"Then the pain subsided," Allecra continued, she could barely look at me. "And suddenly I was thrown into a new wave of sensation. It was an impulsive need that had just broken free of its shell, and it was like my mind was switched off. I turned and pushed Nattia back onto the bed. She went from being confused to very frightened when my tattoos and eyes went aglow. I begged her and begged her, yet I still forced myself on her. She tried to call out my name, to make me stop, but I didn't hear anything other than my thumping heart and the throbbing need to be inside her. And that I did."

My breath came to a halt. Allecra looked up with concern.

167

"I will stop now," she said. Her voice was like a rock hitting the bottom of an empty well with a dull thud.

"No, don't." I shook my head vigorously at her. "You must continue the story. No need to hide it from me anymore. There shouldn't be any more secrets between us."

After a moment of contemplation, she nodded.

"Nattia covered her face with her hands and cried a little. I felt sorry for her, but I couldn't make myself leave her body. I felt my new member got even harder like it had set down roots. *'I understand,'* Nattia said to me. *'I won't protest anymore. But I want you to remember this, Allecra, that you are raping me. I like you, but it's not how I wanted it.'* I didn't say a word. I was overcome by my own lust. My hands drew her close to me and my hips started moving, slowly for a while then violently at the end. Nattie closed her eyes and gave herself up to me. Her face was expressionless as she turned her head away from me. I could still see the tears streaming down her cheeks. But gradually, I could sense the pleasure rising up through her body like an extension of myself. I had never felt such a powerful sensation. I remember climaxing over and over until I thought my whole body was melting. It was my first experience of sex. "

I began to feel slightly dizzy as it all got so intense. But Allecra was worse. She seemed to be tormented by the mounting guilt and shame. It was heartbreaking to see her like this.

"And what happened after that?" I tried to sound understanding. It wasn't exactly how she intended to do.

"My brother and sister had known this would happen, but they wanted me to go with it all the way," Allecra said. "After a while, Nattia forgave me, but she wasn't able to conceive a child either and we tried many times after that but nothing. Then Xenon decided it was time to move on. It was part of the plan all along. Once I reached puberty, we would go in search of my potential match. I didn't want to, but I had no choice except to leave Nattia behind."

CHAPTER 22

"I F IT TROUBLES YOU SO MUCH, you can stop," I said as my hand was carding through her unkempt blonde lock. Before I knew it, I was holding Allecra's hunched form in my arms. She stayed quiet in my embrace for a while before she gently wrapped her arms around me.

"You must be disgusted by what I had done," she said in a grave voice. I shook my head.

"It's not entirely your fault. Yes, you have done a terrible thing, but I know you, you're not terrible. You deserve forgiveness," I said. Allecra pulled back and stared at me in discontent. She almost looked angry.

"Would you excuse all rapists in the world the same way?"

"They did it on purpose, but you didn't! It was under different influences."

"That doesn't justify my wrong doings, Nina," she retorted coldly. "I told you I'm no good."

"Your action has a cause of its own," I defended. "I don't know, but something tells me you're not the same like those subhumans. It's just not who you are."

Allecra stared at me for the longest moment. All the twists and turns of the conversation took their tolls. She looked confused, stunned, and hesitant as if she didn't know how to accept what I had said. Had the guilt always been taunting her conscience all these years? I bet it had.

The wind shifted through leaves and flower bushes around us. Allecra lowered her eyes to the ground. A frown still marred her perfect face.

"This is so strange," she said at last. "Speaking to you like this gave me an odd kind of relief. You didn't scream or became hysterical about any of it. I wonder if you're even human."

There was a thin smile on her lips, which relaxed me.

"You keep it all inside for too long," I said. Allecra stayed silent and then she looked up at me again. Her deep greenish blue eyes sparkled.

"Thank you, Nina," she said. "You are like a black hole absorbing all the torments and unease from me."

"You kind of did the same for me," I told her.

169

I didn't remember who started it, but the next thing we knew, our lips found each other. It was a soft slow kiss. It wasn't even inspired by heated passions but something more innocent.

When our mouths disconnected, I looked into her dazzling eyes. There was a slow spark of brightness in her irises. I could see the gold flecks spreading around the rings much clearer as they shone with gratitude.

"Thank you for bearing with me, Nina," she whispered.

"I want to tell you everything — all my dark, dirty secrets and past mistakes. Will you be alright to listen?" Allecra said.

"I have no objection if it frees both of us from the shadow of a doubt," I told her resolutely. "I was the one who asked you."

"Alright then," Allecra said with a solemn nod.

It took the whole evening for her to tell me about her sexual odyssey with the seven potentials. Even as a summary, it was still a long tale with many detours.

After they left Africa, Allecra and her two siblings traveled to the Middle East. They traveled through most part of Asia, Europe, Latin America and finally North America. The latter was where they were staying now.

Since the experience with Nattia, Allecra learned to distance herself. As her body matured, her desire and untamed need to mate began to take its course. At times, Allecra felt disgusted with her own body. She needed to release that pressure building inside of her. It was more difficult to stay celibate for a long period of time because the dull throb would only worsen.

That was how her 'sister' came to fix it. Xenon was brought up in Arzuria. She was given a task to assist Allecra in finding her Earthling match. But she was also there to take care of Allecra. Allecra was constantly in pain and refusing to have sex with random humans as suggested.

She told her sister she would only sleep with the one that would be the mother of her child. Of course, Allecra had attracted many daring humans, women and men alike. Yet it seemed she was only able to detect and feel attracted to female potentials.

"That's probably what my people had in mind when they created me," she said. "They were not confident that I could be the carrier of a human child so they turned it the other way around."

In this sense, we both agreed that Allecra was still a virgin with her femininity. And she was still unaccustomed to her new member. It had reached a point where she could hardly control it. That one time, Xenon decided to take the matter into her own hands, quite literally.

Allecra remembered how her sister pried her hands away. Regardless of the protest, Allecra was soon locked in a fascinating horror as her sister cradled her 'secret' gently in her hand, the way a doctor took a pulse. With Xenon's soft hand touching her, it felt like there was hot lava surging and springing up inside her body.

"You have to let me help you," her sister said. "Your body was genetically engineered to do this. It's no use fighting it. Let me, Allecra."

At that time, Allecra was crying. She was still an awkward teenager and part of her was still an embarrassed innocent girl. She watched her sister take her in her mouth. It was a strange thing to do, but it sure felt exceedingly incredible.

She despised the wicked yet delicious sensation for it rendered her speechless and vulnerable. But it quickly overrode every thought she harbored in her mind, and Allecra simply let go.

After that day, it had become a convenience to do it with Xenon whenever the need struck hard. Besides, she figured it was her sister and not a random stranger who would come to her with a hint of a sexual invitation. It was just a form of sisterly care, that was all there was to their sexual interactions.

Allecra also studied humans, especially woman anatomy and their behaviors. She discovered the amazing metamorphosis of breeding and the complexity of female psychology. She found out that her potential girls needed security, comfort, and trust. They often had trouble accepting her. Sometimes, the potentials were straight girls. They were unable to accept the fact that Allecra was also a girl. Yet it didn't take long for their hesitation to vanish. I guessed no straight girls who had seen Allecra would still continue being straight. She was born to awaken their sexuality. Her whole existence was made to intrigue them. It was encoded in her DNA.

Allecra had mastered her confident stare, the elegant grace, and all the qualities that women were instinctively attracted to. It melted their resistance and unleashed their hidden desire.

"Once a potential meets me, it's like two magnets drawing towards each other," Allecra told me. "But with you, it's different. You seemed to repel from me instead. Xenon had to plays her part in that."

"What does it have to do with her?" I asked.

"She would mentally prepare you to subconsciously adjust to my presence," she said. "You were an odd one, Nina. That's why Xenon got curious."

Then it was the story of the seven. Allecra met the second one in the Middle East. Her name was Samira.

"We disguised as tourists. I saw her for the first time in the lobby of a high-class hotel. Samira wasn't wrapped in an immaculate all-black robe and a veil like most women there. When her intense silver eyes lanced at me, it was like a lightning of passion. In that moment, the sexual energy instantly emanated between us. Soon Samira had developed a growing interest in me, although we did not speak a word to each other for a whole week."

One day when the fate shoved them into the same elevator, Samira and the blond were mindful of each other. Then just out of the blue she gestured to Allecra's tattoos and asked in a sweet voice, 'I touch?' Allecra nodded and rolled up her sleeve higher. Samira ran her nimble fingers over the inked skin. Then all their desire was swept up as if by a sand storm. All resolve came undone and the dam broke.

"With just the slight gleam in her eyes, I understood that she wanted me," Allecra said.

She had made sure that this time; it was completely consensual between the two of them. But in the heat of passion, neither minded nor cared. No doubt, Allecra's secret was a shock, but nothing could hold the girl back anymore.

"She was quite amazed by her discovery of me," Allecra said almost coyly. "But she had no hesitation."

Samira was the first to introduce Allecra to contraception. For a while, they had sex with cautious protection.

"But Xenon insisted that we didn't have much time," she said. "So one night, I purposely forgot to bring a condom with me. Samira was irritated by it, but she was on the prowl for sex, and so we decided to do it anyway."

Allecra could feel the burst coming up, as the girl wanted her to pull out. Samira started begging the blonde not to release inside her, but it was too late. Allecra drew all of it so deep that even it wasn't what Samira wanted, the girl moaned loudly with pleasure and held the blonde tighter.

"I remember staring at her in hopeful fascination," Allecra said. "I thought it would work this time but sadly, it didn't."

_*_

Samira could not conceive even after their unprotected sex. But something else had evolved in their short-lived relationship. The potential girl grew more obsessive. In a way, it was the girl who seduced Allecra into having more sex.

"Not that she ever said or did anything overly seductive," Allecra tried to defend. "But by then she had understood my intention, yet she wasn't against the idea and even seemed eager to try, 'I would do everything for you, Allecra, I don't care anymore. Whatever it takes. We could go somewhere else far away and raise our children together,' Samira said to me while we were lying in bed. As much as I wanted it to happen, I just knew it was no fruition in the end."

So even the girl had opened her golden door and agreed to bear an heir for Allecra, it was pointless. Samira was finally forced to forget everything just like Nattia.

"I had to take away her memory of me," Allecra said with a sigh. "It was horrible for both of us, but that's the only way I can settle things with each of my unsuccessful Earthling match."

They left the Middle East and went to South East Asia. Allecra had come to realize that women behave differently from place to place. No wonder, she still felt confused. One thing she didn't understand very well was how women concealed their sexual desire. Theoretically, they surely must have the urges in them— that much she could tell. But when it came to how this desire manifested itself and what it was like, she was at a loss. In Asia, Allecra found the third potential human. The two met during their camping trip in the mountain.

Allecra had just turned fifteen when she found her. She was delighted to have found her. She had almost lost hope in finding any match after leaving Samira. The discovery of the new potential was like a blessing that filled her heart with warmth again.

"Her name is Rami," Allecra said in a nostalgic voice. "She was a tour guide on the mountain. She was the shyest girl I've ever met, but we instantly felt the bond. It was a December day in the southern part of a country called Cambodia. The mountain air was foggy and cold, but the sun would shine through the thin layer of clouds. Rami came to us like a blossomed flower. We camped out in the forest over the green hills. The girl took us to a pristine lake, which used to be the mouth of a dead volcano a long time ago. It looked like a bowl filled up with water. There were plenty of beautiful wildflowers I'd never seen and all kinds of orchids. Rami told me that flowers blossoming is how the earth smiles."

She introduced Allecra to various plants, trees and flowers, and strange earthly animals she had never seen before. Rami also told Allecra of the endangered species and said all of these might be gone someday.

"Her worries of the global warming and the future of this planet were palpable. She said the forest is the breath of the world. I told her that the same thing might have happened back where I came from. Nature just decided to get rid of all future intelligent life there."

Rami just looked at her strangely but she was too shy to ask anything at that time. But Allecra knew that the girl was drawn to her since the first day they met. Still, Rami wasn't showing any sign of such desire. They stayed on the mountain, watching sunrise and sunset together. They went hiking, bathing in the cold waterfall, and sitting around a bonfire under the stars. But nothing sparked until the last day of their trip that something happened.

That night was different from any other nights; Rami came to Allecra's tent. Allecra recalled the moment vividly.

"She told me she couldn't sleep, but the gleam in her eyes had an unmistakable stir of affection. I invited her inside for it was so cold and windy on the mountain."

The two of them lay there in the quiet night. The Earthling girl started telling her the tales and folklores she had never heard of. Allecra tried to listen while the wind softly rustled the canvas. Outside, a night owl hooted from the distant tree. But her mind was mostly occupied by Rami's sleeping form beside her.

"I do remember a strange tale she had told me," Allecra said. "It was a story of a princess who disguised as a man to follow her husband, who had gone to war. As she traveled through the forest, a Yaksani, an ogress, who saw the princess as a handsome young man, fell in love with her. The ogress abducted her to her cave and took the princess as her husband not knowing her captive was also a woman. They lived together for a while until a hermit took pity on the princess, who could not give the Yaksani any child. The hermit then placed the soul of a tiger into the ogress's womb, and she became pregnant and then gave birth to a very powerful son."

She had known many strange things from her planet, but people on Earth still managed to amaze her. There was more to the story, but the ending was lost in the wind as her body was yearning for something else. She vaguely remembered asking the girl if there were still a hermit guy who could do the same for her. Rami laughed and wondered if Allecra wanted an ogress to mother her child. It made them laugh. After they stopped, the two found themselves wrapped in each other's arms. They kissed and kissed. By then Allecra's body was on the verge of exploding.

Rami whispered to her, "I know what you are and how you want me, Allecra."

Some people were like that, Allecra realized. Their minds were so tolerant to bizarre things.

Slowly Allecra revealed her secret to Rami. The blonde girl braced herself for the scream of shock, but nothing came. There was only the constant wind blowing outside their tent.

"Rami stared at me in fascination for a long moment. Then she gingerly reached over to hold me in her hand, as if to see whether I am real," Allecra said with a slight blush on her cheeks. "I asked her if she was afraid of me, but the girl shook her head and said, *'You had come to me in my dream just like this.* .'"

That night was the first night they had sex together. Rami was no doubt a virgin. Allecra turned her face up and began to remove Rami's clothes one piece at a time with the gentlest touch she could manage. Then she took off her own. When Allecra held the girl close to her, she felt her trembling. She kissed until Rami regained her calm and the trembling stopped. The shy girl then mustered up the courage to cradle Allecra's stiff erection. And slowly, Allecra guided it inside her.

"Rami was warm, wet and inviting, yet when I went inside her, she tensed with a flinch," said Allecra. "I had gotten into a careless habit with condoms that I forgot about the pain it could have caused her." Allecra's voice seemed to be coming off from a far distance.

Allecra did make up for Rami's pain of losing her virginity though. She knew how to lengthen their climax and how to make it start again. Sex had turned into something akin to an inborn talent for the blonde. She and her potential girl went at it with their wilder craving for each other's flesh.

It wasn't warm enough inside the tent, but after they were done, the two of them clung to each other's nakedness without a sense of cold.

"It was right before I fell asleep that Rami whispered to me, *'I will never do it with anyone else — never for the rest of my life.'*"

Allecra let out a sigh.

"But no matter how many times we had joined our bodies, there was no result. Yet Rami was the first girl whom I didn't take away her memory before we left. She just accepted the coming and going of my existence."

They left the country and went straight to Japan.

"Why Japan?" Allecra said. "I was slowly falling into a depression and needed distractions."

She went on with her detailed journey.

She and Triton had the same obsession with cars and racing. There was a world tournament held in Tokyo that year so they decided to go unwind there for a while. Little did she know she would find another special Earthling.

"I saw Eriko in the crowd. She was cheering for her boyfriend. He was one of the top racers in the country."

Allecra was in the dilemma. She didn't know whether to steal a stranger's girlfriend or leave Japan. The latter choice was strongly objected by the two siblings. Triton had befriended the boyfriend. And to make a long story short, Allecra had easily charmed her way into Eriko's heart after the end of the tournament.

"We had sex for the first time in her apartment," Allecra said with a bit of a sardonic chuckle. "Eriko was straightforward as she was originally straight. She did not beat around the bush. We had just come back from a party her boyfriend threw that night. She told me she wasn't feeling well and asked me to leave with her. Later, I realized her boyfriend had cheated on her with a car pinup model that she worked with. The two of us left together and went up to the rooftop. Tokyo was lit up at night. It was breathtaking to see all the lights that these people used to illuminate each of their little worlds. We sat on plastic chairs, drinking red wine straight from the bottle. Eriko asked me about love. I asked, *'What is love?'* I was clueless of this. I had heard people talk about it and seen people in love, but it had never concerned me. Eriko explained to me her conception of love. *'Let's say, I tell you I want to eat strawberry shortcake and you drop everything you are doing and run out to buy it for me. That is love.'* Allecra told her if that was love, Eriko would get diabetes. Eriko laughed and said, *'Are you even a normal girl, Allecra? There are times in a girl's life when something like that is incredibly important to her.'*

Then Eriko looked into Allecra's eyes and put her arms around her before she kissed her lips.

It was a soft and gentle kiss, it was meant to be a friendship kiss between two girls, but once it started, they couldn't stop. Eriko was in a state of arousal and half-drunk. She led Allecra by the hand onto her bed and climbed on top of her. The blonde alien tried several times to warn her about some hidden thing, but Eriko was like a kitten in heat.

"Half of her consciousness was probably left at the bottom of the wine bottle at that time," Allecra said. "But everything about her showed her determination to do it with me."

Eriko herself might have forgotten to feel the surprise. She was glistened with her own wetness. Eriko just went and stroked the pulsing length between Allecra's legs until she whimpered and let out heavy moans. Then Eriko mounted on Allecra's hardness. It slid right in, a loud groan elicited from both parties. They gasped, trying to adjust to the wonderful sparks that coursed through their bodies. Eriko gyrating and grounding on Allecra was like the end of the world and all that existed was their joined worlds.

"The morning after, we woke up in each other's arms. Eriko finally found out about my secret. To my surprise, she was more excited than shocked. She asked if we could do it again right after," Allecra's voice almost faded as if the memory exhausted her. "Eriko broke up with her boyfriend. And I spent a year in Japan with her because Eriko actually got pregnant."

CHAPTER 23

"THE NIGHT ERIKO told me she was pregnant," Allecra went on with her story. "Her eyes were shining, her lips parted in a hopeful smile. I imagined that tiny life growing inside her, the tiny embryo with all my cells. So much information was hidden in that little world. My DNA had already determined what hair color the baby was to have, how tall it would grow, even whether it preferred vanilla to chocolate. It was an exciting thought. It was as miraculous as it sounded. Things went smoothly. Everyone was finally relieved that this time our dream didn't get blown away like dandelions in the wind."

But then came the dark storm that shuddered everything. One night, Eriko went into labor prematurely.

"The baby didn't make it," Allecra sighed gravely. "Eriko had two operations. She wouldn't have children anymore. She kept asking for the baby."

It was the saddest voice I'd ever heard from her.

"Was the baby a boy or a girl?" I asked her. Allecra didn't answer, but I had a feeling that she didn't know either. Her face darkened and her bright eyes got dimmer. It was obvious that it left her emotionally scarred, and we left the question hanging in the air then. After the miscarriage, she felt responsible for the loss of her baby and Eriko. Allecra stayed longer with the girl. She wanted to take care of Eriko's emotional health, but they were constantly reminded of their still born baby.

"We were both just depressing each other by being together," Allecra said. "So we decided to move on, and I left Japan at last."

They ended up in Europe after that. Allecra was lost once again. The whole baby incident took a toll on her, and things began to get even shadier. Allecra resented herself and stopped trying to find a potential one for a time. But it wasn't long before they found a new Earthling.

"I met Claire when I was asked to be a freelance model," Allecra said.

"You worked as a model?" I said. A gentle angelic smile lit her expression as she nodded.

The fifth potential was a newly discovered model herself. Allecra was approached in a fancy club in Paris by some clothing company agents. They asked her if she was interested in modeling. Her look fascinated them greatly that they couldn't just ignore such a rare gem.

That was when Claire introduced herself to her.

"She also introduced me to a world of fashion," Allecra said. "In that world, imagination and creativity could have their freedom. *Designing clothes is like my secret closet to Narnia,'* Claire had told me. She didn't like it when people don't know which things go together and which don't. She said I was the first person she met that had everything about me to look right."

It went without saying that the girl was also intrigued by Allecra like the other potentials before her. Once they set their eyes on the blonde, there was no turning back. Allecra needed to forget what happened in Japan and welcomed all distractions. Xenon must have sped up the process, so Allecra was able to attract the Parisian girl in a sexual level.

"It was in a dressing room. It happened so fast, we both felt like being in the middle of a whirlwind. One moment, Claire was fitting me for a new design. The next moment, we were in each other's arms and my body joined with hers," Allecra said, speaking as if she was using someone else's voice, robotic and emotionless. The secret was out in open. Claire was obviously confused, but she was a potential one, she couldn't deny Allecra's touch even if she tried.

They were together for a while. Allecra began to use sex to divert her mind from the baby, even she knew it wouldn't work with Claire. And like all Allecra's relationship, the history repeated itself once again. The same patterns and unhappy-ending. They left Europe and moved to Fiji.

"I lived for several months, in a little village at the foot of a mountain. There was a secluded spring in the cave, and I climbed to swim in it every day."

During that time, Jenera, the new potential girl saw Allecra. For some reason, she was hiding there, watching the blonde swimming in nudity. It was easy to imagine what a striking sight it must be for the human girl. Allecra had known for a while that Jenera was spying on her. She waited until the intrigued girl showed herself to her. The blonde was like sticky pollen attracting the bees. Jenera did come out at last.

Allecra was stark naked when she walked up to her. There was no need for them to speak out their passion. They already knew what the other wanted. And they went at it with no hesitation nor awkwardness at all. Allecra held the end of Jenera's flowing sarong as she spun. Layer after silky layer fell to her feet. They stood before each other, eyeing the other's nude bodies in sexual hunger.

Jenera's gaze was locked on Allecra's long stiffness. The girl lay herself on the rock and parted her shapely legs, conveying what she wanted. Allecra could barely contain her pent up needs. She knelt before the girl, crawling like a graceful leopard over that supine form. As she held herself, Allecra guided her hardness home through that sweet heaven gate. Then they started the passionate rhythm together.

"Jenera was what you would call a *free spirit*, who sought a spiritual peace of mind and body. She told me what we did was how goddesses make love to each other."

At that point, Allecra snorted a little.

They stayed together for a time, but like the others, Jenera could not conceive. Everything went back to square one.

Allecra had already expected that it would end unceremoniously this way.

Then they moved to America for the first time. She was almost eighteen by then.

"I stayed in New York at first," Allecra said. "Then I found Eva. She was a violinist, a rising star in the music industry. I had seen her performance a number of times before we met in person. Triton is still her devoted fan."

With a special arrangement, Allecra got to see the musician. They would go for dinner together and sometimes had a quick drink in a famous bar.

They talked about music. Eva talked about her passion, *My parents gave me a plastic violin when I was five. I instantly felt a natural joy in producing each resonance. I then found pleasure in dividing times and transforming them into an effective row of tones. Whenever I play music, it gives me a sense of control in my life.'*

Allecra realized that all the girls she met always had that special something about them. As the two accidentally touched, all Allecra could think of was that she wanted her. She also knew Eva wanted the same thing. The intensity was pulsing like electricity between them. Without either of them being the first to suggest it, they walked to a nearby hotel.

It went on like that for a while.

"One night, as we lay satiated on the bed in each other's arms, Eva rolled on top of me, her lips smiling as she said three words, "I love you." I felt as if I was betraying her. It was like the sky came down on me. What I did with her had virtually nothing to do with 'love'. All I wanted was to be held in her arms and buried myself inside her, and hopefully, impregnate her. When I said nothing and she didn't find what she looked for in my eyes, Eva settled for hope. She hoped to bear me a baby, so I could stay with her. Thinking back, the same thing also happened with the rest of my potentials. But it wasn't them, it was me. I failed them all."

After the end of the long tale, Allecra looked at me. We sat in a long stretching silence. I should've been repulsed by all this, but with her, it was different. All I felt was sympathy and understanding.

Allecra then took my hand and placed it against her cheek.

"I'm sorry for spilling it out so graphically. I know this probably hurts you, but I believe, in the long run, an honest, detailed account will be the best to clear your doubt," she said softly. "I just want you to know that never in my life had I experienced such a suffocating need for someone. At first, I didn't know what was happening to me, but soon I realized it was something stronger than 'lust'. I still have this violent urge to have you, but it's so different now. Why this need arose in me so suddenly, why it happened with you and not someone else, I have no idea. But the feeling I feel now is impossible to curb. I want you in every way there is to want a person. I might have had sex with other girls before, but moments of intimacy like this... are rare. I had read about 'unbearable desires' in books, but until I met you I could never really imagine what such a thing meant. If I could be anything I wanted; I would be the one that you love."

~*~

I drove through the twilit city streets. Then I got off the highway heading homeward. My mind was still full of Allecra's stories. After I reached my aunt's house, it was after six. I had never been late, but everyone hadn't arrived yet. After I finished washing, I went down and started making *shashlikee* chicken and *pelmeni*, a Russian dish like a dumpling with butter and sour cream.

While I was half way through with the meal, the twins got home. Jay came over and sat down on the island. I heard him talking about random stuff on the phone for a while before I felt his eyes watching me. Then Piper came to join us, which made the awkwardness less unbearable.

"Smell good," Piper said, peering over my cooking pot. "You do have the wife material, Nina, I'm so jealous."

Taken out of context this 'wife material' wasn't a straightforward compliment. Why are girls who have basic survival skills being praised as just someone's wife? But before I could say anything, Jay's voice came to me.

"Nina?" Jay said. "Can I ask you something?"

I swirled around to look at him with a frown.

"Yeah?"

"Did any guy ever hurt you?"

"No, why?" I said.

"Well, I was just wondering maybe some guy broke your heart and you turn to girls instead."

"Did Illamas ever hurt you, Jay?" I asked him. He seemed taken aback by my question.

"What? No," he said with a confused look. "What are you talking about?"

"Then why are you into girls and not llamas?"

Piper barked a laugh. Jay glared at his sister before he turned to me again.

"Well—" he said, blinking. "I just like girls."

"So the same thing with me, no one hurts me. I just like girls," I said and returned to my cooking again.

"But don't you think maybe you just haven't met the right guy yet? How do you know you're a lesbian?" he continued. I turned off the electric stove as the soup was done and walked over to the island and sat down in front of Jay. He leaned away from me as if he was afraid I would slap him, which I kind of considered.

"Can I ask you something, Jay?" I said as he kept looking at me nervously. "Are you sexually attracted to llamas?"

Piper, who was listening to our talk, was trying to hold her laugh beside me.

"What?! No!" Jay squeaked. "Nina, what kind of a question is that?"

"Then how do you know? Maybe you haven't met the right llama yet," I said. Piper burst out laughing again while Jay looked deeply wounded.

"You girls are so mean," he pouted. "I'm not talking to you anymore."

~*~

The next morning, the sky was hazy and overcast, but the weather was not especially cold. I decided to wear a leather jacket and a silk scarf around my neck. Somewhere in my mind, I had noticed the change. I was starting to dress up again. Not that I had been badly dressed before. My fashion sense was no longer the blunt and tasteless one.

After I parked my car at the lot, I expected Allecra to be there, but she wasn't. I waited for her to show up until the first bell sounded, forcing me to leave. This had never happened before, and it left my heart a bit deflated. Did her absence have anything to do with the walk down the memory lane yesterday?

In class, I couldn't concentrate. Allecra must be upset about what she did, or what happened to the baby. I shouldn't have forced her to tell me all this. When I got to Language Arts, the seat she occupied was still empty. I walked listlessly towards our desks and sat down with a sigh. I turned my gaze to the window. The sky was brighter but not enough to brighten my mood.

Just out of nowhere, Xenon walked into the room. She didn't seem astonished to see me as I did. But I tried to react to it with calmness as if our encounter was entirely natural. We exchanged no greetings as if it had all been prearranged. I stared at her face, and she looked at me with a flickering light in her eyes. I just realized her eyes were lighter than Allecra's, like the color of topaz. But they were intense and sharp like the eyes of a snake's.

She wore a white top under a black jacket and a tight skirt. She had some bracelets that matched her small gold earrings and flat platinum necklace. Her face was smooth like a porcelain sculpture. She was beautiful with the same enigmatic gaze just like her sister. Then she sat down next to me and just stared at me some more. I looked back at her topaz eyes. Everyone was looking at us like they were watching a horror movie. I was going to say something when she started first.

"Allecra is in pain," she said.

"Huh?" I said, startled by the news. "Is she okay?"

"Come with me if you want to know," she said and stood to leave. I saw her brother was waiting by the door. There was something about the way she just walked away that made me follow.

The three of us got out of the building together. Triton had disappeared and a moment later, a sleek black open-top Ferrari rolled in. The cushion was covered with glossy red leather, and it smelled brand new. Xenon motioned for me to get into the passenger seat and then she climbed in beside me. Triton got the black roof back on and shifted the gear before driving out of the campus.

"I get that you and my sister haven't done it yet," Xenon spoke. I didn't say anything. I didn't know what to respond. Triton glanced at me through the rearview mirror. Xenon frowned and snapped her head to him. It was as if she reacted to something I couldn't hear.

"Screw her age," she said. "We have no time to waste for this nonsense anymore."

It was as if they had a private conversation, only Triton didn't speak anything. Xenon turned to me again.

"You know everything about us, Nina," she said. "You can have whatever you want, but we only ask you for one thing."

"I want nothing from you," I said. "And you have no right to ask me anything either."

Xenon stared at me. Triton looked a bit surprised but I could see a smile flickered on his lips.

"I know you want my sister. I could see it in your mind."

I remembered what Allecra told me about her sister and her uncanny ability to implant sexual nightmare in my head.

"It was all your doing," I said in accusation.

"Oh, but it seemed like it was part of your wild fantasies with Allecra. I was just adding fuel to the flame," she said with a smirk.

"Allecra and I doing it or not, it doesn't concern you," I said firmly.

"If you still don't consent to it," the dark-hair girl said, this time her voice was lower. "I will make her leave you. Surely there are other potential Earthlings out there. Don't think you're that important to us."

She was looking at me, waiting for me to surrender to her threat.

"If Allecra wants to, then she obviously can," I said. "I'm not stopping her."

Xenon was taken aback by my declaration. Triton let out a quiet chuckle. The girl sighed and then leaned back on the seat.

"Now I see why," was all she said.

The Ferrari was like a time capsule in a way. A space capsule. It went swiftly, taking me through the wormhole of time. Before I knew it, we had reached an outskirt of the city. I should've been worried or gotten a panic attack at the notion of being abducted, but I felt no fear.

They brought me to a private neighborhood. There was only one road that twisted and turned. On both sides lined up huge overhanging trees and walls of granite rock. We turned towards a gate, which opened itself. The car crawled into a heavily wooded estate with pines, oaks, maples and cypress. It did not look like an estate as the rest of the residence there. It was cool, dark and quiet more like a forest.

But after the car drove further inside, the trees were replaced by manicured garden and huge green lawn dotted with palm trees. Then I saw a white house bathed in direct sunlight unbroken by clouds. It was a futuristic two-storey house shaped like Legos stacking on top of each other. The verandas had glass railing and wide glass windows. A pristine swimming pool was right next to the house. Beyond it was the view of the stretching city and the long white beach against the blueness of the Californian sea.

Triton parked the car in front of the house and we got out. There were at least three other cars parking in the garage, a silver Porsche, a red Rolls-Royce and the black Lamborghini.

I was aware that the three siblings were loaded, but I didn't expect them to actually roll in money. It made me uncomfortable knowing that Allecra was so rich.

They led me to the house. As the double doors opened, I was greeted by the most stylish living room I had ever seen in my entire life. The furniture was all splendid. A white sofa blended with yellow crafted floor lamps.

Xenon talked something I didn't understand to Triton, who smiled and nodded. Then the girl turned to me again.

"Go upstairs with Triton," she said. I wanted to say something, but nothing sounded important to utter. At last, I began to walk as Triton led the way. Xenon looked on until we left the living room. It was actually a very big house. There were some green ivy plants growing inside a long glass case. They hung from the ceiling like floating seaweeds. The stairwell made of polished wood snaked around it, leading us to the second floor.

Triton didn't say a word. He just showed me to a room and held up a finger towards me, meaning for me to wait for a moment. He walked to the door, sticking his head in and then out again then signaling me to go inside. Without a word passing between us, I went into the room. The door closed behind me, leaving me alone. And for the first time I had been here, I felt nervous.

It was a very immaculate room. Everything seemed systematical from a wide wooden office desk to the sofa of the sitting area. One of the walls was entirely made of display shelves. I considered myself a neat person, but whoever lived here must have a severe case of OCD. It wasn't just painfully spotless but also artistically organized in precise order.

I began to walk further to the other side and found the bedroom. The blinds on the glass wall were drawn half way down, allowing just enough sunlight to stream onto the varnished wooden floor. A large white bed set at the center. The lamps were still on by the bedside. Then I heard the sound of the bathroom door open, and an elegant figure gracefully walked out into the room half-naked.

My mouth sagged.

Allecra was drying her long blonde mane with a towel. She didn't see me as I just stood there with wide eyes. She wore a white shirt with all her buttons undone. And worse, she had no bra on except a pair of black underwear. Her lean feminine flawless body seemed to glow. It made my cheeks burn hot. I could feel my heart pounding and skipping. And there was a heavy, melting feeling below my belly. The sight of her was quite overwhelming. My gaze traced down to the area below her toned stomach, but what I saw puzzled me.

Even I was a virgin, I would still know the difference.

Where there should have been a bulge, I found none. She didn't look like she had that *'thing'* —between her legs — at all.

CHAPTER 24

WHEN MY THOUGHT PROCESS started working again, I began to realize how awkward it was here in Allecra's bedroom. She was just there, glorious and half-naked. Then her head snapped in my direction as if she was finally aware of my presence.

"Oh, geez, Nina!" Allecra exclaimed in surprise. "What on earth are you doing here?!"

Her words snapped me out of the hypnotic trance. My breath hitched in my throat. I didn't even notice that seeing the tantalizing view of her body had frozen me in place.

"I—I was just—" I stuttered, alarmed with her uncharacteristic shock.

Allecra let out a string of unfamiliar words. I suspected they were Arzurian curse words. She buttoned up her shirt in haste.

"Nina, get out! Now!"

"But...but Xenon said you were..."

"Go!" Allecra hissed again. My blood rushed backward through every vein in my body and my ears turned hot in anger. I bit my lips as tears stung my eyeballs. Who wants to see her anyway? I thought then turned on my heels to run out of the room.

My hand reached for the door and opened it. But before I could exit, a pair of hands grabbed me by the waist and twirled my body around. Allecra swiftly pushed the door shut and pressed me against it. I looked up to find those ardent turquoise eyes burning into mine. I gasped and found her mouth swoop down to kiss me feverishly. Our teeth clashed and her tongue was in my mouth in a heartbeat.

My arms wrapped themselves around her strong body. I felt her hands roaming over my back and squeezing my bum. Desire washed over like a heat wave from a desert. My fingers laced through her blonde hair, pulling at it gently. It caused Allecra to moan in my mouth. It felt as if every atom in my being was on the verge of exploding.

"Oh, Nina..." Allecra groaned in the back of her throat. It reverberated through me.

I felt her hips began to move by instinct between my thighs. And in that moment of blinding passion, it hit me — Allecra wanted me right there. My heart pounded in my chest with a frantic tempo.

Suddenly, Allecra broke off and put me down on my wobbly feet. My mind was reeling. I gasped in the air, trying to pull myself together as the heated blood pumped through my core.

"You need to go, Nina," Allecra half-gasped and half-growled. "Get out before I lose it, go!"

Her shoulders were hunching like a wild predator and her eyes were luminous with lust. She closed her eyes briefly as if to rid the agonizing thoughts in her head.

"Allecra," I said, still panting heavily. "Are you alright? I was worried..."

She cut me off by gripping my elbows hard and pulling me away from the door roughly. Our faces were now inches apart. Her luscious vermilion lips pulled back over her teeth.

"If you don't want me to rip your clothes off and get inside you now, you have to leave!" she hissed.

With those words, I was shocked. Then the shock combined with rage, and I pried myself away from her hands and pushed Allecra off as hard as I could.

"Allecra, you're so mean!" I yelled at her before I opened the door and got out.

I wiped my teary eyes as my feet descended the stairwell. I heard the slamming of the door and thuds of footsteps chasing after me, but I ignored it. When I got downstairs, I didn't see anyone. I had no idea where Xenon and Triton were.

"Nina, wait!" Allecra's silky voice was surprisingly close.

I sprinted through the big house like a mouse running from the cat.

"Antonina!" she called after me again, pronouncing my full name with a hint of frustration. I gritted my teeth as a fury raged through me.

What does she want exactly?

The sunlight stung my eyes once I stepped out of the house. I flinched and paused for a minute to think. If I had to run all the way through this grand estate, then so be it. But then Allecra came from behind me and whisked me off my feet. I let out a startled gasp.

"You come back here!" she hissed and carried me bridal style back into the house.

"What do you want? Put me down!" I was yelling and kicking my legs in protest although my arms went around her neck. To my utter surprise, Allecra leaned over me and joined her lips with mine. The kiss stole the breath out of my lungs.

"Well, that shut you up," Allecra said after she pulled away. Sunlight glinted off her shoulders, turning her hair golden. Her face was dazzling with an ethereal glow. My face flushed as I felt her soft breasts against me. My lips tingled from the kiss.

When we were back in the living room, she put me down on my feet. Xenon and Triton reappeared. The dark-haired girl looked at us with questioning eyes. I felt a growl vibrated from Allecra's chest. She still kept a firm grip on my wrist like a handcuff.

"You stay away from my Nina!" Allecra hissed fiercely at her older siblings. My head turned to her again. The anger evaporated from my system at her words.

Triton raised his brows while Xenon glared at us. By the surprised look from the other two aliens, I realized it was the first time they saw Allecra being like that. Xenon sent a glance at me before averting her topaz eyes back to her sister.

"Very well then," she said quietly at last. "I just hope you still remember why we are here, Allecra."

"I know what I'm doing," Allecra snapped. "Leave us alone."

And without another exchange of words, Allecra pulled me away from them. I thought she was going to take me back to her room and pick up where we had left off. Instead, she led me to another splendid quarter of the house. It turned out to be the cleanest kitchen in the world.

There were mugs and crystal glasses hanging in alignment. Everything from cupboards to the sink and stoves was sparkling. I wondered if the kitchen had ever been used at all. There was a big window that showcased the view of the ocean. I could see a line of white sand beach from here.

Allecra walked us over to the island.

"Sit down," she commanded as she released my hand. I watched her going over to a double-door fridge and took out a bottle of water. Her long slender fingers unscrewed the cap and then she drank the content as if to calm herself down. After that, she heaved a long sigh before turning to face me again like she just remembered I was there.

I stayed quiet, waiting for her to say something. Instead, she just poured a glass of fruit juice and then walked over to me. After setting the drink down in front of me, Allecra took a seat on the next stool. The skin around my wrist was still stinging from her viselike grip. I was rubbing it unconsciously to ease the pain. She noticed it and frowned.

"You're hurt?" she asked, looking at my hand in guilt. Her hands reached over to cradle my wrist, but I pulled away.

"I'm fine," I said in a brash tone. I was still mad at her. Allecra took my hand in hers again, but this time, she brought it to her lips and kissed it.

"I'm sorry," she whispered and kissed my hand one more time. "I was a bad girl."

"Very bad," I agreed, which made her chuckle.

"I know." She smiled as her long beautiful fingers massaged my wrist. The feel of her hands touching me brought a familiar sensation to my body, but I tried to ignore.

"You scared me, too."

Allecra dropped her gaze as if in shame. Her long curved lashes shaded her turquoise eyes from mine. I wondered where her thought had taken her. As for me, my head was still spinning at the whirlwind of our sudden encounter.

"Are you still scared of me right now?"

"I don't think I would like to see you like that again," I said.

"Let me know if there's anything I can do to shoo away your fear," she said. She looked a lot calmer now than when I first saw her a while ago.

"What happened to you, Allecra?" I asked. She just sighed and shrugged.

"This morning, I woke up and felt as if a fire alarm had set off inside my body," she said. "I tried to stop it but I couldn't."

"Your sister came to me at school and said you were in pain," I told her.

"I guess Xenon was a bit overreacted," Allecra said.

"So you didn't let her...you know," I said.

"Of course not!" she said, looking at me in disbelief. "I couldn't bring myself do it with her. I don't know why, but every part of me wants only you, Nina."

Her words sent relief spreading through my chest. It was a strange thing to feel this attached to someone. My mind flashed back to the passionate moment we shared earlier.

"You could have had me," I pointed out.

"Yes, I could have had you right there and then," Allecra said then her eyes locked onto me again. "You don't know how it's tortured me, but I still wouldn't let myself hurt you."

"Allecra, what if I tell you that I'm ready?" I said. Allecra just stared at me. Then she stood up with both of her hands in her messy blonde lock.

"Oh, Nina, I wish you hadn't said that," she sighed in exasperation.

"But...why?" I asked, looking at her pacing back and forth.

"Didn't you see how I could barely refrain myself? When you walked into my room like a lamb wandering into a lion's den, I almost lost my mind. Not having your consent was the only thing that kept me sane from my craving," she said. "Now you make me afraid."

"You're afraid of what?" I stood up, too.

"I'm afraid that once I start having you, I could never get enough of you."

Just like that, I fell in love with her all over again. I loved that she tried to ward her temptation with me, even though it troubled her greatly. I also loved that she was vulnerable and honest with her feelings, even when she didn't realize it. I went over and held Allecra from behind, startling her for a moment. She stopped pacing and wrapped her arms back over mine.

"Then you can take me however you want and whenever you want," I said, surprising both of us. "My body is yours and my heart is yours."

~*~

I breathed in the fragrance of Allecra's slightly damp hair. My hands began to caress her flat stomach, getting under her shirt to feel her smooth skin. Her body was firm with toned muscles and yet her skin was soft and delicate like a baby's skin.

What a perfect healthy flesh!

It provoked something in me. Allecra had nicely shaped breast. I hadn't seen all of her, yet I already knew that Allecra's body was the incomparable pinnacle of perfection. Everything about her came in good shapes and sizes. I found it really distracting to my already messed-up sexuality.

Our bodies turned hot again. Her panting became noticeable. Allecra hadn't moved an inch ever since I declared my submission to her. I kissed her back and her shoulder then landed my lips lightly on her bare neck. My nose nuzzled over her neck and silky blonde strands. Allecra sighed.

"Nina, please..." Her voice was troubled with suppressed needs.

"I know you want to do it with me," I said.

One of my hands mindlessly inched down her stomach, slowly as if to avoid her noticing. My heart was pounding in shell-shocked beats. I had never been so daring like this before. I couldn't stop myself from wanting to feel her there — down there where her *'secret'* was hiding.

I remembered how Allecra didn't appear to have the extra tool on her. Where has it gone? The question wrecked me with the kind of curiosity that could make Hera proud.

"Where is it?" I whispered hotly against her skin. My voice was filled with impatience and longing. She didn't seem to be aware of my hand slithering into her pants, getting closer and closer to her hidden treasure. Then Allecra jumped up as if she had just woken up from a nightmare. But with a little more push of my hand, I found her, warm and soft underneath her underpants. I was puzzled for a moment before it dawned on me that Allecra was just the same as me. Her body bent forward as if she had just received a kick in the stomach.

"What the hell, Nina!" she cried and unwrapped herself from my arms and turned around to face me.

She put her hands on my cheeks, and then I realized how far I had gone. Her piercing turquoise eyes studied mine with a gleam of irritation.

"Nina, snap out of it!" she sneered. "You're losing your mind!"

I stared back at her, blinking.

"What are you talking about? What's wrong with—"

"Xenon...damn it! I should have known!" She hissed with a clench of her jaw. "She's doing this to you just to tick me off."

Then she hissed to herself, looking furious.

"What? I don't understand," I said. "What does this have to do with your sister?"

"Nina, my sister can mess with people's heads the same way the moon messes with horses. Whatever you think you're doing with me is just her projection," she said. A dark expression settled over her enigmatic face.

"You meant she made me say and do all these?" I asked in confusion and started to feel embarrassed with myself. Now that Allecra had mentioned it, I felt kind of awkward and ashamed of what I had done. I was always like that timid, unassuming fisherman's wife.

"I have to get you home," Allecra said urgently. "We can discuss this later. Being alone together here won't do us any good. I might end up taking you right on the dining table or worse on the kitchen floor any times."

My body shivered at the idea, but I nodded vigorously without another word.

A moment later, Allecra led me out of the house and walked towards one of the cars parking in the garage. Instead of taking the Lambo, she clicked a button of the remote control. The Porsche let out two sharp beeps, and she opened the door for me. I got inside. Allecra shut it with a slam and went around the car to the driver seat and then let the top down.

She now had on a black Marc Jacob jacket that stylishly matched her plain white button-up blouse. Allecra started backing the car out with one hand on the wheel while the other placed behind my headrest.

And she managed to look so damn fine all the time.

We drove through the wooded part of the estate. The afternoon sun kissed our skins with its bright light. The sea breeze blew in a constant stream, which contained the salty scent.

"What is going on with me?" I asked as I rubbed my temple. "Will I be normal again?"

"Tell me how you are feeling right now," Allecra said. She looked sideways at me through her dark sunglasses.

"Are you mad at me?" I asked in a small voice. Allecra shook her head.

"It's not your fault," she said. "Sometimes, Xenon did that to my other potentials, too. You're not the first one to molest me." My head turned sharply at her.

"I did not molest you!" I said.

"Then what else can I call that?" Allecra asked.

"I was just curious about the—the—you know. I didn't mean to. Besides, there was nothing down there."

After I said that, I felt my cheeks blush. My eyes instinctively drifted down to the area between her thighs. Allecra caught me staring at her private and closed her legs quickly, shifting herself away from my gaze.

"What did you expect to find? The Empire State Building in my pants?!?" she snapped, giving me a hard scowl.

I bared my teeth, ready to bite back but nothing came out. I crossed my arms and turned away to look at the view through the window. We passed time in the silence. Then I heard Allecra cleared her throat like she wanted to get my attention.

"You really want to know where my boy's part is?"

"Not anymore," I muttered. "Hide it all you want."

Allecra made a noise that sounded like a snort.

"Well, for your record, I did not hide it. I don't even have to," she said. "My anatomy is different from humans. When I get aroused, it comes out."

"How?" I said. "How is that even possible?"

She sighed, but I noticed a slight blush on her cheeks.

"Actually, I'm similar to humans in a way that I was a female first before my Y chromosome kicked in, except that my X chromosome is still activated. That's why I have both sex organs. My male part is also from my female part. Now, go figure!"

Oh, goodness. I should have remembered that from biology class. I sank back into my seat in realization. Everyone on this planet was born female before the sex chromosomes determined who got to stay female and who got to become male. In short, each person was born with an X chromosome. Only when it got paired up with a Y chromosome did that person become a boy. In Allecra's case, she had evolved with both sexes in a strange genetic evolutionary way.

"So it just grows out of your girl's part when you want sex?" I asked coyly.

Allecra gave a stiff nod back.

"You'll know when you see it. It takes years of practice in self-control," she said. "But it's harder now whenever I'm with you."

"Back in the house, you seemed so..."

"I know," Allecra cut me off, and I nodded. "It happened when I go too long without sex. But when you walked away from me, I felt instantly deprived inside and realized I wanted you more than just sex."

This had to be the most unlikely romantic thing I'd ever heard.

"Are you still hot and bothered now?" I asked.

"Yes, but not as much as before."

"Oh." My breath hurled in my chest. Allecra was horny now, but not hella horny like she was back in the house. "So does it mean there is still a chance it would come out?"

"If you shove your hand inside my pants again, then yes."

I felt the heat in my body rise up at an alarming rate.

"What if I kinda wanna see it?"

"No!" she cried with a frown. "If I let it out, I can't guarantee that you could walk straight out of this car!"

My hands went to my mouth, trying to stop a gasp from escaping through my lips. I could feel every part of my body tingle at the thought of us doing the naughty.

"Do you still have any more questions?" Allecra said, looking a bit amused by my reaction.

"Nnnno...no." I gulped.

We stopped. I looked up and realized we were at a traffic light. Another car rolled up beside ours. It was a pink minivan with a bunch of girls and guys inside. They looked like typical beach-goers. One of the boys was playing his ukulele. They glanced at our car and the guys were awestruck by my blonde girl.

"Oh, shoot, now I'm gay," one of the girls blurted while the others giggled to each other. But Allecra acted like she didn't hear, or maybe she just ignored them.

When the light turned green, she stepped on the accelerator and zoomed off with a loud screeching noise from the spinning of the rubber tires.

"Why would you act like that? That was so rude!" I said. Allecra looked at me with a blank expression.

"What?" she asked.

"Just because you are good-looking and rich doesn't mean you should be rude to people," I scolded.

"That's how I put people off," she said casually. "Men are so afraid of confident girls, it's just so funny. And girls...well, they all just want me, whether they realize it or not, sometimes I have to pretend to be mean."

"Well, you are mean!" I said and made a face at her, which made Allecra chuckle.

"Looks like the functional Nina is back!" she said. "No longer wanna get your hands in my pants, sneaky kitten?"

The remark made the heat to rush up my face again. I bit my lips from yelling at her. Allecra smiled handsomely at me. I had to train myself to deal with that tremendous amount of hotness and sexual frustration at the same time.

"Did you call your other potentials that, too?" I murmured. Allecra's cheery smile faded. I wanted to kick myself for ruining the mood.

Allecra swerved the car to the left and went down a quiet lane. We had reached an out of the way restaurant. The label read Steve's Steak House. Allecra parked the car between a black mustang and a beat-up camero. The whole place looked more like a movie set.

"Let's have something to eat. I'm hungry."

We walked inside and sat at a table by the window.

"The steaks here are excellent. They have a special recipe," Allecra said after we settled in.

"You don't normally cook, do you?" I asked.

"Why should I cook when I can always order foods?" she shrugged. "Besides, I don't know how."

I smiled. At least, there was something Allecra Knight was incapable of.

A middle-aged woman came to take our orders. Allecra asked for medium-rare steak with sweet and sour ribs, some mashed potatoes and mixed salad, also some corns and green beans.

When the meal arrived, I began to eat with great appetite. I hadn't realized I was starving, too. John Lennon's Imagine was playing through the speakers.

"Nina, tell me why you asked me that?" Allecra asked all of a sudden. I almost forgot about what I had said.

"I don't know. Since you had been with the other girls before, I guess there must be someone who struck you as more fascinating, or someone whom you enjoyed taking on cute dates, or saying nice things to just like this. Obviously, all the seven girls were special in their own ways — and even better yet, they all wanted to have your babies. I just don't see why I'm worth any more than them."

Allecra listened to my long tirade of low self-esteem and then sighed heavily to herself. A sound of a beach bus pulling up at a gas station across the street stole my attention. Allecra took my hands in hers to make me look at her again.

"How I wish to spank you right now for thinking like that all this time." She exhaled loudly. "Listen to me, Nina, you're not like other girls. Actually, you're nothing like other girls, and that girl you just saw getting off that bus isn't like other girls either. It's not surprising, really, it's almost as if everybody in the world is different from each other. You should stop comparing yourself to anyone else anymore. A flower never compares itself to other flowers. It just blooms in its own right and beauty."

We both looked at each other as the lone bus drove by.

"But I'm afraid I'm not someone you're scared to lose," I murmured.

"Nina," she said in a gentle tone. "I have decided since the first day we met, that even if there are other potential ones out there, I only want you. The moment I felt like a complete being in existence was when I first saw you. And I would never be the same again without you."

I felt a smile tug on my lips then.

"You sound more and more like a human, you know," I said.

"Oh, really?" she raised her blonde brows, but she was also smiling. "Triton used to make me read a story about what humans were like in the ancient time. You want to hear some of it?"

I nodded with eagerness like an engrossed child waiting for a storytime.

"Well, according to the Aristophanes in Plato's *Symposium*, it said that in the ancient times, people weren't just male and female, but one of the three types. In the past, people were male-male, male-female or female-female. In other words, each person was made out of the elements of two people. Everyone was happy with this arrangement and never really gave it much thought. But then the God took a knife and cut everybody in half, right down the middle. So after that, the world was divided just into male and female, the upshot being that people spend their time running around trying to find their other halves. Sometimes, they find each other again; some other times, they get mixed up with someone else's half."

199

My mind was engrossing in the story. Male-male, male-female, and female-female?

"So that meant each of us was separated from our other missing self, who could be a male or a female? It all made sense now," I said.

"I felt like I had been searching for my other half all my life," Allecra said again quietly. "But I don't have to look anymore. My other half is right in front of me. I never could grasp the meaning of complete until I met you. Suddenly, everything makes sense, and each time I spend looking at you, you just take my breath away. "

She took my hands and squeezed them warmly.

"I never knew we were cut in half and got separated so far that you had to travel all the way through time and space to find me," I said.

Allecra laughed and reached over to pinch my cheek in adoration.

"Hello, nice to see you again, my lovely other half," she said and we both burst out laughing.

~*~

At last, we reached my aunt's house. The driveway and the front garage were empty. No one was home. My aunt had left with Robert and would be back late at night. The twins were still in school. I had skipped my entire school day to be at Allecra's house, but now I still didn't want to leave her.

"Do you want to go inside?" I asked her. Allecra smiled sweetly and shook her head.

"I don't think it's a good idea."

"I will be alone for at least a few more hours," I told her. It was a heartfelt plea. Allecra stared at me, considering it.

"Alright," she said afterward. I almost jumped up in joy. We walked into the house together. Allecra looked around with a passive expression.

"Do you want something to drink?" I asked as I led her to the kitchen. Seeing her around the house like that was kind of strange. The two separated worlds were somehow overlapping each other. Allecra just shrugged as if to say she was okay with whatever.

We sat down at the kitchen table together. I had brought out a piece of chocolate ice cream cake and poured us some warm tea. Aunt Vikki couldn't stand coffee just like me. And she preferred to have her favorite brand of teabags well-stocked in the cupboard. Allecra and I ate the cake and washed the sweetness down with the light tea in silence. Then my mind wandered to the afternoon event.

"Allecra, about the thing I offered you back in your house..."

"That's okay," she said.

"No, no, let me finish," I said. "Xenon might have egged me on subconsciously, but I feel like I am also ready. I want to take our relationship to the next level."

"You don't have to rush, Nina. In fact, I pretty much enjoy the way things are now. What we have are genuine emotions with a little mix of deliriously heightened sensation, like this nice cup of warm tea and chocolate cake — sweet, pure, and simple."

With a passionate tug on my heartstring, her words made me rise up and came around the table to her. I then sat on her lap, so that she could do nothing but stared at me with wild eyes. Allecra squirmed underneath me a little, but my hands encompassed her neck.

"Nina...wait..." she half-gasped. Her lower part strained to avoid the intimate contact.

"Tell me something, Allecra," I said. "Do you want to do it with me?"

"You have no idea," she said, her voice thickened with passion.

"Then I want you to do the thing you did with the seven — no restraints, no hesitations," I said. "But I also want you to be patient and really, really gentle. You have to do it with me differently. You know that this is difficult for me to give my intimate part of my being to someone. I don't want you to just have sex with me. I want you to make love to me. Do you understand? —because I love you, Allecra."

"I love you, too," she whispered back. We both sort of lost in each other's eyes after the confession. It was the first time we said the magical words out loud. The three-word declaration was finally signed and sealed by two meeting souls. We couldn't wait to merge and become one again.

"Please take care of me, Allecra," I whispered. "I will be a nervous wreck when the time comes."

"I promise I will never hurt you," Allecra said and smoothed my hair. "When we decide to do it, I will hold your hands while we join our bodies like two long lost halves because then we can be as free as we want with

201

each other. But always remember that me holding your hand is my way of reminding you that I love you gently from my heart."

We kissed.

"After my birthday, we will do it," I said, pulling away from her soft sweet lips.

"Three more weeks," Allecra whispered back breathlessly as we stared into each other's eyes.

CHAPTER 25

So THERE WE WERE, carrying on our temporary platonic relationship. It had been five days of just us sitting side by side and talking about a million little things whenever we had the chance.

Spring had begun to settle over the world. I could see the leaves of the trees slowly changing into bright pigments. Red dragonflies fluttered around the quadrangle, being chased by the neighborhood children with swinging nets.

There were a number of things people plan to do in spring, like drinking apple cider, making a friendship bracelet, or planning a party during spring break. But my plan had taken on a slightly adventurous turn this year. Sometimes, my stomach did a somersault at the thought of how it all was going to unfold.

Long story short, it was now confirmed that I was going to lose my virginity to Allecra Knight in three weeks. The prospect of having my body in sync with hers made me flush all over. In the end, I would rather want it to be with Allecra than anyone else in the world.

I put on my most cozy knitted scarf and tugged my hair out. As the weather was breezy, I wore a denim jacket under a camel wool coat and skinny jeans with my boots. Spring was a perfect time one dressed for looks, as well as for comfort.

Now, I devoted a great deal of time and attention more than usual to my daily appearance. Setting a deadline to plunge into a sexual odyssey had its downside. A small insecure part of me couldn't stop caring about how I looked to Allecra. I wanted to be in my best form for her and only her. And for me, my body was sacred, like a shrine to be kept clean and protected without a speck of dust or the slightest stain.

I left the house and brought along a mason jar, which I had prepared a special parfait filled to the brim with layers of fruits topped with yogurt. When I saw the black car parked in front of the garden, I knew the real world had blended with fantasy before my eyes. The epitome of perfection that was Allecra herself, standing singularly in form and brilliancy with symmetrical grace, caused my heart to swell up like a balloon ready to burst.

Before I could work myself up to a full-blown attack of hyperventilation, I walked over to her with my hands clutching the jar, cold and fresh with delicious fruit aromas. Allecra looked at me and her bright greenish blue eyes lit up. There was this weird pleasure stirring up inside me just by getting raked over by those eyes.

"What's this?" her voice drew me back to my senses.

"I made it especially for you," I said and held up the jar of breakfast-dessert shyly to her like a little school girl. Allecra started smiling. Her smooth fingers came to wrap around mine. Then she unscrewed the lid and took a sniff of the pleasant scent.

"Is this gonna be as sweet as you?" she said good-naturedly.

"You and your teasing need to stop," I said but Allecra leaned over until she was close to my ear. I held my breath.

"My tongue can do a better job of teasing you than my words can," she said.

"Allecra!"

"Alright, alright—just kidding!" she said and laughed as I glared hard at her. "We're gonna be late. Let's get going!"

Recently, Allecra started picking me up more often. It was a good thing that we both were early birds, so no one in the house actually noticed this.

Along the way, I spoon-fed Allecra the parfait while she drove.

"It's official now," she began, "your body is meant to sit in the passenger seat of my car and your hand is meant to hold mine while I drive."

"I can't hold your hand at the moment," I said. "I'm busy feeding a big baby."

"So to fit your description of me, next time you can feed me when I'm in my birthday suit."

I had to pause and think for a moment then I gasped.

"Allecra!"

She laughed out loud, and I tried not to hurt her while she was driving.

"There is a word, 'basorexia' Do you know what it means?"

"No, my English is still poor," I said sulkily. Allecra chuckled again.

"It means an overwhelming desire to kiss,'" she whispered and tried to lean into me, but I pushed her away.

"You better take the traffic seriously, young lady," I scolded her.

"Did you just tell a person who had been on a spaceship to mind her driving?" she said mischievously.

I shot her a look.

When we reached our school, Allecra walked me to my locker as usual. As we were about to leave, I heard some snickering and murmuring around us. Then I saw Jack with some of his friends and some cheerleaders laughing amongst themselves.

"What are they laughing at?" Allecra noticed my reaction to the group. Jack was staring at me with a cold look so Allecra walked up to him and his friends.

"No!" I cried out loud and came to pull her back. "Don't bother with them. Let's go!"

I tried my best to steer Allecra away. Luckily, the school bell rang and the group left. They looked over their shoulders at us and continued to whisper.

"They really gave me a bad vibe," Allecra muttered. "I want to know what that was about."

"I will tell you if you promise not to do anything reckless," I said when we entered science class. Allecra didn't look too happy with the deal, but she agreed nonetheless. By the end of class, I reported to her everything that had to do with Jack Conner.

"On one condition, Nina - if he ever comes within ten feet from you, he'd be on a receiving end of bad luck from me," Allecra declared.

"But you promised!"

"I didn't say I wouldn't break my promise," she said. "All I know is no one messes with my girl."

I wanted to say something but the term of endearment just made me smile.

Allecra promised to see me after class. Today I had a special lecture — the unbiased lesson in sex ed. Luckily, I attended it with Jordan. The rest of the lecture was about abstinence, peer pressure, contraception, abortion, and abuse. It was the same old thing I already knew, but this session was different because, during the Q&A time, it ended with a guy being sent to the nurse office after three girls attacked him with their backpacks and textbooks as their weapons. The whole affair began when he shared his opinion on abortion.

"If girls aren't stupid enough—" He didn't even get to finish his sentence.

The lesson was then carried on as normal. A teacher named Beth, who was strangely unaffected by the bloodshed earlier, simply continued to demonstrate the use of contraception.

The teacher was in her mid-fifties, short and stocky, and from behind, she had a weird sort of gait, like a crustacean. She wore tiny metal-framed glasses, but in contrast to her gentle-looking exterior, her voice was strikingly clear and youthful. It was the kind of voice that would pierce the farthest reaches of any noisy classroom. And she was the first teacher who taught us about homosexuality without batting an eye, unlike other people.

"If sexuality were doors, children, Heterosexual would be a door that swings one way," she explained, "while Homosexual, a door that swings the opposite way. Bisexual, a door that swings both ways. Pansexual is a revolving door. Demisexual, the door is locked, but one person has key; and finally the oddball, Asexual is the door that is actually a wall."

I had had some doubt in the past while I was still dating boys. I didn't know who I was and what was wrong with me. Now I was trying to figure out which door was actually me.

"But whoever you are, it's always important to protect yourself, ladies," the teacher continued, "You don't expect your partner to be careful, therefore you must always carry a condom with you."

She pulled out a foil package of the condom and tore it open. We were staring at her, unblinking, like she was going to set off a bomb.

Instead of using a toy to show us, she brought a big bottle of Pepsi and rolled the condom onto it all the way to the bottom to prove the rubber's elasticity.

"And girls, if a guy tells you he's too big for a condom, you run— you run really fast!" she said.

At the end of the class, she passed a basket of those foil packages around. Awkwardly each student in the room took one, by the time it reached me; I blushed as I stared hesitantly into the basket.

"Nina, it's okay if you don't take them," Jordan said. She was probably thinking I had no need of those, considering the nature of my relationship with Allecra Knight. But she was wrong. There was something she didn't know. And I didn't plan on telling her why I had to look around before grabbing a handful of the condoms and quickly shoving them into my bag.

Jordan's eyes widened as she stared at my redden face, but she didn't say anything.

After class, Jordan walked me to my locker. I was sort of afraid Allecra was already there, but she wasn't.

While I waited for her, Jordan seemed to linger there.

"You don't have any more class?"

"No," I said.

"You're waiting for her?"

I nodded sheepishly.

"Does she treat you well?" she went on, and I looked at her. Jordan murmured, "Sorry."

"That's okay," I said. "She is really nice to me."

"I'm glad to hear that." Jordan smiled, but it seemed a bit forced. "It's just I know you delight in the exotic, and I'm a bit concerned."

"What do you mean?" I asked.

"I meant you get excited and mystified when something or someone different comes along and walks into your life," she said. "Ordinary people are not your match, but that also means you tend to wade deeper into the dangerous water more than normal people, and I don't want anything bad to happen to you, Nina."

"Thank you for your concern, Jordan," I said. "But you don't have to worry about me. I know what I'm doing."

Jordan looked at me for a minute and then she slowly nodded in acceptance. I knew she had meant well. She was the first person since Klara, who had an excellent intuition, and whom I was able to feel anything like an attraction with until I met Allecra. Unfortunately, there had been limits to our friendship.

Then I saw Allecra coming from the other side.

"I gotta go, I'll see you later," I said, but when I was about to turn and walk away, Jordan stopped me.

"Nina," she said and paused for a while. I looked at her and waited. "Just take care, okay."

I gave her a half-hearted smile and waved her goodbye. Maybe I didn't like being told what to do, but it was also because I wanted to keep my outlook on Allecra unsullied.

School day ended at three. It so happened that today, I had to do groceries shopping after school. When Allecra heard that, she wanted to come along with me.

"I want to watch you shop," she said.

"Why?"

"I don't know. I just want to watch you do things, daily human things," she answered.

"So you have never shopped in a supermarket like that before?" I asked and she shook her head 'no'.

"You should learn to cook, Allecra. You can't just eat out all the time."

"I can if you agree," she said and quirked her eyebrow at me. I scowled. "You know what I meant!"

"Why? I have never had any food poisoning so far," she said with a casual shrug.

"You need to live like a human if you want to be with one," I said. She grinned back and pulled me into her arms.

"Right, now that I have my human motivation right here, yes?"

I nudged her back shyly with my shoulder.

We reached our destination. Allecra looked around once we entered the biggest supermarket in town. We went through aisles after aisles. Allecra pushed the cart and followed me. She observed me and listened to my comments on each item we bought.

When we finished, Allecra paid for everything, even though I violently protested it, but it was no use. She simply pulled out a shiny credit card from the inside of her jacket. The cashier, who was a young college-aged girl, stared at her with an awestruck face and accepted her card in a daze. I was pouting all the way to the parking lot until we reached the car.

"I wonder how you could keep a low profile until now," I said, still annoyed as we loaded everything and got into the car. "I mean you all are merely three kids living with no guardians, and nobody wonders where you got the money? No one checks into your account or anything?"

"Oh, the Arzurian wealth is immeasurable," Allecra said as she backed the car out of the lot. "And if you happened to be the last heir, then you inherited everything. You couldn't help but indulge yourself a little. In fact, we came here with just a small portion of our gold and diamonds..."

"Gold and diamonds?"

"Arzuria is rich in gold and diamonds. They are like rocks to us there," she said. "But what I have now is enough to last us many more generations on Earth, well, that if I ever have children."

Silence followed after she said the last part. It automatically became a taboo to talk about breeding between us. Allecra sensed my discomfort and turned on the music. Yann Tiersen's *La Valse d'Amélie* was playing. And I listened to it distractedly for a while without knowing what to say. Then I changed the subject.

"Your brother, Triton, he doesn't seem to talk much, does he?"

"Oh, he does talk, but not in a way you're used to," Allecra said with a meaningful smile.

"What does that mean?"

"You'll see when you get to know him," she just said with a grin that lightened up the mood. I learned later on that Triton had been working on a precise and complicated system to keep their secret safe, with a labyrinth of accounts hidden under layers of camouflage. Once he put his hands on the keyboards, he was the king of the cyber world. That was how no one knew they were still illegal immigrants from outer space.

As it was still too early to go home, we went to her house at the outskirt of the city. Allecra led me straight to her beautiful kitchen. I hesitantly glanced around.

"Don't worry, they're not here," Allecra said. "It's just us now."

"Are you hungry?" I asked.

"A little." She shrugged.

I sensed that we tried not to bring up the incidence that had happened that day, so I decided to make food right away. The house itself was just as bright and elegant as I first saw it. Designed furniture, shelves and sofa were successfully utilized in the living spaces that speak comfort. The contemporary painting and decors of the interiors always enticed me. I could see the glass-framed terrace from Allecra's luxurious bedroom. Just to imagine myself being in that same room with her made my inside warm and gooey.

In the kitchen, I paused to take in the spacious area for a moment. The wooden texture of the cabinets was in contrast with the flawless white color of the concrete wall. There was a sliding glassed door that led to the garden outside in the backyard. Beyond the estate was a small unpaved lane, probably leading down to the beach.

I started working around the electric stove. The cabinets and a bright shiny sink and faucet looked untouched.

"How long have you been living here?" I asked.

"Just a few months before you showed up," Allecra said. "My sister likes the area and I like the design of the house. Triton doesn't care where he is as long as there's enough space to drive around."

"You have way too many cars for a teenager," I pointed out.

"It's the closest thing to the hovercraft we had back on my home planet," she said.

"The hovercraft?"

"It's like a car, but it hovers," she explained, "The roads there are paved with magnets, so you could drive on it. It's like a bullet train in Japan."

"Oh wow, you literally lived in the future, Allecra," I said in amazement. She just chuckled back. I had to turn my focus on finding an aluminum pot and bowl with some ceramic plates. They also looked brand new.

"Where's the juicer?" I asked. Allecra pointed to the left over my head. But then she had to come and help me open the top cupboard when she saw how I was quite vertically challenged. Her tall elegant body pressed against my back and I sort of froze in place. Allecra took the juicer out and put it down on the counter, but she didn't move away. I could hear her breathing softly on my neck. My hands gripped the edge of the counter tightly as my heart started pounding. Her lower half was brushing against my backside, and for a moment, I could almost detect that special heat.

"Allecra..." my voice trembled a little and I felt my body shivered. Then she pulled away abruptly.

"I'm sorry," she said in a rather hoarse tone.

"That's—that's okay," I tried to speak and cleared my throat. "Have a seat while I finish this."

She nodded and retreated back to the stool, watching me from a distance. There were still red tinges on her cheeks, and I was secretly pleased by the fact that she wasn't as in control as I thought.

I went on cooking with my back to her. My heart had returned to normal rate again, and I started preparing to make beef *Stroganov*, which were pieces of sautéed beef in *Smetana* sour cream. The next dish was *Coulibiac*, a kind of salmon fish loaf with rice and hard-boiled eggs with mushrooms and dill. The two dishes would take a long while to make, but we had plenty of time. Cooking was like writing. It was a fascinating process of seeing one flavor complimented another, just like a 'noun' and an 'adjective.' And seeing the things you put together becomes a reality before your very eyes satisfied me. It was truly an effective means of my retreat.

I worked in quick pace, handling more than one cooking procedure at once. After I tasted the boiled dish, I was at the cutting board then took something out of the fridge and piled it on a plate. It was after half an hour later that Allecra came to stand next to me. An engrossed look plastered her face. I smiled at her and continued to work. Soon she was helping me with handing out kitchen utensils. I enjoyed working in her kitchen. It made me even more excited to cook when the person I loved was going to eat what I put on the plates.

I guessed I could do this forever.

"Wow," Allecra said, sounding genuinely impressed. "Watching you cook is like watching a magician pops rabbits out of the hat turns scarf to doves, and juggle flames at the same time — each with perfect time and balance. I'm in awe of you, Nina. Who taught you how to make all these?"

"It's a long story," I said sheepishly.

"You can talk all day. I don't mind," she said. Her eyes never left me. "I want to know every bit of details about you."

Before I left Moscow, Klara had said to me, *"Don't date anyone who doesn't ask you about your childhood and why you are the way you are."* I remembered it like a mantra. Now, it made me happy that I actually found the one who did ask. Allecra kept watching me as I washed the rice, mixed it with a quarter of brown rice, put it in the cooker, and then I turned on the stove. Turning back to her, I drew my eyelashes down a little.

"I taught myself," I answered. "My dad was always busy. When I was little, we mostly ate take-outs or at the deli below our apartment. My dad hated cooking, so he was always like, *'let's order pizza'* or *'let's just buy some croquettes at the butcher shop,'.* I remembered having a big pot of something in the fridge and eating the same thing three days in a row. So when I was in my first year of high school, I decided that we had to have a real meal. I bought an old cookbook from my neighbor's grandma. She wrote it herself. I mastered it from cover to cover: how to choose the right ingredients, how to bone a fish— everything. That's how I learned a lot of Russian traditional dishes that usually surprised grown-ups. Then my dad bought me a complete set of utensils. He couldn't tell the difference between a cauliflower and a broccoli, but he went out and got the best kitchen gadget there was."

"You dad sounds like a nice guy. You're lucky to have him as a father," Allecra said.

"Maybe; maybe not," I replied with a dry smile. She wanted to say something but seemed to change her mind when I looked away.

"Perhaps, you should teach me how to cook some yummy human food?" she said to change the subject.

"Oh, now you're interested," I teased.

I decided to teach her to make a side dish. With very few instructions, Allecra turned out to be a natural at handling knives, almost with expertise. She chopped a lot of ginger to a fine consistency. Then she sliced some celery and mushroom into nice-sized pieces. The Chinese parsley, too, she cut it up finely. Then I watched her peeled the shrimp and washed them at the sink. She spread a paper towel out to absorb the water, and then she laid the shrimp in neat rows, like a troop in formation. Next, she warmed a large frying pan and dribbled in some sesame oil in a spiral pattern before slowly fried the prepared ingredients over a low flame.

"You learned fast!" I couldn't help but admire her talent.

"I just did what you told me," she said with a shrug and a smile. But still, the way she did things was amazingly precise and economical with no mess or wasted time at all. Oftentimes, I simply forgot that she wasn't an ordinary girl.

Allecra's cooking was far better than I had imagined a first-timer could achieve. She even took the time to decorate the plate like a professional chef.

"Well, that was fun," she said after we placed everything on the table in the garden outside. We sat down and began to eat. The early spring sun cast light upon Allecra's blonde hair and the shadow of her lashes danced on her cheeks.

Even a simple activity like holding the knife and fork, Allecra made it fascinating to my eyes. She really got me and I was helplessly drawn to her like Icarus to the sun.

"How is it?" I asked expectantly as I watched Allecra took a mouthful of *Coulibiac*.

"This is delicious!" she said. "If only I knew you were such a great cook, I would have brought you over to cook for me every day!"

"That's all you want me for?"

"Don't be ridiculous Nina," she said. "Why would I do that?"

"It always seems like I want to be with you more," I said.

Allecra sighed.

"Nina, didn't all the things I said to you make any dent on your memory at all?" she said, "Hell, you're damn perfect. You don't even have to know how to cook or do anything special to stay with me."

"No," I said quietly under my breath, "I'm just afraid that when we stay together longer, you discover that I'm not as interesting as you thought I was."

"Nonsense!" Allecra cut me off and then came to sit on the chair next to me. She took my hands in hers. "I don't care how many people are better than you in this world. You're all I see, Nina. I won't look at anyone else or want anyone else but you. I want you - end of story!"

"Really?"

"Yes," she said fervently.

When we were silent, I could hear the faint sound of the sea waves drifted into my ears. Allecra looked into my eyes, and I into hers. I put my arms around her neck and kissed her. The slightest sensation went through me as we closed our eyes and gave in to the motion of our locked lips.

~*~

213

When I got back home, it was six. Fortunately, the cats and the mice hadn't returned home yet. Allecra smiled and her eyes flickered to mine, and then she leaned in to swiftly kiss me just at the corner of my lips. Even so, my heart lurched frantically. I had spent a few precious hours with her until it was time to go back to my other world, more plain and less complicated, and yet less exciting and magical.

Then I saw the back of a black car, the BMW, rolling passed by and then coming to park in front of the house. Stepping out of the car, Aunt Vikki stood with her husband. I guessed I had probably crossed some unknown line.

"I have to go," I said and waved goodbye to Allecra. She seemed to sense my discomfort and nodded. Robert's face was impassive as a stone as I walked out of the Lambo.

"Who's that?" Aunt Vikki said when I reached them.

"She's the friend I told you about," I said. "We work on the science project together."

Robert looked at me then.

"So it's a girl," he said. He hardly spoke, but when he did, I bridled a little at his word 'girl'.

"I would quite like to see that friend of yours some days," my aunt said to my surprise.

After finishing my bath, I reappeared and tried to act normal, which meant doing things like hearing Piper talk about her friends and helping Aunt Vikki arrange lilies and dandelion in the vase. Robert was still in his office. I pretended to be oblivious to my aunt's scrutiny.

After the dinner was ready, we ate together and for the first time, I thought about my father. Normally, I couldn't bear to think of him along with Dominika, but this time, I was genuinely free of that shuddering thought of them. It was as if the things I had been through were just, well, the things I had been through. I wasn't sure whether I was still mad at my father, but what is done, is done. Maybe he had found his other half in a woman like Dominika, even if she was like a witch that came straight out of Shakespeare's Macbeth to me. But what would my dad think if he found out that my other half was an alien hermaphrodite from outer space?

We chitchatted for a while over dessert. Then I excused myself to my room.

That night I dreamed about a place that looked so strange. There were colossal trees that shaped like the Baobab trees in Africa, except they were white and the leaves were crimson. In the sky was an aqua-blue moon. I walked through the strange forest and entered a meadow. Something greeted me there. In the atmosphere hung several levitating islands, floating about with a few coral-shaped trees of various colors on top.

The sky was unevenly blue and pink and a little violet mixing in like a painting of Van Gogh's. In the middle of a clearing was a gigantic flower. It shaped like an opium flower in the shade of dark purple.

I was burned by a curiosity that deprived me of all self-control. Then I heard a voice calling me. I looked around but found no one. The voice kept echoing from somewhere I didn't know. After a while, I realized it was from the inside of a flower.

My feet took me closer to the strange plant, and I began to notice how familiar the voice was.

"Who's that?" I asked, leaning closer. I lifted my hand to touch the soft surface of the outer petal. Suddenly the flower opened itself. I stepped back and watched it blossom slowly until it spread big and wide like a carpet. The exquisite scent emitted in the air. I inhaled and felt my senses heightened. Lying stark naked was a blonde girl in a fetus position. I was even more intrigued by her presence. I stepped into the flower and knelt down to observe the strange girl.

Then the petals of the flower started closing in. I got up in surprise and tried to push back, but to no avail. I screamed and rolled around in panic. Inside the flower was soft like cotton, but everywhere I pushed wouldn't budge. I was trapped. Then I heard a giggling and I turned around to find the girl. When she turned, I realized it was Allecra.

"I've been waiting for you, Nina," she said and then crawled up towards me.

"Why are you here?" I asked, still looking around.

"It's time," she said softly and brought her hand to my cheek. My clothes slowly dissolved from my body as if someone had poured acid on them. Soon I was left with nothing to cover my nakedness.

"We better hurry," Allecra said in a voice that seemed to echo from a cave.

"But we promised to wait until my birthday," I tried to remind her. Allecra didn't answer and came to mash her lips into mine. All senses abuzz. I heard my own first melting moans. Then her soft hand slipped down her tummy and disappeared between her thighs. She then parted her sweet pinkness, stroking herself for a second, before something stirred and sprouted out from her purring sex. The long fleshy length grew out of her sex, already weeping musky juice.

I gasped and squirmed. It was the first time I had seen her thing, primed and drooling, nearly making me swoon at the very sight of it. Then something held me down. I looked and realized there were vines tying around my limbs. The vines were thick and strong, growing out of nowhere and wrapped themselves around my legs, pulling them apart, spreading me wide and defenseless. In my state of disbelief, I screamed.

Allecra didn't seem like herself. She ignored my protest as she inched that rigid member of hers forward. It wasn't too big, yet it wasn't small either. In fact, it was rather slender in a feminine way. The tip was slightly wider like a mushroom with a tiny slit in the middle.

I felt on the verge of throwing up.

"No, Allecra, no, please, no—" I cried again and again. She began rubbing her hot throbbing tip against me and poking lightly into my warmness, swirling about, intently whipping my scent into the crackling air. I choked in pure pleasure. The heavy slippery sensation burned my core like fire. My heart was galloping like a runaway horse. I trembled and shuddered under her blazing bright eyes. There was a look of unquenchable lust in them.

Then she stopped suddenly. I thought she had listened to my objection, but then Allecra rammed herself into me. A burst of piercing cry erupted from my throat. Every muscle in my body lost control for a moment. All the while, Allecra watched me in agony mixed with indiscernible pleasure. Her smile was mean and her eyes were full of sadist thoughts. I shivered and trembled, trying to close my legs, but it was hopeless, Allecra had already been deep into my startled walls.

She began to move inside me.

No, this isn't real. I found myself thinking. Allecra would never hurt me like that. This isn't reality.

As I kept repeating it like a mantra, the vines around my body loosened and fell away. And when I looked up again, there was no Allecra anymore, but a dark-haired girl that was Xenon. That was when I recovered my strength and pushed her away with all my might. The petals of the flower slowly began to open. The light from the outside came piercing in until everything was white and blinding.

When I opened my eyes again, it was in the morning. I woke up and was finally freed from the imprisonment of Xenon's manipulation of my mind. I felt free like there was no fog veiling in the window of my consciousness. She couldn't mess with my mind anymore.

I smiled to myself. I am free.

That morning, Piper and Jay had wedged themselves onto the stools of the island. Aunt Vikki and her husband wouldn't be up until sometime later.

It just dawned on me that the twins had turned me into a mother figure without me realizing it, and I found myself reminding them about schoolwork or schedules just so no one would run into troubles.

I was making light breakfast on the go with oatmeal and some fresh strawberry and bananas, which I had cut into bite-size and added blueberries into the mix with yogurt. The good thing about the twins was they would eat whatever I conjured up onto the plates for them without a single complaint.

Piper was flipping through a magazine while Jay's eyes were glued to his phone.

I opened the windows and let the air in along with the smell of honeysuckle. As I stood there all dreamy and dazed at the pleasant sights in the world, I got to taste what it was like to be truly happy.

It was a time like this when I let my guard down for like half a nanosecond and Piper suddenly stopped eating and looked at me in her usual snoopy way.

"Nina, why are you smiling like a loon all by yourself? Are you in love or something?"

By now, I should have gotten used to the fact that privacy in this house was almost nonexistent. And I thought for a minute about the best way to answer her, but then out of impulse, I just turned back with the silliest smile on my face and said, "Yes I am."

Jay was staring at me with his fork midway to his mouth. I was also taken aback to hear my own honest announcement of romance for the first time. If I ever remembered being asked about being in love with anyone in the past, I was certain that I would always come up with a vague 'I guess so' or a 'maybe', but not this loud and proud 'yes' that was as clean cut as the answer to my math equation. It was impossible to deny it, much like it was impossible to hide the sun with a thin cloud of uncertainty. Piper was looking at me and after a moment, she gave a little happy squeak like a mouse cheer.

"Aw...Nina! That is so sweet, I'm happy for you!" she said. Jay was still in shock as if he had just been dragged out of bed in the middle of the night.

"Wait...what?" he asked, blinking between me and his sister.

"I heard someone is in love?" Aunt Vikki's voice echoed from the living room. We all turned to my aunt, who was still in her pink nightgown as she walked into the kitchen.

"Mom, Nina has a girlfriend," Piper told her excitedly. It snatched the yawn from my aunt's mouth. Aunt Vikki turned to me with a funny look as she was still not fully recovered from her sleep.

For a moment, no one spoke and the awkwardness deepened.

"A girlfriend," my aunt repeated as if it was a foreign word. My aunt took a seat at the table and kept staring at me with steady eyes. I felt like I was naked under her gaze. "Now I'm so looking forward to seeing her. You must bring the girl to your birthday celebration."

"Birthday?" all the three of us echoed.

"I have your birth certification, Nina." My aunt simply smiled. "Besides Robert and I figured we could not miss a more perfect day for a garden-party with our old friends this year. It just so happened that the date we picked coincides with your birthday, so one stone kills two birds."

"That's great!" Piper said. "I will invite all my friends, too."

"Can I bring mine?" Jay asked, sounding equally excited as his twin sister. All the while I wasn't sure how I was going to tell Allecra about all this.

218

CHAPTER 26

THE WEEKS THAT FOLLOWED were unnaturally calm, but the calmness wouldn't last long. My thoughts were like beasts that never get tired and kept on tracking me down wherever I go.

For the first time, I was afraid of my own imagination. I tried to pay attention during classes, did my homework as best as I could and made sure it was neat. I answered the questions the teachers had asked me, but the feeling I got whenever I was close to Allecra was almost aphrodisiac.

It was a Monday morning— a week before my birthday. Birds woke me up a little after six. I went downstairs, brew some jasmine tea for my aunt then set a timer on the coffee machine before I began to make breakfast. It became a custom that I also prepared lunch for Allecra, too.

The sandwich I packed into my lunch box looked delicious with smoked salmon, watercress, and lettuce on soft whole wheat bread. I made sure that the crust was nicely cut. The texture was crunchy with horseradish and butter.

While I waited for the family to get up, I sat on the porch and listened to lively bird songs outside the windows. The sky was splotchy with white puffy clouds—like pieces of floating cottons—the cumulus clouds.

I stared at the veil of light blueness that blended in with a haze of golden ray and I breathed in deeply. The air was floral-scented as it was in an early spring. The weather was ideal. You could not have had a more perfect season for a garden-party. I ran a replay of the last conversation I had with Allecra about the invitation from my aunt.

"She wants to see you," I said a bit repentantly. Allecra was silent for a moment. I wouldn't mind if she refused, but then she looked at me.

"Do you want me to go?" she asked.

"If you're okay with it."

"You sound like you're embarrassed," she said.

"No! Why would I be embarrassed to have you there?" I tried to reassure her. "It's just—it's just that this is the first time I bring someone to see my *family*."

Until then, it had never hit me how our relationship had developed thus far. I guessed I was still in awe that she was mine, and the feeling hadn't sunk in yet. Allecra stared at me for a long moment.

"I see," she said and smiled mischievously, "I'm your first."

I felt my cheeks radiated heat.

"Like it wasn't obvious," I murmured.

"Don't worry about it, Nina," she said. "I won't tell anyone that your girlfriend is an alien."

I gave her a withering look. Allecra chuckled before stealing a peck on my cheek softly.

Even just the memory of it still didn't fail to make me blush. To make things less complicated, Allecra and I agreed that we should only see each other at school until things got settled down.

When everyone was up, we had breakfast in a tranquil mood together.

"Everything okay?" my aunt asked me in Russian. That would only mean she wanted a private conversation with me.

"Yes, everything's fine," I replied.

"Is your friend coming to your birthday party?" she asked. I thought it was nice of her to refer to the garden party as my birthday party even I had begged her not do anything special for me.

"She said she would love to," I answered. My aunt nodded.

"You know, I just want to make sure that you hang out with the right people," she said. Suddenly I felt nervous. "I assume she does well in school, too?"

"Yes, she's a good student," I said but refrained myself from telling Aunt Vikki that aside from hardly ever attending classes, Allecra was an inborn genius.

"Good then." She nodded.

I knew what my aunt wanted from me, although she never said anything about it. I could feel that she trusted me and treated me like an adult. All I wanted was to get school over with as soon as possible. I didn't expect top grades or to be popular or to join social activities like my cousins.

Over the past several months, I tried not to cause any trouble here. My report card surprised me by having all A's. The lowest grade was an A-, but that was in math. The school was not easier than my old school in

Russia so I wondered why my grades were so good. Perhaps, I had a special tutor.

As I entered the hall, my eyes roamed over the school bulletin board. There was a big colorful poster in the midst of others: YOUNG WRITERS CONTEST, 5,000 WORDS MAX TO SHOW YOUR TALENT! JOIN NOW!

I was staring at it for a while.

"You're interested?" a musical voice said behind me. I turned around to find Allecra smiling. And have you ever met someone whose smile looks like it could make flowers grow? I believed I had. My stomach did a flip in excitement when I saw her face.

"Oh, hey you," I said, tugging my hair behind my ear. "Well, I don't think this is for me."

"Why not?" she asked. "You want to be a writer, don't you?"

"I don't want to be a writer!" I protested. I didn't know why I felt embarrassed about this. Perhaps, writing was so intimate and it was supposed to be my secret.

"But you are always scribbling away about bunnies and squirrels and monkeys," Allecra pointed out.

"I don't write about monkeys!" I corrected her.

"Aw, why are you so cranky about it?" she said. "I think you're really good."

"You do?" I said, because coming from Allecra Knight, that counted for something.

"Arzurian's honor," she said and came over to wrap her arms around my waist. The compliment made me smile. That was what I loved about her. Even while she was teasing me, she was also disarmingly sweet when I least expected it.

"Allecra, we're in school," I warned her, squirming in her arms.

"So?" she said and was about to claim my lips when the bell rang. I jumped back and stepped away. Allecra groaned.

"Later, I promise," I said with an amused grin.

In Language Arts, Mrs. Smith was handing back papers. I got 93 on a short story about a baby elephant that lost its mother in the forest. But Allecra got a 98 on her work on some dystopian stuff. Of course, I was the first to read her story, and I admitted that I could never come up with anything better than hers. Yet it bugged me that she didn't seem to even try. It was just something she did to kill time. At the end of the class, Mrs. Smith asked me to stay over. Allecra told me she would wait outside.

"Antonina," she called my full name with a smile and handed me some kind of an entry form. I then realized it was the same writing contest I had seen. "Take a look at it and see if you're interested."

"Oh, thank you, ma'am, I've seen it earlier in the hall," I told her.

"I really think you should go for it. With your writing skill, it's supposed to be a good experience for you."

"But I don't think I would win this."

"Winning or not, it doesn't matter," she said. "You will learn a lot from it."

"Why don't you ask Allecra instead?" I asked curiously. "She can write really well— way better than me."

Mrs. Smith smiled.

"I recognized her talent, but I see your passion," she said. "If you win it, it will open up a lot of opportunities for you. It'll also look good on your college application. Just think about it, Nina."

Mrs. Smith had a solid point with that last part. I nodded and thanked her wholeheartedly.

After school, Allecra asked me what it was about. We were eating our sandwiches under the big pepper tree, enjoying the breeze on a nice spring day. The tall tree provided a melancholy and pleasant shade. I began to tell her everything. Allecra pursed her lips and stopped chewing for a moment.

"I think she's right," she said.

"I'm still not sure about that," I said with a weak shrug. "It's just that there are a lot of people who can write. I'm just a salmon swimming among the dolphins and sharks and whales in this big ocean of literature. I don't think I would even be short-listed. I think I still have a lot to learn."

"You're not confident about your writing," Allecra concluded, nailing it right on the head.

"Yeah, you can say that," I murmured. "Few writers are."

Allecra came and brushed a strand of hair from my face, tracing her fingers over my cheek gently.

"Forget about all the reasons why it won't work and believe in the one reason why it will," she said. "You know, salmons don't give in to the current that easily."

"Oh, Allecra, you're going to make me cry," I said and playfully pushed her shoulder. She giggled.

"Maybe I can make you cry out my name instead," she said.

"Stop being such a perv," I said.

"I can't help it," she said with a mischievous smile. "You're the cutest thing I've ever had — cuter than puppies and prettier than flowers."

I blushed so hard that I had to cover my face. Allecra drew me into her arms and gave me kisses on my temple. After we finished our lunch, she thanked me for the delicious sandwiches. I handed her a bottle of grape juice.

"So what now?" she said, sipping the drink.

"Well, it's worth a try," I said at last. "But first, I will have to read a lot to learn how to write better. That's what every writer says."

"Yes! That's my little Salmon!" Allecra cried, smiling cheekily at me. "Let's go to my house then."

I didn't see the connection between my writing and going to her house immediately, but I didn't argue. I was pretty much willing to be alone with her anyway.

We got into her car and drove off. Along the way, we chatted about nonsense things. I felt more open and less embarrassed about my dorkiness with her. During one of the conversations, it had transpired that Allecra didn't understand why I was obsessed with typewriters.

"A computer would be a lot easier and faster and less noisy," Allecra said. "If you misspell a word on a typewriter, there goes the entire page."

"You don't understand! The keyboards make a mousy tappy tap tappy tap sound... like knitting needles creating a pair of socks," I tried to explain her. "Everything you type on a typewriter sounds grand - the words forming in mini-explosions. It's just fascinating to me. Besides, you have to think about what you're going to write and you have to hit the keys with real purpose. The sound is soothing, like the lullaby of a subway train with beautiful black racing stripes down the sides. I just think I like the solid achievement of tapping words and witness their births on paper. It's like seeing magic happens."

But as I was saying that, I could see her perfect lips curved in some hidden joy.

"What?" I asked.

"Nothing," she said. "I just like the way you talk."

I smiled back.

Then Allecra asked me about my ideal place to visit. When I told her it would be wonderful to sit in a hammock under a palm tree, sipping my drink from a pineapple with a mini parasol in it. Allecra wondered what on earth I wanted a parasol in my drink for.

"Unless you want to protect your drink from the rain!" she said and laughed.

"It's not like that!" I said, but I was laughing, too.

I guessed even though Allecra had seen the world and certainly knew a lot about many things, there was still some simple human natures she didn't have a clue about. But all these talks, unlike arguments, stimulated my brain cells and brought only binding acceptance for us both.

The car came to a crawl. We seemed to be in a traffic jam. We were behind a red trailer truck.

"Looks like we're stuck now," she said. The line of traffic stretched out long and slow.

Suddenly, Allecra groaned.

"Are you okay?" I asked in concern.

"Yeah, I'm fine," she answered a bit too quickly, but I noticed her hand went to her lower abdomen.

"Are you hurt or something?"

"Don't worry about it," she said. "It will go away."

But that uncomfortable scowl still etched on her face like she was secretly hurting. It made me uneasy, not only was it because I might have known the reason behind it but also because I was really worried about Allecra. She was probably under too much stress (yes, you know the kind!).

"Is it too difficult for you?" I asked.

"What?"

"To be like that?"

"Like what?" she asked again, glancing side way at me.

"I mean, do you have to suffer when you don't have...hmm...sex?"

"Well, it's uncomfortable like I said," she said a bit awkwardly. "It's the same like when girls have their period cramps."

I suddenly became curious about her anatomy again.

"Oh, so do you have periods, Allecra?"

"No, I don't," she said quickly, but I could see a tint of red on her face.

"Why not?" I said. "Aren't you half-girl, too?"

"Yeah, but it's more complicated, Nina," she said with some level of difficulty.

"Complicated how?"

She sighed.

"Well, I don't have periods because I...er...you know...helped myself," she said. A tint of red formed on her cheeks.

"Help yourself?"

"Oh gosh, Nina, please change the subject." She was blushing openly now.

"I don't quite understand the connection," I said again.

"You don't have to," she said.

"But I want to know," I insisted. "Please, Allecra!"

"Fine, but don't freak out," she said. "It's a complicated process. If I want to skip my...er...day of the month, I have to get it out of me—my fluid, I mean, otherwise I would have periods like any other girls."

"Oh my god!" I gasped, putting my hands over my gaping mouth. "I'm sorry, you told me not to freak out, but oh my god!"

Allecra shot me a pointed look through her sunglasses.

"If you don't wipe that look off your face, Nina, I swear I'm not telling you anything anymore," she said threateningly.

"No, no, please, I'm sorry," I said. "I mean... I wish I could avoid Mother Nature like that too! That's really cool."

"You think it's cool? You don't find it strange or anything?"

I shook my head back.

"I'm an inner weirdo," I said with a grin. "Strangeness fascinates me."

"So tell me, have you ever touched yourself?" Allecra turned to look at me. I could detect a smirk on her tightly pressed lips. Now the table had turned. I blinked hard.

"Well, that's my privacy," I said. Allecra looked flabbergasted.

"How dare you..." she said but had to groan again. She let a string of curses I didn't understand.

"What's wrong?" I asked again. "You don't look okay to me."

"It's nothing," she said, but she was breathing harder. I began to feel worried about her condition.

"Are you...hard...right now?"

"You mean the sole of my feet?"

"How could you joke at a time like this?" I said and slapped her thigh. "Ow!"

I thought I did it lightly but the impact might have resonated through her body. I didn't know how intense that was.

"Sorry! Are you alright?" I turned to inspect her carefully.

"Uh-huh," she just said, but her face was tensed. She made a low sound in her throat again.

"You know, if it's too hard for you to resist, maybe...maybe I can help," I said faintly. Then I placed my hand on her knee. Allecra glanced down at it and back at my face.

Before she could protest, I unbuckled my seat belt and took her cheeks in my hands, taking her by surprise. I was aware that the windows were black-tinted, and no one could see us.

"Please, let me help you," I whispered. This time, it wasn't because of some mind-control by her sister. It was just my imminent craving for Allecra. Then my lips found hers, moist and soft and delicious.

"Nina...wait..." she couldn't seem to form a sentence between my lips.

"It's okay. You don't have to fight it," I said. My hand slowly snaked down to her belly. When I found the source of her warmth, I felt her body shuddered.

"Oh please, Nina stop!" she whimpered shakily. "You're gonna make me—oh geez—damn it!"

But I could feel her pants tighten under my touch. *Oh my blessed, I can't believe this is really happening.*

Allecra squeezed her eyes shut and gritted her teeth. At the same time, she seemed powerless to stop me. It was a strange thrilling moment to see her like this.

I started moving my hand, stroking her down there gently, so gently that I could feel the bulge in her pants rising. I didn't know what it was at first, but the growing outline between her legs soon became obvious.

"Oh my," I gasped, and we froze at the same time. I looked down and realized her 'secret' rising. Allecra looked as shocked as I was. But suddenly, we heard a loud honk from behind. It made us jump. I withdrew my hand and hurried back into my seat. The traffic was moving again.

"Oh, damn it!" Allecra cursed and stepped on the accelerator. The Lambo roared and jerked forward.

My heart was pounding faster than the speeding car. From the corner of my eyes, I could see her face flushed crimson. Her jaw set tight. We didn't talk again until we arrived at her house. We got out together. I guessed she was probably mad at my sexual advances.

Allecra didn't say anything and just took me by the hand and led me straight to a built-in elevator. I hadn't noticed there was an elevator in her house. It was hidden behind a sliding wall like a secret passage. Then Allecra pulled me by the hips into hers. One of her hands came around my waist while the other tilted my head to look at her.

"You!" she growled.

"I'm sorry," I whimpered.

Her eyes were luminous with desire. Then she buried her nose in my neck and collar bones. My eyes fluttered open and close from the intensity. But before anything could happen, Allecra pushed me away and bent over with her hands on her knees as if to catch a breath.

"For the love of the universe, Nina! I don't know what I should do with you."

I was leaning against the elevator wall. My pulse roared in my ears, trying to calm my riotous heart.

"You're alright?" I asked. "I'm sorry."

"You should be," Allecra said. "I knew what you were doing. I almost pulled over into some quiet lane and bury all my need in you right then and there."

"Oh god," I gulped. If I was religious, I would have crossed my chest for that.

"Yeah," she said, nodding, but after a moment, she started giggling. Then I watched her stand up straight again. She took several deep breaths like she was trying to find her equilibrium. There was a long quietness, except the buzzing of the elevator.

"Are you alright now?" I asked.

"I guess so," she said. "Only if you promise not to provoke me again."

"You mean, provoke that thing," I murmured under my breath.

"Huh?"

"Nothing! So what are we doing here?" I asked instead.

"Oh, I almost forgot," she said and then pressed the button on the panel. "I want to show you something."

We descended to what must be the basement. When the elevator door slid open again, my jaw dropped to the floor. This wasn't an ordinary basement. The first thing I saw was white-painted bookcases that stood proudly around a well-lit room. It was, in fact, a private library, which took up an entire floor. There were books on every shelf. It was impossible not to be excited at the sight of them. I felt like Belle from the Beauty and the Beast.

"You never told me you have a library!" I said as my feet ventured out on their own accord. I went and ran my hand over the book spines. "Allecra, this is so amazing!"

The whiteness of the spacious interior was beautifully lit. The craft fabric lamps hung stylishly from the ceiling. There was a sunken living area that hosted cozy sofa and a wooden coffee table, standing on a white wool rug.

Allecra looked at my animated face and smiled. She seemed to relax again. When we entered the place, she went and sat down on the sofa with her long legs crossed. Her arms spread out on either side in a relaxing posture, but her eyes never left me.

"You like it?" she said.

"Yes," I said. "You built this?"

"Triton and I did. He's a bibliophile," Allecra told me. "Just so you know we're not just some petrol-heads."

"Right, at least you own more books than cars," I said, beaming while drifting around the room. "Have you read all of these?"

"While we were traveling around the world, looking for my potential one, Triton made me read books so that I would learn more about people on this planet," she said and shrugged coolly.

"That's a smart way to understanding humanity," I said with an approval nod.

"You like reading then?"

"What kind of a writer that doesn't like reading?" I said. "I do read quite a lot if I do say so myself."

"Oh really?" Allecra said in a challenging tone. "Have you read Wuthering Heights?"

"No," I said.

"How about Jane Eyre?"

"No."

"Pride and Prejudice?"

"No, but..."

"Gone with the Wind? Hamlet?"

"No and no," I said and started to feel humiliated and irritated as if Allecra had caught me in a lie.

"How come you become a writer if you haven't read those books?"

"I don't read classics, okay? Not in English," I retorted. "Besides, we have our own legendary writers."

"I see," Allecra said. "But you must read widely. Looks like you would have to be here with me more often."

"You think?"

"Yeah, we can form a book club, just you and me, right here on this couch," she said, pointing to the couch and us. I had to admit, this was a brilliant idea, but the way she suggested it sounded so perverted to me. I scowled back at her. I had always dreamed of finding someone whom I could just do things like this with — things like cooking together, reading books together, owning a pet together, or maybe, even having children together.

Oh geez, no no no, my maternal instinct is trying to kick in. You don't want children, Nina, cross that out!

I swept the thought to the corner of my mind before Allecra noticed my inward conflict.

The most interesting part about Allecra's library was how the books were arranged. It was not in alphabetical order but by their colors. It was probably the most alien idea I had ever seen. She also had various decorative objects displaying on the shelves, mostly some expensive toy cars. How could she chastise me for being obsessed with old fashioned typewriters?

Allecra turned on music on the home theater system. A soft heavenly violin song floated into the air like caressing breeze. It was so gentle and melodious that I stopped what I was doing and turned to look at her. Allecra caught me looking and smiled.

"Do you mind?" she asked.

"No, it's beautiful," I said.

"It's one of my favorite songs," Allecra told me.

"Who's the violinist?"

Allecra was silent for a time and I just understood. I might be the most detached girl to other people, but I picked up something subtle like this very quickly. I walked back from the bookshelf.

"It's one of your potentials, isn't it? What's her name? Eva?" I asked. Allecra nodded. I didn't know why my chest felt a little tight when I knew Allecra still had a place in her heart for one of her ex.

"Sorry, if it makes you feel uncomfortable, I'll turn it off," she said.

"No, that's okay," I said. She glanced over at my face and gave me an apologetic look. She walked over to me and her hands reached for my hips. As Allecra drew me closer to her, I looked away from her turquoise eyes without a reason.

"You need to know some people are magic, and others are just the illusion of it," she said.

"How could you be so sure I'm not one of the illusions?" I said.

"I fell in love with the way time seems to exist everywhere but between us, as if the clocks hold their breath when we kiss. That is magic," she said in a voice that was barely a whisper. "I keep getting lost in your smile and I hope I never find my way out. That is magic. And every touch you give me, every kiss, Nina, I hope it's as magical to you as it is to me."

I bit my lips from smiling but my heart was crying tears of joy. Allecra smiled at the funny look on my face, but at that moment, her bright eyes narrowed to my mouth.

"You need help biting those lips?" she asked in a low husky voice that always made me tremble inside. All of a sudden, I found it hard to breathe. A stir of heat went through my body.

"Yes," I whispered back. Allecra's turquoise eyes darkened. She wasted no time and just lunged at me.

Before I knew it, her mouth was hot on mine. She brought her hand to my neck as I felt her sleek long tongue slipped through my lips, filling my mouth. Her other hand snaked around my waist and pulled me into her. I moaned into our insatiable kiss, but I realized, as usual, she was angling her lower half away from touching me. I was annoyed at how careful she was. With a daring impulse, I pressed myself into hers and pushed us onto the couch with me on top.

Our tongues were still twisting around each other, but I sensed Allecra began to squirm as I wedged myself in between her legs. Part of me wanted to push our limits and see how far we could go.

I began to grind into her.

"Nina! Not like that," Allecra moaned. Her voice was raw with impending desire, and I marveled at her desperation. Her hands had found their way into my hair, but then she began to pull away from my mouth soundly.

"We need to stop," she said with heavy panting. "I don't think I could stand it any longer if we keep this up."

Then she shifted herself around uncomfortably. With a strained look on her face, I realized we both blushed scarlet.

"You know, Allecra," I said. "I think if it's so hard on you, maybe...maybe we don't have to wait."

"Of course, I will wait," she protested. And we went silent for a moment.

"Tell you the truth, I already saw it," I said.

"Saw what?"

"Xenon showed me your...er... *secret* ...in my dream," I murmured. "I know what it would look like, or so I think."

Allecra's eyes widened.

"She still enters your subconscious mind?" she said and let out a frustrated growl. "I really have to talk to her about that."

"No, Allecra, you don't have to," I said. "I think she's no longer able to do that to me again."

She looked at me for a long moment.

"What do you mean?"

"I fought it."

"You fought it," she repeated. I smiled with a nod.

"I just want you to know that I'm not easily frightened by what you are anymore. Xenon might have tried to manipulate my mind, but after all, she was only speeding up the progression of my feelings. Now, I just wish I could be one with you."

"But I'm a masochist and have to keep us waiting for a while," she said. "I like the taste of this sweet anticipation."

"It's just a matter of time, right?" I asked.

"Not today, but soon, I promise," she said. "Now come here and sleep on my chest so I can whisper into your ear how happy you make me feel."

CHAPTER 27

LIFE WAS GOOD AFTER ALL, or at least as good as it could get while co-existing with someone from another planet. The three days before my birthday, I found that spending time with Allecra after school was a matter of self-disciplines coupling with a great deal of concentration. The amount of sexual tension between us was still insane. Some of the times we had to find something to distract ourselves from each other.

As in the case of today, Allecra decided to cook some special dishes she'd learned on her own. Even though she had just picked up the skill, it seemed she excelled at it already. In fact, she could do just about anything, but she usually didn't. She called this being *laid-back*.

Allecra pulled her Lamborghini into the driveway. The tires traced a silent arc over the pavement. It came to a stop in the designated spot exactly the same spot with the same arc every time. I guessed it was just Allecra's way of doing things —precisely and flawlessly.

As we got out of the car, I watched her took two shopping bags full of groceries out of the trunk. Embraced by Allecra Knight, even these ordinary paper bags from the supermarket looked elegant and artistic in her arms. Maybe the blonde had some special manner of holding them.

Her whole face lit up when she turned to me again. It was a marvelous smile as if she had just emerged from a deep cavern. I offered to help her, but she shook her head 'no'.

We entered the house together.

Allecra proceeded to take the groceries out of the bags. She put them away in plastic containers and loaded them into the fridge. She stocked each item according to their sections in arranged order. Allecra worked in spectacular nimbleness without wasted movement. I offered to lend her a hand, but she only smiled and shook her head again.

"Just sit down," she said. "I'll be through in a minute."

The rest of the supplies we bought, she set them aside for cooking. I looked at the ingredients: lemongrass, turmeric, galangal, and kaffir muss.

"You're making curry?"

"Hey, it's not just a normal curry," she said, feigning offense. "It's a Cambodian curry."

"What's the difference?"

"It has distinct exotic flavors and aromas, and it's not too spicy," she explained.

As she went about her household tasks, I became engrossed and convinced that everything would progress far more elegantly and smoothly if she did it alone. I could stare at her like that all day.

Her immaculate house was quite huge, yet it never got particularly dirty or untidy. I would notice the simple act of cleanliness from the blonde. Allecra arranged the dishes in the china cabinets after taking a few of them out. All the pots were lined up according to size. She adjusted the pots and the edges of the linen towels then pointed all coffee cups' handles in the same direction. When she walked past the sink, she repositioned a bottle of hand soap and even changed the towels even if they showed no sign of having been used.

If it were someone else, I would have felt perturbed and intimidated by such compulsive routines, but Allecra gave none of the impression of any obsessive behavior. She just seemed to be doing only what was natural and right. Perhaps in her mind, there was a fastidious map of the way things should be. I guessed disarrayed things bothered her if they weren't in correct orders. I had tested it by moving the salt shaker apart from the pepper shaker. The next time I looked, Allecra was moving the salt shaker back to its original position.

After a short while, it seemed she had garnished the intended dishes. She gave a sprig of parsley and sliced limes and a drizzle of sauce, and everything looked delicious on the plates like magic.

The last dish was the curry.

Allecra stirred the reddish yellow soup with a wooden ladle, then put the cover back on and lowered the heat. As we waited for the curry to boil, I suddenly remembered the deadline for our science report. Allecra and I had almost finished. It would be due next Monday. I went to sit on the stool of the island and pulled up my bag. I took out the blue spiral-bound notebook and opened it.

"I thought you were done with the report," Allecra said, noticing me skimming through the notes.

"Almost, but not quite," I said.

Apart from learning that her planet would take 450 days to rotate around its sun and the length of a day lasted more than twenty-four hours, and the people rode hovercraft over magnet-paved streets and ate nutritious packed foods from the genetic engineered products, the report seemed to lack some other crucial details.

"What else do you want to add?" she asked.

"I still see some loopholes here and there," I said. "So I want you to answer me a few more questions, Miss. Allecra Knight."

Allecra came to sit in front of me.

"Alright, Miss Antonina Black, whatever you want," she replied with a mild annoyance. I giggled at her adorable face and grabbed my black ink pen like I was going to interview a criminal.

"What was it like on Arzuria before you came here?" I asked. Allecra pursed her lips as if to think for the right words.

"Well, we had a peaceful, advanced and harmonious society," she said. "One continent, one government, no borders or the need to divide people into different races. Everyone lived equally according to his or her profession."

"That sounds like an ideal communist state," I told her. "Stalin would be so proud to know his dream is achieved elsewhere."

"You know, though the practice is evil, the theory is actually perfect. I don't know but it worked in Arzuria," she said. "We, too, had science, knowledge of the universe and the mind. Our technology was far more advanced that it would seem like magic to you."

"Then how come you became...er...the Endling?" I said and suddenly was afraid I might offend her, but Allecra just shrugged.

"There are theories about our race dying out," she said casually. "There's the Natural Mutation that caused a mysterious sterilization in our DNA. Nature just prevents us from reproducing."

"You mean it's a natural cause?" I asked. "But why?"

"I don't know. We're still not sure about what has caused our extinction," she said. "Perhaps, we were too intelligent, too seamless, that it tipped off the balance in our world. And gradually, it was like we were being sterilized year after year until there wasn't a single baby born on our planet. The Government was alarmed by the terrifying drop in population. Of course, they had tried everything they could think of to change that. They encouraged polygamy, banned divorces and abortions, provided excellent childcare and everything, but nothing could stop the declining birth rate that acted like a plague. People grew old and died off day after day. No babies were born again — nothing. That was when the Arzurians decided to find another species to hybridize with. And the human race became our best choice."

"Are there other intelligent life forms apart from us they have tried to crossbreed with?" I asked.

"Of course, many of them," Allecra said. "You're not the only one in the universe. There are more planets like Earth in this galaxy than the grains of sand on any beaches in the world. Don't forget that what you see isn't all there is."

"I know that!" I retorted. "I'm just asking."

Allecra chuckled at me.

"Anyway, humans are like our distant cousins," she added. "But they are the stuck-up and immature ones. They are capable of doing things the Arzurians couldn't. The more I got to observe them, the more I am forced to conclude that they are in fact selfish and greedy creatures with so much of their potentials wasted. They forget that they are brothers and sisters and became delusional and imagined invisible boundaries, social structures, and differences in beliefs and religions that separate them instead of just living, sharing, creating, and evolving together."

"Not all of us are like that," I protested for the sake of our global dignity. She looked at me with her head cocked to the side and her perfectly shaped blonde brow arched. Then she smiled.

"You're right," she said. "There are people like you. Nothing would be the same if you do not exist. You make Earth feels like home away from home to me."

That brought a smile back to my face.

We set the food on the dining table after it was done. But then Allecra froze and turned towards the doorway. She seemed to sense something or someone. Then I heard the sound of footsteps, and Xenon and Triton came into the room.

I quickly got up from my chair and went around to Allecra. She stood up and put a protective arm around my waist and whispered into my ear.

"It's alright, Nina," she said and then turned to her siblings as if to say 'what now?'

Triton smiled and just shrugged. Xenon frowned at the look her little sister gave her. Within a few seconds, I could feel some sort of nonverbal dialogue being exchanged between them.

"I'm just checking to see how you've been," Xenon said at last, still maintaining an air of superiority.

Allecra frowned. "As you can see, everything is perfect."

"That's an exaggeration," her sister said with an edge in her tone and then her eyes rested on me. Her topaz eyes looked at me as if they knew me but didn't like me very much. I recoiled and almost hid my face into Allecra's chest.

"Cut it out, Xenon. I'm not a child anymore," Allecra said as she rubbed my back soothingly. I felt Xenon was going to say something, but Triton stepped in. He raised a hand up in the air, halting the conversation. Then he pointed to the steaming food on the table. Without actually saying a word, we all understood what he meant, *'Everyone needs to sit down and talk things out. Nothing can't be solved with good food.'*

It was remarkable how he did it, and soon, Allecra relaxed and slowly released her hand from my back.

"Fine," she breathed. "It's better we stop dodging each other."

Xenon didn't respond, but she didn't object either. When each of us settled down around the long table, Triton was the first to dig in. The rest of us simply sat in silence.

Triton spoke to me or rather gestured with his hand to me. He held his fingers up near his face and moved them slowly like tracing a picture in the air without complicated motions. And the message just transmitted into my mind. I had no trouble understanding the words he conveyed.

'The food is delicious,' he seemed to be saying and then he smiled again. *'You cooked?'*

I was transfixed by this strange communication. As Allecra had said, Triton had a special way of speaking. Oh well, one of them entered my dreams, another had tried to erase my memory, and now this one had spoken to me with just his thoughts.

"No, Allecra made them," I told him. Triton smiled brightly at his sister with an amused look.

"Oh, shut up and just stuff your face, Triton," Allecra said, looking embarrassed and irritated.

Xenon turned to stare at me, for a moment, I could almost see an impressed look flashed across her face, but it was over too quickly.

"You changed a lot, Alle. Next thing we know you might forget that you're one of us," Xenon said, sarcasm dripping like venom from her words. At the same time, I noticed that she had also used her sister's nickname purposely, indicating to me that she was still closer to Allecra than anyone else.

"I would change anything for Nina," Allecra said without batting an eye. "I realize that it's better to be more human than the ones like our kind." She put her hand on mine to emphasize her meaning. Despite the suffocating tension in the atmosphere, I felt the warmth pooling inside me at her affection, but I was also dreading Xenon's antagonism that projected towards us. I wished Triton would do something, but at the moment, he was obsessed with his bowl of curry.

"Are you taking sides now?" Xenon said in a bitter voice.

"No, but don't make me, or you won't like my choice," Allecra said brusquely. The dark-haired girl stood up, knocking the chair away. I flinched and almost begged for the two of them to stop. Her penetrating eyes looked between me and her sister and then back at me again.

"I want to talk to the girl," Xenon finally said.

"No," was Allecra's terse reply. They did a staring contest for a moment before Triton came to break it off with a burp. Then he turned to Allecra. I couldn't catch what they were conversing about but then Allecra sighed and reluctantly nodded. She looked at me and gave a reassuring squeeze on my hand and got up.

"Allecra?" I said.

"Don't worry, you'll be fine. I'm still around here," she said then leaned in to kiss my temple softly before leaving with Triton.

There left only me and Xenon in the room. The girl took a seat again. I tried to hold her gaze to show that I wasn't afraid.

"You know you're being selfish," she said.

"Selfish?" I echoed her word.

"You got Allecra wrapped around your fingers," she went on. "She has a responsibility to carry out for her people, but you keep her from doing her job."

"She made her choice to stay with me," I said to remind her again.

"Allecra doesn't have a choice," Xenon said coldly. "You don't understand, do you? She loves you. This love thing—" she said and grimaced, as if the word tasted bad in her mouth, "—is what ties her down. You're selfish to stand in the way and shatter her dream."

"I..." I tried to protest, to say something back but nothing came out. A part of me knew that Xenon was trying to guilt-trip me. She was trying to make me yield to their will, but I also knew she was right. I only thought about myself and forgot about what Allecra wanted. I was crippled by my own fear that I hindered her and brought her down with me like an anchor.

My eyes dropped to my hands in defeat.

"I want you to think about it," Xenon said, "while you still can."

I didn't know what she meant by that, but when I looked up again, Xenon was gone. A moment later, Allecra came into the room. She walked quickly over to me as I sat there.

"Are you alright?" she asked. I gave her a bright smile and nodded.

"I'm fine," I said. She stared at my face for a while, trying to see if Xenon had done any damages to my brain.

"Don't listen to her— whatever it is," Allecra said. "We'll be fine."

She pulled me into her arms.

"I love you, Allecra," I whispered.

"I love you, too."

CHAPTER 28

I FOLLOWED THE ROUTINES so religiously that I almost forgot about my birthday. As the last week dragged on, schoolwork did its best to take my mind off certain things. Exams and quizzes kept coming like World War II's bombardment, and my mind could hardly find time to wander off.

I tried to forget about what Xenon had said and thought only about what would happen on my first night with Allecra. The very thought still made butterflies burst inside my stomach even I had imagined it a million times before.

Soon, I would be eighteen. I was going to be a legal adult, capable of making my own decisions. But never in my life had I ever thought I would put 'lose your virginity' on the list of things to do when you're eighteen. Sometimes, I was too anxious that I was afraid my aunt would figure out my dirty little secret.

At school, I met Jordan after class. She wore a white baseball jersey with a catcher's mitt and a tiny ball tucked under her arm.

"Hey, Nina, heading to lunch?" she said with a smile lit on her face. I had joined the regular PE three days a week as required by this school's extra curriculum activity. I would be running laps and playing softballs with the other unathletic girls.

"Oh, Jordan, you never told me you play sport," I said, immediately feeling impressed. Her white baseball pants fitted her nice curves and long legs. She looked impressive in a sports gear like this.

"Well, you never asked," she said, "I've been on the girl baseball team since sophomore year." Then she shrugged as if it was no big deal.

"You look so cool in the uniform," I said. "What are you playing?"

"Ever heard of baseball?" she asked.

"Of course!" I said with a giggle, "It's an American sport, but I've never seen it except on TV. I still don't know why they have to run and catch the ball and all that. It's just we don't watch it in Russia."

"What?" Jordan cried in shock. "There's no baseball game there?"

"We don't even have McDonald's, Coca-Cola or Nutella," I said.

"Oh my god, how do you people survive?" she said. I had to laugh.

"I don't know—with healthier foods, I guess?" I answered, but when I saw the look of horror in her eyes, I added, "I'm just kidding."

This time, Jordan burst out laughing.

"Oh Nina, you got me there," she said. "Well, maybe I can show you how to play baseball."

"Baseball?!" I exclaimed. "Did you mean...playing baseball?"

"Yeah," she said with an easy smile. "It's good for your health and teamwork skills, too."

Jordan tossed the white ball into the air and caught it back in front of me. I had to admit it was really tempting. No one had asked me to join any game since they knew I wasn't made for rough-and-tumble sports.

"I'm sorry, Jordan," I said, "I don't think I can. I have to see someone after school."

"Oh, I see." Jordan breathed and nodded slowly. "Looks like she's got you on a very short leash, huh?"

And to prove that I wasn't tied to anyone, I decided I would give baseball a try.

"Alright, I'll go," I said.

"Really? Are you sure she wouldn't mind?" Jordan asked teasingly.

"No," I said, giving her a look. "She wouldn't."

"Okay, cool," she said. "See you on the baseball field after school then."

Later, I had lunch as usual with Allecra. I told her I would be going to play baseball with Jordan and that I couldn't go to her house today. Allecra stopped chewing suddenly and looked at me.

"You're going to play baseball?" she said. "You?"

"Yeah, I'm going to play baseball."

"With Jordan?"

"With Jordan," I confirmed. Allecra went silent, thinking to herself.

"Can I go?" I asked.

"Of course," she said, but there was tautness in her voice I had not heard before.

"You can come along with me if you want," I offered her an option.

"No," she said.

Yet I saw the tightness in her eyes. Jealousy was new to her, but she did not know how to frame this feeling. I felt cruel, suddenly, for bringing this up into our conversation. I didn't know why it had ended up like this.

"Maybe I shouldn't go," I said.

"No, you should go—have some fun," Allecra said and she continued eating. I didn't know what else to say.

After school, I made my way towards the baseball field, which was among other sport fields. Boys and girls were running, passing, kicking and hitting everywhere. All of them wore smart sports gears. Someone called out to me. It was my friend.

"Nina, over here," Jordan said, waving her baseball cap at me. I smiled and walked towards her.

At the pitcher's mound, there was a machine that shot balls out at a not-so-frightening speed, so that the players could practice batting. I saw some girls running and sliding themselves over white plates on the grounds.

"What are they doing?" I asked.

"Warm-up homerun drills," she said. "Want to try?"

"Oh no, I don't think I can," I said. "It actually looks scary to throw yourself down like that."

Jordan laughed. Then she handed her ball to me.

"Alright then, let's play catch first," she said.

She let me wear her cap and baseball jacket and a mitt. After that, she showed me how to raise my shoulder, my left leg and swing my hips before throwing. Jordan taught me how to hit the ball with a baseball bat. I'd never held a baseball bat before, and I was excited.

"Okay, this is how you stand, Nina," Jordan said and came behind me to demonstrate. She patted the back of my knees to make me crouch down a little and then wrapped her arms over mine to show how high I should lift the bat and swing. I was too excited that I wasn't aware much of the physical contact we made.

At the center of the field was a pitching machine. Jordan went to turn it on.

"Ready for some game?" she called out. My palms sweated as I shifted myself nervously.

I nodded back because I didn't trust my voice to carry any confidence in it. Then the ball popped out from the machine like a canon. I looked at it like it was a grenade and swung my bat with a yelp. I heard Jordan giggled. I missed the ball completely.

"Just concentrate," she encouraged. And I lifted my hands again. This time, the ball landed on the ground with a thud behind me.

"I'm so hopeless," I sighed with my shoulders slumped.

"You're new at this," Jordan said, still smiling. She came and gave my shoulder a squeeze. Then she stepped aside a bit farther away from me. I guessed she was probably trying to avoid getting brained out by my bat. But the next round, I actually hit the ball. The sound was marvelous in my ears. I cried in triumphant joy as we watched the ball sailed high into the sky. It flew in a large arc and then dropped again—nailing another player in the head.

"Oh, dear," I gasped. "Did I hurt her?"

Jordan laughed when she saw who my victim was. The girl with a high ponytail wearing a baseball uniform picked up the ball and headed towards us. Her cheeks were flaming red.

"I'm sorry about that," I said with an apologetic smile. The girl tossed the ball to Jordan, who caught it with her glove.

"Who's this?" she growled and glared at the still-grinning Jordan.

"My friend, Nina," Jordan said. "I'm teaching her how to bat."

"She doesn't look like she belongs on the baseball field," the girl said with a judgmental look. "Why don't you take her to a cheerleader squad or something?"

Despite the annoyed look she displayed to me, I could detect something else that smelled like jealousy. Then the girl tossed her ponytail and walked away.

"Sorry, that's Rachel. Don't mind her, Nina," Jordan said with a sheepish smile. "You did me a favor by boinking her with the ball. She's kind of annoying sometimes."

"She's kind of cute, though," I told her.

"Oh please, she's a real pain in the rear," Jordan said with an eye roll. "She's a lot less cute when you miss a homerun."

"So you admit that she's cute?" I teased my friend. Jordan's cheeks reddened a little.

"Well, I didn't mean it that way...not that she isn't pretty or anything. I mean, she's fast and a good pitcher and all, but I don't think she's batting for our team."

Then she grinned at me. It took me a moment to get it and we both laughed.

"You know, Jordan," I said, "You've definitely got crush potential. Who knows, maybe she secretly has a crush on you."

"As in crush you into pieces is more like it," she said and I giggled again. "Anyway, how about a homerun now?"

"Huh?"

"You hit the ball! In the game, you must run over those home plates," she said.

"Oh!" I said.

"Go! Go!" Jordan urged.

And I dropped my bat and sprinted as fast as I could, pretending that I was in the real game. Jordan cheered me on. I got carried away and when I made the round, I was running too fast. Jordan was standing only a few feet in front of me.

"Brake, Nina! Brake!" she cried. I tried to skid to a stop but couldn't. My body collided into hers. Jordan tried to catch me, but we stumbled backward and fell to the ground together.

"Oh my god, are you okay?" I cried a moment later.

"I'm fine. You okay?" she said. We helped each other up and burst out giggling. But then I saw Allecra standing on the bleachers, staring at us.

"Uh oh," Jordan said. My stomach did a flip.

"I'm sorry Jordan, but I think I should go," I said urgently

She saw the nervous look on my face and merely nodded. I returned her jacket and cap before I ran out of the field. My eyes darted around, searching over the bleachers, but Allecra was nowhere in sight. I didn't know what she must've thought when she saw me and Jordan, but I had a pretty good guess that it wasn't good.

I looked for her everywhere. I even went to the parking lot. Luckily, her car was still there. She hadn't left the school. She wasn't waiting under the pepper tree either, but where had she gone to? Then I remembered the one place.

Climbing the metal stairs up to the attic, I realized I hadn't been up here for quite a while. I looked at the rusty door, which was slightly ajar, then I pushed myself inside the gloomy darkness.

"Allecra, are you here?" I whispered. Then a pair of bright turquoise eyes lit up like jewels in a dark corner. I had seen them like that before, but they never ceased to amaze me with their intensity. Before I could open my mouth to speak, I felt hands cupping my cheeks. My back was against the wall and Allecra's face towered inches from mine.

"Allecra, please, don't be mad at me. It was just an accident," I said in a nervous voice, peeking up at her through my lashes, and she was just gazing at me. Her expression was difficult to read in the dark.

"You're my girl, remember?" she growled in a low voice. "Or do you need a reminder that you're mine, hmm?"

I just stood there in agonizing silence. The anticipation before the kiss mirrored my shaking lips. After a moment, she brought her lips roughly over mine. The breath hitched in my fluttering chest. I felt so unprepared for this.

It was different from any other times when we made out. Allecra's lips were now like galaxy's edges, rough and hungry. They burned as if she was trying to engrave her claim on my mouth. My hands went up to grip her black jacket to maintain some sort of leverage in my melting body. I felt my knees weaken, and I could barely breathe.

"Wait..." I tried to gasp but trailed off when she ran her lips to my heated cheek and nestled my neck. My fingers found their ways into her silken unruly blonde lock. She and I sighed heavily at the same time.

"Shh, I don't want to hear it," she said and then claimed my lips again and unleashed her tongue into my mouth. Her long probing expert tongue coaxing my own to come and play. After a moment, I couldn't take it anymore and tilted my head away to break her fierce kiss. Besides, I needed air.

"Please, don't do that," I said and pushed at her chest.

"Why? You want someone else to do it instead?" Allecra said. Her face was hard like stone. Her eyes glowed with light. I felt my own anger flaring up.

"What are you talking about, Allecra?" I cried. Seeing the pointed look on my face, Allecra seemed to come back to her senses again. She stepped back, blinking.

"Nina," she said, frowning in trepidation and surprise. "I just...couldn't help myself."

"Allecra, why are you being like this again?" I asked. She looked at me in the eyes. Her jaw tightened.

"I was just freaking out when someone tried to snatch you away from me," she said. "I love you, Nina, and I want every goddamn ounce of you all to myself. I can lose anything in the world, but not you."

"I'm sorry for putting you in this state," I said. "But you need to know that I'm not anybody else's. You don't believe in me?"

My voice cracked with anger.

"I know you're like the sea that nobody can own," Allecra said in a softer tone again. "I fell deeply and madly in love with you, as in drowning, you have to understand this, too."

We stared at each other. But Allecra looked so sad, it broke my heart.

"Allecra," I breathed and then stepped forward to card her hair gently. I pulled her into my arms, and we shared a tight understanding hug.

"You know that I'm yours, but I also want to be my own," I whispered and she nodded over my shoulder.

"I'm sorry for acting like this," she said again.

"It's okay." My hands rubbed over her back to shoo away her guilt. "I still love you no matter what."

"Same," she said.

_*_

Afterward, Allecra took me shopping to make up for it. We went to H&H Center, a major shopping complex along the Hollywood Walk of Fame. I had never been to that place before. I watched the sights of buildings passing by the window. Allecra took me into a boutique that sold designer's clothes.

"You don't have to do that," I said.

Allecra scowled.

"Isn't that what girlfriends do? They go shopping together," she said as if I hadn't known it before. "And don't worry. You just help me spend my spare change."

"Ugh, spoiled rich alien kids," I muttered under my breath.

Inside the shop, she picked out two dresses for me, both made of silk material, one in pastel pink and the other in white with black designs—the kind of dress I could never afford. They even felt expensive. She bought an orange boxy jacket, a textured mini skirt, and a chambray shirt for women, and some other outfits.

Allecra seemed to have a clear image in her mind of how I would look in them. It took her no time to pick out what she liked. I would have spent more time at a stationary store choosing a new eraser. But I had to admit that her taste in clothes was short of astonishing and classy. The color and style of every shirt and dress she chose were all stylishly coordinated.

Allecra paid with her credit card.

"Now, it's your turn to pick out my outfits," she said, grinning at me.

"Can't you do it by yourself?" I asked.

"I want you to dress me," she said. "Or you want your family to see me in this?"

She gestured to her clothes. Allecra was always stylish, but she had a point that it would be an element of surprise if she dressed the way she dressed to meet Aunt Vikki and Robert.

"Okay, but don't mind me, I'm very picky," I said. It was just my excuse for being indecisive. I had never shopped for anyone before, not for a boyfriend and especially not for a girlfriend.

Yet I knew Allecra preferred androgynous fashion. I chose some tomboy apparel for spring. I got her a black tuxedo-like blazer with a white button-up oxford blouse. It came with a pair of oxford feminine loafers. I could imagine her looking all refined and elegant in them already.

But I also picked some ridiculous outfits just to annoy her. I made her wear a floral patterned jacket and leopard-print pants, and a hot pink tee, but when she got out of the dressing room, Allecra still looked like art.

I forgot that she used to be a model.

"Nice choice," Allecra complimented my taste, but I could see her smirk. I stuck my tongue out at her, and she chuckled back.

"You don't want to try yours on?" she asked.

"No," I said. "If I look ugly, it'll be your fault."

She came to wrap her arms around my waist.

"How could you ever be ugly when you make the world so beautiful?" she said. Allecra made me shy like an idiot, and I had to bury my face into her neck.

"Aw, Allecra, stop," I said. She laughed again and held me closer in her arms. She gave me a kiss, and I didn't care that the sale persons and other shoppers were staring at us.

~*~

Regardless of our almost-fight yesterday, this morning I woke up with a start. Today was Saturday and also my birthday. I could barely contain the thrilling sensation that coursed through my body. With a newfound energy and enthusiasm, I got out of bed and got ready for the brand new day.

I was relieved that Allecra and I had worked it out in the end. It would be terrible if we got mad at each other just before I turned eighteen.

Breakfast was not yet over before men came to put up the marquee. The hired gardener had been up since dawn, mowing the lawns and sweeping them until the grass and the dark flat rosettes where the daisy plants had been seemed to shine.

Soon the florist van pulled up and brought over the roses. Everyone agreed upon roses because they were the only flowers that everybody would recognize. Hundreds, yes, hundreds of them had been delivered to the house. I had never seen roses in such profusion.

The vase stands were loaded out of a red truck to be arranged on the garden lawn.

"Where do you want the marquee at, madam?" one of the workers asked Aunt Vikki when we came out to inspect the progress. Robert came down in his silk kimono jacket.

"What do you think, darling?" my aunt asked her husband, who scratched the back of his bald head.

"You're the organizer. It's no use asking me," he said. Then Piper flew in, still in a turban of a white towel.

"Whoa, are they starting already?" she asked. "Mom, dad, you can leave it to me. I'm determined to get everything right. I love to arrange parties!"

"Only if you don't go out looking like that, honey," Aunt Vikki said and then shoved her back inside to get dressed.

Four men in their short-sleeves arrived in a group to the garden. They carried staves covered in rolls of canvas, and they had big tool-bags slung over their shoulders.

A moment later, Piper came back out in her pink tank top and white short shorts. Some of the men pretended not to notice as she walked around, bending over to sniff the roses. Aunt Vikki was busy talking to the hired servants and managers on the phone. I had to follow my cousin around.

"What about the lily-lawn? Would that do, miss?" said a muscular sandy-haired dude. His smile was so easy and too friendly that Piper blushed.

"Yeah, that's a good spot," she said. The men went off to set up the marquee. My cousin turned to me and smiled.

"What nice eyes he has! So blue!" she said. "Isn't he hot?"

I rolled my eyes at her. "Lukewarm, maybe."

"Oh come on, Nina," Piper said. "You've dated guys before."

"What does it have to do with that?" I asked her, but my boy-crazed cousin just went on and on about it.

"Gosh, he's sizzling! He's explosive! He's—"

"Girl, show some class!" I cut her off. "I know he can be a nuclear meltdown, but control yourself!"

Piper pouted heavily at me. Her face emanated hurt. I almost felt bad about it, but sometimes, she needed a mental slap.

"Listen, Piper, you don't have to chase after people. A person who appreciates you will come to you," I said. "They need to know that you're real and you're important. Don't run around to prove that you matter. You deserve someone who is crazy about you too, and who can make you forget what it feels like to be heartbroken and lonely."

Piper teared up.

"Oh Nina," she said. "I think I want to cry."

"Well, don't," I said. "We need help arranging these flowers later."

While we were watching the workers put up a small stage where the band was going to perform, Aunt Vikki appeared. Then my aunt paused and looked at Piper up and down with a sour face.

"Have you forgotten your pants?" she asked. "Go back inside now and find something to wear."

"Mom! I haven't forgotten my pants. I am wearing shorts," Piper protested.

"Go change them immediately, young lady," my aunt said sternly. "Why can't you just be like your cousin?"

"Gosh! I feel like I have two moms now!" Piper groaned and then stomped off.

"I don't get kids these days, they might as well walk naked," Aunt Vikki scoffed and then turned to me.

"Hmm...Anything I can help?" I asked. My aunt smiled and handed me a name card.

"Can you go with John to pick up someone at the airport for me? I have so many errands to run before the party starts," she said.

"Oh yes, no problem," I said. "But who is it?"

"She's a daughter of Robert's closest friend. He sent regrets that he couldn't make it to the party. But his daughter could come on his behalf. I heard that she's a talented violinist in New York, and she came here as a visiting music teacher at UCLA music department. It's nice that she offered to perform for us tonight too."

My aunt was a classical music lover. Several times I had heard her humming along to *Nessun Dorma*. A person who could more or less manage a good rendition of *Puccini* and *Turandot* would never miss a guest performance like this. Aunt Vikki already seemed excited about it.

"So what time will she arrive?"

"Around ten, I supposed," she said.

I nodded and reassured her that I would get ready soon. Then I went back inside the house and looked at the sleek-looking card with its glossy creamy color. The address and name printed on it were in cursive style, but what made me freeze was the name, Eva Shapiro.

Piper insisted on coming along after she found out that I was going to pick up a rather famous person. At the airport, we saw the violinist the second she stepped out of the aisle. She was hard to miss, considering she was wearing a black jacket, black capri pants, and chic brown ankle boots. On her head was a brilliant red over-sized beret. She was holding a violin case in one hand while the other dragging a wheeled pink luggage from behind. Immediately, I felt kind of dorky wearing just my jeans and a white button-up shirt with my old jacket.

She was even more gorgeous outside, still in her early twenty. Her almond eyes were the color of the forest. They sparkled pleasantly as she smiled when we introduced ourselves to her. I had no problems meeting new people, but even so, I had my moment of anxiety when facing this young woman. I had done a little internet search, and there was only one Eva Shapiro, who was a rising music prodigy.

Could she be Allecra's last potential?

I tried not to jump into conclusion, but the question kept pricking like needles in my mind.

After a few cordial pleasantries, we left the airport. She had already booked a room at a fancy hotel. I sat in the front with John while Piper and Eva occupied the back seats.

"I haven't been here in a long time," she breathed, absorbing the Californian sunshine through the half-open window. Then she caught me staring through the rear view mirror and smiled.

"Thanks for coming to pick me up," she said.

"No problem," Piper said.

"Are you from here?" Eva asked me.

"No," I said. "I..."

"She just moved here about four months ago," Piper answered for me.

"Oh, I see." The violinist nodded.

"I live with her parents. They are my aunt and uncle-in-law," I answered so that I didn't seem rude by not talking.

"I'm guessing you're from Russia, am I right?" the young woman said as if daring me to say otherwise.

"Yes." I nodded.

"Well, I could tell by your accent. Your Russian lilt is mild but unmistakable, like a trace of incense in the air. Which part of the country are you from?"

"Moscow," I said inelegantly. In the back of my mind, I was wondering why she tried to engage me in a conversation even though she already had Piper.

"Oh I love Moscow," she said. "I was asked to join a music performance at Bolshoi Theater last year. I took that opportunity to explore Moscow. It was a fantastic city indeed, full of history and wonderful arts, not to mention people's incredible taste in music. One of my favorite Russian composers is Nikolai Rimsky-Korsakov. Have you ever heard of him?"

Even as a former citizen of Russia, I had never heard of him until now.

"No, I haven't," I admitted, and I had never felt so uncultured.

"Oh, he was best known for his tone poem Scheherazade—a legendary Persian queen and the storyteller of Arabian Nights," Eva said. "But I understand that young people like you probably don't care about classical music anyway."

"So you play classical or contemporary?" Piper asked her.

"It's a bit of both actually. I've brought some of my CDs along," Eva said. I heard her unzip her shoulder bag and pull it out.

"Cool, I wanna hear it," Piper said eagerly and handed the CD to me.

"Alright," I said and inserted the disc into the player.

The music started flooding the car like a flower in full bloom releasing its fragrance. Even John seemed to be listening to the beautiful song as he drove.

But why had I instantly recognized the piece of this music? The moment I heard the first opening bars, all I remembered was Allecra's story of the last potential. It came to me like a flock of birds swooping through an open window.

"Wow, even I'm not a classical music fan, I pretty much enjoyed this one," Piper said honestly. "This piece isn't boring like I had expected. Well...not that I expected your music to be boring, don't get me wrong."

Eva laughed.

"Well, I want to create music that could be enjoyed by people of all ages," Eva said. "Music is a universal thing. It's like love."

Then she went quiet as if distracted by something in her mind. I could see a cloud of memories fogging her dark green eyes for a second before it cleared away. No one noticed it but me. Eva let out a nervous giggle.

"You guys probably think I sound ridiculous."

"No, I think it's beautiful!" Piper said admiringly. "I know artists like you always talk funny, but I love your outlook on love. You're just like my cousin Nina. Oh, by the way, today is also her birthday. Right, Nina?"

"So the party is yours?" Eva asked me.

"Er...no, it's not entirely my event," I told her. "It just happened that the date matches."

"I see," the violinist said. "But I would still love to play a birthday song for you."

"Thank you," I said. I realized she wasn't just beautiful and talented, but she was also nice.

We dropped her off at the hotel where Eva would be staying. She said she needed a power nap after the flight and promised to meet us at the party. We bade her goodbye.

On the way back, I couldn't stop thinking about the young musician. She was indeed the same person Allecra once shared a bed with.

CHAPTER 29

I STOOD IN THE MIDDLE of my bedroom and swirled around before a full-length mirror in a slow spin. My eyes took in every inch of the dress Allecra had bought me. I had to admit, I really loved it. The color of the fabric suited my skin tone. And not just that, but the shoes and the jacket seemed like they were made to compliment me.

She even knew the right size and chose exactly the design I liked. I guessed everything had to be perfect in Allecra's world. She was like an ideal communist. The thought made me chuckle to myself. To be honest, I was beyond excited about tonight more than anything in my seventeen, now turning eighteen, years of living. My previous birthdays had never been such an exalted moment like this.

Klara had sent me a birthday card prior to today. We had talked a few times on Skype, but it wasn't long enough for me to tell her about Allecra. I didn't give her any details either. All my best friend could pick up on was that for the first time, I was truly in love. But a tiny fraction of my mind still drifted back to that afternoon with Eva.

What will Allecra think of her former Earthling fling? What would happen when they meet? What should I do? What should I say? And how would I feel?

I could find no pleasure in trying to answer these questions, so I let the mystery unfold itself.

In the garden, the tall vase stands stood in two scarlet and white promenades, leading through the lawn like paths of an ancient shrine. The blooming cherry trees near the garden's ornamental basin dropped their petals every now and then.

Lots of cars had pulled up into the driveway and along the sidewalk in front of the house. People kept arriving. Family friends arrived and were walking up the pavement. There were also a few children with bright faces, tripping along merrily beside their middle-aged parents. Everyone seemed to deck out in their dignifying party dresses.

Aunt Vikki and her husband were busy welcoming their friends and colleagues into the main area. Jay was herding his pack of buddies around the marquee. Piper hadn't come out yet. She was probably still changing into her eighteenth dress.

I wandered around for a while, admiring the ice sculptures of dolphins and mermaids and a fountain of wine with orange slices bobbing in a red pool. The sun was setting behind the mountain. The purple sky slowly darkened into night. Yellow lamps went up on the trees, and the garden was full of cool, blue florescent light.

"Nina!" Piper called me from across the green lawn. I turned to my cousin, who was trudging through the well-trimmed grass in high heels. I wondered if she knew that she could easily land on her face. Piper wore a tight sparkly purple dress. When she reached me, Piper gave me a once over look.

"Dude, why does everything you put on seems so classy?" she said as she gestured to my dress. I was wearing a white cropped jacket over a scoop-necked pink pastel Dior dress.

"And you look hmm...sexy," I complimented her back with a smile.

"What? You think I'm showing too much skin?" she said, gazing down at herself in panic.

"No no! That's not what I meant," I said. "You look lovely, Piper."

"Oh, I do?"

"Believe me, girl, you're beautiful," I reassured her. "And you don't dress for anybody's entertainment, you dress for you. If you are happy with it, then wear it."

She was chewing her bottom lip, as if considering whether to believe me.

"You know, Nina, sometimes I just want to have that intellectual air like you," she said. "I want people to see pass my blondness. You get what I mean?"

I giggled and nodded that I understood her.

"You can be elegant and sexy and still be smart, Piper," I told her. "That's what girls are made of, you know? Salt and spice and everything nice?"

"It's sugar and spice and everything nice," Piper corrected me and let out a giggle, too. Then she paused and looked passed me beyond the garden.

I turned around and caught a distant glimpse of a spotless white Cadillac rolling in. The car was four-door long with tinted windows. Some of the party guests, who had just arrived, turned their faces to look in curious awe.

"Wow," my cousin breathed, unruly impressed. "Who is that?"

After she said that, one of the car doors at the back swung open, and I saw the crown of a blonde head emerged. My heart skipped and perked up like crazy.

I felt my lips tugged into a helpless grin for I knew who that was.

"Oh my goodness," Piper gasped beside me. "Nina, I swear, you're practically dating a modern day Aphrodite or something."

"She's a hermaphrodite," I corrected her under my breath.

"Excuse me?"

"Nothing," I said. "Well, I think I have to...er..."

Piper laughed and waved me off.

"I know you're dying to meet her," she said, "Just go and tell Allecra I said 'hi.'"

I nodded and quickly maneuvered through the garden.

My feet half-ran and half-walked in welling excitement. Allecra was looking around, probably trying to find me. Of all the people, she only searched for one person. The very prospect made my inside tingly and melting. Her angelic face seemed to light up the whole world. And when those turquoise eyes found mine, the same marvelous smile took my breath away.

As usual, I couldn't help being moved by the sight of her. In that moment, everything felt like a dream came true. The world was all right from where Allecra stood.

I noticed with some surprise that her usual messy blonde lock was now tied up in a stylish half-ponytail. Her frings fell over one side of her face and the rest of the silky strands brushed around her shoulders.

She was wearing the very outfit I had picked for her. The black tuxedo blazer and white button-up feminine dress shirt fit her elegantly. Allecra's skinny black jeans also showed off her curves and endless legs. She looked more like she could be on the Red Carpet instead.

I slowed my pace as she also walked up towards me. We stopped just a step away from each other, as if trying to take it all in.

This is it. Finally, the day has come.

We both were smiling like some shy lovers. After a while, Allecra was the first to break the silent spell.

"You look beautiful," she said, giving me a handsome lopsided smile.

"You, too," I murmured back with the blush on my cheeks.

I realized her face even showed a little hint of subtle make-up. It was just the basic feline eyeliners and light lipstick and nothing more since she didn't need extra help. Allecra was beautiful, and I found her strikingly alluring than ever tonight. The thought of her making an effort to look good for the event was heart-warming. It showed that she cared about all this enough to lose her alienness and let herself mingle with my ordinary world.

Then the driver's window rolled down and Triton greeted me from inside the big vehicle with a friendly smile. I waved back.

"Sorry if the presentation was a bit overboard," Allecra said, gesturing in the general direction of the car. "I tried to talk him out of it but..."

She ended with a shrug. I just giggled back and shook my head.

"Don't worry, you're not the only one here who is trying to show off," I said, pointing to a black limousine of some tycoon parking on the other side.

"Hey, that's not helping!" Allecra said and pretended to pout. "Why can't you be on my side like a good girlfriend does?"

"I'm always on your side!" I giggled.

"Then come right over here," Allecra said and opened her hands out for me. I laughed and went to wrap my arms around her elegant body. She smelled exquisite and it drew me into her even more. Allecra smiled down at me as I looked up at her in love-daze.

"What are we gonna do now—standing here and staring at each other all night?" she said. I laughed again and leaned in to kiss her adorable cheek.

"Sorry," I said, "Please come with me. I'll introduce you to my aunt."

"Just give me a moment," she said and then made a show of doing unnecessary adjustments to her clothes and immaculate hair. I watched her with an amused smile.

"Are you that nervous?" I asked.

"Nah, I only wish Triton gave me a bullet-proof vest just in case," she pretended to say.

257

"I thought you feared kryptonite, not bullets," I teased, making Allecra chuckle.

"I'm from Arzuria, not Krypton!"

"Alright, alright, let's go!"

Inside the big ornated marquee in the middle of the garden, I found Aunt Vikki's table. She was sitting with Robert in perfect timing. They were looking in our direction. Now, I felt like the role had been reversed, and I was the one who was nervous.

When we reached my aunt, everyone turned their heads to us, but more especially to Allecra. It seemed as though the blonde was the sun rising at the wrong time of day. I swear, everything was sort of silent for a moment before Aunt Vikki rose up from her seat with a bright smile.

"Nina," she said. "Come and have a seat with us."

I stole a glance at Robert. He looked more like a mafia boss Al Capone than a businessman in his white formal suit my aunt had donned him in. They shook hands and tried not to be awkward. Allecra seemed quite relaxed beside me. She'd even got a casual smile plastered on her lips.

The seats were reserved for just the four of us. We both took our seats opposite them. The waiters placed two porcelain plates between a set of silver utensils. On the long silk-covered table, foods were being served by hired waiters. We had oysters on iced trays and lobsters and roasted ducks for the main course. There were men and women in expensive dresses and suits filling almost every space in the garden. They were eating, chatting, and laughing with gusto.

Around our table, everyone stopped staring at Allecra and went back to their conversation.

"Aren't you going to introduce this beautiful young lady to us, Nina?" my aunt spoke to break the ice. I realized I had forgotten about the whole introduction thing due to my anxiety. But when I was about to speak up, Allecra cleared her throat and started with a soft smile.

"My apologies," she said cordially. "I should have introduced myself earlier. My name's Allecra. Thank you for inviting me. It's a great pleasure to be here."

The tone she used was surprisingly tender and enthralling. It was like melting honey dripping from the beehive on a lovely spring day. Allecra's melodious voice turned several female heads to her direction. Now I had witnessed how Allecra used her inborn ability to sway the heart of ladies. Even my aunt, who was critical of people, was now blinking under her charm. But Robert didn't look too comfortable about that. His face seemed guarded and even suspicious. I couldn't tell what they were thinking and didn't want to know for now.

"What a lovely name," Aunt Vikki said, smiling back. "I'm glad you came to our event. It's also Nina's birthday celebration."

"I wouldn't miss it for the world," Allecra said politely and returned the smile. "Nina's birthday is as important a milestone to her as it is to me."

My aunt arched her eyebrow at the brutally honest remark. At the same time, she looked mildly amused by Allecra's enigmatic sincerity. I noticed her and Robert made a discreet look at the blonde as she elegantly held a tall crystal glass of champagne to her lips.

"Hmm...is that so?" my aunt said slowly. "Are you two planning something special together?"

I felt a piece of cinnamon bun stuck in my throat and coughed a little. My aunt looked on as I reached for a glass of water.

"Yes," Allecra said, still smiling. I felt my breath halt, but soon she added, "We are planning to go to college together."

I didn't see that coming.

"Oh really, Nina?" Aunt Vikki said. "That's great you're thinking ahead already."

I nodded back with a smile.

"Well, I know this isn't the place to talk about family matter," my aunt began and looked at Allecra again. "But we only have this time to spare. Let's cut out the boring part. I have to know something to be certain about you two."

"As you please."

"You seem to do a lot of good to my niece," Aunt Vikki said. "She looks less angry and lonely now than when she first came here. But as her guardian and aunt, I'm very protective of her, and I want what her mother would want for her. Yet I can't control every aspect of her life. I just hope that you don't mistake my trust for carelessness and do something that would disappoint us."

My aunt was hinting a motherly message. Had she sense something abnormal about my alien girlfriend?

"Your concern is well-understood," Allecra said. "I will make sure Nina is happy with me in every way and as much as humanly possible. You can have my words."

She turned to smile at me. I smiled awkwardly back.

"Such a gentlewoman," Aunt Vikki murmured with an approval smile. By then some of the adults at the nearby tables might have picked up on our relationship status. I could spot a variety of reactions. A few men were amused while others were barely interested. Only one heavy weight lady to the right looked disgusted and shook her head.

But none of their reactions bothered Allecra. If anything at all, her hassle-free posture and her graceful body language impressed them.

Robert shifted himself in his chair a little and paid more attention to the napkin on his lap. But the silence reigned on as nobody said anything further.

"Are you both certain that you truly are what you claim to be and not just a phase?" My aunt asked, but it was me she was looking at. I didn't blame her for asking that. She just wanted me to be a hundred percent sure that I really knew what I wanted.

"It's been so as long as I can remember," I said. "If it was a phase, I should have outgrown it by now."

She nodded solemnly back.

"I see," my aunt said and turned to Allecra again. "So how old are you?"

"I'm nineteen."

"And you study with Nina?"

"Yes, sometimes."

"Sometimes?" Aunt Vikki frowned in confusion.

"I take some college courses online at Harvard and UCLA," Allecra said, surprising both me and my aunt.

"Harvard and UCLA?" this time Robert asked. I guessed he'd been secretly underestimating Allecra by her looks.

"Yes, sir," Allecra said with a polite nod. "Business and economics major."

"Oh, really?" Robert said, looking doubtful like all good businessmen would. When his favorite interest popped up, he began to show some sign of mild curiosity. "Then can you tell me a little about what you think of economics?"

I could tell that Robert wouldn't pass an opportunity to test Allecra — to see if she really had what it takes to earn his recognition.

"Do you know the difference between a doctor and an economist?" Allecra asked him back.

Robert raised his brows, not expecting a stimulating question to be fired back at him like that. His lips twitched in fascinated surprise.

"Well, you tell me," he said.

"A doctor saves people one at a time while a good economist saves millions of people at a time."

Robert smiled and nodded.

"But people are still complaining about job losses."

"An economist would look at the issue as a silver lining," Allecra said and raised her glass for a leisure sip. She was waiting for the effect to sink in. Sure enough, now Robert was leaning forward on the table. His attention was fully fixed on her. I noticed Allecra smiled knowingly to herself. Nothing was more accomplished than having an upper hand over a self-righteous man.

"And why is that?" Robert decided to ask. He couldn't curb his curiosity any longer. Allecra just had this mesmerizing aura.

"One thing I learned during my time in this country is that it once took ninety percent of the population to grow food chains. Now it takes only three percent. Pardon me, sir, but are we really worse off because of job losses in agriculture? Some of the would-have-been farmers are now sitting here enjoying their champagne with you. That is a silver lining."

Robert burst out laughing. His face went red. I had never seen him like that before.

"I can see your point," he said and nodded in agreement. "But what would you suggest we do other than complaining?"

By now, some of the men at the other tables were eavesdropping intensely as if Allecra held the answer to the global crisis. She gave a charming smile, the kind of smile that reminded me of a young intelligent character in the Great Gatsby.

"I suggest instead of counting jobs, we should make every jobs count," she said like an articulate expert. "Whether it be farming, sewing, engineering, fixing human body parts. By benefiting from the variety of abilities in a society and trading with another that is specializing in whatever they do best, everyone in the world can all be better off and enjoy a decent life. It's the good old win-win solution."

"Ah...good one," Robert said with an approving smile. The look he gave Allecra was one I had never seen before, which said, *'You're still a strange concept to me, but at least, you have my respect*.

I didn't know what negative mindset he had been nourishing, but I was relieved that everything turned out surprisingly well. It was amazing how Allecra did it. She made no effort to hone the edges of her manner, or to try to fit into the framework of everyone else's expectation.

Allecra just stood out by being her own unapologetic self and that was truly bold and intriguing to many. They now talked and shared some laugh like old friends.

Then my uncle-in-law turned to his wife and spoke in a low voice, "I wish Jason would wake up from his delusional dream about being a silly football star and start working his butt off in school instead. And Piper, too — I don't even know what she wants in life."

"Oh honey, you promised that you would let your children follow their dreams," my aunt reminded him crossly.

"I know, I know," her husband said in a resigned tone.

Aunt Vikki turned to Allecra and me again.

"So what do your parents do, Allecra?" she asked. As innocent as it was, I found myself going stiff at the question. I wondered how Allecra would respond to that.

"Well, I can only tell you that they are not in the same world with me," Allecra said. For a moment, I could feel the silence flooded back again.

Obviously, Allecra wasn't lying and neither was she telling the truth. But my sensitive aunt looked heartbroken at the thought of a bright girl like her being deprived of the family warmth.

"Oh dear lord," Aunt Vikki said. "I'm so sorry to hear that."

"There's no need to be sorry, madam. It's been a long time ago," Allecra said politely.

"Please, just call me Viktoriya," my aunt said. "I'm not big on titles actually, and I think we're family now."

Just like that, they were on first name basis and even became family.

"Thank you, Viktoriya," Allecra said and highlighted it with a charismatic smile again. Her vibrant attitude must have done wonders on the other potentials the same way. I reckoned it with a sting of irritation. My aunt sort of blushed. Robert cleared his throat at my aunt.

"Oh come on, Rob," my aunt scoffed and gave her husband a chastising pat on his arm. I guessed Robert and I were experiencing a little dose of jealousy. I, too, rewarded Allecra with a pinch on her left thigh under the table.

"Ow," she yelped and turned to me as if to say *'what was that for?*. I just scowled back.

The band was playing some acoustic love songs. Then we saw Piper walking over with someone. I realized with a pounding heart that it was the violinist.

"Mom, dad, looks who's here?" Piper said.

"Oh, there she is!" Aunt Vikki exclaimed. Everything was like a slow motion. Allecra looked up to find Eva sauntering in some flowing elegant white dress. It vibrantly hung from her curvaceous figure to the floor making her looked like a fairytale princess. Her glossy perfect hair cascaded in silken waves down her feminine shoulders. She moved towards our table delicately. As expected, Allecra stiffened her usual tranquil pose when she saw her former potential.

Eva greeted everyone around the table with a charming smile. My aunt and uncle-in-law exchanged a few questions before the girl finally turned to us. In that brief moment, I saw Eva's emerald eyes immediately locked with Allecra's turquoise stare.

From my peripheral vision, the blonde quickly tore her gaze away a second later and looked at something else. The violinist's face went blank for a short while. Then she became herself again and smiled politely as usual. Allecra took a gulp of her wine from the glass and no longer seemed at ease.

"Are you okay?" I asked. She looked back and tried to give me a cheery smile.

"Yeah, o'course...I'm fine," she said. I continued to stare at her face, trying to insinuate that I knew what was happening, but she refused to look at me in the eyes.

"Nina?" My aunt's voice called out me. I jumped back from my silent observation and realized Eva was gone.

"Yes?"

"Eva is going to performance for us, including a birthday song for you," she told me. "Isn't it great?"

"That's really nice of her," I said with a thankful smile. Everyone was moving up to the seats in the front of the stage, waiting for the special spectacular. A while later, we heard Eva's voice coming from the speakers.

"It's a great pleasure to meet everyone here," she said into the mic. "At this point, I'm just going to go through relatively famous violin concerti."

There was a round of applause and whistling from the audience.

"Mozart loved the violin," Eva said. "It was an instrument that fit his capricious character. I can't think of another composer, who so effortlessly and often changes his mood like this man."

A chorus of laughter rang in the air. It wasn't often you got to see a beautiful and talented musician with a sense of humor.

"If you like this piece, please also check out my improvised Mozart's *Sinfonia Concertante*. Now, I hope you enjoy this performance tonight." She then rested her violin on her shoulder and a bow poised over the bridge of the instrument. The wondrous music began to drift off to grace the air. The audience was soon transfixed by that phenomenal fingerwork of the skilled musician.

Allecra and I listened in silence. After the first song ended five minutes later, Eva received an enthusiastic cheer.

"The next song I composed a long time ago," she said. "I dedicate this work to those, whom we couldn't forget, and their memories, that will be cherished forever in our hearts."

Then I saw her eyes landed where Allecra was. It was quick but obvious enough for me to catch.

Allecra was sitting like an angel sculpture beside me. She wasn't looking at the stage now. I noticed her eyes paid more attention to her wine glass instead. I heard her audibly swallow the alcohol. It made my heart clench and the air clogged my lungs for no reason.

"You're sure you're alright?" I tried again.

"Why do you like to ask me that?" she said.

"Because I know you're lying, Allecra," I told her. The words just came out of my mouth and I couldn't take them back. Allecra's head snapped to me. She looked startled as if I had jabbed her with a needle.

"What are you talking about?" she said.

I scowled in disbelief. Why did she still want to hide it from me? Is it because she still has feelings for Eva? Of course, she must have. The way Allecra looked at the young violinist only showed how deep their bond used to be. Although I never knew what happened between them in details, but who wouldn't want someone like Eva? I saw no reasons not to like her myself. If it wasn't for the quest of making babies that failed, Allecra and her would have been perfect together. I knew it was ridiculous of me to think that way, but I couldn't help it.

"You still miss her, don't you?" I said and turned my head to the stage. Eva was incomparably captivating on that glowing spotlight. Then I looked back at Allecra again. Those brilliant eyes turned away from me once more. I realized she couldn't hold my gaze this time. My hands clutched the hem of my dress tightly.

"So you know who she is then," Allecra finally said in a quiet voice.

"It doesn't take a rocket scientist to figure that out, Allecra. I'm not stupid. Don't underestimate me like that," I said coldly back. She sat up straight and looked at me in total surprise.

"Nina, what the hell!"

"Isn't it obvious for you?" I snapped back, ignoring her outburst. "She seems to recognize you, Allecra. Stop acting like you have no clue about it."

"Fine, you know about Eva, so what? Whether she remembers me or not, it doesn't change anything. It's in the past now and I couldn't change that. What do you want me to do, Nina? Re-erase her memory? Make her stop feeling? Tell her to go home and live an empty life?"

"I don't want you to do any of that!" I snapped at her and rose from my seat. Allecra looked taken aback.

"Nina...?"

"What kind of a person would I be to wish something like that on someone?" I said then turned to walk away. Allecra got up and followed me out to the garden.

Her ignorant words made hot painful anger bubble inside my chest like magma. I felt my tears of frustration spring up in my eyes. She, of all people, should have known that was not my intention. I could stand anything, but I couldn't stand having my heart misinterpreted by the person who should have understood me the most.

"Nina, stop walking away from me," Allecra said, but I continued my angry stride across the lawn. "I'm sorry for whatever I said. I'm a dumbass, okay? Please don't do that."

I didn't know why I had become oversensitive about this. Perhaps it was because I wanted her to know that I wasn't that kind of girlfriend that antagonizes every ex she sees. Also, some part of me just wanted her to console me, even though I knew it was childish.

The night air was chilling and goosebumps spread over my arms. I realized I had left my jacket at the table.

When we reached the nearby man-made pond, I crossed the bridge to the other side. Allecra kept her pace after me. I walked over to another smaller island garden. I stopped by the bank under a willow tree. There was nowhere else to go except turning back. The pond's surface rippled, reflecting the tiny yellow lights hanging from the trees like little suns.

The cold wind blew again, making me shiver. For a moment, we just stood there in silence.

Allecra walked up to me and draped her blazer over my shoulders. I made a fuss of trying to shrug off her attempt to rescue me, but Allecra wrapped her arms around me, locking my body in her warm embrace.

"It's times like this that I wish I could read your mind, Nina, so that I would know what mistakes I have done to you," she murmured apologetically into my bare neck. Her breath was warm against my cold skin.

"You could erase people's memory but couldn't read their mind?" I asked, but now my rage had softened a little with just her touch.

"I was never trained to do that," she said, "Maybe I should start from now on. It would be so useful to read you like an open book, hmm?"

"Eva," I said in a dry tone. "I could tell she still remembers you."

"Some people just cling to the past more than others. Eva is a musician. She can't forget emotions. She might forget the things we did, but not how I made her feel."

I turned around to face her. Allecra looked at me with searching eyes.

"She must have loved you so much then," I said. "That's why her heart tries to fight for the memory of you. I could see that in her eyes."

Allecra dropped her gaze from mine. Her sculpted face seemed to blush with shame and guilt. Sympathy permeated my chest again, but I couldn't bring myself to stop wondering how Allecra felt towards the violinist.

"Eva and I are over, Nina," she said as if to remind me. "I feel bad for what I had done to her, but it was for the best."

"But she's a wonderful woman, isn't she?" I said again. "That's why you acted like that when you saw her, because you still—"

"Stop it, Nina!" Allecra turned to stare at me with those piercing turquoise eyes. "I never forget anyone I left behind, no matter how much I wanted to. But the only person I want to remember forever is you."

"I don't see why you gave up all that just for this," I said, gesturing to myself. Allecra's brows knitted together. Concerns seared through the façade of her gorgeous face immediately. But then her frown smoothed back again. It seemed she finally understood what must have taunted me.

"Just this?" she echoed my word in apprehension. For a minute there, she almost looked angry and upset and even disappointed. "Nina, tell me how you feel about this. I want to hear everything."

The faint sound of classical music continued to pervade the tranquil ambiance.

"You might think this is stupid," I said in a small helpless voice. "But I can't help feeling this way. I'm afraid that one day I'll wake up and you'll be gone, that you won't be mine anymore, just like how it happened to the other potentials. Because only in my dreams do good things happen and then I wake up disappointed with reality. You're too good to be true, the best thing that's happened to me. I don't want you to be gone like the people in my life. Because I love you so very much, Allecra."

My voice broke at the end.

"Oh, silly girl," Allecra breathed and held me into her tighter. She stroked my hair and kissed the top of my head gently. She seemed flabbergasted and speechless at what I just said. Her hand went up to the bridge of her nose and she squeezed her eyes shut.

"I'm sorry," I said, feeling quite alarmed by her tormented demeanor. "I told you this is stupid. I know I should believe in us more."

"Tell me how it all boiled down to this," she whispered softly. Her voice was strained with emotions.

"When I saw Eva and discovered how wonderful and nice she is, it just doesn't make any sense that you don't feel anything for her. It makes me wonder why. She's beautiful, talented and mature — a real woman. I'm just a simple girl. Not that I think of it as a competition or anything. Clearly, I know myself enough to see that I could never top that..."

"Please no more of that now," Allecra said gravely. "I am so mad and disappointed at myself for failing to make you feel special. This is all my fault, Nina. But I want you to know you don't have to be beautiful and talented like her. You are beautiful and talented like *you*."

Then she took my hands in hers and brought them to her soft lips.

"You need to know that loving you gives me life and all the joy in the world. You mean more to me than you'll ever know. I love you, Nina. I freaking told you that from the start."

I met Allecra's eyes again. We stared at each other's face for a moment.

"I'm sorry for being so difficult about all of it," I said.

"No, you don't have to apologize," she said. "What I dread the most is you being too scared to tell me how you feel."

"Don't you think I'm annoying?" I asked. This time Allecra let out a chuckle.

"I wish I could get you away from here right now and punish you for asking me that," she said, but she was smiling again. My lips also curved up at the corners.

"Tell me what you're thinking right now, Allecra," I said.

"You really wanna to hear?" she said and I nodded. She pursed her lips and stared off into a distance for a second. Then she leaned in and whispered in my ear. "I want to get down on my knees and make it hard for you to think about anyone else but us."

I pinched her arm hard.

"Ow!" she cried. "You need to stop pinching me, woman!"

I laughed. Her hurt look did not match her playful eyes.

"You deserve it." I stuck my tongue at her.

"By the way, I have prepared a special gift for you," she said.

"Oh yeah?"

"I'll show you afterward," she said. "But for now I need your sweet lips on mine."

The heat rushed back to my face.

"We're not doing that here." I gave a warning glare.

"Oh yes, we are," she said and pulled me against her. The inside of my body was already churning with need. Leaning forward, our mouths found each other in a fierce kiss. Her fingers curved around the side of my neck while mine tangling over her blonde strands. She drew me closer by the waist, feeling my back softly with her hands. Our tongues clasped and braided in furious need.

"I could barely wait for the night to be over," she moaned hotly into my mouth. This was what I wanted the most for my birthday. A kiss that riled up my inside, making my stomach turn with butterflies. A kiss that sent jolts of electricity up my spine, making my heart skip. Kissing someone should not be like a burning candle, it should be like fireworks going off.

Just like this.

All of a sudden, Piper appeared from behind the tree.

"There you are!" she called from a distance. We were both startled by the interruption and broke away from each other's lips. The smacking sound was too loud for Piper not to know what we were doing.

"Oh sorry!" She covered her face with her hands and then peeked at us through her fingers. "Are you done?"

"What is it, Piper?" I asked, a bit annoyed.

"Come on, it's time to cut the cake!" she said excitedly.

I didn't realize the music had ended. Eva was no longer playing the violin. My cousin came over to pull our hands and brought us back to the marquee.

CHAPTER 30

WHEN WE ARRIVED, Piper yelled at the top of her lungs, "I've got the birthday girl!"

In the middle of the table was a square cake with white frosting. Number-shaped candles of a one and an eight were already lit on top. Then the birthday song was played by the same violin. My aunt came to me while Robert remained talking with some black-suited old men.

"Happy birthday, Nina," my aunt said.

"You didn't have to do this," I said.

"Don't be silly. It's your eighteenth birthday, just enjoy it," she scoffed. A sweet birthday song streamed out from Eva's violin, controlled by those lithe musical fingers of hers. All the while, Allecra stood behind me.

After the song ended and the candles were blown out, I was urged to make a wish and then cut the cake. Everyone might not know me personally, but they enjoyed the extra dessert. The children gathered around the table as I placed each piece of the sweet treat on their plates.

I noticed Jay and his friends were standing beside the stage, flirting with the young musician. A bunch of girls stood nearby, probably Piper's friends. They were giggling among themselves as they stared at Allecra.

"Gosh, she's so hot," I heard one of them gossiped to the others. "I would go gay for that blonde girl in a heartbeat."

"I heard that Piper's cousin is her girlfriend. Her name is Nina," a girl in a yellow dress said.

"Her cousin is a lesbian?" a guy wearing black-framed hipster glasses asked. "Aw...I thought she was straight. She's pretty cute, though. Well, that's sad."

"Yeah, why a lot of pretty girls are lesbians these days?" another guy chimed in, "What a waste!"

I sighed. They didn't know I could hear them. Then I noticed an adorable shy girl in a pink dress staring at the remaining cake with hungry blue eyes. I handed out a piece for her, but she shook her head.

"Mom told me I shouldn't eat your cake," she said to my surprise.

"Er...why, sweetie?" I said.

"Because she said you're gay and that is a sin," she said. My face blushed scarlet.

It pained me how parents would indoctrinate their children this way. Out of the corner, Allecra came over to me.

"What's wrong?" she asked and then turned to the little girl. "Who is this pre-human?"

The kid stared at Allecra with her bright steady eyes. I was afraid she would cry. Instead, the girl looked as though she was awestruck. Then she opened her tiny arms to Allecra.

"I want 'up'," she said. Allecra raised her eyebrows and turned to me.

"Oh my," I gasped in astonishment and started giggling at this unexpected request. Allecra shrugged and then scooped the little kid into her arms. I was amazed at how at ease and graceful she was holding the child. It seemed so...*natural*.

"You tell your mom that being gay isn't a sin," she said to the kid. "But stopping people from being gay is."

"Allecra," I said. "You can't just tell children that."

"Why not?" she said and then turned her face to the girl again with a bright wicked smile. "They need to know what is what."

"What does *'gay'* mean?" the little girl asked.

"Oh, it means 'happy'," she said, smiling at her.

"So God doesn't like it when people are happy?" she said. "I don't get it. What's wrong with being gay?"

Allecra pursed her lips as if she was trying to find the right answer.

"Well, being gay is like eating a chocolate cookie, and everybody trying to take it from you and replace it with a peanut-butter cookie, even though you're allergic to peanuts."

It just struck me how amazing Allecra was with children. She made me wonder what our child would be if we ever had one. The baby would be made up of half of her, the very person I loved, and half of me. What an utterly and truly beautiful thing to imagine.

"Oh, that is so mean," the kid said. "It's like when my mom won't let me eat my favorite candies."

"That's right," Allecra said. "And do you like girls or boys?"

"Allecra!" I warned her.

"I don't like boys!" The girl answered and shook her head vehemently. "They're nasty and dumb and always leave a mess behind. They can't do anything by themselves. That's what my mom said about my dad. But I like you—you smell good. You're not a boy, are you?"

I had to laugh at that. Allecra shot me a look.

"Why do you think I'm a boy?"

"Because you don't dress like a girl, and you're handsome," the girl said.

"Alright, I'll take that as a compliment, pre-human," Allecra said, smiling smugly at me. "So tell me what you think love is?"

"I think you're supposed to get shot with an arrow or something," the girl said. "Then you can flutter your eyelashes with little hearts flying out."

Allecra blinked as if she was unable to grasp this strange human concept.

"O...kaay..." she said slowly, "I guess...that might be the case."

"Are you two in love?" the girl asked us. Sometimes, children could be very observant.

"Yes," Allecra said without a pause. "Why did you ask?"

"Because you shouldn't say 'I love you' to each other unless you really mean it," the little girl went on. "But if you really really mean it, you must say it out loud a lot."

"Oh, why?" Allecra seemed genuinely interested.

"Because people forget," the kid replied.

We both were stunned by this simple wisdom of a little girl.

"That is...a very beautiful insight, little human," Allecra said and rewarded the girl with a soft kiss on her cheek and a piece of cake. The child looked pleased with the affection. For a while, we both goofed around each other good-naturedly. If anyone didn't know, we actually looked like a family. Until her mother showed up.

"Natalie!" a woman called. "I've been looking for you everywhere. Now come back here."

"That's my mom," the girl said. Allecra quickly put the girl down, and the kid ran off to the middle-aged woman in red satin dress with big hair. The woman gave us each a disgusted look before taking the girl by the hand and walked off with her. I was suddenly saddened by that.

How many narrow-minded parents are there planting hatred in the wonderful garden of their children's mind? Allecra sighed beside me. She was probably thinking the same thing. Then her arms wrapped around my waist from the side.

"Will you feed me the cake? I feel kind of sad," she said. I smiled and scooped a spoonful of frosty cake into her waiting mouth.

"You're like a big baby," I giggled and wiped the cream off her lips.

"It's your birthday. I can't wait to see you in your birthday suit, too," she said. I smacked her arm.

"Will you stop?"

Then Jay appeared with a frown.

"Can you just tune it down a little?" he said with a disapproving look. "I don't mind your girlfriend here but just stop this disturbing PDA. You can go groping and tonguing each other somewhere else. "

Allecra's jaw tightened. Her face turned hard as she glared back at Jay.

"Jay, we didn't do anything..." I said, but Allecra stepped up to him. She was the same height as my quarterback cousin.

"And what about you and your pack of lewd friends perving around the ladies?" Allecra said. Jay stared at her from head to toes. He tried to act tough, but I had a pretty good guess of who would fall first in the fight.

"Is this the famous Allecra Knight?" he said. "I can see why my cousin is crazy about you. Well, like my dad said, at least you can't get my cousin pregnant."

Allecra balled her fists.

"That's enough!" I said and pushed Jay away.

"I hope your internal organs won't see the light of day anytime soon," Allecra muttered.

"What?" Jay looked puzzled. I almost forgot he had the IQ of a lettuce.

"You're a jerk, Jason," I said and pulled Allecra away. "Come on, ignore him."

Someone turned on some loud disco music. The guests began to escort their partners to the dance floor.

"This is why I don't want to be around people!" Allecra growled furiously. "Humans are hypocrites, believing in things like God and heaven, all the while hating each other and hurting each other!"

"Calm down, Allecra. It's alright," I said as I rubbed her back gently, hoping to dissipate her anger. As we moved through the crowd, I noticed Eva was looking at us while being locked in a circle of her music admirers.

Then my phone vibrated in my dress pocket. I took it out and slid it open to see an international number. It could only be one person.

"I need to take the call, Allecra," I told her, and she just nodded. I guessed she was still worked up about what happened with my cousin. "I'll see you at the table later."

It gave me a knotty feeling in my stomach but I tried not to think about it. The other people had gathered at the front of the stage, dancing to the music. I walked out of the party area and went to the other side of the garden to be away from all the noises.

"Hello?" my dad's voice said from the other side of the world. I could hear a faint baby babbling in the background. He was holding his new apple.

"Hi, Dad," I said. I could feel that he was quite surprised to hear no hostility in my tone.

"I'm just calling to wish you a happy birthday," he said. "Happy birthday, Nina."

For some reason, I felt a familiar feeling I hadn't felt for a long time. It was the father's warmth. He still remembered it.

"Thank you," I said.

"So how have you been?"

"I'm alright," I said and then I didn't want to sound generic and added, "Aunt Vikki threw me a birthday party."

"Oh really?" he said. "I wish we could all be there to celebrate it together."

"Is Dominika included?" my words were still bitter even when I tried not to.

"Nina, please," my dad said. "Can we just get through one conversation without you fighting with me?"

"I'm not..." I was about to protest but decided it wasn't worth the effort.

"Hey you want to talk to your little brother, Boris?" he asked, clearly trying to change the subject. I didn't know what to say to that, so I was silent. Then I heard him coaxing at the baby, and I could hear a tiny cry through the phone. Of course, the baby still couldn't talk, but he made bubbly noises and his voice was so innocent and pure. It was hard to relate him to my evil step-mother. Without realizing myself, I was smiling at the beautiful meaningless sounds coming through the phone.

"He said happy birthday to you big sister!" my dad translated. I couldn't help giggling at that.

"You're an expert in the baby language now, Dad?"

He laughed.

"And a champion of babysitting, too," he bragged and we laughed again. We talked for a little while until I heard a door opened in the background and some female voices.

"Alright, I have to go now," my dad said. "I'll call you again later, Nina."

"Okay," I said.

"Goodbye, girl."

"Bye, Dad."

We hung up. I felt as though a weight had been lifted off my chest. I didn't even know I had been carrying it around with me. Was that how it felt when we forgive? I wasn't sure, but it did make me feel a lot better.

I turned, but to my surprise I saw Jordan, walking across the lawn.

"Jordan!"

"Nina." She smiled.

"I thought you didn't come," I said when I reached her halfway.

"Sorry, I'm late," she said and handed me a nicely wrapped present. "Happy birthday, Nina."

"Thank you, but you don't have to get me anything," I said. "Please come inside. The party isn't over yet."

"No, that's okay," she said with a wave of her hand. "Actually, I was just dropping by to congratulate you."

"Oh, why?" My face dropped.

"Well...I...er...kind of have to pick up someone for a movie," she said coyly. Then I understood.

"Jordan!" I gasped. "You're going on a date?"

"Well yeah," she said with a sheepish nod. "Rachel just asked me out."

"Oh my god, did she?" I squealed in excitement. Maybe our encounter at the baseball field made Rachel realized that she needed to step up her game. I found it so funny and yet so adorable. "I'm happy for you, Jordan."

And I went to give her a big hug, which she returned.

"Come on, it's just the first date," my friend said with an eye roll.

I laughed. "There will be a second and third and so on."

"You're too optimistic," Jordan chastised. "Alright, enjoy your party. I guess I better go now."

"Okay, good luck," I said, smiling. She waved and then turned to leave. I watched her until she got into her car and waved again.

When she was gone, I got back to the party. Allecra was not at the same spot I had left her. I looked around for a while. Then I saw Piper sitting alone, looking wretched for some reason. I began to feel worried and went to check on her.

"Hey, Piper, are you okay?" I said as I took a seat.

"Yeah, I'm alright," she said but shrugged dejectedly.

"Tell me what's wrong?"

"Nothing, you can't just blame your brother for having cabbage for a brain, can you?"

"What did Jay do again?"

"Just being a stupid and inconsiderate twin brother. He knows that I hated him, but...ah never mind," she said and then got up. "Now will you excuse me, I need another fruit punch since dad wouldn't allow me to drink."

I looked around for Jay and saw him with his group of friends, having a good time dancing with the ladies. I wanted to ask Piper again, she already walked away. My head did a quick scan but still no Allecra.

I walked out to the garden, searching for her. After a while, I gave up and took the gift Jordan gave me to my room.

But through the window, I saw Allecra standing behind an oak tree, half-hidden by rhododendron bushes. I smiled and got out of the house again to where she was.

Once I got there, she appeared to be talking to someone. I didn't know what stopped me from going up to her. Then my heart dropped to my stomach. The other person was Eva. I couldn't hear what they were saying, but the violinist seemed to be crying. Allecra looked sympathetic at her and put her hands around the violinist awkwardly, but Eva leaned herself over to kiss Allecra. My eyes widened in shock.

My hands went to my mouth. I felt my throat closed up. My lips clamped together from an invisible stabbing pain in my gut. Unable to witness it any longer, I turned around and ran out of there. As my feet picked up speed, the image of Allecra kissing Eva in a dark corner of the garden receded into the distance, yet the memory had already engraved on my mind.

How could she do this to me after all the things she said?

I ran until I couldn't find anywhere else to go. It seemed that I was pretty good at running away from things tonight. My stomach heaved from the burning acid. I rushed to a nearby bush and doubled over.

I threw up.

Everything was a lie. Allecra made me believe she loved me with her sweet words and charm, but then she went out and did what I would never do.

After I was done, I tried not to cry. Wiping my lips with the sleeve of my jacket, I turned to a wooden bench and sat down. My lungs belched like exhaust pipes. I dropped my face in my hands and forced back the tears.

This was the reality I was afraid to wake up to because the real world would swallow me with its teeth of disappointment and tongue of hopelessness.

CHAPTER 31

THE PAIN SEEMED DIFFUSE as though by an anesthetic. I began to feel the numbness of the aftermath seeping through my bones along with the night chill. I could still feel the blood rushing with a dull ache in my chest.

As I was sinking into the heartbreak after being cheated by my non-human girlfriend, there was this thought that maybe I hadn't been enough in the first place. I couldn't blame Allecra. Xenon had warned me before. By being stuck with me, Allecra would be hindered from fulfilling her role. Maybe she could give Eva a second chance.

I sat on the cold bench and waited for the pain to pass. I forced myself once again to consider the timeless virtues of resilience.

Resilience had rescued me all my life. Between maternal absence and paternal incompetence, I learned the tender secret of being strong. I learned to endure the hurricanes of life's unfortunate events.

But this raging emotional storm took too long to pass. I felt like I was still in the eye of it.

After a few deep breaths, I tried to regain my grip on the rationale. I wiped my misty eyes and pulled myself together again.

The sun would still rise again in the blue skies, and the flowers would still bloom no matter what. I could do this.

I looked around, trying to focus my mind on the purple hyacinths and blue lilacs. But their vibrant greenish blue only reminded me of those turquoise eyes.

"Stop it!" I growled at my undisciplined heart and shook my head like a complete nutcase in the dark. My chest still ached for the tall blonde, who was the center of my problem and passion. I was so screwed.

"Hello, Nina," someone said behind me. My head snapped around to find Jack Conner. He was smiling wolfishly under the shadow of a cypress. I stood up to greet him with a deep scowl.

"What are you doing here?"

"Well, it's a pleasure to see you, too," he said, still wearing that stupid smile of his. His eyes gleamed from the dark as he stared at me.

"The pleasure is all yours," I replied. "Who invited you here?"

"Didn't Piper tell you? Her father works with my old man," he said smugly. "Besides, Jay and I are buds again."

"Excuse me?" I said in disbelief. I remembered the distressed state Piper was in and realized she was right about her twin brother. Jay was an even bigger idiot than I initially thought.

"Well." Jack shrugged haughtily. "Guys throw punches at each other and say things girls would never think of saying, but when it all blows over, we play football together again."

Jack Conner took a few steps closer towards me. I backed away from him. The charged air between us was filled with austere chill and unease.

"I have nothing to talk to you. Please leave me alone." I felt like I was in the face of a rogue wolf that could smell my fear. Without wasting any more time with my cousin's ex, I turned around and began to walk away quickly, but Jack came to block my path. His face was unnervingly close to mine.

"You mocked me, Nina, and you humiliated me by doing this," Jack hissed like a maniac. All of a sudden, he seemed intimidating and maybe a little unstable.

"I don't know what you're talking about, Jack. Stay away from me!" I said and sidestepped him, but he grabbed my hand and swirled me around. I tried to pry his grip off my elbow but to no avail.

"Let me go right now, Jack, or I'll scream," I said in threatening voice. He still didn't seem to show any sign of backing off.

"This is ridiculous. You both are girls! What does she have that I don't have, Nina?" he growled.

"Everything!" I snapped back and pushed Jack's broad chest away as hard as I could with both hands. He stumbled but gripped me back by the waist and hurled me against the wall of his muscular body.

"I love you, Nina. She can't make you happy like I can," Jack said desperately and tightened his hold around me.

"No! Let go of me!"

I was thinking about what was the best angle to kick his nuts and how much strength it would require me to do so. One kick that could deliver a tremendous jolt of sharp pain to make him think it was the end of the world.

But I noticed he was wearing jeans and I couldn't get a clear opening.

"Let me show you what pleasure with a guy feels like, Nina. You won't regret it," he said.

I struggled against his barbarous advancement, but he was too strong. I screamed as loud as any panicky girl would scream. Yet I was so far away from people. The music was booming too loudly in a distance. No one would hear me. Jack knew this and he took full advantage of it. He held me with iron hands that would bruise my skin.

"Let me go, Jack!" I cried and struggled against his vise-like grip. "Help! Somebody, help me!"

In that moment, the only person I wanted my cries to be heard was Allecra. But she was probably still shoving her tongue down Eva's throat. Jack nuzzled my neck with his nose. His unshaven face scratched my skin. My mind raced in tandem with my heart.

If I couldn't run or kick his balls or head-butt him, my last solution would be to bite the hell out of Jack. Bite like a frenzy pit-bull that wouldn't let go. My father told me that you could take a man off guard if you inflict real pain on him. At least, you have a small chance of escape. I was about to open my mouth and bite Jack when a fierce powerful voice came from behind us.

"Let go of her immediately!" Allecra growled, which sent relief spreading through my pounding chest. Like an answer to my prayer, she had come to save me like I knew she would. Deep down even in my moments of panic, I knew that I would be safe as long as Allecra was near. She had an almost clairvoyant knowledge of where to find me.

I turned my head and saw her stomping towards us. This time, my heart leaped to my mouth. Allecra looked terrifying...and breathtakingly beautiful. She marched forward with a deadly air of the grim reaper. I had seen her like that once.

"Allecra," I breathed. Jack released me, but still kept a firm hold on my wrist.

"What are you gonna do about that, blondie?" he challenged. I knew he was trying to look equally frightening, but it fell short. He was no match for the grace and power Allecra possessed within her. It was like watching a kitten snarling at a lioness. I could feel him shifting on his feet. Without a response, Allecra's eyes went ablaze in turquoise light. I gasped as she turned those pair of stirring galaxies to Jack.

The guy dropped his jaw and stumbled back in a shocking bewilderment. He tripped over himself and fell.

"Holy shhh...! What the hell is that?" Jack cried in obvious fear. Allecra's glowing eyes had not dimmed back. They still burned in a frightening death glare. Jack was now panting on the ground, speechless and pale like a ghost.

I went up to Allecra, but she only turned me away as gently as she could. Her face was purposeful. Her gaze never left the gaping and voiceless Jack Conner.

"Allecra, no! Please, don't," I tried to speak to her and pull her back, but she didn't budge at my plea. I realized Jack was no longer making any sound. He was just kneeling there, staring back with the blankest look on his blood-drained face.

"I have put up with this one long enough," Allecra growled from the depth of her chest. "I'm going to take away his memory, scattering everything in his brain. I'm gonna make him live in a vegetative state!"

"Allecra, no!" I cried. "Please, Allecra, don't do that."

She didn't listen and just held Jack's empty stare. His body started trembling like he was having a seizure.

"Goodbye, asshole," Allecra muttered icily. "You might be as good as dead."

Jack's pale face contorted. His hands went up to clutch his head and rake his hair. The guy threw his head back and screamed in a strangled choking voice. It was horrible to watch. He was being punished in the most unusual way.

Whatever Allecra was projecting was probably so painful. And now Jack was on the receiving end of this highest form of brutality. I didn't know Allecra was capable of doing such things.

"Allecra, stop!" I cried again and came to put myself between her and the tortured man. My tears flowed freely over my frightened face.

Only when she heard me sobbing that she blinked again and turned to look at me. Her eyes were still glowing, burning with unnatural light. Jack finally collapsed onto the ground, unconscious.

"Why are you doing this?!" I cried and pounded her chest with my small fist. She held me back arm-length by the shoulders. Her gaze searched mine with deep concerns and confusion.

"Nina, what's wrong with you? Can't you see that he was trying to do bad things to you?" she said. "What would happen if I hadn't found you first? He deserves more than this. I should have toasted that hollow head of his for what he did to you!"

"No, Allecra! You're being cruel!" I yelled and shrugged her hands off me. And as if I needed a sweet reminder, the thought of her and Eva streamed back into my mind again. It fueled my rage, coupling with disappointment and heartache to rage like a feral storm. "You did worse to me than him. You're so mean, and I hate you!"

"What?" She looked at me long and hard, like she didn't have the slightest clue of what I said.

"You know what you did!"

Just like that, Allecra's strong arms wrapped around me and forced me to walk away with her from the spot. I tried to shrug off her again, but she wouldn't let go of me.

"Where are you taking me?" I cried.

"Shh...be quiet," she said. "We need to talk."

"Don't tell me to be quiet!"

"Nina, please!"

"Don't you *Nina* me!"

Allecra grunted in her throat and kept speed-walking even faster. We skirted around the garden and came out again on the other side. I realized she had brought me back to the pond. She released me and now pulled me by the hand instead. Then we came over the bridge to the island garden, and she stopped us under the same willow tree.

Allecra turned me around to her at last.

"Now tell me what the hell was that about?" she demanded as if I was the one who almost killed a man and kissed her ex. "I don't know why you're so angry at me. I was just saving you from that sorry piece of trash!"

"It's not just about him! You knew what you did," I spat and turned my back to her like a sulking child.

She came around to face me again. "Nina, for the sake of all things good, just tell me what the heck did I do to make you upset?"

"You want me to tell you? Alright, first of all, you need to know that it's wrong to kill a person. It's a crime against humanity..."

"Are you using humanity to protect that beastly man?" she said.

"Second," I went on, ignoring her defense, "if you didn't mean all the things you said to me, you don't have to lie to me anymore."

"Lie about what?"

"That you love me and care about me!"

"But I really do!" she snapped. "How else should I tell you that? Damn it!"

"You're a liar, Allecra," I said. "Your actions proved otherwise. I saw what you did with Eva."

Allecra looked stunned. "You did?"

"Yes, you kissed her! Don't you lie to me about not having feelings for her," I cried and stared at her through my hot tears. "Why did you do that? You told me you both were over. And now look at what you've done to me!"

There was a long pause between us. I was waiting for her to say something and to explain to me what was going on, that I got it all wrong, but my heart fell further downward when Allecra remained silent. Her lips pressed into a thin line. Then she closed her eyes and turned away from me. My mouth fell open and closed again like I was a goldfish.

"I see," she sighed a moment later.

"Is that all you've got to say?" I asked with a glare. Allecra didn't answer. She pressed her fingers to the bridge of her nose and heaved another loud sigh. I was still waiting, but she only walked towards a nearby bench under the tree and sat down. I watched her in confusion mixed with rising anger. Unable to tell what she was thinking, I just stood there. At last, Allecra turned her face to me again. Her bright eyes dimmed down from the light overhead.

"Come here and sit on my lap," she said to me. Her voice was calm and collected.

The nerves!

I wanted to scream from all the coursing frustration in every cell of my body, but at the same time, my feet were inching forward, pulling me to her with an irresistible force.

Please give me the strength not to sit on her lap.

A moment later, I dumped myself on Allecra. She wound her arms securely around my waist like an octopus's tentacles. Then she shifted her body a little to the side, swaying me along with her as she dug her right hand into her hip pocket. Allecra pulled out a sleek black leather box. It was wrapped with a sumptuous purple ribbon.

She proffered it to me. "Happy birthday, Nina."

I stared at her in disbelief. And after a moment, I took the small box from her hand and threw it to the ground. It landed without a sound on the grass beneath our feet. I wanted Allecra to see that I was still mad at her.

"I don't want your gift anymore," I said fumingly. Allecra looked back at me with her penetrating brilliant eyes.

"Pick it up," she said in a tone that made my body shiver.

How I wanted to cry and do something drastic in that moment, but in the end, I stooped down to retrieve the box from the ground. I shoved the gift back into her hand.

"Are you happy now?" I said with a grumpy look.

"You spelled trouble, Nina, you know that? Adorable, sweet, and sassy—yet my very special trouble," she said.

"Then why don't you go back to Eva?" I snapped back. I couldn't help it. Allecra gave me a look that was enough to shut me up.

She turned away again and held the little box in her hand. Allecra began to untie the knot of the purple ribbon while her other hand still wound around my waist. The black lid soon popped open.

Most girls would squeal just at the sight of diamonds, but not me. I had never felt any desire towards any gem-related objects before. Partly it was because I knew I could never afford one.

Yet whatever sparking inside the tiny box made me gasp in astonishment. It was the most beautiful piece of a rare-looking jewel ever. The gem was shaped like a raindrop fashioned into a white platinum necklace.

"Erytus stone from Arzuria," Allecra told me as I stared unblinkingly at it. My head turned to look at her with wider eyes.

"It's from your planet?" I gasped. Allecra nodded with a smile.

"Erytus is the most precious and rarest of gems in our world," she said. "It's harder than diamonds and changes color from blue-green in the daylight to purple at night. Its incandescent light is what makes it special."

I watched her slender fingers delicately pick the gem out of the box and held it by the string. The stone swayed in the air and sparkled like a twinkling star. It was the most beautiful reflection I had ever seen.

"Erytus was formed inside a mountain where it crystallized under low pressure and a high temperature of the volcanic rhyolitic magma," Allecra told me again. "This one was said to be unearthed among the skeletons of a half-ton elephant-bird in my planet. Very few specimens like this exist."

She fluidly fastened the necklace around my neck and pulled my hair gently back around my shoulders. I looked down at the gem that sparkled lustrously on my chest.

"I know people on earth like to give diamonds to their loved ones as a precious token of love," she said. "In Arzuria, Erytus stones were only given to those you would cherish for life. Once you give it to someone, you're bound to them forever."

"Allecra..." I tried to say something but amazement stole my power of speech.

"I want our love to be like this jewel, tested by fire and ice yet unbreakable and beautiful in the end."

"You're so confusing. Why do you give it to me?" I said.

"This is the only way I can hope to make you understand how much I need you in my life, Nina," she told me.

I tried hard not to give in.

"No, I don't think I'm worthy of it," I said with all the detachment of an exhausted heart. "You should give it to someone else."

I didn't want to specify who I was referring to. She couldn't expect me to accept the gift and disregard what had happened like it was a wrapper on a candy bar.

"What do you mean, you're not worthy? You're more precious to me than all the gems in the universe," Allecra said.

"What about Eva?" I asked.

Allecra scowled back at me.

"I can make you forget about everything in a blink of an eye, but I won't do that, you know why? Because whatever you think you saw between me and Eva was just a scratch on the surface, the tip of an iceberg."

"You mean my mind played tricks on me and that my girlfriend kissing her ex isn't real?"

285

"Eva understands that I can't go back to her," Allecra said, "but she needed some memory to remember me by. She doesn't want to feel like there is something missing and not knowing what it is. I want her to move on with her life."

"So you kissed her," I said sarcastically. "How's that supposed to help her move on?"

"She needed me to break up with her like a normal human lover would do," Allecra said. "All Eva wanted was for me to say it out loud without memory erase and my disappearance like a coward. It's still hard for her, but that's the only way she can convince herself that our relationship was real; it did happen, and it had ended, so it's time to let go. It's like an unfinished play that has to be curtained. Our kiss was just to signal it. That is the least I could do for her, Nina. I hope you understand."

Now I couldn't decide whom I should feel sorrier for, myself or the violinist. Eva was so brave and strong to be able to confront this. Knowing what she must have felt made me feel bad for her. I also felt guilty for my hasty judgment and misunderstanding.

"Is that true? It's nothing but a goodbye kiss?" I finally asked, even though I already believed everything. I wanted it to be true so I could forgive Allecra, and I was more than happy to do that because I couldn't stand not having her back in my life.

Allecra took my face in her soft hand and stroked my cheek gently.

"Sometimes, I feel like we both are fellow criminals, fearing one another, who might kill the thing that is our love."

"You started it," I said. "I just need constant reassurance that you still need me."

Allecra smiled.

"I'll make sure you'll go to bed feeling you're loved and needed every single night," she said. "I just want you to look at me and think that you're my happy ending, Nina. I want you to fantasize about kissing me as much as I do about kissing you. I want to be loved by you and craved by you. This is the truth. You have to believe me."

Her face leaned forward and she pressed her luscious lips over mine. I deepened the kiss. And I found myself falling in love with this blonde alien all over again.

"I believe you," I whispered.

"Thank you," she whispered back between our laps of tongues and heavy breaths. "It feels like heaven when you kiss me. It makes me forget all the times you put me through hell."

"Excuse me? I'm the one who puts you through hell?" I said and broke our joined lips. Allecra groaned in dissatisfaction by the separation.

"Yes, you are! You know how many times you drove me crazy? The first time you rejected me, those times when you were with Jordan, when you were being so stubborn, and just tonight alone you almost made me die from all my worries by disappearing. Maybe I just wanted you to fight for me instead of giving up and walking away," she said. "It hurts, Nina. How I wish you think 'she's mine' when you look at me because I always think of you that way every time I look at you."

After all that had been said, I stared at her and finally understood. My arms went around her neck and she held me closer to her.

"I'm sorry," I said in remorseful voice.

"Please don't be. It's not your fault. It's okay," Allecra said and shook her blonde head over my shoulder. "You don't know how I am absolutely infatuated with the way you play with my heart and still don't know it. But I love you, Nina. I really do."

"I love you, too," I whispered. I was afraid I would cry from the outburst of happiness inside my chest.

Allecra said softly, "I'll tell you how much I love you again if you forget."

I giggled when I heard that. We pulled away and looked into each other's eyes for a long moment.

"You know, I'm eighteen now," I said shyly as if to remind her what it meant. She smiled.

"We don't have to rush."

"I'm not rushing."

"You're not Russian?"

I slapped her arm.

"You're impossible!" I said.

Allecra just giggled and kissed my cheek again as if in apology.

"I'm just kidding," she said. "My sweet Nina looks too adorable not to be teased."

A blush returned to my face.

"Allecra," I called her name and bit my lips.

"Yes?"

How do you tell someone that you want to make love to them?

"It's about time we—we—you know," I said, all the while blushing like an idiot. Allecra had a small smile flickered on her perfect lips.

"Are you sure about it?" she asked. "I can wait until you feel alright again after all this."

"I would feel more alright when we become one. It will reassure me that you belong only to me."

"I don't want to pressure you this way."

"Gosh Allecra, if we don't do it now, I might change my mind," I said. That came out more like a threat. I wasn't sure if I was the one pressuring my girlfriend into sex.

Allecra was silent like she was mulling over the options.

"You can always change your mind, Nina," she said. I groaned with an eye roll at her. Allecra chuckled back.

"You're still mean," I said. "Fine, if you don't want to. Let's not have sex...forever."

"Aw...why are you so blunt?" she said. "I know you're not a very verbal person. If we decide to do it tonight, I would just have to pay close attention to what you want and need. So it's better to take it slow. One step at a time."

"Does it hurt?" I asked uncertainly.

"I show better than tell, Nina," she said.

"Will you show me right now?"

"In this garden?" she said with an arched eyebrow. "How kinky."

"No, not here!"

"Then where?"

I looked in the direction of my room, but it would be awkward to have sex in my aunt's house. It felt like I was being disrespectful of her hospitality or something.

"I don't know," I said, feeling my heart started to drum against my ribs in nervousness. Although I had anticipated it, I wasn't prepared for our agreement to be met so soon and so overwhelmingly smooth.

I remembered some parts of a poem about the goddess of flowers.

'Persephone is having sex in hell.
She is lying in the bed of Hades.
What is in her mind?
Is she afraid?
Is she afraid of her first time?'

Will I be afraid during mine with Allecra, I wondered.

"Let's go to my place then," Allecra suggested after a while.

"Are we sneaking out?"

"Not if you get permission."

"What?"

"Leave it to me, Nina, I can handle it."

Suddenly, her voice sounded thick with desire and needs. Her intense eyes made the heat pooling inside my body become more pronounced.

Allecra also wanted me.

Yet at the same time, I couldn't help but wonder, with a tingling anxiety and cowardice of a virgin, if I would return home stained with red juice like the character in Scarlet Letter.

All of a sudden, I felt dizzy. From all the emotional roller-coaster of the night to getting our relationship consummated in just half an hour apart seemed a bit much. Allecra had to hold me in her arms. Her darkened eyes stirred with concerns.

"Nina, are you alright?" she asked. "You know if you're not well, we don't have to do it. It's totally fine."

What happened tonight had set my suspicion astray and dragged back all questions and doubts in its filthy jaw. But I fought those thoughts and shooed away my doubts.

After tonight, I also knew I would not be what is called a girl any longer. But this is Allecra, my Allecra. And I wanted it to be with her.

"No." I shook my head resolutely. "I want to. I want it with you. Just take care of me."

Allecra still didn't look confident about that.

"Please," I said again in a pleading tone. It broke her resolves at last.

"Alright then, let's go," she said, and together we rose from the bench and walked hand in hand out of the garden.

CHAPTER 32

I WAS TOLD TO WAIT when Allecra went over to my aunt and her tipsy-looking husband inside the marquee. She talked for a few moments before walking back to me and saying, "You're a free elf now. Let's go!"

I asked her with a shell-shocked face what had just happened, and she merely smirked in mirth and shrugged.

"Don't worry, they won't think about you at least for another 24 hours."

"Are you kidding me? Tell me what you said to them exactly."

"I told them we would like you to have a sleepover at my house tonight since it's your birthday."

"Just like that? And they agreed?" I stared at her in suspicion and disbelief.

"Well, in case you didn't notice, I can be very persuasive," Allecra said with a mischievous grin.

"Tell me what you did to them, Allecra," I demanded. "I won't leave with you until I know the truth."

Allecra rolled her eyes.

"Oh Nina, it's nothing harmful," she said. "I was just—you know—channeling some good thoughts here and there — that's all."

"How could you do that?" I cried in accusation. "I meant—of course, I know you could do that, but still, how could you do that?"

She stared at me with a chiding scowl.

"Are we really going to talk about this now?"

I was silent for a moment then Allecra came to hold me by the waist and pulled me gently into her embrace.

"Please, just relax and let the moment take care of itself," she said consolingly. "I promise everything will be fine."

I bit my lips in consideration. But it wasn't a hard decision to make. I guessed the real problem was I always expected it to be difficult, so when things worked out far too easily, I chickened out and was afraid to take the chance. Perhaps I had to get used to life being simple and effortless with Allecra. Besides, I was the one who initiated the whole idea.

"Fine, let's go then," I finally said.

Allecra grinned back and steered us out of the garden.

When we got inside her car, Triton was grinning widely at us.

"Oh stop it, brother," Allecra said. "Just go as fast as you could."

Triton simply raised two fingers in a salute like a knight pulling on a visor and then drove off.

"Wait, what about Jack?" I asked.

"Jack who?" Allecra said indifferently.

"The guy you almost turned into a turnip earlier!" I said. As soon as she was reminded of him, Allecra's face darkened and her eyes looked slightly murderous again.

"Let the ants eat his head!" she snarled back. "Why do you care about that idiot?"

"I don't care about him," I tried to tell her, "but what if he tells someone what happened?"

"He can't," was all she said. "From now on he won't bother you anymore."

"Oh my god, please don't tell me you already..."

"No, not yet," Allecra said, still sounding not so pleased about it, "I wish I had, though. Anyway, I did select a special drawer in his brain and scattered the files of his memory, altered and shuffled them around. Now he won't remember anything. And I made sure to instill in his brain an unidentifiable terror of tonight."

"What does that mean?" I asked in total confusion.

"Well, I give him this fear that if he dares to get near my girl again, his life will be hell."

"Now, he couldn't recognize me anymore?"

She nodded back, and I sank into my seat in amazement.

"Are you okay?" Allecra asked me in concern. "If you're still in shock, maybe I can just..."

"No, I'm fine. I'm not that emotionally fragile," I said with a wave. "Believe me, I recover from unpleasant things pretty fast. In fact, I feel surprisingly detached from all that."

"It can be because you're still in denial after a trauma," she said. "and your subconscious mind decided that you need me as a distraction."

"What are you talking about? I wouldn't think that way about you," I protested in vehemence. "I have already prepared for tonight. Besides, I knew you would come to my rescue. Deep down, I still believe in us. Even though I had thought all the light was sucked out of this world when I saw you and Eva, I'm still in love with you."

It made her smile and shook her head.

"Nina, how could I ever be with anyone else when every beat of my heart is only meant for you?" Allecra said. "I'd still choose you; in a hundred lifetimes, in a hundred dimensions, in any version of reality, I'd find you and I'd love you— always."

Her words brought joyful tears to my eyes.

"I love you, too, Allecra," I said, my voice broke with sheer emotion. Then we reached for one another and stayed tangled up in each other like that for the rest of the car ride.

The long Cadillac pulled into Allecra's estate half an hour later. After he parked the car, Triton shot out of his driver's seat like a lightning bolt to open the door for me. The whole time he was smiling. I felt my cheeks flushed at his strange enthusiasm. Could he know what we were up to? They were all some psychic interstellars after all.

Allecra gave her brother a nudge in his ribs after she got out.

"Go, Triton, you started to creep her out," she said, which earned a playful pout from him. He turned to wave at me and said without making a verbal sound and much to my embarrassment, *'I wish you a long blissful goodnight!'*

I blushed openly this time.

"Triton, just go!" Allecra growled at him. The tall quiet guy snickered as he turned to leave. When Triton was gone, we entered the house together. The air around us seemed to be charged more than usual. Maybe it was because this visit was different from any other visits.

"Alone at last," Allecra sighed in relief.

She took off her blazer and laid it neatly on the back of the sofa. I watched her slender hand went up to pop two buttons off her collar and deftly rolled up her sleeves. The gesture was subconscious and a natural thing to do, but it struck a chord with me as a balance between boyish charm and voluptuously feminine elegance. This didn't fail to make the temperature in my body grow more ardent. It felt different from any other time I was here and alone with her.

She led me through the living room towards the kitchen.

"Would you like something to drink?" Allecra asked after she sat me down at the island and went over to the fridge.

"Just water please," I said. "I like water."

But the way I said it made Allecra turn around to look at me.

"You're sure you're alright? Am I putting any pressure on you?"

"No!" I reassured her. "It's not you, Allecra, really. Just give me a moment to adjust to this, that's all."

She flashed me a gentle smile and then set two wine glasses on the island in front of me.

"Maybe this might help you relax a little," she said and poured a well-chilled white wine into both glasses. She slid one over to me.

"Sorry, I'm a bit nervous," I said.

"Would you believe me if I tell you it feels like my first time, too?" Allecra said.

"Oh, I wouldn't have guessed," I said.

"Trust me, you have no idea what effect you have on me," she said. I didn't know what else to say to that but it sure did make me feel a whole lot better.

We both took a swig of our drinks in silence. The smooth sweetness of the wine calmed me down a bit. Allecra's hand reached over to mine and rubbed it lightly like she was petting a frightened kitten.

"Nina, I just want you to know that you don't have to pressure yourself into this. You can just come here and cuddle up with me. We can talk. We can ramble about meaningless things like we always do. Then you can fall asleep in my arms. And I promise you that before darkness swallows this already darkened world, I'll whisper in your ear just how beautiful and precious you are to me, and how much I love you with all my heart."

Oh, Allecra...

I shook my head vigorously with joyous tears in my eyes.

"You're everything I've ever wanted, and I want this with you. I really do."

"Me, too," she said softly. "But it's not necessary if you..."

I leaned over to kiss her lips, cutting her off mid-sentence.

"Believe me," I whispered afterward. "I really really want you."

A slow brilliant smile lit up on Allecra's face. For a moment, she seemed flattered by my honest declaration. She placed her soft hands on both sides of my cheeks and joined our foreheads together.

"Then we can have a goodnight sex, a middle of the night sex, and a good morning sex if you want," she said in a low husky voice. "Or we can do all of the three until you can't possibly walk right the next day. Everyone will know I got a hold on you tonight and everyone will know you are mine — my Nina, my other half, my one and only."

I chuckled. "I still don't know what I'm supposed to do."

Allecra grinned with a playful gleam in her turquoise eyes.

"You don't have to do anything. Just watch how I make you come," she said, which earned a smack on her arm from me.

"Allecra!" I said. My cheeks were blushing from her words. She giggled back at me like a goofy school girl. When she stopped, she let out a contented sigh and poured us a second glass of wine.

"I'm going to freak you out a little, though," she said.

"Why? You mean—with your—*thing?*" I asked before I could stop myself. The wine must have gotten to me. As expected, Allecra frowned at my word choice. I knew she didn't like it when I called her secret member that, but good grief, she seemed even more appealing and utterly adorable when she got annoyed.

"Do you still think having sex with my thing is disgusting?"

"No, I don't!" I protested with a slight blush. "You know I'm not a straight girl. I never thought it was possible for me to feel this way. Sex with a guy, in my mind, always seems like letting an eel from the river take liberties with me. It's just unthinkable."

"So what makes it different with me?"

"When I'm with you, I feel safe," I said. "To me; you're not a hermaphrodite alien anymore. You're just Allecra, my Allecra."

I could feel her smile before I saw it on her chiseled face. Her eyes had a look of gratitude and pride.

"And when did you realize you have an affinity for women?"

I took another sip from the glass.

"I liked looking at Renaissance paintings of naked maidens when I was young. As I grew older, I realized there was something different about me. Most of my friends started talking about boys and I was just there unimpressed. When I started dating boys, I had no real sexual appetite. It was never easy for me to reveal the intimacies of my soul to another person. At one point, I suspected myself to perhaps be a door that was actually a wall."

I let out a dry chuckle at my own inside joke, but Allecra seemed to understand what I meant. I remembered how hard it was before I came out. No matter how long the queue of hopefuls or how vicious the slander that I was an arrogant snob, who had her legs welded together, or an implacable iron maiden, who denied men pleasure, I would never betray myself.

"I thought there was no one in this world specifically made for me. And I was right, depends on how you look at it now." My eyes lanced at her as I said it. "I was right because it takes you all the way here to show me what love feels like."

When looking into her enigmatic eyes, that familiar unutterable connection began to push and pull with our beating hearts again.

"Being with you makes me feel special. I just never want to share my body with anyone like this. It's the first time in my life that I've felt this way," I went on. "If I have ever given you an impression that I'm hesitant or having a second thought, it can only be that I have never experienced such an intense intimacy before, and it overwhelms me. But I still want you. I just don't want to ruin this special moment."

"Don't worry, Nina. Everything will be perfect. Everything will be beautiful," Allecra said, looking back to match my gaze. "In fact, as long as it's with you, it will be more than all the joys in the world for me."

A smile slowly found its way to my lips again.

"I love you," I said for the hundredth time.

"I love you, too," she replied with an impish smile. We stared at each other like that for a moment, just soaking up the comfortable silence and basking in an empyrean glow of our love.

Allecra leaned forward and our lips locked like they are meant for each other.

As if to signal the anticipated moment, Allecra pulled away and emptied her wine in one swoop before putting the glass down in an urgent manner.

"Alright," she exhaled. "Let's make love tonight."

It made me giggle at the blonde's straightforwardness. At the same time, her very words churned up my inside with accumulative heat. I felt my heart clenched in the midst of anticipation and nervousness.

As we climbed the stairs up to the second floor, Allecra wouldn't let go of my hand. She drew me behind her like a comet drawing its tail of fire. I gingerly followed her, passing the evergreen plants in the glowing glass case. We reached her room and entered it. Soon, I was surrounded by her wonderful smell. I almost felt dizzy with the intoxicating feeling that was inspired by Allecra herself.

Once again, my heart started drumming in an excited rhythm in my ears. When we finally reached her enormous bed, Allecra turned slowly back to me. Her hypnotic gaze raked over me as if to savor the moment. I could see those bright turquoise eyes glowing with a profound passion.

Like a seed of desire that was planted and ready to sprout, she stepped forward and tipped my chin up. I looked into those stirring galaxies. My head swam with suppressed longing and hunger. It was like reality elaborating with fantasies, and I was seduced by the knowledge that I could be this lucky to have this person. I felt my heart swoon and my breath shortened beyond control.

Allecra ran a hand through my hair and trailed her fingers down my heated cheek then over to my throat and collarbones. I shivered under her electrifying touch. She was patient with me. Every move was no faster than a slow motion of a sea diver.

"Just relax," Allecra whispered and leaned her tall handsome figure over me. Then we aligned our mouths. Our tongues entwined as we slowly slipped into the uncensored world of craving.

Here we were, the two of us in the semi-darkness, after months of fantasizing and dreaming, now within tantalizing reach.

Her hands caressed my sides gently and slithered over to my hips and back. My breath hitched in my throat. Her warm sleek tongue wedged between my teeth as I parted my lips and let it delved deeply inside my mouth. My whimpers grew louder until they turned into occasional moans. Allecra held me even closer in her arms, and I could detect the coursing warmth in her body.

She reached down to undo the buttons at the back of my dress. Her lithe fingers let them loose easily with no awkwardness at all. It made my head spin, and I had to tilt my head away from her kiss to collect myself.

"Am I going too fast?" she asked in a worried tone. I shook my head and swallowed hard. For some reason, it felt like the cat had gotten my tongue and I couldn't speak.

"Shh...It's okay. It's okay," Allecra soothed me, smoothing my hair and rubbing my back gently. Then she coaxed me to sit on the bed with her. My body curled up into her perfect form as she wrapped her arms around me. Allecra was giving me butterfly kisses over my hair and temple until I relaxed again.

"Allecra," I whispered.

"Yes?" Her voice came out like gentle melodies in my ears.

"Can you take off your clothes first?"

There was a short pause before she answered.

"Okay."

She untangled herself from my arms then stood up and took two steps away from the bed. After that, Allecra turned and brought her hands up, calmly undoing the buttons of her shirt. With intense fascination, I sat there watching her svelte fingers unfastening the buttons one by one. There were five in all.

Gradually, her beautiful skin was revealed from its hiding. She slipped the fabric off her shoulders in an agile motion and dropped it to the floor. Her hands rose up behind her head to untie her blonde strands, releasing them from their bond. Her hair came loose like a golden waterfall.

Allecra lifted her gaze to me again. In the dimly lit room, her bright eyes gleamed like a pair of gems. My breath came to a halt as I gawked at her, transfixed by her slim and toned bicep. I could see her Arzurian tattoos snaking along her arms and shoulders. Her black silk bra even made her breathtakingly and utterly sexy. My eyes feasted on her lovely curves, her shapely shoulders and the gentle movement with each breath of that flat tone belly.

Allecra ran her slender fingers through her silken blonde hair leisurely. Even this subconscious gesture seemed elegant and seductive. All of a sudden, the room felt too hot, or maybe it was just the blood rushing and singing in my feverish veins. It aroused me and I was swept along by a gigantic force. I had to swallow the deluging saliva in my mouth. My jaw went practically unhinged.

As expected, Allecra's proportional body was the finest creation. The swelling roundness of her breasts, the indentation of her navel, her refined hipbones, they were all marvelous and enthralling. I almost felt intimidated by such perfection.

"Breathe, Nina," she said, slightly amused. It made my face grow hotter. Then Allecra became concerned and added, "Don't be afraid."

"No," I managed a faint reassurance. "I'm not afraid. Not at all."

Allecra nodded slowly. "Good then."

She continued to unfasten the button of her jeans. Then she began to unzip her fly. I almost got attacked by a sudden hyperventilation.

"Wait, Allecra!" I said and stood up from the bed, too. The movement made me realize that a certain place of my body had become evidently wet. Her action stopped as she looked at me with a quizzical arch of her brows.

"Hmm?"

"Where's the bathroom?" I asked.

Allecra frowned at me. She looked confused by my request.

"I'll be right back," I said and strode off on my wobbly feet towards the bathroom. But I turned to look over my shoulder at her. "Please don't get me wrong. I just want to freshen up a little for you."

Allecra blinked and then she groaned.

"Oh, Nina. I don't mind that," she said. "Your scent can shame all the flowers in Netherland, and I want you now!"

Her words almost melted away my resolve. Yet no matter how much my body was burning and screaming to be taken by the blonde, I couldn't risk causing any disappointment.

"Just keep those pants on for me," I said with a smile before running off to the bathroom.

"Nina!"

I could still feel Allecra's perplexed stare after me.

Once I locked the door, I took a deep slow breath. After a minute of recollecting myself, I walked around Allecra's large untarnished contemporary bathroom in awe. Instead of a normal bathtub, she had a mini-sunken pool by the glass window facing the cliff with a view of the ocean.

There were white pots of decorative plants in the corners along with bamboo baskets and a small linen closet with clean towels and bathrobes. Everywhere was systematic and sparkling.

I reached the sink and opened up some wooden cabinets. They contained all kinds of cleansing products, mostly hair products. The bottles were all aligned like disciplined soldiers. Allecra really took a great care of her messy blonde mane. She had more hair products than any girl I had ever known. I felt so ungirly compared to her.

Strangely enough, I found no shaving cream or women razors. I guessed Allecra had no need of those. Even though I wasn't a hairy person, I still felt nervous about what she would think. She was suspiciously a germaphobe and a neat freak for crying out loud!

Well, if she doesn't appreciate your imperfection, boo her! My inner voice said, and I nodded in agreement.

I undressed and got into the shower. I twisted my dark brown lock into a bun to keep it dry. It took me a few minutes to figure out how to operate the futuristic shower head. The lukewarm droplets hit my skin in a gentle pleasant flow. I sighed, feeling my tensed muscles unwound.

Then there was a knock at the door.

"Nina?" Allecra's impatient voice came through the pitter-patter. "Really, you don't have to take a shower or anything."

I suppressed my own chuckle. When I reached for the bar of soap, another urgent knock came again.

"Nina, don't wash yourself with anything!"

I froze. That was a strange request.

"I want your scent unadulterated," was her quick response like she could read my mind. My body tingled with goosebumps at her amorous intention. My stomach did a fluttering somersault. And she could do this to me even from behind a closed door!

It took a few moments before I was done. Stepping out of the shower again, I wrapped myself in one of her bathrobes and went over to the sink.

Allecra had an abundance of various toothbrushes in all colors and brands. They were stored in the drawer, all lying in neat rows.

Shaking my head in amusement, I picked out a new toothbrush and applied a pea-size toothpaste onto the bristles. I knew it was a ridiculous thing to do. Allecra had been sucking my face off without a single complaint, but I just couldn't help it.

When I tentatively stepped out of the bathroom again, I noticed she wasn't by the door anymore. But as I walked back to the bedroom, I heard the sound of a blow dryer. I found her blowing her wet blonde strands. It seemed she also had a quick shower herself. When she heard me clear my throat, she switched off the dryer and turned around.

She had her old shirt back on, but this time, I could tell her bra were gone. The outlines of her perfect mounds caused the heat to course through my tummy. Once again, my own wetness was evident between my thighs. I wore nothing else underneath my bathrobe.

"What took you so long?" she said, pouting, "I decided to cool off before you drove me crazy with the wait."

She frowned and crossed her arms in sulk.

"Now we're even," I said and stuck my tongue out at her.

"I'm going to bite that tongue of yours if you do that one more time," she said. With a mischievous intent, I pressed my lips together and let just a tiny tip of my tongue out again. Allecra narrowed her eyes at me and then she rushed over. I screamed and ran around the bed.

"Come back here!" she shouted, but she was also giggling.

"No!"

"I'm gonna spank your butt for that."

"If you can catch me," I said.

In a blink, she jumped over the bed like a flexible cat and grabbed my body before swirling us around. I yelped and laughed in her arms. When she put me down again, Allecra gave me pestering kisses over my face before landed a peck on my lips.

"It's my birthday, don't spank me," I begged, batting my eyelashes at her.

"Okay, but you still have to be punished," she said.

"How?"

"You'll know," she said in wickedness. "Ready now?"

I looked back into her slightly blazing turquoise eyes and nodded. She claimed my mouth once again with my arms wrapped around her neck. The wagging of her tongue collided with mine, and the warmth of her breath fanned my hot cheeks.

I felt more daring this time. My hands felt their ways down to her chest, unbuttoning her shirt once again. My body trembled at the touch of her soft breasts. Allecra pulled away to watch me undressing her. After the shirt came undone, I stroked her flat stomach with my hesitant hands, going upward slowly. Our eyes met again. I could feel Allecra panting against my palms as I was reaching for her breasts.

I stopped as if seeking her permission. Allecra simply took my hands and placed them on her chest. I gasped inwardly at the delicious soft mounds. Allecra made me squeeze her while her mouth claimed my lips again. There was something about that last gesture that seemed to tell me she was also mine.

"Take off my jeans too, please," she murmured between kisses. I didn't need to be told twice.

Feeling my way down, I found the button and undid it. Then I held my breath and slowly unzipped her fly. In that moment, I realized Allecra had allowed me to take charge. And it emboldened me, making me more eager. Her nose nuzzled my neck. Her mouth suckled and nibbled on my skin, causing my eyeballs to roll back at the sensation.

Allecra stepped back suddenly and pulled her jeans down in a swift motion. She tossed it aside. In spite of her shirt, which barely rolled off her feminine shoulders, she was now left with only her black underwear.

I didn't know I could feel both, but to my disappointment and relief, there was still no bulge.

Allecra seemed to read my mind. She chuckled and wrapped her arms around me, gently holding my body closer to her.

"I've been waiting for us to have this moment. Waiting for the time you're ready to accept me," Allecra whispered in a raspy tone.

Her hands came to untie the knot on my robe, but I stopped her. Allecra's face turned apologetic like she was worried she had overwhelmed me. I gave her a small smile to reassure her. Then I tugged on the butterfly knot with a rapid pounding in my chest. When the fabric came loose, Allecra stepped back, almost in astonishment.

I slowly parted my robe, and her eyes were ablaze with suppressed hunger and heated passion. I couldn't look her in the eyes anymore because of their intensity.

"Nina," she breathed. Her luminous gaze still glued to my exposed nudity with longing. "You're so beautiful."

I was flattered by her words, but I wasn't sure if she simply said that to please me. Then Allecra came to embrace my body. It was as if she couldn't hold back her desire anymore.

"You're so beautiful," she said again. "You should be kissed every day and every hour. It blows my mind how you could be unaffected by your own beauty. I feel so lucky to have you all to myself tonight."

All verses ceased from my mouth when she suckled on my lips. Quickly discarding my robe, she hoisted me up and tightened her arms around my body. I instinctively wrapped my legs around her waist in return. She swirled us around towards the bed. Then I felt my back softly landed on the bouncy mattress. We giggled at the collision of our soft bodies. Our mouths reconnected with more craving. There was no awkwardness for us now. Nothing could stop this from happening, except—

"Wait, wait," I cried breathlessly, unhooking my lips from Allecra's. "You have a condom?"

She paused as if she had just remembered it, too. "Well, I don't think—"

"No, you have to!" I said firmly.

"I don't mean I won't use it, Nina," she said. "I just don't have the need of it for now."

"Why?"

"This is just for you," she said and winked at me.

"So you're not gonna...you know...deflower me or anything?"

"I can do it another way," Allecra chuckled and then pursed her lips in contemplation. "When a woman only concerns about another woman's pleasure, it's just beautiful. Now I feel like I only want to pleasure you, and that's more than enough for me."

I didn't know what I should feel about that. Allecra wasn't going to join bodies with me. But I couldn't insist on it for fear that I would come off as needy and desperate.

She seemed to read my mind.

"Do you want me to?" she asked.

"It's up to you," I said with a weak shrug. Allecra didn't mind my indecisiveness and only smiled.

"We'll see," she said. We kissed again, tenderly at first but then more passionately. My lips were swollen from all the kisses we had.

Her hands stroked my thighs and went over to squeeze my bum in a sensual motion. My hips buckled softly against her smooth stomach. I was throbbing and burning inside; I could barely breathe evenly anymore. When Allecra lifted my hips a bit, I felt the slipperiness between my legs smearing her skin. My face reddened in embarrassment. I realized how ridiculously wet I had become, but Allecra didn't seem to mind. Instead, she just moaned at the contact. She seemed pleased with herself even. Her body started moving and rubbing my sensitive rosebud. Pleasuring jolts of electricity surged through my being. I gasped and moaned in tandem to the thumping of my heart. The blood rushed up and down in accordance with the blissful friction. It was hard to believe I could be touching someone else in this manner. I was just glad that I was doing it with Allecra.

"Do you like it?" she asked with a slight smirk on her sculpted lips.

"Can't you tell?" I said, panting while trying to scowl at her, but failed miserably. My face must have looked funny that Allecra giggled back.

"Maybe we can just do this," she said to my dismay.

For a person who was born with an intense libido, Allecra seemed to have more restraint than I did.

"Allecra, please," I pleaded.

"What?" she said and then buried her face in my breasts. I gasped sharply as she sucked on my nipples.

"Can I see your secret?" I asked, making her stop.

"No," she whispered back. "Not yet."

"Allecra!" I cried, tugging at her shirt collar like a little whiny girl. She giggled again and dipped into my neck, licking and nipping. I tried to form words, but they all dissolved like ashes to the sensual swirling of her expert tongue.

"Remember when you asked me why my tongue seems so long?" she murmured, tracing her lips over my chest and down to my left nipple. Her warm mouth took it in and grazed it with her teeth. I moaned unabashedly, and my back arched over the bed. "I was just waiting for this moment to show you the answer."

I felt her tongue rolling my nipple around until it was embarrassingly hard. She moved it to my right breast and paid the same amount of attention. Her hands squeezed and stroked all over my body, stirring up something from my depths.

Before I knew it, Allecra was kissing her way down my stomach.

"Wha—what are you doing?" I asked, gasping.

"Showing you my answer, why?" she said. I finally understood.

"Don't!"

"Why?" Allecra asked, genuinely shocked to hear that.

"I don't think you would like it."

"Nina, you're as pink and delicate as a flower!" she said.

"But…it's a bit new."

"Nina, you're so damn beautiful," she said. "My mouth watered just thinking about doing this to you. Let me have it, please."

She almost growled in a feverish hunger, and I sort of pitied her. Besides, I couldn't deny that puppy-look on her face. I took a deep breath and finally succumbed to her raw passion.

"Alright," I said in a faint voice.

She smiled in triumph and restarted her ministration. Her lips moved over each sensitive spots. I lay perfectly still like a Japanese *nyotaimori* woman, who serves foods on her naked body. Allecra's head moved down my panting stomach until she got between my thighs. Her eyes got even brighter as she stared intensely. I had to look away in embarrassment. My legs tried to close themselves by instinct, but Allecra pushed them further apart.

For a long moment, she didn't do anything but stared. I shivered at the prospect of having my private exposed and gazed at with those piercing turquoise eyes. My sex was clearly soaked from within. I could feel the cold moistness when Allecra's breath fanned on me.

I squeezed my eyes shut, bracing and waiting. She made me anticipate it. She knew it would spark every carnal nerve ending and make me more sensitive. And deep down, I reveled at the way her burning gaze pouring over every naked inch of my virgin femininity.

"This is mine," Allecra murmured longingly to herself.

Then she spread my legs wider. I took a peek through my eyelashes and saw her long sleek velvety tongue slithered over my inner thighs. The sensation made my breath falter. I felt her going around the edges of my overheated core, but never to the exact spots. She wanted me to want it. She wanted me desperate and burning.

And she had succeeded. Before I knew myself, my hand reached down to the silky blonde lock and my hips began to churn instinctively.

I could see Allecra was smiling to herself. She looked up at me with unwavering eyes.

"Please," I begged her.

Allecra smiled wider and then her face buried in my sopping core. Her tongue swirled and lips nibbled away at my blushed nub.

I gasped loudly in pleasure, twisting my body over the bed. I forgot how powerful her long ravenous tongue was. It felt like a wet kindle setting a fire ablaze inside my trembling body. Her glowing eyes watched my face contorted in overwhelming bliss.

I felt her nimble fingers parted my slippery lips. Her slithering tongue elongated, moving up and down the oozing opening before slipping inside my wetted cleft. The entering motion felt endless through my walls. It was like a long octopus's tentacle going down deeper and feasting on the juices of my temperate hive. My mouth flung open in a strangling joy. The pleasure that was raging inside me made my eyes teary.

Allecra had to lock my rolling hips with both hands over my thighs, keeping me open and still. My back arched off the bed accompanied by soft whimpers. My nipples hardened in arousal.

She was licking me from inside out, vibrating my pelvic bones with her own moans which she unleashed right into my womb. I had never thought anyone would be so obsessed with another person's flesh like this. Allecra was actually making out with my girlhood. Her tongue was in me so deeply, she could have tickled my lungs. As she continued feeding herself the juice of my innocence, my mind and body felt like they were melting away.

Swollen, drenched and on white liquid fire, I sensed an indescribable building up. It was an unstoppable sensation rolling like tidal waves from my depths.

"Allecra...I..." I tried to cry out a warning, but somehow Allecra sensed what was about to happen through my writhing form. She neither slowed down nor sped up. Instead, she brought me steadily to the edge of oblivion. My fingers tangled up in her hair, tugging at it harder as I finally exploded, climaxing in such succession that it surprised even me. My inner walls tightened like I was trying to keep a firm grip on Allecra's ravishing tongue, refusing to let her leave my body. Allecra helped me ride the blissful tide by stroking my quivering tummy.

I buried my head into a pillow and muffled my scream as I came undone in her mouth again and again.

When the mind-blowing pleasure receded, I lay back in a delightful daze. My chest heaved loudly while I tried to catch my breath again.

Allecra kissed my slippery region and continued to lap up the overflowing juices from me. I was too far gone to notice until there was the shift of weight as Allecra crawled up over my limb body. She planted kisses on my chest and neck as if to apologize for causing this shocking eruption.

"You're alright?" she whispered. I tried to say something but I couldn't. My throat just closed up. There was this flood of emotions inside me. My chest tightened like I was about to cry.

"Shhh...it's okay, baby girl," Allecra consoled me and smoothed my hair gently. "You'll recover soon."

She kissed me until I could gather my thoughts again. I tilted my head up to her, and she understood what I sought. Our mouths locked one more time and I tasted myself on her luscious lips. Nothing felt more intimate than this.

After a moment, we pulled apart.

"Do you want it, too?" I whispered although my body was still buzzing from the gripping sensation.

Allecra smiled and shook her head. She slid off me and lay by my side. Propping her head on her elbow, she kept staring at me in fascination.

"It's late, and you're tired," she said. "Let's go to sleep."

"But...you haven't..." I tried to protest, yet it seemed I still had trouble forming coherent sentences.

"Shh...don't worry about me," Allecra said and stroked my cheek with the back of her fingers. "Like I said, this is for you. I just feel more satisfied knowing I was the reason you came so hard."

I giggled and smacked her arm weakly, which made her giggle back. Then she pulled the soft blanket over us. We snuggled up into each other.

Allecra played with my hair as I slept on her chest, tracing meaningless patterns over her bare stomach.

"There is something I want to tell you, Nina," she said softly.

"Yes?" I asked.

"I can now see why humans are special," she whispered. "I used to think that we might have landed on the wrong planet after seeing the defects and flaws in them. But you show me the other side of what being human truly is. I began to see the kindness and compassion, the courage to face your inner fear and endless emotional strength. And because of you, now I have learned another important thing."

"What is it?" I looked up at her.

"That love is indeed the force of the universe. It makes the world go around and come alive. The only energy that is unique in all reality. It's what unites us in this beautiful collective consciousness called life. And it makes me tremble at the thought that I've found such a beautiful and powerful thing with you."

CHAPTER 33

I LAY IN BED BESIDE ALLECRA, staring at her. I realized she was already asleep for her breathing had changed. Her face was youthful and smooth under the dimmest light in the room. It was the first time I saw her sleeping. This indeed was her best face of all, bright and innocent with a graceful boyish charm.

It surprised me to see that at first. How she could be so lovely and intriguing even in her slumber. I gazed at the small contented smile tugged on those tender lips. Her long curved lashes cast shadows on her cheeks. This was her truest self — earnest, guileless and loving. The only face that gave back to me the emotions and the sense of relief that made life bearable.

I could just stare at her like this all night.

My hand came up slowly to stroke her soft cheek, the velvety skin of a sleeping angel in this bed. Whenever I woke up in the middle of the night, a face like this could save me. By day, too, I could shield myself from the dark thoughts by resting my eyes on it. Grief and fear could be repudiated by the sight of this face. This person lying next to me was indeed the finest assurance and the safest refuge for my heart.

I prayed Allecra was not merely an illusion or my own imagination. I would be damned for the feelings I kept amassing for her days and nights. I just wanted to be able to kiss those tempting lips, to share her palpable cravings and be embraced in a burst of her affection each and every day.

My besotted heart was deeply mesmerized by her presence. And I found myself drowning in the ocean of this love and desire. It was exhilarating and comforting at the same time. It was where love raged and passion aspired, making me twist and ache in sweet pain. Allecra had tried to describe it to me before. The pain that ached so sweetly she could die if she no longer felt it. I now understood.

"You're the best birthday gift ever, Allecra," I whispered softly. "I love you."

Delving myself deeper into the comfort of her body, I could hear the air traveling through her chest as she breathed. The beating of her heart was so solacing; it was now my favorite lullaby. At last, my mind slowly slipped into a luring serene sleep.

The next morning, I awoke again, feeling the soft tingles on my cheeks and forehead. My heavy eyelids struggled to open, but they couldn't fight back the spell-bound doziness. I heard myself groaning inside my chest. My brain was still refusing to function, but the tender sensation of soft lips smacking over my skin was too ticklish to bear. Goosebumps rose like waves over my body. My mind was forced to snap into the conscious world again.

Above a pair of crystalline turquoise eyes twinkled with mirth and mischief. Allecra giggled and buried her face against my neck. Her arms tightened around my nude form, pulling me closer to her. She kept nuzzling me and that tickled.

"Allecra...stop," I groaned and made a feeble attempt to push her away. Yet she continued to plant butterfly kisses down my throat and over my bare chest. Another wave of goose bumps raided my skin.

"Wake up, sleepyhead," she whispered and chuckled at my sour expression. "Come on, I know you love me more than sleep."

"Don't flatter yourself," I grumbled and tried to pout. I ended up gasping instead when Allecra's lips wrapped around my left nipple and suckled it hard. "Oh, my..."

"Hmm? What did you say?" she murmured against my breast, but continue to torture me gently.

"I said..." I struggled to put coherent words together and failed miserably. Her velvety tongue went over to another breast and began the same assault there. I whimpered again.

"Your face looks so cute when you sleep, but I think it looks way cuter when you come," she said.

"No...Allecra, I have to go to the bathroom," I tried to whine in protest.

"Do you really, *lapochka*?" The Russian term of endearment was so heart-melting, especially coming from her sultry voice. I almost lost my resolve right there. The cozy cover was too comfortable to leave, but Allecra's slender legs begin to entangle over mine. I thought my body wasn't ready for this yet, but Allecra proved me wrong. To my surprise and embarrassment, the wetness had already collected itself promisingly between my thighs.

Oh the things she could do to me!

"Allecra..."

"Yes?" she said, lips brushing over my stomach to my navel. My legs nearly fell open on their own accord. All my life, I had never experienced the loss of body control like this. It was astonishing how your body could betray you.

"I need to go to the bathroom, please," I said and wiggled away from under her. Allecra looked up and pouted, but then her brows smoothed back.

"Nature's call?"

"No, just...to get cleaned," I said.

"Okay," she said. "Then I'm coming with you."

"No!"

"Yes," she said.

"Allecra, no!"

"Nina, yes," she said and chuckled. "Or I'll have my cupcake right now."

"You're evil!" I cried.

Allecra just laughed and then got off me. The cold morning made me shiver after the absence of her warmth. She held out her hand for me to take, but when I sat up, I realized my problem.

"Er...Allecra...I'm still naked," I said coyly. Allecra raised a perfectly arched brow at me.

"Nina, you do understand that we already had sex, and there's nothing I haven't seen," she said.

"I just can't walk around like that!" I snapped.

"Geez, you're such a woman," she grumbled. But when she saw me rubbing my arms from the chill, she came to envelop me into her warm body again. She pulled the blanket over me.

"Give me a minute," Allecra said and kissed my lips once before she turned away and disappeared from the bedroom. I gathered the sheet around me and got up from the bed. A moment later, Allecra reemerged, holding a white silky satin kimono. It was framed in a mix of beautiful Chantilly lace and soft chiffon. She shrugged it off its hanger and walked up to me.

Without saying anything, Allecra turned me around. I reluctantly let go of the sheet, which silently fell to the floor. I felt Allecra's heated stare like a laser beam from behind. She took her time to savor my naked backside before she shrouded me with the robe. I let out a soft sigh as I embraced the silken gentleness of the fabric around my body. But I felt ghostly hands grazing my bum. Out of shyness, I jerked away and turned to face Allecra again. She looked like a kid getting caught with her hand in the cookie jar.

"Sorry," she murmured with a sheepish look.

"It's okay," I said and blushed.

"I bought it, thinking it would look perfect on you, and I was right."

She smiled as her hands came to tie the strings into a butterfly knot for me. Her bright eyes traveled over my body in satisfaction. The lovely robe reached at mid-thigh, and I felt like I was shrouded in cloud.

"You're spoiling me rotten," I said. She just smiled and kissed my forehead.

"You're worth spoiling with all the best things I have," she said and tugged my hair back. But then she frowned. "Where's your necklace?"

"Oh!" I breathed and then I remembered I had taken it off when I took a shower last night. "I must have put it into my dress's pocket."

Allecra grunted and then walked me towards the bathroom. She found my dress again and fished out the tiny black box from the pocket. Then she took the necklace out and proceeded to fasten it back on my neck. The Eytus gem blinked with its radiant light.

"Promise me not to take it off again," she said softly. I nodded as I fingered the beautiful rock. Every time I looked at it, it seemed to sparkle in different colors. "You're the first human to be bound to an Arzurian by the Erytus stone, you understand?"

"Is the bond breakable?" I asked.

Although I believed her vow wholeheartedly, the fear of abandonment was still hidden in the deepest part of my being.

"Why did you ask that?" Concerns laced in her turquoise eyes.

"Nothing, I'm just curious." I shrugged.

Allecra smiled and was about to claim my lips when I turned away. I didn't know why I did that. I tried to shrug it off by pretending to cover my mouth with my hands.

"What's wrong?"

"I need to brush my teeth," I said, my voice muffled. Allecra gave me an eye roll and groaned again. I giggled back and turned towards the sink, towing her along by the hand. All the while, I tried to dispel those bleak thoughts from my head. I must believe in Allecra and me, like my father's favorite quote of Confucius's, *If you look into your own heart and you find nothing wrong there, what is there to worry about? What is there to fear?'*

Inside the immaculate bathroom, I stood beside her in front of the twin rectangular ceramic sinks and an enormous mirror. Then we both started brushing our teeth like twin sisters with mirroring motions. When I rinsed, she also rinsed. Suddenly, it became a game of mimicking each other. When I took a shot of mouthwash, Allecra did the same. And when I looked at her, she looked back at me. We both looked like a pair of puffer fish. We burst out laughing like children, spilling the green liquid all over our chins.

After we finished cleaning up, Allecra turned to me.

"Let's take a bath together," she said, which made my body freeze.

"Together?"

Some part of me still hadn't gotten used to doing intimate things like this.

"Yeah, why?" she asked. I shook my head.

"Nothing."

"Good then," she said.

While Allecra prepared the bath, I went to relieve myself. Although the toilet was at the other side of this big bathroom, I had to hold my breath so that it wouldn't sound like a waterfall. I wondered whether Allecra did it like me or like boys. I shook my head. I needed to stop questioning everything. It was getting unhealthy for me.

After I cleaned myself up, I came to sit on a vanity chair and watched Allecra worked. As usual, she was meticulous about everything she did. It was always graceful and efficient. I loved watching her doing household stuff like this. The process was like making a perfect cup of tea or preparing an amazing dinner. I was in awe of how such a vibrant person could be so domestic, too.

Allecra poured a cup of Epsom salt in while the water was running to help dissolve it. Then she added a box of dried herbs of rosemary and chamomile. They spread all over the bubbling water. She made sure the bath was at the right temperature. When she was done, she turned to me.

"Come here," she said.

I got up and walked towards her. She took my hand, brought it to her lips and kissed it. My heart fluttered again at the unexpected affection. I didn't know why I still felt nervous when her hands came to untie my robe. Maybe it was the way her intense eyes looked at me.

"Stop looking at me like that, Allecra," I murmured out loud. My face blushed under her stare again.

"Like what?" she asked innocently, but the corners of her perfect lips curved up.

"Like you want to see me naked," I said. Allecra burst out laughing.

"Damn right I do!" she admitted.

"Stop, you make me nervous," I told her. She leaned in to steal a peck on my lips.

"Oh, don't be," she said. "I imagine you naked all the times."

"You're so perverted," I said and gave a playful cuff on her shoulder.

"Why, thank you." She grinned back.

When Allecra got rid of the knots, the light in her eyes shifted and got darker with the familiar longing. Her hands came to peel the silk fabric off my shoulders, slowly letting her fingers brush over my skin and down my arms. I cast my eyes to the floor. My body shivered from both the exhilarating touch and the early morning air.

When I was completely bare again, Allecra kept exploring my body with her dazzling eyes. I heard her swallowed loudly just like the first time she saw me.

"Nina, how you manage to take my breath away every time is beyond me," she said.

Allecra leaned towards me. I thought she was going to kiss me, but she only touched our foreheads together and smiled. Her hands went to cup my cheeks in her soft palms. Even my own face felt strange to me as if something about me had changed overnight. I could feel the tiny thread of life connected us. It was like our essence and energy were trying to mingle together like floating stardust in space.

My heart picked up speed when she drew me in by the waist, and I slipped my hand under her shirt to feel her soft bare skin. Our eyes still bore into each other, and I marveled at the notion that all of her was mine as much as all of me was hers. Our passion shrouded around us like a warm cocoon.

My hands began to unbutton her dress shirt. Allecra then shrugged it off as my hands went over to the soft supple roundness of her breasts. They filled my palms deliciously and were both firm and delicate against my fingers. I could feel her heart beating in tandem with mine. I was so engrossed that I didn't notice she had slipped off her panties. There was no hesitation. It was just something she felt comfortable doing.

I stepped back like she had done the night before, to feast on every inch of her in fascination and hunger. My eyes traveled from her toes to her shapely legs to her slender thighs and round hips. But something stopped my gaze there. It was the fact that Allecra was made no different than me. Between her endless legs was the same bare pinkish femininity just like mine. For a long moment, I could do nothing but stare.

Allecra watched me watching her. Then she put her hands on her hips and tilted her head to the side.

"You're alright?" she asked.

"Allecra, you're..." I whispered back, but the shocking beauty of her innocent flower made me speechless.

"I know, I'm flawless," she said with a smirk. Her pompous remark caused me to scowl at her in irritation.

"I wasn't going to say that," I lied. "I think you're...well...human-like...like a human."

Allecra chuckled and then narrowed her eyes at me suggestively. "So you're not curious at all?"

"Well, where is it then?" I said.

"Where is what?"

"You know what!" I said, almost stomping my feet in a childish tantrum. Allecra laughed, throwing her head back like a nude goddess in mirth. Her skin glowed against the rising sun, peeking over the sea. Then she came to hold me again.

"Okay, let's just get into the water first," she just said and guided me by the hand towards the nicely prepared bath in the sunken bathtub. I dipped my leg in and then the other before I squatted down. As my body submerged in the water, Allecra followed suite. Her blonde hair swayed to the ripples. Our eyes locked for a moment. Then she came over and turned my body around wordlessly. My back was pressed against her front. I reveled at the tingling sensation when the tenderness of our skins touched. Her lips found the nape of my neck and her hands roamed my belly with gentle strokes. Despite the pleasant warmth of the bath, I shivered at the sensation.

I turned my head around and our lips found each other again. This time, it was the light sensual kiss instead of the one that contained fire and ice. But soon my breathing changed as there was a battle of entwined tongues, yearning for the sweet victory. Allecra let out a soft chuckle from the depth of her chest when I began to fight back for dominance. Then her hand went up to cup my chin and forcibly shoved her entire tongue into my mouth. I broke off from the kiss and pulled away, nearly gagging.

"You're an animal!" I cried and splashed water at her. Allecra shielded her face with her hand while laughing.

"I thought you liked my tongue after last night," she said, grinning playfully back. I shot her a look.

"I don't like it when you're rough," I said.

"Oh, I'm sorry, okay?" she turned to apologize. "Please come back here, I need you!"

I bit my lips from smiling. She reached out her hand to take mine, pulling me back towards her. I felt her hands behind my bum, hoisting my body over to straddle her lap. I stared at that lovely face and couldn't help smiling at last.

I wrapped my arms around Allecra's neck while she ran her hands over my sides. Allecra wrapped my legs around her waist and leaned back against the edge of the pool. My heart pounded as I felt the sweet slipperiness between my thighs on her. The water was lapping our entwined bodies languidly. The sweet flowers that emitted an escapist fragrance brushed our noses.

"How long is your tongue exactly, Allecra?" I asked.

"Not as long as you might think, but longer than yours," she said smugly, her hands kept caressing my back.

"But it felt endless when you—when you went down on me," I said.

"If you suspect that I might be part-lizard, I'll show you," she said. I watched her as she slowly unrolled that pinky flexible muscle from her mouth. But the tip barely went past her chin like I had expected. In fact, it kind of looked normal like any human tongue.

"That's all?" I said. "I thought it was longer than that."

"The average human tongue is four inches long. Mine was just a tad bit longer," she said. "Trust me, the part of me that is longer than that is something else."

A flirtatious gleam flickered in her eyes. I felt my face reddened with heat again. I guessed her unfiltered sexual innuendos were going to ruin my sanity one of these days.

Allecra giggled at the look on my face and pulled me in for another round of tongue-wrestling. Everywhere she touched began to burn. I felt myself moving against her while my hands kept fondling her breast. The only feeling that mattered to me.

"Can you show me the longer part of you then?" I asked.

"You mean my legs?" she asked.

"Stop it!" I said which made her laugh. Then she claimed my pouting lips again.

"Nina," she whispered huskily against my mouth. "Will you sit by the window for me?"

"Why?" I said, pulling away and frowning at her illogical suggestion.

"You know why," she said and motioned for me to stand up. I wasn't sure what she was planning to do until she rose with me still clinging like a baby koala from the water and walked in complete ease before setting me back down by the glass window. Then she kneeled before me with her face leveled with my private. I realized with an accelerated heartbeat what was on her mind. Without a word, her lithe fingers went over to my thighs, ready to spread them apart.

"No, Allecra!" I said and clamped my legs together tightly. She looked at me.

"What's wrong?" she asked. "You didn't enjoy it last night?"

"I did! I—I enjoyed it a lot," I said, blushing harder. "And that's the problem."

"Why?"

"I don't know," I said and shook my head. "It's just kind of scary to me—to enjoy something like this so much."

Allecra squinted her eyes at me and then nodded like a doctor recognizing a patient's symptom

"I see, you have a fear of sexual perversion."

"A fear of sexual perversion?" I echoed her words.

"You're afraid that you might be perverted by liking sexual activities," she said. "I remember you used to recoil just from my touch alone. It's bordering on a fear of intimacy, which is often tied to a fear of engulfment and abandonment."

I blinked back at her. It amazed me how Allecra always had answers to my complicated tendencies.

"How do you know all that?" I asked.

"Observations, and well, I am a psychology major," she said and shrugged casually like it was nothing.

"I thought you majored in economics," I said.

"I just wanted to impress your uncle," Allecra said and smiled. "Anyway, I can still be your sex therapist, so you will learn to enjoy a wide range of sexual experiences like any normal human beings."

"Said by an alien girl," I mocked. "So what are you going to treat this phobia with?"

"With this." She grinned, pointing to herself, "I'm the best medication you can find. We can start the session right about now."

She crawled over to me again.

"No, wait!" I said.

"What is it again?" she asked impatiently.

"Can I touch you back afterward?"

Allecra thought it over but then shook her head.

"No, I don't think it's the right time yet."

When does she think is the right time for crying out loud?

"Fine," I said and folded my arms over my chest. "Then you can't touch me either."

"Aw, Nina!" Allecra whined.

"You have to be fair, Allecra," I said. "It's my turn now."

She gave me a sore look.

"Alright," she said. My heart perked up and pounded in an eager rhythm.

"Really? You're gonna let me?" I asked, almost unable to believe what I had just heard. She was really going to let me do it. This was as exciting as it was nerve-wracking. I had never done it with another girl before, but Allecra wasn't that different from me, at least for the most part.

"But you have to promise me that you won't go too far, okay?"

"Why..."

"Don't ask any question," she cut me off, "or I'll just dive right in there, and you won't be able to say another word."

"You can't just do that," I said and scowled back.

"Oh, try me," she challenged.

"Fine," I said. Allecra smiled again and came forward. Her breath tickled my skin. I wriggled a little.

"Don't move," she said and took her time to stroke my legs then raised one up. Her fingers massaged my ankle for a moment before she planted her lips on my toes. It sent a jolt of stirring shock up my spine. I tried to jerk my leg away, but Allecra wouldn't let go. Her lips and tongue traveled up my shin and knee, setting a trail of fire over my skin. My hands gripped tightly onto the window ledge. I bit my bottom lip to muffle the moans. Allecra's head went in between my thighs as she kissed and licked around the inner sides. My eyelids fluttered and closed to the rapid panting of my chest.

Allecra leaned me further back against the glass window, my hips raised a bit more outward. I almost cried out from the intensity of this outpouring of passion. Then that strong expert tongue slid out and gave its first lap on my sensitivity. I whimpered. Allecra's slender fingers came to aid by opening the outer petals of my flower. My body trembled as the heat pooled around my belly.

I was throbbing and slippery, but Allecra was devoted to her meticulous way of doing things. She rubbed the pads of her fingertips gently around my slick folds. My breath hitched in my throat from the incredible blazing sensation. She pulled the hood back and her lips and tongue came down and brushed softly over my wetness, going along the canyon of my ecstasy. I moaned out loud, unable to suppress my burning need anymore. My hips moved in response to the hot probing tongue along my drooling lips. Her penetrating eyes watched my euphoric expression with stirring heat. I let out a whiny sound when it was almost to the point I could scream. She pulled away, leaving me to my great disappointment and pending build-up tension.

Allecra came up to kiss me with my juices coating her chin.

"You want my fingers?" her whispered. The question came as a shock to me, but when she licked her beautiful deft fingers, wetting them with saliva and juices from my inside, there was no holding back. Allecra's blazing eyes never left mine as her hand went down between my legs again. The first touch of her fingers made me gasp and tremble out of control.

"Close your eyes," Allecra instructed and I did as I was told. After a moment, I felt a delicious sliding of one digit into my wet cave. My jaw clenched from the sweet rhapsodic filling. I inhaled deeply. Allecra nibbled on my bare chest and over my heaving breasts. She took my nipple into her mouth and teased it with her tongue while expertly entering me at the same time. I sighed when she pulled her finger out again, but only to come back with another one.

"Oh my," I gasped, my jaw slackened.

"Did I hurt you?" Allecra asked. I shook my head vigorously.

"No," I panted. "It feels...amazing."

"I know," she said and giggled softly. Allecra kneeled down again and began to work her fingers through my entrance. The motion was smooth without any resistance at all. I squeezed my eyes shut as I felt them going through my sopping passage. The process was so slow as if Allecra was trying to sneak in without being noticed.

"You're so soft," Allecra whispered once she couldn't go any deeper, then started moving. Just the prospect of having Allecra's nimble fingers in me almost pushed me over the edge. My hips shuddered. I was almost on the verge of exploding when she rubbed the pads of her fingers over my sensitive area, as if stirring up honey from the hive. She distracted me by leaning over slowly to lick my hardened pink pearl. Her tongue circled around it sensually. I moaned at the intoxicating bliss that coursed through my quivering form. My head swam deliriously in pure sexual ecstasy. Allecra stroked the roof of my walls until every atom in my entire being sparked with flaming pleasures.

"Allecra..." I gasped.

My legs shook violently. I knew neither where nor who I was anymore. All I wanted was Allecra between my legs doing what no one in the world could have done to me. The walls began to crumble and close in. I felt myself slowly breaking piece by piece then so dramatically and blissfully all at once.

My breath halted and I came on her with a demanding grip. She could feel it, too. It was a hard and slow eruption. My hand gripped her wrist and I clamped my legs together while my inside clenched and unclenched in a shocking orgasm. After a moment, it subsided. Allecra kept her hand still and only massaged me gently until the tightened muscle unwound again, and I was able to come all the way down. I was swollen and very sensitive. I wasn't ready for her to slip out of me yet. She understood and stroked my trembling legs with her free hand to soothe me.

Another moment passed and Allecra softly slipped her hand out. I winced, though it wasn't from pain but rather from the feeling of sudden hollowness. My eyes were dazed and unfocused. I felt Allecra's lips came to release mine from my own biting.

We kissed quietly. I was lured back into the water by her gentle hands. When my hand brushed her fingers, I could feel they were still coated in slipperiness. Allecra kissed my neck and shoulders until I came back to my senses again.

"Do you have any stinging feeling?" she asked. I didn't know why she asked me that, she was so gentle and expert with her hand. There was barely any thrusting, only the sweet burning probing and stroking. It was like a clever thief coming into a dark house, turning on the light, taking a look around and then turning the light off again before leaving the interior unscathed.

I felt no pain and I told her so.

"Good," she said and released me then floated away on her back.

"Wait, it's my turn now," I said.

"Gosh, I thought I could make you forget it," she groaned.

"You promised," I said, which made her roll her eyes.

"Alright, *kotik*," she said, using the Russian word for 'kitten' on me. "But you have to close your eyes and don't ask."

I bit my lips from uttering another *why*. I did as was told and started feeling blindly over the water. I tried to locate Allecra again, but she wasn't there where I last saw her.

"Hey you!" I called.

"Don't open your eyes," she said.

"Why must you always make it difficult for me?" I whined. Suddenly it turned into a hide-and-seek game. I heard her chuckle and went towards the direction of her voice. Allecra was swift and light with her movement like a slithering snake. She moved away just before I touched her.

"Right here," she said behind me. I turned around and found her shoulders and arms. She leaned back and I followed her. We reached the edge again, and she turned my body around once more. We were in the same position like we were before. Her soft chest squashed gently against my shoulder blades.

"Can I open my eyes now?" I asked.

"No," she whispered, but this time her voice sounded thick and heavy. I realized she was panting. Then I felt her hand over mine, bringing it downward. I held my breath as my brain tried to register what she was doing. My fingers brushed over her smooth inner thigh. My heart pounded harder. At last, I understood her action. She let me feel over her lower abdomen and then further down. I felt the soft sleek velvety skin. It was like delicate petals.

I gasped and opened my eyes, but Allecra held me from turning around. Her breathing was getting laborious over my shoulder. All my life I had never touched any girl like this, except myself. She was so much like me that I felt the familiarity almost welcoming. I couldn't believe I was doing this to Allecra. The feeling was stupefying and surreal and overwhelming.

"Touch me, but be gentle please," Allecra whispered behind my ear. And I did, slowly and gently. She was so soft and silken down there, also slippery. For a moment, I was afraid I would hurt her, but Allecra just sighed. Her breath was loud and her heartbeat hastened. As our fingers laced over her private, I could feel the growing tension rising from within her core, specifically her tiny little rosebud. It seemed to swell under the pads of my fingers.

"Oh Nina, Nina wait..." she whimpered. "Please...stop..." I began to feel her body tremble against mine.

I removed my hand from her girlhood and turned myself around to face her. Allecra's dilated eyes brightened as she looked at me. Her cheeks turned rosy and hot. There was another side of me that wanted to see her in the same euphoria like I was earlier. She looked relieved only for a moment until I came to wrap my arm around her shoulders firmly. My other hand went down to her sex again. She was warm and invitingly wet even under the water.

Allecra took a sharp breath. When I began to caress her once again, I felt her legs quivered at either side of me. Her eyebrows furrowed in conflicted pleasure and desperation. She told me not to go too far, which made me even more curious about what would happen if I did.

Allecra gritted her teeth and seethed, but at the same time, she was powerless under my touch. Touching her like this wasn't that much different from touching myself.

"Nina...if you keep doing it, it... it'll come out," she gasped. Her chest heaved laboriously.

"Then let it out," I whispered and leaned in to nuzzle her smooth neck. Allecra tilted her head back and shut her eyes. She was even more beautiful this way, I realized. I wanted to see her like this often. I wondered if that was how she also felt about me.

When I slowly and gently nestled my middle finger inside her, Allecra arched her back. I sensed the wave of coursing heat pulsating around her little girly nub. To my amazement, it suddenly began to swell up against the base of my palm.

"Oh damn it, Nina!" Allecra growled and gasped.

I looked down and saw her little bud growing and hardening until it sprouted out like a time-lapse mushroom. I jumped with a surprised gasp.

There it was— Allecra's long-awaited secret member.

CHAPTER 34

IT WAS THE MOST ALIEN THING I'd ever encountered since I'd known Allecra. Considering her bizarre anatomy, I would be lying if I said I wasn't freaked out at all. A tiny part of me wanted to fall in a hysterical shock like normal people would, but the rest of me was completely spellbound by the fascinating sight. The actual meeting of the new member was neither any different nor was it scary.

I wasn't that innocent. I knew what it would look like and what such a thing could do, but it was the first time I ever got to see a real one. And ironically, it was from another girl.

We were both quiet. Allecra looked at me with wide heated eyes. She was guessing my expression as my stare was still transfixed on her revealed secret.

In a strange indefinable way, I found her pulsating length familiar and approachable like an adorable pet that would never harm me. Allecra was just like how I had seen her in my dream. The one thing that hit me harder was the word I thought I would never use to describe a male sex organ ever in my life. But this was an exception. There was no denying it — she was surprisingly and unarguably... beautiful. That slender member almost possessed a feminine touch. How it stood poised and perfect just like the rest of her. It even appeared to be completely natural, as if it belonged there. How it could be possible I would never understand.

For a long moment, neither one of us knew what to do. It was getting more awkward as Allecra was waiting. I realized she was giving me a chance to decide for myself whether this was what I really signed up for. I took several deep breaths to calm the pounding heart in my chest. My tongue was still glued to the roof of my mouth.

But I had to do something or it would give the impression that I was afraid. I wanted to show Allecra that it didn't change anything between us. I still wanted her regardless of what she was born with. She was still the same girl I had come to love so deeply. And that was all that mattered.

With that in mind, I surprised myself, and probably Allecra as well, by reaching my hand out to her. At this very gesture, Allecra recoiled like a frightened deer. I paused and looked up at her again. She bashfully turned her face away from my searching gaze, but I could see a visible tinge of red on her lovely cheeks. Her bright eyes seemed conflicted but not hostile. It was a wonder how her attitude reversed in accordance with her physical transformation. One moment, Allecra was the confident tomboy, and the next moment, she was just a shy little girl. What a mind-boggling contrast that was!

"It's okay," I whispered. "I'm not afraid of you."

I wasn't even aware of my own breathing as I reached over to her again. This time without prolonging the tension, I went for it. My fingers swiftly wrapped themselves around her hardness. A spontaneous sharp intake of air was loud amidst the silence.

I marveled at the fact that it was real and that it was really happening. My jaw went unhinged by itself. Allecra's white teeth bit down on her maroon lip to keep from whimpering. Her feet jerked a little under the water. I could faintly feel her pulse through my hand.

It's alive!

"Nina, please..." Allecra spoke in a strangled voice. "You're...squeezing me."

I realized I had unintentionally gripped her a bit too hard. I quickly relaxed my hand and almost retreated then. I was afraid that I had hurt her, but a glimpse of that sweet tortured look on Allecra's face intrigued and emboldened me.

She was soft and flexible, yet surprisingly firm and warm. It amazed me how a certain part of her body could turn this hard. And in the depth of my darkest desire, I wanted her this way — captured and surrendered in my hand. A slow shudder evidently went through her. It looked like Allecra was struggling to keep still.

"Are you okay?" I asked, but my hand already started to feel her up, cradling her stiffness and brushing my fingers over her sleek pinkish tip.

Allecra groaned in her throat. I was thrilled to discover how my caress could affect her entire being.

"Nina—please—stop moving—I can't..."

Ignoring her plea, I continued my curious advancement. My mind was too engrossed in the act of caressing that elongated *'girl nub'*. It caused

Allecra to throw her head back and moan louder. Her hands gripped her knees to support herself.

A lot of questions floated around in my head. Does this fleshy hardness give the same worldly pleasure just like mine? Can she really feel the mounting intensity from my touch?

It was weird and at the same time captivating with the thing I was doing, and perhaps a tad bit dirty, but nothing about Allecra felt unnatural or disgusting to me.

I heard a low hiss and Allecra suddenly rose from the water to embrace me. I had to release her when our bodies pressed together once again. Her strong arms roamed over my skin almost too roughly as she kissed me in earnest. Her supple tender lips moving over mine in pronounced desperation and hunger. We both moaned audibly at the same time. I felt her hardness nestling against my belly. Then Allecra's hips began to flex as if by sheer mating instinct. My heart fluttered and skipped so many convulsing beats.

"Oh god..." I huffed out loud, breaking from the kiss for needed air. Obviously, I should have known better by now. Yet I couldn't seem to stop from reacting exactly as Allecra had predicted the night before. She drew her face back to have a look at me. I could sense the extra amount of effort it took for her to tear herself away.

"I'm sorry," she apologized like she had just realized what she was doing. A spark of guilt and shame ignited in her eyes. I knew something had crossed her mind, but before I could open my mouth to speak, Allecra turned around and got out of the pool in such haste that a minute later she was out of the bathroom. I blinked in shock, unable to figure out what I had done wrong.

It was so silent in the room. I was left with the question of what had pushed Allecra away. The look I spotted on her face was a haunting mask of self-hate and disgust. She must have misinterpreted my startled response as a form of rejection. I wondered what had transpired this conclusion. There was only once I had seen her like that— the day she confessed about her past mistakes. I realized with a flash of emotion, Allecra had scars from her first relationship with Nattia. The memory matched the thing we were doing. How it had felt similar to her, and she might have thought I was repelled by it the same way.

I was so stupid!

After what seemed like a long wandering thought, I got out of the bath and readied myself before I went after her. I must tell her that she had gotten it all wrong.

A moment later, I found Allecra sitting alone on a loveseat at the portico. I slid open the glass door soundlessly and stepped outside. The winds blowing from the sea were less chilling and growing more pleasant after the sunrise. Allecra was drying her wet hair with a bath towel. She was now in a plain white t-shirt and a pair of black panties, yet looking completely stunning under the glow of the morning sun. I walked up to her quite nervously. Thinking about what we had done in the pool and how it had ended made the situation a lot more awkward than I had anticipated.

"Hey," I called out to her. Allecra turned around and then a small smile lit her face.

"Hi," she said. I was relieved when she held out her hand to me. I took it as she scooted over to let me sit down beside her.

"What's wrong?" I decided to ask, staring at her face with steady eyes. Allecra looked away again.

"Nothing," she said with a weak shrug.

"I'm sorry if I have upset you," I said. "I didn't mean to..."

"No, it wasn't you," she replied but didn't say anything further. I waited for a while.

"Tell me, Allecra."

"I'm just...upset with myself," she finally admitted. "If you want to change your mind, there's still time. I totally understand."

"What are you talking about? I'm not going to change my mind about anything," I said with vehemence. "I know what you're thinking, Allecra, and you're wrong. You're gentle, patient, and more in control than I could ever be."

"I might have believed all that until this stupid *thing* happened," she scoffed begrudgingly with a vague motion at herself.

It pained me that I had caused her to hate something about her body. I brought my hand to card through her soft blonde strands and then coaxed her into my embrace. She wrapped her arms back around my waist and sighed.

"I won't back out just because you're different," I said softly. "I know what you've gone through and the tormenting guilt you keep buried deep inside, but I'm not Nattia. I'm aware of the choice I made and I chose you. I want you just the same — every single part of you. You're still my Allecra, and nothing has changed that."

She was quiet for a long moment. I kissed the crown of her head gently. Allecra smelled like the fragrant bath we had shared. I inhaled her scent again.

"You were a naughty kitten," she murmured against my chest, which made me giggle.

"Sorry, but if I hadn't outed your secret, it would take you forever!" I said. "In fact, I started to wonder whether it was because you didn't find me desirable or something."

Allecra let out a melodious laugh and pulled away. I was glad she had brightened up again.

"You're probably right about the last part," she said. I shot her a look and then pinched her bare leg.

"Ow, Nina! Not again!" she yelped.

I giggled back and stuck my tongue out like I was five.

"Serve you right," I said. Allecra scowled at me.

"You're feisty," she muttered. "Let's go down for breakfast before I do something really naughty here."

She got up and pulled me along by the hand.

In the kitchen, Allecra and I helped each other prepare our first breakfast together. I cut the avocados while she buttered the well-toasted bagels. I made scrambled egg and mixed salad and cherry tomatoes with olive oil, and she sliced up the salmon.

She was so expert with the knife that I had to stop what I was doing to watch her. All of the slices were cut evenly like a row of fallen dominoes. She laid the salmon on bagel slices neatly along with the avocados, salad, and my scrambled egg.

It didn't take us long to assemble everything onto the plates. After that, we sat down at the table and ate in a peaceful ambiance of the house. Allecra fed me a forkful of mixed salad, and I let her take a bite of my own bagel. It was the typical love-crazed couple scenario, but I knew how much effort we had put into it and how many barriers we had broken just to get us to this point.

"I miss you already," Allecra said as she brought a napkin to wipe the corner of my lips.

"But I'm still here," I reminded her.

"Yeah, but soon you'll return to your human world, and I will be left alone to miss my sweet kitten every minute that ticks by," she tried to sound pitiful. I gripped her jaw and gave it a little shake out of adoration.

"Don't be a baby. I'll see you again tomorrow."

Then I leaned in to kiss her on the lips. She tasted of butter and salmon.

"Ew...gross!" I grimaced, which made Allecra laugh. I handed her a glass of orange juice as I took a sip from mine.

"You could stay with me longer, or better yet — forever," she said. "I'll feed you well."

"With cat foods?" I laughed.

"Probably," she giggled along.

"You know how boring my reality is," I said. "I need to run off from your palace like Cinderella at midnight, or I might be in trouble."

Allecra pursed her lips as if to think of something. After a moment, her eyes lit up with a hint of excitement. She leaned towards me like she was afraid of being eavesdropped.

"What if I really want to take you away from here? Will you come with me?"

"What are you talking about?" I asked with a suspicious frown. "Don't tell me your sister's plan to kidnap me is still on."

"Don't be ridiculous," she said. "You'll just come on your own anyway."

"That's not true!" I protested. "I have my free will."

"Then where do you want to go for spring break?"

"Why you ask?"

"Just answer me, Nina."

"I don't know," I said. "I only want to be with you all the time."

"Great, would you like to travel the world with me then?" Allecra said easily with an impish smile.

"You know I can't just travel the world with you," I said.

"Why not? I want to look at you seeing the world with me."

I blinked. Something about the way she said it made me almost cave in.

"Maybe someday," I decided. "I don't think it's the right time yet."

"Aw, why not?" Allecra raised blonde brows like she had no concepts of a human dilemma, which might be the case.

"You don't understand," I said. "I still live with my aunt. I can't just flap my wings and go anywhere I want like a bird."

Allecra rolled her eyes. "You forgot who I am."

"Oh right, speaking of which, you need to know that in the human world, we deem it morally wrong to compel other people with your alien mind tricks," I told her with a chastising look.

"I didn't compel them," she said. "I just switched off some neurons in their brains and transferred some new information—"

"Whatever it is," I cut her off. "You can't twist their mind to get your way."

"Of course, I can!" Allecra defended.

"No, you can't!" I said again. "I meant — yes, you can, but you shouldn't do that, alright?"

"So can you ask them next time?" she said.

"I can't."

"See? That means I should and I can," Allecra said and quirked her brows at me.

I groaned.

"You haven't answered my question yet," she said. "If you could go anywhere you want, where would it be?"

I had no idea why she insisted on me answering that, but I finally complied with an annoying sigh.

"Well," I said, "I want to see the aurora in Alaska."

"What happens to relaxing by the beach with a parasol to protect your drink from the rain?"

"Half of the population on earth probably have it written down on their bucket list already," I said. "Besides, I think this is just one of my unattainable wishes. It doesn't matter."

"Whatever you want matters to me, Nina," Allecra said.

"What are you, a Genie?" I looked at her.

She bit back a smile.

"What if I told you I could take you anywhere you want without you actually leaving here?"

"You lost me at the entire question," I said, staring hard at her.

"Triton and Xenon don't like me doing this, but screw that. I'll do it for you. Besides, quantum jumping is so damn fun."

"Wait, quantum what?"

"You go into another physical world," Allecra simply said with a casual shrug. "Similar to a parallel world. Ever heard of that?"

"Yes! In science fiction!" I answered bewilderingly.

"Really, Nina? Look at me! Am I a fictional character, too?"

"You might as well be," I murmured. "Only fictional character is that perfect."

Allecra gave me one of her trademark scowls.

"Aw...you hurt my feelings. If I exist in your mind, then I'm real!"

"Okay, let's suppose that the parallel universe exists," I said. "What does it have to do with me wishing to see the aurora?"

"I could bring you to Alaska in an alternate world, so you don't have to deal with the complicated stuff in this one." She made it sound as easy as a snap of her fingers.

"How are you going to do that?" I asked with a blank face.

"You pull in all your metaphysical energy inside your brain and then turn it inside out."

"You mean visualize it and make it real?" I simplified.

Her extraterrestrial concept was a riddle in itself.

Allecra nodded.

"Do you know how we aliens navigate through space?"

"With your flashy blinking spaceship," I said.

"Well yeah, there is a ship all right, but not exactly how you think it works," she told me. "It is more like a capsule to protect us from the subzero temperature in outer-space. The ship took about an hour to get us here because it was a long distance trip."

"An hour?!" I gasped. "Are you freaking kidding me? I thought it took you years!"

"Oh well, I forgot you humans are still primitive," Allecra said as if to herself. I shot her a withering look.

"Enlighten me then," I muttered.

"Alright, let just think of the universe as a fabric or a canvas instead of an empty space. Then imagine you own a machine so powerful that it could draw energy from the stars."

"You mean like time-machine or a portal?"

"Almost but not quite," she said. "On my home planet, we had like hundreds of Teslas to build that special machine. It could pull in the fabric of the universe like a frog catching a fly with its sticky tongue."

"Do I look stupid if I said I don't get it?" I asked.

Allecra paused for a second before she got up to grab a sheet of blank paper from the island counter. When she sat back down, she began to draw two dots at opposite ends of the stationary.

"Okay, imagine the universe as this sheet of paper, and these two little dots as the Earth and my planet Arzuria. Now tell me how you would connect these dots?"

"I would draw a line between them, why?" I said. Allecra snorted as if I had said something funny.

"If you take a spaceship and travel in a straight line like that, by the time you've reached Earth, you'll be a long-dead skeleton," she said.

"Then how did you do it?"

"I'll show you," Allecra said. She pulled one end of the paper and folded it over in half, touching the dots together. "See? That is our secret of space traveling. The same way I'm gonna take you on our quantum traveling. You don't have to leave here. We'll just bend the fabric of reality and then jump in."

"This still sounds like something out of a horrible science fiction," I said.

"Oh, humans." Allecra sighed in defeat. "Alright then, let me show you how our modern technology works."

She took my hand and got up from the table. Allecra walked me to the hidden elevator in the house. I thought we were going down to her underground library, but it seemed to go even deeper. The doors dinged and slid open. I gasped in total awe at what I saw once again.

"Welcome to our playground," Allecra said, walking backward and pulling me along by the hands.

My eyes scanned around at the white clean place hooked up with transparent monitor screens and metal cases with blinking lights. It looked like a set of Star Wars movies.

"You also have a science lab?" I breathed.

"What kind of an alien who doesn't have a science lab?" she asked with mock horrors.

"How cliché." I scoffed, but she just giggled at me then walked us down the hall to another room. It was getting colder. In fact, it was almost freezing in here. Allecra came to wrap her arms around me and rubbed my shoulders.

"Sorry," she said. "The room has to be kept at this temperature or the computers would heat up and jam."

"What do you hide down here?" I asked curiously. "A flying saucer?"

"Now you're being cliché," Allecra said and rolled her eyes.

When we stopped, we were greeted by a white plastic cover that seemed to hide something. I couldn't tell what it was underneath until Allecra walked to it and pulled the cover off. It fell easily and noisily to the floor, revealing a strange-looking piece of machinery like nothing I had ever seen. It was shaped like a giant ring made of shiny steel.

"What's this?" I asked while my eyes kept staring at the weird object in amazement.

"Triton and I remodeled it after the one that got us here," she told me, "—except this machine is not as powerful as the original one. We can only do short-distant traveling—well—unless my brother and sister join the force. But I know you wouldn't want that, would you?"

I just shrugged and slowly walked around to inspect the object with an intense interest.

"And what does it do?" I finally asked.

"We call it the 'Spindle'," she said. "It spins and manifests your quantum universe into reality— like turning raw cotton into clothes."

"What are you even talking about?" I said with a clueless frown. Allecra gave me a smile before she walked up to me.

"Imagine your thoughts are like fine threads of silk and this machine can weave them into the fabric of reality. Whatever designs your imagination concocts, it will become real."

"What?—How could you materialize something out of nothing?"

"The same way a writer creates a story from nothing. It is the consciousness that creates the material universe, not the other way around," she said. "Come on, Nina, why is it so strange to you? Your people also do stuff like that, only you call it 'magic'."

"You're not an alien version of Doraemon, are you?"

Allecra frowned. "Who is Doraemon?"

"You never heard of him?" I said. "Doraemon is a future cat robot. He has a 4-D pouch on his tummy that he can pull out all sorts of inventions. Come on, you spent a year in Japan!"

"Really? He has a fourth-dimension pouch?" she said, looking perplexed and rather impressed with the notion of a gadget cat. "Well, I didn't know that."

"Maybe you were too busy working in the baby factory," I murmured.

"I'm sorry?"

"Nothing," I said and changed the subject. "So tell me about your machine!"

"Oh, well, we can use the Spindle to teleport us from one dimension to another or just within our own realm."

"There are other dimensions?" I asked with wide eyes.

"Didn't you learn anything in science class at all?" she said.

"Excuse me, Allecra. I've never been taught anything unrealistic like parallel worlds, portals, time machines, or any bizarre alien concepts at all," I pointed out.

"It's because humans are still learning about the universe, but the Arzurians already passed this stage."

"Well then, I just hope that no one knows about your existence," I said. "or they will take you to the NASA lab and put you in a jar."

"They can try," she said with a confident shrug. "I don't know about other aliens, but we, Arzurians, are impossible to track. You know why?"

"Why?"

"Because we're super cool," she said with a smirk. Then she pointed her thumb to the Spindle. "Besides, we've got this magic carpet we used as our private transportation. With the machine, we could jump from one space to another. It was convenient during my days searching for the potential one. That's why nobody was aware of our trespassing. But now that I won't need it anymore, we just keep it here."

"Oh," I breathed, realizing that I was the reason Allecra no longer trotted around the globe, trying to breed with an Earthling. I didn't know whether I should feel flattered or self-conscious about it.

"Do you want to see how it works?" Allecra asked, sounding excited all of a sudden.

"Well...mhmm...I guess," I said with a little hesitance.

"Don't be afraid, it's perfectly safe," she said. "It's like a Hieronymous Machine your people created. All it takes is your faith. If you don't put your mind into it, then it won't work. You must believe with all your heart that it will."

"I have to pretend that it works?"

"Not pretend — believe," she said. "When you believe, your brain sends out a magnetic wave to the universe. In turns, it will start to change things around because your energy is powerful enough to alter the cosmic energy since you're a part of it."

I had to admit I was blown away by Allecra's logic. Finally, I nodded for I trusted her, and I was also eager enough to find out what her alien technology could do.

She took me to the middle of the ring where there was a metal platform to stand on. I couldn't believe all this was actually possible. Maybe it was like turning on a television. We all know how to switch it on and change channels and stuff, but we don't know how it works.

I didn't see Allecra going all over anything like she was supposed to. Instead, she just stood staring at me as if expecting something to happen by itself.

"Aren't you going to turn the lever or push the button or anything, Allecra?" I asked in a whisper.

She just laughed.

"The power source is here," she said and tapped a finger on her temple. "The Spindle operates through mental energy. Something has to connect between your mind and the machine. Now Nina, use your imagination and think of where you want to be."

"I don't know...I can't decide..."

"Just concentrate—visualize it until it feels as real as can be like you are already living it inside your head," she instructed in a calm tone. "You're a writer, right? I believe your mind can picture everything vividly."

"But..."

"Just breathe and close your eyes."

"Okay," I said and then did as I was told.

I couldn't think of anything at first, but I didn't what to disappoint Allecra, so I tried to envision the place I wanted to see. Not Alaska though, since I'd never seen what it was like there. My vision kept slipping away, straying from my grasp. Then I felt Allecra's forehead touched mine. Just like that, it seemed to still my disarrayed thoughts. I pictured the only place I could think of, drawing every fiber in my brain for this make-believe.

I heard whooshing sounds and I realized the giant ring was spinning around us. The temperature in the room seemed to drop even lower. Freezing winds began to whirl in the room. I felt a strange weightlessness in my body. I got panicked at the sensation for a second, but I knew Allecra was there to make sure I was safe. The grip of my arms around her tightened.

A moment later, I opened my eyes to find hers ablaze with bright turquoise light. Even her tattoos glowed. All around us, the blur of the spinning ring began to slow down again. As it stopped, I finally got a glimpse of our surrounding and gasped in utter shock.

We weren't in the lab anymore. I stared wide-eyed. It didn't take me long to recognize where I was because this was exactly how I pictured it in my mind. It was like waking up to a dream rather than reality.

Above me, the azure skies were steep and low with thin white clouds painted on the vault of the blue canvas. Faint twinkling stars lit through the veil that covered the frozen land. Slowly, as if being lured by the view, I broke away from Allecra's hold and walked off to what laid before me. At the far end of the earth's corner stood the taiga forest of birch, fir, and larch. Their leafy branches parted gently, like theater curtains.

Stretching far in front of us was snow-capped mountains so perfect they looked like stage scenery. It was the world unlike the monochrome one we'd just left. Everything all danced in aqua-blue light, shimmering blindingly like heaven. Here stood the mystical, revered, sacred Lake Baikal — one of the most spectacular places on earth.

I could hardly believe my own eyes. Even the chilling fresh air that brushed passed my thin clothes and the freezing cold biting through my slippers felt so real. Under my feet was ice and snow dotted with raised glaciers like jagged crystals. They glowed in bright green hue.

"Oh my god," I whispered. "It's not an illusion, is it?"

"No," Allecra's voice said softly beside me. I still looked about us in disbelief and awe.

"How could you do that?"

"No, you did it. You brought us here. All I did was just to get a hold of your brain signals and let the machine print out your imagination. It's the same as a film role and a projector."

Allecra then came to place her arms around me protectively. It was like she wanted to ward off the cold, but it also seemed she was trying to lock me from drifting away.

"By the way, what is this place?" she asked, "I have never seen it before."

"This is Lake Baikal of Siberia," I told her. "It's where the ice queen cast her spell and where the angels come down to dance. The very name fills Russian hearts with joy. I have always wanted to see it since I was a child. I can't believe we are here now."

"It's beautiful, isn't it?" Allecra whispered into my ear.

"Yes, and phenomenal, too."

"Just like you, Nina," she said and kissed my neck. "You're the first girl who could make it happen, you know that?" Her breath was warm on my skin. I turned around to face her.

"No other potentials have ever done it with you before?" I asked.

"No," she said. "I never felt like showing the world to anyone until you."

I could feel the moisture brimming in my eyes. I smiled and leaned in to kiss her cheek.

"So all of it is truly real?" I said. "Nothing has gone amok in my head? Tell me I'm not hallucinating or going crazy."

"Nina, to all your questions—no," she answered with an amused smile. "You create your own reality. Humans do it all the times. We just do it Arzurian style. Everything's manifested instantly. That's why it's called quantum traveling or jumping. After all, your mind is already a portal to another universe in itself."

"You know, Allecra, you're like my very own Aladdin on the magic carpet," I said, and she chuckled back.

"I thought I was your Doraemon, the robot cat," she said and we both burst out laughing. The cold wind blew again, and she felt my body shivered. "Alright, let's get back before you freeze to death in my arms."

We turned to the Spindle, but I didn't see it anywhere.

"Where's the machine?" I asked, bewildered.

"Don't panic. It's there but back in the lab where we left it," Allecra told me casually. "I know where it is. Just come with me."

"Why wasn't it brought along with us?" I asked.

"It only acts as a gateway transporting you to another place. Just like a good book does to a reader. The physical book is no longer relevant except the world it projects from the pages. And in this sense, so is my machine."

"I see," I said slowly, trying to get my mind around it.

Allecra walked me a few more steps and stopped. I looked around and saw a faint circle mark on the icy ground beneath our feet.

"This reminds me of the crop circles," I said. Allecra just rolled her eyes, which now began to glow again. Before long, I heard the familiar whooshing sound and then the ring slowly reappeared out of thin air. By then, we were transported back to our old world.

CHAPTER 35

I CAME HOME AGAIN with a pounding heart. Though Allecra reassured me that no one would remember I went missing, I was still expecting the worst.

To my relief, the house looked empty. Nobody was standing by the door, waiting to grill me. For that I was grateful, but then I became curious about where everyone had gone to. They probably were still asleep since it was still noon. The party must have taken a toll on them.

I went up to my room. After Allecra showed me her secret toy (no, not that one!), it was like the world wasn't consistent and logical anymore. It was like you put the macaroni cheese in a bowl and shoved it into the microwave then expected to get it back after it was done. You think it's reasonable and normal to find whatever you put into the microwave, but in my case, the macaroni cheese turned into rice pudding.

I guessed from now on, I would have to get used to this new illogical reality while being with Allecra Knight. The blonde alien literally turned my world upside down.

After I closed the door, Piper almost gave me a heart attack by sitting primly on my bed, smiling.

"Piper!" I gasped. "You scared the hell out of me!"

My cousin just stared back with a silly grin on her face and said. "Tell me!"

I blinked hard. "Tell you what?"

"That you just had sex," she said.

My face reddened. I tried to hide my embarrassment by quickly turning to walk towards my closet. I put away Allecra's silk robe she gave me this morning. But my silence seemed to confirm whatever Piper thought I did.

"I can't believe it!" Piper cried and jumped from the bed towards me. "You did?"

"What are you talking about?"

"You know—bumper to bumper? Horizontal tango? Do you understand—*sex?*"

I opened my mouth and closed it again, not wanting to lie or telling the truth at the same time, which made it worse.

"So where are your parents?" I asked to sidetrack her instead.

"They've gone on an urgent business trip for a few days. Dad got promoted as the head of the board so mom has to work closely with him, too," Piper said. "Don't worry. No one is here to chew you out for sneaking off with your hot girlfriend last night."

"I didn't sneak out. It was just a sleepover. We did ask for your parents' permission," I protested lamely.

"Really?" Piper asked in surprise. "That's unfair! How come they never let me do that often?"

My tactic only worked for a moment before Piper's nosiness about my newborn sex life boomeranged at me again.

"So Nina, how was it being with a girl, not to mention Allecra Knight?" she said with an annoying leer. I felt the need to cover my face at that.

"Piper..."

"Oh for god's sake, stop acting like a virgin anymore!" she said. "Tell me, was she good? Did she make you come?"

"Gosh! Piper, you need Jesus!"

"What? I'm just curious! I might come down with a rash if I don't know."

"Well, good doesn't even begin to cover it, okay?" I admitted. Piper pressed her hands to her cheeks like a screaming man on the bridge in the Munch picture. I had a feeling that she was about to scream, too.

"Please, don't do that," I said pointedly.

"Aw, Nina!" Piper squealed. "I'm so amazed and proud of you! What was it like sleeping with a girl?"

I should have seen this coming, and I knew I couldn't escape this anymore.

"Sex is sex. Doesn't matter what gender you do it with," I said. She seemed to mold the idea in her head for a moment.

"So did she use a strap-on?"

"Not all lesbians prefer toys, Piper," I said. "I don't."

Besides, Allecra has a real one, I just wanted to say for the heck of it, but didn't. For the next two hours, Piper fired off a hundred more questions at once accompanied by gasps and squeals over my first time.

I hadn't anticipated this kind of enthusiasm. Why do we all have that one person? I deserved a reward for not digging a hole and crawl into it because of that. Piper only surrendered when I stopped answering her and told her I had homework to finish.

The next day, the heart in me leaped when I saw the black Lamborghini hovered outside. I quickly got out of the house. Allecra was sitting inside her car, staring at me through her dark sunglasses. She took some time to look at me from head to toes, like at any moment she would whip out a measuring tape and start measuring me everywhere. It made me blush.

"Don't look at me with that face, Allecra," I said after I got into the car.

"Well, good morning to you, too," she mocked.

"Stop it," I said crossly.

"Why does my girlfriend become a grumpy old lady all of a sudden?" she asked.

"Nothing," I said. She narrowed her eyes at me. "Well, it's just Piper really got on my nerves last night."

"What was it about?"

"Oh, you know."

"Okay," Allecra said and grinned back as she started the car. "I wouldn't mind if you told her I'm a sex goddess."

I shot her daggers, which made her chuckle as she started to drive away.

In the class, I found myself on the brink of sexual tension all over again. It was felt like an egg balanced on the edge of a table, set to topple over at any moment. I had never felt a strong sexual urge with another person beyond all reasons like that.

Allecra and I weren't a touchy-feely couple, but what we had between us was transcendent. The upshot was that I was burning with a fierce desire for her like a thirst that couldn't be quenched.

We studied ancient Greek plays. *Euripides*, one of the Greek tragedy marked his work by the way things get so mixed up that the characters become trapped. They've all got their own situations and reasons and excuses. Each one was pursuing his or her own brand of happiness and as a result chaos and conflicts take place.

Mrs. Smith was explaining, "In Euripides, there's almost always a point where a god appears in the end and starts directing traffic like this: 'You go over there, you come over here, you get together with her, and you just sit still for a while.' This is called *deus ex machina* ."

"De sex machine?" Michael said.

Mary Jones shot him a disgusted look.

"It's *'deus ex machina'* you immature idiot," she said before flipping her hair and turned back to the teacher.

"But you can no longer write like that, everyone," Mrs. Smith went on, unaware of the dirty joke.

"Why is that?" someone asked.

"Because it's not realistic," she said. "It's a weak plot and doesn't reflect real life at all. Think about it — everything would be so easy in real life if some force would swing down and solve all your problems. You have to make your own choices and mistakes and receive the consequences at the end, whatever it is."

Afterward, we had science class. Our report about Arzuria came back with an A-. There was a teacher's compliment written on it saying it was creative, although it was strange to have floating islands in the air.

Allecra was defensive about it when I said we shouldn't have added that part.

"There were actually islands that floated on my planet," she said. "They contained magnesium and other minerals that created the magnetic force."

"I believe you," I said. "I had seen that in my dream when Xenon tried to manipulate me."

Allecra looked at me with concern. "Has she entered your dream again lately?"

"No," I said.

"Good then," she said with a nod.

After class, I spotted Jordan walking with Rachel, the girl whose head I bonked with a ball. The way Rachel looked at her was obvious that she was in love. I smiled, feeling happy for my Jordan. She deserved someone who loved her back.

I didn't see Jack anywhere though and wouldn't want to either. I was hoping that the *deus ex machina* would just order him to stay out of my life forever. Perhaps, Allecra had already assumed the role and put him in his deserved place.

At lunch, Allecra said she had a surprise for me. Instead of sitting under the Pepper tree, as usual, she brought me to the parking lot and into her car. Then she drove us to a quiet wooded area near the school. She brought out a neatly wrapped bento lunch box and opened the lid.

No wonder she told me not to pack anything today.

Inside was filled with decorated foods. I gasped in utter joy. She even made a cat face out of rice and nori. It was, of course, the wonder cat, Doraemon. I giggled so hard when I saw it. There were also octopi made from hotdogs and star-shaped bread and fish-shaped omelet framed with salad.

"Oh, my...this is so adorable!" I cried. "How long did it take you to finish this?"

"Long enough," she said. "You know why?"

"Why?"

"Because the most important thing about making a bento is to make it with love," she said.

"You're so cheesy," I said, "but so sweet."

Allecra gave me a brilliant smile.

That smile, though, that goddamn smile of hers was my undoing. It made me long to bite her cheeks, though I wouldn't do that. To satisfy my craving, I grabbed her face and kissed her hard on the lips. All the tension that kept mounting up inside me began to melt and flow in a form of heated passion. It enveloped us slowly. Allecra ran her fingers through my hair and pulled my head to her, causing me to moan. Our shortened breaths matched as if we were breathing for one another.

"I've been thinking about it all day, Nina," she whispered hotly into my gasping mouth. "Can I have your taste again?"

It took me a second to understand what she meant. Her hand went up to my thigh, stroking my skin. I was wearing a short black skirt, and now it seemed that it might or might not be a terrible idea.

"Allecra, we're in the car," I said. "People might see us."

"No one's around. If there is, I would know," she said and dipped down to my exposed neck. "Nina, just a little, please?"

My heart melted at her plea, but it would seem I was too easy if I surrendered that quickly.

"But...what about our lunch...?" I tried to speak after her face buried in between my breasts and nuzzled them like she was a wild boar.

"We can eat it later," she said. "Now I'm starving for something else."

My heart rate went crazy at that, and I could feel the wetness seeped through my panties as the heat stirred from the pulsing lust between my legs.

She slipped her hands under my skirt and pulled down my panties. Then I felt her fingers touching me. My jaw dropped and eyes fluttered at the wonderful motions of her sensual caress. Allecra's lips curled in a smile at the generous amount of my juices.

"Open your legs, please," she said with a hint of teasing.

"Nnhh..." It was hard to get out another protest when my mind went haywire by the electrifying sensation. Allecra chuckled.

"Your body already said 'yes' to me," she whispered in a sultry voice and grinned at me. "Come on...be a good girl."

I bit my bottom lip and coyly granted her what she wanted. My body did need this release. It was a surprise that I wanted it already. I didn't have to say anything. Allecra just understood. With her lust-filled eyes, she turned me gently so that my back was against the locked door of the car.

Once I was facing her, she began to roll up my skirt and parted my legs. Her unapologetic action made me blush scarlet. I was still embarrassed about having my femininity exposed that my hands went to cover my private immediately.

"Aw Nina, why?" Allecra said and pulled back to look at me with a miserable face. She was not pleased about it. But then she leaned back in and kissed my inner thighs over and over. Her soft lips nibbled over my hands as if seeking access to my girlhood. Despite my shyness, it made me giggle at the ticklish feeling. I knew what she was looking for, and pity filled my heart.

Slowly, I loosened my clamping hands and let Allecra dig her way in like an eager butterfly finding her favorite flower. Her tongue reached out to suckle on the nectar from my heated core. It sent my mind reeling. I whimpered aloud at the shocking pleasures.

After a while, Allecra took no prisoners. She was devouring every hidden depth of me. Within a few minutes, I was on the verge of coming with overflowing joy. One of my hands gripped over the handle on the ceiling while the other twisted in those silky blonde strands. My hips buckled and legs trembled uncontrollably to the ravenous tongue going in and all over me. I felt my juices trickling down her car seat. But it seemed Allecra wanted me hanging over the cliff of blissfulness a while longer.

"You taste so amazingly sweet," Allecra murmured against my excited sex. It sent a vibration up my shivering walls.

Seeing Allecra's face between my parted thighs, feasting on me like I was something delicious made my body shudder in both ecstasy and happiness.

The gripping convulsion burst in my throbbing core. My body arched as I cried out from worldly pleasures.

"Mmmh...good girl," Allecra said and smacked her lips as she pulled away. Her lips and chin were coated with my arousal. Then she got some tissues to clean me up. I sat straight again and watched her intimately take care of me with such affection and love.

When she finished, I pulled up my panties and smoothed back my skirt. I looked back at Allecra, who was already staring at me with twinkling dilated eyes.

"Sorry," she said, which surprised me.

"For what?" I said.

"I just love seeing your face when I make you come. You looked sexy."

"Don't you think it's a bit unfair that I couldn't see yours like that, too?" I said. "You think I'm uncomfortable with this, but you don't let me do it to you."

Allecra seems to be caught off guard with my words.

I leaned towards her slowly, afraid that I might scare her away again. My hands coaxed her back to her seat. Our eyes locked. Allecra swallowed hard at the seriousness on my face.

"Nina..."

My hand went over to her private and stroked her. I heard Allecra took in a sharp breath. A familiar stirring pressure and heat coursed through her body. I began to notice the growing bulge of her hidden member. Allecra's chest heaved louder as my fingers began to unzip her pants. Slithering inside like an eel, I found her secret already straining to get out. Then it sprang up into the open air. I suppressed my gasp this time. Not that I was scared, but I was more awestruck and driven by the same old curiosity. Her pinkish tip was already slick with clear juices. It was obvious she got real hard right away. Allecra's turquoise eyes found mine again. I could see the same look of nervousness in them. Her hands clutched onto the seat firmly, as if to refrain herself from moving.

"Sorry," she said, her voice was hoarse and thick with struggles. "I didn't mean to."

"It's okay," I said. "I understand how it is. Nothing you can do about it."

I cradled her erection gently, feeling her over like it was the most curious thing in the world, which was probably the case.

"Nina, you don't have to do anything," she said again, but her face contorted in concealed pleasures. "It will go away eventually."

"But I want to," I said. "You said if you don't help yourself, you will be visited by Mother Nature, do you want me to help out?"

"Maybe."

"Maybe?"

My hand grasped her a little harder. Allecra groaned deep in her throat.

"Yes!" she corrected herself. "I want you to. I can't even tell you how badly I want it."

I smiled and began to move my hand along her pulsating length. I had never done this, but it didn't take a rocket scientist to figure out what pleasures look like on a lover's face.

I couldn't believe we were actually doing the dirty inside the car. It was a strange new feeling. It seemed desperate and yet also arousing. I felt like we were two sneaky lovers that couldn't keep their hands off each other.

"Just so you know, I'm not giving you head," I said. "But this I can do for you."

Allecra smiled.

"I know."

"You do?"

"You have class. You are too cool for that," she said.

"Or maybe I'm just too gay for that," I said.

She giggled a little.

"I can't believe you're actually doing this to me," Allecra said, breathless.

"Me, too," I replied with a hot blush. "How is it?"

"Indescribable," she said. "But you can stop if you don't like it. I'm not forcing you."

"No, not until you're finished," I said. "Just let me know when you're about to come, okay?"

"Okay," she said and let out a big sigh. I could feel the trembling in her body. I reached my free hand out to card through her hair. She turned her cheek into my palm and I went to kiss her lips.

A minute later, Allecra had to pull away and told me she was coming. I quickly grabbed some tissue from the compartment between our seats. The blonde shuddered in my hand and hot thick gooey juices spurted out.

"Oh, Nina!"

Allecra came over and over. There was so much juice coming out of her. It was like it was squirted out from a water pistol. I was afraid the tissues weren't enough to catch it all. Not that I minded.

A little while later Allecra finished, but she grabbed the heavy tissue away from me and opened the window before tossing it outside. She looked at me again to see my confused and quite disappointed face. I wanted to ask her why she did that.

"Don't worry," she said. "It doesn't glow in the dark."

"I'm not..." I was about to say, but Allecra sealed my lips with hers.

"I love you, Nina," she said against my mouth. "I love you so much."

I smiled into our kiss.

After it was all over and everything got cleaned up properly, we began to eat our lunch together with *Nouvelle Vague* playing in the background.

CHAPTER 36

THE NEXT DAY, Allecra took me to a bookshop after school. I told her I wanted to buy a few books that I must read for a book report in Mrs. Smith's class.

"You don't have to buy any more books," Allecra complained during the ride. "I have a whole library for you."

"Those are *your* books," I said.

"Nina, you should know by now that everything I have is yours," she said, "including me."

My lips stretched into a wide smile. I savored her every move and then looked at our joined hands that rested on her lap as she drove. And once again, I was drunk by the intoxicating richness of her love. I wondered if at any moment, she might explode into pixie dust because of too much cuteness packed inside her. I giggled to myself, and Allecra turned sideways at me.

"What's so funny?" she asked quizzically. I shook my head back.

"Nothing," I said and bit my lips from smiling like a silly lovesick girl. Allecra frowned at me behind her dark sunglasses. We stopped at the traffic light.

"With that cheeky attitude, I'm not sure if we should go to the bookstore or somewhere else quiet," she said. Then she gave me a wicked half smile that sent my thoughts scattered in all directions.

"Allecra...yes...I meant...no...we...should go to the bookstore. I just want some books that are age-appropriate for me," I said, trying to collect my marbles back. "You don't have the ones I want to read."

"You think my literary taste is dull?" she said.

"Not dull, just cringe-worthy," I said. "I don't think I would want to torture myself reading War and Peace, or Ulysses like you."

"Hey, at least half of the War and Peace is good," she protested. "And though Ulysses seems like it was written by a perverted lunatic, the rude passages make sense."

"Just so you know, that kind of books put my sanity at risk," I said with a grimace, "All the more reason to find my own genre."

"Okay, whatever you want, kitten," she said.

I smiled at her, feeling all mushy again.

We found a nice bookshop and decided to go in. It was rather spacious inside and very cozy, the nicest bookstore I'd been in. The interior was lit with craft lamps from the high ceilings. The floor was carpeted. There were bestsellers displays and rows of shelves marked with labels. A few middle-age men were browsing through self-help books at the non-fiction section. An elderly couple was at the counter, already checking out. There were also a couple of children lingering about at the children lit section.

We walked past the two siblings, a girl and a boy who were sitting on the floor, engrossed with the illustrations of Charlotte's Web. I smiled at them when they looked up. They returned the smile sweetly, which was the most heart-warming gesture ever. And for a flitting moment, I imagined having those little humans I could read bed-time stories to. But when the kids saw Allecra, they quickly closed the book and skedaddled off to their parents. It wasn't the impression that something about the blonde scared them away, but it was more like a childish shyness. Allecra just had this strange effect on children, and I didn't know why. I looked at Allecra, who gave a one-shoulder shrug.

"Human kids are weird," she murmured. "I don't know how I could handle them if I ever had one."

"You don't want a mini-you running around anymore?" I asked, half-teasing and half-serious.

"Well, I still do," she said. "But if you're not the mother, then never mind."

My heart faltered at that. Maybe it was because of a slight tone of longing in her voice and the wishful look in her eyes that exuded a turbulent change of mood.

"Allecra, we've talked about this before," I said with a low sigh and then cast my eyes down. It was funny that somehow I still felt guilty for something I had every right not to. Allecra put her arms around me and gave a little rub on my back as if to simmer down the awkwardness between us.

"I'm sorry," she whispered. "I didn't mean to. Let's not think about it again, okay?"

I nodded.

We strolled along the aisle of Young Adult Fiction. The graphic designs of a few works caught my eyes. I picked one up to read its previews. Allecra did the same with the other, flipping through the fresh yellowish pages.

"This book is kinda boring," she said after a while later. "Don't bother wasting your time or money on this one. The trees that died to make the paper for this book would never rest in peace."

I was shocked at Allecra's brutal comment.

"How do you know?!"

"I've just finished one-third of it," she said casually.

"You what?" I said. "You only picked it up like ten seconds ago! How could you tell it's boring?"

She pointed to herself and said, "Alien."

I realized then that aside from being a literary prodigy, Allecra also had super reading speed. That was probably the only thing I envied about her.

"Anyway, you shouldn't be so rude like that, Allecra," I said, "Maybe you should read some of these books. They can be really good, you never know."

"Why?" she said skeptically. "I only read from authors that are already dead."

"Seriously?" I asked in bewilderment.

"I just find the recent works unrealistic and ridiculous," she said and shrugged.

"Don't judge a book by its cover, or in this case, its cliché," I defended. "Sometimes it tells a unique story entirely."

"Oh really?" Allecra said then she held up the copy and flipped through it. "How about writing something more realistic than *'a bookworm girl falling in love with a hot young billionaire orphan with a desire to beat women up so that he could get off'*?" Then she threw her hands in the air as a sign of disbelief, "I mean, really? The girl should call the police!"

"Hmm," I said and squinted my eyes at her. "Should I be worried about some hot rich alien girl, too?"

"Excuse me?"

"Never mind," I said. "So what kind of story ideas do you think are realistic anyway?"

Allecra pursed her lips to think.

"Well, how about, *'A geeky girl goes out with a jock only to learn that he has no hidden depth. ?'*"

It made me burst out laughing. "You're unbelievable!"

"Oh, here's another one," Allecra continued, "*'A cheerleader meets a football captain. There's no sexual tension. The captain already has a boyfriend.'*"

"That sounds like the kind of books I would much prefer to buy," I said between giggles.

"Or better yet, *'A girl kisses a boy, doesn't like it. Kisses another girl, likes it much more.'*"

This time I laughed harder, causing a few passersby to glance at us.

"How about, *'an openly gay girl falling in love with a hot blonde girl, who turns out to be an alien hermaphrodite'*?" I said.

"That's not realistic," Allecra said with a frown then hurled my body against hers roughly. "That's fantastic, and I sensed you're being a sarcastic kitten again, aren't you?"

"Allecra, there are people around here," I whispered.

"I can tell you a dozen more realistic themes," she said. "Maybe you can write a love story with your nails on my back, and I'll write love poems with my tongue on your skin."

"Allecra, stop..."I said. But her enamored words did send a chilling tingling up my backbone in such an inappropriate time and place that I had to wriggle myself out of her arms.

"Feel free to shut me up with your lips anytime, gorgeous," she murmured huskily and leaned over towards me, but I pushed her back and walked away. She just chuckled.

At the center of the bookshop, I found a table where they displayed typewriters. I gasped and fell immediately head over heels.

"Allecra, they have typewriters!" I said. Allecra followed behind me. There were about a dozen of them, ranking from old to modern-looking ones. They came in different sizes and colors, from vintage black to lustrous pink! My hands felt over the round-shaped keys with characters printed on. I was itching to hit one or two, but dared not.

"Which one you like?" Allecra asked. "The pink one?"

"I don't know," I said, intrigued. "They're all unique."

Then my eyes caught sight with a red Remington Starfire. It was the most beautiful one among the rest —small and slim. Its sleek color looked like a bright red rose with black keyboard set like empty theater seats.

"You like this one?" Allecra asked again. My eyes glanced at the price and suddenly felt deflated. It was over five hundred dollar.

"No," I said and shook my head. "It's fine."

"You know, Nina, you can have all of them if you just give me a nod," she said. I turned to her sharply.

"What am I going to do with all of them?!" I said. "I don't want you to spend your money on me. Besides, I already have a laptop at home."

It made her roll her eyes, but I ignored her.

When we were done browsing, we went to the check-out counter with my chosen books. There were a few other customers there, so we had to wait in line. I got myself a copy of *The Martian Chronicle, Fahrenheit 451*, and *1984*, which was the second book I read by George Orwell after *Animal Farm*. Not everyone knows Animal Farm is a satire of the Russian Revolution. All of the books were recommended by Allecra. I figured they suited her extraterrestrial taste better.

"Hand me the books and wait here," she said. I gave her the copies and she left. An infatuated male cashier stared at her in obvious awe as she approached. I snickered at the comical scene.

While Allecra was checking out the books for me, the bell dinged as the glass door of the bookstore opened. By reflex, I glanced up and saw someone I didn't expect to see.

"Hey, Nina!" her surprised voice was clear and melodious in my ear, but I still hadn't prepared for this encounter yet. There were a few nanoseconds before I could make myself speak.

"Hello, Eva," I greeted the violinist. "Nice to see you again."

"You too," she said. "You're here by yourself?"

"Oh no, I'm not...I'm with...er..." I said and then paused, not sure how to tell her.

"I'm done, let's go," Allecra's voice called out. Eva and I turned to her at the same time. The blonde froze in her track as she stared at us. A spark of surprise ignited in her turquoise eyes. There was a moment of silence as the three of us stood in the middle of the shop, staring at each other awkwardly.

"Hey," Eva finally said in a quiet tone, clearly didn't expect this incidence as well.

"Hi," Allecra said with a cordial smile.

"I didn't expect to see you two here," Eva breathed again. Under a white jacket she wore a yellow silk blouse, which were finely tailored and looked stylish, yet at the same time sophisticated. She definitely knew how to dress. And in that instance, the violinist was the second sight that stood out the moment she stepped in. The first was, of course, the quiet blonde beside me. I felt the need to say something to break the tension.

"Yeah, so how's everything with you so far?" I asked Eva. "You settle in well?"

"Oh so far so good," she said. "I just moved into an apartment with a good friend of mine. I'm here to find some music books before the term start."

"Oh, I see," I said, "By the way, I didn't get a chance to thank you personally. Thank you for the beautiful performance the other night. Everyone loved it."

Eva smiled shyly.

"My pleasure, Nina," she said, "I think we should hang out sometimes, maybe go shopping or see a movie. Piper should come along. What do you think?"

"We would love to," I said because there was no way I could reject that. I gave a brief glance at Allecra, who paid more attention to her shoes than usual.

"What about you, Allecra?" Eva said, which caused her to look up again.

"Yes?—Oh no, I'm good," she said with a shake of her head. "You both can go and have fun. Thanks for asking."

There was another pause before Eva turned to me and her smile brightened again.

"I hope to get in touch with you soon," she said. "Have a good day both of you."

"You too, Eva, take care," I said with a small wave and the violinist moved inside and we turned towards the door. I looked at Allecra again. She seemed particularly distracted.

We got into our car a while later.

"You're alright?" I decided to ask her.

"I'm fine," she replied casually. "Why?"

"I'm just worried about you," I told her honestly, "Seeing Eva again might trouble you, I know."

She turned and studied my face.

"There's no reason to look back when you have so much to look forward to, Nina," she said, staring into my eyes. Then Allecra leaned it and kissed my forehead. After that, she started the car and drove off.

But instead of going to my home, she took me to a place by the beach and parked the Lambo near the cliff.

"Why did you bring me here?" I asked.

"To get some fresh air," Allecra said.

We got out of the car, and she brought out a blue blanket from the trunk. Allecra took me by the hand as we hiked down the grassy hill. When we reached the beach, I had to take off my heels, because the sand was so soft. There were no other people there. The evening sun began to hung lower beyond the ocean. Allecra and I found a good spot by a big rock and lay the blanket on the white sand. We made a nest for ourselves and lay side by side, looking up at the pale blue sky. As the sun began to set, the clouds turned bright pink and orange over the sea. All we could hear was the sound of seagulls and the splashing of waves.

"It's beautiful here," I said as I took in a deep breath of fresh air. My words hovered in the gentle winds that brushed against our skin.

"My favorite place," Allecra said.

"You seem quiet," I noted. She glanced over at me and laced our fingers together.

"The thing about Eva," she said. "I want to make it clear to you that there's nothing romantic between us anymore."

"I know. I just don't understand how you two could do it," I said. "I can't imagine seeing you with another girl. It must have hurt a lot. And it seems to me you both haven't forgotten about each other yet."

"Nina, moving on doesn't mean you forget about things," Allecra said. "It just means you have to accept what happened and continue living."

"You're right," I said, but this meaningless response floated in the air like a drifting cloud above us. I felt her hand came up to my cheek and turned my face to her.

353

"The Japanese say you have three faces," she said. "The first face, you show to the whole world. The second face, you show to your close friends and family. The third face, you never show to anyone. That face is the truest reflection of who you are."

"Why are you telling me this?" I asked, propping myself on one elbow to look at her. Allecra stared at me. The evening light made her turquoise eyes shone like purple galaxy. I could see the gold flicks spreading like stardust in them.

"I want to tell you that sometimes when you're not guarding yourself against the world, I can see your innermost face," she said. "It's the most beautiful one, the most brilliant and compassionate one, but it's always hidden. It's hidden because it has flaws. Among all the beautiful things it can show, there are also fears, insecurities, vulnerabilities, and doubts."

"I know that I'm not perfect," I whispered. Then her hands pulled me down into her embrace. I wrapped my arm around her and curled up into her body.

"Nina, when I first saw you, I thought that you were perfect, so I fell in love with you," she said. "And now that I see you're not perfect, I love you even more."

I heard a seagull squeaked in the distance. I guessed the gulls might cry if we were apart.

"I love you, too, Allecra," I said and brought my lips to hers.

We kissed and listened to the sound of waves and whistling sea breeze, and nothing was more wonderful than this.

At home, I bathed and prepared a simple dinner for the twins. Jay came home at 7:30 followed by Piper five minutes later. It was unusual for either of them to be this early when their parents were away. They would be back at least around eleven or twelve at night the last time we were on our own.

I went to the kitchen and brought beef sautéed in butter with a Caesar salad and chicken soup. Jay sat at the island a moment later. He and I hadn't talked to each other since the party night. I should be mad at his insolent remark to Allecra, but now I just pitied him for having a brain stuffed with so much ignorance.

Jay cleared his throat to get my attention.

"Nina," he said. I looked up. "I—I just wanna say I'm sorry for dissing out on your girlfriend that night. I was drunk and..."

"That's alright, I'm not mad," I said without looking as I put the salad into a bowl.

"Really?" he said, looking relieved.

"I know that the brain has two sides, left and right. Unfortunately, your right one is lost and the left is also out looking for it."

He thought for a second and then burst out laughing.

"Aww, Nina, that's a good one!" he said and laughed some more. It's kind of irritating when people are so dented to be offended by your insult that they find it humorous instead. I rolled my eyes.

"Hey, what's so funny?" Piper said as she appeared into the kitchen. Before she said anything more, the phone rang. My cousin went to answer it.

"Robert Black's residence," she said and then after a pause, she exclaimed, "Oh, hey Eva!"

My head turned at the sound of her name.

"Yeah, I'm free tomorrow," she was saying, "...oh shopping? Sure!—We can just do that."

Then my cousin glanced at me and nodded to the voice on the other side.

"Of course, I'll let her know," Piper said and then ended the conversation.

"Who are you talking to?" Jay asked.

"It's Eva Shapiro, the famous violinist!" she said and turned to me. "She doesn't have your number, and she asked if we would like to hang out with her tomorrow."

"Can I go with you, too?" Jay said, looking hopeful.

"No, just girls only," Piper said. "Guys are gross testosterone lumps, and speaking of which I'm still mad at you for inviting Jack to the party."

"Aw!" her brother cried. "I thought he wanted to make up with you."

"No, he's an idiot and so are you," Piper said.

"How is he now?" I asked Jay.

"He's alright," he said. "Why?"

The twins turned to look at me. I realized they didn't know what really happened that night, so I turned back to my cooking.

"Anyway, I don't want anything to do with him again, like ever," Piper said.

"Well," Jay said and scratched his neck, "He's kinda acting weird lately. He seems paranoid of something and is hinting that he wants to change school."

"Really?" I said in surprise. Jay just shrugged back.

"Whatever," Piper said. "It's not my concern."

Clearly, I didn't know how bad Allecra had damaged his poor nerves, and I felt a bit sorry for Jack Conner.

"So when does Eva want to meet?" I asked Piper to change the topic.

"Tomorrow afternoon," she said, looking excited again. "I just hope we get paparazzi following us."

But I had an awkward feeling stirring inside me. It was obvious that Eva wanted to meet me for some reason. Although things between Allecra and I had reached a new high, I just didn't know if I was ready to face her ex alone. What was Eva thinking about?

The next morning at school, I decided not to tell Allecra about it. I felt like it was best not to bring back the spark to the old flame. Not that I was hiding from her, but I was not in the position to be certain what it was going down that lane. Piper awaited me in front of the house when Allecra dropped me off. I prayed so hard for my cousin to stay where she was.

"I'll see you tomorrow," I said to Allecra. She nodded with a smile, but still had a strange gleam in her eyes I couldn't tell why. After briefly kissing her cheek, I walked out of the car. The blonde drove away, and I walked towards the house.

"Come on, Eva is waiting inside," Piper said.

"She's here?" I asked in shock and turned over my shoulder to see if Allecra was really gone. My cousin just nodded. When we entered the house, I saw the violinist sitting in the living room, talking to Jay, or rather being flirted with by him.

"Eva, Nina's here," Piper called out. "Her hot girlfriend just dropped her off."

I almost wanted to cover her mouth. I didn't know why Piper had to overstate things like she was a herald of my love life. Eva turned around and stood up with a sweet smile. She wore a cotton top with a brown leather jacket and a flowing mini skirt. As usual, she was stunning. Jay didn't look too pleased to be interrupted. He was probably trying to get scored with the violinist.

"See you again, Nina," Eva said with a cordial smile.

"Hi," I said with a small wave back.

"I hope you don't mind going out today?" she said.

"Not at all," I said.

"Okay," Piper said. "You go get ready then."

After I showered and got dressed in the best clothes I owned, I went down stairs again. I had no time to pounder over how to look effortless like Eva. Piper suggested we ride in her car since Eva didn't have a car yet, and mine felt too small for us three.

When we got into the Porsche with its roof down, Eva announced that she would like to go to a certain shop, whose owner was one of her good friends. During the ride, I watched the sights of Los Angeles passing by and felt a pang of homesickness in my gut. Moscow wasn't so fancy and vibrant as this city, but to me, it was just grand.

We went to a boutique that sold designer brands. There Piper bought a new bag and some jeans. I even got myself a new leather jacket. Eva bought two dresses, both of thin materials and four pairs of Jimmy Choo's and Dr. Martens's. She paid with a gold credit card and asked for the items to be delivered to her address. We hang around from store to store for a while.

Afterward, we went to a hair salon. The place was like a dance studio, with shiny wooden floors and mirrors covering the walls. There were two rows of revolving chairs, and everywhere beauticians were coming and going with dryers and hairspray and whatnot.

I didn't intend to get myself primped up, but it was impossible once you get inside a salon. Piper was getting her manicure at the other side of the room. Eva and I sat beside each other on the chairs while I pretended everything wasn't awkward between us.

I realized she didn't ask to do anything for herself, just a bit of trimming up.

"You really have beautiful hair, Nina," Eva suddenly said, which surprised me. She was looking at me through the mirror.

"Thank you," I said and blushed a little at her compliment.

The man who was to take care of my hair said, "Honey, there's nothing more I can do to this hair. But whatever you do, don't cut it, okay? Like ever."

"Why?"

"Girl, I wish I had your hair. It's this thick and bouncy and shiny," he said. "Men love it."

"I'm not into men, though," I said.

"Oh my my! One of us!" the hairdresser said, and he looked totally happy to hear that. "Alright, I'll turn you into an instant knock-out in no time, baby."

Eva and I caught eyes with each other and muffled our giggle.

Afterward, Piper came to us and declared that she wanted to get her platinum blonde hair dyed.

"Are you sure?" I asked.

"I want something that makes me look more mature," she said.

"Piper, you look mature when you act mature, not because of the color of your hair," I said.

"No, I also think that it's time for a change," she said. "I want the new-me look."

Eva leaned towards me and whispered, "What happened to her?"

"Some idiot broke her heart," I whispered back. Eva nodded with a small 'oh'.

While we had to wait for Piper, Eva suggested we went to a café next to the salon.

"You want something to eat, Piper?" I asked.

"Just get me a hot latte. I could use some caffeine now," she said while her head was covered with foils.

When we entered the expensive-looking café, Eva did a quick circuit. She seemed to look for a place quiet enough for us to sit. I thought we were only here to order and get back again, but it looked like it wasn't what she had in mind. I realized Eva wanted to have a moment with me.

We took a seat opposite each other. Then a waiter with a Pompadour hairdo, wearing a black bow and a long apron around his waist, came to take our orders. I asked if they had non-caffeine beverages, which he suggested a glass of lemon tea. Eva ordered an espresso and a Perrier. The waiter apologized that they had no Perrier and asked if he could bring tonic water instead. Eva thought about this for a second before she accepted. I had never known a woman who knew exactly what she wanted. I couldn't even see the difference. She reminded me of Allecra. But Eva was more of how she was brought up as a refined sophisticated lady while the blonde was naturally particular about everything.

After the waiter left, the silence descended on the two of us. Eva had an air of deep thought. Her forest green eyes stared at me with a gentle curiosity. In that moment, my imagination suddenly ran riot, and I thought about all the intimate things Allecra and the violinist must have done together in the past. It was unbearable to picture Allecra had bodily pleasures with this beautiful girl. I knew it was ridiculous of me to think of their past, but I just couldn't stop feeling that way when I looked at Eva.

Soft ambient music floated into the room. Everything seemed to go slower in here than the world outside. It was like the time flowed in different speed from where we were sitting.

"I love this song," Eva suddenly said. "Do you know it, Nina?"

I shook my head 'no'. But it didn't matter because she seemed to already expect the answer. She just smiled brightly.

"This is Canon by Pachelbel in D major," she said.

Although I knew Eva was a musician, I was still amazed at how she could tell a music by ears so precisely. Sitting with her, I felt like my own talent was nonexistent. In fact, I didn't even know if I was good at anything at all.

"It's beautiful," I said, and I meant it. Then a different waiter arrived. He looked a bit older than the last with sideburns and mustache.

"Miss Shapiro?"

"Yes?"

"My apology for our service earlier," he said politely. "We've just got for you the Perrier you requested, and all your beverages today will not be charged, so please enjoy your drinks in our café."

"Oh, thank you!" Eva said sweetly. "That's really kind of you."

"For a special guest like yourself, you're most welcome," he said with a smile at both of us before placing our drinks on the table. When he left, Eva took her first sip of the coffee.

"Does it happen often?" I asked. Eva just smiled sheepishly.

"No, just a few times," she said. "Café owners are mostly music lovers. In fact, a lot of my fans know me because of places like this, too."

"I see," I said and drank my tea as well.

"You don't drink coffee, do you?" Eva said just to be conversational, but I felt a little embarrassed to answer her.

"No, I have a low caffeine tolerance," I said. The violinist was probably thinking, how Allecra ended up with a highschool girl, who had no elegant class nor special talents, or trendy taste, whatsoever.

"Oh, lucky you!" she said. "I'm a caffeine addict. I can't live without coffee."

"If I had a dollar for every time I heard this," I said, which made the violinist chuckle. I beamed back. She put her cup down and took out a handkerchief to dab at her lips.

"You know, we people find happiness in something petty like that," she said and then sighed, "But happiness is just a denial reaction to life."

"A denial reaction?" I asked.

"You're probably still too young to get it, but as a musician, melancholy is a sign of considerable self-awareness for me," she went on. "Have you ever noticed? Those who have embraced sadness have produced some of our finest art. Had Beethoven started taking Prozac, we might never have heard the 'Eroica' symphony. Had Van Gogh found his satisfaction, we'd never have seen his masterpieces to brighten up our own little lives. Beethoven, Franz Kafka, Mussorgsky, all miserable, but the sad people make the world a happier place. There's an Arabic *saying 'Sunshine all the time makes a desert.'* Happiness is like the phases of the moon."

"I'm sorry, I'm afraid I don't quite understand what you're trying to say," I said.

"Let's cut to the chase then," she said. "I know how you must feel having me around. But before you get suspicious of my intention, I must make it clear that I mean you no harm."

I was silent as I waited to see she was getting at.

"What I'm saying is, I know about your relationship with Allecra, and I believe you have some basic of knowledge about our past as well. Yet that's not the sole reason why I wanted to have a talk with you. As a girl to another girl, I have to tell you what you should know."

"What is it that I should know?" I said.

"It's about Allecra," she said with a soft sigh. "She gives you all sort of things you wish for, doesn't she? She has this knack of making you feel special, so special, that you start to believe you're the only one that matters most in the world. And believe me, in a way, you are special. That's why she chose you. You're not like any other girls out there, Nina. There's an endless depth in your eyes. But this should not feed your optimistic innocence and steer you away from the truth."

"What do you mean by that?"

"You know what Allecra is, and what she wants from you," she said. "I don't need to go into details."

"If it's like what I think you meant, I can tell you that Allecra doesn't care about it anymore," I told her. Eva's face showed a little of surprise when she heard it, but then it smoothed out again.

"Yes, I can tell how much she has changed," she said. "It's like seeing a different person now. Not that she wasn't a great lover when we were together. She was perfect in every way. I'm sure you can agree on that. She was everything I could ever wish for as a life partner. But then one day, she just left. To put it plainly, I envy you, Nina. I envy you for getting a hold of her heart now. I saw that much in her eyes. The way she stared at you. It's something I wish I had. I'm sorry for feeling this way. I couldn't help it. But then again, I pity you more."

"Why?" I said in a voice barely above a whisper.

"I'm not saying that you don't deserve all these. In fact, I'm just worried about you. I want you to know that you shouldn't entrust your happiness entirely on her. One day she might leave you just like she did with me."

The thing is when I'm really angry, I don't rage. I go all cold and apparently that freaks people out. And now I could see that Eva seem to back paddle.

"Nina, I care about you," she said. "You're a wonderful person. You make people feel at ease in your company. I like you, like a sister the instant we met. But this is the truth you must accept."

Her voice was sincere enough that it made me realize that anger wouldn't solve anything.

"Allecra will never leave me," I said at last.

"You might be right, Nina, but things are not that simple," she sighed, "Her siblings will not take it lightly. They are here to make sure they have what they aim for. They won't allow their plan to go barren. You're a smart girl. You must know what would happen. I don't want this thing to ruin your life."

I sat quiet, staring at the ice melting inside the glass. My chest tightened, and I felt the lump swelled up in my throat.

"Nina, you still have many days ahead of you, your future, your passions and many more," Eva continued, almost in an atoning voice. "I don't want to see you get hurt like me. That's all I want to say."

Then she stood up. It seemed she wanted to say something more to me but, in the end, decided against it.

"I'll get Piper the coffee," she said. Then with a low sigh, she walked away. I closed my eyes and the darkness began to blend, and I felt the silence burrowed its way into my brain and the shell that held me.

CHAPTER 37

THAT NIGHT, Eva's words made sleeping difficult for me. Seconds turned to minutes, and minutes to hours. I lied in bed and clutched the pillow with my thoughts scattered around like leaves falling from a dead tree.

I should have been worrying about something else, something sensible like homework, SAT test, college applications, part-time jobs, or even the so-called writing contest, which I hadn't even started yet. Those were the things normal teenagers should be worried about. Not sex or the risk of unwanted pregnancy or the threat of someone you love leaving you. But now, there wasn't a single person in the world knew how this private burden weighted me down.

Allecra loved me, no room for doubt about it. But Xenon would never turn a blind eye on this for long. I could feel her patience wearing thin. She had warned me the last time we talked. How I should reconsider my position while I still could. That was perfectly clear that she would end things between Allecra and me if I remained unbent.

But I wasn't the kind of person who would deceive myself. It was not what I wanted from the start, and no one could make me. That was the stubbornness, the hidden rebellion that had sent me all the way across the ocean in the first place. My father would call it 'impenetrable heart'.

Not that it hadn't crossed my mind about giving what Allecra wanted. In fact, it'd always been tugged in the back of my head the whole time. Yet I still believed that our relationship didn't have to be this way.

Eva was right about one thing. I was going to throw my life and future away if the breeding worked between me and Allecra. If it didn't, I would be too selfish to keep her with me. Although she loved and respected my decision, was the blonde alien truly happy knowing her ultimate dream and life mission would never be fulfilled because of me?

And if I agreed to have her baby, it could only complicate my life even more. So many changes and uncertainties I would have to face that I wasn't ready for. I honestly didn't know what to do.

All those thoughts drifted like fog in my mind. I fell asleep a few times and woke up just as often. These were short, unsettled snatches of sleep. It was one of those nights where you question everything and nothing feels right. Time wobbled by like a wagon with a loose axle until the light changed outside the window.

I was late when I woke up. Allecra had already been waiting outside. Concerned about her patience, I showered and dressed in haste. White clouds hung low at the horizon. The spring morning breeze seemed to carry excessive pollen in the air.

Inside the car, Allecra stared at me with an unusual scrutiny. It was as if she was detecting something behind the smiling mask of my face. I gave her a sloppy kiss on the lips. After all these times, she still looked a bit startled at my enthusiastic show of affection.

"What?" I asked.

"You're in a good mood despite looking like a panda," she noted.

"Oh," I breathed and touched my face in alarm. "I was up late doing some writing last night."

A blatant lie.

Allecra sighed and shook her head at me. She reached her hands out and smoothed the skin under my eyes, which felt slightly puffy.

"How was your night out with the girls?" she asked, but she sounded like I had just got back from a battle rather than a time with Eva and Piper. For a moment, I thought I had seen the worry in her eyes like she was expecting some bad news.

"It was nice," I said, which was partly true. "I bought a few clothes. Oh! And Piper dyed her hair. Guess what color she picked?"

"Huh?" she said.

"Dark brown with dip-dyed turquoise! But don't worry. It turned out great, though," I said, "Piper's definitely flaunting it now."

"Glad you didn't do anything to yours," Allecra just said, running her fingers through my hair. "Don't ever dye it, okay? I love your hair natural like that."

"Okay, mamochka."

"Aw, don't call me that." She grimaced.

"What do I call you then?"

"Call me daddy," she said.

I gasped at her.

"I will never *ever* call you that, Allecra," I said and cringed to myself. She chuckled back.

"Alright, alright, I'm just kidding," she said and then started the car.

As we drove to school, we chattered about other things. I was just relieved that she seemed to have forgotten about the subject of last night. I didn't want her to dig into the details. I knew I would have to tell her at some point, but I just couldn't do it now. Allecra wouldn't be pleased about it. I didn't like putting Eva in a bad light. The violinist was just looking out for me, as a fellow potential.

But even Allecra and I were hopelessly in love with each other, I wondered how long my overthinking mind would creep back to overwhelm me again. The worst thing was feeling like I had a dream that I was happy with someone, when in fact, I just hadn't woken up yet. I tried to keep up my bearing and acted normal for Allecra's sake.

She walked me through the campus after we arrived. Lately, she had been alone with me instead of with Xenon and Triton. I had no idea where the other two were nor what they were doing now.

Allecra saw me off to class afterward. I was glad nothing seemed out of ordinary to her. But for me, Eva's voice still echoed from the deep darkness I tried to ignore.

During bio II, we studied about butterflies. Miss. Peterson was talking about how butterflies taste with their feet. Taste receptors on a butterfly's feet help it find its host plant. A female butterfly lands on different plants, drumming the leaves with her feet to make the plant release its juices and detect the right match of plant chemicals. When she finally identifies the right flower, she lays her eggs.

I was only half-listening for the rest of the lesson. Jordan noticed my spacing out while we were supposed to name different body's parts of a Monarch butterfly in the book.

After the bell rang and class was dismissed, she looked at me and said, "Hey, Nina, what's wrong? You're alright?"

I didn't know how she knew it, but Jordan seemed to have radar for a troubled mind. And when she asked, *'what's wrong'* she really did care. Because I felt like I needed to talk to someone, I asked her straight out.

"Jordan, what would you do if you were so bent on loving someone, just to have your heart torn out by them at the end?"

"Wait, don't tell me that you and Allecra—?"

"No, no, we're fine," I reassured her. "I'm just asking."

She looked relieved, but at the same time confused and curious at my question.

"Nina," Jordan said with a low sigh. "If she ever dumps you, I'll let her know she's the stupidest person in the world."

"She's really nice to me, don't worry," I told her again and smiled half-heartedly back.

"Well then, I'm happy to hear that. I can't imagine how anyone could have possibly tasted your lips and let you go."

I felt the blush creeping up my neck.

"You haven't answered me yet." I changed the subject.

She pursed her lips for a moment.

"It depends on how deeply you love that person," she said.

"Would you still be with that person even if things get more complicated, either by choice or by default?"

"You shouldn't be in a relationship with the mindset that something bad will happen, Nina," she said. "If it's meant to be, it will be."

I molded it over and over in my head.

"You mean — you would decide to go for it anyway?" I asked. "What if it's not meant to be. What if it's not the right decision?"

"Love is a feeling, not a decision," Jordan said. "Just like a butterfly, it will fly away if you try so hard to chase it, but if it comes to you on its own, you best appreciate that moment."

That was a serendipitous discovery for me. I felt as though the hidden weight was lifted off my chest, and I was able to breathe freely again. Then I felt Jordan's hand on mine. I looked at my friend.

"Nina, if you're wondering what the direction your relationship is going right now, follow your heart. It always knows where it wants to go," she said. "I know it's scary at the beginning and ending can be heartbreaking, but if what happens in between makes you feel more alive than any time in your life, I think it's worth it."

"Thank you, Jordan," I said.

Indeed, Eva might be right about what she said, but she didn't know me, and how tough I could be. She underestimated my strength, thinking I might not have the courage to face complications and see things through. Now whatever happens let it happen, I was done worrying and overthinking. I wasn't going to run away like a coward anymore. I was willing to fight for this love. I was going to fight for Allecra.

Down the hallway, I ran so fast, everyone else had to make way for me. When I reached the Pepper tree, I spotted the sight of tousled blonde hair. My heart pumped faster than my feet. She was standing there, waiting to have lunch with me as always. I called her name. Allecra turned around and I jumped right into her arms with my legs wound around her like a baby koala. She was strong enough to catch me. I leaned in and kissed her hard on the lips then pulled away.

"Whoa!" Allecra said, looking surprised and confused. "What is it, monkey?"

I giggled and got down on my feet again. We stood gazing at each other.

Of course, Allecra was like a butterfly. Her love had come to me. I was the flower she wanted, the right match of chemicals, not Eva or the other potentials. I was different, and I believed that we would get through anything as long as we had each other, whatever it might be.

"Allecra," I said softly, holding her hands in mine and staring into her deep brilliant eyes.

"Yes?" she said.

"Can we see the aurora tonight?"

~*~

The two of us arrived in a white plain of Alaska through the portal-like spinning machine. This time, it was Allecra who projected the threads of thoughts into reality. All around us was a vast snow-covered area bordered by tall hemlocks, cedars, and pines. It was already dusk here, but there was no aurora in the sky.

"It will appear soon enough," Allecra whispered like she could read my mind. "You're lucky. Aurora Borealis is frequent in spring and winter."

She pointed to a distance. I followed her hand and saw a small cottage with a spinning waterwheel about a hundred feet away. It stood near the bank of a running creek. Far behind was miles and miles of snow-peaked mountains where the sun had just set.

"It's so beautiful! Does someone live there?" I asked.

"Nobody lives around here," Allecra said. "That's my cottage."

"Your cottage?"

"Let's get inside and find you some warm clothes," she said. "It'll get colder when night falls."

There were a few pots of plants on the stairs on the front porch. The light on the door was on. Allecra opened it and we got inside. Everything was made of varnished wood. It had a small living area with a rug under a white couch and a fireplace. There was a kitchenette at one side with a glass window facing the view of the mountains. I saw a ladder going right up to the bed in the attic.

"We'll have to wait for a while," Allecra said. "How about a nice hot mug of chocolate?"

"That would be perfect," I said with a smile.

As the night drew in, we both sat by the burning fireplace on the couch with our legs under a warm blanket. We cupped our cold hands around the warm mugs. The marshmallows floated in the browny drink. Then Allecra clicked on a button of a remote control, which she fished out of a bowl on a nightstand. Then the roof above us opened, revealing a skylight. I gasped at the perfect canvas of diamond-like constellation above us. I saw more stars than I ever thought possible.

"Amazing!"

"I know." Allecra smirked charmingly at me. "I designed it myself, and Triton helped me build it. Impressive?"

"Very! How do you get the electricity in the middle of nowhere anyway?"

"Hydropower," she told me. "That waterwheel isn't just for decoration, you know."

Under the glow of the fire, we snuggled into each other and sipped the warm beverage in contentment.

"Can we live like this every day?" I asked, resting my head on Allecra's shoulder. She put her arm around me and smoothed my hair.

"If you want to, we can start from now," she said. I loved this about her. She always made everything sound possible no matter how far-fetched it was.

"I wish," I said.

"Maybe someday," she said. "Did you know we're facing Russia right now?"

"Oh really?"

"Yeah." She nodded.

"It's breathtaking here," I said. "Russia still regrets selling Alaska till these days."

"Oh please," Allecra scoffed and rolled her eyes. "You're all still in the illusion of what belongs to whom. But no one has brought anything into the world, and everyone will leave it the same way. We're just passing through for a short time. Who cares?"

"Alright, Miss. Philosopher." I smiled and leaned to kiss her cheek. She tilted my head back and met my lips with hers. She tasted like sweet chocolate, literally.

Then we felt a gentle glow in the distance. I opened my eyes and turned. There I finally saw it — the greenish light taking on a yellowish and reddish cast in the sky. It was even better than a double rainbow.

"Here it comes, Nina," Allecra whispered in my ear, "the northern lights."

"Oh my god," I breathed. "It's happening!"

"You want to get a better look outside?"

I nodded eagerly. Allecra brought me a pair of gloves and a wool scarf. She wrapped the scarf around my neck. Yet her meticulousness only made my impatience grow, and I couldn't keep still.

"Stay still! It's not going away," she said with a scolding frown. "It's cold out there. I don't want you to get sick and blame me."

We both put on our coats and finally went outside to the field. I was almost running in excitement. Allecra followed after me with a blanket in hand.

There were glowing rays in greenish tinge. The beams of the beautiful corona formed an aurora. They seemed to gather in a starlit sky. In the spectacular flame-like greenish blue, the tongue of rays rippled and flickered in curving bands like magical draperies.

"Oh Allecra, this is beautiful! I feel as if I'm in a fantasy world!" I said and laughed in delight.

"You would really love Arzuria, too, then," she said. "Auroras appeared almost every night there."

"Oh, really?" I turned to her. "You got to see aurora every night?!"

"Almost," she said. "Sometimes just meteor showers."

"What?" I was awestruck again. "No wonder why you people are so dreamy. You're literally from a magical realm!"

She laughed.

We walked farther into the white field. I kept spinning myself around and around, trying to take in every angle of the beautiful night. Allecra stood watching me in silence. A content smile plastered on her face.

"Allecra, this is too beautiful. I think I'm going to cry," I said, my voice quivered. She came to me and put her arms around my waist from behind.

"Let's sit down and watch it together," she suggested. Allecra spread the blanket on the frozen ground. She smoothed out the corners and then beckoned for me to sit with her. Then we both looked up at the glowing draperies fluttering above us. After a while, Allecra shifted and lay our bodies on the blanket. I turned my head to look at the blonde girl beside me. Her beautiful turquoise eyes shimmered like the aurora above us.

"I love you, Allecra," I whispered. She quickly tilted her head to me and smiled.

"I love you, too."

We gazed into each other's face before drawing in to have a sweet light kiss.

"Out of anyone in the world, why am I the one for you?" I asked after we pulled away.

"Because the wind carries your scent and the stars sing your name at night," she said.

I laughed, and she laughed along.

"Stop doing that! I'm serious," I said. Allecra took a deep breath and looked at me again.

"Well, I don't know Nina. I was scared as hell to want you," she admitted. "But here I am —wanting you anyway. The greatest gift you have ever given me is yourself. You're just like aurora to delight my world."

My heart fluttered as I listened to her.

Our eyes met again, and the silence deepened. Flickers of blissful electric currents charged the atmosphere around us as she gazed unrelentingly into my eyes. My heart swelled up so big inside my chest, I almost couldn't breathe. I grabbed her face and kissed her almost forcefully. She reciprocated my fierce burning kiss with equal passion. We both had to draw in a jagged breath and broke away.

"It's getting cold now," she said breathlessly. "Let's get inside and talk about the universe and make out more."

I knew Allecra tried to avert the sexual tension for my sake, but I wouldn't have it anymore.

"Can we do more than that?" I asked.

"What do you want to do?"

"I want you," I whispered back.

There was a long dragging silence after I said that. But Allecra understood. She understood perfectly.

"Are you sure, Nina?" she asked.

"I couldn't be any surer of anything than this."

Allecra's eyes heated up, glowing brightly turquoise in response. I could sense her resistance slipping away. We both couldn't hold it back anymore.

And finally, without another word, Allecra nodded.

We walked back into the house together. After we each freshened up in the small bathroom, we changed into comfortable clothing. Allecra gave me a sleeping shirt that barely reached my thighs. When I asked for a pair of pants, she said it was warm enough inside that I didn't need them.

"Besides you look far lovelier with no pants on," she added, causing the heat to rush up my body.

Allecra was in her white loose t-shirt and black spandex shorts, yet she could be in one of those underwear commercials.

She climbed up the ladder to the attic then held her hand out for me. I followed afterward. The white puffy mattress was spread on the floor there. Soft cozy pillows lay around the bedding. There was a tiny lamp by the corner.

"Come here," Allecra said and patted the bed for me. My heart skipped a beat. She whipped off the blanket as I got in. Then we both lay side by side, staring up the ceiling for the first time with nothing to say. After a moment, Allecra shifted her head.

"Wanna see another surprise?"

I stared at her and then narrowed my eyes down to the bulging blanket.

"No, little perv! That's not what I meant," she cried and then turned around and pressed on a switch. Suddenly the roof once again slid open showing three paralleled skylights above us. I could see the remnants of light from the aurora along with the twinkling stars flickered over us.

"Oh my goodness, Allecra," I gasped. She grinned back at me.

No wonder, Eva couldn't forget the emotions the blonde gave her. I could never for the life of me forget this. But I tossed the thought of Eva aside. This moment wasn't about anyone else but us.

When I turned to look at Allecra again, she was on her side, watching me. I had not heard her turn. Her unwavering greenish blues stirred like the northern light itself. She reached for my hand. Her fingers were smooth and slender and always gentle, lacing with mine.

"Nina," she whispered my name.

The quietness enveloped us. Then she pulled the cover away, exposing us into the cold Alaskan night. Allecra leaned toward me. Our mouths opened for each other, and the warmth of her sweetened desire poured into my soul. I couldn't think of anything, except feeling the softness of her lips. It was magical.

The kiss deepened and grew more ardent. Then Allecra pulled her lips away from mine soundly. She got onto her knees and began to doff of her clothes. I went after to help while joining our months again.

Without the blanket, I was a little cold, but I was burning inside from the torrid heat of our longing. I could feel that Allecra was growing tense, fighting the impulse she had been fighting since our first night together.

As soon as her shirt and shorts were removed, Allecra's hands went to get rid of mine. It was easy to undress me, and she did not waste time being gentle about it, although she tried. When my shirt was gone, she leaned me back onto the bed and took off my panties. I raised my hips and let her pull it down my legs.

Allecra was also stark naked, unabashed and goddess-like just as I first saw her. That elegant lithe form lacked no lush feminine curves. When I lowered my gaze to the area of her sex, she traced a hand down to touch it.

She bit her bottom lip and let out a low groan and then slowly revealed her lone aspect of her nature that complimented the ideal of archetypal beauty. Allecra slid her hand away and let that slender appendage atop her girlhood sprung outward, fully erected between her thighs.

I would never get used to seeing this bizarre process of her bodily function.

Like a lioness, she crawled towards me until she hovered over my body. Her lips found mine in a hot deep kiss again. Now there was only our naked skin hot and cold flushed up against each other on the bed. Allecra tenderly stroked my cheek with the back of her fingers. I reached down and got a hold of her pulsing length. She breathed sharply when she felt my fingers wrapped around her. I heard her whimper as I let her blushed tip rub against my stomach and gently cradled her. Allecra sighed in response to that pleasant touch of my hand. Her head tilted to mine, plunging her tongue deeper into my mouth. I could feel her beginning to harden and expand even more. The feeling of Allecra coming to life in my grip made me flush all over.

"Nina...wait..." Allecra gasped in my mouth and pulled away.

"What..." I said, gazing up at her in confusion.

"I have to get you ready for me," she said and went with all her supine form down over the valley of my breasts. She suckled them until every nerve in my body raged with needs. Allecra trailed butterfly kisses over my tummy and farther down. When she reached my sex, I moaned softly at the sensitive feeling brought by that ravaging tongue. She rekindled the flame of my passion and pent-up craving, nibbling and flicking away at the little bit of my throbbing bud. I was hot and oozing with my own arousal and her saliva. But before the sudden surge of pleasure could be reached, Allecra pulled away, leaving me wanting for more. I realized the anticipated moment had come. She lay over my body again. Her eyes were glowing with heated desire.

"Are you going to do it now?" I asked in a whisper.

"If you want me to," she said, but her voice a little strained and her breath was heavy.

"Will it hurt me?"

"You've grown into a woman, Nina," she said and kissed my nose and cheek over and over soothingly. "You'll be fine. I'll take care of you, I promise."

"Okay," I replied. "But first, you must put on a condom."

"Oh," Allecra breathed and rose up a bit. "Damn, I don't think I have one with me. I didn't know we were going to."

I quickly shook my head to show that she didn't have to worry.

"I have some in my bag," I said a bit sheepishly, causing her blonde brows to rise at me

"I didn't know my girl's been carrying condoms around," she teased.

I smacked her arm.

"I got it from sex Ed class," I told her honestly, "I just had a feeling that we would need them."

Allecra grinned back then dipped down to kiss my lips.

"And you're right," she said, "We need them...a lot of them."

She turned to the corner of the attic where my bag was sitting by a small glass window. After she fished it out, Allecra tore open the foil with her teeth urgently. I sat up to watch her work in fascination.

"You have to pinch the tip before you put it on," I instructed her.

"Which tip?"

I blinked and then understood.

"Oh my god, Allecra!" I cried and threw a pillow at her. She dodged it and burst out laughing.

"Sorry!"

I gave her a scowl. Allecra crawled back toward the bed with an apologetic look.

"Oh, Nina," she coaxed as she came to place her soft lips on my bare shoulder and neck. "I'm a little nervous. I make bad jokes when I get too excited."

"Alright then," I said, "Now just put it on."

"Aw...bossy Nina, I like," she said and sat back on the mattress. The whole time, I couldn't take my eyes off her elongated member that stood up against her belly. I became engrossed again when she started to put the condom on. But then she stopped and frowned at me.

"Don't look, I'm shy!" she said and turned her back on me. I bit my lips from smiling.

Once she was done, Allecra quickly covered us both in the puffy blanket and reached over to switch the light off. The darkness was thick around us until slowly, our eyes adjusted. Lying naked beneath Allecra's warm body, I could look over her shoulder to the night stars. It felt like nothing else existed except the two of us and the constellation with traces of floating aurora.

Allecra reached down to feel me. When she found I was still hot and slippery, still waiting and throbbing for her, she kissed me again until my mouth was swollen from our kisses. I could feel her hardness pressed up between us. It was an odd feeling, both foreign and familiar. My heart leaped forward and began racing when Allecra shifted her body.

"I love you," she whispered before gently spreading my legs. Those three words relaxed me and enthralled me all at once.

"Hmm," I replied with a nod, giving her the unspoken permission. I pressed my cheek to the pillow and squeezed my eyes shut, waiting for whatever Allecra was going to do. But I snapped back to attention, though when I finally felt her erection hot and hard against my sex.

I looked down to see Allecra was kneeling between my spread thighs, throbbing length in hand, rubbing herself against me slowly and sensually. I could tell that she was fighting the urge to just plunge herself into the depth of my trembling softness. But she tried to nestle her way in as gently and slowly as she could. She had to withdraw herself because I still didn't seem to yield, and Allecra must've been afraid to hurt me. I was holding my breath every time I thought she would press into me.

"Keep breathing, Nina," Allecra said. "I don't want you to pass out on me."

She moved away and stretched down over me again. Her lips nibbled on my breasts and suckled my nipples deeply.

"Why are you stopping?" I asked.

"You're still not fully open for me yet," she said and just continued her ministration.

"How do I open?"

"That's okay. We don't need to rush. Take your time and just relax," she whispered back. She kept kissing and licking everywhere until I forgot about the tension. This time her hands scratched and stroked my skin and the prospect of joining our bodies in pleasure got me craving again.

Allecra seemed to understand what I wanted. Our eyes locked. I watched the stirring pools of galaxies glowed brighter. The tip of her hardness was parting my wet lips slowly, very slowly that I almost couldn't tell it at first. I looked down speechless and wide-eyed at the sight of Allecra finally entering me.

Then there was a tightness as I stretched around her. The head spread me wide, then wider, like it tried to squeeze its way in as she slid into me. I let out a long exhale while she kept going. It was a beautiful feeling, having her inside me, hard and pulsing with warmth. But it also terrified me. Then there was a fast slipping followed by a buzzing dull sting.

It startled me and my chest panted again.

"Shh...it's okay, it's okay," Allecra coaxed softly. "Did it hurt?"

Just like that, the stinging feeling faded away. I shook my head to reassure her that I was fine. In fact, I was surprised that there was actually no real pain. It was all too easy.

"Good," Allecra said and began to push forward again. But this time, it was faster and easier. I could feel her curve up inside me and her faint pulse in the warm softness of my womb. By reflex, my hip muscles tightened to the sweet invasion, causing jolts of blissful sparks to burst through every hollow of my bones.

"Oh geez, Nina," Allecra gasped.

I realized our pelvic bones had touched at last. Allecra went as far as she could go. And now, she was also panting hard against me. She closed her eyes and let out a moan into my neck.

After every inch of her had buried deep inside my core, I began to feel the tingling going around me.

She slid herself back out again. We both moaned together at the delicious friction. Then she went back in. She did that over and over, creating a slow sensual rhythm. It was short but repetitive strokes. They sent jolts after jolts of frenzy lightning. Her stiffness started wagging storm all over my shivering form.

Allecra hissed my name again, gritting her teeth. Her eyes aglow and her breath quickened as her hips moved.

The fullness between my thighs made my thoughts jumbled and my nerve haywire. I could barely string two words together. Allecra's turquoise eyes met mine, and we shared a moment of acknowledgment — this was really happening. We were actually making love.

Snapping back, I looked down between us as Allecra kept plunging herself into my depth. My juices lubricated her thrusting, making her grow harder with new vigor. It seemed like gentleness wasn't necessary anymore at that point. I moaned to the brutality of intense pleasure. It spread from my toes to my skull and going back to the region of our joined parts. Allecra pressed her mouth against mine, letting our tongues lashing at each other in time with those steady powerful thrusts. My fingers found her blonde hair. There was a gathering feeling inside me. I began gasping each time her hardness pierced my being, sending pleasure with the essence of deepest love.

My whole trembling body felt like it was disintegrating and then sticking back together atom by atom. I thought I would lose my mind from the euphoric intensity that wrecked through me, and I tried to cling to her. Allecra pressed her face against my breasts. She was groaning. My back arched against her, taking more of what she was giving. I dug my nails into her back harder, scoring her skin. She seemed pleased with my response, her eyes lighting in triumph at the changes in my breath. But she was also surprisingly hard and full inside me. Allecra grabbed my hips and began to rock us more violently, turning those little humping passes into deep hard strokes that made me scream. I greedily urged onward with every shake of my hips to meet hers.

I wondered if this was love-making feels like — with us using the other's body to reach the apex of sensual bliss together.

A few more of her thrusts, I felt myself bursting. My walls fluttered around Allecra in a powerful contraction I had never felt in my life. Every part of my body clenched and taunt as I wailed in a release, letting myself fall into a blessed delirium. It didn't take long, but the moments seemed like an eternity of joy. Moments later, Allecra also shuddered in my arms. I could feel her length pulsating inside my gripping walls. She hissed out loud and found her own release soon after.

Allecra collapsed weakly onto me. She no longer had the strength to support herself, but her hips continued a few more clumsy thrusts. When her climax began to ebb, she finally slowed down to a stop. For a long moment, we both lay there in each other's arms, thighs soaked with wetness. Our hearts hammered rapidly against one another. The scent of our love juices filled the air.

Allecra carefully withdrew herself from me. I was amazed to feel a dull pain afterward, but it wasn't irritating. She threw the condom away into a tiny bin at the corner. I caught a glimpse of her potent alien seed. There was a lot of it — white and seemingly gooey like whip cream and able to bring new life with it. Then Allecra came to the bed with a wet clean towel and proceeded to clean me. She was very thorough about it that I had to clamp my legs from her.

She smiled. After it was all done, she came back and wrapped her arms around my body, tenderly holding me close to her. But I felt my chest grew heavy and I couldn't breathe. Allecra was surprised to see a tear roll down my cheek.

"Nina, are you alright?" she asked in alarm. "Are you hurt?"

"No," I said, my voice croaked in an effort to speak again. "I'm fine...I don't know why I'm crying."

"You're just a little overwhelmed after sex," she said. "It's understandable."

"I guess so," I said and cried a little in her arms. Maybe it was the fact that I had just lost my virginity. But I was glad that I lost it to the person I loved.

"Oh baby girl..." she said and stroked my hair. "Shh...It's okay. I'm right here."

She wiped away the tears from my face and kissed my cheek.

"I just... can't believe we finally did it," I said.

"Me too," she whispered back.

"I thought I wouldn't be able to bring myself to...you know?"

"I know."

"I love you, Allecra."

"I love you more."

And we lay there, kissing and cuddling each other with all the stars in the sky witnessing us.

CHAPTER 38

IT WAS 9:30 IN THE MORNING by the time I awoke. The bed was empty, but I could still feel the warmth that Allecra left behind. Beyond the skylights overhead, the Alaskan sun framed the clouds with an ethereal glow.

I squinted against the late-morning light, but my head was clear from a wonderful thick sleep. I sat up and looked around. Most of the clothes from the night before scattered beside the bed, and I was actually naked. There was a trace of that special feeling in my lower half, the sweet lassitude that comes after having your insides powerfully churned.

So this wasn't a dream.

I was glad that it did happen. At last, Antonina Volkova, or Nina Black if you prefer, is able to lose herself to the wonder of sex. But to be honest, I still didn't know how to take this new status yet. Anyway, having sex or not having sex doesn't define who you are. I was still me.

I got up to get dressed in my old night shirt and hurried down the ladder. Then I heard the sound of running water and the jangling of pots and pans in the kitchen. When I reached where the noises came from, I realized Allecra was making breakfast. Her back was turned as she stood in front of a stove. There was a potful of boiling spaghetti and a whistling kettle.

The windows were open, letting all the good spring smells float in with the fresh icy scent of the mountains.

I watched Allecra in contented silence for a while. She had on a loose sleeveless tee that revealed those curving inks on her arms and a pair of black panties. The sight of her backside alone caused a shiver in my body.

Allecra's hair was tied up in a messy ponytail. I had hardly ever seen her wearing her hair up like that. The sunlight that shone through the window seemed to make a golden frame around her whole body. The view of the snow-peaked crystalline mountains at the backdrop was shockingly perfect with Allecra in it.

She was also moving around barefoot, and I couldn't stop staring at her smooth slender legs. She held her postures like a principal dancer in the tiny space, all grace with refined movements and strength.

Then Allecra turned around and caught me staring at her. She smiled and walked up to me. Then we both stood, looking at each other's face again. For a moment, we just gave shy and weird grins, as if we were at loss for words or not knowing how to begin. There were too many things to say. But maybe because of our ridiculous awkwardness, the two of us burst out giggling at the same time. Allecra came to pull me into her arms and spun me around in our light-filled cottage. I laughed and wrapped my arms around her neck.

"You sneaky kitten," she said.

"You should've put some pants on." I giggled.

"Look who's talking!"

She put me down and gave me a peck on my lips. Her breath smelled like fresh mint, like mountain air and snow and sunshine.

"Well, someone didn't give me any last night," I said.

"Because I knew you would wake up beautiful without them."

"Gosh, you and your sugary words," I said.

"Can't blame me. I've been eating something sweet lately."

"What is it?"

"Your lips," she said and smiled. I smiled back, but then she leaned over to whisper in my ear. "All of them."

I gasped and shoved her away.

"Why are you being such a pervert all the times?" I said with a glare.

"Only with you," she laughed back.

"Did you say that to the other potentials, too?"

It made Allecra scowl at me. My breath hitched when I realized what I'd just said, fearing that I had offended her about her past lovers, but Allecra just pinched both of my cheeks and stretched them hard.

I yelped.

"Don't spoil my morning mood, or else..." she said and then went, "Oh shoot!" before going over to the stove and lifted the cover off the spaghetti pot. A cloud of steam emitted into the air.

"You're making spaghetti?" I asked, rubbing my cheeks and also attempting to change the subject.

"There's nothing else in the house except some cans of Bolognese sauce and pasta," Allecra replied while stirring the boiling pot with a wooden ladle. "I remember you didn't have any dinner last night. You must be hungry."

As if on cue, my stomach growled. I clutched it in embarrassment.

"That's really thoughtful of you," I said. "But give me a moment to wash up first, okay?"

"Okay," she said.

In the small bathroom, I showered with lukewarm water that was probably heated by the hydropower from the creek. Then I came to stand in the big mirror and began to brush my teeth. But then I let out a gasp after a closer inspection. There were a few little red bruises around my neck and collar bones and several tiny ones above my breasts like dead rose petals. Though they weren't big, they were still pretty much visible and could last for days.

"Allecra!" I yelled as I got out of the bathroom and headed towards the kitchen again.

She was arranging the silverware on the table when I went over to her.

"What's wrong?" she asked in alarm.

"Look!" I said, yanking the collar of my shirt to show her. She glanced down my chest and then back at me.

"Well, you have beautiful breasts," Allecra said.

I pinched her bare arm. She jumped away with a yelp.

"That's not what I meant!" I hissed. "Tell me who gave me these hickeys?"

Allecra put her hand over her heart with a fake gasp.

"You think it could be me?" she said. I pinched her again.

"You're not funny, Allecra!"

She pouted and peered over my shirt to check the bruises.

"Oh wow," she said. "Oopsy!"

"Oopsy?!" I glowered at her in accusation. "If Piper sees these, she'll put me on a trail again."

"If she wants to know, let her know," Allecra said with a casual shrug. "Why do you need to be embarrassed about it?"

"You don't understand," I said. "This is like me holding up a sign that says, *I just had sex*."

"And a great one at that," she added, quirking a perfectly arched eyebrow at me.

"Oh stop it," I muttered.

"Come on, Nina, I thought that was what humans like to do," she said. "They mark each other during sex, isn't that right?"

"Right, and I'm dead if my aunt sees this," I grumbled.

"Okay, okay, I'm sorry, *lapochka*. No more marking from me then, I promise," she said. "Now let's sit down and eat your breakfast before we get back."

She pulled the chair for me, and I grumpily sat down. Allecra settled on another one opposite mine. She placed a plate of steaming spaghetti with Bolognese sauce in front of me.

I dug up a forkful of the pasta, gave it a few air blows and shoved it into my mouth. It tasted strangely delicious, or maybe I was just hungry, or both.

Allecra had also made us some hot chocolate. I watched her curling the pasta around her fork tines until it formed a tiny neat ball of spaghetti and put it into her mouth. No mess. I loved watching her delicacy and effortless maneuvers towards things. It never ceased to amaze me. Sitting together in a small kitchen facing the view of the mountains with the sunlight streamed through the windows, I realized this was what I wanted to wake up to every day for the rest of my life.

"I still don't want to go home yet," I said out loud.

"We can always come here again," Allecra said.

"I know. But this moment is too perfect; I just don't want to leave it. It feels like living my dream already."

"Your dream is living in a cottage and watch auroras?" she asked. It made me chuckle.

"Well, no, not exactly, but I heard someone said, *'If you have a garden and a library, you have everything you need.'* And I thought to myself I would make it happen and that would be my life. I don't want a big house or any fancy cars. If I can have a small patch of garden and a little library, if my kitchen is nice and filled with necessary utensils, and my fridge never runs out of foods, my tiny car can get me places with no problems, then I have all that I want."

"It sounds perfect, Nina," she said with a soft smile then she placed her palm on my cheek and brushed it with her thumb. I put my hand over hers.

"What about you?" I asked. "What is your dream?"

"I don't have any dream," she said, eyes studying my face. "Because I have you. You are better than a thousand dreams. You are real."

My fork dropped from my hand, and just like that, I got up from my chair and rushed towards her. Allecra promptly welcomed me into her arms and settled me on her lap. I put my palms on her soft cheeks and stared into her eyes. Her long lashes looked like one of those glossy ads for mascara, so thick and curved.

"Will you stay with me, Allecra, for the rest of my life?" I said. My voice quivered with emotions.

"Why do you have to ask when you already know the answer?"

"I just want you to confirm it," I said.

"Nina, I will be with you, forever and always, I promise."

"Don't break your promise, okay?"

"I won't."

"What if you're forced to leave me?" I demanded. Allecra furrowed her brows at me at those words.

"What makes you think I would be forced to leave you?"

I bit my lower lip before I spoke.

"Eva talked with me the other day when we went out..." I started. "She said that you might break my heart by leaving me someday—just like you did with her. And even you don't want to, your siblings would make you. I remember what Xenon said to me. She wouldn't allow it, at least not for long."

Allecra sighed.

"Is that why I felt a strange kind of hesitation the morning before we came here?" she said.

I looked down, guilty.

"I just had too many questions about us."

"So what changed?"

"It came in spontaneity and also in perfect clarity that I know whatever happens, loving you is still worth everything in the end."

"I won't let anyone break us apart, Antonina," she said, using my full name as if in finality. "Not even Xenon and Triton. I had never known what I really wanted. It'd always been for my people, for the future generation of Arzuria, but now for the first time, I realized what I wanted for myself — and I want you. I do not take it lightly when I say that. No one can take you away from me."

It was in that moment that I gained a perfect understanding of both her heart and mine.

Allecra and I were quiet for a long time. The feeling of craving from last night flying between us in a crazy jagged way of a bird caught in a room. The feeling was so strong it made us unable to resist it anymore. Allecra narrowed her gaze to my lips then leaned forward until our lips joined in kisses. It always started gently and sweetly, but then growing more urgently, soft lips moving against each other, exchanging breaths and moans. It was crazy how we wanted each other again already. Every single inch of me became alive with the same starving need. Allecra seemed to feel the same way. That was the feeling I loved best in the world.

I got off Allecra so that she could run to my bag and grab a foil package. There was something wanton about all of it, but neither of us cared. Allecra returned to me. Her lips found mine amidst the passion.

She hoisted me onto the table and got between my legs. Her hands feverishly worked over the buttons of my shirt before stripped it off my shoulders though not all the way. We were in a hurry, and nothing was sexier and sensual than that. I was emboldened after everything was no longer tangled between us. It was the first time amongst other first-times as long as I could remember that this desire wasn't out of sexual perversion.

It was simply a way of being in love and showing it when all verses failed.

Allecra's secret member reappeared, springing forth from her panties when she pulled down the waistband. I shivered at the sight of it. She immediately put on a condom, not bothering to hide from me anymore. She kneeled over between my legs and eased my panties down and then off. Her roughness made my heart go nuts inside my chest. It was like she couldn't wait to taste me. All I felt was her velvety tongue and soft lips going all over my sensitive flesh, slipping in and out like something curious and hungry. Until my bloodstream turned to hot lava and my brain and body was on the verge of eruption that Allecra stood up to hold my trembling form in her arms. She took my hand and wrapped my fingers around her stiffness. It felt harder than the last time, miraculously hard.

We kissed again as our hands traveled even farther down to her girlhood. It was slippery just like mine. Allecra was very soft, too. I was amazed how it could be possible to be so soft and so hard at the same time.

After a while of this, she helped me off the table. I stood up, feeling my own wetness smeared on my inner thighs. Allecra sat down on the chair again.

"Come over here," she said, gesturing towards her.

Those words were like a casting spell over my body, and I did as I was told. She pulled off her panties all the way down, leaving only her tee. Then she pulled me over by the waist. I didn't know what she was doing, but as her hands helped to balance me, I automatically raised my leg and straddled her.

I felt the burning need intensified once I was spread, moving closer to Allecra's pinkish head. Her eyes once again took on a shade or two lighter.

"Allecra..." Our eyes traced one another's face.

"Trust me," she whispered.

I took in a sharp intake of air when I felt her tip poised right at my glistened entrance.

Without any more word passed, she let me sink into her. I was so wet that her hardness slipped right in, ending to the base and with no resistance at all. My walls quivered and tingled at the sweet impaling sensation. I whimpered while Allecra bit her lips and knitted her brows together in pleasure. Her breaths were hot and heavy on my chest. Now that I was completely sitting on her lap with every inch of her buried inside me, I didn't know what else to do.

I waited for Allecra to take action, but she only sucked on my breasts earnestly and stayed silent.

"Allecra..." I said in a coy tone.

"Hmm?" she said, still obsessing over my perked nipples. I was losing my patience.

"Shouldn't we start now?"

"If you want to, you start it," she said. Then I understood what she was doing. Allecra wanted me to be in charge, to break through my fear of sexual intimacy. She really took her sex therapy seriously. I was hot and embarrassed and desperate at the same time.

"Allecra please," I said and shook her a little. Instead, it sent a rush of blissful havoc up my inner depth and throughout my body. I gasped and felt her smile over my blushed skin.

Allecra flexed her hips a little under me, I moaned louder. And soon by sheer sexual instinct, my own hips began to stir like they had a life of their own. I tried to refrain myself, but it was fruitless once it started. Allecra seemed to enjoy seeing my growing enthusiasm. Her lips curved up at the corners smugly. I just wanted to wipe that smile off her face. I wrapped my mouth around hers instead. She helped me gyrating against herself. I gave up feeling shy. I gave up being self-conscious and thinking and just becoming one with her.

We were perfectly fit into each other.

With Allecra tightening her hold around my waist, I clung to her neck like I was drowning. I began rocking myself harder, grounding onto her and clenching and swallowing her again and again until Allecra threw her head back and moaned with me. I kissed her neck but then had to let my back arch as the motion and intensity were taking us into a perfect limbo where nothing could stop us.

~*~

After we got back home, I tried to adjust to our old reality again. My head felt like it was having a hangover, a good kind of hangover. And the second-round was probably a mistake, not that Allecra didn't make me come, because she did, and it was really hard and powerful and all-consuming that I thought I had forgotten what universe I was in during that solid blissful moment, but it resulted in me walking home like a duck.

Piper was having some friends over when she caught me climbing up the stairs.

"Hey Nina, you're back?" she said. "How was the sleepover last night?"

386

I had texted her before we left to Alaska that I was going to have a sleepover at Allecra's house. She had been cool about it, and only replied with *'Have fun, gal!'* and an emoji of two girls and a bed and some hearts.

"It was alright," I lied. "We studied for SAT test."

Piper cringed.

"You guys are nerds," she said. "So nothing else? No eating tacos afterward?"

I shot her a look.

"Don't you have things to do with your friends, Piper?"

"Oh we're about to go out soon," she said. "Wait, is that a hickey?"

"No, it's not!" I said and then started to run up the stairs to my room as quickly as my feet could go. I heard Piper burst out laughing from below.

"You go, Nina!" she yelled.

Once inside my room, I closed the door behind me and leaned my back against it. A tiny smile on my lips began to stretch wider, and then I was giggling to myself.

Aunt Vikki and her husband had returned from their trip that same day. I was relieved that I was already home before them. Piper was still out with her friends while Jay was busy filling his role as a quarterback. I wore a button-up shirt to hide my bruises and tried to walk less funny when I met my aunt and Robert. Aunt Vikki, keen as she was, didn't notice any change in me, or that I was good at hiding it.

The next day after school, I drove in my car to Allecra's house by myself. She said she had a surprise for me. I saw her waiting by the front gate and picked her up from there. Every time I saw her face, I found myself anticipating the coming of new excitement and maybe a little of the sexual side as well.

"Why didn't you just wait for me inside the house?" I asked her.

"You took donkey years to show up," she just said and pushed her sunglasses back. I made a face at her, but I also found it sweet of her, waiting eagerly for me.

Once we got inside, Allecra took me straight to the library. After we got there, she blindfolded me.

"What are you doing?"

"Don't worry, Nina, I'm not into that," she said and walked me forward. When we stopped, Allecra sat me down on the sofa and removed my blindfold. There, sitting on the coffee table in front of me was a glossy red typewriter.

I gasped with my hands over my mouth.

"The Remington Starfire!" I said and went over to touch the machine like a bright-eyed kid in Christmas.

"It's for you," Allecra said, smiling down at me. "Do you like it?"

"Oh Allecra, I love it!"

It even had our initials N&A on one side. I got up to give her a bone-crushing hug.

"Thank you, Allecra," I said and pecked her on the lips. "Can I try it?"

"Of course, it's yours," she said, "Type away."

I grinned and sat down again, continuing to admire the typewriter for a while before putting a blank sheet of paper, which Allecra had already prepared for me. Then I put my fingers over the keys and slowly pressed on a character at a time. It startled me how easily the metal keys hit the ribbon and a fully created letter already appeared on the paper, also how sweetly it sounded in my ears. It wasn't as loud as I expected, in fact, its noises were like the rattling sound of coins. It was soothing to hear.

Allecra sat behind me and leaned over my shoulders.

"What are you writing, sweetheart?" she whispered while nuzzling my neck.

"Have a look," I said and turned the typewriter towards her.

Written on the page was the three words *I love you*.

Allecra smiled and looked at me again.

"I love you, too," she said and then we kissed.

During that week, Allecra and I spent time together at her house. I kept the typewriter there. I didn't want my nosy cousins to know or worse, my aunt to find out what we'd been doing. Not that I expected them to solely think we both spent time knitting together all day, but it was best to keep it that way.

My aunt had insisted I invite Allecra for dinner again. I almost got a panic attack, trying to find an excuse. She just said she wanted to get to know Allecra more and that she found her a bit too fascinating. Although my aunt seemed genuine about it, I was glad Robert wasn't there to hear her saying that.

But things started getting wilder (in a good way) between Allecra and me, regardless our cautious behaviors.

It only lasted for a while when the restraints broke again, and we developed what became an increasingly intimate pattern.

After school, we would speed off to her house because there were this constant buzzing and ringing in us. It happened after a stolen kiss or even a slight brush of our knees or fingers, and just like that, we couldn't wait to try again and again to get enough of each other, but sometimes, as led by impulsive impatience of our teenage hormones, we just slipped into our good old attic above the storage room or drove the car into the quietest area of the wood by the beach where we tried to quiet that buzzing and ringing until we had to stop from exhaustion and rawness, but it was like some curse for the more we tried to suppress it, the stronger it became.

Yet I no longer locked myself in the prison of doubt and fear. There is nothing more dreadful than the habit of doubt. It's a sword that kills relationships. It had bothered me terribly, like a fishbone stuck in my throat. But now I was free. I could enjoy my freedom to love and to give as much as I wanted.

When the cherry blossoms had all fallen and in their place, misty green leaves had begun to grow, I felt like a bird that has flown out of its cage into the open sky.

It was the beginning of summer.

CHAPTER 39

The FIRST TWO WEEKS before summer was the busiest. I had been working ahead of my classes. If I passed all the exams, I could earn my required credits and be able to take SAT college admission test before graduation.

But for now, I just wanted to make sure my transcript was decent enough for a scholarship. If I needed to get out and go to college, I had to work extra hard. Although my aunt said she wouldn't mind paying for my tuition, I couldn't just rely everything on her or Robert. And of course, Allecra had offered to cover up my entire life's expenses if I ever let her, I didn't want that either.

To make up for that, I agreed to let Allecra plan on our secret quantum adventure this summer. Sadly our sexual rendezvouses had to be postponed until school let out. It was mainly my idea. I needed my mind to stay focused on schoolwork. Allecra respected my decision. I could tell she didn't want to pressure me. Also, I had to submit my entry to the writing contest despite starting just two days before the deadline.

Sitting on the wool carpet of Allecra's library, I was typing away on the branch new Starfire. Needless to say, I was enjoying every bit of it, the typing, actually. It made me feel as though I was a real writer. Yet I had to pause several times to think of what to say or try to find the right word. It was a bittersweet process.

Allecra was lying leisurely on the couch, flipping through the Holy Bible. That's right. After I told her that we were going to have dinner with my aunt and my Christian uncle-in-law again, the Bible was the first book she grabbed when she came down here.

Aunt Vikki insisted she hadn't gotten acquainted enough with Allecra during the garden party. She would like to get to know more about her. Robert would even get off work for the very occasion. So I couldn't just say 'no'.

"What are you reading?" I asked Allecra after I decided to take a break when I was stuck on my writing.

"Funny stuff," she replied casually.

"Don't be so blasphemous, Allecra!" I said. "It's the Holy Bible. You must not disrespect."

"Well, I'm trying! But how could you not find it funny?" she said and then proceeded to read a passage to me. "It says here, 'Early in the morning, as Jesus was on his way back to the city, he was hungry. Seeing a fig tree by the road, he went up to it but found nothing on it except leaves. Then he said to it, *May you never bear fruit again!*' Immediately the tree withered. Matthew 21:18-22."

Then she burst out laughing.

"Why are you laughing?" I said with a disapproving look.

"Why are you not laughing?" Allecra said and continued to chuckle some more. "It's too funny. I think I kinda like Jesus more knowing this side of him."

"You seem to enjoy your Bible reading way too much," I said.

She sat up from the couch and put the big book away. Then she leaned over and gave me a kiss on the cheek and looked at my unfinished writing.

"What are you writing about?"

"I can't tell you yet," I said.

"Nina, I could read everything you've written with just a glance and you're still hiding from me?"

"I'm almost done!" I told her and tried to cover the page with my hands. "I have to close it on a perfect note. That's why I'm stuck. I need more time."

"Or you could just put *The End*," she said.

"Allecra, writing the ending is like saying goodbye to a lover," I said. "You can't just be blunt and impassionate like that."

"Okay, at least tell me the summary," she said while trailing kisses on my neck softly.

"Well, if you insist, it's a story about a white raven."

"A white raven?" she said. A spark of interest lit up in her eyes.

"Did you know there are actually white ravens?" I asked. "They're not albinos either. There's simply no melanin in their body. They actually exist."

Allecra raised her perfect brows and said, "So how does the story go then?"

I got up and sat down on the couch, pulling my knees to my chest. Allecra followed suit.

"The white raven is the protagonist, who miraculously escapes death before his mother eats him after he hatches."

"His mother tries to eat him?"

"Because he's white and considered as ugly and worthless," I told her. "Though he grows up to adulthood, he gets bullied from the other black ravens because he's different from them. He feels lonely and confused. He doesn't understand why everyone hates him so much. He believes in his heart that he's just like any other ravens, but no one likes him, so he never finds his mate and stays on his own for the rest of his life."

"Sounds like a very sad allegory," Allecra mused. "Now that you mentioned it, it just reminds me of a Greek myth."

"Oh, another myth?" I said. "Tell me."

"Well, at first, all ravens were white," Allecra started. "They were messengers of the god Apollo, but one day, they failed to inform the god about an affair of his mistress, a princess of Thessaly. He cursed the ravens so furiously that their feathers were scorched, and all ravens have been black ever since."

"Oh, I didn't know that!" I said,

"Maybe you can elaborate this for you ending."

"What should I say?" I murmured to myself. "The white raven is excluded from the society of the black ravens because of the color of his features, but they don't know he's just the same as them. They're indeed the same species, but they forget that they are one."

"That seems like a perfect ending," Allecra said.

"Thank you!" I kissed her cheek and added one on her lips. But before I could break away, she gripped my chin and deepened the kiss. We held each other and fell back onto the sofa with me on top.

"I can't stop thinking about kissing you, by the way," she murmured against my lips. Her sweet, gentle mouth, her strong, lean arms enveloped me.

I felt her hands feeling over my back then slithering inside my shirt. I made a soft sigh. The second I did Allecra got bolder. Her mouth moved over mine in a rough urgent need, so fast it was as if she was trying to create fire with our lips.

I grabbed her face between both my hands to stop the madness, but she took it as a sigh of enthusiasm. And before I knew it, her velvety long tongue unraveled and filled my mouth with its hunger. Allecra was going to get more into it, but I unhooked my lips from hers with a wet smacking sound.

"Allecra, I can't do it now," I said apologetically and wriggled away from her grasp

"Oh why?" she asked.

"Well, I'm afraid I'll forget the perfect lines if I don't write them down quickly," I said and pushed myself up again.

"Yep, every freaking writer ever," she scoffed. I bit back a smile and gave her another kiss on the lips before I got back to my writing.

_*_

Aunt Vikki was on the doorstep waiting for us. She looked elegantly sophisticated in a creamy white dress. Behind her was Jay, chest puffed and chin up like he was a house guard ready to throw people out.

When we reached them, Allecra exchanged pleasantries with my aunt, who was obviously dazzled by her. Even Jay studied Allecra from head to toes with gawking eyes. She was wearing a white button-up shirt and a black checked Polo sweater with khaki pants. She even tied up her blonde mane nicely. Everything seemed plain yet still elegantly well-put. She wasn't extravagant or trendy or stylish. She was just flawless. Her simplicity was indeed pure perfection.

We went to the living room. Piper was there, smiling from ear to ear at us.

"Aw! Look at you two, so coupley!" Piper said.

Even in my extraordinary state of queasy embarrassment, I felt the warmth of her approval.

"Piper," Aunt Vikki warned.

"Hello, Piper," Allecra said.

"Hi, Allecra," she replied quickly and enthusiastically. If I wasn't mistaken, my straight cousin was subtly checking my girlfriend out.

We saw Robert stood up from the sofa.

"Mr. Black," Allecra greeted him politely. "Nice to see you again."

"You, too," Robert said with a tone of formality back. I felt my stomach churn from the tension.

"Thank you for inviting me," Allecra said and smiled easily, looking between him and my aunt.

"It's nothing, my dear," Aunt Vikki said as she came to stand with her husband, and I saw her gave him a pinch. "We're all family now, aren't we?"

Robert made an awkward shift and glanced to his wife, but he didn't say anything.

After a few cordial words, we moved on to the dining room. A nice dinner was already prepared on the table, completed with expensive bottles of wine.

We all began to take our seat. Robert sat at the head of the table. Aunt Vikki sat beside her husband. Jay and Piper were facing us.

Allecra pulled a chair for me.

"Drink?" Robert said to her. He was already holding the uncorked wine bottle towards her glass.

"Yes, please," Allecra said.

Afterward, we began to eat. Aunt Vikki asked us about our plan for college and stuff. I told her we were preparing to take the admission test after the summer.

"What are you going to do during the vacation then?" My aunt turned to Allecra.

"It depends on what Nina wants to do," she answered unabashedly. I felt my throat tighten.

"Oh," Aunt Vikki said, "but we're going to Florida to visit Robert's parents, would you like to join us?"

By 'we, she also included me. Allecra and I exchanged a look. I didn't know about my aunt's plan.

"Actually, if you don't mind, we both want to spend time studying for SAT here," I said, and it wasn't a complete lie.

"Oh, is that so?" My aunt said. "Well, that's good. But are you sure, you want to stay behind, Nina? I don't know if it's a good idea to leave you all by yourself."

"Don't worry, Aunt Vikki, I'm eighteen now. I can take care of myself."

"Indeed," Allecra said with a voice like a casting spell. "We'll just do a lot of studying together."

From across the table, Piper wiggled her eyebrows at me. I pretended not to notice her. Aunt Vikki was silent for a while. But Allecra left no room for doubt with the way she said it.

"Alright then," my aunt said. "After all, I should give Nina some independent time."

I wasn't sure if Allecra was using her mind-control thing or not. But either way, I wasn't going to complain.

"Mom, can I have some independent time at home, too?" Jay asked. "I don't want to go all the way there to listen to grandpa's talk of the Cold War or the Great Depression all day."

"Me too," Piper said. "Gram's gonna make me eat until I turn into a regular hippo."

"You kids know they're getting old now. You should spend some times with them," Aunt Vikki said.

"Yes, no excuse," Robert added.

The twin just groaned at exact the same time.

Robert seemed less poised now after a few glasses of wine. His face was slightly red when he turned to Allecra.

"Say I would like to ask you about a certain topic to stimulate our brain cells, do you mind?"

Aunt Vikki murmured, "Here we go again."

"Not at all, sir," Allecra said.

"Well then," Robert cleared his throat. "How are you two going to have children?"

"Rob! You can't just ask them like that," my aunt cried and looked apologetic at us.

"Why not? If we are family, we better be frank with each other," Robert said with a shrug.

Allecra just smiled.

"It's alright," she said. "Actually, Mr. Black, I think there's a chance Nina and I can have children."

I gave Allecra a *what are you doing?* look. But she ignored me. Robert burst out laughing.

"But I didn't mean the artificial procedures. I refer to natural procreation. Since your relationship isn't natural, I don't think it's the same thing, isn't it?"

That was when I realized that, deep down, we were still different from them, just like the white ravens in the society that values black. The bridge of understanding would be so difficult to build as long as people still held this false belief.

But Allecra didn't show any sigh of disdain. If at all, she looked amused.

"What is 'natural' exactly, Mr. Black?" she said. "If you reject something that is unnatural, then you should've rejected your cars, computers, or your smartphones because only animals, plants, and people are natural, even bacteria are natural. So why a child born from a same-sex couple that can grow into a person isn't?"

Robert blinked.

"Well, but straight marriage is the most valid because they produce children. And gay couples might raise gay children."

"If gay parents will raise gay children, so straight parents only raise straight children?"

Robert blinked again. Everyone was looking between the two of them like they were seeing a tennis match.

"At least, they have been around for a long time and are supported by God."

"No wonder Solomon had three hundred wives, and a bride who could not prove her virginity must be stoned to death, and a girl who is raped must be married to the rapist."

There was a long silence. My aunt and Piper were clearly disgusted by what the Bible said. Jay scratched his neck in discomfort.

"Man, that is not cool at all," he said.

"How could people do that?" Piper agreed and grimaced.

Aunt Vikki was looking pointedly at her husband.

"Oh come on, darling, don't look at me like that. I'm not the one who wrote the Bible!" Robert protested.

"That's enough for now," my aunt said, "or you can sleep in your office tonight."

Robert raised his hands up in surrender.

"Mr. Black, my apologies if what I said has offended you," Allecra said. "I don't claim that everything in the Bible is fallacious. But there are some parts that no longer serve the greater good in the modern world. Things change and people change, it's just the way it is."

"Don't apologize," Robert said and then he smiled a genuine smile, which surprised me. "I haven't had such an interesting debate for a long time. You really opened my eyes."

I could feel the air return to my lungs and relief flooded through me. Allecra reached under the table to grab my hand and squeezed it.

After we finished dinner, Piper and I helped bring in desserts, apple pie and ice cream with a little mix of vodka. Later, Allecra told some joke at the table, and they laughed. One of them was a riddle, *'why a man jumps into the water, but his hair isn't wet?'* The answer was it's because the man is bald. Robert laughed so hard, his whole face reddened like a tomato. Even Jay was laughing his head off.

It was dusk when I walked Allecra out of the house to her car.

"Thank you for coming, Allecra," I said. "I owe you this one."

"Nina, don't say that," she said.

I smiled.

"You're amazing, you know."

"I know," she said, making me giggle. Then there was a long pause as we stared at each other.

"When school is over, I'm all yours," I said. Her turquoise eyes gleamed at my words.

"All mine," she said, giving me a meaningful grin.

I nodded again, and we kissed each other goodnight.

~*~

At last, I finished all my exams, term papers, and class projects and still came out in good shape. I had worked so hard for my grades, I hardly thought of anything else for the past few weeks. I had also submitted my entry to the writing contest. The school was closed for the summer vacation at last. Everyone had their plans. Mine was just a bit more miraculous.

Allecra and I were talking about all the places we would see in her library when we heard the ding of the elevator. We both turned to see Xenon and Triton walking in.

"Damn it, I should've changed the security password," Allecra muttered to herself. She got up from the couch. I stood up, too. Allecra she went out to greet her brother and sister with a sour look. Xenon dressed far more simply than usual. Her outfit had nothing idiosyncratic about it anymore, just a white blouse, tight jeans, and no accessories to speak of. Except probably her heels, which were thin and sharp as a pencil lead, they could be a weapon in a spy movie.

"Why are you here?" Allecra asked her sister.

"I wouldn't be here if I didn't deem it important for you," Xenon said. But she sounded less hostile than the last time I saw her. Well, at least, she wasn't while speaking to Allecra.

"Is that it?" Allecra said.

"Please stop doing that, Alle," her sister said sternly. Then her topaz eyes glinted when they drifted to mine. "Can I have a moment of privacy with my sister?"

I looked at Allecra, who finally tore her gaze away from Xenon to give me a small nod. I was reluctant to go at first, but Triton came to escort me out of the room, telling with his bright smile that seemed to say, *'It wouldn't take long.'* I got into the elevator with him. Before the door shut, I could hear Xenon started to speak in their own language.

Triton and I got up to the living room. He showed me to the sofa and gestured for me to sit down. Then he took a seat on a bean bag nearby. For a few long minutes, we didn't talk. I tried to notice other things, the hem of my shirt or my shoes or the carpet. Triton just smiled as he observed me. His staring strangely didn't feel creepy at all. It didn't even give me the slightest discomfort. It was more like a curious friendly bear looking at you, and you know there would be no harm.

'You have anything to eat?' He suddenly asked in his own unique telepathic way. I had to make sure it wasn't my own thought when he was speaking to me. Triton rubbed his tummy to indicate that I heard him right. He was hungry.

"Oh!" I blinked. "Well...er...I can fix you a sandwich if you want."

Triton raised a hand up with big eyes as if to say, *'It's alright if it bothers you.'*

I blinked again. I still hadn't gotten a hang of this kind of communication, to be honest. But Triton didn't seem to mind my slow response.

"It's nothing," I reassured him and gave him a smile back. "Don't stand on ceremony. I'm good at making snacks and like to do it all the times."

He grinned and nodded at last. In fact, I was grateful for the task as I finally had an excuse to do something rather than sitting still. We got up and went to the kitchen. I opened the fridge, but to my surprise, there wasn't anything left in there, except a few fresh cucumbers and a package of seaweed, which Allecra must have bought to make me a Bento lunch. We hadn't been to the grocery shop for a while, so no wonder.

"Sorry, Triton, there's nothing here," I said apologetically, turning to him. He gave me a smile and an *'it's okay'* shrug. For some reason, it broke my heart to see that. It was like I had disappointed a child when he asked for some cookies. I decided to do something out of the cucumbers. "Well, you know what, how about a healthy snack instead?"

Triton raised an eyebrow. I just got the fruits out (yes, cucumbers are technically fruits) from the fridge, washed them and cut them on the chopping board into bite-size. I tore open the nori package and wrapped a strip over each sliced cucumber before stabbing it with a toothpick. I gathered the cucumber pieces on a plate and poured some soy sauce into a dipping bowl then brought everything to the table.

Triton stared at my invention in amused curiosity. He took one piece from the plate and dipped it into the sauce. Triton crunched down on the fresh cucumber. The sound echoed in the quiet room. He swallowed and took two more and gobbled them. In just a moment later, he polished off everything, even the soy sauce. I brought him a cup of tea and poured myself some, too.

'Delicious cucumbers! Thank you!' He smiled quite childishly at me.

"They were organic," I said and returned his smile. Triton laughed a quiet laugh.

'No wonder our sister is crazy about you,' he said. I felt my face blush.

Then my eyes glanced at the clock. Xenon had been talking to Allecra quite a long while now. I wondered what they were possibly talking about.

Although I had an inkling that it wasn't something I would like to know, I was still curious.

'Don't worry, they're just talking.' Triton said with an amused look.

"I'm not worried," I told him.

'Good.'

He leaned back on the chair, putting his hands behind his head. His hair was like silver and his eyes were the same, I just noticed them.

"Can you tell me why you drop by all of a sudden?"

'We are here today because of the Elders.'

"The Elders?"

Triton didn't respond for a few long minutes. I thought he didn't hear me.

"Who are the Elders?" I asked again.

'Our homeworld's remaining Arzurians.' He said. I looked at him in puzzlement.

"I thought you were the last Arzurians," I said.

'No.' Triton gave a little shake of his head.

"But Allecra said, she is the Endling," I told him.

'She is.'

"What about you and Xenon?"

'We don't matter.'

I remembered what Allecra told me about her two interstellar siblings. They were cloned or created, or whatever it was called, but they weren't like Allecra. Yet, everything Triton said didn't add up.

"What do the Elders want?"

Triton seemed to pause for a moment. It was the first time I sensed a jumbling wave of his thoughts between us. It was like a static noise when a TV was unable to reach the right frequency and the images came disoriented and wrinkling. Triton sat up and resumed his original position. There seemed to be a conflict as he looked at me, but for a split second, it all cleared up again. Maybe having fed him had earned me a fragment of his trust or kindness of some sort. Without actually saying it, he told me so quietly:

'They are waiting.'

I was silent for a while, trying to grasp my mind around this piece of information. But nothing made any sense.

"Waiting for what?"

We heard the elevator's door bell. Allecra and Xenon walked into the room afterward. I got up from the table with Triton. Xenon gave him a small nod and the two of them turned to leave. There was no awkward goodbye, which I was thankful for.

After they left, I went up to Allecra again. She wasn't looking at me, but at the retreating car outside.

"Everything okay?" I asked her. For a moment, it was as though the Allecra I was holding was replaced by someone else. "Allecra?"

"Yeah, everything's perfect," she said and smiled brightly at me.

"But why Xenon..."

"She's just being Xenon, don't pay her any mind," she said. "Shouldn't we prepare to go on our holiday now?"

I nodded, but the whole time, the flow of her attention seemed to be channeled in different directions. A great transparent wall that wasn't there before suddenly appeared between us. I sensed a kind of uncertainty in her, a sense of dread even. I wanted to ask her more, but I didn't want to sound demanding. When I had my moment of doubt, Allecra had let me walk through it myself. I should do the same for her. When she was ready to tell me, she would let me know what was going on.

CHAPTER 40

"YOU'RE SURE THIS IS anywhere closer to where we're heading?" I asked Allecra, who was walking in front of me with surprising ease.

The ground was slightly damped and covered with dead leaves. I was not used to such physical exertion, and it was only out of will that I didn't ask Allecra to slow down or take a break. I didn't want her to think I couldn't handle outdoor activities. We'd been hiking through an unknown forest for almost half an hour now.

I watched Allecra's long legs flitting through a rough path without any problem. It made me jealous at how easily she moved regardless of the steep terrain. I hurried to keep up with her and found myself running short of breath.

"You want to hitch a ride on my back?" Allecra said as she looked over her shoulder to me. I shook my head back.

"No, I'm fine," I said. She just smiled and shrugged.

"Well, let me know when you want to ride me," she said and quirked her eyebrows. I scowled back at her. I had to concentrate on walking and ignore her sexual innuendo at the same time.

But deep down, I was glad to see Allecra being her usual carefree herself again. After her siblings' visit, it seemed something was bothering her. Then just like that, she decided we should start our summer trip right away. I still couldn't understand what Triton had hinted to me, but soon I gave up trying to figure out the answer. It was difficult to pinpoint something that I had no clue of. Besides if Allecra wanted me to know something, she would tell me in her own time.

The field around us was filled with white and blue and yellow flowers. I was busy looking and admiring the nature when I lost my footing and skied over the ground until my hands grabbed a hold of a baby tree to stop the momentum, Allecra turned around quickly.

"You're alright, Nina?" she asked, concerned. I reassured her I was okay, but she insisted on giving me a piggyback ride from there. I tried to protest, but she just wrapped my arms around her neck as she hoisted me onto her back.

"Oh geez! You're as heavy as a sack of potatoes," Allecra pretended to complain, but she got moving so swiftly over the slope.

"I didn't ask you to carry me!" I pointed out crossly.

"Well, blame it on my love for you," she said, which shut me up.

Along the way, I kept pointing out flowers and trees on both sides of us. Allecra even stopped to pick a wild orchid I wanted. And she didn't mind when I put the flower in her hair. She seemed to find relish in my childish excitement as we hiked through the forest.

After a while, we came to a little path which seemed to lead up to a small hill. The hill was covered with a mass of green foliage. At the foot of the path was paved with pebbles and sand. Allecra chose the route of least evergreens to go down to the shore.

A moment later, we saw the view of a lake ahead of us. It seemed to appear out of nowhere.

"Here we are," she told me and then put me down again. I was speechless.

The sky was a fresh-swept blue, with only a trace of white cloud clinging like a streak of test paint.

The other side of the lake cast the reflection of tall pine trees and white-peaked mountains on its pristine water. The lake was shallow and glistened different shades of turquoise and blue. Its floor was visible, and I could see multicolored pebbles worn smooth right at the place where the water met land. The area around the shore was surrounded by flowerbeds and clusters of bushes and trees.

We stopped a few feet away from the lake and the two of us looked out toward the magnificent view together.

"It looks like a giant mirror, the most beautiful lake I've ever seen," I breathed. Allecra looked at me and smiled.

"I want you to see nature in its most gentle form like this."

"Where is this place, anyway?"

"Somewhere in New Zealand," she said.

"Oh my god!" I cried, "Really? We're in New Zealand?"

"Yeah," she chuckled. "I love it here. The trees and flowers reflect their uncomplicated seamlessness. Unlike Arzuria, Earth has this sophisticated charm that makes the planet so special. I guess it's just like the way you are to me."

I turned my head to look at her and she was already staring at me. It was the best feeling in the world.

"Thank you for bringing me here," I said.

"You deserve to see all the beauty there is to see, Nina," she said. "I always picture us in strange places, holding hands and looking at all the beautiful things together, always us."

I went to embrace her from the side. She kissed the top of my head lovingly.

We walked about a few more feet to the shoreline and found a big white tent made of canvases by a chestnut tree. The tent was round with pointed roof in an Indian style. There was even a campfire nearby.

"Whose tent is this?" I asked Allecra.

"Ours."

"Oh, are we camping here tonight?" I said in an excited voice.

"You have never camped out before?"

"No," I said. "I had always wanted to go camping as a kid. But my dad was always busy. I remember building a fort inside my apartment alone and pretended that it was in a forest. Sometimes I scared myself so bad, I stayed inside the fort until my dad found me asleep in it."

"You sound adorable," Allecra said. "We can play fort together here. Let's go and check it out."

We went inside the tent together. It was quite spacious and high enough for us not to hunch over, and it had a small mattress with pillows and a white blanket at the center. I was impressed. Allecra grinned proudly at me.

"We can spend a night or two here," she said.

"So what are we going to do now?" I asked.

"It's up to you," she said. "We can do whatever we want."

There was a silence. Both tried to act like there were no other 'special' activities in mind except to enjoy the nature.

"Okay, well..." I said. "The lake looks so pleasant outside."

"You want to take a swim in it?" She asked.

"I don't have any swimsuit with me."

"You can swim nude," Allecra said. "It's so quiet here."

I gave her a pointed look.

"Thanks for your suggestion, but I would rather not."

"Suit yourself," she said with a shrug. "But I'm going to."

"Huh?"

Allecra just smiled and went outside again. I followed after and watched her removing her clothes in astonishment. She stepped out of her underwear before glancing back at me with a smirk. I was no doubt blushing as I watched her from behind.

The length of Allecra's tattooed body sent a shiver up my spine. I didn't pretend not to look anymore. Allecra, all naked and carved to perfection, stepped into the water like an ancient goddess taking her bath — one foot after another until her body was submerged in the water.

I felt quite disappointed being left behind. I wanted to see more of her and caress her in my arms. Allecra turned around and looked at me again, her ample chest covered by her long blonde lock. My blood pounded in my ears as I stood there. The look in her eyes beckoned to me like a siren's call. I felt the heat in my body rose up ardently, telling me to go to her at once.

What was to be embarrassed about when every fiber of my being was in need of her?

Without further hesitation, I slowly took off my clothes, too. At the same time, Allecra wedged her way back through the water towards me.

Allecra helped me out of my clothes faster than I could do it myself. She got down, and I felt her lips pressed against my lower stomach as she rolled down my panties. Then she kissed my hipbone, my belly and then down there. I bit my lips from whimpering and tried to keep still. It happened just like that.

The whole thing was oddly enthralling, to say the least - us being naked in the wildness under the open sky, but it was the oddness that made it much more arousing.

The dipping sun only brightened the lake's surface with its clear turquoise color. Then Allecra swept me off my feet and carried me into the water. I clung to her and squealed as the first cold splash hit my skin.

Allecra laughed and put me down. I swam away and she swam after me. When she caught me again, our mouths went for each other. We kissed with our arms wound around the other's body. Allecra's long ravenous tongue licked the sensitive spots on my neck and down to my breasts. I felt her body's heat seeped into mine, burning up my desire and moisturizing my secret place. She caressed my breasts earnestly and brought them to her warm mouth. I gasped in pleasure. Then Allecra wrapped my legs around her waist, her hands went to my back and bum, hurling me against her body.

The thrusting was only teasing, but it was the magical position, and if stimulated intently, would make me weep in lustful tears. I tightened my hold on her shoulders and allowed myself to be carried by the motion. I just couldn't help but move my hips against her.

The water mixed with my own arousal was overwhelmingly slippery. Allecra devoured my lips and squeezed my backside. I closed my eyes, mouth gaping apart, moans slithering out of my throat.

Feeling the movement of her hand going downward while her other arm went around me in support. I thought she was going to use her fingers.

"I'm... sensitive right now," I said. "Be gentle, please."

"You're such a tease, Nina, it's your fault."

Our gazes locked again. There was a determined glint in Allecra's turquoise eyes. The strength of her grip was suddenly apparent. I could feel the unmistakable tension wrecking within her lower region. I looked down and to my surprise, her secret member sprang out. Allecra got a hold of herself and rubbed her erection against my heated core unapologetically. It made me jump in shock.

"Allecra, wait!" I cried out. "You don't have a condom on yet."

"Nina please, I want you now," Allecra said between her heavy breaths. The affection in her blazing eyes mingled with a new kind of lust. She brushed and caressed my exposed lips with the tip of her rigidness. The sensual feeling it brought caused blissful havoc to wag in my startled body. It was pure maddening.

"No, please don't do that...Allecra..." I said in protest, trying to wriggle away from her grip. The constant stimulation of our sensitive parts against each other was consuming my mind, and the more I moved, the farther my legs inevitably parted in the process as Allecra wouldn't let me go.

My sensitivity could not escape the pleasurable contact of that eager slippery tip. A wave of stirring desire washed over me, stripping me off my willpower. I didn't know what to do. Allecra was like a different person. Her angelic face shone with hunger. Under a normal circumstance, I would have willingly welcomed her passion, but this wasn't what I had in mind.

Her hot lips burned trials of kisses over my skin. Allecra slipped herself inside me. Her member went through my startled depth in a single stroke effortlessly. My jaw dropped at the electrifying sensation. It shocked me to my core. Allecra moaned at the same time. She held me still as I convulsed around her, trying to adjust to the intoxicating feeling.

My heart drummed inside my chest. I felt her in my belly, filling the hollowness of my heated walls. The sensation of our joined bodies was extraordinary. It felt like nothing we had ever done before, but after the pleasuring shock wore off, a flare of anger rushed through my veins. This wasn't what I wanted. Allecra couldn't force me into this. When she tried to kiss me again, I recoiled away from her.

"I said no!" I cried. Not until I said it that my tears started rolling off my cheeks. Allecra froze as she stared at me with wide eyes.

"Nina..."

"Take it out now before you start raping me," I said in a quivering voice.

Allecra's mouth fell open. Shock and guilt shone through her bright turquoise eyes. Quickly but gently, Allecra eased out of me again. I hugged my naked self and turned away from her like a wounded animal.

"Wait! Nina, I'm so sorry. I didn't mean to." She tried to pull me back into her arms again, but I shrugged her off and ran back towards the shore.

I gathered my clothes and went inside the tent. After I got dressed, I climbed onto the bed and covered myself with the blanket. My heart was still pounding in my ears. I heard Allecra's footsteps coming towards the tent. Her shadow cast over the canvas before she entered. I felt a weight on the mattress. Then Allecra's hand placed on my shoulder gently.

"I'm sorry I was impatient with you," she said in a pleading tone. "I got carried away."

"You knew I didn't want any of that," I said. "Why did you do it?"

"I just wanted to bring us closer together," Allecra said. "I want us to be one with no barrier between us."

I sat up and glared at her.

"Didn't you think of the consequence at all?"

"Nina, I love you. You don't have to be afraid of anything. I'll take great care of you, I promise."

"You don't get it, do you?" I said with a disappointing shake of my head. "It's not just about my fear of you getting me pregnant. It's about us respecting each other!"

Allecra looked quite surprised to see my emotional outburst.

"Maybe it doesn't cause anything anyway," she said. "You shouldn't be so worried."

"I'm not like other girls, Allecra. I can't do this for you. I'm scared! Why don't you understand? Why can't you try to understand my feelings?"

I covered my face in my hands and burst into tears. Allecra came to hold me, but I pulled away from her grasp.

"Please, leave me," I said in a tear-coated voice. "I want to be alone."

Then I dropped myself back onto the pillow with my back turned to her again. It was pointless to say anything more. Allecra let out a heavy sigh.

"Alright," she said and leaned over to kiss my hair softly.

I closed my eyes and burrowed my head into the blanket, trying not to think what had just happened. I didn't know what to make out of this circumstance. I was too upset to cry and just lying there, staring and unseeing.

The sun must have already set. The tent was growing dark, but I didn't turn on the lamp. The sounds of crickets and wild birds orchestrated from the trees.

I woke up again with a start. I didn't realize I had fallen asleep. A bright light came through the tent from the outside. I realized Allecra had built the campfire. And the first feeling that wagged in my gut was an intent hunger. I hadn't eaten since we were in Allecra's house and hiking had exhausted me.

My nose instinctively caught on a delicious aroma. It made my stomach growl. Outside were the crackling sounds of burning wood. Allecra must have built the campfire for cooking. That was where the delicious smell came from. I wished I could have something to eat, but I didn't want to face the blonde alien again. Why did things go downward spiral? We were having fun and enjoying each other's company, and all of a sudden, we were not in speaking term. The whole situation made me even more miserable. I rolled back on the bed and curled up into a fetus position, hoping my stomach would quiet down.

A moment later, the canvas flap pulled open and Allecra came inside.

"Nina, are you awake?"

I stayed silent. She came to sit beside me. The strong delicious smell brushed past my nose again. It awoke all my senses, causing my eyes to open. I realized she had barbecued some skewer meats.

"You must be hungry," she said. "Get up and eat something."

"I'm not hungry," I said, but the moment I said it, my stomach growled treacherously. Damn it!

Allecra chuckled. "Come on, stop being a sulking baby. I made a lot of kebabs for you."

"I don't like kebabs," I murmured again.

"Really?" she said. "Have you ever tried it? It's so delicious."

Allecra picked up one of the stick meats and started eating it.

"Hmm...juicy and fresh," she moaned. "Are you sure you're not hungry?"

My mouth watered until it almost choked me to death as I was lying down. Why the heck does it have to smell so good?

I sat up with an annoyed frown. Allecra looked from her plate, still chewing the barbecued meat wholeheartedly. Her lips glistened with grease, and there was a suppressed mirth in her eyes. Then she handed me the plate.

"Want some?" she asked.

"No." I gazed at the food longingly. The beef was cut nicely in even cubes and stack with green peppers, onions, and mushrooms. The meat dripped with a honey teriyaki sauce. I licked my lips before I could stop myself.

"Alright, if you say so," Allecra said and then began to get up again.

"No, wait!" I cried and pulled her by the hand. She sat down again.

"Pardon?"

"I want to try it," I said tersely.

"Okay." Allecra put the plate down. "Tell me which one you like."

"The biggest one, please," I told her. "but take the mushrooms out."

She smiled and did as was told, picking out the mushrooms for me then handed me the skewers.

At first, I nibbled it, trying to act indifferent, but once I discovered how delicious it tasted, I started gobbling everything greedily. Allecra went outside and brought me a few more. She watched me eat until I was satisfied. Then she poured me some tea from a thermos bottle into a cup. I must have looked barbaric, but I was too starving to care.

"You're done?" she asked. I nodded back, feeling a little embarrassed afterward. She took the plate out and came back a while later.

I sat, sipping the warm tea in my hands. I was trying to convey the message that, just because she fed me doesn't mean we have made up. But then Allecra moved over towards me.

"What are you doing?" I asked, leaning away.

"You look like a cat with whiskers, let me clean your face," she said, holding a wet towel. Gently she wiped the sticky sauce off my face. After she was done, she stared at me. Her eyes sparkled under the dimming light.

"I'm sorry," she said.

I dropped my gaze from hers. Allecra took my hand and kissed it.

"You could have asked me first," I murmured.

"I know," she said. "I wanted you so bad, I got greedy and forgot myself. Let's not fight. It feels horrible when we fight."

"I wasn't the one who started it," I said. Allecra rubbed her eyes with her thumb and index finger and sighed.

"Nina, I don't have the energy to do this anymore," she sighed.

"I know I'm difficult to love. You shouldn't waste your energy with me," I said bitterly and looked away.

Allecra gently tipped my chin and made me look at her again.

"Nina, if you loved yourself just as much as I love you, you would love yourself endlessly."

I let my heart soak in the tingling warmth of her words. It filled me with pleasant joy and washed away the chagrins between us. I put the cup down and went out to embrace Allecra in my arms. She held me back tightly.

"Maybe we can work it out another way," I suggested. "I can take pills if you want."

"We can talk about it later," she said. "Now just come and cuddle with me. I want to hold you until the sun rises. I don't want to see you cry because of me, Nina."

I nodded and then we got into the blanket together. Allecra pulled me to her as I curled myself up into her body.

At last, we came back to each other's arms again.

CHAPTER 41

I OPENED MY EYES and realized it was already morning. Inside the tent was brightened by the sunlight. But something felt different, and I found the bed deprived of Allecra's form.

I got up and changed into a clean shirt I had packed with me. Then I went outside, expecting to find Allecra doing whatever she was doing. But all I saw was the faint smoke drifting from the campfire of last night.

The sunshine glared down the pristine turquoise lake. The tranquil view was pleasant to the eye. But I was more concerned about finding Allecra than to enjoy the landscape.

I searched around the campsite, looking for her, but she seemed to disappear out of sight.

"Allecra? Where are you?" I called out to her as I walked down towards the pebbled shore. Where had she gone? I tried calling her, only to be answered by the cries of birds on their way to their early hunts.

Unlike yesterday the forest seemed dark and deep with the towering trees. They formed thick walls around me. It was also eerily quiet without Allecra.

I decided to go down to the lake again and gathered the water to wash myself. Through my own reflection, a strayed unwanted thought came into my mind. What if she was hurt because of my rejection? I shouldn't have been so harsh on her. After all, Allecra was born with this instinct, something that was akin to thirst. And she'd been patient and understanding this whole time while all I cared about was what I wanted. Now that I thought it over, I felt a smidgen of guilt with how I reacted towards her.

I came back to the tent and sat down on a log, waiting for Allecra to return. The intense loneliness began to seep in and overwhelm me. I knew it was silly to be scared. She wouldn't have left without me, not like that. But her sudden disappearance made me anxious and slightly deranged. All kinds of dark thoughts battled their way into my head.

I tried not to panic as I sat there alone. Then I heard the stomping of boots of someone's footsteps from a grove of pines. My heart skipped. I turned around. To my immense relief, it was Allecra. She was holding an armload of dry twigs and branches.

"Allecra!" I cried and ran to her.

The moment she saw my distraught face, she dropped everything to the ground and came to meet me half way. I threw my arms around her, and she held me back tightly.

"Nina, what's wrong? Are you okay?" She asked.

I pulled away to look at her.

"I woke up, and I didn't see you," I said. "Where have you been?"

"I'm sorry. I thought you were still sleeping," she said with an apologetic look. "I just went out to pick some apples and berries then gathered some wood for cooking."

"What are you? A hunter-gatherer from Stone Age?" I said in frustration. "Don't you leave me alone like that!"

"I'm so sorry. I didn't know," she said and kissed my forehead to soothe me. "I just wanted you to rest and make you breakfast before you wake up."

Seeing her guilt-ridden face, I decided to let it slide.

"Never mind," I said in a small voice. "I just got scared without you."

"Now let's sit down," she said and moved us back to the tent. We both sat on the log before the campfire. "By the way, I brought back some of these for you."

She opened her leather bag hanging from her shoulder and pulled out a bunch of wildflowers. I had never seen flowers like these. They looked similar to lavenders, but bigger with bell-like petals and came in blue and purple hue. They were truly beautiful.

"It's lupins," Allecra told me. "There's a field of them nearby. You want to go and see it with me?"

I looked at the flowers then back at her. So she'd been busy picking flowers for me.

"They're so lovely, thank you," I said and took them from her. "And yes, I'd love to."

"Good, but first help me with the breakfast." She smiled and kissed my temple again.

Allecra rekindled the embers until the flame burst to life again and then set out to work. Everything she needed was packed in Tupperware. She seemed to know what we would do out here in the wild. It was like she had planned it beforehand.

I helped her whisking the egg with milk and cinnamon in a bowl. Allecra stirred mascarpone in another pot then spread it over bread slices. I liked watching her cook. It was so adorable.

She placed the maple syrup and berries in a small covered saucepan and swirled it over the fire. I dipped sandwiches in egg mixture then cooked them until crisp and brown.

When it was all done, Allecra poured over the toasties with warm syrup. It looked like the kind of thing you ordered from a luxurious restaurant. It tasted even better with the view of the sunrise over the turquoise lake.

"Hmm...if there's anything finer than this, I have not encountered it yet," I moaned after a big bite of the toast, feeling the cheese melted in my mouth.

"Am I not the finest thing you have encountered so far?" Allecra said.

"Well, you're a tad better than this toast."

Allecra laughed and reached her hand out to wipe the syrup off the corner of my lips with her thumb.

"Sorry for leaving you alone earlier," she said again.

"It's fine," I said. "I think I was just a bundle of nerves. I shouldn't have been so harsh on you."

"Nina," she said with her eyes looking at me. "Both of us have a lot of feelings we need to sort out once in a while."

"I promise I won't be like that with you again," I said.

Allecra smiled at me and pulled me to her.

We finished our breakfast, cleaned up the place and put out the fire.

Then we set out for a short hike to the lupin field.

Allecra and I traversed the through the green forest. Sunlight shot down through the branches of the trees like spotlights. The slope gave out after a while, and we entered a level plateau. The trail reached a gentle waving thicket of plume grass. Allecra would reach for my hand whenever she thought I was having weak footing.

At last, we arrived at the blooming field. The view of the flowers carpeted the earth took my breath away. It was like standing before a fairyland. The lupins blossomed in various shades of blue, yellow, purple, and pink. The turquoise lake stretched out to the horizon. The mountain's snow-white peaks looked incandescent against the blue sky.

"This place is so beautiful," I whispered in awe.

We walked down the field together and found a nice spot among the swaying flowers. We sat down and let the faint warmth of sunlight washed over us. Allecra lay down on the soft grass.

"Come over here, Nina," she said and I moved towards her. The lupins surrounding us danced against the breeze. Allecra was soft and warm against me. We snuggled into each other. Then we kissed. Our lips moved with growing ardor.

"Tell me something Allecra," I whispered.

"Yes?"

"Do you really want to have kids with me?"

Her eyes lit up at my question. She turned to me in surprise as if she couldn't believe what she just heard. After a moment, she nodded.

"Of course, I do," she told me. There were vehemence and sincerity in her voice that made my heart clench.

"I don't know if I can do this yet," I said. "I couldn't help but have a dreadful feeling about the sharing and nurturing a new life. But my heart is not made of stone or steel to remain unmoved by your entreaties."

Despite her extraterrestrial intelligence, Allecra's eyes still fixed on me in confusion.

"What do you mean?"

"I want to be emotionally and physically ready, that I'm capable of being a mother of your child."

I watched Allecra's mouth fell open.

"Oh Nina, that would the most wonderful thing in the world to me!"

I smiled nervously at her hopeful enthusiasm.

"Allecra," I said again. "There are too many things I have to deal with right now. I still haven't found my place in the world yet. What if you have to wait ten years or twenty years for me?"

"Whenever you're ready." She leaned in to kiss my forehead.

"But I might never recover from this chronic fear," I said. "Will you wait for me forever?"

This time, she didn't answer me right away, and my heart pounded at the notion that she was disappointed about it.

"You overthink things too much," she said at last. "Stop letting yourself be scared by what hasn't happened yet. Throw away the worse-case scenarios and doubts. I will protect you and comfort you if things get tough."

"Can you promise me that?"

"I promise," she said and smiled sweetly back. We kissed again.

~*~

Our next trip was to a pleasant Greek island. It was a small town of whitewashed houses that huddled up over the cliffs like sugar cubes.

After I told her I just wanted to walk around some foreign villages and gaze at authentic people and sit in a local café somewhere overlooking the ocean, she brought me to the island where it had the bluest of the sky and the widest of the sea. Our rented villa stood on the rugged landscapes, overlooking the white shore.

I still marveled at the rush of excitement when my eyes opened to the breathtaking view. The ocean gleamed from our secluded balcony. Its aqua-blue water rippled like jelly in a giant bowl. I could hear a faint ship bell from a distance. The dreamy scenery looked like it came straight out of a postcard. And I couldn't wait to get out there and see things.

Since Allecra was familiar with the area and even spoke fluent Greek, she took me for a stroll around the village. We went through winding isles of houses and antique shops before we decided to take a break at a local café.

Sitting by the beach, we sipped our tea and watched pedestrians passing by tumultuously.

"I had never dreamed of going anywhere like this," I said to Allecra. "I thought I was going to be wrapped up in the layers of my ordinary existence forever, never allowed to venture outside into the world for the rest of my insipid life."

She gave me a marvelous smile.

"I can take you everywhere, Nina, just like that robot cat you told me."

It made me giggle.

"Anyway, did you bring it with you?" I asked in a low voice even I knew there was no chance of people would understand what I referred to.

"Yep, in my bag," Allecra reassured me. "But you don't have to rush, Nina, unless you want us to—you know—very soon."

"That's not it!" I said. "I'm just being cautious. I'm on the first day of my menstrual cycle. The protection will start right away if I take it now."

"Okay, okay, I'm just kidding," she said and fished a package out of her bag. I took it and opened it up discreetly and popped a pill into my mouth. I washed it down with a glass of water. Allecra was watching me with contemplating eyes.

"What?" I asked her.

"Nothing." She shrugged. Her eyes emanated something else, but I couldn't grasp what was behind them. Before I could say anything, she called the waiter and paid the bill.

"What are we going to do next?" I asked.

"Let's go on another stroll before we get back."

She took my hand, and together we walked out of the place. Strolling through the cobbled road, we heard a faint music. It seemed to be coming from the village's church at the top of the hill followed by the bell chiming. As we got closer, the melodies became louder. It was a wedding song. When we went past the church, I spotted the bride and groom surrounding by relatives and friends. They dressed in formal suits and beautiful gowns ready for a photograph.

I was suddenly gripped by a longing I had never known before. Marriages had never been in the uppermost of my mind. I always thought of wedding like a cage to a wing-clipped bird. My heart would sink at the thought of a faceless person on the altar with me. I just couldn't picture anyone I would want to spend the rest of my life with.

Not until now.

Holding Allecra's tender hand in mine, I felt like I was one of those girls who fantasized about wedding dresses and saying 'I do. And that made me feel stupid. I was embarrassed for wanting something symbolic like that. Allecra wouldn't conform herself to this silly norm, would she?

As we continued to walk, Allecra noticed my absent stupor— probably through our touch alone. She stopped and turned around to look at me.

"Are you alright, Nina?"

Her voice brought me back from my reverie.

"Yeah—yeah, I'm alright," I said. "I'm just a little tired."

"Maybe we should go back to the villa and rest," she suggested.

I just nodded back.

Once we arrived, Allecra led me to our room. The ocean breeze flickered through the silk curtains of our balcony.

"How about we take a bath together, Nina?" Allecra said with a mischievous look.

"How about no?"

"Aw, I miss taking a bath with you!" she whined at me like a little girl. "Come on, I'll scrub your back."

"Well only if you don't do anything silly again," I said.

"You're on the pill now. What's to worry about?"

"Pills are not always effective."

Allecra just rolled her eyes and then she forcibly carried me off to the bathroom. Despite my protesting screams, I wasn't really trying to stop her.

The bath lasted only half an hour because neither of us could wait anymore. The familiar look of craving had returned to those brilliant turquoise eyes. I shivered from their glowing intensity, coupling with my own aching need. We miraculously found our way back to the bedroom, blindly wrapped in each other's passion.

"Shouldn't we need a back-up in case the pill hasn't kicked in yet?" I whispered breathlessly as her hot mouth ravaging my throat.

"But Nina..." Allecra's strained voice was desperate. She looked up at me with pleading eyes. I knew she dared not refuse if it was what I wanted. Yet the look on her face could reduce even a tiger to tears. Her gaze pierced through me with yearning heat.

It felt like a lifetime ago since we had been intimate. We restricted ourselves from each other for the sake of keeping ourselves sane. But now, holding this desire back was almost physically impossible for us both.

"Never mind then," I said and gave in to the fierce kisses that scorched my skin with love and lust.

My back landed on the soft bed with Allecra between my legs. The bathrobes soon got tossed aside as our naked bodies burned for each other. Our skins rubbed, making my blood sing through my veins. I traced the tattoos on her arms and shoulders.

Allecra's hands skimmed over my sides and down to my hips and thighs. I could feel my pulse quickened and my breaths shallowed. The tension in my belly reached a melting point where I would beg Allecra to do something if it came to that.

"You're ready?" Allecra whispered, all the while she never removed her lips from my trembling body.

I tried to speak but could only manage a weak *'yes'* since there was a lump of excitement stuck in my throat. Allecra broke her kiss and rose to her knees. Our eyes met in an intense gaze.

She reached her hand down between her thighs and sort of groaned a little. This was probably the most spectacular part of our love-making. I watched her touched herself until that lean delicate erection grew instantly to its full length. My heart faltered for a flitting moment before it started to race again. I still found it astonishing how her anatomy was so different. It never failed to amaze me. Allecra wrapped her fingers around herself and absentmindedly moved it. My jaw slacked at the sight.

"Allecra, wait..." I blurted.

She stopped and looked perplexedly at me.

"Yes?"

I got up onto my knees so that we were face to face with each other.

"I'm not sure how to describe it," I said, feeling my face blush coyly. "It's like a curious wanting feeling. Please, don't touch yourself. Let me do it."

Allecra's perfect brows arched in question. I felt extra stupid, but then she smiled.

"Okay."

I moved closer to her. We sat back with our legs wrapped around the other's waist. My hand went straight to her secret and cradled it gently. Allecra whimpered through her clenched teeth as our stares entwined. Her blonde brows furrowed at the first sensation of my touch. We leaned in and kissed again with probing tongues. I moved my hand.

"Oh geez, Nina—" She gasped. She was growing harder. "If you keep it like that, I—I'm going to..."

But she couldn't finish. I enjoyed seeing her trying to fight it. Allecra briefly licked her fingers and brought them to the area of my femininity.

"Allecra...what are you doing?!"

"It's only fair," she said and inserted two digits slowly inside me.

"Stop it," I gasped.

"Stop?" She made small movements with her fingers. Electricity shot through me. It felt so incredible.

"Oh my." I changed my mind.

"What did you say?"

"Stop—talking."

"You're quite strange for a human. Some girls like to talk during sex, oh, and they scream, too."

"Haven't you had enough of screaming girls already?" I said, trying to mock her but failed miserably. As I was lost in the gripping pleasure, my hand around her hardness loosened, and I fell back onto the bed.

"Gotcha!" she said.

"You're so immature!" I told her between heavy breaths.

"But you love me," Allecra giggled. She withdrew her hand and crawled on top of me. "You've always been quiet, but I'll make sure you'll be quite vocal this time."

The glint in her turquoise eyes made me shiver. All those times we made love had exceeded the level of pleasure I hadn't expected. Now to go even beyond that was unimaginable. Before I had any more time to think, Allecra teased my breasts with her tongue and teeth until my body writhed.

And without further foreplay, her hands splayed my legs apart. I felt the cold scented wetness accumulated there. Allecra finally eased her slippery hard tip into my softness. My nerves went buzzing like a colony of bees. She tried to make it slow and gentle, seeing it as my first time going natural. That handsome chiseled jawline tightened with internal restraints. But I was already soaking profusely and invitingly. Allecra ended up sliding herself into me in one swift move. Both of us let out a guttural groan. My back arched off the bed, and my inside quivered with sensual sparks bursting within my body. Allecra was hard like a rock and even slightly bigger than usual.

"Oh my goodness...Allecra," I whimpered, feeling every inch of her everywhere.

"Sorry, you're just so very soft," she moaned and inhaled sharply. "Be still, Nina please and let me savor you."

My mind got sucked into a euphoric world as I roamed her smooth tattooed back with my hands to distract myself. I thought I might come just by having her in me. I guessed Allecra was the same. She rested her head on my breasts and nibbling away at my nipples.

"It's getting easier now, isn't it?" she whispered.

"I guess."

"It feels better, too, no?"

"Allecra, just shut up," I groaned.

"Only if you say please."

"Please shut up."

She laughed, and her laughter vibrated blissfully my waiting depth. I let out a long sigh, tilting my head back from this stolen pleasure.

"I'm moving now, is that okay?" Allecra asked. It felt like our first time all over again. Somehow it was kind of sweet and special.

I nodded back, granting her permission to bring me to whichever state she desired. Allecra stirred her hips, which caused my breath to halt in my throat.

Then she started flexing cautiously. Her lips sought mine again with more craving. I felt my heart resumed its wild rhythm when she made little jolts of feral pleasure in my core.

My slippery arousal coated us both, giving the motion more freedom and ease. Allecra held me against her body like she was trying to merge us together. She began to moan louder. Her blushing angelic visage contorted with bliss. My fingers glided into her hair while my body felt like it was being engulfed by an internal flame.

Allecra was going deeply and more feverishly now, and not before long that I started screaming into her shoulder. My toes curled from the ragging ecstasy as I took every powerful thrust. Each one made me shudder.

The tide within my trembling form was rising and falling. I was caught between the current, unable to anchor myself in the world any longer. My eyes fluttered open and close at the rising wave of electrifying pleasures.

Spontaneously, Allecra cried out and her body shuddered. Her lips pulled back over her teeth with her eyes squeezed shut. The outlines of tattoos brightened in a turquoise glow. I almost started to worry for her, but then I felt a sudden spurt of thick warmth rushing through my walls. I gasped, realizing that Allecra was coming. She released herself inside me. The feeling of her potent seeds powerfully filling my womb was indescribable. I could feel her coming again and again, causing my mind to spin and my heart to stop. I lost every care in the world. It was more than anything I ever had with her. The pure rawness of her pleasure was enough to push me over the brink of oblivion.

My core tightened around Allecra as I found my own release, coming undone beneath her. Her powerful spurts still kept going in me. My walls constricted, gathering all her juice. I clutched her body to my chest and moaned helplessly in her arms. The climax was far more intense than I was prepared for. My mind swirled out of the present reality and time.

After it was all over, there was this peaceful contentment I felt in Allera's embrace. We panted and stayed in the same position for a while, listening to each other's heartbeat.

At last, we separated our joined bodies. Allecra pulled out of me so slowly as if she was afraid to make a mess, and even that gave me a delicious sensation. I was surprised to feel her juice filling up so thickly in there, and not a single drop of it oozed out. It was so warm and heavy inside my twitching womb. Allecra had come so much, I had never felt anything like this. I was so satiated and so full. It was the best sex we'd ever had.

But this time, Allecra didn't clean me up like she normally did. And some part of me didn't want her to. It was deliriously wonderful to know that she had left part of her behind. Allecra curled up into me with her arms wounded around my waist. Her soft sleepy sighs followed. I smiled and turned my head to face my lover.

Our eyes met. I traced my fingers over her lovely cheek, feeling the delicate skin on my palm. The wind ruffled our twisted sheet. Allecra soon opened her dazzling eyes again. They greeted me with sweet tenderness.

Always.

CHAPTER 42

TRAVELING WITH ALLECRA was like browsing through a catalog of your fantasies and actually got teleported there at the speed of your thought. Our quantum adventure continued from one city to another as summer days passed slowly by.

Sometimes, we would find ourselves waking up in the vibrant beach city of Rio de Janeiro, or roaming the boisterous fair in Munich, or going to Van Gogh Museum in Amsterdam, or riding the London Eye. Some other times, we went on a dinner date, drinking red wine while watching flamenco dancers in Bueno Aires, or listening to a live orchestra in the Colosseum of Rome at night.

I wished our summertime would never end. We could keep trotting around the world like this forever. Just the two of us.

The sun rose high in the morning sky, signaling our new day in a new city. I felt tingles running up my spine when I awoke. Allecra was nuzzling my neck from behind.

"Morning kitten," she purred in my ear. Her breath tickled me, causing my skin to prickle with goosebumps. I turned around to meet that angelic face.

"Stop it! You're tickling me," I giggled.

"I love your smell," she said. "It's intoxicating."

"Yeah, I use something called 'shampoo '."

"I don't think that's just it," she disagreed, inhaling my skin again. "It's your natural scent."

"My natural scent?"

"You don't know? Human women's natural scent is more seductive than any perfume in the world," Allecra said. "It can arouse your partner and only happens when you are ovulating."

"Oh," I said and frowned a little at that. If it was the case, that meant now my female hormones were busy at work preparing me for a possible pregnancy. I immediately grimaced to myself. Whenever we took a break from traveling or were alone, Allecra and I would do the wicked deeds like any lovesick couple would do.

It didn't matter that I could be trying to make dinner for us or in the middle of something mundane. The next thing I knew, I ended up in her arms — us kissing urgently and me being hoisted onto the counter or the dinner table with Allecra doing naughty things between my legs.

Though one thing I came to notice was that Allecra loved releasing herself in me. I sometimes complained about the huge mess afterward. But secretly I quite enjoyed the sensation of her filling up my youthful womb with the powerful spurts of her potent juices. Her intense climaxing made my head spin in sweet delirium. I was just glad that I was protected from the shuddering possibility of getting pregnant.

Sometimes, we would just stay in bed and be at it all day. I couldn't resist the pleasure of Allecra undressing me, caressing my skin, holding me close as her breathing turned ragged. It was all so feverish and blissful. I still marveled at the rapturous feeling of her going inside me, having every inch of her everywhere. The mounting sensation was like tidal waves crashing on the shore. It shattered my world with overflowing warmth. Our love-making wasn't a mere physical pleasure but a natural extension of ourselves.

"How are you feeling?" Allecra suddenly asked.

It was kind of funny to hear her asking me like that. Perhaps she was worried that last night's fun was too taxing for me. I reassured her with a peck on her nose.

"I'm feeling great," I said, smiling. "How about you?"

She studied my face in silence for a minute. In that moment, I noticed her eyes were seemingly veiled by a shadow. It was as though they were guarding something inside her mind. Before I could grasp what that look signified, her gaze returned to its glorious shine again. A slow drowsy smile reappeared on her angelic face.

"Not so well actually," she said, stretching herself and spread her arms over her head.

"Are you still tired?"

"Well, my back is a little stiff."

My face reddened in guilt. Allecra must have worked too hard last night.

"Maybe I can give you a massage," I offered.

"Nah, I just need a little hip exercise with you," she said. Her amused smile directed at me suggestively.

"Oh, for goodness's sake, Allecra!"

"What? It's good for us both, scientifically proven," she argued. "Besides I'm at your mercy now if you take a look at me."

Then her eyes moved down. I took it as a cue to look under the cover and had to gasp. She was hard already!

"You're insatiable!" I cried and was about to get out of bed when she grabbed my waist from behind and pulled me back to her again. Her arms locked me securely in a firm embrace.

"Yep, take note, Nina, especially in the morning," Allecra chuckled mischievously.

"But we're having sex almost every day!" I groaned.

"And you loved it every time, didn't you?" she mocked. "And it's your fault. No one should look so pretty waking up in the morning."

I opened my mouth to protest but found myself unable to deny it. It was true. Allecra was born fully equipped. She knew exactly what being a girl feels like and cleverly used it to her advantage. In fact, ever since we left the island in Greece, sex with Allecra was like a domino effect which you can't stop once it starts. My face was blushing so hot. I felt her rigidness brushing up against my backside, and a hot wave of need rode over my tingling body once again. I turned my head around to look at her. She looked back at me.

She leaned to kiss my cheek then moved down to wrap her mouth around my nipple. I moaned in my throat as she sucked it hard.

"Gosh, how do I deal with an alien who wants sex all the times?" I murmured.

Allecra pulled away with a smacking sound and frowned at me.

"I don't want sex all the times," she protested, "I just want sex with you all the times. And you deal with me by being a good girl."

It sent electric sparks down to the region of my longing. Then she moved down and buried her face into my stomach then my private. One of her hands sensually roamed over the valley of my breasts while the other parted my thighs. Her first lap made my hip jerk with bliss.

"Allecra, at least let me take the pill first," I said breathlessly.

"You've been taking it for weeks now. You can do it later," she said, "it's still fine, trust me."

Her lips and long slick tongue kept harassing my swelling femininity, tracing over the opening of my desire and making it difficult for me to speak.

"We can never be too careful," I replied with heavy breaths.

But Allecra delved her strong ravaging tongue deeper, causing my thoughts to shatter like glass.

"Allecra, please, just wait a minute," I said apologetically. And with great effort, I managed to untangle myself from her arms and got out of bed. She rolled onto her back. I thought I heard Allecra sighed to herself. I went to the nightstand and popped the pill with a glass of water. When I returned to bed, Allecra was lying on her back with her secret stood gloriously. My heart fluttered at the sight.

"Can you have a little decency to cover yourself? You're being narcissistic," I said.

"What? Don't you like what you see?"

"I'm gay, and that still looks like a banana to me."

"Ouch!" Allecra said. "You need to come here right now to be punished."

I laughed and went over to her. She took me into her arms, and we kissed each other desperately. Allecra lay back down and left me straddling on her stomach. I pinned her hands above her head. Those dazzling eyes stared up at me with glowing heat.

"I want you to take me, Nina," she whispered, slowly moving my body up a little and adjusting herself beneath me. "Take me all you want."

The slick pink head was already coated in slipperiness, which seemed to come from both of us.

I took a deep breath, biting my lip and quietly sheathing myself onto her. Her body tensed up from under me once I took her all the way. Allecra made a seething sound through her teeth. Her blonde brows furrowed at the sweet feeling of our unison. My hands rested on her ample breasts, rolling those firm and perfect mounds in my palms. Allecra closed her eyes and tilted her head with a deep sigh to savor us.

Every inch of her felt beautiful.

And then we started making sweet love together.

When we climaxed, Allecra unleashed herself with such a force and velocity that I could feel it flicking wildly against my walls. My core burned hot as it twitched around Allecra. Then I couldn't hold it anymore. I let out a sharp gasp and reached my own climax. Some of her thick potent seeds dripped out of me, making quite a mess between my thighs, but neither of us stopped. We couldn't stop ourselves until we were completely melted like a candle from the inside out. I was still amazed at how it could feel this wonderful every time.

~*~

Aside from all the traveling and slipping between the sheets whenever we could, I also insisted we took sometimes off to study. That way I wouldn't feel like a complete liar to my aunt.

Allecra wasn't so thrilled with this nerdy idea, but it was clearly my need of education. Besides she had to be my private tutor, or else, I had threatened her; there would be no sex. It might sound unscrupulous of me to use this card against Allecra, but I thought we shouldn't be all play and no work. We would stay in our hotel suite or go to a public library, or a small pleasant cafe in the city we happened to be in, and then we would study.

With great patience and sharp clarity, she could explain anything I wanted to know. She seemed to have no trouble going over the answers. It still took me by surprise how intelligent and wise she could be, but what bugged me a little was her being frivolous most of the times. Yet it sometimes made me wonder if she ever had a kid, would her son or daughter be smart and lovely and mischievous just like her? I bet they would.

But then I was gripped by a sordid feeling that Allecra might never continue her legacy because of me. I still couldn't find the courage to fulfill her dream. It made me feel like a horrible person to her. I could only do what I always did best— by trying not to ruminate too much about this shady thought

It was raining one evening. We were huddled up together at a quiet corner of a restaurant in Prague. Allecra and I had just spent a two-day tour in Istanbul before we decided to come here. It was strangely beautiful outside, seeing the city through droplets of rains on the glass window.

426

"I wonder what ants do on rainy days," I said out of the blue. "How do they keep their nest dry?"

"Well, they're hard-workers," Allecra said. "They probably spend the day cleaning their houses and putting buckets under the leaks."

It made me laugh.

"Probably so," I agreed.

"All joke aside, you know that when the queen of the ant colony dies, the colony can only survive for a few months," Allecra said. "Queens are rarely replaced and the workers are not able to reproduce. So their perfect civilization will collapse, too."

"Oh, that's so sad that they can't do anything about it, isn't it?" I said.

"Similar to the Arzurian civilization," she said. Perhaps it was the calming effect of the rain that made us feel like talking about it again. "You know a similar fate might have happened to the Martians on their planet."

"Oh really? Isn't it what scientists today still debating about?" I asked, "Once there was life on Mars and now it's all gone?"

"That's right," she said. "Before we came to earth, we had also studied possible earth-like planets in your solar system. The Arzurian Elders used to have some hopes that Mars was the answer since all evidence suggested a sign of life there. There were river deltas, flood plains, and oceans. Mars was a wet fertile place, but it was later discovered that the planet was all bone dry now. The red planet, that's what they call it today. Something bad must have happened on Mars."

"You mentioned the Arzurian Elders, who are they to you?" I asked the same question I had asked Triton.

Allecra looked at my face like she just realized what she'd just said. Her eyes locked with mine steadily.

"Well they are the highly respected scientists who gave birth to me," she said. "They're like my parents in a way."

"They're still alive?" I asked curiously.

"Yes, you can say that for now." She shrugged.

I realized that the Elders she spoke of were probably the important figures that Triton and Xenon took the order from and came to earth with Allecra. The last time her siblings came to see her, it was something about the Elders. Triton told me they were waiting. I felt a chill rushing through

427

my bones. I was too stupid not to realize this soon enough. Now I might have known what they were waiting for.

"Nina?" Allecra called me. "You're okay? You look kind of sad."

"I'm alright," I said and tried to change the subject. "Do you really think there used to be a Martian civilization before earth in the past?"

"Not just on Mars, but on Venus too. Those two worlds are the example of a planet gone bad," Allecra answered. "Your civilization is probably the youngest among them in the solar system. But by the time we discovered Mars, the Martians had already vanished for billions of years. Good thing, the Arzurians found earth afterward."

"Really?" I was only half-listening.

"Yeah, you only knew about the ancient civilizations on earth that used to exist but not anymore," she said. "Like Mars, Arzuria is also coming to the final doom. The Arzurians will meet no different fate from the Martians."

Allecra sighed softly at that. It was the first time she showed her true sadness.

"Unless you succeed in reproducing the next generation and continue their bloodline."

"Right," she said with a weak shrug. Now I felt like I was the reminder of her failure, and that saddened me even more.

I decided to steer the conversation away from the subject again. I was good at dodging it.

"I wonder why people on Mars didn't try to save their race like the Arzurians."

"Maybe back then when Mars was alive, the earth was still an infant planet, merely a lump of rock and hot lava. They couldn't find a new host planet in time," Allecra said. "But there's a theory that asteroids that hit Mars had cast rocks into space and sent them all the way to earth. So if Mars had life billions of years before this planet, it could be possible that the bacteria that clung to the rocks were the beginning of life transferred to the virgin earth to start anew. And if that is the case, then you're considered as the descendant of the Martians."

"You're not kidding!" I cried with a surprised face.

"It's a plausible idea, Nina," she said with a laugh. "This hypothesis is called *Panspermia*, much like bees pollinating the flowers, except with asteroids, comets, meteoroids and even spacecraft."

"Spacecraft!" I breathed in realization. "That is how your own civilization is now trying to pollinate life to another planet. They did it through you!"

"I thought we already went through it before," Allecra said. "That's why I'm here."

"No, it just hit me harder this time," I said, suddenly feeling bad. "So you don't procreate, your people...what are they going to do?"

Allecra didn't speak for a long moment. I felt the familiar sharp pang of pity pierced through me as I looked at her. I reached my hand out to card her soft blonde hair.

"I guess now you know why my siblings are always pressuring me," she said with a low sigh. "You can think of us as the society of ants."

"If the queen dies, so does the colony," I said grimly.

"Yes," she sighed. "The same with my people if I'm gone."

Allecra was the Endling, I shouldn't have forgotten that.

The sorrow spread through my heart like poison. I couldn't fathom the hidden grief Allecra must have harbored all these times. Seeing the loss of brilliancy and mirth in her eyes now caused tears to well up in my own. I went to embrace her, and she held me back.

I was at a loss to know how I could ease her pain. Now I had tasted the terrible bitterness of her hidden responsibility.

"I'm so sorry," I whispered. My hand clutched the front of her shirt. "If only I were stronger and braver...If only..."

I shut my eyes tightly in frustration and helplessness, silently cursing my cowardice that held me back. Allecra kissed the top of head to soothe me.

"Shh...it's alright, sweetheart," she said. "You don't own us anything. It should be me to say sorry. It should be me."

We sat like that for a while. I didn't notice her words at first, but then they seemed to resonate some subtle hint in my ears. I looked up to meet her eyes again.

"Why did you say that?"

Allecra kept staring back at me in silence

"Nina," she began slowly.

I thought I saw a flash of unsettling emotion stirring in those turquoise pools, but something else seemed to dim it back as soon as it started.

"Well, you must be tired now. It's been a long day," she said, breaking from my gaze, "Let's go back to the hotel."

The look on her face was hard to read, and her tone of voice gave its finality that I had to nod, forcing a passive smile in response. It was the first time I was certain that Allecra was clearly hiding something from me.

~*~

Soon cities slowly bored us. Allecra took me to a more natural and grandeur place for a change of view. After the talk that day, I could feel something was coming loose slowly. I was waiting for it to crumble down on top of me. But I tried to forget about this ominous feeling and just enjoy the time I spent with Allecra.

She took me to see the Niagara Fall, which just took the breath out of my lungs, and so did the White Cliffs of Normandy where we stood in each other's arms and looked down at the sea below us.

But the most memorable trip was when I got to hear my voice echoed off the curvy walls of the Grand Canyon.

"It feels like we're walking on Mars!" I said excitedly.

We were deep in the slot canyon. The power of water and time over the years had created deep, gorgeous passageways that we could walk through. Allecra was smiling at me as we sauntered around the labyrinthine place.

"Well looks like you have found your nostalgic spot, little Martian," she teased.

"Allecra, you can't prove we're really originated from the bacteria on Mars, okay?" I said. "Stop teasing me about it."

She raised her hands up in surrender. "Alright, little Earthling."

I couldn't decide whether I should hurt her or kiss her, so I turned to walk again. We kept moving farther.

"It is so quiet down here," I said. "I could even hear the earth breathing!"

"Nina, it's just the wind," Allecra said. My eyes turned into slits back at her.

"You literalist alien are a pain in the neck, you should know that," I said. It made her chuckle.

"If you think I'm making the place boring, let's play hide and seek here," Allecra suggested.

"Wait, what? No!" I said.

"Are you still a scaredy cat?"

"I'm not a..."

"Good," Allecra said. "Then find me."

She started walking backward with a mischievous grin. Then she turned to run.

"Allecra, I'm not in a mood!"

"Come and get me, kitten!" she called back.

I followed after her, but I couldn't keep up on the small path. The next moment, Allecra was out of my sight.

"Allecra, stop doing this! We don't know the place," I said, scanning around the cave-like passages for her.

"Meow!"

Her voice drifted from a narrowed space somewhere. I tried to follow it, but everywhere down here looked the same and different all at once.

"If you don't come out, I will not talk to you anymore!" I cried.

There was a silence. I waited, but nothing. I sighed in irritation and decided to stay where I was until she returned. After a long moment passed, I felt a pair of hands grabbed me from behind.

"Boo!" Allecra said behind my ear, but I didn't stir. "Why didn't you scream?"

"I already knew it was you."

"Oh, are you really mad at me now?" she said and then kissed my cheek over and over. "I like it when you scream, though."

"You're so sadistic and mean," I muttered, tilting my head away while trying to shrug her hands off.

"Aw, I thought I was fun."

"Stop it!" I said. She turned me around and planted a kiss on my forehead and another one on my pouted lips.

"Forgive me, *kotik*," she said. "I just wanted to train you not to be scared when being left alone."

"Do you also push people into the water to teach them how to swim?"

"If it works, why not?" she said.

I pinched her arm.

"Bad Allecra!"

She giggled and pulled me into a hug.

"I want to show you something, come with me," she said and just took my hand.

We walked to another passage through the reddish walls some ten feet away and turned the corner. At the end of the path, we saw a spot where golden sunlight beamed down through the canyon.

"Oh my god, it looks like the light shining from a descending angel!"

"Do you always have to describe things in a funny way all the time?" she said with a soft snort.

"Excuse you, I'm a writer," I said. "You can't expect me to see the world as plain as you do."

Allecra burst out laughing.

"You think I'm boring?"

"No, just too blunt to my liking," I said, but suddenly an idea came to my mind. "Hey, can we go to stand under the sun ray for a moment?"

"Why?"

"I just want to!" I insisted.

She rolled her eyes, but we went over to the sunlit spot and stepped into it together. The light enveloped us with its brilliance.

"Oh my goodness, look at you, all golden!" I gasped, staring at the radiant girl in front of me. The beam drenched over her seamless features like ethereal glow. I reached out to brush my fingers on her dazzling face. Her blonde hair turned completely golden, too.

"You could be a real angel coming to earth, Allecra," I told her.

"If I were an angel coming down to earth, you must be the one who keeps my wings."

I laughed.

"Don't you want to go back?" I said.

She frowned.

"To where?"

"I don't know, some other worlds, Olympus, or Meru, or Asgard, or Arzuria?"

"Arzuria?"

"To me, it sounds like one of those mythical realms." I shrugged.

"I belong to Earth now. Here is better than any other worlds in any universe," she said in a soft voice. "Here I'm with you."

I smiled. My eyes entwined with hers. We both leaned forward until our lips mashed together in tenderness and endless love.

CHAPTER 43

Allecra took me practically everywhere; even for an absurd reason as eating ice cream in Copenhagen, or visiting the famed chocolate factory in Switzerland. But one thing became clear to me, she never took us to the places she had found her former potentials.

It had been hovering in the back of my mind. Was she afraid we would run into her ex-lovers? Or maybe those places would awaken some poignant memories of them. I couldn't tell for sure, but I had had coincidence tapped me on the shoulder before, I meant how else you explain my encounter with Eva? Of all the fifty states in America, she decided to land right in the middle of my aunt's garden party. What a small world. And although I didn't hold any grudge against Allecra's exs, I still didn't want to be reminded of their past romance either.

Besides, there was this tiny insecure part of me that she might chance upon a new Earthling match. The scenario made my inside twist into uncomfortable knots. I knew Allecra loved me with every fiber of her being, but sometimes the thought of someone else could make her happier than I could trouble me.

However, there was another new question. I just started thinking seriously about it, especially after all the talking about her people and her siblings. I had tried probing Allecra lightly, but she would close the pearl of truth like a clam. I tried to respect her privacy by giving her space and some peace of mind, but it became increasingly vexatious for me being out of the loop too long.

Good grief! Is it possible for me to achieve a perfect understanding of my interstellar girlfriend?

I brooded about all this while I was standing on the balcony of our hotel suite in Salzburg, Austria. It was breezy outside with the view of the Alps. The city was divided by a river with medieval and baroque buildings and mountain vistas. The wind pleasantly ruffled my hair, chilling through my comfy shirt. I rubbed my bare legs together to dissipate the cold as my torso leaned over the chest-high marble railing. Suddenly I noticed something strange, a strange tenderness. I indiscreetly peered down my own shirt. My breasts seemed a little rounder and a tad bigger than usual. Maybe I shouldn't let Allecra indulge herself with them so much, I thought with a hint of blush on my cheeks.

The sun continued to light up the sky like a giant candle over the city. A few moments passed while gazing at the sunrise, I heard the balcony door slid opened. My head turned around to find Allecra scuffled out of the room, stretching herself languorously. Her hand tousled that messy blonde mane in sleepiness. I chuckled at her adorable entrance. Allecra wore only a baggy white t-shirt and panties. I still couldn't get used to how shockingly hot she could be even early in the morning.

"Why are you up so early, Nina?" she said. "You should be sleeping in my arms. Don't you know I have a need to squeeze and hug cute things when I wake up?"

I laughed, but Allecra came forward and threw her arms around my shoulders, dropping half of her body weight on me in the process. I whined a little, trying to hold us both upright.

"Geez, be careful, we can fall to our death!"

She snickered and straightened herself back a little.

"Don't worry, I won't let you go even if we fall," she said and kissed my forehead softly.

"And what's good?" I chastised back. My fingers itched to run through her unruly bed hair, and I let them.

Allecra gently turned me around and slide her hands around my waist. I leaned my back into her chest snugly. The warmth of her body was surprisingly comforting in the chilly morning.

"So where shall we go next?" She asked.

"Oh, I haven't thought about it yet," I said. "How long have we been here?"

"Two or three days, I suppose," she said. "Time jumbles up when you travel like that."

"You're right," I said.

"So any particular place you want to see?"

I thought for a moment then told her out of randomness that I would like to walk along some beautiful rows of trees that formed a tunnel.

"Why tree tunnels of all things?"

"I don't know." I shrugged. "I just think it would be like walking through a magical kingdom or something."

"You are that kind of girl, aren't you, Nina?"

I frowned and tilted my head to look at her.

"What kind of girl?"

"The kind who is full of rainbows and flying unicorns fantasies."

"Well, that's the perk of dating a homo sapiens, emphasize on the word 'homo'."

"Oh please, kill me."

I slapped her hand. It made Allecra giggle softly over my shoulder.

"I think I know such a place that fits your description," she said at last. "It's a very small town in Spain called *Sena De Luna*."

"Sena De Luna?" I said, "What an adorable name!"

"Yeah, the village has a very famous tree tunnel and also mountains, farmlands, ponds and creeks and stuff, a great place for peace and quiet," she told me. "I used to stay there in autumn and then spent my winter in Sierra Nevada, where I spent every weekend watching the duck family."

"The duck family?"

Allecra laughed and nodded.

"I know it's a weird expression." She said. "There's a pretty big pond, where I discovered the duck family. Sometimes I fed them bread I brought with me. They were pleasant people to see. I spent hours sitting under an oak tree or a chestnut tree all by myself, watching them. The ducks had these flat orange feet that were really cute like they were wearing little kids' rain boots. But in winter, the pond froze up, and they would come flapping through the air and land on the ice. Their webbed feet are not made for walking on ice, so they lost balance and went sliding across the surface of a frozen pond. Sometimes, they even fell on their butts! And I watched them skidding and tumbling all over the place. It made me laugh. The duck family was like a live comedy!"

I couldn't help giggling along as I listened and imagined the duck family in my head.

"They must have hated the winter so much then."

"I think they didn't hate it all that much," Allecra said. "The duck family looked like they were living happily together. I'd never seen them fighting, so they must have gotten along well. And even if winter comes, they would just grumble to themselves, *'Oi, ice again!'* But then they move on and forget all about it and just do their best to live their happy little duck lives."

Listening to Allecra talk about ducks like that, I understood why I fell in love with her and kept falling for her every single day. I got this warm, contented feeling melting inside my body, and it dawned on me that we had to be together like this.

I leaned in to peck at the corner of her lips.

"I can't wait to meet the duck family with you," I said. Allecra smiled and kissed me back.

"Alright, but first we need to do a little shopping," she said. "The town is a bit remote by the way."

After that, we were walking down the streets of the old city, which was extremely picturesque and full of stone houses that looked like they were originally from the twelfth century.

"This city reminds me of Moscow," I said. "Only a lot smaller."

"Speaking of which, I wonder why you haven't suggested we go to Russia yet," Allecra said. "Maybe we should go there afterward?"

"There's nothing interesting to see there."

"You've got to be kidding me!" Allecra exclaimed. "I know you were born and raised there, but I haven't seen it yet. How strange? Why haven't I been to Russia for all these years? I could have met you sooner!"

"If we met there, hell would break loose with my step-mom," I told Allecra. "Dominika is bad as my aunt is good. And don't you know homosexuality is banned in Russia? Also, most Russians are homophobic. We probably can't even hold hands in public without being scorned or verbally harassed."

"What?!" Allecra cried in disgust. "That is ridiculous! If that happens, I will teach them some lesson about respect."

"Now I really don't think it's a good idea to go there."

"But don't you miss your father, Nina?"

I was quiet for a moment. The last time I talked with my dad, I could feel the man I used to know resurface. It had been a long time since Dominika happened.

"It's alright." I shrugged nonchalantly. "Besides how can I explain why in the world we're standing at his front door anyway?"

"I can," Allecra said casually. "You know how I did it with your aunt?"
I shot her daggers.

"How about we go to Japan instead?" I said. "You keep extolling the country, then why don't we go there?"

"Japan?" Her expression seemed to change a little.

"Yeah, I saw a picture of the Cherry blossom tunnel there. The branches burst into millions of delicate pink flowers. It's so beautiful. I want to see it."

"It's already passed spring now," Allecra simply said.

"Well, how about going to Africa instead? We can go on a Safari and see the animal kingdom," I suggested. "Or we can go to Cambodia and visit a thousand temples there! I have always wanted to see the land, and we haven't gone to see the Pyramid too, but maybe we should drop by in France first. Why haven't we visited Paris yet? It's a city of romance for crying out loud! Then we can go to Fiji afterward. What do you think, Allecra?"

Allecra merely adjusted her sunglasses on the bridge of her nose. I couldn't read her face as she only looked straight ahead. She didn't respond for a moment, but when she looked at me, her face was as smooth as a lifeless mannequin on the window shop we just walked past. I couldn't tell what she was thinking. Her blank stare had frozen my brain. I started to regret bringing up the idea.

"Nina," she said, but there was grimness in her tone. "You can pick anywhere you want, but not those said countries, okay?"

"Why?" I said.

"These are places I couldn't go back to, and you should've known why."

"Of course," I said softly. We continued to walk in silence. It wasn't the kind of silence I liked. It was like we were fighting but also not. I hated this silent fight.

Allecra reached her hand out to brush a strand of hair from my face. I realized she didn't like being this way with me either.

"Maybe someday, Nina," she said at last. "But not now."

I nodded back.

We reached a cobbled square where the market appeared.

Allecra led us to a store. Inside, we strolled through the aisles and picked out some canned foods and other necessities we might need. But when I dropped two packs of tampons into the cart, Allecra frowned, as if it was the most unusual thing she'd ever seen.

"You need these?" she asked.

"What else do you think I need them for?" I said with a slight blush. I almost forgot she was unfamiliar with this kind of stuff. Her otherworldly perfect system worked so well that she didn't have to suffer like a human girl. But I needed to be prepared before my period was on its way.

Oddly, Allecra seemed to be lost in thought for a moment. Then she looked deep into my eyes. Hers were strangely lit and transparent like turquoise crystal, unblinking and thinking. For a flitting second, I somehow peered into their depths, but there was nothing I could see.

"Alright, let's go," she simply said after a while. I thought nothing of it after that.

_*_

The breeze blew over the branches of trees, its dampness sharp against my skin. We continued along the road, where the forest ended, and we came out to an open green farmland spread in all directions. A single thread of white smoke rose in the distance.

Allecra and I wandered into the Spanish town of Sena De Luna. It was a beautiful quiet town indeed. I could see stone houses with red-tiled roofs clustered around the green scenery. Some houses had laundry drying in the sun. Others had pots of plants and flowers on every windowsill. I saw a yellow cat sunbathing on one of the stone walls. Then there was a red and yellow feathered parrot, who screamed, *'Holaaaa!'* from a birdhouse under an olive tree in someone's yard. At first, I thought it was a person. I couldn't resist stopping and having a little chat with the cute parrot, but apparently, the bird spoke only Spanish.

"He said *'Hello* .'" Allecra translated for me.

"Yes, I know that one," I said, rolling my eyes at her.

"*Besameeee!*" The parrot spoke again, and this time, I was lost.

"Kiss me," Allecra said.

"Allecra, we're not doing that in the public," I said, blushing in shyness.

"No Nina, that's what the parrot said."

"Oh."

"Come on, let's find the tunnel," Allecra said and turned to walk again. I didn't know why I felt a little jab in my heart. Normally she would tease me or try to flirt with me at every chance she got, but it seemed she wasn't feeling it today.

Once we arrived at the tree tunnel, I was practically turning my head around like a crane, gawking delightfully at the dense foliage and colorful flowers that almost blocked the sun above us. The trees formed a tunnel that snaked out like a pathway of an ancient enchanted forest. The ground was covered with fallen flowers and leaves in bright pink and purple hue. The sounds of birds chirping resonated in the sky. Allecra and I walked hand in hand through the tunnel in relaxing quiescence.

"It's so magical here. I feel like we're in Wonderland!" I said in amazement then looked at Allecra. But she wasn't listening. Her face was blank like a mask, and her mind seemed to be led astray by some private pondering.

Strangely ever since we left Salzburg, I sometimes spotted her with that same faraway look when she thought I wasn't looking, but when I asked, she would brush it aside with a bright smile and a sweet response that made me believe everything was alright.

"Allecra?" I called her name to get her attention. "What are you thinking about?"

"Yeah?" she turned to me.

"Are you okay?"

"Yeah, sure," she said and beamed sweetly back, but the twinkle of her voice didn't seem to match her eyes. Yet I nodded; besides it was hard not to be distracted by the beauty of her smile and everything around me. I made us walk through the tunnel twice just to savor the feeling.

We went to find the pond. But when we got there, there were no ducks to be found. I was secretly crestfallen since we had stumbled our way through the overgrowth towards the place.

"I believe they will appear soon," Allecra said like she had a special way of reading my mind.

To my surprise, we found a small wooden hut, probably built for travelers. It was amazingly cozy and actually beautiful by the view of the pond. And I felt as if we'd suddenly come across a five-star hotel.

When we got inside the hut, Allecra opened up her backpack, which had a copious amount of foods for the two of us. I helped to lie out the blankets then I went out picking flowers to put in our new home like we were going to stay there for years. Allecra watched me for a moment and then she came to help me pick them. We sat down again, and I started making a flower crown for her.

When I looked up, Allecra was all the time gazing at me, and though I didn't think much about it at the time, I noticed her eyes were stirring deeply than usual. She just smiled back and turned to pick the petals that fell on my lap to sniff.

As the afternoon drew in, we unpacked our lunch of bread, pickled olives and some cheese. We ate our simple lunch contently and then had some cherries for dessert. After that, there was nothing else to do except enjoying each other's company until the world started crashing with thunder. And it wasn't long before the rain starting pour down from the sky. The raindrops were gentle and soothing on the sun-drenched earth. The trees swayed in the wind, but amazingly our little hut turned out to be watertight. We only had to huddle together to avoid getting soaked. Allecra wrapped us like a burrito with the picnic blanket when it got colder.

I leaned into her body and rested my head on the crook of her neck. She held me in her arms comfortably, telling me how much she loved me without saying anything out loud. If there ever was a more perfect day than this in the history of time, it wasn't one I'd heard about. I could just spend eternity under this hut with her.

"Nina, look!" Allecra whispered into my ear, pointing to the pond. I followed her hand, and there I saw a flock of ducks swimming in a formation across the water. There were a mother duck and her ducklings, about six or seven of them in total. They were so fluffy and yellow. It was like seeing balls of cotton floating around the pond.

"Oh my gosh, they're so cute!" I said gleefully. Allecra laughed at my animated face.

"There used to be many of them around here before," she said.

"Where are the rest now?"

"Well, some might've moved away, some gone to college or visited their in-laws."

I chuckled and gave her a good-natured shoulder-nudge. We watched the duck family paddling about, bathing and drinking in the rain joyously.

I looked back at Allecra again. The film of moisture from the rain clung to her skin. I reached out to wipe her face, relishing in the softness of her skin.

"I wish we could stay here," I said, "and live happily ever after like the duck family."

"Right, maybe we should live here!" Allecra said, suddenly sounding excited at the idea. "You have no idea how much it's tempting me."

"You didn't just say that, Allecra."

"No seriously, let's do that now!" she said, her brilliant eyes were looking at me expectantly. "I can get the nicest house for us to live in, and you can have a big kitchen and a beautiful garden and a library. We don't have to go back to anything or worry about anyone."

Her eyes were sparkling with so much hope that I realized she was actually meant what she said.

"Well, even I would love to be with you so badly here, I can't just leave everything and everyone behind," I told her. "There are so many things I'm not yet ready for. We both are still too young for this."

"What else do you care, Nina?" She said. "I'm here with you now. We can live like two happy soulmates in between dreams and reality, and no one will bother us."

"Allecra," I said, studying her face with concerns. "Where did this come from?"

She was silent for a moment then looked away from my searching eyes. I was sitting right next to her, but in that instant, I felt like we were thousands of miles away from each other. My hand came up to stroke her cheek gently in my palm and turned her face back to me. She gave an exasperated sigh. I rested my forehead against hers and locked our gaze.

"I know there's something you're not telling me," I said in a soft voice. "I have always known that it's there, and I could feel it eating away at you. It worries me seeing you not being yourself. Tell me what is going on."

Allecra stared at me. Her look was like a sharply pointed icicle piercing deep into my soul.

"Will you forgive me if I tell you something, Nina?" she said at last. My heart was pounding as I stared at her, immediately regretted that I had asked. I was beginning to get nervous and scared of what I might hear. The charming spell of the summer rain had vanished. The duck family was gone.

"What is it?" I said as calmly as I could, but my voice quivered with dread. Allecra swallowed hard before she opened her mouth to speak again. I felt like a frightened deer, waiting for her words.

"I lied to you about the pills."

I could feel my heart sink deeply into the void of emptiness. My hands went back for her face to cover my mouth, yet a small gasp escaped my lips. For a long moment, I couldn't find my voice to speak. All I could do was staring back at Allecra through the brimming unshed tears. I thought I knew what heartache felt like. But there was nothing compared to this. The pain in your chest, the ache behind your eyes, the knowing that things would never be the same.

"What...?" I breathed shakily. My face tensed with internal pain that coursed hot and cold inside my body. I felt a slight dizziness but tried to keep my composure.

"I had to, Nina," Allecra said quietly. "I'm sorry."

Something inside me had crumbled away, and nothing came in to fill the cavern. There was an abnormal lightness in my head, and sounds had a hollow echo in my ears.

"You've planned it all along?" I struggled to speak through my tight throat. "All these trips and everything...to get what you want from me?"

"No! It's nothing like that, Nina," she said in a panicky voice when she heard that. "Listen...you don't understand...I..."

I turned away from her, not wanting to look into her eyes anymore. Then I buried my face in my hands. It felt like the weight of a mountain had dropped on my shoulders. My throat burned as I began to cry. I felt Allecra's hands reached for me, but I pushed her away. My whole body was trembling.

"All those times I was a fool thinking I was enough for you, thinking you only wanted me and loved me for me," I said between sobs. "And all those times I thought we were genuinely making love."

"No Nina, damn it! You got it all wrong!" Allecra cried, pulling me into her arms. "I truly am in love with you. When we were intimately together, it was all real and magical. I swear it over my life. I didn't fake a single moment of it. You can't disregard how I feel about you like that!"

"Then what do promises mean to you?" I said in a trembling voice, "Something that you can break when you want to? You don't understand, it's not that I'm not trying. I try so very hard to change my mind about it, to be strong enough for your sake and deserving of your love, and all I ask of you is to give me time!"

Allecra shook her head, closing her eyes in defeat. My breath was burning in my lungs, and I wondered when I was going to choke.

"I know, Nina, believe me, I really do," she said. "I'm so sorry, but I had no choice."

I had never seen Allecra crying, but now her eyes glittered with tears as she looked at me.

"I can't believe you did that to me, Allecra," I whispered in disappointment. "I thought you would never hurt me again."

"Do you think I wanted all this?!" she yelled back loudly. "I didn't even ask to be born the way I am, or carry the responsibility I probably couldn't fulfill!"

"Right! Then go ahead and choose the greater good over my stupid feelings!" I cried and covered my face in tears again.

A deep silence like the shadow of a cloud settled around us. The only sound I heard was my pounding heart and ragged breaths. We were quiet for a long moment. Then I heard Allecra took a deep breath.

"I know you hate me now," she whispered. "But if you were me, you would understand."

I wiped the tears off my face with my hand roughly.

"And if you were me, if you killed your mother by being born and were scared senseless of the unexpected, you would understand me. You can't tell a depressed person to be happy or a scared person to be brave. But I don't hate you, Allecra. In fact, I can't even hate you. Not one bit, not even at all, but I do hate what you did to me. I was too intoxicated with happiness that I left no room in my heart for the unimaginable."

Allecra winced at my words. Pain and guilt were written all over her face. I almost felt pity for her.

"They insisted on knowing about you," she said in a low voice. "That whether or not you're the one."

I looked up at her, but she dropped her gaze from mine. Allecra let the word hung in the air, and I just knew what she meant by the hopelessness in her voice.

"But I'm not the one, am I?" I asked softly. Allecra didn't reply. "It doesn't work with me, does it? That's what troubles you all this time."

I didn't know what was worse, being lied to by someone you valued above all else or being told you're not the one for them. I felt as if I had been walking through a storm, numb and soaked to the bones with emotions.

"Nina," she said. "I could be wrong, maybe you need more time. I will ask them to wait a little longer. We just have to try harder..."

"But I can't give you what you want now, you get it?" I said. "I just can't! I just can't!"

"You don't know how long the Elders have been waiting for me," Allecra said, taking my hands in hers. "Their patience is wearing thin. I am powerless against my creators. They threatened me unless the breeding is done."

It took a great deal of effort for me to say it out loud.

"Are you going to leave me like the others, too?"

She looked stunned when she heard it.

"What on earth are you talking about?" she said. "All I know is I can't live without you. Everything that I did, I did it so that we could be together. I'm not giving up on you. I know we can make it through this. I'm scared too, but I trust you that you can do it. Don't let us go, Nina."

I shook my head and closed my eyes, summoning all the strength I had left to speak.

"What are they threatening you with?" I asked.

"Xenon talked to the Elders and reported on our progress. They are not pleased with my inactivity. If you're not conceived..." she said and paused to look at me, and for the first time, I saw her face marred with distraught and fear.

"If I'm not conceived, then what?" I whispered.

"They will take me back to Arzuria."

Like a tree struck by lightning, I sat dumbfounded with the buds of hope and dreams scorched and blackened to ashes. The thought of losing her already filled my heart with foreseeable grief. If Allecra was taken away from me, all things joyous and beautiful and bright would be gone with her. I could not live like this.

One big tear spilled from my eye, ran down my cheek and splattered like a raindrop on our joined hands. The others followed in an unbroken stream. I bent forward and pressed my face into Allecra's chest, sobbing with an intensity I'd never felt before.

Allecra held me tightly in her arms, rubbing my back and said nothing. I was physically and emotionally drained that no matter how hard I tried to cling to her, I could still feel as if Allecra was slowly slipping away from my grasp like a dream.

CHAPTER 44

Moonlight and the sound of wind ruffling leaves filled the dark quiet room. In the stillness of the night, I was lying in bed, not knowing what country or city we were in, but I didn't care anymore. My tears had dried up like an exhausted spring. No thoughts formed in my hazy mind. I felt as if my body was melting away, like a candle burned out with its own heat. The hysterical bouts of crying had driven me into sickness and Allecra into depression. Albeit the motive to secure the vestige of trust, things had taken a drastic turn after the whole truth was revealed.

The Azurian Elders had found a new world for Allecra — a civilization whose people were more compatible with her kind than the humans. Allecra would be taken to that Earth-like planet, millions of light-year away from me. She could carry the hybridization and have a better chance of succeeding with the new race.

It was one thing to lie to me, but to leave me after making me believe in what we had together was salt on the wound.

Allecra was now sitting on a cushioned armchair by the open window. I hadn't spoken a word to her since we left the pond. The night-blooming jasmine floated in through the lace curtains. Her face in the moonbeam as stunning as it was, reminded me of the marble statue of a mourning angel in the museum.

In the darkness, I heard her sigh gravely to herself. She was contrite and demented by guilt. Her breaths resonated in my ears every now and then. I could almost feel her heartbeat in the small empty space between us, waiting for me to forgive her for her faults, yet she knew she couldn't ask that of me anymore. What she did was too heavy to lift with my forgiveness alone. It needed time. But time was now slowly flowing like desert sand into a bottomless abyss.

In the end, it was like someone had taken a gigantic knife and cut through our joined souls all over again. I thought I had known this girl, whose smile was as bright as the summer sun and eyes that twinkled like the winter stars. The way her hair looked like a field of golden wheat. How her face lit up when she looked at me. Her stare, solemn like a wise owl's at midnight. I thought I would recognize her by touch alone, by the way, she breathes against my skin, but that person I knew was gone, replaced by someone else new.

Was there anything that could eclipse the stain of this betrayal and bring my Allecra back to me? A familiar forgotten thought crawled like a stalking beast from the darkness of my mind.

Perhaps we were not meant to be together.

The realization caused a pang of heartache to stir inside me again. Hot tears surged up from the back of my eyes, burning their way like unclogged pipes until they spilled ceaselessly down my cheeks. So many innocent moments of us spent in the pinnacle of happiness, crowding forward inside my heart but slowly dissolving away into dust. My shoulders shook despite my muffled sob.

"Nina?" Allecra's voice came to me. It was as gentle as a river breeze upon my skin, but I didn't answer. Her calling was only a sound beyond range. She got up and walked over to my side quickly.

Allecra cleared her throat. There were tears in her voice, but I turned away so that I wouldn't see that beautiful face. It would break my heart all over again. A heavy sigh issued from her lungs.

"Please Nina, don't do this," she pleaded, "I could bear anything but seeing you broken and hurt. It makes me hate everything about myself even more. I'm so very sorry for everything I did to cause you this much pain."

My throat burned from swallowing the lump that was still stuck there. Every part of my body felt limb and heavy and useless, as though it would turn to stone and crumble to dust in despair.

Allecra came to the other side and sat on the bed with me. Her shimmering turquoise eyes searched for mine in the shadow. She put her soft hand on my forehead as if to feel me.

"Nina, you're burning up," Allecra said worriedly.

Then she swiftly got off the bed and went out of the room. She came back with a glass of water and two cold medicines in a small plastic cup. Allecra tried to get me to take them, but I pushed her hand away, spilling half of the water onto the bed sheet. She froze with a frown etched on her perfect face.

"If you think this is a clever way of punishing me, well, it's working, Nina," Allecra said, her voice rose with frustration. "I receive it ten folds, hundreds of thousand folds! I don't think I could take it anymore. Tell me what I should do to make it stop! How can I make it up to you?"

I was silent. All thoughts fell away from my mind like snowflakes dropping silently in the dark.

"I know what I did to you was utterly selfish and unforgivable — because I am selfish," Allecra continued. "But this greed and selfishness sprang from my desire to keep you with me, to be showered with your love, your touch, your smile and laughter each and every day. I wouldn't trade it for anything in the world. You have no idea how grief threatened to tear away at my heart. It blinded me with fear and drove me half-mad. When Xenon told me they wanted to take me back, I was shell-shocked. In my moment of weakness, I mistreated your trust and made that stupid mistake. But if I lost you, Nina, I'd lose everything in me too!"

Her speech struck a sympathetic chord, but of course, my mind was numb. Her words, her touch, her eyes all spoke in different tongues at me, and all I could respond was an inscrutable stare as empty as my soul.

"Nina, please, just say something," Allecra whispered pleadingly. She turned to kneel by the bedside, looking at me in the eyes. Her face was once I had not seen, full of pain and sorrow mixed with other unrevealed feelings. My heart faltered as I opened my mouth to speak.

"I have nothing to say, Allecra," I said, my voice turned hoarse and scratchy from crying.

"Why? Why do you look at me like you want me to disappear like you want to erase me, erase our memories?" she said. "You said you would always love me no matter what."

"You can't use love as a chain to put around people's neck and enslave them to your will."

I could feel my words bite at her heart like vicious snakes. Allecra's face contorted with instant pain. Her gaze flickered. Her whole body tensed like something inside her was breaking. I watched her face shone luminous and impossibly pale as if the moon had drunk color out of it. A moment passed in deafening silence then another and another.

At last, she stood up and slowly turned away from me. Those glowing turquoise eyes were all glassy and distant. Without a sound, she walked back to the window again. Her face stared off into the black starless sky. From her reflection on the glass, I thought I saw a single drop of a tear rolling down her cheek, but it could have been just the night dew outside.

"I thought what we had with each other was strong enough," she said softly as if speaking more to herself. "But maybe I'm the only one who really believes our love could free you."

The wind blew and night birds fluttered their wings over the treetops. Then Allecra turned to look at me one more time. I wanted to run to her and hold her in my arms and kiss her, asking her not to go, but I couldn't.

And she left the room.

Silence shrouded itself over me like a black mist. I wanted to cry, but no tears came out, and all I did was staring blankly at the spot where Allecra stood, listening to my own heart breaking into pieces. It was the most painful cry I ever had. I didn't know hearts could feel so empty but so heavy at the same time.

*

In the kitchen, the next morning, Allecra and I sat down together at the table quietly. In front of me, a white porcelain bowl of warm soup emitted steam in the air. It shifted about and drifted like little ghosts in the morning light. Tendrils of it swirled up into my lungs as I breathed deeply the good savory scent, a strong hint of ginger and cinnamon. Beside it, a small bowl of white rice and a cup of hot lemon tea. I relished in the warmth of it, but I wasn't hungry.

Allecra sat looking at my face while I was staring at the food.

"You can't go without eating all day, Nina," she said.

I missed those mornings when we woke in each other's arms. When I was in her lap, kissing her, our bodies entwined skin on skin, memorizing the shape of the other's lips and getting lost in each other's gaze, and my fingers running through her silky hair, and when I pulled away just to see the ardency, passion, love and fire in her glowing eyes.

Now we sat and talked like two strangers.

I let out a low sigh and made an effort to pick up the spoon and began to eat. My hand kept feeding my mouth mechanically. Allecra's soup was a perfect blend of flavors as expected. Its saltiness immediately eased the rawness of my throat.

450

"Where are we now?" I asked without looking up.

"Somewhere no one could find us," Allecra said.

I lifted my head to scan around the place for the first time. It was a beautiful house with a nice and well-equipped kitchen. There was even a red vintage refrigerator. A wrap-around porch faced a lively garden outside. I could see the blades of grass glowed with a deep green luster. There were rose bushes and flowerbeds of white daisies and moonshines and sunflowers and even a row of tulips in the garden. The sky was blue, and there were little sheep clouds up high.

Everything I saw was better than what I could have imagined. I wouldn't be surprised if we were actually living inside a painting of some artist. And I bet there was even a small library somewhere in this small dreamy house. But for some reason, I didn't feel enlivened by any of it. It was all too good to be true.

Allecra reached over for my hand with her soft fingers. Her action was cautious as if she was afraid I would break from her touch.

"We can stay here as long as we want, Nina, even forever," she said, "We can be here and create a world removed from reality, from all responsibilities and unwanted future."

I held her gaze, staring into her sparkling turquoise eyes.

"Tell me we're not hiding from them."

She didn't answer me.

"Allecra."

"I'm doing everything I can. I'm willing to fight for us."

"What's the point of fighting if we know we're going to lose anyway?"

"No, I haven't lost you yet."

"I'm not the right match for you, Allecra," I said in a hollow voice. "You've tested it for yourself, haven't you?"

"Please, don't say it like that, Nina," she said. "You made it sound like everything we did was a pretense. What I feel for you is valid...every single damn emotion and thought of you."

"But I can't be what you want anymore."

"Screw everything! I don't care!" She snapped back, "I refuse to stand by and watch myself lose you. All I know is I'm not giving up! I will try my goddamn hardest to make things work for us. We're not broken yet, Nina. And I will mend us back again."

"It's too late, don't you think?" I said, "We're running out of time. I can feel it in my bones. Something is going to tear us apart. And I've been subconsciously thinking about it. How long will we hold onto this tiny sliver of hope? Perhaps I shouldn't stand in your way anymore."

Allecra stared at me for a long stretching moment. Her mouth opened in shock.

"Nina, are you breaking up with me?" she asked softly.

"It's the only way..."

"No!" She got up from her chair and walked over to me purposely. Getting down on the floor, she took my hands in hers, making me looking into her glistening bright eyes.

"Why do you do this?" she asked, her voice faltered a little with emotions. "We can work it out together. We can bring everything back the way it was, the joy, the happiness."

I reached my hand to her cheek and caressed her soft skin gently.

"You'll get all of that, but with someone else," I said, "And you are right, Allecra. You can't free me. I have to free myself."

She stared deep into my eyes, her face blank, a kind of blank that was full of anxiety, nervousness, and fear.

"Are you not in love with me anymore?"

"I love you with everything I am, and I will always love you that way," I said, "but I've always felt like I was going to lose you, like two planets obit towards different directions. Maybe we just fell in love at the wrong time. I can't move on if you're still standing there. Maybe it's best for you and me to let it go."

"No! I won't allow it!" Allecra said, shaking her head in disbelief and desperation. "After all the things we have been through, how could you do that to me?... Please don't, Nina, I'm not letting you go!"

To my amazement and heart-brokenness, fine crystalline tears rolled down Allecra's face. She kept wiping them away roughly with her hand as if she was not used to them. My heart stuttered into pieces seeing her cry.

"Allecra, shh...it's okay," I said and wiped her smooth cheeks gently with my thumbs. When she calmed down a little, I cupped her face in my hands and leaned in to kiss her lips. "Listen to me, you have to fulfill your destiny. Your people are counting on you to save their hope and dream. Please don't let me hold you back from doing what is more important."

Allecra shook her head back disapprovingly.

"Stop it, please," she begged, her body trembling. "I'm so sorry I broke your heart but don't push me away like that. I'd do anything, whatever it takes to make you forgive me. Please just let me stay with you for the rest of my life. I don't want anything anymore, just you and me."

Then she pressed her face to my breasts and held me in her arms. I stroked her head. My longing hands went over to her slender shoulders, squeezing the taut muscles that looked as though they would snap at the mounting misery. I could feel her growing frustration and despair as they coursed through her feverish body like heat-waves. But my heart had turned cold and dark, mostly hopeless, I couldn't even tell if it was beating or bleeding.

"It has nothing to do with what happened. I understand perfectly why you did what you did," I said and smoothed her hair like I'd done hundreds of times before. "If anything, it only made me realize that our relationship isn't a fairytale. It seemed like one, but without the predictable happy-ending. And the most unfortunate thing is it has reached a dead end for us now. We have to accept the truth."

"If we're not together, Nina, how the hell do you expect me to live my life when I can't even find the shattered pieces that make me whole again?" She said as she looked up at me with tearful eyes. Those clear galaxies ablaze with pain and desperation were too heart-wrenching to see.

Looking at her distraught face caused the anguish to bubble up like boiling lava inside my chest. I turned my head away for a moment to collect my bearing. Then with a deep shaky breath, I spoke again.

"There will be dark emptiness for both of us, but it won't last forever," I said, "and I hope one day you find a love that can fill the void with all the things ours couldn't be."

This time, Allecra let out a dry humorless laugh amidst her tears.

"This hope of yours will be in vain, Nina," she said in a grim voice, faint and bleak with emotions. "Living will be a slow suicide for me if I go back. Even if they sent me to the alternate universe, thinking I could have loved another you, in another body, in different time and space, and surely you would have loved me back, but the thing is, that person wouldn't have been the real you — the only Nina I want this with."

I bit my lips from breaking down and took another deep breath.

"I'm sure you love me more, Allecra, but I will love you longer. When this is over, you will have the same passion for another girl who deserves it. And I will still be here, loving you just the same."

Allecra stared at me for the longest time, as if she'd lost the power of speech. But when she spoke, her words were slow and lifeless like echoes from a cave.

"I was cognitive enough to know that this love would be my ruin, but I chose to let it consume me anyway," she said nostalgically, "Because I realized that the thing I was afraid the most was the thing that set me free. And now you want to shove me back to the prison I built for myself, leaving me to rot in the cell of my guilt and loneliness. Is that what you want for me, Nina?"

I was gripped by shock hearing Allecra's bitter words. Her pain reached through to me like a thousand needles piercing into my own heart. Suddenly the desire to hold her and caress her strike me, but she already got up and stepped away from my grasp. Her face hardened and her stare seemed far away.

I rose from my chair to grab her tightly clenched fists, trying to uncurl them and lace our fingers together, telling her wordlessly how much I was hurting too, but she would not let me. In the midst of intense hopelessness, I pulled her stiff body into my arms and cried with my face buried into her chest. The exquisite scent of her skin filled my lungs with familiarity and sweet memories of us.

We stood like that for what seemed like an eternity.

Then all of a sudden, there were strong gusts of wind wagging around the house. The air grew thin with statics like it was before a thunderstorm.

Allecra looked around us in confusion. It wasn't her own doing, I realized, but after a second we seemed to understand what was happening.

I used to be excited about this phenomenon, but this time, it felt different. My intuition told me that something was wrong. Sparks of electricity formed and danced about us. The walls of the room were peeled away one by one. Our little utopian reality sank like the water of a giant fishbowl had been drained out.

"They've found us," she whispered, causing my heart to drop a little farther downward.

The house and its lovely garden and everything else I thought would be permanent were swept clean by the Spindle machine.

A burst of blinding light drenched us harshly. I felt Allecra's strong arms curled around my waist and gathered me to herself. Breathing through sobs, I had a sickeningly feeling that this was the last time we would be embracing each other. Our grip was desperate. And even after everything stopped, we still held on tightly like we would break, not like that of glass that still with pieces remained. This brokenness left nothing for it was of the heart. I felt as if we were in a shipwreck, clinging to the wreckage of ourselves.

We were now returned to the laboratory back in Allecra's house, and we weren't alone.

"About time you come back," Xenon's sharp voice startled me. "You think we couldn't find you, little sister?"

Allecra and I turned around to find her and Triton standing before us.

"Xenon," Allecra said even she seemed to be aware of their being here already.

Her eyes were still tearing after the effect of our conversation. Her sister came forward. Allecra pulled me to stand behind her.

"We're leaving Earth today," she said.

"What?" Allecra said in surprise.

"It's an order from Arzuria," Xenon told her, and her face turned to me. "Earth has offered us nothing but disappointment and false hope."

"No!" Allecra protested, "I won't leave with you."

"Stop being a fool with this human girl," her sister snapped back, "You know she's not the one. We all knew it from the start."

"I don't care if she's the one or not. If you want to take me back, you will have to kill me and bring my body to Arzuria."

Xenon was taken aback by this fierce threat from her sister.

"Allecra..." I whispered in alarm. My hand tugged at her hand, but she ignored me.

Triton looked between us as he stayed guarded behind. His chiseled face was not like the one I'd known. There was no expression or twinkle in his dark eyes anymore.

"We just learned that another Elder has died, Allecra," Xenon muttered through her teeth, "How long does it take for you to wake up and stop this stupid delusion? We can't afford to wait for nothing anymore. You're not one of them. How could you sit back and watch our entire race disappear from the face of the universe? You can speak human language, be with them and dress like them, but there's still Arzurian blood in your veins. You have a responsibility to fulfill, Allecra. You bear our people's wish. And now you want to let a girl shutter it and destroy what our people have worked so hard for?"

Allecra snickered darkly.

"What do we have in our own world of perfection and superiority?" She asked. "Besides our noble and intelligent race that can't be touched or broken with emotions? Now I only hear their withdrawn heartbeats and melancholy breaths, drifting in a darkened plain of space. Maybe that is the reason we can't create life because we don't create love. When was the last time any of our kind know how to love deeply and helplessly like the humans? We are the superior race who forgot to live ordinarily. Do you even notice there's dew on the grass in the morning?"

"What?" Xenon said, staring at her sister in confusion.

"Tell me Xenon, have you ever wanted to walk through a tunnel of trees just to feel it, or run through a field of poppies and notice a moving snail and say 'oh she's probably set sail to China'?" Allecra said. "Do you giggle when you blow on a dandelion and think they drift in the air like tiny white parachutes? Because these are the joy and wonders Nina has taught me to feel."

"This is stupid!" her sister growled, her face squeezed itself out of shape with anger.

"You don't know what I'm talking about, do you?" Allecra said sarcastically. Then she turned her face to me again, making our eyes lock amidst the tension. "That's what happens when the love on Earth lights up your whole being, blowing your mind with colors and sounds and sensations, and all you have to do is gazing into the other person's eyes and seeing not only constellations but an entire galaxy of everything you've ever wanted and needed. I've tripped and fallen into a depth like no other, a black hole in itself. I have fallen in love with her, Xenon, and you can never bring me back from it."

The whole time, I was staring unblinkingly at Allecra. From the corner of my eye, Xenon looked as stunned as I was.

456

"But does she feel the same for you?" Xenon said. The very question snapped us back to reality. It was the question Allecra had no clear answer to. "You have heard what she said, haven't you? She wants you out of her life. Her love is just a good for nothing emotion that weakens you. It's just a sweet illusion. Maybe she doesn't even love you at all. She only wanted you because you're exciting, even exotic to her dark desire, a mere curiosity to her human mind."

I shook my head vigorously, trying to tell Allecra that it wasn't true, but everything Xenon said was too convincing that I lost hope in trying to deny it. But given what had transpired our tempestuous breakup, Allecra might as well believe every word. Perhaps, it was better for her to think of me this way. I loved her so dearly, but she deserved better than a ridiculously difficult girl like me.

"Our mother ship is waiting for us behind the moon," Xenon spoke again, "Like it or not, you have to leave Earth now."

Then she motioned with her hand to Triton.

Triton seemed hesitated to obey Xenon's order. Allecra pushed me out of the way and moved forward. At the same time, her eyes went ablaze, glowing like fire in a bright turquoise light.

"Triton!" Xenon yelled. "Get her!"

Finally, the tall alien man shifted his feet, but before he could even take a step forward, his knees buckled and his bulky body dropped to the floor with a thud. I muffled a gasp with my hand. Triton didn't move. His eyes froze like a dead fish's.

"Now you turn yourself against us because of her?" Xenon hissed.

"You made me do it, Xenon," Allecra sneered back, causing her sister's topaz eyes to glow in fury. Instead of lashing out, Xenon turned her stare in my direction. Suddenly I felt a sharp pain piercing through my head, freezing every nerve in my body. I screamed and my legs gave out from under me. Allecra's startled face turned around and found me lying paralyzed on the floor.

"Nina!" she cried and came to me. With a combination of telepathy and hypnosis, my body had lost its function. My eyes were blinking with tears of fear and confusion as all words died on my lips.

Allecra picked me up from the floor and held my limp body into her chest. She wiped the tears from my cheeks frantically. From the corner of my eyes, Xenon awoke Triton again and gave him an order with her pointed stare, and this time, the tall guy moved obediently and swiftly to Allecra. When his hands found her shoulders, she gave him an elbow to his stomach and tossed her brother like a sandbag to the floor once again.

Another burst of pain erupted in my head. I screamed again.

"Nina!"

"If you don't come with us, Allecra, I'll make sure she will never be the same girl you so cherish ever again," Xenon said.

Allecra's face seemed to be seized by fear as she was staring at me helplessly.

"Don't you dare harm her, Xenon," Allecra muttered fiercely.

"I will let her go only if you agree to return to Arzuria."

There was a long agonizing silence. Allecra looked as though she was debating with herself, but another sharp burning pain seemed to crawl from every neuron in my brain like insects. I gasped and cried out. My skull tightened like it was going to slit open. Tears burst out from my eyes to the sheering agony.

"No!" Allecra cried. "Stop!"

"Give her up, Allecra."

"I can't..." she sobbed helplessly.

"Yes, you can, or I'm going to rip apart all her memories of you, everything she's ever known will go up in a smoke," Xenon said. "She can even be brain-dead if I see fit."

"NO!" Allecra cried. Rage clouded her mind, filling her eyes with fire. Allecra rose up and turned to Xenon, intending to lunge at her, but before she could reach her sister, Allecra keeled over onto her knees.

"You think they created me to protect you without giving me the power to control you, Allecra?" Xenon said. "Maybe I should take away your memories of her instead."

"No..." I said faintly, trying to crawl my way towards Allecra. The pain in my head was gone as soon as Xenon's attention focused on her sister. Allecra was motionless, completely lost in a state of unconsciousness.

Her sister walked over to her and put her fingers to Allecra's temples. The glow of their eyes intensified like miniature suns. I heard Allecra screamed in pain. My hand outstretched in protest.

"No!" I cried.

In just a short moment, I watched her body lolled and dropped to the floor. My mouth gaped and eyes widened in shock. I quickly crawled over to her feeble body. My hands gently pulled her into my embrace. Her face was ashen like a pale moon. Her breath went in and out faintly like the fluttering of a dying butterfly's wings. I touched her cold cheek as my tears flowed incessantly.

Xenon stood, looking over us in silence.

"If you love her, let her go," she said. "Allecra is better off without you as a burden. She will find a new home and everything that happened on Earth is no longer her concern. She isn't yours to claim. She belongs to us. Don't make everything even more difficult than it already is. I know it's hard for you, but you must leave the room and this house and live a new life. We won't be your problem anymore."

I was still sobbing quietly to the unresponsive girl in my arms. Though I always had an inkling of how it might end, I just didn't think I would lose her so soon. It was the saddest thing that life was full of sudden goodbyes.

Now I understood when star-crossed lovers die, there is a parting swan song. Perhaps it was the greatest grief known to man, to be left on earth when another was gone. My hand was ceaseless now, stroking and tracing the elegant base of that slender neck, drew softly across the pulse and down to her beating heart. I would miss this the most. This, this and this. Her eyes, her lips, her hands and everywhere.

In a tremendous surge of sorrow and loss, I held Allecra close to my broken-heart. I kissed her soft lips and whispered a soft goodbye.

Xenon called for Triton, who had recovered and was now standing beside us. His face as empty as ever, but there was a dull glint of sadness in his eyes as he stared at me.

"Get rid of everything before we leave, Triton," Xenon ordered him, "We don't want any trace of us left behind."

Triton nodded and then turned to all the ultramodern equipment and computer system around the lab. He spread his hands wide, like a music conductor about to start the first bar of notes. His fingers moved like the way he talked to me, but whatever he projected made everything in the room tremble and hiss with mechanical noises. Then all things went dead and slowly fell apart, becoming loose piece by piece, atom by atom. It was as if they demolecularized themselves into tiny grains of black sand flooding to the floor. Soon what was left was crumbled meaningless heaps of black dust. The only thing remained was the Spindle. It needed no power to run but the force of the mind.

"It's time," Xenon's voice said. "Take her away."

Triton wordlessly and apologetically lifted Allecra from my arms. I was reluctant to let her go, yet I had no strength left to protest. My mind was numb with pain. My body was empty and hollow and as light as a feather. Allecra's form curled limply to her brother's broad chest, and I watched them slowly turned to walk away, taking the last glimpse of her face with them.

When they reached the giant machine, Xenon's head drifted back to me again. Through my tears, I saw a flash of mild concern ignited in her eyes.

"Wait," she spoke, narrowing her gaze on me. Triton stopped for a moment. They didn't say a word, but then the girl just shook her head. "Never mind, let's go."

As I watched them standing inside the spinning ring, the brilliant pool of light shot up straight to the sky. I shaded my face with my hand. Their silhouettes began to fade away slowly until they were gone. The Spindle itself crumbled into a million pieces afterward. All that remained was a pile of disintegrated metallic sand.

In the end, I was left all alone with the emptiness as big as the whole sky.

CHAPTER 45

I LAY UNMOVING ON the floor for hours. At this point, I had lost the will to even think. My eyes opened with tears streaming as though from a river. It seemed like the sun and the moon had fallen from the sky. Everything had gone dark right to every nook and cranny of my heart. The event of what just happened wouldn't stop rewinding itself until the images were now hung permanently in the gallery of my skull.

As I remained weeping in silence, the feeling of utter desolation overtook my consciousness. I felt myself slipping away like ebbing water into a deep dark gloom.

It must have been a long time since I passed out. I woke up again with a start and found myself in the tomb-like darkness. For a moment, I didn't know where I was. Until my fingers brushed over the sandy floor, and all the memories came rushing back to me like a flood. It brought along an unfulfilled desire to hold Allecra again, to touch her soft lustrous skin, to feel the warmth of fresh blood coursing through her, to hear her heart beating those blessed beats. But all of these were no longer in the world with me.

My chest grew tight like it was shrinking and collapsing on itself. I wished my body had withered like everything else in this room.

I cried again, harder and sadder. It was difficult to breathe without choking with tears.

But wasn't that what I wanted for Allecra?

Some part of me was happy that she would be free from all this unwieldy burden and pressure and torment of conscience. Perhaps someone else could give her everything that I couldn't. And I had to go on living. Allecra would be starting a new life. I should begin mine and quench this thirst that wouldn't quit, and a premonition of despair that awaited me. The best antidote now was to shut off that stream of memories, though deep down in my heart of heart, I knew it would be the longest fight.

Making a painstaking attempt to get up, I rose from the ruin of my soul like a phoenix rising from its ash and slowly left the demolished laboratory. My heart was still in recovery, still struggling to accept the inevitable weight of this loss. But I was determined to take one step after another and leave the narrative of my brokenness behind.

My feet unconsciously took me up to the library. It was silent, cavernous and empty. The bookshelves looked like white skeletons without a single spine of books. They had taken everything away.

The floor echoed from the sound of my footsteps. I ran my hand over the shelves and looked around the room in nostalgia. Like dark, soft shadow, sadness once again reigned over my heart with no warning. I closed my eyes and immersed myself in the depth of deprivation and loneliness, giving myself up to grief, letting the pain pour over me, choking me like strangling hands around my neck.

My knees buckled under the invisible weight of despair. I was crying on all four with the force of a person vomiting. I had never cried this hard in my life.

After a while, I calmed down again and sat back, leaning myself against the shelf in exhaustion. That was when my eyes landed on something glinting under the table. I recognized the object immediately. My heart pumped with surprise as I went over to retrieve it.

My typewriter was still here in Allecra's deserted library.

They did not throw it away. I figured it must be Triton who left it behind. He left it for me to keep. One of the two things Xenon didn't know Allecra gave me. The typewriter felt cold and heavy in my feeble hands. Placing it on the table, I kept staring at it like I couldn't believe it was real. It was like everything in this house could vanish in a blink of an eye. Then I pulled my necklace out from the collar of my shirt. The stone's sparkling resplendence seemed to grow oddly dark and dull as if it was too mourning with me. The bittersweet remembrance of the old days resurfaced like a humongous iceberg in the ocean. Now Allecra wasn't going to read to me or tell me a story, or rush to hold me and give me peppering kisses ever again.

But I willed myself not to give into tears this time. Then a sudden urge to write struck me afresh. I began setting up the typewriter and pulling out some papers I found from the drawer of the nightstand. I started to write. At least, it gave me something to be occupied with during this emotional ordeal.

When the first word was punched onto the paper, another came flowing from my head, I wrote without stopping, all sort of words that describe my pain and loss. The sound of my fingers tapping on the keyboard was mercilessly loud and furious, yet also increasingly soothing. I wrote about the state of my broken heart. One fragmented sentence after another. Tears flowed down my cheeks without me realizing. It was the longest letters I had ever written. Then the papers ran out. And I stopped. I would have gone on forever if there were still words that could portray all my feelings. But I knew no amount of words that had ever existed in the world could express how I felt.

I stared at my own writing for a very long time. Then I plucked the paper out and piled them together, making a three-fold.

Call it coping mechanism or whatever it was, but after pouring out all my thoughts onto the papers, I made a conscious promise to myself that I would not go back to these feelings again. It would take a huge effort of will, but it was a start.

The sky was already pitch-black, in contrast to the morning sunlight from where I came from. Walking out of the house, I looked around the place for the last time. The silence made everything else seemed to come alive— the chirping of birds, the cries of all sorts of insects, and the distant sound of ocean waves. But what rang in my ears the loudest was an indescribable sound I couldn't explain — the sounds of hollowness that came from deep within me.

With my typewriter tugged under my arm and the folded letters I wrote, I finally turned to leave. My car was still in the garage with the key dangling from the driver's door. I knew Triton had prepared all this for me, but the black Lambo and the rest of their cars were gone.

Without another delay, I got inside my own car, started the engine and then drove off. My tear-stained face reflected on the rear-view mirror as I took the last glance at Allecra's beautiful house. I imagined it crumbling into fine powdery dust along with pieces of my heart.

_*_

When I reached home, I went up to my room. Time itself slogged along in rhythm with my faltering steps. I closed all the curtains and locked the door, but even so, there was no escape from that haunting sound inside my chest.

I got out the music box which Jordan had given me on my birthday. It was made of polished wood with very nice inlaid work and hand painted images on the exterior. It was even lockable with its key.

I opened the lid, letting the melodious music float harmoniously in the quiet room. I put my letters into the box. Inside also had a small compartment, which I used to store the Erytus stone, too. I didn't know what twisted fate that had made Jordan give me this kind of gift, and how ironically fitting that was to have it now, but like Pandora's Box full of diseases and evils that plagued mortals, this was the box of my grief and sorrow.

I closed the lid and locked it with the key, storing all my wounded feelings away. Afterward, I curled up on my bed and tried to numb every part of my body, as if by doing so, I could disappear from the world, too. The hollowness would come again soon enough when I had no choice but to welcome it, and when it arrived I would take a good long time to fill the void, like dropping pebbles down a deep dark pit — one pebble at a time. Not now, though, not yet.

I stayed up all night until there was light in the sky. I couldn't sleep and just spent the next morning watching the garden and the green hill with trees stroking the belly of the sun as it rose. I felt completely drained, but I couldn't fall asleep regardless. I went on staring at the cherry trees that stopped blooming since last spring.

I wondered how Allecra was, what she was doing. Had she arrived at her planet yet? What would they do to her? I tried to picture what would happen.

The return of the Endling with her unfruitful results from Earth.

The Elders sat around like a trial in disappointment.

Soon, they would make her a newly arranged journey to another place more promising. Of course, Allecra would follow their order. Allecra was not the same anymore. She would find a new potential because she couldn't remember me.

She won't be coming back. My heart's clenched at the thought as if every bone in my body was suddenly creaking and screaming. My eternal longing for her presence felt like hungry parasites sucking with their ferocious appetites, selfish and starving for love and passion. It caused an unbearable swell of pain as if my heart and body were being ripped to shreds.

The afternoon deepened, twilight approached, and the bluish shadows enveloped the garden. The sky was covered from one end to the other with clouds, blocking the moon.

The second night, I was able to drift to sleep. But once I did, I dreamed.

I saw Allecra walking through a flower-filled meadow somewhere. The mountains were crystal blue. She smiled at me brightly. I was overjoyed to see her again. Tears sprang from my eyes in relief. But when I rushed over to her, our bodies fell through each other like mist. My hands tried to grasp for her again, yet she just disappeared. I turned myself around in panic, calling out to her over and over until I woke up screaming her name.

That was the most sadistic and cruelest dream in the world. I felt like dying.

Other nights it was just impossible to sleep. The thoughts of Allecra would come back. There was no way I could stop them from entering my muddled mind. As soon as one more of them found the slightest opening, the rest would force their way in, cramming inside my head — an unstoppable torrent of memories: Allecra gracefully stepping out of her car to rescue me from the top of the hill. Allecra peering at me with those incredibly clear eyes of hers as we sat under the pepper tree. Allecra standing with her beautiful smile on my birthday. Allecra sitting on the school windowsill with her blonde hair swaying against the wind.

There were also those helpless moments of our joining bodies for the first time, our first climax, our confessions, hopes, and promises.

I felt all this with such clarity that I could just reach out and touch her, as if she was right there in my bed, except her body and soul was no longer in the same reality.

It was the same fashion the following week. I hadn't tasted anything but water and whatever I found in the fridge to nibble on, bread, crackers or nothing. I discovered in the mirror that I was becoming emaciated. I could hardly recognize myself. My hair was a matted mess. There were dark circles under my eyes.

I was looking out of the window when a flock of wild ducks flew from a pond in the neighborhood park. The ducks reminded me of the duck family Allecra had told me back in Austria.

When the world gives them ice to slip on, they would just do their best not to fall, even if they fall, they would still try to get up and continue their happy little duck lives.

From that moment on, I decided to try and see whether or not I could regain the courage to return to the real world, leaving the illusory castle that I had built on the fragile dream. I would have to do something to reclaim my footing.

As my survival instinct kicked in, I began to get up and went around the house. Everything still felt strange to me. I felt like I was a ghost wandering about from room to room. Then I started doing the cleaning I hadn't paid much attention during my absence. The maid had come once a week to tidy things up, but I still took it upon myself to do it. I just wanted something to distract myself, to block all thoughts and memories that threaten to intrude my mind. I still felt like I was walking in the bottom of the sea, but I would have to adapt myself to this new situation.

Like Pandora's Box, there was one thing left. When granted, a person would use it as fuel, as a guiding star to life. That thing was hope. Right, I still had hope, not for anyone else, but for myself.

~*~

In the morning I did laundry and reorganized my own room. Then I went grocery shopping for the first time in weeks and made myself a decent meal for a change. It felt like a lifetime ago.

Once my days fell into a pattern, I tried my best to keep them that way. I didn't know why, but it seemed important to me. One hour followed the next like rhythm of the songs miners sang. Nighttime was the most dreaded time. All sort of pain and grief tried to get out of the box. They would slam at me like the waves of ceaseless tides, sweeping me along to a nostalgic place — a place of the past where I still lived happily with Allecra. I would try to fight back and cling to hope and hold on until the morning came again.

One day, three days, another week passed by. Surprisingly I didn't find it painful to be shut away, living a monotonous, solitary existence. If anything it gave me an abundance of alone time to heal.

Now I was able to get up every day and had a simple breakfast of bread and jam with a cup of jasmine tea. Then I would spend an hour or so, doing things like ironing, or vacuuming and even gardening. When I ran out of stuff to do, I brought all my textbooks to the big living room and did an exuberant self-study until I felt like passing out. But for once, I could indulge myself in something logical, definitive, and could be proven in life.

Lunch was usually green salad and fruit. The afternoon was spent sitting on the sofa and reading the books I owned. Sometimes, I reread the same sentence over and over, trying to imagine the scenes depicted in the story, but it was as if my brain had trouble catching the meaning.

It took me a long time until I would be able to get out on the balcony. I would sit on a wooden chair, keeping my stare at the night sky. The stars reminded me of Allecra the same way people looked at Orion and thought about the Greek legend.

But at this point, I no longer forbade myself not to think of her. She had become a part of everything that I was. She was my breaths, my heartbeats, my senses and agony and happiness. It was pointless to try and forget her. I let my mind conjured up the familiar feeling of being held in her arms again. Looking at the stars hovering over the darkened world, I closed my eyes and immersed myself in that phantom warmth of her love. No matter how far we were away from each other, I knew I was still going to love her for the rest of my life.

Autumn was quietly lurking as summer faded away day after day. It suddenly hit me that ever since I had been back, I hadn't had my period yet. I tried to convince myself that maybe it was due to the body's hormonal reaction to my emotional state. But it was late, very late. Time was a little tricky in my mind. I was too caught up with distractions that I forgot all about it. How long had it been? Two weeks? A month?

Now, however, for the first time in my life, I saw something different in myself. I was able to sit in front of the mirror longer than before and examine my face more thoroughly. I wasn't being narcissistic, but for some reason, the unrecognizable girl was gone. I inspected my face from a number of angles like it weren't mine. My skin was glowing and became more lustrous. I looked a lot better than ever before, and which was kind of strange. Or at least it felt like I was taking on a late transformation of a mature woman. Probably.

I closed my eyes and stopped thinking about it.

One windy day, as I lay wrapping in the blanket, the house phone rang. It took about five rings for me to actually register the sound. I got up and slowly went down to the living room.

It was from my aunt. During my time traveling, Allecra had piggybacked our home line. It redirected her calls to my phone so I could talk with Aunt Vikki anywhere without her being suspicious. She would call me once or twice a week. I only missed it a couple times but immediately called her back after I got home. I did a good job at concealing my secret after all.

I greeted her as I picked up the receiver. We talked for a moment before she told me the family would return from Florida soon. Robert needed to get back to his work. I said it was great to have them back and reported what I had been doing as I normally did when she asked. I had rehearsed how I would respond if she asked about Allecra, but fortunately, she didn't. After we hung up, I went to my room and sat down on the edge of my bed. Outside the tree leaves began to change color.

Summer was coming to an end.

~*~

I woke up with bleared eyes. The ceiling spun above me in haziness. There was an awful bitter taste in the back of my throat, burning up my tongue like surging acid. I gagged and struggled to get up. Another bout of nausea hit. It was sickening and exigent. I had to stumble my way blindly to the bathroom. A fraction of my foggy mind wondered what I had eaten the night before. But food poisoning was out of the question. It had been like this for several days now. My legs felt wobbly, but I managed to get into the bathroom. And once the light was on, I felt my stomach recoil and erupt uncontrollably. My shaky hands grabbed the edge of the sink, and I doubled over and wretched.

The disgusting taste of stomach acid and some foul unidentified fluid made me tear up. I couldn't hear anything but the ringing sound in my ears as my head twirled and throbbed.

What is happening?

I rinsed my mouth and stared at myself in the mirror again. My face was paler under the light. I wiped the tears from the corners of my eyes. Something was wrong with me. My body had become strangely different. I ran my hands over to my breasts. Aside from the tender and heavy-feeling, they had grown sore to the point that just putting on my bra was like mild torture, and those random cramps, headache and back pain, not to mention my missed period. I had suspected what these signs could be. But this made me shudder at the frightful possibility.

No, it can't be.

Maybe I was just sick.

The next day, I went to the drugstore. The cashier looked me and one essential item before indiscreetly sighed to herself. I tried to keep a straight face and got out as soon as possible.

The pregnancy kit came in a long white packet. I bought two different brands just in case. Locked in my bathroom, I sat on the cold toilet seat and opened the pack. It included a small plastic cup and a strip of litmus paper. On the lid of the plastic vial was an indicator, a small but profound blue minus sign. In the case of pregnancy, a vertical line would emerge to transect that line, turning the minus into a plus.

I did everything as instructed then sat there, hardly able to make myself look down at the tiny vial. My heart was pounding as fast as a bird's, my future hanging on this simple line segment. I told myself to breathe as I waited. A minute had gone by, a full minute in which I didn't know whether to cry or to flush the vial down the toilet.

I was scared and shaking like a leave.

Glancing down again, I saw with great relief that there had been no change. No vertical line had come to complete the cross. My heart slowed down a little. I wiped my sweaty cold hands on my shirt. The heat from my face made me realize I was raging with nerves. Two minutes, I prayed for two more little minutes, and the old chronic fear would leave my miserable life alone.

I waited, breathless. As two minutes expired, tears formed in my eyes and my body began to tremble. I was looking down at the indicator in my frozen hand, and now I couldn't take my eyes off it. My grip was so tight I might break the vial.

"Oh no...oh god no..."

There it was, appearing, materializing. A faint blue line. I rubbed my thumb across it, hoping it might be erased. A vertical crossbar. My heart beat all the way to my throat and the dropped down to my ankle. I was gasping for air. The line grew stronger, adopting a life of its own.

Finally, I dropped the vial from my hand. It rolled away from me and went immobile on the floor. From the reflection in the mirror, I had become as blue as the line. My knees turned to jelly, and I let myself sink to the floor, too. A chill spread through my being. I began to shiver as if my body was going to freeze all over. I hugged myself for a time, listening to my labored breathing.

How ironic the fate could be.

It was undeniable now. I was indeed pregnant with Allecra's child.

CHAPTER 46

THE WARMTH OF WATER seeped into every pore of my skin as I sank lower into the bathtub. I did the test again, and the result was the same. I was obviously pregnant, and my thoughts of Allecra being far away, farther than any human could ever dream of, had become my only companion. I put my hands on my abdomen. It was still barely swollen, but I knew there was a little one hidden inside me.

The little one.

That was what I was going to call my child, still tiny — nothing more than a hint of life. But eventually, my belly would grow bigger. The little one would take nutrition from me. In the dark, heavy liquid of my womb, the little one would grow steadily, unceasingly like a seed sprouting in a fertile field.

Am I seeing this pregnancy as something good, something to be welcomed as it's supposed to be? Or as a twisted fortune that singled me out for being the coward I am?

I couldn't draw a conclusion no matter how hard I thought about the questions. I was still in a state of shock. My emotions mixed up, jumbled like a jar of trapped moths. I was confused, unprepared and utterly scared. In another word, I felt split in two, and I was still struggling to swallow this life-changing realization.

Yet I also had to recognize this tiny one as the force of my new hope. The only thing closest to Allecra I had left inside me, like a sudden flash of light in the dark.

When I thought of it this way, I could feel my fear evaporated, though not completely. I relished knowing that a part of her stayed with me now. The very prospect just warmed my heart and calmed me down again. The feeling was something to hold onto. I would try my hardest to become strong, for myself and the little one.

At night, I started writing letters to Allecra, telling her about my life on Earth. And when I lay in bed with my cheek against the tear-stained pillow, I would talk to her about our baby.

"I'm having your baby now, Allecra," I said. "I still don't know how to go through this yet, but I'm carrying the little one inside me for you. Can you hear me?"

Sometimes in the middle of my rambling monolog, I would break down crying, telling her how scared I was and how I wished I was enveloped in her arms and to be protected from this harsh world.

Perhaps, it was because of my desperation, I got this ambiguous feeling that Allecra was there listening to me. It was as if I'd conjured her from thin air, pulling her out from whichever corner of the universe she might be, except she couldn't touch me or wipe away my tears. This feeling comforted me; even it was all just my imagination.

The moonlight bathed the bare branches of the trees. I listened to the beats of my own heart, soon there would be two hearts beating. Eventually, as if led by that monotonous rhythm, the soft blanket of sleep wrapped itself around me. It was the deepest sleep I had ever had in many weeks. Also, I did not dream.

~*~

The family came back from their summer vacation at last. The car pulled up in the driveway with John and Jason helping out with the luggage. I was waiting for them by the door, eyes squinted at the bright sunlight shining over the large garden. Piper's sun-tanned skin made her look even better as she bounced up the steps.

My aunt came to hug me, but after a moment, she seemed to notice something on my face.

"You don't look well, Nina, are you okay?" she said as the rest of the family entered the house.

I reassured her that I was fine and tried keeping the concealment of the fact that I was lying.

"You're sure?"

"Yes, I just feel a bit under the weather. So how was your summer?"

"Oh it was delightful apart from the heat," she told me. "I felt like turning into a chicken barbecue on the beach. We both know we're not meant for a hot climate, aren't we?"

"How about we spend our summer in the middle of the Siberian tundra next year, darling?" Robert mocked his wife good-naturedly. It just made me smile.

"Hey Nina, I've got you some gorgeous dress I found while shopping. Now come with me, I want to show it to you," Piper said and took my hand. I guessed she just wanted to have a moment with me for some reason.

When we were inside my room, she put the bag down on my bed and twirled around.

"You won't guess what I'm about to tell you now," she said energetically. "So I met this guy at the beach..."

"And he's a surfer, right?" I said. Piper's baby blue eyes widened.

"How do you know?!"

"It's the most cliche thing I could think of."

Her face pouted at me.

"Well, you've got it right, though," she said. "And you know what? His last name is King. Can't you believe it?"

Then she giggled to herself.

"So you met him," I said, just because it felt like I should say something.

"Yes, and he's planning to start college here once he graduates," she said. "He told me he wants a change of scenery, but still want the sun and the beach. Then he asked me for my number, and who would deny a guy named King? We exchanged our snapchat, too. You won't believe how sexy his golden curly hair was. I'll show you his picture later."

"So you just brought me up here to talk about your newborn romance?"

"No!" Piper laughed. "Maybe part of it, but anyway, how was your summer? I knew you didn't spend all day knitting with Allecra obviously."

I had expected this kind of question from Piper, but the mention of Allecra still caused a twinge in my chest. My jaw clenched as I tried to mask the pain, but my face must have said it all since Piper's brows furrowed in concern.

"Something wrong, Nina?"

I dropped my gaze, unable to meet her curious stare.

"We broke up," I said at last

"What?" Piper said. Her mouth opened. "But you girls seemed inseparable...what happened? Did she cheat on you?"

"No, nothing like that," I said. "It just didn't work for us. I'm sorry, but I don't really want to talk about it right now."

Piper stared at my face for a moment before she nodded.

"Okay, I understand exactly how you feel. I'm sorry to hear that," Piper said and we both fell silent. Then she turned to the bag, "Well, let's forget about the dumbass people. I've got this cute dress for you, you'll love it, come try it on."

She unzipped the back and picked out a lovely purplish gown, holding it at arm's length towards me. But when she put it over my body, she frowned.

"Wait, are you gaining weight, Nina?" she asked me. I looked down at myself and had to admit that she was right.

"Er...I guess so," I said, but in my mind, I was almost thrown into a panic with her question.

"Don't worry," she said, "Maybe you can keep the dress until it fits you again."

I nodded with a smile and thanked her for the present. However, it was inevitable to reveal what I was hiding. Eventually, my belly would swell and everything would break loose no matter how hard I tried to keep it secret. It was in that moment that I realized I couldn't dodge the truth for long.

At dinner, I thought about telling them right then that I was pregnant, but I realized how shocking it had sounded the last time I told them I was gay. Now imagine me telling them I was pregnant. It was impossible it was for me to announce this contradictory news. It was still difficult even for me to digest, let alone everyone else.

Just think how they would react if they knew I was now carrying a baby made my palm sweat. What would Aunt Vikki say if I told her I got pregnant without a partner? She would think I was a victim of some hideous catastrophe. Robert might see it as a terrible sin against his faith, or simply a human-shaped embarrassment to his name. What about my dad? It would confirm him that I was a certified failure in the family, the rotten apple that fell far from the tree.

And what about my cousins? The Nina who acted like she was always the mature one, thinking and speaking like she was above them. Now look at what she had done to herself, look at who she had turned out to be — a knocked-up and abandoned and soon to be a high school dropped-out.

I even wondered what Jordan would say if she knew. Would she give me her wise words *I told you so*?

I shook my head to shoo away these unkind thoughts. They made me even more anxious and disheartened.

While the family was talking and sharing stories of their vacation, the hired maid brought out a dish of grilled salmon. The whiff of its smell sent a wave of nausea up my throat. I covered my mouth with my hand to silence my gag, but it was too late. Everyone froze to look at me from their plate. I wished the queasiness would go away, but it only got stronger and more insistent.

"Nina, are you alright?" Aunt Vikki asked worriedly.

With another gagging sound, I bolted out of my chair towards the hallway bathroom.

I threw up whatever I had eaten. If this kept going, they would find me more suspicious, what could I do?

When I was done, I heard Piper's voice called from behind the locked door.

"Nina?" she said, "Mom asked me to check if you're not feeling well. You need any help?"

I cleaned up thoroughly and wiped my mouth then opened the door again.

"I'm alright, just an upset stomach," I said.

"You look kind of pale," Piper noted. "Are you sure?"

"Yeah, don't worry."

My cousin gave me a long look before she nodded.

~*~

A few days passed, my morning sickness began to get worse. I realized that I couldn't keep doing this any longer. I was helpless and in need of help, but I was also terrified to tell anyone. The morass of my conflicted mind was deep and sticky like it was going to sink me down as time moved forward. I felt as though I was walking through the mud, exhausted and everywhere I looked was an endless muddy field. In front of me, behind me, I could see nothing but a swampy darkness.

I had to reach out for help. I couldn't do this alone. My selfish damage would cause the little one to suffer with me. I would have to swallow my pride and face my fear, giving myself up to the current of fate and see where it would take me from here.

One night I knocked on my aunt's office door. She was still working while Robert would be late because of some meeting.

"Oh Nina, come on in," she said with a smile. I was led to sit down on her couch like the last time. As expected, my aunt put aside her work and sat down with me. But when she saw my face and noticed the look in my eyes, her smile faded and replaced by a look of concerns.

"Nina, what's wrong? Are you sick?"

"I have something to tell you," I said softly.

My aunt stiffened a little from the tone of my voice. She seemed to have some sort of inkling that I had a weighty speech to deliver, but she waited.

I had worked so hard to build the courage to come up to her after days of silent contemplation over words. But I suddenly found my throat closed up and mouth clamped shut. Everything in my mind just crumbled at that critical moment.

When my eyes glanced at the framed picture of my mother smiling with my aunt in Moscow, the suppressing tears began to break free, becoming unrelenting until my whole body shook. My aunt came to hold me, asking what happened in a frantic voice. But I couldn't answer as emotions choked the words out of me. She let me cry for a few more minutes until I calmed down again. Now my aunt looked really worried and anxious with my state.

"Tell me, Nina, what's going on?" she asked.

"I'm so sorry, Aunt Vikki, I didn't mean it to happen," I sobbed. "I'm so sorry."

"What is it?"

It was probably every parent's nightmare, and my aunt seemed to figure it out from a woman's intuition, solving the equation of my situation from all the subtle hints she gathered as she looked at me.

"Oh Nina, please, don't tell me you're..." she breathed, but couldn't finish. Her hand was over her heart.

I nodded to confirm her suspicion.

"I'm pregnant."

Aunt Vikki's eyes widened, her jaw dropped in speechlessness. I felt even more horrible with myself for everything that I had caused her. I wasn't just disappointing her but also hurting her feeling and disrespecting her trust. It was like the world had stopped revolving, and I was frozen in this difficult time forever.

"Nina, how did that happen?" She whispered.

"I can't tell you, I'm so sorry," I said tearfully.

"But what about Allecra?—Does she know about it?"

I understood why she asked this question, assuming the pregnancy was no way caused by Allecra.

"No," I said quietly, trying to maintain some level of control with my surging emotions.

I could detect what thoughts that were running inside her mind with the power of my observation alone. The look on her face told me she didn't believe I would be passionately making love with a man while being in a relationship with Allecra. It was not only because I was a homosexual, but because it just wasn't me.

She might have thought of this and worried that I had been taken advantage of, that it might have been the result of a heinous act of a pervert. It was normal for her to be worried with this horrific assumption. Obviously, I couldn't get pregnant by myself, and the only person I had a deep affection for was Allecra, so why did this happen?

But it was a lot less complicated if my aunt didn't know the hidden part of the story, that in fact, it was Allecra herself who impregnated me.

"Nina, I'm asking this again. Do you have any idea who or where the father is? You don't have to be afraid. We will protect you. Tell me who did it?"

"I'm sorry, I can't tell...please don't ask me again, I'm so sorry," I said with my head in my hands like a lunatic.

My aunt sighed softly to herself.

"Alright, Nina, it's alright, I understand," she soothed me, rubbing my back gently. "You must have had enough stress to shoulder right now. Let's think about the child. I have to ask you a very forward question. Do you plan to have the baby?"

I was silent.

"You know I won't pressure you into anything, Nina," Aunt Vikki said again. "It's your choice. Whatever you decide, I understand and will support you every step of the way."

"Thank you, Aunt Vikki, I don't know what to expect yet," I said honestly. "I'm so scared, but still, I'm going to bring this child into the world."

"Are you certain that this is what you really want?"

"Yes," I said. "I haven't reached the stage where I can love the tiny embryo now, but having this inside me makes me feel special. I'm someone whose mother died from giving birth to her, so it's hard for me to imagine what it will be like when I go through it with my own child. I have no clue of what to do. But if things go smoothly, the due date will be between June and July of next year, and I will try to finish school before I give birth to this little one."

"The little one," my aunt repeated as if to try the words for herself. Then for the first time since we started talking, my aunt gave me a faint sad smile.

"Which means we will have to make some changes for the baby," she agreed. "You can still finish school later if you want. It's more important to get a specialist to check you up and get medical attention as required, you understand this, right?"

"Yes, I do. I'm sorry, Aunt Vikki," I said. "I didn't mean to bring all of this trouble to you."

"Please, do not apologize, Nina," Aunt Vikki said. "We have to stick together in a time like this."

We were wrapped in quietness for a time.

"I assume you haven't told your dad yet?"

I shook my head 'no'. She sighed and rubbed her forehead with her fingers. I felt bad for making things difficult for her, but I didn't know what else to do.

"So when are you going to tell him?" she asked again.

"I was about to ask you a favor about that too...can you...can you please tell him for me?" I said. "I don't think I could do it."

Aunt Vikki nodded. She knew how I must have felt.

"Alright, I'll call him tomorrow, is that okay with you?" she said. I nodded.

"Aunt Vikki?" I said.

"Hmm?"

"Did it hurt when you gave birth to Jason and Piper?" I asked.

My aunt smiled sadly again and smoothed my hair as if she was sorry for me that I had to face all this too soon.

"I don't want to scare you with my labor story," she said, looking at me with empathic eyes. "All I can say is, every woman is different. Yes, there will be pain, a lot of it, but you'll forget all about that the moment you baby is born, and they're all you can think about. The pain just disappears."

_*_

The next day, Aunt Vikki sat her family down for the most shocking news. Now everyone knew about my being pregnant. As my aunt explained what happened, I was holed up in my room. The talk was done in an atmosphere of mortifying silence, yet I could faintly hear the conversation from downstairs.

"Mom, you mean Nina is having a bun in the oven, seriously? Nina?" Piper asked in shock. "Geez, no wonder why she's been acting kinda weird lately."

"How could that happen?" Jay asked.

"So who's the father?" Robert said to get to the point.

"She won't tell me a thing," my aunt answered. "At least, she didn't show any sign of being a victim of that unspeakable crime or anything, but she wouldn't tell who did it either."

"Well, it's impossible that she got knocked up by her girlfriend, isn't it?" Jay said. "I wonder how the hot blondie of hers takes this news."

"Actually, they broke up," Piper said. "I still don't know what really happened between them. Nina just doesn't want to talk about it."

"Maybe she went out to a party and was drunk and..."

"Jason, shut up, you have no idea what she's been through," Aunt Vikki said. "She's not that kind of girl."

But her voice was drained of vehemence as she spoke.

"So what are you going to do with her?" Robert asked. "Is she going to keep the baby anyway?"

"She has the right to decide whether to keep the child or not, Rob," my aunt said. "And I feel responsible for what happened to her. We have to help Nina getting through this. She's a good girl. She wouldn't need us if she didn't have to."

"Well, I'm just asking, honey," he replied.

But I knew Robert was more relieved that none of his kids got pregnant or got someone pregnant.

"Why did I even agree to let her stay home alone in the first place?" Aunt Vikki blamed herself. "I thought she would be with Allecra, and the girl should've protected her."

"Mom, I told you, you were bewitched by that Allecra girl," Jay said.

I felt guilty all over again, and I didn't want them to blame Allecra alone. Everything was just a terrible mess.

"We have to give Nina some space," Robert said again. "When she's ready, she will open up more."

"You're right," my aunt said. "Now I have to make a call with Pyotr about it. It will be a great shock to him, but I guess it can't be helped."

My heart fluttered at that. I felt the shivering chill went through me at the thought of my dad finally discovered what happened to his daughter.

Another ten minutes later, we heard Aunt Vikki talking to my dad in Russian, and it didn't sound good. I was standing at the top of the stairs, listening.

"No, it's not the case of sexual abuse....Yes, I'm sure of it...No, she won't tell me—calm down I...sorry...I know how you feel, brother, but you're not going to come to America to kill anyone who did it, okay?...I'm sorry if you don't calm the hell down, I'll hang up now..."

A long pause later, they started talking again. I didn't even know I was shaking until then. I decided to stop listening and ran back to my room.

Without turning on the light, I sat on the floor by my bed and hugged myself, wishing the trembling to go away.

Surely, my dad was gravely disappointed in me. I thought of his difficulty raising a child alone since my mom died. I should've understood how lucky I was for his loving care. And now look at how I repaid him.

A soft knock on my door startled me. I got up to open it and saw my aunt there. She looked at me apologetically and held up her phone to me.

"He wants to talk with you," she said.

I was reluctant to take it, but she encouraged me with a nod.

"Don't worry, he just wants to talk," she said.

I finally took the phone from her and pressed it against my ear. My hand shook.

"Nina?" came my father's voice. It was not hostile and furious like I had expected. In fact, he sounded worried.

"Dad," I said.

My aunt let me have some privacy and left the room.

"It's all my fault," my dad spoke to my surprise. "My little Nina doesn't deserve this. I shouldn't have let you go to that country. I've made a big mistake, Nina, I'm sorry."

I was stunned. Tears spilled down my cheeks at the tormented voice of my father. I started to cry.

"No, dad, don't say that," I sobbed. "I'm sorry. I'm so sorry."

He didn't ask me anything else. He knew it was pointless. All I told him was I didn't want to him to come over, that I would be fine with my aunt's care. We talked for a while before we decided to say goodbye.

But before we hung up, I told my dad for the first time since I came here that I loved him.

CHAPTER 47

SCHOOL STARTED AFTER SUMMER folded itself over and left the world. Piper let me ride with her on the first day. I didn't think I could do it. My hands couldn't stop trembling, and once I was there, I was even more shaken by all the noises.

The first period, I was late because I forgot the combinations of my locker and had to try again and again. I convinced myself that no one would notice me and know I was carrying a baby.

It wasn't that I was ashamed of having the little one. I was still ambivalent with the things that had transformed in my life. It felt like I was living in a parallel world where I saw myself and Allecra from everywhere I looked — the parking lot, the hallways, the Pepper tree, or the window seat.

Outside the building, it was raining the first autumn rain. It poured straight down without any wind, soaking every single tree. I was sitting in my desk in Advanced Language Arts, looking at the rainfall. The seat next to mine was empty, and I came to accept that one period of my life was over forever.

When I opened my notebook, it was like an arrow of lightning had struck my heart. Nothing could prepare me for this immense pain. The cartoon drawing I did of Allecra with her frowning brows and the seagulls crying 'boohoo' made my eyes burn with tears.

A student walked passed my desk, and I turned away to hide my face. My throat ached from the swelling lump. I flipped the page and wished I could feel numb again, but another wave of nostalgia hit me as the post-it note contained Allecra's poem glared at me.

Don't fall in love with a sailor boy,
He won't set your heart free,
O don't fall in love with a sailor boy,
He'll take your heart to sea.

They were just words strung together like pearls and soundless on a page, but their power could rip and tear the heart to pieces, burning it to a cinder. I covered my mouth to muffle the sound of my grievous whimper. A few students noticed me, but I quickly wiped my eyes and closed the book. I felt the curious stares, but I ignored them.

After class, a familiar voice called my name. It was Jordan. I hardly recognized her at first. She'd a new look. I remembered her corn-silk hair was long and straight. Now it had nice waves and fell over her shoulders elegantly. Her skin too was glowing like most girls after the summer. I was glad to see her again. She came right up and hugged me with a big smile on her face, saying it was nice to see me. I told her the same.

"How are you?" she asked.

"Fine," I said, but the word sounded weak. I tried to mask it with a bright smile. "I like your new hair, Jordan."

"Oh really?" Her face lit up.

"Yeah, I think you look great."

"Great enough to melt all the girls in the world into puddles?" Jordan teased. I giggled back. Then I was amazed that I could do it genuinely and easily with her. Jordan seemed to have a knack of making people feel better even when they were secretly sad. And I knew at least I still had a friend with me. My day began to have a little sunshine in it. And that was when I thought to myself *'If a flower could bloom again after winter passed, then so could I*. For my little one and for me, there was no time to be crippled by a broken-heart anymore.

"You look different, Nina," Jordan said. She might have noticed that I had put on some weight since I had always been skinny. "So how's everything with you?"

"Everything's okay," I said and quickly asked about other trivial things, trying to avert the conversation from talking about me. Jordan got the hint that something was off, but she didn't try to pry.

"Oh by the way, congrats on winning the contest," she said.

"What contest?" I was surprised.

"Didn't you join a creative writing contest?" Jordan raised an eyebrow at me. "I saw your picture on the bulletin board! You got first place!"

"Oh I didn't know," I said, even more surprised. "I thought I wouldn't even get short-listed to be honest."

"You should be proud! So many entries this years, and you got it. What is your story? The White Raven? It sounds interesting. I can't wait to read it on our school newspaper."

I blushed.

"Thanks for letting me know about my unaware fame," I tried to joke.

"Then can I be the first to get your autograph, Miss. Antonina Black?" She replied.

We both burst out laughing. It was nice to laugh with someone again.

The school bell rang, and we had to leave for our other classes. I promised to catch up with her later.

The next few days, everything began to get better. All those thoughts of Allecra were like the unexpected guests. I would welcome them and then let them leave in their own time.

In fact, a lot had changed over the summer. I heard from Jay that Jack Conner had transferred to another school for real. So I wasn't afraid someone would bother me anymore. Even that crazy guy who at one point tried to assault me was gone.

Between classes, Piper would text me to see if I was okay. Piper and Jay were told to keep an eye on me, and they did. But people started noticing the absence of the Knight siblings. Everybody began looking at me as if they could find the answer on my face.

To satisfy their curiosity, a few brave souls even came up to me and asked about Allecra, *the ancient goddess with blonde hair, where is she?* I told them I didn't know. Soon they gave up, assuming Allecra had dumped me and left, like all gods and their affairs with mortals or just how a cheesy teenage love should end these days.

By the time I met Jordan again in biology class that week, she already knew what had happened. One day when she didn't have lunch with her girlfriend Rachel, she found me eating alone on a bend outside the cafeteria.

I decided it was time she should know about me and Allecra. Of course, I didn't tell her of the little one inside me or the whole Arzurians and my extraterrestrial love life. Just some stuff that I was sure my friend could humanly accept. Jordan listened and didn't ask questions. She knew I would tell her things only if I wanted to.

"I couldn't imagine anyone would want to let you go, Nina," Jordan said at last.

"She didn't," I said. "I let her go."

My friend stayed silent. She looked at me for a long moment before she spoke again.

"Why?"

"Everything between us was like a poor imitation of the twisted plot in Shakespeare's play," I said with a dry chuckle. "It's not just about two people being madly in love and life is complete. The ending is a lot less glamorous in reality. It can be a tragedy. But no matter what, I regretted nothing."

"I know there's more to it," Jordan said. "But if you feel like crying, I have a fairly soft shoulder to lean on."

I smiled, but the sadness still lingered on my face.

"Thank you, Jordan, I have cried enough," I said with a shake of my head. "Then again love is always short, isn't it? A weakling heart like mine would take longer to recover."

Jordan reached across the table for my hands and squeezed them.

"Having a soft heart in a cruel world is not weakness, Nina, it's a sign of courage," she said. "And I admire you for that."

I smiled again a little brighter this time.

"Thank you, Jordan."

~*~

Although people at school ignored me as they got on with their lives, I had other problems to deal with. Aunt Vikki had talked to the principal and reassured the school counselors under my request about my situation. They must have had pregnant teens before that everything went smoothly. Now I could continue my studies as I wished.

My aunt no longer allowed me to do anything but rest, because I had a lot of morning sickness that went on for two or three weeks. I would projectile vomit like never before. It got that bad to the point I thought I might lose the little one. I wasn't keeping anything down, not even water.

I began getting sent to the nurse office at school. Twice I was put on IV as I was very dehydrated.

Some days, my feet could swell so much that I wished I could wear bathroom slippers to school instead. My hips displaced, and I tried to walk without crying when I awoke. I was also recommended a series of medical tests to check my weight, blood pressure, uterus growth, and baby's heartbeat.

But during that time, I didn't remember feeling anything other than shock and fear that I had to look after my baby and begged the little one to stay with me.

I missed school for several days on end. Jordan called to check on me. She was worried. I told her I was just sick and asked her about any class work we might have. She was getting suspicious. I was sick so often. My attendance went downward spiral.

I was feeling lonely and scared. Sometimes, I walked around the room crying to myself, unable to lie down because of my back pain and emotional stress. I didn't know what to do. But when my dad called during the weekends, I told him everything was alright, and I was doing fine. I didn't want to worry him even more.

But the third months into my pregnancy, I felt the new change in me. It started with a pleasant wave of calmness that washed over my entire body like a warm blanket.

The mental fog and stress I'd been carrying around vanished slowly. The sounds that didn't even register before began to make sense again. Soon, I reached a level of alertness and concentration I needed. It was like walking around on a winter day after it just snowed.

I started going back to school and did my schoolwork as best as I could. I paid close attention in class. Everything else just drifted by like background noises. Jordan started paying more attention to me. After the end of each class, she walked me through the hallway until Rachel showed up, and we said goodbye.

I felt a lot better by the end of the third month. The morning sickness was eventually fading away, giving in a rush of food cravings. Aunt Vikki had hired the cook back. She made sure I had plenty of fruits and vegetables and foods rich in high fiber in my diet. She only wanted me to rest and exercise and not to study too much.

Piper sometimes took me shopping for baby clothes. And she seemed even more excited browsing for infant items than I was.

Although Robert and Jay mostly avoided awkwardness with me around the house, they helped setting up a crib in my room for the little one, too.

On top of that, there was a plethora of advises and suggestions from our gynecologist. When I had times, I tried to read to my baby or listen to Mozart's soothing clarinet concertos, which the doctor had recommended for pregnant mothers. At night, I wrote letters to Allecra and stared at the dazzling stars in the sky.

That was how my life was at that time.

~*~

The autumn sun glared down brightly through the clouds, but the arrival of nights became noticeably early as it was the transition from summer to winter. Halloween drew in. My maternal emotions were so affected when I saw those little kids trotting in their monster or hero customs up our garden for 'trick or treat'. They just seized my heart with adoration and joy.

In Thanksgiving, Robert and my aunt had a big dinner with our neighbors while I stayed in my room. I told them I wasn't feeling well, but I just didn't feel like meeting anyone.

Towards the end of the year, my stomach had grown bigger week by week. I wore dresses that wouldn't make me look too obvious, but it was like the proverbial elephant in the room.

At the hallway and in class, I started getting stared at and hearing whispers behind my back.

'Is she?'
'Sure is! Look at her bump.'
'She's too young, gosh, how silly."
'Typical, that's what they said about Russian girls.'

Some of the teachers expressed their disappointments by ignoring me, acting like I was a ghost of their former student.

But they didn't know my story.

I told myself that in a few more weeks, I would take my exams and would be graduated. Now it was more important to have my credits and SAT score in order then I would be out of here. Yet it wasn't easy being

487

pregnant while trying to endure all the criticism. I felt like it was going on forever.

One particular evening, Piper brought home a book called *A Hundred Baby Names*, which listed names and their meaning.

Piper read a lot of names out loud. Many of them would not do at all. Philbert, which means "superior", sounded good for a boy, but Jay said, at school, boys would call him a nut. My aunt suggested names that were Russian like Ekaterina or Elizaveta for a girl. Robert thought they were too fancy and quite a mouthful. However, I appreciated that the family was slowly accepting my baby in the most subtle ways. I was truly lucky.

In the end, we couldn't agree on any name since we weren't sure whether the baby would be a boy or a girl. I had decided not to find out my baby's gender anyway.

What if the little one was born like Allecra? I thought to myself.

Now I realized I had never considered the full complication of the birth. I never visualized my baby would be anything other than normal and that he or she definitely deserved a chance at a normal human life.

The next day after school ended, Jordan confronted me. There was no better term to put it when she came up to me, looking into my eyes for a few seconds before she spoke.

"Can I talk with you for a moment, Nina?" she asked.

I knew something was up, but I nodded.

In total silence, Jordan walked me to the baseball field. It was empty. Then she asked me to sit down on the bench.

"Why did you bring me here?" I asked her. She sat down beside me, looking slightly uncomfortable and stressed. Her expression became more worrisome every passing minute. But then she had no choice but to tell me whatever had bothering her.

"Nina, are you pregnant?" she asked at last.

I couldn't stand the agony of anticipation, so I was glad she made it straightforward. With a deep sigh, I turned away from her imploring gaze. Jordan saw that I was worn out by all the secret. My answer would mean a full confession, and she braced herself for it.

"Took you long enough to figure out," I said. To stop myself from crying, I put my hand on my stomach, but my tactic failed when I was actually confirming my answer to her.

"How...how could that be..." for the first time, Jordan the wise, could barely form a proper sentence.

"It doesn't matter how, does it?"

"It does! Nina, it does matter to me!"

I looked at her through my tears, stunned by her outburst.

"Jordan..."

"I know. I know," she said. "But I just don't understand. You were in love with her, weren't you?"

"I still am."

"Then what happened?"

"Don't worry, nothing heinous happened to me, but I would rather not talk about it."

Jordan didn't speak for a time. Her eyes never left my face.

"The real father isn't around, is he?"

I didn't know what made me say this, but maybe the truth was too big and slippery, it had to come out one way or the other.

"It's not a he."

She stared at me, stunned.

"What?"

"I've got to go," I declared and got up to leave.

"Nina, wait!" Jordan came from behind me. She wrapped her arms around my shoulders to stop me. Then I realized she was crying.

"I'm sorry," she said tearfully.

"Why did you say that?" I asked.

"I wished I were there to protect you. I wished I had fought for you so that this wouldn't have happened."

I touched her arms and turned around to face her, wiping my friend's tears with my thumbs.

"No, Jordan, it's a lot different than what you think, and there's nothing you could have changed. I would have chosen it the same way."

"Nina...tell me what really happened?"

I smiled at her saddened face.

"It's best for you not to know," I said. "Trust me."

~*~

I started noticing *flutters'* inside me. It felt like butterflies in my stomach or popcorn popping. It was a very strange feeling but also amazing. I told Allecra our child started moving quite a lot recently. Half of me was growing excited, but another half was also petrified. I didn't know how the little one would come out. I could either face this fear head-on or continue to let it be a major part of my life. But I could say I now began to overcome it, slowly.

At last, I finished all my credits for high school and took SAT test and graduated a few months early. Then I spent the remaining time, preparing for my childbirth. Soon Piper and Jay started talking about their prom and graduation day, both of which I wasn't going to attend.

Week after week passed by like a train wagon. I was nine months pregnant. My stomach had grown to the size of a watermelon and quite heavy for my small frame.

It was almost eleven at night, and I was wide awake, still staring at the ceiling. Suddenly, there was like the crest of a wave of a period cramp. I lay there with my mind racing for a while. Then I got up and took long deep breaths the way I had done often during my pregnancy.

The whole house was sleeping. I had another wave—another rolling cramp. I grimaced at my swollen stomach.

No, could it be?

But it hadn't reached my due date yet.

I went slowly to have a hot bath, still feeling jittery with this new sense of discomfort. After half an hour, I felt better and wondered if it was just a normal cramp.

But as I grabbed the towel rack, another one shot up from my belly.

"Ow!" I cried out loud and hugged my stomach. The pain was as sharp as when you stub your toes.

Then I felt a popping sensation followed by a gush of fluid from between my thighs, spilling all over the bathroom floor.

My water broke.

I gasped in a shocking realization.

As I suspected and feared, I knew I was going to go into labor soon.

I tried to put on my bathrobe and reached for my phone. My trembling hand dialed Piper as she was the last a person I had contacted. After a long ringing, she finally picked up. Her voice sounded groggy.

"King?"

"Piper, it's me," I said between gasps. "Please I need your help..."

"Nina, are you okay? You sound like you're going into labor..."

"Actually I am."

"Oh snap!" she said. "Wait right there, Nina! I'll go get mom."

The phone went dead and a few moments later, Aunt Vikki and Piper found me clutching my stomach on the wet floor.

"Oh god," Piper gasped.

"Piper, go wake Jason to get the car. Your dad isn't home," my aunt ordered as she came to me. "We need to get Nina to hospital."

"Oh right, okay!"

"Nina, don't worry, we'll take you to the hospital. Can you stand?"

I nodded and bit my lips from crying as she helped me up.

In the hospital, I was being moved around the corridor and everything blurred like I was being airlifted between boroughs like a whale.

Inside the delivery room, I had a gripping panic attack when the nurse was preparing the needle. The other lubed me up and strapped monitors to me, and a chorus of fetal heart tones beeped out in the room like a horse galloping. I felt embarrassed like I was having my first period when they started to open my legs. The first time I lay there, I started to cry with some kind of panic and mixed emotions. My aunt tried to calm me down, stroking my head and telling me not to be afraid.

"Your body will know what to do, it's in your nature, Nina, you're going to be fine," she said. Of course, I couldn't tell her how the evaluation had failed us in this aspect.

"No, no, I can't do this," I sobbed.

I had spent my entire nine month scared to death of the tray covered in sharp sterilized tools and the doctor trying to cut me. Now this nightmare was one I couldn't wake up from, because it was real.

"Nina, calm down, the doctor will give you epidural to help with the pain, just stay calm," Aunt Vikki soothed me.

When the doctor walked in, they did give me the drug.

It didn't work.

I had two failed epidurals and still felt the pain. The anesthesiologist gave me the saddest look and told me that for some women, it just wouldn't work. I was going into labor naturally.

The contractions were getting worse. Every time a contraction would come, my lower back would slowly begin to seize up as though it would snap. I felt the muscles inside me were slowly twisting harder and harder like a clenched fist until it became almost unbearable. I let out a strangled scream. It was the most horrible pain I had ever experienced. I thought I had imagined the worst of it, but I was wrong.

Sweat-beaten and trembling with chills, I cried and prayed to my mother to help me.

"She's seven centimeters dilated," the doctor said. "I could see the head now."

When they told me to push, I did as hard I could. The pain was like having my insides twisted, pulled, and wrangled out like a wet rag. If I fought it, the pain became worse. It was like my whole pelvis was made of breaking glass, piercing my own womb with its shards. The pain was so bad that in the middle of one push I wished I could walk away from my body. I lost my breaths several times and thought I was going to die.

"The mother needs oxygen."

"Should we perform the caesarean..." one of the nurses suggested.

"No, the baby is crowning," the doctor said. "She can make it."

"Nina, you can do it," my aunt's voice said. "Just a little more."

Hot tears streamed from my eyes, mixing with cold sweat. I was caught in the undertow of a tidal wave of pain and being trapped under it, terrified and helpless — like I was drowning and dying.

But in the intense moment of my labor, my feverish mind thought of Allecra, and how she would be here to comfort me if she could.

I bit my bottom lip and tried to push with all my remaining strength.

For our little one, the voice in my head said.

I wasn't going to let go of us.

Suddenly, I felt a sheering burn and a slow slip of my baby's head outside, and I knew the wave had released me back to the surface. The doctor pulled my newborn out. The sight of the fluid and blood-covered tiny thing made my heart burst with relief and joy.

"Nina, it's a girl!" My aunt told me.

But a few seconds went by in silence. I didn't hear the crying as it was supposed to be. Instead the doctor and nurses were fumbling around my little one on the other table, where they seemed to perform a certain medical procedure.

"What's wrong?" I asked weakly, noticing my aunt's frozen face. I had forgotten about the agony I had just gone through and was staring wild eyes for the answer. Why didn't they give me my child?

After about fifteen minutes, new fear entered my heart. It wasn't the kind of fear I had ever known. This one was the worst of all fear. The doctor shook her head and sighed.

She walked towards me.

"The baby didn't make it," she said. "I'm so sorry."

I felt like the air was knocked out of my lungs. My body went cold all over, and I was almost on the verge of passing out when I heard it.

No, this can't be happening.

"I want to see my baby, my baby, give me my baby!" I demanded.

"Nina..."

"Give me my little one...please!"

The doctor nodded to the nurse, who had cleaned up and wrapped my daughter in a white blanket. She came to place my girl in my waiting arms.

I stared at my daughter—at Allecra's daughter for the first time.

God, she's so beautiful.

But her tiny nose didn't breathe, and her tiny hands didn't move.

She was my only hope in this world.

How could this be?

I burst out crying. I wished it were me instead. My aunt wiped her tears as she watched me held my baby to my breast. I removed the blanket and held my little girl against my chest to warm her tiny body. Her skin was cold and pale.

Then I found myself humming a song I didn't even know. I touched her little fingers, making little tunes and leaning my cheek against her head with tears flowing ceaselessly.

My daughter had come to earth perfect in every way. Why had she not opened her eyes? Was I being punished for my crime of being born difficult to my mother that I deserved to lose this child?

I was tormented with grief to see my baby this way. I had never wished for anything harder than I wished that little heart to palpitate with life.

493

My forehead rested against my daughter's as if in supersensible communication.

"Please," I begged over and over.

Then a sensation prickled in my bones, and I felt I had discovered a delicate link of interaction somewhere. It was a clairvoyance that new mothers possess but which had taken me awhile to discover. At last, I closed my eyes and was able to understand an esoteric language from my little one.

My face broke into a shining smile and more tears slide down my cheeks. A soft nasal cry cut through the silence as the first angelic heartbeat sounded in my daughter's chest. Another cry, and I gasped in pure joy. In that moment, I received a tacit confirmation from my little girl that she would soon be ready to claim her glorious presence on this planet.

~*~

For three days, they had kept my baby in an incubator. In the cocoon of a closed hygienic atmosphere, everything was being done to encourage the steady progress of my precious little thing.

I sat with my gloved hand on the side of plastic capsule, never taking my eyes off the tiny movement. The heart monitor showed green peaks at regular intervals.

Throughout the long nights I would talk to her in an empathetic voice of a mother, about how much she meant to me in the unparalleled world. I also told Allecra about our baby.

"Our baby is born now, Allecra," I whispered. "I wish you were here to see your baby. She's in a capsule like she just arrived from outerspace, and she looks just like you."

Those were the times I missed Allecra so intensely and with such a passion I just wanted to scream for her.

The doctor finally let me breastfed the little one after they took the last examination. I was relieved and overjoyed that they found nothing wrong with her. The little one woke up and opened those sparkling bright eyes for the first time.

Oh how they just took my breath away!

"This child is miraculous," the doctor said with her kind smile. "She's a gift to earth from heaven."

I smiled back. My aunt and Piper came to see me.

"Oh geez, mom, look at her eyes!" Piper exclaimed with a fascinated look. "They're...wait...blue? Green?"

"Turquoise," I said without taking my stare off my child.

"She really is a beautiful pumpkin," Aunt Vikki said, smiling. "Well, she kind of reminds me of someone."

"Yeah, I think so too, mom," Piper agreed.

But I didn't say anything and let their mind wander.

After the breastfeeding, they took turn holding the little one. The doctor came again and said we could go home if we wanted to. A while later, Robert and Jay arrived. When they spoke now, it was with the penitential tones of the humbled. It seemed like somehow my daughter had affected them and made them respect me, being a mother and all.

Jay took a look at my baby's face and raised his brows.

"How come your baby has a head full of blonde hair already?" He said. "And she looks a lot like your ex-girlfriend, too. Those eyes..."

Piper gave him a nudge in the rip.

"Can you stop being an insensitive jerk and shut up for once?"

"It's alright Piper," I said, smiling. Actually I was pleased they all thought that way.

"So you got a name for the baby already?" This time Robert asked.

"I talked to my dad yesterday," I said. "We both agreed that we should call her after my mom."

"Elvira?" my aunt said. "That's a good name, Nina. I should have thought of that."

"Yes, we will call her Elvira," I said, turning my gaze back at the now sleeping angel in my arms.

"Aw...that's an adorable name!" Piper said. "Or we can call her Ella or Little El."

"Sounds like a cool rapper name, you know, Lil El?" Jay chimed in.

My aunt shook her head and then turned to me.

"Your mom would have been so proud of you," Aunt Vikki said and stroked my hair. "You are such a very strong and brave woman just like her."

I had always thought of myself as a coward, but now to hear someone telling I was brave made me tear up with gratitude.

"Thank you, Aunt Vikki, and everyone for everything," I said. "I couldn't do this without you all."

That evening we returned home with Elvira in my arms. She slept most of the times and only awoke for me to breastfeed her. I could hardly believe my own heart that it could love this much when I looked at those bright galactic eyes.

What was this actual creation of divine miracle that somehow this universe allowed to be organized inside me? And now here she was in my arms like magic. It was like the whole universe had opened up to me again.

I wondered how Allecra would have felt if she knew that she was now a—daddy? A mommy? But whatever she was, I was sure she would have been just as overwhelmed with all this joy like me.

After I finished feeding my little girl, I went to my closet and pulled out the Pandora's box. The sadness and grief stuck inside it no longer bothered me. I had one thing that protected me now.

Taking out Allecra's necklace, I stared at the dull sparks of the Erytus stone. Then I came back to the crib and held it up for our baby to see. She seemed to look at it and cooed adorably back. Her soft little hands jerked as if delighted. The stone swayed around, amusing her. My heart just melted at the sight.

"See that, honey?" I said softly to her. "Your...mom-dad gave it to me on my birthday. Now I want you to have it. Thank you for bringing hope back into my life. I love you so much."

Then I fastened the necklace around her neck. Elvira looked at me with some sort of intellectual flash in her gaze.

All of a sudden, an iridescent light lit up from the stone as well as those celestial turquoise eyes of my daughter.

I gasped and covered my mouth at the strange, yet familiar happening.

The bright glow lasted only a second before it ceased, but I knew something special had taken place.

Elvira yawned as if in oblivion. I touched her face and a strong surge of reassurance washed over me.

It was a faint sign of promise.

CHAPTER 48

AFTER GIVING BIRTH to my daughter, I had a vivid dream of Allecra for the first time. Before a wide arched window, Allecra stood watching the winged-whales sailed through the sky like zeppelins. A school of mothers and their babies flapped their wings in the air, sending gusts of the wind against the crystal dome of the city towers.

A dark violet moon hung low by the edge of the sleeping sea. Another silver moon rose high among the stars, constellations upon constellations of bright twinkles spreading across the silent auroric night. Bellow sprawled authentic buildings, their porous pocket, and bubble windows lit with golden light. Circling metal-paved streets within transparent tubes glinted like silver snakes under the moon glow.

Yet despite all its outlandish beauty, the city was more of an immense tomb, too quiet and seemingly empty of life.

Allecra gazed up at the silver moon. Then her turquoise eyes closed as if she was trying to summon a thought in her mind. But nothing came. She gave herself an imperceptible shake of her head.

'Sister?'

A soundless male voice came from the dark where a tall figure stood poised by the wall. The word was in another language, but it still made perfect sense in the dream.

Allecra let out a soft sigh.

"You know why I like to stare through this window?" she said, still observing the fish soaring passed the moonlit clouds. "It seems to remind me of someone. The window and strange things floating about somewhere. And I seemed to like the company of that person a lot."

She turned herself around to look at the tall figure in the shadow.

"Last night, I woke up with a lingering sensation," she said. "A very outlandish feeling, like a distant calling though I didn't hear anything. And I felt this intense need to answer it, but I couldn't. Then I sat up grasping at the air. My hands trembled with disappointment, and there was a sharp gripping ache in my chest. I have no idea what it is."

'It's called 'sadness'.'

"Sadness," Allecra repeated as if trying a new word in her mouth. She fell quiet for the longest moment before she spoke again. "Triton, how long have we been back?"

'A month.'

"That means a year has passed on the Blue Planet," she said and sighed to herself. "I tried to remember things from that world, but my memory feels like mist, foggy and shifting. Xenon...she erased something important in my mind, didn't she? But I still feel these vague jumbled feelings in my heart. It doesn't seem to go away, and now it dawned on me that I do not want to live with this—this sharp nagging pain in my chest. Do you know what kind of pain it is, brother?"

She waited for a long moment until at last Triton spoke.

'You miss an Earth girl.'

"I miss an Earth girl? This gnawing feeling in every hollow of my bones is because I miss someone on Earth?" Allecra said, frowning to herself in contemplation. "Tell me, Triton, why do I miss her? What was she to me?"

Her brother sighed and stepped into the light. His angular face bore a look of remorse as he stared at Allecra.

'Because of your love for her.'

"But now I can't remember anything about this love!" Allecra looked frustrated as she was trying to figure something in her mind. "Why did Xenon do this to me? Why!?"

Triton didn't respond. They stood bathing in the moonlight for a while. Allecra put her slender hands and forehead against the glass and closed her eyes again. She was trying hard to remember the feeling she had lost.

"Can you tell me what the girl was like?"

'I already disobeyed the order by telling you this much. I'm sorry.'

Allecra turned to her brother.

"I want to go back to Earth," she said suddenly. "Something is calling me back to that planet. I feel like I have to go there, Triton."

But the sliding sound of the triangular door stopped their conversation. Xenon strode into the room.

"Our aerospace technicians said they will take at least four months to prepare for the transferring. They had used up the power bringing us back from Earth," she informed them. "Anyway, their satellite has sent a report that the new world's habitability is still active, and the environment is perfectly safe for us to stay. The Elders would like to send you there as soon as possible."

Triton turned to Allecra, but she didn't look away from the window. Xenon looked at him. A short exchange of private dialogue seemed to issue from their meeting eyes. Then the dark-haired girl sighed before coming to stand beside Allecra.

"You haven't said a word to me since we're back in Arzuria," she said. "I know you're angry at me, for reasons you can't even remember, but you have to understand that whatever I did, it was for the best. In the New World, you will find a more suitable potential—"

"I think I have a child," Allecra spoke up all of a sudden. Her eyes gleamed like midnight dew under the moonshine. As soon as the words came out of her mouth, there was a long stretching pause among them.

"What?" Xenon asked, looking perplexed.

"I can't explain it to you, even I don't know it myself, but I just know that I have a baby now, Xenon," she said again, finally turning from the window to her sister. "They have to take me back to Earth. My child is waiting for me!"

"Allecra, you know it is a very serious matter..."

"I have to see the Elders." Allecra turned to walk out of the room, but Xenon grabbed her hand.

"Allecra, no!" Xenon said her. "You can't jump into conclusion and let them know about it."

"I do not jump into conclusion!" she yelled back. "You don't understand this feeling because you're not a parent!"

"Of course I don't! And I never will," she said. "But assuming what you said is true, I believe the child is better off on Earth."

Allecra looked at her sister in disbelief and disgust.

"Did you intend for it to happen all along?" she asked.

"Don't be ridiculous," Xenon replied sternly through her clenched teeth. "Though I admit I had a slight suspicion that the girl was conceived by you, but a suspicion is just a suspicion. I could not rely on some vague hint like that."

"Even if you could, you wouldn't!" Allecra growled. "Were you jealous of us? You separated me from my unborn baby and the human girl because I loved an Earthling and not you?"

Xenon gave her a slap that sounded sharply in the too quiet room. Allecra's face turned to the side from the blow.

"I only wanted to protect you!" Xenon cried. "It would be easier with someone you had no feeling for, but I knew you loved that girl so much that you couldn't think of the future consequence. I just don't want you to go through it. If the Elders know that you actually have an heir, they will claim the baby."

"They can't do that!"

"Yes, they can and they will," Xenon said. "This is what the whole operation is all about. Do you think they would let you live happily ever after with your human lover on Earth? Think again, Allecra, you know they would want your baby here in Arzuria. And what do you think they would do to the child? Look at Triton and me and you! What are we exactly? They only wanted you to use the female earthling as a host for our genetic reproductive purposes. They have no interest in your human love!"

Allecra was stunned to hear what Xenon said. She ran both hands through her hair at the sickening realization.

"Then what am I going to do?!" Allecra cried and started pacing in hysteria. "I can't stay here. I want to go back. I have to go back! They need me!"

"Even if you could return to Earth, years would have passed between the two planets. Time goes backward or forward when navigating through space. And if you could find the human girl and her baby again, eventually the Elders would find you and take the child back with them, then what will become of the earthling mother? How would she feel having her child ripped from her arms and being left behind to grieve once again?"

Allecra growled and turned to the window, repeatedly pounding the wall of thick glass with both hands.

"It has to be a way out of this! It has to be!" Allecra cried with more blows. She was now like an imprisoned bird trying to break free from the cage.

Her sister looked at her with conflicted eyes. After a while, she gestured to Triton.

"Stop her."

"No, leave me! Get out! Get out!"

Then Allecra slid down onto her knees and began weeping.

Xenon couldn't look at her anymore and simply nodded to Triton. The two Arzurians turned and left through the door, leaving Allecra alone with her grief.

I woke up from the dream and heard my daughter's siren wailing in her crib. I quickly leaped out of bed and went to her. Her whole face blushed red from crying.

I checked her temperature and peeked in her diaper, but everything seemed fine. I picked my baby up and cradled her in my arms. I thought she might be thirsty and tried to feed her, but she tilted her head away.

Fearing that the noise would wake the whole house, I brought her to the balcony, humming a soft lullaby to soothe her. Elvira wouldn't stop crying. She had never been like this. I didn't know what to do.

The dream had bothered me but at the moment my daughter was all I cared about. She seemed to be so upset with something, and her crying just broke my heart. Before I knew it, my own tears spilled onto her soft blanket. I was silently crying, too.

~*~

Allecra strode along the corridor with Xenon and Triton escorted by a number of soldiers in white uniform.

They came to a large burnished silver room. In a vast pool of moonlight coming through the crystal ceiling, men and women sat at a long stone table around the hall. In the large chamber illuminated by light from the transparent pillars, everyone regarded the three young Arzurians with scrutinizing stares.

The Elders looked at them with their eyes glowing. There were dark purplish shadows under their cheekbones. Despite their impressive violet cloaks, they were old and withering with age. Allecra stepped forward and bowed to them.

"Are you prepared for the journey to the new home?" one of the Elders with bald egg-shaped head and silvery eyes asked.

"No, sir," Allecra said. "I have come here to talk with you about Earth."

The older Arzurians frowned and looked at each other.

"The hybridization program on that planet has failed. What is there to discuss about?"

"What if I tell you, I have found the cure to our barren world?"

A chorus of gasps and murmurs echoed around the chamber. A female blue-eyed Elder leaned forward and spoke up.

"What did you just say, young one?"

"I want you to listen first to what I've learned from the human race," Allecra answered.

"There's nothing they know that we haven't already known in our world."

"That's not true," Allecra said. "They might not be intelligent and advanced like us, but we lack what the humans have. It has been programmed in their brain since birth by the evolution. They inherently and spontaneously know what it means to their survival and reproduction. Since the first moment they are born, their kind possesses an unwavering force within them. It's what makes life possible."

"And what is it?"

"Love."

The murmuring of the word erupted among the Arzurians again, as if they'd only heard of it for the first time.

"Love?"

"Yes, the force that's driven life," Allecra said with a solemn nod. "Our civilization has grown too advanced, we're like thinking machines. We were not born, but harvested, taken from our mother's womb early and placed into tubes, artificially nurturing until an appropriate time, because everyone preferred it over the nine months." She paused and looked at everyone's attentive faces directed at her. "We went to school at three, finished at twelve and were trained to become perfect citizens with desired professions in our society. We'd never been shown love to or taught how to love because we hardly saw our family or friends or even spouses face-to-face except their holographs. Life was too busy we stopped eating real foods but energy pills. We were interested in a fast and open relationship more than a committed one. We stopped showing real feelings for fear of being called 'weak, no sadness nor joy, let alone true love. Needless to say, our minds are full but our hearts are empty. That's how the evolution made us evolve into a barren species because nature knows we're incapable of sustaining life."

A wave of shock washed over the room. An Elder raised her bony hand to silence the noises.

"So what do you suggest we solve this inherited problem?"

"Learn to feel like humans," Allecra said. "On Earth, there's a man who jumped into a frozen river to save a drowning deer. There's a woman who took the place of a friend in a car accident. If we learn to form such emotions like that, our race can gain the ability to love and create life again."

The Elders listened. Some nodded, but some did not.

"If you said we've never been shown love to or taught how to love since we were young, how did you come to learn about love yourself?"

"While I was on Earth, someone taught me how to feel this special thing. I don't remember who she was or what she did, but I never forget how she made me feel. Now I know I have found the answer. If there is love, there is life. It's just that simple."

The Elders were silent for a long while.

"You want us to feel like the Earth people," A violet-eyed Elder said. "That's like telling adults to act like toddlers again. Our civilization has gone this far, battling countless disasters and wars and failed governments to build a peaceful and orderly world. Now you tell us, we should follow the inferior race?

"If you said love is the cure to the Arzurians, and you have been taught to love, why did you not succeed in the end? Who knows whether your theory works or not? If everything turns out fruitless as it's been before, it would be a waste of our time. By then you would have lost your potent fertility for breeding, and we can't risk that. You all know time is crucial to our mission."

Allecra was tongue-tied between keeping the secret and telling the truth about the baby. Her hands balled into fists. She knew she had been cornered. Xenon and Triton glanced at each other.

"I have given you the cure to saving our dying world. Whether you believe it or not, it's not my concern anymore. I won't go anywhere. I want to go back to Earth."

"Nonsense!" another Elder said. "You shall be sent to the new planet with no further delay. You're the last one of us. You're born to ensure that our future generation can continue our bloodline. We are not the humans!"

Allecra's body trembled in suppressed rage. She wanted to say something back, but Xenon gripped her arm.

"Allecra, don't," she whispered. "We have tried."

Hopelessness had settled over her once again. She closed her eyes and a tear rolled down her cheek. The sight of her vulnerability seemed to cause a stir of surprise among the Arzurians.

"Our civilization is collapsing because of you," Allecra said quietly at last, "You don't know what love is. Maybe we're better off going extinct!"

The Elders's glowing eyes widened in shock.

"Allecra, please," Xenon whispered again and tugged at her hand. The gesture stopped her with immediate calm. Then the dark-haired girl turned back the Elders. "We will proceed as planned, respected Elders."

The old men and women nodded curtly, but some of them still looked unsettled by Allecra's bitter words.

The floor split apart and a large machine emerged, looking much like the Spindle except it was much grander and with a spaceship in the middle. Then the ceiling above them opened like lotus petals, revealing the starlit dome of the multi-colored sky. Everything was prepared and ready to launch at a moment's notice.

The technicians' fingers flew over transparent keyboards. Their voices murmured codes and directives in a continuous stream. Symbols scrolled, and vanished, and flickered, jumping from screen to screen. The light power surged from the bottom of the great equipment.

Allecra and her siblings were escorted to the enormous machine and ordered to get into the spaceship.

Communication between the Arzurian scientists rang around the room.

"The location command codes have been entered. We will send them directly to the New Planet in sixty seconds."

The brightness of the light intensified.

"Wait, there seems to be a problem!" someone cried. "The message has been intercepted by an unknown source, repeat the message has been intercepted...!"

"What's happened?" The Elder said.

"Sir, someone altered the location. They are not going to Planet Tarael," a technician answered. "They're going to Earth!"

"Stop the machine!"

Sparks burst from every screen like bright rain. All equipment began to melt into sand.

"We can't stop it, sir! They're destroying the main circuit!"

"Get them!"

A troop of uniform soldiers sprinted towards the Spindle. Xenon turned to Allecra and grabbed her face before she kissed her on the lips.

"She's waiting for you," she said. "Go find her."

And before Allecra could respond, her sister jumped out of the spaceship again. Triton's hands moved over buttons and switches.

The giant ring began to spin.

'Keep the machine going, sister. They're trying to pull us back.' Triton reminded Allecra.

The whole place was trembling as the Spindle spun faster. Winds blew and a great column of light burst into the sky. The last time Allecra looked at Xenon, she was standing among the piles of fallen soldiers on the floor. Her sister turned around to her before giving her a farewell smile. Then everything went blinding and silent.

~*~

I made a turn at the corner of the street and came to a stop by the sidewalk. I saw other people went through the gate. The chatters and laughter filled the air as I entered the playground where they set up a stage.

There was the sound of applause each time the name was called. I was a bit late. I had to finish an urgent article that needed to be sent to my editor. But my daughter's graduation was always on the forefront of my mind the whole time.

I came to sit next to a couple of parents at the back row and scanned eagerly for her. The teacher continued to call out names and each pupil came up to receive a certificate in their adorable white gown and cap. I didn't have to look for long. Elvira's unruly blonde hair stood out from the crowd.

As if she could feel my eyes on her, my daughter looked up and glanced over to my direction. The angelic face that wasn't smiling a moment ago now resembled a bright sunshine with her toothy grin. It made my heart melt with pure joy. She waved animatedly at me, and I waved back with a soft giggle to myself.

"A lovely young lady, isn't she?" the woman sitting beside me said cordially while we watched my daughter moved onto the stage.

"She is," I replied, beaming back.

"Are you her aunt or her sister?" She asked innocently. I turned to the woman and shook my head with a smile.

"No, she's my daughter," I said.

"Oh," she breathed and tried to hide her surprise. "Well, now I can see the resemblance, but I think she must take after her father more, eh?"

"I guess so." I nodded back. I had gotten used to this kind of questions by now.

The announcer called out my daughter's name through the microphone. She went up to receive her certificate and looked over to me and smiled, waving her little hand at me. I got tears in my eyes as I clapped proudly.

Looking at her, I was in constant awe that my baby girl had grown so fast. She was just a bundle of joy in my arms the other day. I still remembered all those moments seeing her crawling for the first time, trying to get stuff from her mouth when she was teething, holding her when she took her first baby step. It was all the best times in my life.

After the certificate-handing and photo-taking were done, El ran up to me. In that moment, I was awestruck once again at how she was like a mini replica of Allecra.

"Mommy!" My daughter yelled in her lovely chiming voice. Her arms opened wide. That wild blonde hair bounced softly over her small frame. I welcomed her into my firm embrace then picked her up. She wrapped her little arms and legs around me, and we both giggled together. I noticed she had grown heavier too. My little one wasn't so little anymore.

"Look who's just graduated here!" I said, kissing her cheek again and again. She smelled like strawberry and chocolate chip cookies they served in this event. "Congratulation, sweetheart! Sorry, I was a bit late."

"'s okay," she said, beaming cutely back. "It's only a preschool graduation."

"Why you don't sound so excited?" I asked. Her turquoise eyes stared into mine as she considered her feelings.

"Well, I'm just glad that it's over now," she said at last.

I knew how hard it was for her blend in with other human kids. Being in school was just to make life easier for both of us. I had to work all day and couldn't look after her.

My daughter was obviously different from other five-year-olds. She was ferociously intelligent. I remembered everyone was a bit concerned when she wouldn't start talking like other toddlers her age, but one day during dinner, Robert cheekily asked her, "Can you speak?" and she went, "Yes great-uncle, I can speak, why?", which surprised everyone. It was just her way of learning things. She wouldn't show it until she got it all right. She never started with trial and error.

During her third year, I taught her both the English and Russian alphabets, and that was all it took from there for my daughter to excel in both languages. She spoke fluent Russian with my dad and Aunt Vikki. She even taught herself mathematics, which I found later to my amazement that she could already understand basic algebra.

El also loved music. I had no idea where she got her musical side from. She only listened once and was able to play it on her baby keyboard. My aunt was thrilled that at last someone in the family shared her passion, and in fact, my own mother was also a music lover. Aunt Vikki bought a real piano she had always wanted then the two of them went through Mozart, Beethoven or Rachmaninov almost every weekend. Since then our house had never been livelier.

My daughter also loved tinkering with complicated machinery. She enjoyed taking clocks or broken toys apart and fixing them.

Now that we lived on our own, I had bought a complete collection of professional manual books about cars and plumbing and even household electronics, which I thought would come in handy. It turned out Elvira read them all and was able to tell me how to fix simple appliances without going to the repairer.

I could not recall ever having had to force her to do anything or scold her for misbehaving. She would decide for herself what she had to do and then she would do it, flawlessly.

Just like Allecra, I thought.

"I know you struggle with boredom a little, sweetheart," I said and reached my hand to brush those sweaty blonde strands from her forehead, "But I can't let you be alone at home all day either. It makes me feel better knowing you're safe."

Elvira nodded and hugged me.

"If this makes you happy, it makes me happy too."

I held her back and kissed her hair, wishing I could just squeeze her to my heart's content.

"Mommy, you can put me down. I'm too heavy for you," El said after a while. I chuckled back and kissed her cheek hard.

"You're always so considerate," I said. "Okay, let's go home."

I put her down, and we walked happily hand in hand back to our car.

During the drive, I asked her about her thought on the elementary school.

"You know they have cool science class and art and music," I told her. "You can learn a lot of interesting things in elementary school."

"I don't know about that yet, but preschool only taught me easy maths or spellingy games or punctuationy things," El said while her eyes wandering outside the window, "And to be honest, Mrs. Wilson is not my most favorite person on the planet of Earth. She said I have an attention span of a goldfish. I wondered if she ever taught a goldfish before. Doesn't she know goldfish sleep with their eyes open? How could she know if they don't pay attention in class?"

"I'm pretty sure you just proved her point and honey, even she's not your favorite people on Earth, you're from Earth and she's your teacher, so you must respect her," I said. "I know you're too smart for the stuff they taught you, but I just thought you would make friends in school and have fun with other kids."

"But mommy, I would rather know someone who can build a robot from tin cans than someone who can spell grapefruit."

Even I disapproved with what she said, I had to laugh.

"Okay," I said with a chuckle. "Let's not talk about school now. How about we have some ice cream before we get home?"

"Sounds great!"

I smiled to myself. After all, my little girl was still a kid.

When El was four years old, I decided to move out of my aunt's house. Aunt Vikki wouldn't hear of it at first. She said she would miss my daughter so terribly since everyone had gone to college, but I reassured her that it was about time I learned to stand on my own. Besides, we didn't move anywhere far, just the outskirt of the city. And we would visit her often.

With all my saving over the years, working several odd jobs after graduation and a little help from my dad, who had put aside a small sum of money for me without Dominika knowing and my aunt's baby fund for us, I was able to buy a small house. It was old, but it was made of solid brick. The first time I saw the place, it gave me a sense of stability and warmth. It used to belong to an old English couple, but they had moved back to their homeland and had no children to live there, so they sold it at a reasonable price.

The area was a lot quieter there since most people didn't want to be that far from all the exciting places in the city. Our neighbors were gentle people, mostly those who seek peace and quiet.

Robert helped to hire people to fix the tiles on the roof and repainted the house anew. I also spent a quarter of a year refurbishing everything little by little. There was a lively front garden that bloomed in all corners and a backyard big enough to host a magnolia tree and a sugar maple and an ancient oak tree with a swing. And every morning always started with birdsongs.

I was glad I had found a perfect house for my daughter and me.

On the way home, we stopped at the local grocery store. El enjoyed shopping with me. She was very particular about what we bought and always helped to remind me what we really needed at home. And while saving a dollar here and there didn't seem like much, my daughter was the answer to our financial prayer. She would figure out how to buy everything in economical price, and although I didn't want her to worry about money, it seemed I could rely on her help sometimes.

At the cashier counter, Ben, the store owner's son smiled at us.

"And how much did you get?" He asked El.

"$49.90," she answered smugly.

Ben scanned the items, and El was right. It had become a tradition that he had to ask her, because one time his machine miscalculated our grocery's price, and my daughter had lost her trust since.

"But that didn't include the discount yet," Ben said and handed her a 20% discount card. "You can use it until next month."

"Ben, you don't have to do that," I said.

"That's no big deal at all. You are one of my favorite customers...I mean, our faithful customers," he said and smiled sheepishly at me. I smiled back and turned to my daughter.

"El, say thank you to Uncle Ben," I said.

"Thank you," she said, without looking up.

In the car, El was a little quiet. Her strawberry-vanilla flavor ice cream was slowly melting the cup.

"Your ice cream is melting. Need some help?"

She mechanically scooped a spoonful of it and reached over to feed me.

"Mmm...delicious," I said then I glanced sideways at her again. "Are you alright?"

"Do you like Uncle Ben, mommy?" She asked me back. Her turquoise eyes looked at me imploringly. I was startled with her straightforward question.

"What makes you ask me like that?"

"He seems to like you, like in a special way," she said, "I just wonder if you like him, too."

El was sensitive and observant sometimes. Something I would confidently say, she took after me.

"I like him as a friend, honey," I told her, "He's a nice guy, isn't he?"

"So you're not going to marry him one day or anything?"

My eyes widened at her question. I didn't know how much a five-year-old knows about marriage and adult relationship already. On top of that, I never told her about my sexual orientation. I figured I didn't want El to be exposed to gender preference too early. But I guessed it wasn't too early to explain your children about it when they asked.

"Sweetheart, there's something you need to know about me," I said. "I hope you don't find it so strange."

"What's that?"

"Well," I said and licked my lips before I went on, "the thing is your mommy doesn't like men...not in that 'special' way. So you don't have to worry about me marrying any man."

"Not even a woman?" El said to my surprise.

"Wait a minute...you do understand what you're asking me, don't you?"

"O'course!" she said. "Beatrice has two moms, and she complains that every time she needs something, she often gets this reply, *'Go ask your mom'* and she doesn't know which one."

I was amazed how children these days seemed to accept the concept so easily.

"Well...don't you worry, I don't think I would marry anyone in the future."

"Phew, that's a relief!" She breathed and seemed to cheer up again.

"Why is that?" I said in amusement at my daughter's reaction. Something seemed to flash in her bright eyes, but it lasted only for a moment before she smiled again and shrugged.

"Because, mommy, I'm gonna marry you when I grow up!"

I laughed and shook my head at her adorable declaration. Most little girls would only say that to their fathers, *'Daddy, I'm going to marry you when I grow up.'* because when they grow older, they would look for a man that could treat them right like the way their father did. But that wasn't the case with my daughter. Even El might not understand it now; I kind of guessed who she might be attracted to in the future.

~*~

"Time for a bath?"

El smiled, knowing that it was a special occasion since I hardly had the time to do it like before. And though my daughter had learned to do a lot of things all by herself, we both still enjoyed spending quality time together whenever we could.

"Okay!" She nodded and put her schoolbag down before we went to the bathroom together.

While we waited for the water to fill the bathtub, I got my daughter out of her clothes. Her necklace gleamed brightly in the light. But when she turned around, I spotted a little pale spiral-shaped bruise on her left shoulder blade. It looked more like a birthmark than a bruise, but I remembered she wasn't born with any birthmark.

It was very much similar to the Arzurian mark on Allecra's back. Looking at the darkening of the pigment, the mark would only grow more visible as my daughter grew older.

There were times when I was contemplating about letting her know who she really was, but I was afraid it would be too soon, and she wasn't ready. Imagine being told who your other parent was...an alien. Life was hard enough as it was.

"Mommy?" El turned around with a questioning look. "You okay?"

I snapped out of my thought and smiled at her.

"Yes, sweetheart, I'm alright," I said and held her hand as she got into the bathtub.

After the bath, I dried her up with a towel and brushed the tangles of her sandy lock. I wrapped her in the towel and carried her out to get dressed.

After we were done, we went to the kitchen. El helped me prepare for the cooking. Then the doorbell rang.

"Can you see who's at the door for me?" I said while I was busy stir-frying broccoli with ground beef.

El quickly went to the hallway. She would be now standing on the mini chair, looking out the front window to check who was ringing our doorbell. I heard my daughter's cute voice speaking.

"Mommy!"

"Yes, who is it?"

"It's the delivery man," she replied.

"Oh, wait a minute," I said and turned off the stove then wiped my hand on the apron before heading out to open the door.

"Please sign here, miss," the man in a bright yellow jacket said. I did as I was told, and he handed a big box to me.

"What's in the box?" My daughter asked.

"A big surprise!" I said in a singsong voice.

We set it on the table of our living area. I turned to El and smiled.

"This is for you, honey," I said. "To celebrate your preschool graduation."

"Wow, for me?"

I nodded with a smile. "Open it."

And she did. I knew she had been obsessed with learning about stars and galaxies. She was always telling me facts about this and that — do you know it rains diamonds in Jupiter? Or do you know we can see Venus from Earth? Or that the rings of Saturn are made up of millions of ice crystals as big as houses?!

"Oh! It's a Galileo Telescope!" she cried with wide eyes. "Amazing!"

"I knew you wanted it the last time you saw it at the mall."

Then she turned to me.

"It must've cost you a lot," she said, looking guilty. I shook my head and pulled her onto my lap.

"You never asked me for anything, honey," I said and breathed in the shampoo smell in her hair. "This is just a small gift. I would give you the moon if I could."

El turned around to hold my face in her small hands then kissed me on the lips.

"Mommy, I love you!" she said.

"I love you too, sweetie." I smiled.

"Oh wait, I almost forgot. I also have something to give you," she said and then ran off to her room. She got back and handed me a piece of paper. It was a lovely drawing done in colorful crayons. I was taken aback at how wonderful and artistic the picture looked.

"You drew this?" I asked. Elvira nodded with a grin. I stared at the landscape a bit longer and realized it wasn't one of the ordinary scenery. The trees had different shades of colors. What even unusual was there were fishes hovering in the sky. She didn't draw just one moon, but four of them in different phases with defined color and details. I felt like I was staring at a stranger version of Van Gogh's Starry Night.

My eyes moved down and found three little human figures holding hand with the smallest one stood in the middle. It was indeed the picture of a loving family.

"That's you and me," El explained, pointing with her tiny finger to the little one with blonde hair and the one with long brown hair.

"But who is the other one?" I asked, eyeing the taller figure that seemed to resemble my own daughter.

"That's Mamochka," she said casually.

"Mamochka?" I said, looking up at her with tears started to glisten in my eyes. El nodded quietly.

"I saw her in my dream last night," she said. "She told me she's coming to see us, and that I could call her, *'Mamochka*.*"

Tears finally fell from my eyes. I pulled my daughter into my arms, and I wept as we held each other.

The sky had been clouding up. A grumble of thunder sounded in a distance. But all I could hear now was my own thought, telling me:

She's coming home.

⁓*⁓

Elvira's head lolled sleepily over my shoulder as I carried her to bed. The rain fell gently against the window. I tucked my daughter in and kissed her forehead like I had done every night.

I came back to the living room again and tried to sit down in front of my typewriter and write, but no word came out of my mind. I was staring at the blank page for a long time before I decided to give up. My hand picked up El's drawing that lay on the table. I sat down and brushed my fingers over the picture then hovered on the one with blonde hair beside my daughter. My eyes turned misty again. I put down the drawing before I ruined it with my tears.

Walking to the window, I looked out to the backyard and the swaying trees. The heavy rain came with a faintest promise in the atmosphere. Everywhere shifted with shadows and lightning.

Somewhere in the house, the grandfather clock kept ticking away. I stood there, looking at the storm like a sailor's wife waiting for her lover to return from the sea.

A bright flash of lightning illuminated the world, and I heard my breath hitched in my throat. I did not pause to think of reasons or logic or whether it was just the work of my own delusion.

I ran out of the house and flung the backyard's door open. Facing the hill and the field of aspen trees, I cried out against the pounding rain. Then my feet tripped and I fell on my knees. My breathing turned ragged with sobs. I strained my eyes towards the darkness but saw no one. Nothing.

Silly you and your imagination! I scolded myself.

Raindrops washed away my tears, but I kept kneeling on the ground crying. Mud spattered on my nightgown.

Then my body stiffened. The feeling came through the earth. A soft footstep one after another. Closer and clearer.

"Nina?" a soft familiar voice spoke.

My heart just stopped.

For a moment, I thought I imagined that golden voice in my head.

But when I raised my face to find its source, my mouth fell open in utter shock.

Oh my goodness...

My lips trembled as I tried to make a sound, any sound at all.

But nothing came out.

The person I thought I could only see in my dream and in every fragment of my thoughts was now right in front of me. Not even the slightest change had touched her. It was as if she had never left.

Reality and dream seemed to merge together before my eyes. I didn't know whether I existed in one or the other.

Gathering all my strength, I rose slowly to stand on my wobbly feet. My eyes took in all of her. Then after a long frozen moment, my hands went forward to wind around that slender figure in front of me, as though on their own accord.

Allecra was still there. She wasn't vanishing as I kept squeezing her harder and closer. She was warm and as real as could be. She was breathing, sighing softly into my hair while holding me back in her strong arms. I could smell her familiar exquisite scent in my nose and feel the ecstatic sensation of her touch on my body. It was like time had frozen and the world had come to a standstill.

"Allecra," I sobbed shakily, tightening my embrace around her, as though I was afraid she was about to fade. The sudden sound of her name struck me as I had never said her name out loud for many years. I felt so overwhelmed but also revivified for the sound of it. It resonated through my body and mended my broken heart. "Is that really you?"

My face buried into her neck. Hot streams of tears smeared her skin. I could hear her heart beating against mine. Our pantings came in tandem.

"Yes, it's me."

Allecra rubbed my back gently. Then she pulled away, and we finally looked at each other's face again.

"Is this real?" I whispered. I still couldn't believe my own eyes though all senses suggested otherwise. My trembling hands came to cup her face, warm and soft, brushing my thumbs over her wet cheeks in awe. "Am I not dreaming? Please, don't be a dream again. Don't go away when I wake up, please."

"No, Nina," she answered softly. "I have come back for you. This is not a dream."

It was too much, too many emotions and questions and confusion and relief all at once. I felt like I was about to fall off the edge of reality. But I wanted to believe it was true.

Allecra stared at me with those brilliant eyes in the same wonderment and speechlessness. How I miss those beautiful eyes! I remembered them too well. They always shone with longing and passion as they rested on me. They too had not changed.

I reached up to touch the smooth velvety skin of her face like a blind person. A burst of warmth flooded my whole being, and I was bewildered with happiness.

"It's you," I whimpered.

But a sudden realization made my body tense. My hands dropped from her face, and I took a step back, hands went to my chest in nervousness.

How can she still remember me?

My stomach twisted in despair once again, preparing to mourn the loss of the old Allecra, the one who loved me before she was gone. The immense joy at seeing her again had clouded my mind that I just forgot about this one forgotten fact.

She looked at me, analyzing the tightness of my stare in confusion.

"Nina, it's really me," she said in the same the voice I longed to hear more than anything.

"You still recognized me?"

"Yes, I remember you now. I remember everything about you. The girl my heart ached to see for all these times."

"How...? How...could that be possible?" I whispered.

"All my memories came back to me the moment I saw you. It all became clear now like a new burst of flames catching the wind. I just know you're the one I'm looking for."

My heart fluttered. Then her lips curled into that familiar beautiful smile.

It took me a few second before I allowed myself to accept that this was indeed happening. I threw my arms around her again. Tears of joy ran hot down my cheeks.

"Finally, you're here," I sobbed. "You have brought my heart back."

"I'm sorry it took me so long," she whispered apologetically. I shook my head.

"No," I said, closing my eyes with a contented sigh. "Just in the right time."

We pulled away. Then our heads tilted towards each other and mashed our lips together, molding them softly with great longing. Our tongues darted out and collided in the midst of gentle rain.

Suddenly, it was like we were transferred back in time like all those lonely years apart didn't exist. My sadness and despair were all gone, replaced by our timeless passion and love that rekindled into ardency, and right there in that moment, we fell in love once again.

CHAPTER 49

"NINA, OPEN YOUR EYES," Allecra whispered, and I opened my eyes again. Time began to flow in the world once more. The rain had ceased. I raised my face and looked up at the sky. The clouds had parted and beyond the bare branches of the aspen trees I could make out the moon. The bright glow on the ground felt like someone had covered the earth with silver cloths.

I turned now to look at Allecra standing before me. This was truly Allecra and no one else. Her eyes, brimming with her own emotions, were the same, bright, unclouded, sparkling turquoises. Eyes that knew exactly what they longed for. And those eyes were looking right into my heart.

I had spent the last five years thinking of her being somewhere unknown to me. During those times, I had engraved her image in my mind. She absorbed all places, and all marrows, she became a part of me. Now she was real, and she was mine again.

Allecra looked at the moon and then back at me as if to make sure of something.

"I need to know this, too," she whispered like she knew what I was thinking. "That there's just one moon, the familiar, solitary silver moon, beaming that tranquil beam, that we're in the same world and seeing the same thing."

I smiled, realizing I wasn't the only one who found it hard to believe. I leaned over to put my forehead against hers and breath in the fragrance of her unique scent. She had sailed through the sea of galaxies and the dark empty space to find me. It was such a long time waiting for her, but it had all passed by in a blink of an eye. Now I could feel the wholeness of her body in my arms. I felt like we were a complete entity rather than two divided souls.

"Welcome home."

Inside the comforting warmth of our living room, Allecra sat on the couch staring at everything around her in fascination. I looked over to her every few minutes while preparing us some hot Chamomile tea. Sitting in my oversize t-shirt and a dry towel hung over her neck, Allecra looked a lot more corporeal, more earthly than a moment ago. Maybe deep down, I was still reassuring myself that she wouldn't disappear on me in a puff of smoke, the way it always happened in my dreams.

The night had caught me by surprise. The prospect of having Allecra returned to me made me light-headed with happiness like I was lying on a bed of clouds. I had pinched and slapped myself to try and wake me up, but it seemed I was fully awake.

When I put the tray of hot tea down, she was still there in flesh and bone, and what happened earlier wasn't sprung out of my vivid imagination. I tried to convince myself that this was really happening, in the real world and the real time where she was sitting there, and I was sitting here not so far away.

Allecra seemed to understand what went through my mind. She leaned across the coffee table and kissed my forehead. My skin tingled after she retreated; taking my hand with her and making me come to sit on her lap.

"I really am here, Nina, stop doubting it," she said, arms wrapping around my waist like she had always done before.

I put my hand to her cheek and felt the smooth warm skin under my palm.

"How did you find me?"

"What do you think leads me to you?" she said.

"The Erytus stone you gave me?"

She laughed. My heart swelled up just at the sound of that musical laugh.

"No, it's love," she said. "Love brought me back through time and space to be with you again. I don't think finding you on Earth is that big of a problem anymore."

I felt my smile widened as I stared longingly at the chiseled face in front of me. She was still the same, always the sweet and charming Allecra I once knew. Looking at her now was like seeing the sun shining through the darkness of the world for the first time.

"I thought you would never come back," I said, my voice quivered with emotions. Then I brought her face closer until our lips touched again, more reassured this time. Her eyelids fluttered close with a soft sigh. When I pulled away, her lips followed me in yearning. I had to push her shoulders back.

We both giggled.

"I am home," she sighed with her eyes staring at me.

"I've missed you Allecra," I whispered back. "I missed you every single moment of every day."

"I would say it wasn't that different on my end," she said. "Even my mind didn't remember anything back in Arzuria, my heart did remember you. It knew what it was missing. Every single beat of it missed you."

Her hand searched for mine and brought it to her lips before she kissed it gently. Allecra's gaze came back to entwine with my own as she spoke again.

"You know I almost gave up on my life. Just a little more and I would have died from the tangled mess of my feelings. A couple millimeters more I would lose all hope and let go. But something kept me going, something very special that I couldn't explain. It was a strange calling to me. Do you understand what I'm saying?"

"I do," I said and felt saddened at the thought of her own immense sorrow.

"I had no memory of you, yet I knew you had our little one."

My jaw dropped in bewilderment. She knew about our child. She even used the same nickname I used to call our baby when I was first pregnant.

"Allecra, you knew about our little one?" I asked, amazed.

"I had this feeling," she said. "A mother's intuitive feeling when her children need her the most. I had only heard it from humans. Now I realized how strong this feeling is myself. I couldn't eat nor sleep. All I could think of was coming back to Earth. Do you believe me?"

"Yes, I believe you," I said. "I know exactly how it feels from the bottom of my own mother's heart."

"Me too." She smiled. But then she froze, her smile slid off her lips. She looked like she just realized something.

"What's wrong?"

"Oh Nina, I missed your childbirth!" she said, eyes filled with disappointment and remorse. "I missed the most critical time. Damn it!"

"Allecra, relax!" I laughed and kissed her temple gently to calm her. "It's alright. It's been five years."

"Were you alright, Nina?"

"Well, I did have a bit of a complication during my labor, but it was worth all my pain."

"A complication?" She asked with a worried frown. I sighed, knowing my childbirth story would upset Allecra a little.

"I had a bit of a trouble giving birth, and when they told me our child wouldn't make it, I thought the world had ended, too," I told her, feeling my throat tighten and my body shiver at the dreadful memory. "But I believe in miracles and the power of love, and we both were fine."

"Oh...my goodness," Allecra whispered, putting her head against my chest. "I should have been there for you...I'm terribly sorry you had to go through it alone. I know you must have been so scared. I should've been there with you and our baby... "

"Allecra, calm down." I rubbed her back gently. "It's alright. We're doing just fine."

"How is our baby now?"

I chuckled.

"She's not a baby anymore," I said. "She's grown up...well...a little bit."

"She? Nina, I have a daughter?!"

"Oh sorry, I thought you already knew!" I laughed. "And your daughter just graduated from kindergarten today."

Her mouth fell open. She looked daze for a moment, as if she couldn't wrap her mind around it.

"Oh gosh...all those years lost! I missed that too!"

"It's alright, Allecra, don't beat yourself up because of it," I consoled her. "You can still start being a mom-dad from now on."

"A...mom-dad?" Allecra stared at me with the funniest look on her face.

"What do you prefer to be called then?"

"How about, 'Mamochka'?" she said and smiled, her eyes gleamed brightly in the dark.

"Oh," I breathed in realization. "Now that makes a lot of sense."

"Can I see our daughter?" she asked.

"She's asleep now," I told her. "You can meet her tomorrow, that if you're not my imagination and disappear the next morning."

"How can I prove it to make you believe I'm real?"

I smiled and cupped her cheeks with my hands again and kissed her forehead.

"You really want to see her now?"

"Of course!" she said with a vigorous nod. "I have come across the universe for this moment. I want to see what our daughter looks like more than anything."

"You don't know what she looks like yet?"

"No! How could I know?"

"Well, I just thought maybe you have seen her because she told me she dreamed of you."

"I did too! But I thought it was just my own imagination."

"Maybe our dreams are visible and could be the link between worlds?" I said, smiling. "I believe you two have some sort of a special bond."

"You think we do?"

"She's your daughter," I said. "You'll know it when you see her. She's special."

Allecra nodded and then brushed my cheek with the back of her fingers.

"I'm nervous," she admitted. I shook my head back with a smile.

"Don't be."

Allecra looked into my eyes in awe and gratitude.

"You've changed, Nina," she noted.

"Five years as a single-mother would change anyone."

"No, it's not just that," she said. "You're a lot more than you were before. There's equanimity in you, a lot more serene, more sophisticated and even more beautiful."

I smiled at her.

"Maybe it's because the thing I feared the most had already happened to me, and going through it has set me free," I said honestly. "There are times when I was so exhausted by the endless struggle that I was on the verge of surrender, but then I thought of you and our daughter, and immediately I felt lighter, excited, and hopeful, like I could overcome anything in life."

"You are a really brave woman, you know that?" Allecra whispered. Her eyes glittered with tears. "Beyond the simple words, I thank you, for waiting for me, for everything you have gone through because of me, for everything that you are. I thank you from the depth of my heart. And I love you, Nina, I love you with all I have in me."

Tears formed and flowed from my eyes.

"I love you, too," I said.

Allecra wiped the tears away and pulled my body against hers desperately like she couldn't stand any more distance between us. No words were needed to tell me how she felt. I understood her perfectly. We held each other and stayed like that for a long while.

After that, I pulled away.

"Come on, let's go to El's room."

"El?"

"Elvira," I told her. "That's our daughter's name. It's taken after my mother's. Do you like it?"

"Elvira," Allecra repeated. She thought for a second and then she smiled. "I like it a lot...Elvira Knight. What a perfect name."

"Who said she has your last name?" I chastised.

"Aw, why not?"

"She's a Black at the moment."

"Well, she will be a Knight eventually."

I frowned at her, but Allecra just smiled and grabbed my face before she kissed me again. Lips moving feverishly with all her tongue slithered inside my mouth, and I couldn't speak. We both missed this so terribly. My mind twirled again, spinning into a blissful universe.

I slipped my hand down her back while my other hand roamed her chest through her shirt. Her soft breasts filled my palm. Heat coursed through me as our kissing intensified. I could hear her breathed caught in her throat. Her moan vibrated through my lips. My own heart pounded as her fingers wandered over the thin fabric of my sleeping gown.

Then Allecra's hands made their ways through the hem and squeezed my leg earnestly. A moan slipped from our lips at the same time. She pulled me closer, and I straddled her, gently nudging her with my pelvic bone. Something stirred within me, something hot and familiar that I almost forgot it was there. It started to crawl back to the surface of my desire, spreading like wildfire through every part of my body. I heard myself begin to pant, and then—

"Mommy?"

My eyes snapped open and I turned around to find my daughter standing there looking at us. Allecra and I both froze in our current positions. My legs still entangled around her waist while her hand wound over my body as the other went inside my gown.

"Oh!—oh god," I gasped and quickly pulled away from Allecra, who looked as disoriented as I was. Then we all stood, eyes wide in shock and embarrassment at Elvira's curious stare. But when I cast a glance at Allecra again, she looked like she had never seen anything more miraculous and wonderful than the little girl in front of her. I would have found this moment magical if I wasn't concerned about what my daughter had seen.

I decided to break the silence and sucked in a lungful of air before I went to El.

"Hey...honey!" I said with a bright smile, kneeling beside her. My hand stroked her unkempt blonde hair awkwardly. "What are you doing here up late, sweetheart?"

But El didn't seem to hear me. Her stare was still transfixed on Allecra, who was standing there like a statue in the middle of our living room. She was also looking back at El in astonishment.

"Who's that?" my daughter finally asked. A few minutes of palpable silence went by, and yet no one spoke. But as I struggled to answer her question, Allecra came forward slowly. She looked rather daze with pent up emotions.

"Elvira," she spoke softly. Her voice seemed to have a mysterious effect on my daughter. They both kept staring at each other. I was holding my breath, afraid to interrupt this precious moment. Then Allecra kneeled down before El, too.

"It's me," she said. There were tears as she stared at our girl. I could only imagine how Allecra must have felt seeing her child for the first time. Coming from a race that had no heir for generations, she was overwhelmed by this blessing in front of her. My own heart was also seized by the euphoric joy and contentment at seeing the two of them together, the sight I had always dreamed of for many years.

All the while, their shimmering eyes never broke contact. Instead, those turquoises seemed to glow brighter like the depth of the galactic seas. I felt like I was witnessing some unexplainable connection between the two. Allecra reached her hands out to touch Elvira's tiny cheeks, and a look of recognition registered on El's face. Then my daughter stepped forward and put her hands back on both sides of Allecra's cheeks.

"Mamochka?" she asked.

Allecra smiled widely in both relief and gratification.

"Yes," she breathed. "Yes, it's me."

Then El surprised me by throwing her little arms around Allecra's neck. The older blonde quickly wrapped hers around our child back. A sigh issued from her lungs.

"We've been waiting for you," Elvira said. "Mommy never stopped looking at the stars. She did it every night. I knew she was waiting for someone. I knew one day you would come to us."

Allecra's shoulders shook as she began to cry. I watched them with tears streaming down my cheeks. Allecra held out a hand to me, and I went over and embraced them in my arms.

In the deepest of night where the hard edges of reality were softened and fantasy lurking in the real world, everything in my life was right again.

~*~

With all the lights turned off, leaving only the moon to gleam through the window, I pulled Allecra by the hand to my room. The night deepened, but time seemed to hold still for the two of us. There was a lot we needed to talk about, but that could wait. Our ordeal was over. We had other priorities. Without a word passing between us, I grabbed the hem of my gown and lifted it over my head. Allecra was sitting on the edge of my bed, looking at me with heated eyes. I walked over to her and straddled her lap. She wound her arms around me. I could faintly hear her heart thumping wildly against my bare chest.

With nimble fingers, she traced her hands over my sides slowly, causing goosebumps to prickle over my skin. I sighed, all restraints melting away. My own hands went to her shirt and she let me take it off. After we both got undressed and got into bed, we held each other tight, mingling our limbs together. Our hands leisurely explored each other's bodies in the dark. With gentle caress of my wandering hands, one by one, I checked where everything was. My palms brushed over her breasts. They were still in the same beautiful roundness. The velvety skin of her stomach and the feminine curves of her waist, and the familiar bulge between her thighs.

Nothing changed.

Allecra was whole and perfect just as I remembered her. She exhaled loudly as I touched her. She touched me back, slowly and gently like it was her first time touching me like she was on a treasure hunt over my body. And once she found where she liked most, she would kiss that part with a seal of approval and promise.

She kissed my forehead, my lips, my breasts and stomach and everywhere her lips found my flesh. The craving exuded from her eyes made my breath falter, and once again I felt the long forgotten excitement and the burning passion surging through my body.

After we had satisfied our curiosity of each other's existence, we locked lips again. My heart almost burst with utter elation. I noted the sparks in her eyes as I rolled Allecra onto her back and held her hard erection in my hand. She whimpered softly in her throat. My hand cradled her in gentleness. She felt warm and hard, almost harder than I had remembered.

"Allecra?"

"Hmm?"

"Tell me how you came back."

"Triton destroyed the main portal machine of our planet before we left. Now the bridge between the two worlds is broken," Allecra said simply. "And competent as they are, it would take the Arzurian scientists at least a decade to rebuild it."

My hand moved to her femininity and traced over it gently like it was a delicate flower. Allecra breathed sharply.

"But if they succeeded after ten or so years, don't you worry that they would come after you?"

"I spent only five months in my planet, but five years already passed on Earth," she said, "Imagine a decade in Arzuria, how many years will slip away by then considering the different flows of time in the universe? Even if they succeeded in reinventing the new machine, it would be pointless to try and find us now. They might as well work on a *'love campaign* .'"

"A love campaign?"

"That's the cure to life for our world, and maybe for every civilization that ever exists in the universe," Allecra said with a smile. "The same as the one you have given me."

A small heartfelt tear of joy rolled down my cheek. Allecra wiped it away from my cheek before planting a soft kiss there.

"Now you can rest assured that no one will take me away from you and our child again," she said, looking at me with loving eyes.

I nodded and kissed her back on the lips, but only briefly.

"What about your siblings?"

"Only Triton is back with me," she said. "Now he's somewhere in Europe living his dream as a racer."

"And Xenon?"

This time I saw a look of sadness crossed her face.

"She sacrificed herself for us," she said. "I couldn't have done it without her. I just hope they spare her for future guidance. She's the closest thing to the knowledge of love they've got now."

"I'm so sorry," I said.

But Allecra shook her head back and smiled again.

"I think that's what she would want for us. We have to move on and live the life we deserve and for those we love."

I nodded and returned the smile.

I spread my legs and moved over her, closing on in and slowly letting Allecra join me in sweetness and ecstasy. Bliss rode over my spine and down my toes. The sensation shrouded me like a cloak of happiness and warmth. I hadn't felt this way in so long I had forgotten how wonderful it was. Like a lost piece to a jigsaw puzzle, everything was complete. With my eyes fluttered closed, I gulped and took a long sharp intake of air. Then ever so slowly, I exhaled, leaning over the sleeping angel before me. My hair flowed over my shoulders and brushed over her naked form.

Allecra's blonde brows knitted from the torrent of pleasure and emotions as we stared into each other's eyes. The night was cold after the rain, but her touch reignited the fire within the depth of my being. It was almost too much to handle. I felt like I was already going to come apart and needed to distract myself.

"Speaking of those we love, how do you feel after meeting our daughter?" I asked, which brought a pleasant smile back to her face.

I was relieved that Elvira and Allecra seemed to have recognized each other almost in a spiritual level.

"Now I know why you seemed amused when I wondered what she looked like."

"Like a mini-you, right?"

Allecra chuckled quietly, causing another wave of tingling vibration between us. I swallowed the moan in my throat, but I could feel my self-control slipping. It took all my willpower not to start moving, at least not yet. I wanted to savor this, the feeling of having Allecra back with me and in this way again.

"It's like meeting my five-year old self."

We giggled together.

"Sometimes I was afraid that my aunt and cousins would suspect it. I guess if it wasn't too mindboggling to think, they would have believed Elvira is actually your biological child."

"And they would've been so damn right!" Allecra said. "No DNA test needed."

"I wonder what they will think if they see you both together," I said again.

She grinned back.

"Well, we'll let their minds wander."

"Do you think Elvira will be like you?" I asked. I was subtly moving at this point. I couldn't help it.

"I'm not sure about that. She has half of the Arzurian blood, but she's also half-Earthling," Allecra said, "Does it worry you?"

"No, not at all," I reassured her. "She'll still be perfect in my eyes, and I will always love her no matter what — just as I love her mamochka."

Allecra smiled widely. She put her hands on my hips and stirred us a little. Her face tensed with stolen pleasures.

"Don't you want your mini-me, too? Another one with beautiful brown hair and gorgeous brown eyes like you?" She asked rather breathlessly, "I just got lucky this time. Who knows you might get lucky next."

"No! I haven't forgotten about my labor pain yet," I said and smacked her arm playfully. "And don't get your hope up. I always use birth control pills to regularize my period."

"Aw, I'm just kidding!"

In return, she flexed her hips harder. I gasped, and my body went weak all of a sudden. I lay atop her with a shivering sensation everywhere. Allecra giggled into my hair and held me tighter.

"Shh...our daughter just fell asleep," she whispered and kissed my forehead, her hands stroked my back sensually. "I think we'll have to learn how to be very very quiet at night from now, because I will make up to you for all the lost times. I'm afraid it'll have to take me infinity to make up for it."

I pinched her nose with a smile and leaned to whisper into her ear.

"Then let's start our forever from tonight," I said.

Allecra kissed me back. And my mind got lost in those ardent stormy turquoises again. I knew without a doubt, that those eyes spoke a special language that needed no words. Just by the way she looked at me, I knew whatever we felt for each other would be forever.

We began the sweet rhythm of lovemaking, breathing quietly, listening to our own frantic heartbeats. I clung to her and she to me. All thought, all ability to think but feel and respond, vanished as our lovemaking intensified. I gave up the past and distanced myself from the future and just became one with each other at the moment. We quickened and then we climaxed, and I held onto Allecra, meeting her, joining her in the ecstatic world and beyond.

When morning came, we slipped on out of bed and stood by the window, enjoying the sky glowing to our hearts' content. The dawn moon had moved quite a distance, though it still hovered just above the earth.

The new sunrise approached, but neither of us wanted to move from each other's arm. Allecra rested her chin over my shoulder and kissed my neck. I kissed her cheek back as her hands encompassed my body softly.

The two of us stood, witnessing the beauty of life until the newly risen sun graced the world again, and there was just a white paper moon hanging in the sky.

EPILOQUE

I WAS STILL ADJUSTING to the surprising twists and turns in my life. But I was also grateful to the people who had entered it and each helped shaped my story. Aunt Vikki had shown me kindness and acceptance. My dad had taught me the meaning of family love. Also Robert and the twins and Jordan for their innocent impacts on me, and even Dominika for being the catalyst of everything that led up to this. But most importantly, I was grateful for my mother, who saved me with her motherly compassion and made me who I was today.

Allecra and I decided to settle in our current house permanently. It had everything we needed.

"It's a really beautiful little house," Allecra admitted. "It's just perfect for our little family."

The word *'family'* struck a chord with me and warmed my whole being with pure bliss. It was what I had been seeking all my life.

Now, I had my own family.

For the past few weeks, I had watched Allecra and our daughter grew closer together. Every day, I could hear their laughter coming from the living room or the backyard as they played. It made my heart swell with contentment watching them.

They always had some sort of adventures or projects together. And it wasn't long before I found our house crawling with dusting and laundry-collecting robots, or spidery window-washers with their suction rubber feet, and other strange inventions the pair conjured up just for fun. With her mamochka, El was enjoying her new freedom of creativity and imagination, something I hadn't granted her due to safety reasons.

Sometimes they would read storybooks together in our little library or play cheery *'Fur Elise'* in twelve different versions on our small piano Allecra had bought for El. She showered our daughter with so affection enough to spoil any child rotten, but Elvira was a wonderful girl and never abused the power she had over us. I told Allecra that it was because she matured emotionally even when she was still in my womb. El never wanted to cause me any trouble. Sometimes I could see the plainest twinkle of joy in her eyes as she looked at us. And when our gazes met, her whole face lit up even brighter.

Allecra also homeschooled El as she saw more benefits that way. Besides, she wanted to spend time with our daughter. And every day, they would get up to make creative breakfast together and pack my lunch and prepare our dinner.

Each morning, I would drive to work with them waving from the house and my face still tingled with their kisses.

And the best feeling in the world was coming back home and walking through the door to find my two favorite girls waiting for my return. They would put off whatever they were doing to welcome me.

Some nights, when El fell asleep, exhausted from the day's activities, Allecra and I would quietly take that moment to tend the embers of our love with endless passion and longing.

Triton came to visit us one harmonious evening.

I saw him smiling in front of our house, and I never knew how much I had missed him until then. I gave Triton a bear hug. We didn't talk, but I understood how much he was sorry for what happened in the past. I told him it didn't matter anymore and how happy I was to see him again.

Then Triton was awestruck, like an artist seeing the great work of Da Vinci or Michelangelo for the first time when he saw our daughter.

'The first of our kind!' he said. *'A true miracle!'*

To our surprise, once El knew how Triton communicated, she started talking to him in the same telepathic way through her mind. Even Allecra couldn't do that. And I wondered if there was a limit to what Elvira was capable of.

That night, as we had dinner together, we did not talk about their sister, or about Arzuria. We all knew we had found what we lived for in life. And Xenon would be happy for us. Triton left with a promise that he would visit us often.

A few months later, two remarkable things happened in my life. The first was a novella that I had finished writing based on the story of the White Raven. It got reviewed for the publication as a children's book, and I couldn't be more thrilled. Although it would be too unrealistic of me if I quit my day job to write novels now, that was nothing wrong with having a little dream.

But nothing compared to the second thing that happened to me.

It was on a warm August day when our daughter insisted we drive up the hill near the beach for star-gazing with her telescope.

There the three of us sat down side by side with El in the middle, looking through the telescope's lens. It wasn't a cold night, but we huddled together closely. Then Elvira cupped her hand over her mouth and whispered into Allecra's ear, but she did it too loudly that I could hear everything.

"Momachka, did you have it ready?" she asked. Allecra nodded, and for some reasons, she seemed a bit nervous.

"What's the matter?" I asked them.

"Nothing, there will be a *'celestial firework'* soon!" My daughter told me with a sweet smile. Celestial firework was what she referred to the meteor shower.

After a long moment, it did happen. We saw streaks of bright light went across the sky. Their tails were big and flashy against the night. There were so many of them, and we relished in the brightness of the shooting stars that took our breath away.

"Mommy, make a wish! Make a wish!" Elvira cried to me. I looked over at Allecra, and I smiled before I did as I was told. My wish was simple.

I just wanted our family happy together like this always.

Then in the middle of the fantastic show, Allecra leaned over me. I thought she was going to kiss me, but she merely whispered.

"Do you believe I can catch one of the stars for you?" she said. I looked back at her with a skeptical grin. But she pointed to the sky, and I followed her finger, and then she waved her hand across it as if to snatch one of the fallen stars from the black fabric.

"Look what I've got for you," she said, and I had to gasp out loud because between her fingers appeared a sparkling diamond ring. The gem glittered as bright as the stars above us. El was giggling excitedly.

Allecra turned to me with a smile. Her bright turquoise eyes bore into mine.

"Nina," she said softly. "Will you marry me?"

I was trying to hold my tears as I impressed every detail on my mind, relishing this magical moment. To savor it. Happiness filled my heart, and it was beating so fast, I thought it would burst from my chest.

"Yes," I said, barely control the tremor in my voice. "Yes, I will."

Allecra's eyes brightened with joy. She smiled widely as she proceeded to put the ring on my finger. Then our heads leaned forward for a kiss to seal this promise, all the while, our daughter was our faithful witness.

"Yay, mommy, mamochka! Let's get married tomorrow!" she cried.

We laughed together then kissed our beloved daughter on her cheeks.

ABOUT THE AUTHOR

Svetlana Ivanova first started writing as a hobby. As her passion is in creative writing grows stronger, she likes to create bizarre stories for fabulous girls seeking love and passion from other girls. She likes to think of herself as a writer version of a mad scientist, who enjoys creating a world where people's suppressed sexuality and fantasies can roam freely. If she isn't writing her stories, she's in class daydreaming about writing her stories.

OTHER BOOKS BY SVETLANA IVANOVA:

THE ROMANOV PRINCESS
ANASTASIA ROMANOV THE SEQUEL
CURSED BLOOD
DAUGHTER OF THE NAGA (COMING SOON)

49026592R00334

Made in the USA
San Bernardino, CA
10 May 2017